READER'S DIGEST CONDENSED BOOKS

The Barrow
by Marion Davis

READER'S DIGEST® CONDENSED BOOKS

Volume 1
1987

THE READER'S DIGEST ASSOCIATION
Pleasantville, New York

Reader's Digest Condensed Books are published every two to three months at Pleasantville, N.Y.

The condensations in this volume have been created by The Reader's Digest Association, Inc., and are used by permission of and special arrangement with the publishers and the holders of the respective copyrights.

With the exception of actual personages identified as such, the characters and incidents in the fictional selections in this volume are entirely the products of the authors' imaginations and have no relation to any person or event in real life.

The original editions of the books in this volume are published and copyrighted as follows:
A Matter of Honor, published at $18.95 by Linden Press/Simon & Schuster

The Golden Cup, published at $17.95 by Delacorte Press

Stepping Down from the Star: A Soviet Defector's Story, published at $16.95 by G. P. Putnam's Sons

A Deadly Presence, published at R21.90 by David Philip, Publisher (Pty) Ltd.

FIRST EDITION
169

Library of Congress Catalog Card Number: 50-12721

Printed in the United States of America

CONTENTS

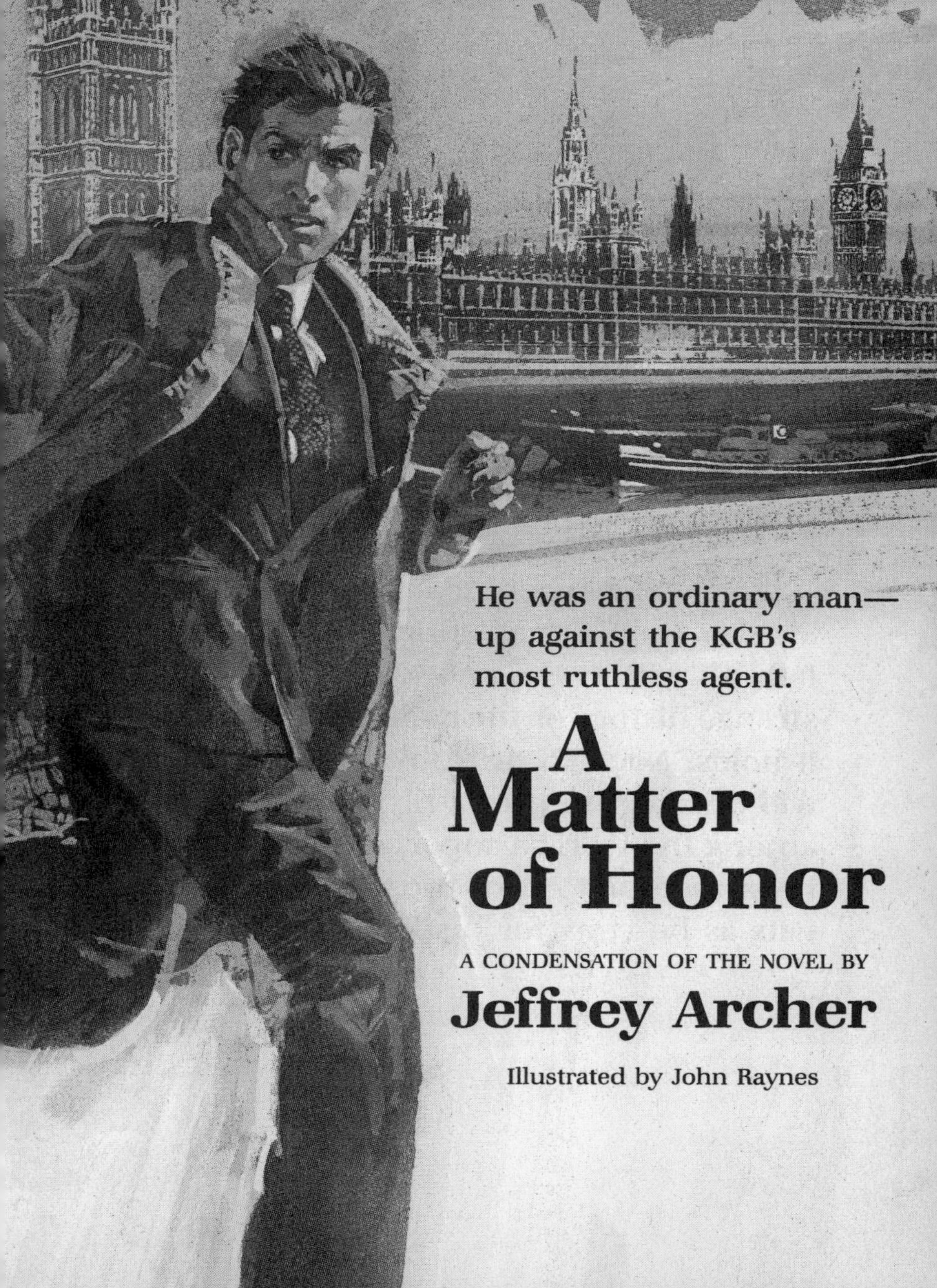

He was an ordinary man—
up against the KGB's
most ruthless agent.

A Matter of Honor

A CONDENSATION OF THE NOVEL BY

Jeffrey Archer

Illustrated by John Raynes

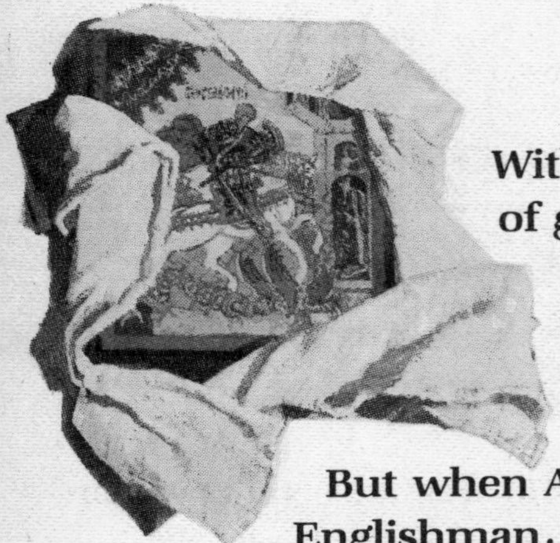

With its dazzling shades of gold and red and blue, the exquisite Russian icon of Saint George and the dragon is a small masterpiece.

But when Adam Scott, a young Englishman, inherits the icon in his father's will, he has no way of knowing its strange history or the dangerous secret that it holds. Nor can he know how swiftly he will be caught up in a high-stakes race among the world's superpowers to possess it—a race that Adam must win by his wits as he runs for his life. . . .

1

The Kremlin, Moscow
May 19, 1966

"It's a fake," said the Russian leader, staring down at the small, exquisite painting he held in his hands.

"That can't be possible," replied his Politburo colleague. "The czar's icon of Saint George and the dragon has been in the Winter Palace at Leningrad under heavy guard for almost fifty years."

"True, Comrade Zaborski," said the older man, "but for fifty years we've been guarding a fake. The czar must have removed the original before the Red Army overran the Winter Palace."

The head of the Committee on State Security moved restlessly in his chair as the cat-and-mouse game continued. Yuri Zaborski knew, after years of running the KGB, who had been cast as the mouse the moment his phone had rung at four that morning to say that General Secretary Brezhnev required him to report to the Kremlin office—immediately.

"How can you be so sure it's a fake, Leonid Ilyich?"

"Because, my dear Zaborski, during the past eighteen months the age of all the treasures in the Winter Palace has been tested by the modern scientific carbon-dating process," said Brezhnev. "And what we have always thought to be one of the nation's masterpieces turns out to have been painted five hundred years after Rublev's original."

"But by whom and for what purpose?" asked the chairman of the KGB, his voice incredulous.

"The experts tell me it was probably a court painter," replied the Russian leader, "who must have been commissioned to execute the copy only months before the Revolution took place. It has always worried the curator at the Winter Palace that the czar's traditional silver crown was not attached to the back of the frame, as it was to all his other masterpieces."

"But what can the czar have done with the original?" said Zaborski, almost as if he were asking himself the question.

"That is exactly what I want to know, comrade," said Brezhnev, resting his hands on the desk. "And you are the one who has been chosen to come up with the answer."

For the first time Zaborski looked unsure of himself. "Do you have anything for me to go on?"

"Very little," admitted the General Secretary, flicking open a file. He read aloud, " 'Around the time of the Revolution, Czar Nicholas the Second obviously saw Rublev's masterpiece as his passport to freedom in the West. He must have had a copy made, which he left on his study wall where the original had previously hung.' "

The head of the KGB remained puzzled. Why should his leader want state security involved in investigating the theft of a minor masterpiece? "And how important is it that we find the original?" he asked, trying to pick up a further clue.

Leonid Brezhnev stared down at his diminutive colleague. "Nothing could be more important, comrade," came back the reply. "And I shall grant you any resources you may consider necessary in terms of people and finance in your quest to discover the whereabouts of the czar's icon."

"But if I were to take you at your word, Comrade General Secretary," said Zaborski, trying to disguise his disbelief, "I could end up spending far more than the painting is worth."

"That would not be possible," said Brezhnev, "because it's not the icon itself that I'm after." He paused for effect. "The money the czar might have raised from selling such a masterpiece would only have kept him in his accustomed life-style for a matter of months. No, it's what we feel certain the czar had secreted *inside* the icon that would have guaranteed security for himself and his family for the rest of their days."

"What could possibly be that valuable?" asked Zaborski.

"Do you remember, comrade, what the czar promised Lenin in exchange for his life?"

"Yes, but it turned out to be a bluff, because no such document was hidden—" He stopped.

Brezhnev smiled triumphantly. "You see, comrade, the document was hidden in the icon all the time. We just had the wrong icon." The Russian leader passed a single sheet of paper to his colleague. "This is the czar's testimony, indicating what we would find in the icon. At the time, nothing was discovered, which only convinced Lenin that it had been a pathetic bluff by the czar to save his family from execution."

Zaborski slowly read the handwritten testimony that had been signed by the czar hours before his execution. His hands began to tremble, and a bead of sweat appeared on his forehead. He looked at the tiny painting, no larger than a book, that rested on the General Secretary's desk.

"Not since the death of Lenin," continued Brezhnev, "has anyone believed the czar's claim, but now, if we are able to locate the genuine masterpiece, we will undoubtedly also be in possession of the promised document."

"And with the authority of those who signed that document, no one could question our legal claim," said Zaborski.

"I also feel confident," replied the Russian leader, "that we would receive the backing of the United Nations and the World Court if the Americans tried to deny us our right. But I fear time is now against us."

"Why?"

"Look at the completion date in the czar's testimony, and you will see how little time we have left to honor our part of the agreement."

Zaborski stared at the date—June 20, 1966. He handed back the testimony as he considered the enormity of the task with which his leader had entrusted him.

Brezhnev continued. "So you can see, Comrade Zaborski, we have one month before the deadline. But if you can discover the whereabouts of the original icon, President Johnson's defense strategy will be rendered virtually useless, and the United States will become a pawn on the Russian chessboard."

2

Appleshaw, Hampshire, England
June 8, 1966

" 'AND to my dearly beloved son, Captain Adam Scott, I bequeath the sum of five hundred pounds.' "

The old lawyer glanced over his half-moon spectacles at the handsome young man before him. Adam put a hand nervously through his thick black hair, conscious of the lawyer's stare. Then Mr. Holbrooke's eyes returned to the papers in front of him.

" 'And to my dearly beloved daughter, Margaret Scott, I bequeath the sum of four hundred pounds.' " Adam was unable to prevent a small grin from spreading across his face. Even in his final act Father had remained a chauvinist.

" 'To the Hampshire County Cricket Club, twenty-five pounds. To the Appleshaw Parish Church,' " droned on Mr. Holbrooke, " 'ten pounds. And finally, to my dearly beloved wife, Susan, our marital home and the remainder of my estate.' " This pronouncement made Adam want to laugh, because he doubted if the remainder of Pa's estate amounted to more than a thousand pounds.

Mr. Holbrooke looked up once more and cleared his throat, as if he were about to announce who was to be left the Goya or the Hapsburg diamonds. The three surviving members of the Scott family sat in silence. What could he have to add? thought Adam.

" 'And I also leave to my son' "—Mr. Holbrooke paused— " 'the enclosed envelope, which I can only hope will bring him greater happiness than it did me. Should he decide to open the envelope, it must be on the condition that he will never divulge its contents to any other living person.' " Adam glanced toward his mother, who looked shocked. Was it fear, or was it distress?

Without another word Mr. Holbrooke passed the yellowed envelope over to the late colonel's only son.

Everyone in the room remained seated as Mr. Holbrooke closed the thin file marked "Col. Gerald Scott, D.S.O., O.B.E., M.C.," pushed back his chair, and walked slowly over to the widow. The two shook hands, and she said, "Thank you."

Once they all had left the office and Adam had ensured that his mother and sister were seated comfortably in the back of the family Morris Minor, he took his place behind the steering wheel. Even before he had switched on the ignition, his mother offered matter-of-factly, "We'll have to get rid of this, you know. I can't afford to run it now, not with petrol costing what it does."

"Don't let's worry about that today," said Margaret consolingly. "I wonder what can be in that envelope, though," she added, wanting to change the subject.

"Detailed instructions on how to invest my five hundred pounds, no doubt," said Adam, attempting to lighten their mood.

The earlier look of fear returned to his mother's face. "I begged your father to destroy that envelope," she said in a whisper.

Adam's lips pursed as he realized this must be *the* envelope his father had referred to all those years ago when Adam had witnessed the one row he would ever see his parents have. Adam still remembered their angry words, spoken just a few days after his father had returned from Germany.

"I have to open it, don't you understand?" Pa had insisted.

"Never," his mother had replied. "After all the sacrifices I have made, you at least owe me that."

Almost twenty years had passed since that confrontation, and Adam had never heard the subject referred to again. The only time he ever mentioned it to his sister she could throw no light on what the dispute might have been over.

A mile or so down a winding country lane Adam brought the old Morris Minor to a halt outside a trellised gate. A path led through a neat lawn to a little thatched cottage.

"I'm sure you ought to be getting back to London," were his mother's first words as she entered the drawing room.

"I'm in no hurry, Mother."

"Just as you wish, my dear, but don't worry yourself over me," his mother continued. She stared up at the tall young man who reminded her so much of Gerald. The same dark hair and deep brown eyes, the same open, honest face, even the same gentle approach to everyone he came across. But most of all the same high standards of morality that had brought them to their present state. "I've always got Margaret to take care of me," she added.

Adam looked at his sister and wondered how she would cope.

Margaret had recently become engaged to a stockbroker, and she would be wanting to start a life of her own. Her fiancé had already put a down payment on a little house only fourteen miles away.

After tea and a sad, uninterrupted monologue from their mother on the virtues and misfortunes of their father, Margaret cleared away and left the two of them alone.

"Now that you're no longer in the army, my dear, I do hope you'll be able to find a worthwhile job," his mother said uneasily as she recalled how difficult that had proved to be for his father.

"I'm sure everything will be just fine, Mother," he replied. "The Foreign Office has asked to see me again."

"Still, you've got five hundred pounds of your own," she said. "That should make things a little easier for you." Adam smiled fondly at her, wondering when she had last spent a day in London. She looked up at the clock on the mantelpiece and said, "You'd better be getting along, my dear. I don't like the thought of you on that motorbike after dark."

Adam bent down to kiss her on the cheek. "I'll give you a call tomorrow," he said. On his way out he stuck his head around the kitchen door and shouted to his sister, "I'm off. I'll be sending you a check for fifty pounds."

"Why?" asked Margaret, looking up from the sink.

"Let's say it's my blow for women's rights." He shut the door smartly to avoid the dishcloth that was hurled in his direction.

Outside, Adam revved up his motorbike and drove toward London and his flat on Ifield Road. He had decided to wait until he had reached the privacy of his own room to open the envelope. Lately his life had not been such that he could be blasé about the little ceremony. After all, in a way, he had waited most of his life to discover what was in the envelope he had inherited.

Adam had asked his father about the family tragedy a thousand times. "It's all a matter of honor, old chap," his father would say, lifting his chin and squaring his shoulders. He had spent the rest of his life suffering the sidelong glances of lesser men, who had made sure they were not seen too regularly in his company. Petty men with petty minds. Adam knew his father far too well to believe even for a moment that he could have been involved in such treachery as was whispered.

Now Adam took one hand off the handlebars and fingered the envelope in his inside pocket, like a schoolboy the day before his birthday feeling the shape of a present in the hope of discovering some clue as to its contents.

He tried to piece together the few facts he had been told over the years. In 1946, within a year of his fiftieth birthday, his father, whom *The Times* had described as a brilliant tactical officer with a courageous war record, had resigned his commission from the army. His resignation had astonished his family and shocked his regiment, as it had been assumed by all who knew him that it was only a matter of months before a general's crossed sword and baton would have been sewn onto his epaulets.

When asked, all the colonel would offer was that he had had enough of war, and felt the time had come to make a little money on which Susan and he could retire before it was too late. Few people found his story credible, and that credibility was not helped when the only job the colonel managed to secure for himself was as secretary of the local golf club.

It was only through the generosity of his late grandfather that Adam had been able to remain in school at Wellington and thus continue the family tradition and pursue a military career.

After leaving there, Adam was offered a place at the Royal Military Academy, Sandhurst. He diligently studied military history, tactics, and battle procedure, but his greatest success came on weekends, when he ran cross-country races. For two years panting cadets saw only his mud-spattered back as Adam went on to become the Inter-Services champion.

When he graduated from Sandhurst he stood ninth in his class, but his leadership was such that no one was surprised that he was awarded the Sword of Honor. Adam never doubted from then on that he would follow his father and command the regiment.

The Royal Wessex Regiment accepted the colonel's son soon after he had been awarded his regular commission. Adam quickly gained the respect of his fellow soldiers. As a tactical officer he had no equal, and it was clear he had inherited his father's courage. Yet when the War Office published the names of those subalterns who had been promoted to captain, Lieutenant Adam Scott was not to be found on the list. To Adam it was becoming abundantly clear that he was not to be allowed to atone for whatever it was his father was thought to have done.

Eventually Adam was promoted to captain, but not before he had distinguished himself in the Malayan jungle in hand-to-hand fighting against the Chinese. Captured and held prisoner by the Communists, he endured the kind of solitude and torture that no amount of training could have prepared him for. He escaped after eight months, only to discover on returning to the front line that he had been awarded a posthumous Military Cross. When at the age of twenty-nine Captain Scott passed his staff exam but still failed to be offered a regimental place at the staff college, he finally accepted that he could never hope to command the regiment. He resigned his commission a few weeks later.

While serving his last few months Adam learned from his mother that Pa only had weeks to live. He made the decision not to inform his father of his resignation. He was at least thankful that his father had died without being aware of the stigma that had become part of his son's life.

The sight of the outskirts of London made Adam's thoughts return to the pressing problem of finding employment. It was true that he had another meeting lined up with the Foreign Office, but he had been impressed by the other candidates he had encountered and was only too aware of his lack of a university degree.

As he swung the motorbike into King's Road, Adam once again fingered the envelope in his inside jacket pocket, hoping, uncharitably, that Lawrence would not yet have returned from the bank. Not that he could complain; his old school friend had been extremely generous in offering him such a pleasant room in his spacious flat for only four pounds a week.

Adam parked his motorbike, aware that, like his mother's old Morris, it would have to be sold if the Foreign Office job didn't materialize. He ran up the stairs to the flat and was on the fifth floor, pushing his key into the lock, when a voice from inside shouted, "It's open."

"Damn," Adam said under his breath.

"How did it go?" said Lawrence as Adam entered.

"Very well, considering," Adam replied.

Lawrence had already changed from his banker's clothes into a blazer and gray flannels. He was slightly shorter and stockier than Adam, with a head of wavy fair hair and thoughtful gray eyes that always seemed to be inquiring.

"I admired your father so much," he added. Adam had introduced Lawrence to his father, and they had become friends immediately. But Lawrence was not a man who dealt in rumors.

"Able to retire on the family fortune, are we?" asked Lawrence in a lighter vein.

"Only if that dubious bank you work for has found a way of converting five hundred pounds into five thousand."

"Can't manage it at the present time, old chum."

Adam smiled as he looked across at his friend. Although taller than Lawrence now, he could still recall those days at Wellington when Lawrence seemed to him like a giant. "Late again, Scott," he would say as Adam scampered past him in the corridor. Adam had looked forward to the time when he could do everything in the same relaxed, superior style. Or was it just that Lawrence *was* superior? His suits always seemed to be well pressed, his shoes always shone, and he never had a hair out of place. Adam still hadn't figured out how he did it all so effortlessly.

"I've discovered this Italian restaurant that's just opened on Fulham Road, and I'm going to meet my friend Carolyn there. Care to join us for a meal?" asked Lawrence.

"Maybe later," said Adam, "but I still have one or two papers left over from this afternoon that I ought to check through."

"Well, come along if you feel you can," said Lawrence as he left.

Adam didn't move until he was sure he could no longer hear footsteps echoing on the staircase. Satisfied, he retreated to his bedroom and locked himself in. He sat down and pulled his father's envelope out of his inside pocket. It was the heavy, expensive type of stationery Pa had always used.

Adam opened the envelope carefully and extracted a letter in his father's unmistakable hand and a smaller envelope that was faded with time. Written on the old envelope in an unfamiliar hand were the words Colonel Gerald Scott. Adam placed the old envelope on the little table by his side and, unfolding his father's letter, began to read.

My dear Adam,

Over the years, you will have heard many explanations for my sudden departure from the regiment, some of them farcical, a few of them slanderous. I always considered it better for all concerned to keep my own counsel. I feel, however, that I owe you a fuller explanation, and that is what this letter will set out to do.

As you know, my last posting before I resigned my commission was at Nuremberg, from May 1945 to October 1946. I was given the task of commanding the British section responsible for those senior-ranking Nazis awaiting trial for war crimes. I came to know the imprisoned officers quite well, and after a year or so I had even grown to tolerate some of them. Such views were considered unacceptable at the time.

Among the senior Nazis with whom I came into daily contact was Reichsmarschall Hermann Göring. Here was a man I detested from the first moment I came across him: arrogant, overbearing, and totally without shame about his barbaric role in the war.

The night before Göring was due to be executed, he requested a private meeting with me. It was a Monday, and I can still recall every detail of that encounter. I received the request when I took over the watch from the Russian major Vladimir Kosky. In fact, Kosky personally handed me the written request. As soon as I had inspected the guard I went along with the duty corporal to see the Reichsmarschall in his cell. Göring stood to attention by his small, low bed and saluted as I entered the room.

"You asked to see me?" I said. I never could bring myself to address him by his name or rank.

"Yes, Colonel," he replied. "I simply wish to make the last request of a man condemned to death. Would it be possible for the corporal to leave us?"

Imagining it was something highly personal, I asked the corporal to wait outside. After the door closed, Göring passed over the envelope you now have in your possession. As I took it, all he said was, "Be kind enough not to open this until after my execution tomorrow. I can only hope it will compensate for any blame that might later be placed on your shoulders." I had no idea what he could be alluding to at the time. Many of the prisoners confided in me during their last days, and toward the end some of them were undoubtedly on the verge of madness.

Göring's final words to me as I left his cell were simply, "Be assured it is a masterpiece." Then he lit up a cigar, as if he were relaxing after a rather good dinner. We all had different theories as to who smuggled the cigars in for him.

I placed the envelope in my jacket pocket and returned to my office to make out my report. I left the envelope in the jacket pocket of my uniform, with every intention of opening it immediately after Göring's execution the following morning. I was checking over the orders of the day when the corporal rushed into my office. "It's Göring, sir. It's Göring," he said. From the panic on the man's face I didn't need to ask for any details. We both ran all the way back to the Reichsmarschall's cell.

I found Göring lying face downward on his bunk. He was already dead. In the commotion that immediately followed, I quite forgot Göring's letter. An autopsy a few days later showed that he had died from cyanide poisoning.

As I had been the last to see him alone, my name was linked with his death. There was, of course, no truth in the accusations, but so stung was I by them that I felt the only thing to do in the circumstances was to resign my commission immediately, for fear of bringing further dishonor to the regiment.

When I returned to England, and finally decided to throw out my old uniform, I came across the envelope again. I explained to your mother the details of the incident, and she begged me to destroy the envelope, as she considered the matter had brought enough dishonor to our family already, and even if it did point to whoever had been responsible for helping Göring to his suicide, in her opinion such knowledge could no longer do anyone any good. I agreed to comply with her wishes, but although I never opened the envelope, I could not bring myself to destroy it, remembering that last sentence Göring had uttered about its being a masterpiece. Finally I hid it among my personal papers.

However, since the imagined sins of the father are inevitably visited upon the next generation, I feel no such qualms should influence you. If there is therefore anything to be gained from the contents of this envelope, I make only one request, namely that your mother should be the first to benefit from it.

But if you open the envelope only to discover its purpose is to involve you in some dishonorable enterprise, be rid of it without a second thought. I feel confident that I can leave you to make the correct decision.

Your loving father,
Gerald Scott

Adam read the letter once again, realizing how much trust his father had placed in him. When he had finished reading the missive for a third time he folded it up neatly and slipped it back into the envelope.

He then picked up the second envelope from the side table and slowly began to slit it open. He hesitated for a moment before extracting two pieces of paper, both yellowed with age. One appeared to be a letter, while the other was some sort of document. The crest of the Third Reich was embossed at the head of the letter, above the printed name of Reichsmarschall Hermann Göring. Adam's hands began to tremble as he read the first line.

It began, *"Sehr geehrter Herr Oberst Scott . . ."*

3

As THE black Chaika limousine drove out onto Red Square, two Kremlin guards sprang to attention and presented arms.

Zaborski touched the front of his black felt hat in acknowledgment, although his thoughts were elsewhere. The first decision he had to make was which of his senior operatives should be charged with the task of heading the team to find the czar's icon.

Within moments of leaving his leader, the chairman of the KGB had formed in his own mind a shortlist of two. Which of those two, Valchek or Romanov, should be given the nod still taxed him, but the deadline of June 20 left him with no option. He would have to make the choice even before he reached his office.

The car came to an abrupt halt outside KGB headquarters. The driver ran around and opened the back door for his master, but Zaborski didn't move. The man who rarely changed his mind had already done so twice on the route back to Dzerzhinsky Square.

His professional intuition told him to select Yuri Valchek. Slow and methodical, Valchek had completed ten years as an agent in the field before confining himself largely to a desk job.

In contrast, Alex Romanov, who had only recently become head of his own section, had shown flashes of brilliance in the field, but they had often been outweighed by a lack of personal judgment. At twenty-nine he was the youngest and without question the most ambitious of the chairman's select team.

Finally Zaborski stepped out onto the pavement and walked toward another door held open for him. He strode across the marble floor to the elevator. Several silent men and women were also waiting for it, but when it returned to the ground floor and the chairman stepped into the little cage, none of them made any attempt to join him. Zaborski traveled slowly up toward his office. By the time he had reached the top floor he had made up his mind. It would be Valchek.

A secretary helped him off with his long black coat and took his hat. Zaborski walked quickly to his desk. The two files he had asked for were awaiting him. He sat down and began to pore over Valchek's file. When he had completed it he barked out an order to his hovering secretary. "Find Romanov."

Comrade Romanov lay on his back, his left arm behind his head and his opponent's right arm over his throat.

An attendant came rushing over to them and bent down to whisper in the coach's ear. The coach reluctantly released his pupil, who rose slowly, as if in a daze, bowed, and then in one movement of right arm and left leg took his coach's legs from under him and left him flat on the gymnasium floor before making his way quickly to the phone in the office.

Romanov didn't notice the girl who handed him the phone. "I'll be with him as soon as I have had a shower," was all she heard him say. The girl had seen him in the gymnasium a hundred times. Six feet tall, with that long blond hair—he resembled a Western film star. And those piercing blue eyes.

Zaborski meanwhile had opened Romanov's personal file for a second time and was perusing the details.

> Aleksandr Petrovich Romanov. Born Leningrad, March 12, 1937. Elected full party member 1958.
>
> Father: Pëtr Nikolaevich Romanov. Served on the eastern front in 1942. On returning to Russia in 1945 refused to join Communist Party. After several reports of antistate activities, supplied by his son, he was sentenced to ten years in prison. Died in jail October 20, 1948.

Grandfather: Nikolai Aleksandrovich Romanov. Merchant, and one of the wealthiest landowners in Petrograd. Shot and killed on May 11, 1918, while attempting to escape from the Red Army.

Alex, as he preferred to be known, had enrolled for the party's Pioneer organization at the age of nine. By the age of eleven he had been offered a place at a special school at Smolensk—to the disgust of some lesser party workers, who considered such privileges should be reserved for the sons of loyal officials. Romanov immediately excelled in the classroom, and at fourteen he was made a member of the Komsomol.

By the age of sixteen Romanov had won the Lenin language medal and the junior gymnastics prize and was allowed to take a place at a university. As an undergraduate, he continued to excel in languages, specializing in English, French, and German. He also continued to pursue his gymnastics, until the university coach wrote in bold letters across one of his reports, "This student is too tall to be considered for Olympic competition." So Romanov took up judo. Within two years he had been selected for the 1956 Eastern bloc games in Budapest. After his victory at the Second Soviet games in Moscow, the Western press crudely described him as "the Axe."

Once Romanov had completed his final year at the university and obtained his diploma (with distinction), he joined the diplomatic service. That was when Zaborski had first come across the self-confident young man. Each year the KGB was able to choose for assignment from the diplomatic service any person it considered to be of exceptional talent. Romanov was an obvious candidate. He had always wanted to be an officer of the KGB.

Zaborski began to read some of the comments he himself had added to the report during the last eight years. As an operative, Romanov had reached the rank of major, having served successfully in the field before being appointed head of a department. Two red dots—indicating successful missions—were placed by his name. Romanov's most significant achievement, however, had been the recruitment of an agent from the British Foreign Office, whose rise through the ranks had assisted Romanov's own career. Romanov's appointment as head of a department had surprised no one, although it soon became clear that he missed the raw excitement of fieldwork.

Zaborski turned to the last page, a character assessment: "ambitious, sophisticated, ruthless, but not always reliable."

There was an assertive rap on the door. The chairman closed the file and pressed a button under his desk. The doors clicked open to allow Aleksandr Petrovich Romanov to enter the room.

"Good morning, Comrade Chairman," said the elegant young man who now stood at attention in front of him. Zaborski looked up and felt a little envy that the gods had bestowed so much on one so young. Still, it was he who understood how to use such a man to the state's best advantage. "You called for me," added Romanov.

The chairman nodded. "The General Secretary has entrusted us with a particularly sensitive project of great importance to the state." Zaborski paused. "So sensitive in fact that you will report only to me. You can hand-select your own team, and no resources will be denied you."

"I am honored," said Romanov, sounding unusually sincere.

"You will be," replied the chairman, "if you succeed in discovering the whereabouts of the czar's icon."

Adam placed the faded envelope between the pages of the Bible his mother had given him as a confirmation present. Then he strolled to the kitchen, fried himself an egg, and warmed up the other half of the previous day's tinned beans. After he had finished this unwholesome meal, he returned to his room and lay on his bed thinking. Would the contents of the faded envelope finally prove his father's innocence?

The clock chimed ten as he rose and pulled the Bible off the bookshelf. With some apprehension he removed the envelope. He switched on the reading light on the small writing desk, unfolded the two pieces of paper, and put them in front of him.

One appeared to be a personal letter from Göring to Adam's father, while the other had the look of an older, more official document. Adam placed this second document to one side and began to go over the letter line by line. It didn't help.

He tore a blank piece of paper from a notepad and copied down

the text of Göring's letter, leaving out the greeting and the large, bold signature. He checked over the copy carefully before replacing the original in its envelope. The document was not as simple to copy as the letter had been, because this time the hand it was written in was spidery and cramped.

The work took a surprisingly long time. Adam wrote out each word in block capitals, and when he wasn't certain of the spelling he put down the possible alternative letters below. He wanted to be sure of any translation the first time.

He had just finished when he heard a key turning in the front door. Quickly he switched off the light and felt his way to bed.

THE first action Romanov took on leaving the chairman's office that morning was to handpick a team of twelve researchers. From the moment they had been briefed, they studied in pairs, on four-hour shifts, so that the work could continue night and day.

The early information had come in almost by the hour, and the researchers had quickly been able to establish that the czar's icon had remained in the Winter Palace until December 1914. Romanov studied a photo of the small, delicate painting—Saint George in a tiny mosaic pattern of blue and gold, and the dragon in red and yellow. Romanov could well understand why people might be moved by the little masterpiece, but as he continued to read about the icon he still couldn't work out why it was so important to the state. He wondered if Zaborski even knew the reason.

A royal servant who had testified before the people's court after the Revolution claimed that the czar's icon had disappeared for a few days in 1915 after the visit of Ernst Ludwig, Grand Duke of Hesse. At the time, the court had taken scant interest in the misplaced icon, because it was still on the wall of the czar's study when they had stormed the Winter Palace. What concerned the court more was why, in the middle of a fierce war between Germany and Russia, the grand duke had come at all. It was thought he had been on a secret visit to his sister Alexandra, the czarina. Historians now believed that it had been his intention to secure a cease-fire.

There was no proof that the czar had made any promises on behalf of his people, but the grand duke, it seemed, did not return to Germany empty-handed. Reports showed that another palace servant had been instructed to wrap up the czar's icon and pack it with the grand duke's belongings. However, no one on the palace staff could explain to the court how a few days later the icon reappeared in its rightful place on the wall of the czar's study.

Romanov's chief researcher had underlined his conclusion in red ink: "The czar must have replaced the original painting with a copy, having handed over the real icon for safekeeping to his brother-in-law, the grand duke."

But why, Romanov wondered, when the czar had a palace full of Goyas, El Grecos, Titians, and Rubenses, did he bother to smuggle out one icon, and why did Brezhnev so badly want it back?

Romanov instructed his researchers to turn their talents to the royal house of Hesse, in the hope of tracing what had then happened to the original icon. Within ten days they possessed more information about the grand duke and his family than any university professor had managed to gather in a lifetime. But Romanov came to an abrupt end when, after the grand duke's death, the painting had been left to his son, who was tragically killed in a plane crash. Nothing had been seen or heard of the icon after that day.

By the beginning of the third week Romanov had reluctantly reached the conclusion that there was nothing new to be discovered. He was preparing his final report for Zaborski, when one researcher, Comrade Petrova, stumbled across an article in the London *Times* of Wednesday, November 17, 1937. It read:

> Grand Duke George of Hesse and four members of his family were killed this morning when a Sabena aircraft carrying them from Darmstadt to London crashed in thick fog over the Belgian countryside. The grand duke had been on his way to England to attend the wedding of his younger brother, Prince Louis.

It was the next paragraph that the researcher had circled.

> Some of the late grand duke's personal belongings, including several wedding presents for Prince Louis and his bride, were scattered for miles in the vicinity of the crashed aircraft. The German government announced this morning that a senior German general has been appointed to lead a team of salvage experts to ensure the recovery of any family possessions.

Romanov called for the young researcher. When Anna Petrova arrived a few minutes later she gave no impression of being overawed by her department head. She accepted that it would be hard to make any impression on him with the clothes she could afford. However, she had cut her hair in the style of the American actress Mia Farrow. She hoped Romanov would notice.

"I want you to scour *The Times* for the six months following November 17, 1937, and also check the German and Belgian press during the same period for anything that would show what the salvage experts discovered." He dismissed her with a smile.

Within twenty-four hours Comrade Petrova barged back into Romanov's office without bothering to knock. Romanov merely raised his eyebrows before devouring an article she had discovered in the Berlin *Zeitung* of Saturday, January 29, 1938.

> The investigation into the crash last November of the Sabena aircraft that was carrying the Hesse royal family to London has now been concluded. All personal possessions that were discovered in the vicinity of the wreckage have been returned to the grand duke, Prince Louis, who, it is understood, was saddened by the loss of a family heirloom that was to have been a wedding gift from his brother, the late grand duke. The gift, a painting known as "the czar's icon," had once belonged to his uncle, Czar Nicholas II. The icon of Saint George and the dragon, although only a copy of Rublev's masterpiece, was considered to be one of the finest examples of early twentieth-century craftsmanship to come out of Russia since the Revolution.

Romanov looked up at the researcher. "Twentieth-century copy be damned," he said. "It was the fifteenth-century original, and none of them realized it at the time—perhaps not even the old grand duke himself. No doubt the czar had plans for the icon, had he managed to escape."

Romanov stared down at the photograph above the newspaper report. The young grand duke, Louis, was shaking hands with the general in charge of the salvage team that had been successful in returning so many of the prince's family possessions. "But did he return them all?" Romanov said out loud.

"What do you mean?" asked the young researcher. Romanov continued to stare at the faded prewar photograph of the two men. Although the general was unnamed, every schoolboy in Germany would have recognized the large, impassive face, with the chilling eyes, that would become infamous to the Allied powers.

Romanov looked up again. "You can forget the grand duke from now on, Comrade Petrova. Concentrate your efforts on Reichsmarschall Hermann Göring."

WHEN Adam awoke he jumped out of bed and walked over to his desk. Everything was in place, exactly as he had left it. It was ten to seven. Although he felt as fit as he had been the day he left the army some seven weeks before, he still completed a punishing routine of exercise every morning. He intended to be at his peak when the Foreign Office put him through a physical. In moments he was dressed in running shorts and gym shoes.

He tiptoed out of the flat and pounded along the pavement to the Embankment, across Albert Bridge, and through Battersea Park, to return by way of Chelsea Bridge. Only one thought was going through his mind. After twenty years of gossip and innuendo, this was going to be the chance to clear his father's name.

Back in the flat, Lawrence, smart in a gray pin-striped suit, was preparing breakfast while glancing at the cricket scores in the *Daily Telegraph*. Adam took a shower. Minutes later he joined his friend in the kitchen. Lawrence was now seated at the table, concentrating hard on a bowl of cornflakes while running a finger down the foreign exchange rates in the *Financial Times*.

Adam checked his watch: already ten past eight. "Won't you be late for the office?" he asked.

"Dear boy," said Lawrence. "I am not a lackey who works at the kind of bank where the customers keep shop hours. But I will have to be shackled to my desk by nine thirty. Alas, they don't send a driver for me nowadays."

Adam started to make his breakfast. "I could give you a lift."

"Can you imagine a man in my position arriving at the headquarters of Barclays Bank on a motorbike?" said Lawrence. He collected his rolled umbrella from the hatstand. "See you tonight, then, glorious, unwashed, and unemployed."

Adam cleared away, happy to act as housekeeper while he was out of work. All he had planned before his interview with the Foreign Office that afternoon was a long bath and a slow shave. Then he remembered Reichsmarschall Göring.

"HAVE you come up with anything that would indicate Göring might have kept the icon for himself?" asked Romanov, turning hopefully to the researcher.

"Only the obvious," Anna Petrova replied offhandedly.

Romanov considered reprimanding the girl for such insolence but said nothing on this occasion. After all, Comrade Petrova had proved to be by far the most innovative of his team of researchers.

"And what was so obvious?" inquired Romanov.

"It's common knowledge that Hitler put Göring in charge of all the art treasures seized on behalf of the Third Reich. But as the Führer had fixed personal opinions as to what constituted quality, many of the world's masterpieces were judged 'depraved.' Hitler ordered them to be destroyed. Among them were works by such masters as van Gogh, Manet, Monet—"

"You are not suggesting Göring could have stolen the czar's icon," Romanov asked, staring up at the ceiling, "only to burn it?"

"No, no," said the young researcher in a tone that indicated she believed herself to be indispensable, at least for the moment. "Göring was not that stupid. As we now know, he didn't always obey the Führer's every word. Göring held some public burnings in Berlin and Düsseldorf of lesser-known German artists, but the masterpieces, the real works of genius, were moved discreetly over the border and deposited in the vaults of Swiss banks. Unfortunately, no one has been able to discover how many aliases he used. Since the end of the war many of the paintings have been found and restored to their rightful owners, but my guess is that a large number still remain lodged in Swiss banks."

"How can you be so certain?" demanded Romanov.

"Because the Swiss banks only return valuables when they can be sure of a nation's or individual's right of possession. In the case of the icon, there was no proof of ownership, as the last official owner was Czar Nicholas the Second, and he, as every good Russian knows, had no successors."

"Then I must retrace Göring's steps by going to the banks. What has been their disclosure policy to date?" asked Romanov.

"That differs from establishment to establishment," said Petrova. "Some banks wait for twenty years or more and then try—by research or advertising—to contact the owners or their next of kin. In the case of the Jews who lost their lives under the Nazis, it has often proved impossible to trace a legitimate owner."

Romanov proceeded to show that he had also been doing some research. "In fact, when the banks have been unable to discover the rightful owner of any treasure left with them, they have handed that treasure over to the Swiss Red Cross for auction."

"But if the czar's icon had ever been auctioned, wouldn't we have heard about it through one of our agents?"

"Precisely. Our operatives have combed Europe. They have spoken to nearly every major curator, keeper, dealer, and crook in the art world, and they still haven't come up with a single lead."

"Then," Petrova said, "that can only mean some unscrupulous bankers disposed of the icon privately once they felt sure no one was going to make a claim."

"A false premise, I suspect, Comrade Petrova."

"Why do you say that?" the young researcher asked.

"For one reason. Swiss bankers make so much money dealing with honest people that it has never been in their best interests to become involved with crooks. There are remarkably few exceptions to this rule, which is why so many people are willing to do business with the Swiss. No. I'm convinced," Romanov concluded, "that while the rest of the world is under the illusion that the original icon still hangs in the Winter Palace, it has since 1938 been lodged in a Swiss bank, waiting for someone to claim it."

"A long shot," said the researcher.

"I am quite aware of that," said Romanov sharply, "but don't forget that many Swiss banks have a twenty-five-year rule before disclosure, some thirty. One or two even have no deadline at all, as long as enough money has been deposited to cover the housing of the treasure. It is those that we must check."

"Who knows how many banks there might be who fall into that category?" Petrova sighed.

"You will, by nine o'clock tomorrow morning," said Romanov. "And then it will be necessary for me to pay a visit to the one man in this country who knows everything about banking."

"Am I expected to start straightaway, Comrade Major?" the researcher asked coyly.

Romanov smiled and looked down into the girl's green eyes. She really was quite magnificent. He leaned over until their lips nearly met.

"You'll have to rise very early, Anna. But for now, just turn out the light."

4

It took Adam only a few more minutes before he had checked over both documents. He put the originals back into the Bible on his bookshelf. Then he cut his copy of Göring's letter into three separate pieces, which he placed in a clean envelope. His next problem was how to obtain a translation of the document and Göring's letter without arousing unnecessary curiosity. He quickly dismissed the German embassy, the German tourist board, and the German press agency, as all three were too official and therefore likely to ask unwanted questions. Once he was dressed, he went to the telephone directory in the hall and flicked through the listings for German organizations until his eye stopped at a promising entry. The address was given as Bayswater House, 35 Craven Terrace, W2.

Adam left the flat a few minutes before ten, the three pieces of the letter now safely lodged in the inside pocket of his blazer. He strolled down Edith Grove and onto King's Road, enjoying the morning sun. He reached the Sloane Square station of the London underground, paid for a ticket, and, installed in a half-empty carriage, again went over his plan. When he emerged at Paddington he checked his bearings and walked in the direction of Craven Terrace.

A few minutes later Adam found himself standing at the end of a short drive, looking up at a bold green-and-yellow sign that read THE GERMAN YOUNG MEN'S CHRISTIAN ASSOCIATION.

He went up the drive and strode confidently through the front door. He was stopped by a porter standing in the hallway. "Can I help you, guv'nor?"

Adam put on an exaggerated military accent and explained that he was looking for a young man called Hans Kramer.

"Never 'eard of 'im, sir," said the porter, almost standing to attention when he recognized the regimental tie. He turned to a book that lay open on the desk. " 'E isn't registered," he added, a tobacco-stained thumb running down the list of names in front of him. "Why don't you try the lounge or the game room?" he suggested, gesturing with his thumb to a door on the right.

"Thank you," said Adam. He walked smartly across the hall, went through the swinging doors, and glanced around the room. Several students were lounging about, reading German papers and magazines. He wasn't sure where to start, until he spotted a studious-looking girl on her own in a corner, poring over a copy of *Time* magazine. Leonid Brezhnev's face stared out from the cover. Adam took the seat beside her. "I wonder if you could assist me?" he asked. "I need to have something translated."

She put down the magazine. "I will see if I can help."

"I hope it isn't too difficult," Adam said as he took the envelope from his inside pocket and extracted the first paragraph of Göring's letter. Then he put the envelope back into his pocket, took out a little notebook, and waited expectantly.

She read the paragraph over two or three times, then seemed to hesitate. "Is anything wrong?" he inquired.

"Not exactly," she replied, still concentrating on the words in front of her. "It's just that it's a little bit old-fashioned, so I might not be able to give you the exact sense."

She repeated each sentence slowly, first in German and then in English, as if wanting to feel the meaning as well as just translating the words. " 'Over the last . . . past year we have come to know . . . each other somewhat . . .' No, no," she said, " 'quite well.' "

Adam wrote each word down as the girl translated it. " 'You have never disguised'—perhaps a better meaning is 'hidden,' " she added, " 'your distaste for the National Socialist Party. . . .' " She raised her head and stared at Adam.

"It's only out of a book," he assured her.

She didn't look convinced but nevertheless continued. " 'But you have at every time . . .' No, 'at all times, behaved with the courtesy of an officer and a gentleman.' "

The girl looked up, even more puzzled, as she had now reached the last word. "Is that all?" she asked. "It doesn't make sense."

"No, that's it," said Adam, quickly taking back the sheet of paper. "Thank you," he added. "It was most kind of you to help." He left the girl and was relieved to see her shrug resignedly and return to her magazine. Adam went in search of the game room.

When he swung the door open he found a young man in a T-shirt and brown suede shorts. He was tapping a table-tennis ball up and down listlessly.

"Care for a game?" said the boy, not looking at all hopeful.

"Sure," said Adam, removing his jacket and picking up the racket at his end of the table. For twenty minutes Adam had to go all out to make sure he lost. As he congratulated his opponent he felt certain he had gained the young man's confidence.

"You put up good fight," said the German. "Give me good game."

Adam joined him at his end of the table. "I wonder if you could help me with something," he said.

"Your backhand?" said the young man.

"No, thank you," said Adam. "I just need a paragraph of German translated." He handed over the middle paragraph of the letter. Once again, the would-be translator looked puzzled.

"It's from a book, so it may seem out of context," Adam added.

"Okay, I try." As the boy began to study the paragraph, the girl who had already translated the first section came into the game room. She made her way toward them.

"This hard to make out. I am not good translation for," the young man said. "My girlfriend better, I think. I ask her. *Liebling, kannst du dies für den Herrn ins Englische Übersetzen*?"

Without looking at Adam, he passed the second paragraph over to the girl, who immediately said, "I knew there was more."

"No, no, don't bother," said Adam, and grabbed the piece of paper away from the girl. He turned back to the boy and said, "Thank you for the game. Sorry to have bothered you," and walked hurriedly out into the corridor, heading for the front door.

"Did you find 'im, sir?"

"Find him?" said Adam.

"Hans Kramer," said the porter.

"Oh, yes, thank you," said Adam. As he turned to leave, he saw the young boy and his girlfriend following close behind.

Adam ran down the drive and hailed a passing taxi.

"Where to?" said the cabbie.

"The Royal Lancaster Hotel."

As the cab moved off, Adam peered out of the back window to see his table-tennis opponent in conversation with the porter. The girl stood alongside them, pointing at the taxi.

Adam relaxed when the cab turned the corner and they were out of sight. In less than a minute the taxi had drawn up outside the Royal Lancaster. Adam checked his watch: twelve thirty. Enough time for lunch before going on to his interview with the Foreign Office.

As he headed for a pub Adam recalled the table-tennis match. Damn, he thought. I should have thrashed him. At least that would have given him something else to think about.

ROMANOV'S EYE RAN DOWN THE list of fourteen banks. There was still an outside chance that one of them might be in possession of the czar's icon, but the names meant nothing to him. He knew he would now have to seek advice from an expert.

He unlocked the top drawer of his desk and consulted the red book held only by the most senior-ranking officers in the KGB. He dialed a number and asked to be put through to Aleksei Andreyevich Poskonov, the chairman of Gosbank, the Soviet Union's central state bank. It was some time before another voice came on the line. "Comrade Romanov, what can I do for you?"

"I urgently need to see you," said Romanov.

"Really?" The gravelly tones on the other end of the line sounded distinctly unimpressed. Romanov could hear pages being flicked over. "I could manage Tuesday, say eleven thirty?"

"I said it was urgent," repeated Romanov.

"We are the nation's bankers and do have one or two problems of our own, you might be surprised to hear," came back the unrepentant voice. "Well, I suppose I could fit you in at three forty-five today, for fifteen minutes." The phone went dead.

Romanov began to write down the questions he needed answered. He couldn't afford to waste even a minute of his fifteen. An hour later he asked to see the chairman of the KGB. This time he was not kept waiting.

"Trying to play the capitalists at their own game, are we?" said Zaborski, once Romanov had outlined his intentions. "Be careful. They've been at it a lot longer than we have."

"I realize that," said Romanov. "But if the icon is in the West, I have little choice but to use their methods to get my hands on it."

"Perhaps," said the chairman. "Don't worry, I'll give you all the backing you need—although I've never had a request quite like this one before."

"Am I allowed to know why the icon is so important?"

The chairman of the KGB frowned. "I do not have the authority to answer that question, but as Comrade Brezhnev's lack of enthusiasm for the arts is well known, you must have been able to work out that it is not the painting itself that we are after." He rose from his desk, walked over to the wall, and tore a page from the calendar. "And we've only eleven days left to find the thing."

At three forty-five precisely, Romanov was ushered into Poskonov's office. The young KGB major was momentarily taken aback by the opulence of the room: the red velvet curtains, the marble floor, the delicate French furniture. He was reminded not for the first time that money still remained the most important commodity in the world—even in the Communist world. He stared at the old, stooped man, with the thinning gray hair and bushy walrus mustache, who controlled the nation's money.

"What can I do for you, Comrade Romanov?" inquired the banker with a sigh, as if addressing a tiresome customer.

"I require one hundred million American dollars' worth of gold bullion immediately," Romanov announced evenly.

The chairman's bored expression suddenly changed. He took several short, sharp breaths before pulling open a drawer, taking out a square box, and extracting a large white pill from it. It took fully a minute before he seemed calm again.

"Have you gone out of your mind, comrade?" the old man said. "You ask for an appointment, then charge into my office and demand one hundred million American dollars in gold. For what reason do you make such a preposterous suggestion?"

"That is the business of the state," said Romanov. "But since you have inquired, I intend to deposit equal amounts in a series of numbered accounts across Switzerland."

"And on whose authority do you make such a request?" the banker asked in a level tone.

"The General Secretary of the party."

Without another word Poskonov rose from behind his desk and walked around to Romanov's side. He ushered the young man into a comfortable chair below a bay window on the far side of the room and took the seat opposite him.

"I knew your grandfather," he said in a calm, matter-of-fact tone. "I was a junior commodity clerk when I first met him. I had just left school, and he was very kind to me, but he was just as impatient as you are."

Romanov laughed. He had never known his grandfather, and the few books that referred to him had long ago been destroyed. His father talked openly of his wealth and position, which had only given the authorities ammunition to destroy him.

"You'll forgive my curiosity, Major, but if I am to hand over one hundred million dollars in gold, I should like to know what it is to be spent on. I thought only the CIA put in chits for those sorts of expenses without explanation."

Romanov laughed again and explained to the chairman of Gosbank how they had discovered the czar's icon was a fake and how he had been set the task of recovering the original. When he had completed his story he handed over the names of the fourteen banks. The banker studied the list closely while Romanov outlined the course of action he proposed to take.

There was an exasperated grunt from the other chair when Romanov had finished. "Let me see if I understand your requirements," the old man said, pausing to light a cigarette. "Now, you suspect that lodged in one of these fourteen Swiss banks"—he tapped the list with his index finger—"is the original czar's icon. You therefore want me to deposit large amounts of gold with each bank, in the hope that it will give you immediate access to the chairman. You will then offer the chairmen the chance to control the entire hundred million—if they promise to cooperate?"

"Yes," said Romanov. "Bribery is surely something the West has always understood."

"How much do you imagine is a lot of money to a major Swiss bank?"

Romanov considered. "Ten million, twenty million?"

"To the Moscow Narodny Bank, perhaps," said Poskonov. "But every one of the banks you hope to deal with will have several customers with deposits of over a hundred million each. No, we must approach the problem from a different standpoint. You do not catch a poacher by offering him rabbit stew."

"But if the Swiss are not moved by the offer of vast amounts of money, what *will* move them?"

"The simple suggestion that their bank has been used for criminal activity," said the chairman. "Let me explain. Why not tell each of the fourteen banks that, after extensive research, we have reason to believe that one of the nation's most valuable treasures has been deposited in their bank? And rather than cause a diplomatic incident—the one thing every Swiss banker wishes to avoid at any cost—perhaps they would consider checking in their vaults items that have not been claimed for over twenty years."

Romanov looked straight at the old man, realizing why he had survived several purges. "I owe you an apology, comrade."

"We each have our own little skills. Now, if you will allow me to contact each of the chairmen on this list and tell them no more than the truth—namely that I suspect the czar's icon is in *their* bank—most of them will be disinclined to hold on to the masterpiece if they believe that in so doing a crime is being perpetrated against a sovereign state."

"I cannot overstress the urgency," said Romanov.

"Just like your grandfather," Poskonov said. "So be it. I shall speak to every one of them. Be assured I shall be in touch with you the moment I have any news."

"Thank you," said Romanov, rising to leave. "You have been most helpful."

The chairman of Gosbank closed the door behind him. I couldn't have supplied you with the one hundred million in gold bullion anyway, he thought to himself. I doubt if I have ten million dollars' worth of gold left in the vaults. The General Secretary has already ordered me to fly every available ounce to the Bank of New York. Of course, the CIA was informed about the deposit within an hour of its arrival. It's hard to hide over seven hundred million dollars in gold, even in America. The chairman returned to his desk and began to phone the fourteen banks.

ADAM headed past the Hyde Park Hotel toward the Royal Thames Yacht Club. It seemed a strange place for the Foreign Office to hold an interview, but so far everything connected with the application had been somewhat mysterious.

He arrived a few minutes early and waited for the elevator. The doors opened immediately and Adam stepped in. A rather overweight, bespectacled man of roughly his own age joined him. Neither man spoke on the journey up to the sixth floor. The large man stepped out of the elevator in front of Adam.

"Wainwright's the name," he informed the receptionist.

"Yes, sir," said the girl. "You're a little early, but do have a seat." Then her eyes moved on to Adam, and she smiled.

"Scott," he informed her.

"Could you join the other gentleman?" she said. "They will be seeing you next." Adam went over and settled down next to Wainwright, who was already filling in the *Telegraph* crossword.

Adam took a more careful look at Wainwright. "Do you by any chance speak German?" he asked him suddenly.

"German, French, Italian, and Spanish," Wainwright replied somewhat smugly.

"Then perhaps you could translate a paragraph from a German letter for me?"

"Delighted, old fellow." He waited as Adam extracted the middle paragraph of the letter from his envelope.

"Now let me see," Wainwright said, taking the little slip of paper. "Quite a challenge. I say, old fellow, you're not part of the interviewing team by any chance?"

"No, no," said Adam, smiling. "I'm in the same position as you—except I don't speak German, French, Italian, or Spanish."

Wainwright seemed to relax. "Now let me see," he repeated as Adam took the small notebook from his inside pocket. " 'During the year you cannot have failed to . . . notice that I have been receiving from one of the guards a regular . . . regular supply,' " he said. "Yes, 'supply of Havana cigars. One of the few pleasures I have been allocated.' No, 'allowed'; better still, 'permitted—despite my . . . incarceration.' That's the nearest I can get," Wainwright added. " 'The cigars themselves have also served another purpose,' " Wainwright continued, obviously enjoying himself. " 'One contained a capsule . . .' "

"Mr. Scott, the board will see you now," said the receptionist.

"Do you want me to finish it off while they're finishing you off, old chap?" said Wainwright.

"Thank you," Adam replied. "If it's not too much trouble."

"Far easier than the crossword," Wainwright added, leaving on one side the little half-filled matrix of squares.

WHILE Alex Romanov waited impatiently for the results of Poskonov's inquiries, he reread the research papers and checked any new intelligence sent in by his agents.

Then the chairman of the bank called.

On this occasion Romanov was driven straight over to Gosbank and ushered up to the finely furnished room without a moment's delay. "You must have wondered if I had forgotten you," were Poskonov's opening words as he guided Romanov to the comfortable chair. "But I wanted to have some positive news to give you rather than waste your time," he added.

A secretary entered the room and placed two empty glasses, a frosted flask, and a plate of caviar in front of them.

Romanov waited in silence.

"I have managed to talk to the chairmen of twelve of the banks on your list," Poskonov began as he poured the vodka. "It will please you to know that they have agreed to cooperate with us. Five have in fact already phoned back. Four to say they have run a thorough check but have come up with nothing that remotely resembles an icon."

"And the fifth?" inquired Romanov.

"Now that, I suspect, may be our first breakthrough," continued Poskonov, referring to the file in front of him. "Herr Dieter Bischoff, of Bischoff et Cie, an honorable man whom I have dealt with many times in the past, has come up with something that was left with the bank in 1938. It is unquestionably an icon, but he has no way of knowing if it is the one we are looking for."

Romanov leaped up from his seat in excitement. "Then I had better go and see for myself," he said. "I could fly out today."

The bank chairman waved him back into his chair. "The plane you require does not leave Sheremetyevo Airport until four thirty-five. In any case I have already booked two seats on it for you."

"Two?" inquired Romanov.

"You will obviously need an expert to accompany you, unless you know considerably more about icons than you do about banking," Poskonov added. "I took the liberty of booking you on the Swissair flight. One should never fly Aeroflot if it can be avoided. It has managed only one aviation record, namely that of losing the most passengers per mile flown. I have fixed an appointment for you to see Herr Bischoff at ten o'clock tomorrow morning."

Romanov smiled.

"I note from your file that you have never served in Switzerland, so may I also recommend," said the old man, showing off, "that you stay at the St. Gotthard while you are in Zurich. And that brings my little investigation up to date. All I can do now is wish you luck."

"Thank you," said Romanov. "May I be permitted to add how much I appreciate your thoroughness."

"My pleasure, comrade. Let's just say that I still owe your grandfather a favor, and perhaps one day you will find you owe me one, and leave it at that."

Romanov tried in vain to fathom the meaning of the old man's words as he descended the wide marble staircase.

WHEN Romanov returned to Dzerzhinsky Square he went to see the chairman of the KGB to brief him on his meeting with the head of Gosbank.

"Thank heaven," said Zaborski. "With only nine days left, at least you've given me something to discuss with the General Secretary when he calls. He has taken to phoning me at one o'clock every morning. Let us fervently hope that you will soon be able to return the masterpiece to the walls of the Winter Palace."

"If it is in that bank, it will soon be in your hands," said Romanov.

When he walked into his own office he found Petrova waiting for him. "You called for me, comrade?"

"Yes. We're going to Zurich." Romanov looked at his watch. "In three hours' time."

5

WHEN Adam emerged from the interview he felt quietly confident. The interviewer's final words had been to ask him if he would be available for a physical shortly. In the waiting room, Wainwright looked up and handed over his piece of paper.

"Thank you very much," said Adam, trying to look casual by slipping it into his inside pocket without looking at the results.

"What was it like, old chap?" his companion asked cautiously.

"No trouble for a man who has German, French, Spanish, and Italian as part of his armory," Adam assured him. "Best of luck."

Adam took the elevator to the ground floor and decided to walk home, stopping at the corner to buy a bag of apples from a pushcart. Farther on, he came to a sudden halt. What had attracted his attention was a sign that read THE GERMAN FOOD CENTRE. An attractive girl with a cheerful smile and laughing eyes was sitting at the cash register by the doorway. Adam strode into the shop and went straight over to her.

"I wondered," he asked her, "do you speak German?"

"Most girls from Mainz do," she replied, grinning.

"Yes, I suppose they would," said Adam, looking at the girl more carefully. She must have been in her early twenties. Her shiny dark hair was done up in a ponytail, with a big red bow, and her white sweater and neat pleated skirt would have made any man take a second look. "I wonder if you would be kind enough to translate a short paragraph for me?"

"I try," she said, still smiling.

Adam took the envelope containing the final section of the letter out of his pocket and handed it over to her.

"The style is a bit old-fashioned," she said, looking serious. "It may take a little time."

"I'll go and do some shopping," he told her, and started walking slowly around the long, stacked shelves. He selected a little salami, frankfurters, bacon, and some German mustard, looking up now and then to see how the girl was progressing. She was continually interrupted by customers, and nearly twenty minutes passed before he saw her stop writing and put the piece of paper to one side. Adam immediately went over to the cash register and placed his purchases on the counter.

"One pound two shillings," she said. Adam handed over two pounds, and she returned his change and the little piece of paper. "This is a rough translation, but I think the meaning is clear."

"I don't know how to thank you," said Adam.

"You could invite me to share your frankfurters." She laughed.

"What a nice idea," said Adam. "Why don't you join me for dinner tonight?"

"I was not serious," she said.

"I was," said Adam, smiling. He grabbed a leaflet from the counter, scribbled down his name, address, and phone number, then handed the leaflet to her.

"What's this?" the girl asked innocently.

"I've put my name and address on the center page," Adam said. "I will expect you for dinner at about eight this evening."

She looked at the leaflet and laughed. "I'll think about it."

Adam strolled out onto the road, whistling. Once he was back at the flat, he put the food into the refrigerator and went into his bedroom to assemble the full text of the Göring letter. He took out his notepad and began to copy out the translations in order: first the paragraph supplied by the girl from the YMCA, then Wainwright's handwritten words from the notepad, and finally the section of the letter translated by the lovely girl from Mainz. He read the completed draft through slowly.

Nuremberg
October 14, 1946

Dear Colonel Scott,

Over the past year we have come to know each other quite well. You have never disguised your distaste for the National Socialist Party, but you have at all times behaved with the courtesy of an officer and a gentleman.

During the year you cannot have failed to notice that I have been receiving from one of the guards a regular supply of Havana cigars—one of the few pleasures I have been permitted, despite my incarceration. The cigars themselves have also served another purpose. One contained a capsule with a small amount of poison, enough to ensure that I shall cheat the executioner.

My only regret is that you, as the officer in charge of the watch, may be held responsible for something to which you were never a party. To make amends for this, I enclose a document in the name of one Emmanuel Rosenbaum, which should help with any financial difficulties you face in the near future.

All that will be required of you . . .

"Anyone at home?" Lawrence shouted. Adam collected the pieces of paper, walked quickly over to the bookcase, and inserted them alongside the other documents in the Bible, seconds before Lawrence put his head around the door.

They headed for the kitchen, where Adam started removing food from the refrigerator. "Who's coming to dinner?" asked Lawrence as each new delicacy appeared.

"A rather attractive German girl, I hope," said Adam.

"What do you mean, 'hope'?"

"Well, it could hardly have been described as a formal invitation, so I'm not certain she'll turn up."

"If that's the situation, I'll hang around in case you need someone to help you eat that lot. How did you meet your *Fräulein?*"

"She was working at a food store in Knightsbridge. I have no idea what she is, or even what her name is, come to think of it," said Adam. "But I am hoping to find out tonight."

When eight o'clock chimed, the table was set and Adam had everything ready on the boil. By eight thirty both of them stopped pretending, and Adam served up two plates of frankfurters, salami, and lettuce, with a baked potato and sauerkraut. As Lawrence began pouring the wine there was a loud knock on the front door. The two men stared at each other before Adam leaped up to open it. Standing in the doorway was a man well over six feet, with shoulders like a professional bouncer's. By his side, dwarfed by him, was the girl Adam had invited to dinner.

"This is my brother, Jochen," she explained. Adam was immediately struck by how beautiful she looked in a dark blue patterned blouse and pleated blue skirt that fell just below the knee. Her long dark hair, now hanging loose, shone even under the forty-watt light bulb that hung in the hall.

"Welcome," said Adam, more than a little taken aback.

"Jochen is just dropping me off."

"Yes, of course," said Adam. "Do come in, Jochen."

"No, I thank you. I have a date as well, but I will pick up Heidi at eleven o'clock, if all right by you?"

"Fine by me," said Adam, at last learning her name.

The giant bent down and kissed his sister on both cheeks. He then shook hands with Adam before leaving them both.

"I am sorry to be late," said Heidi.

"It was no problem," said Adam, leading her into the flat. "By the way, this is my flatmate, Lawrence Pemberton."

"In England the men also need a chaperon?" said Heidi.

Both men laughed. "No, no," said Lawrence. "I was just on my way out. As you can see, the table is only laid for two. I'll be back around eleven, Adam, just to make sure you're safe." He smiled at Heidi, put on his coat, and closed the door behind him.

"So I *am* going to eat my own sausages, after all," she said, laughing. And the laughter didn't stop for the rest of the evening as Adam learned about Heidi's life in Germany.

"My parents only allow me to come to England for a holiday job because my brother is already in London. It is to help my languages course at the university in Mainz."

"So how long will you be here?" Adam found himself asking.

"Another two months," she said. "If I can stand the job."

"I hope you stay the full two months," said Adam.

"So do I," she replied.

When Jochen arrived back punctually at eleven he found them doing the dishes. "Thank you for a most interesting evening," Heidi said to Adam.

"Not a good word," reprimanded Jochen. "Lovely, happy, delightful, enjoyable, perhaps, but not interesting."

"It was all those things," said Adam, "but it was also interesting. May I come and buy some more sausages tomorrow?"

"I would like that," said Heidi, smiling. "By the way, you never tell me why you needed the strange paragraph translated. I have been wondering who is this Rosenbaum and what it is he left to someone."

"Next time perhaps," said Adam, looking a little embarrassed.

After Heidi had left, Adam sat down and finished off the last glass of wine, aware that he hadn't spent such a lovely, happy, delightful, enjoyable, and interesting evening for a long time.

IT WAS already dark when the black limousine drew up outside the St. Gotthard Hotel in Zurich. The only words Romanov spoke to the driver were, "I shall return to Moscow on the Tuesday morning flight."

Jacques Pontin, the manager of the hotel, was stationed at the door, waiting to greet the new arrivals, Major Romanov and Anna Petrova. He introduced himself immediately, and as soon as he had checked them in, he banged a little bell to summon a porter.

"Suite seventy-three," Jacques instructed the porter before turning back to Romanov. "I do hope your stay here in Zurich will prove to be worthwhile, Herr Romanov," he said. "Please do not hesitate to call upon me if there is anything you need."

On the seventh floor, the porter led the way down a long corridor to a corner suite. He turned the key in the lock. The suite was, as Romanov had expected, in a different league from the finest hotels in either Moscow or Leningrad.

"Your room is through there, madame," the porter informed the researcher, and unlocked an adjoining door. Although smaller in size, the room maintained the same unassuming elegance. The porter gave a slight bow and, closing the door behind him, left Romanov to unpack, while Anna Petrova went to her room.

By the time Romanov had undressed, he could hear the shower beating down in the adjoining bathroom. He crept over to the door and edged it open. He smiled, noiselessly moved across the thick carpet, and slipped into the bed.

Adam stepped out of the freezing shower. Within minutes he had dressed and joined Lawrence in the kitchen for breakfast.

"Sorry to rush off before you've had your cornflakes," said Lawrence, picking up his briefcase.

Left on his own, Adam boiled himself an egg and burned some toast. At this rate, he decided, he wasn't going to win the *Daily Mail's* Housewife of the Year competition. He eventually cleared away in the kitchen, made his bed, and then settled down at his desk to consider how to get the official document translated without arousing further suspicion.

Almost absentmindedly he removed the Bible from the bookshelf and extracted the letter. The final paragraph still puzzled him. He considered Heidi's translation once again.

> All that will be required of you is to present yourself at the address printed on the top right-hand corner of the enclosed document, with some proof that you are Colonel Gerald Scott. A passport should prove sufficient. You will then be given a bequest that I have left to you, in the name of Emmanuel Rosenbaum. I hope it will bring you good fortune.

Adam turned his attention back to the document. He was still quite unable to discern what the bequest could possibly be, let alone whether it was of any value.

Romanov hailed a passing taxi. "Bischoff et Cie," he said as he waited for Petrova to join him. They had left the hotel by a circuitous route in order to avoid the CIA agent Romanov had spotted in the dining room at breakfast.

The cab wound in and out of the morning traffic until it came to a halt in front of a large brown granite building. Romanov walked up to the imposing doors, which were made of thick glass and covered in welded wrought iron. By the side of the doors, carved into the stone and inlaid with gilt, were the words Bischoff et Cie.

Romanov turned the heavy wrought-iron knob, and the two Russians stepped into a spacious hall. To their left a smartly dressed young man was seated behind a solitary desk.

"Good morning," said Romanov. "We have an appointment with Herr Dieter Bischoff."

"Yes, Herr Romanov," said the receptionist, checking the list of names in front of him. He directed the Russians to the fifth floor, where a secretary escorted them to a reception room that looked as if it belonged in an elegant country house.

"Herr Bischoff will be with you in a moment," she said, withdrawing. The room was dominated by a magnificent oval Louis Quatorze table, with eight carved mahogany chairs. Romanov felt a twinge of envy at the thought that he could never hope to live in such style.

The door opened, and a man in his mid-sixties, followed by three other men in dark gray suits, entered the room.

"What an honor for our little bank, Mr. Romanov," were Bischoff's first words as he bowed and shook the Russian's hand. Romanov nodded and introduced his assistant, who received the same courteous bow and handshake. "May I in turn present my son and two of my partners, Herr Müller and Herr Weizkopf." The three men bowed in unison but remained standing while Bischoff took his seat at the head of the table. At his gesture Romanov and Anna sat down beside him.

"I wonder if I might be permitted to check your passport?" asked Bischoff. Romanov took out the little blue passport from his inside pocket and handed it over. Bischoff studied it closely and decided it was mint. "Thank you," he said as he returned it.

Bischoff raised his hand, and his son left them. "It will only take a moment for my son to fetch the icon," he confided. "Meanwhile, perhaps some coffee—Russian," he added.

"Thank you," said Petrova, clearly a little overawed. Romanov didn't speak again until Herr Bischoff's son reappeared with a small box and handed it over to his father.

"You understand," the old man confided, "the icon may not turn out to be the one your government is searching for."

"I understand," said Romanov.

"This magnificent example of Russian art has been in our possession since 1938 and was deposited with the bank on behalf of a Mr. Emmanuel Rosenbaum."

Both visitors looked shocked. "*Nevozmozhno*," said Anna, turning to her master. "He would never . . ."

"I suspect that's exactly why the name was chosen," Romanov said curtly to Anna, annoyed at her indiscretion. "May I see the icon now?" he went on, turning back to the bank's chairman.

Herr Bischoff placed the box in the center of the table. The three men in gray suits took a pace forward. "Under Swiss law we must have three witnesses when opening a box in someone else's name," explained the old man.

Romanov nodded.

Herr Bischoff proceeded to unlock the metal box with a key he produced from his pocket, while his son leaned over and undid a second lock with a different key. The little ceremony completed, Herr Bischoff pushed up the lid of the box and turned it around to face his guests. Romanov reached into the box and drew out the icon. The painting he held in his hand was quite magnificent. A small wooden rectangle that was covered in tiny pieces of red, gold, and blue, making up the mosaic of a man who looked as if he had all the worries of the world on his shoulders. The face, although sad, evoked a feeling of serenity.

It was Anna who finally spoke. "A masterpiece it is," she said, "and undoubtedly fifteenth century, but it's not Saint George and the dragon. It is the icon of Saint Peter. You see, he holds the keys. . . . Painted by Dionisy in 1471. It is not the czar's icon."

"But does it belong to the Russian people?" asked Romanov, still hopeful of some reward for all his trouble.

"No, Comrade Major," said the researcher emphatically. "It

belongs in Munich, from where it has been missing since the day Hitler was appointed Reichschancellor."

Herr Bischoff scribbled a note on a piece of paper in front of him. At least one bank in Munich was going to be happy to do business with him in the future.

Romanov reluctantly handed back the icon to Herr Bischoff, only just managing to say, "Thank you."

"Not at all," said Herr Bischoff, replacing the icon in the box and turning his key in his lock. His son completed the same routine with his own key and then departed with the unclaimed treasure. Romanov rose from the meeting. At least he had discovered Göring's alias—or one of them.

"Herr Romanov, I wonder if I might be permitted to have a word with you," asked the elderly banker. "It is rather a delicate matter, so perhaps you might prefer your associate to leave us."

"That won't be necessary," said Romanov, unable to think of anything Bischoff might have to say that he wouldn't later need to discuss with Petrova.

"As you wish," said Bischoff. "But I felt perhaps I knew the real reason you had selected this bank in particular to start your inquiry."

"I didn't select you," said Romanov. "You were only one of—" He stopped himself.

"I see," said Bischoff, looking bemused. "Then may I be permitted to ask you a few questions?"

"Yes, if you must," said Romanov, now impatient to get away.

"You are Aleksandr Petrovich Romanov, the son of Pëtr Nikolaevich Romanov?"

"Yes."

"And grandson of Count Nikolai Aleksandrovich Romanov?"

"Is this to be a lesson on my family tree?" asked Romanov, making his irritation visible.

"No. I just wanted to be sure of my facts," said Bischoff. He glanced quickly at Anna before continuing. "You are your father's only surviving child?"

"I am," confirmed Romanov.

"In which case this bank is in possession . . ." Bischoff hesitated as a file was put in front of him by one of the men in gray. He placed a pair of gold half-moon spectacles on his nose, taking as long as he could over the little exercise.

"Don't say anything more," said Romanov quietly.

Bischoff looked up. Petrova was sitting on the edge of her seat, enjoying every moment of the unfolding drama. She was disappointed when Romanov turned to her. "You will wait outside," he said. Petrova pouted and left reluctantly.

When he was certain the door was closed, Bischoff slid the file across the table. Romanov opened it gingerly. On the top of the first page was his grandfather's name. Below were printed row upon row of incomprehensible figures.

"I think you will find that we have carried out your grandfather's instructions in maintaining a conservative portfolio of investments with his funds."

"What does this figure at the bottom represent?" asked Romanov.

"The total value of your stocks, bonds, and cash at nine o'clock this morning. It has been updated every Monday since your grandfather opened an account with this bank in 1916."

Romanov was speechless.

"We are also in possession of several boxes, which your father deposited with us soon after the war. He assured me that he would return, but we never heard from him again. We were saddened to learn of his death. You might prefer, in the circumstances, to return and investigate the boxes at another time."

"Yes," said Romanov. "Perhaps I could come back this afternoon?"

"The bank will always be at your service, Your Excellency," replied Herr Bischoff.

No one had addressed a Romanov by this title since the Revolution. The Russian sat in silence for some time.

When Romanov and his companion left the bank he was still so overcome by what he had learned that he failed to notice that the man he had so deftly avoided at the hotel was now standing in a streetcar line on the far side of the road.

IT WAS a stark room, dominated by a wooden table and several wooden chairs. A small black crucifix was the only ornament on the whitewashed walls. Adam sat bolt upright while the man of God, clad in a black cassock, stared down at the copy of the document. When he had heard Adam's request he had invited the young man into the privacy of his little office at the back of the German Lutheran church.

After some considerable time, without raising his eyes, the pastor offered, "This is a receipt, if I am not mistaken. Roget et Cie, who must be Swiss bankers based in Geneva, have in their possession an object described herein as 'the czar's icon.' It appears," he continued, his eyes still fixed on the document, "that if the holder of this receipt presents himself in Geneva, he will be able to claim the aforementioned icon of Saint George and the dragon, deposited there by a Mr. Emmanuel Rosenbaum in 1938. I confess," said the pastor, looking up for the first time, "that I've never seen anything like it before." He handed the document back to Adam.

"Thank you," said Adam. "That has been most helpful. Do you happen to know if icons are at all valuable?"

"I am not the best man from whom to seek an opinion. No doubt the art auctioneers Sotheby's or Christie's could help you."

"I'll pay them a visit next," said Adam as he rose from his chair. "You have been most kind."

"Not at all," said the pastor. "I was only too pleased to assist you. It makes a change from Frau Gerber's marital problems and the size of the deacon's squashes."

ADAM took a bus up to Hyde Park Corner and walked briskly down Piccadilly toward the Ritz. He had read somewhere that Sotheby's was on Bond Street. As he passed Gucci, Cartier, and Asprey he was beginning to wonder if his memory had failed him, but finally he spotted the gold lettering on the far side of the road.

He crossed the street and entered the front door of the building. He felt like a boy on his first day at school, unsure of his surroundings, as he walked along to the reception area.

"May I help you, sir?" asked a girl behind the counter.

"I need some advice concerning an icon," began Adam.

"Have you brought the piece with you, sir?"

"No. It's still abroad at the moment."

"Do you have any details? Artist's name, date, size? Or better still, do you have a photograph of the piece?"

"No," said Adam sheepishly. "I only know its title. But I do have some documentation," he added, handing over the receipt he had shown the pastor.

"Not a lot to go on," said the girl, studying the German transcript. "But I'll ask Mr. Sedgwick, the head of our Russian and Greek icon department, if he can help you."

"Thank you," said Adam, and while he waited for Mr. Sedgwick he studied several photos of items that had come under the auctioneer's hammer in recent sales.

"My name is Sedgwick," announced a donnish voice behind him. Adam turned to face a tall, cadaverous figure with a ginger mustache. His suit hung on him as if from a coat hanger.

"Scott," said Adam, offering his hand.

"Well, Mr. Scott, why don't we sit over here, and then you can let me know how I can help you."

"I'm not sure you can," admitted Adam, taking the seat opposite him. "It's just that I have been left an icon in a will, and I was hoping it might turn out to be valuable."

"A good start," said Sedgwick, unfolding a pair of spectacles he had removed from his top pocket. "Now, am I to understand you do not have a photograph of this particular icon?"

"That's right," said Adam. "To be honest, I've never laid eyes on it. All I know is that it is known as the czar's icon, and the subject is Saint George and the dragon."

"How strange," said Sedgwick. "Someone else was inquiring after that particular painting only last week, but he wouldn't leave his name."

"Someone else wanted to know about the czar's icon?"

"Yes. A Russian gentleman, if I wasn't mistaken." Sedgwick tapped his glasses on his knee. "He wondered if it had ever passed through our hands. I was able to explain to him that the great work by Rublev remains in the Winter Palace for all to see. One can always be certain that it's an original from the Winter Palace, because the czar's silver crown will be embedded in the back of the frame. Do you have any documentation on your icon?" Sedgwick inquired.

"I have a copy of the receipt that was left to me in the will," said Adam, and handed it over.

Mr. Sedgwick studied the paper. "Excellent, quite excellent," he said eventually. "It seems to me that a copy of the czar's icon, painted by the court painter of the time, belongs to you. But you will have to go and pick it up yourself, that's for certain."

"But is it worth all that trouble?" asked Adam. "Can you give me any idea of its value?"

"Hard to be precise without actually seeing it," Sedgwick said.

"So what is the lowest figure I might expect to get for it?"

The older man frowned. "Ten," he said after considerable thought. "Perhaps fifteen, but with an absolute top of twenty."

"Twenty pounds," said Adam, unable to hide his disappointment. "I'm sorry to have wasted your time, Mr. Sedgwick."

"No, no, no, Mr. Scott. You misunderstand me. I meant twenty *thousand* pounds."

6

"A LITTLE more caviar, comrade?" inquired Petrova across the lunch table.

Romanov frowned. His excuse about "strictly confidential information only to be passed on at the highest level" had merely elicited a knowing smile from his companion, who also did not believe that her boss's pressing appointment was at the consulate that afternoon.

Anna held out a spoon brimming with caviar and pushed it toward Romanov, as if to feed a reluctant baby.

"Thank you—*no*," said Romanov firmly. He called for the bill. "I'll see you back in the hotel later."

"Of course," said Petrova, still lingering over her coffee. "What time shall I expect you?"

Romanov frowned again. "Not before seven," he replied. He paid the bill and left the table without further word.

By three o'clock he was once again seated in the private room of Bischoff et Cie, with Herr Bischoff sitting opposite him and his son standing behind him.

"We are in possession of five boxes, which have remained unopened since your father visited us in 1945," began Herr Bischoff. "Should it be your desire to inspect the contents . . ."

"Why else would I have returned?" asked Romanov, already made impatient by the measured voice and studied ritual.

"Indeed," said Herr Bischoff, seemingly unaware of any discourtesy. "Then all we require is that you sign a disclaimer. It is only a formality." He slid a paper across the table. There were over twenty clauses of German in small print. Romanov scrawled his signature between the two X's. He made no attempt to discover what he was signing. If they hadn't stolen his grandfather's heritage already, why should they be bothering to try now?

"Perhaps you will be kind enough to accompany me," said Herr Bischoff, quickly passing the paper to his son, who left immediately. Then he rose and led Romanov silently back to the corridor. But on this occasion they traveled down in the chairman's private elevator all the way to the basement.

When the doors opened, Romanov might have thought they had entered a jail had the bars not been made of highly polished steel. A man seated behind a desk on the far side of the bars jumped up and with a long-shafted key turned the lock on the steel door. Romanov followed Herr Bischoff through the open door, then waited until they were both locked inside. The guard preceded them down a corridor, not unlike that of a wine cellar, with temperature and humidity gauges every few yards.

At the end of the corridor they found Herr Bischoff's son waiting in front of a vast circular steel door. The old man nodded, and the younger Herr Bischoff placed a key in a lock and turned it. Then the chairman stepped forward and undid a second lock. Father and son pushed open the nine-inch-thick door, but neither made any attempt to enter the vault.

"You are in possession of five boxes. Numbers seventeen twenty-one through seventeen twenty-five." Herr Bischoff removed a small envelope from his pocket and added, "The key inside this will open all five boxes." Romanov took the envelope and turned toward the open cavern.

"Once we have left," said the old man, "we shall pull the door closed. When you require it to be opened, you have only to press the red button on the side wall to alert us. But I must warn you that at five o'clock the vault locks automatically, and it cannot be reopened until nine the following morning. A warning alarm will sound at four forty-five." Romanov checked the clock on the wall: three seventeen. The two Herr Bischoffs bowed and left.

Romanov waited impatiently for the vast door to close behind him. Alone in Aladdin's cave, he looked around the room and estimated there were two or three thousand safes lining the four walls. He suspected there was more private wealth in that one vault than most countries on earth could call on.

He checked the numbers of his own boxes, three small ones above two large ones, and decided to start with one of the small boxes. It was full of papers. He flicked through them, to find they were deeds to many large tracts of land in Bohemia and Bulgaria—once worth millions, now controlled by the Socialist state. In the second box he discovered the bond certificates of companies once managed by his grandfather. The last time they had declared a profit was in 1914. He cursed as he moved on to the third box, which contained only one document, his grandfather's will. It meant that he was the lawful owner of everything—and nothing.

Dismayed, Romanov knelt down to study the two larger boxes, each of which looked big enough to hold a cello. He hesitated before placing the key in one of the locks, turning it, and pulling out the vast container. It was empty. He could only presume that it had been that way for over twenty years. He quickly unlocked the fifth box and in desperation pulled it open.

The box was split into twelve equal compartments. He raised the lid of the first compartment and stared down in wonder. Before him lay precious stones of such size, variety, and color that they would have made anyone who was not royal gasp.

It took Romanov a further hour to go through the contents of the remaining eleven compartments. When he reached the last one—almost an anticlimax, in that it contained nothing but gold coins—he felt thoroughly exhausted. He checked the clock on the wall: four thirty. He began to replace the lids on each of the compartments, but during the treasure hunt he had come across one object of such magnificence that he could not resist removing it. He paused as he held up a heavy solid-gold chain, which was weighted by a medallion that hung from it. On one side was an engraved picture of his grandfather—Count Nikolai Aleksandrovich Romanov—while on the other was a profile of his grand-

mother, so beautiful that she surely could have worn any of the jewelry in that treasure trove with distinction.

Romanov slipped the chain over his head and tucked the medallion under his shirt. When he had replaced the lid on the last compartment he slid the box back into place and locked it.

His mind turned to Poskonov. Had the old banker known all along, or was it a coincidence that Poskonov had sent him to this bank first? Members of his profession didn't survive if they believed in coincidence.

A false move, and the state would not hesitate to send him to the same grave as his father and grandfather. He would have to be at his most skillful when he next came into contact with the old banker, otherwise he might not live to choose between power in his homeland and wealth in the West.

"After I have found the czar's icon, I will return," he said quite audibly. Suddenly the alarm bell rang out. He was surprised at how much time he had spent in the locked room. He walked toward the vault door and pressed the red button. The great door swung open to reveal two anxious-looking Herr Bischoffs.

"We were beginning to get worried about the time," said the old man. "I hope you found everything to your satisfaction."

"Entirely," said Romanov. "But what happens if I am unable to return for some considerable time?"

"It's of no importance," Herr Bischoff replied. "The boxes will not be touched again until you come back."

"What temperature are they kept at?"

"Fifty degrees Fahrenheit," said Herr Bischoff, somewhat puzzled by the question.

"Are they airtight?"

"Certainly," replied the banker. "They are hermetically sealed. And anything left in them is safe from any investigation."

"Excellent," said Romanov. "There is a possibility that I shall return tomorrow morning with a package of my own to deposit."

"CAN you put me through to Mr. Pemberton?" said Adam.

There was a long pause. "We don't have a Mr. Pemberton working here, sir."

"That is Barclays Bank International, isn't it?"

"Yes, sir."

"Mr. Lawrence Pemberton. I know I've got the right branch."

The silence was even longer this time. "Ah, yes," came the eventual reply. "Now I see which department he works in. I'll see if he's in." Adam heard a phone ringing in the background.

"He doesn't seem to be at his desk at the moment, sir. Would you like to leave a message?"

"No, thank you," said Adam, and replaced the receiver. He sat thinking. If he was to carry through the idea, he needed some information that Lawrence as a banker should find easy to supply.

A key turned in the door, and Lawrence entered the flat. "How does one open a Swiss bank account?" were Adam's first words.

"Well," said Lawrence, looking at him in surprise, "anyone can open a Swiss bank account as long as they have a worthwhile sum to deposit. And by that I mean at least ten thousand pounds."

"And how would you go about getting the money out?"

"That can be done over the phone or in person. Few customers, however, would risk the phone, unless they're resident in a country where there are no tax laws to break."

"What would someone need to do if they had inherited money in a Swiss açcount?"

"They would have to prove that they were the person entitled to inherit the deposit. That's not a problem if you're in possession of the correct documentation, such as a will and proof of identity."

"So, if I were entitled to a million pounds' worth of gold in a Swiss bank, left to me by an Argentinean uncle, and I was in possession of the right legal documents to prove I was the beneficiary, all I would have to do is go and claim it?"

"Nothing to stop you," said Lawrence. "Although under the law as it currently stands, you would have to bring it back to this country and sell the gold to the Bank of England for the sum they deem correct, and then pay death duty on that sum."

"Thanks for the information," said Adam, and he disappeared into the bedroom.

The pieces of the jigsaw were beginning to fit into place. All he needed was a copy of the will to show that the Roget et Cie receipt had been left to him. He could then prove that he was the owner of a worthless—or priceless—copy of the czar's icon.

When Romanov returned to the hotel he found Petrova in her room, sitting in a corner reading. "I hope you had a fruitful afternoon?" she inquired politely.

"I did, my little one. Why don't we have a quiet supper in my room, so I can tell you all about it while we celebrate in style?"

"What a magnificent idea," said the researcher. She dropped her book and began to concentrate on the extensive à la carte menu on the bedside table.

Romanov was impressed when their banquet finally appeared. Anna had chosen as an appetizer slivers of gravlax edged with dill sauce. Accompanying it was a half bottle of *premier cru* Chablis. Between mouthfuls Romanov told her of his family inheritance, and as he described each new treasure the researcher's eyes grew larger and larger.

Romanov's monologue was only once interrupted, by a waiter who wheeled in a trolley on which sat a rack of lamb surrounded by zucchini and tiny new potatoes. To accompany this particular dish, the hotel had provided a Gevrey-Chambertin.

The final course, a fluffy raspberry soufflé, required in the researcher's view the finest Château d'Yquem, but it only made her lapse into singing Russian folk songs, which Romanov felt, given the circumstances, was somewhat inappropriate.

After she drained her glass, he suggested it might be time for them to go to bed, as they had to catch the first flight back to Moscow the following morning. He wheeled the trolley out into the corridor and placed a DO NOT DISTURB sign over the doorknob.

"A memorable evening," said the researcher, smiling as she flicked off her shoes. Then Romanov unbuttoned his shirt, and she let out a gasp of surprise. "It's magnificent," she said in awe.

Romanov held up the medallion. "A bauble, compared with the treasures I left behind," he assured her.

"Comrade lover," Anna said in a childlike voice, pulling him toward the bed, "do you realize how much I adore you?"

"Um," said Romanov.

"Well, if that gold chain is nothing more than a mere bauble, perhaps you might allow me to wear it occasionally?"

"Why not permanently, my darling?" said Romanov, and without another word he removed the gold chain from around his neck and placed it over the young woman's head. Anna sighed as she fingered the thick chain, which Romanov didn't let go of.

"You're hurting me, Alex," she said with a little laugh. "Please let go." But Romanov only pulled the chain a little tighter. "I can't breathe properly," gasped the researcher. "Please stop teasing." Romanov continued to tighten the chain around her throat.

"You wouldn't tell anyone about the windfall, would you, my little one?"

"No, never, Alex. No one. You can rely on me," she said, choking.

"Can I feel certain?" he asked.

"Yes, yes, of course. Please stop now," she piped, her delicate hands now clutching desperately at his blond hair. Romanov merely continued to twist the chain tighter and tighter. "I'm sure you understand that I must be absolutely certain that you wouldn't share our secret—with anyone," he explained to her. But she did not hear his plea, because the vertebrae in her neck had already snapped.

On his run along the Embankment on Monday morning Adam mulled over the task that still needed to be carried out.

If he took the morning flight out of Heathrow on Wednesday, he could be back in London by the same evening, or Thursday at the latest. But there were still several things that had to be completed before he could leave for Geneva.

He stopped on the pavement outside his block and checked his pulse before climbing the stairs to the flat.

"Three letters for you," said Lawrence. "Mind you," he added as his flatmate joined him in the kitchen, "two of them are in buff envelopes." Adam picked up the letters and left them on the end of his bed en route to the shower.

Once he was dressed, he opened the letters. He began with the white one, which turned out to be a note from Heidi, thanking him for dinner and hoping she would see him again soon. He smiled and tore open the first of the buff envelopes, which was from the Foreign Office. He was requested to attend a physical at 122 Harley Street at three o'clock the following Monday.

Finally he opened the other buff envelope and pulled out a

letter from his bank on Pall Mall, informing him that they were in receipt of a check for five hundred pounds from Holbrooke, Holbrooke and Gascoigne. This covered an overdraft he had run up, and left his account in credit to the sum of £272.18.4d.

He rejoined Lawrence, asking, "So what are you up to today?"

"I shouldn't let you in on this," said Lawrence, "but the governor of the Bank of England wants my views on whether we should devalue the pound from two eighty to two forty."

"And what are your views?"

"I've already explained to the fellow that the only two forty I know is the bus that runs between Golder's Green and Edgware, and if I don't get a move on, I'll miss my own," he said. Adam laughed as he watched his friend disappear out the door.

Lawrence had changed considerably over the years since he had left school. He had seemed so serious in those days, and certainly destined for greater things. No one would have thought it possible that he would end up as an investment analyst at Barclays. At Oxford, contemporaries half joked about his being a cabinet minister. Was it possible that one expected too much of those idols who were a couple of years older than oneself?

Adam fried himself an egg and a couple of rashers of bacon, then sat down to scribble a note to his sister, enclosing a check for fifty pounds. At nine thirty he made a phone call. Mr. Holbrooke sounded surprised by his request but agreed to put a copy of his father's will in the post immediately.

Adam's other requirements could not be carried out over the phone, so he locked up the flat and went to catch a bus. His first stop was at his bank, where he joined a line at the foreign exchange counter.

"I would like fifty pounds in Swiss francs, fifty pounds in cash, and a hundred pounds in traveler's checks, please," said Adam when he finally reached the front.

The girl entered some calculations on a large desktop machine. The transaction would leave Adam with about twenty pounds in his account, once his sister presented her check. He began to hope that the Foreign Office paid by the week; otherwise it would have to be another frugal month. Unless of course . . .

Adam signed the traveler's checks in the cashier's presence, and she handed over the Swiss francs and the fifty pounds in cash.

Another bus journey took Adam to the British European Airways office, where he asked the girl to book him a round-trip ticket to Geneva. "Economy," said Adam.

"That will be thirty-one pounds, please, sir." Adam paid in cash and returned to the flat for a light lunch. During the afternoon he called Heidi, who agreed to join him for dinner at the Chelsea Kitchen at eight o'clock.

Romanov awoke to the ringing of the phone. "Yes," he said.

"Good morning, Comrade Romanov. It's Melinac, the second secretary at the embassy."

"Good morning, comrade. What can I do for you?"

"It's about Comrade Petrova. Have you come across the girl since you reported her missing?"

"No," replied Romanov. "And she didn't sleep in her bed last night."

"I see," said the second secretary. "Then your suspicions that she might have defected are beginning to look serious."

"I fear so," said Romanov. "And I shall make a full report to my superiors in Moscow, pointing out that you have done everything possible to assist me with this problem, Comrade Second Secretary."

"Thank you, Comrade Major."

"And brief me the moment you come up with any information that might lead us to where she is."

"Of course, Comrade Major."

Romanov replaced the phone and walked across to the bathroom adjoining Anna's room. He stared down at the body hunched up in the tub. After locking the door, he went into his own bathroom for an unusually long shower.

He then ordered breakfast, which arrived fifteen minutes later. Once he had finished the orange juice and croissants, he returned to the phone to call Jacques Pontin, the hotel manager.

"Good morning, Herr Romanov."

"I have a delicate problem that I was hoping you might be able to help me with. I am in possession of a rather valuable object that I wish to deposit with my bank, and I wouldn't want . . ."

"I understand your dilemma entirely," said the manager. "How can I be of assistance?"

"I require a large container in which to place the object."

"Would a laundry basket be large enough?"

"Ideal, but does it have a secure lid?"

"Oh, yes," replied Jacques. "We often have to drop them down laundry chutes."

"Perfect," said Romanov.

"Then it will be with you in a moment," said Jacques. "I shall send a porter to assist you. May I suggest that it be taken down in the freight elevator, thus ensuring that no one will see you leave. Will a car be calling to collect you?"

"No," said Romanov. "I—"

"Then I shall arrange for a taxi to be waiting. When will you require it?"

"In half an hour. Perhaps you would be good enough to have my account prepared so that there will be no holdup."

"Certainly, Herr Romanov."

Romanov put the phone down, wishing he could export such service to Moscow. Next, he made two local calls. As he replaced the phone, there was a gentle tap on the door. Romanov went to answer it. A young porter stood in the corridor, a large laundry basket by his side. "Please return as soon as the taxi has arrived," said Romanov, pulling in the basket. The porter bowed slightly and left. Romanov locked the door. He wheeled the laundry basket into Petrova's bedroom, undid the leather straps, and threw open the lid. Then he went into the bathroom, lifted Petrova's body in his arms, and crammed it into the basket.

Romanov then gathered the researcher's belongings and tossed them into the basket. Once he had removed the gold medallion from around her neck, he covered up the body with a hotel bath towel and sprayed it with a liberal amount of Chanel No. 5 that had been left, courtesy of the hotel. Finally he strapped the lid down securely, wheeled the creaking basket back into his room, and left it by the door.

Romanov began to pack his own suitcase. There was a knock just as he finished, and he opened the door.

The porter entered, nodded to him, and began to tug at the

laundry basket, but it took a firm shove from Romanov's foot before it got moving. The porter sweated his way down the corridor as Romanov walked by the side of the basket, carrying his suitcase. When they reached the rear of the hotel Romanov watched as the basket was wheeled safely into the freight elevator, before he stepped in himself.

When the ground-floor doors opened, Romanov was relieved to be greeted by the hotel manager. Waiting outside was a large Mercedes with its trunk already open. The taxi driver and the porter lifted up the laundry basket and placed it in the trunk.

"I do hope everything has worked out to your satisfaction," said Jacques as he held open the back door of the Mercedes for his departing guest.

"Entirely," said Romanov.

"Good, good. And will your young colleague be joining you?"

"No, she won't. She has already gone ahead to the airport."

"Of course," said Jacques. "I am sorry to have missed her. Do please pass on my best wishes."

"I certainly will," said Romanov. With that, he slipped into the back seat, leaving Jacques to close the door behind him.

Romanov checked his suitcase at the Swissair office and then asked to be driven to Bischoff et Cie. Herr Bischoff's son, accompanied by another man, was waiting in the hall to greet him. "How pleasant to see you again so soon," he volunteered.

The taxi driver waited by the open trunk while Herr Bischoff's companion, a heavily built man of at least six feet four, lifted out the laundry basket as if it were a sponge cake. Romanov paid the fare and followed Herr Bischoff into the elevator.

"We have fully prepared for your deposit, following your phone call," said Herr Bischoff. "My father was only sorry not to be present personally. He had a long-standing engagement and hopes you will understand." Romanov waved his hand.

The elevator traveled to the basement, where the guard unlocked the massive steel cage. Romanov and young Herr Bischoff proceeded at a leisurely pace down the corridor, while the giant carried the basket in their wake.

Standing by the vault door was another of the Bischoff et Cie partners. Without a word the partner placed his key in the top lock. Herr Bischoff then turned the second lock, and together they pushed open the great steel door. The giant placed the laundry basket on the floor beside Romanov's five boxes.

"Will you require any assistance?" asked Herr Bischoff as he handed the Russian the key in his personal sealed envelope.

"No, thank you," Romanov assured him. He did not relax until he had seen the vast door close behind him, and all of the Swiss helpers were left invisibly on the other side.

He stared down at the one large box he knew to be empty; it was smaller than he had recalled. Beads of sweat appeared on his forehead as he unlocked it, pulled it out, and raised the lid. It was going to be a tight fit. Romanov unstrapped the laundry basket, lifted the researcher up, and dropped her into the box. He stuffed the girl's belongings down the sides of her body, leaving only the Chanel-covered towel behind in the laundry basket.

He replaced the lid on the airtight box before pushing it securely into place and locking it. Satisfied, he strapped down the lid of the laundry basket and wheeled it back to the entrance of the vault. He pressed the little red button.

"I do hope you found everything in order," said the young Herr Bischoff once the door had opened.

"Yes, thank you," said Romanov. "But would it be possible for someone to return the laundry basket to the St. Gotthard Hotel?"

"Of course," said the banker.

"And I can be assured that the boxes will not be touched in my absence?" he asked as they walked down the corridor.

"Naturally, Your Excellency," said Herr Bischoff, looking somewhat aggrieved at such a suggestion. "When you return," he continued, "you will find everything exactly as you left it."

Well, not exactly, Romanov thought to himself.

When they reached the entrance to the bank the young Herr Bischoff bowed. "We shall look forward to seeing you again when you are next in Zurich, Your Excellency," he said.

"Thank you," said Romanov, who shook hands with the young man and walked out onto the pavement, to find the anonymous black car waiting to take him to the airport.

He cursed. This time he did spot the agent, standing by the streetcar line on the far side of the road.

The chairman of the KGB studied the report on the desk in front of him. Something didn't ring true. He looked up at Romanov. "Your reason for visiting Bischoff et Cie was because they claimed to be in possession of a fifteenth-century icon that might have fitted the description of the one we are searching for?"

"That is correct, Comrade Chairman."

"But the icon turned out to be of Saint Peter, and not of Saint George and the dragon."

"Also confirmed by Comrade Petrova in her report."

"Ah, yes, Comrade Petrova," said Zaborski, his eyes returning to the file. "And later that evening Comrade Petrova mysteriously failed to keep an appointment with you?"

"Inexplicably," said Romanov. "When she did not turn up by breakfast I went to her room, to find all her personal belongings were gone."

"Which convinced you she had defected."

"Yes, sir," said Romanov.

"But the Swiss police can find no trace of her," said Zaborski. "So I keep asking myself, Why would she defect? Her immediate family lives in Moscow. They are all employed by the state. And it is not as if this were Comrade Petrova's first visit to the West."

Romanov didn't offer an opinion.

"Perhaps Petrova disappeared because she might have been able to tell us something you didn't want us to hear."

Romanov felt a shiver of fear as he wondered how much Zaborski really knew. "Perhaps," Zaborski went on, "she could tell us why you felt it necessary to go to Bischoff et Cie a second time." He paused. "I think I may have to open an inquiry into the disappearance of Comrade Petrova. Because, Comrade Romanov, by the time you went to the bank a third time, every second-rate spy from here to Istanbul knew we were searching for something."

Romanov remained silent. He began to feel confident that Zaborski was only guessing. If he had suspected the truth, the interview would have taken place in the basement, where a less intellectual approach would have been carried out.

Zaborski now rose from his chair. "The General Secretary informed me that he is not impressed by your latest efforts. All he is interested in, however, is finding the czar's icon, and so for the time being, comrade, he has decided there will be no investigation. But if you ever act in such an irresponsible way again, it will not be an inquiry you are facing, but a tribunal, and we all know what happened to the last Romanov who faced a tribunal. Do I make myself clear, comrade?" he barked.

"Very clear, Comrade Chairman," said Romanov, and turning smartly on his heel, he quickly left the room.

The chairman of the KGB waited for the door to close before his eyes settled back on the file. What was Romanov up to? He flicked down a switch on the little console by his side. "Find Major Valchek," he ordered.

"I'VE never actually had champagne and caviar," admitted Adam as he looked up at the beautiful girl who sat opposite him in the restaurant.

"Well, don't get frightened, because I can't imagine caviar will ever find its place on this particular menu," teased Heidi. "But perhaps soon, when you are the proud owner of the czar's icon, that is, if Mr. Rosenbaum—"

Adam put a finger to his lips. "No one else knows about that, not even Lawrence."

"That may be wise," Heidi whispered. "He will only expect you to invest all the money from the sale in his boring bank."

"Funnily enough," said Adam, "the one time I rang Lawrence at the bank, the operator couldn't immediately locate him."

"What's so surprising about that?" asked Heidi.

"It was as if they had never heard of him," replied Adam.

"A bank that size must have over a thousand employees. You could go years without knowing everyone who worked there."

"I suppose you're right," Adam said as the waiter cleared their table and placed two coffees in front of them.

"When do you plan on going to Geneva?" Heidi asked.

"Early Wednesday morning. I hope to be back that evening."

"Not very romantic of you to choose my one day off to fly away," she said.

"Then why not come with me?" he asked, leaning across the table to take her hand.

"That might be more significant than sharing your sausages."

"I would hope so, and you could be most useful. I don't speak German or French, and I've never been to Switzerland other than on a school skiing trip—and then I kept falling over."

Heidi sipped her coffee. "The Swiss speak perfect English," she said eventually, "and should you have any problem with the bank, you can always get in touch with Lawrence."

"It would only be for the day," said Adam. "Think about it."

"You really mean it, don't you?" Heidi sounded serious for the first time. "I'll come—on one condition. If the icon turns out to be worthless, you will let me refund the price of my ticket."

"I agree to your terms," said Adam. He leaned over and kissed Heidi on the lips. "Perhaps it will take more than one day," he added. "Then what would you say?"

"I would demand separate hotels . . ." replied Heidi, "if it wasn't for the high cost of the Swiss franc."

"How was Zurich?" the banker asked as he lit a cigarette.

"Like a Polish tractor. The bits that worked were fine," replied Romanov. He wondered if Poskonov's doctor realized how much the old man smoked.

"From that I assume the bits that didn't work failed to produce the czar's icon," Poskonov said.

"Correct. But Bischoff turned out to be most helpful. My every need was catered to."

"Good man, Bischoff," said the banker. "That's why I sent you to him first."

Romanov studied the old man carefully, looking for a hint that he knew exactly what had been awaiting him at the bank. "Was there any other reason you sent me to him first?" he asked.

"Lots of other reasons," said Poskonov, "but we'll not bother with them now. I've outlived two generations of Romanovs, and I wouldn't want to outlive a third. I'm sure we can come to an understanding after you have found your icon."

Romanov nodded.

"Well, you will be pleased to learn that I have not been idle in your absence." The banker waved Romanov to a seat before he reopened his file. "Originally," he began, "you presented me with a list of fourteen banks, twelve of which have now confirmed that they are not in possession of the czar's icon. But the other two have refused to cooperate in any way."

"Why is it your influence does not extend to them?"

"The most obvious of reasons," replied Poskonov. "Other interests exert a stronger influence. That being the case, there is a chance that one of these two banks is in possession of the icon you seek. As they are never going to admit as much to Mother Russia, I am not sure what I can recommend you do next."

The banker sat back and waited for Romanov to take in this news. "You are unusually silent," he ventured after he had lit another cigarette.

"You have given me an idea," said Romanov. "I think the Americans would describe it as a long shot."

"I suspect you will need this, whatever your long shot," Poskonov said as he removed a piece of paper from his file and handed it to Romanov. On it were the words Daumier et Cie, Zurich (refused); Roget et Cie, Geneva (refused).

"No doubt you will be returning to Switzerland very soon," Poskonov observed. "I wouldn't recommend you visit Bischoff et Cie on this trip, Alex. There will be time for that in the future."

Romanov stared at the banker.

The old man returned his look. "Just remember, you won't find me as easy to get rid of as Anna Petrova," he added.

7

The elderly-looking man took his place at the back of the taxi line on the Zurich street. It was hard to estimate his height, because he looked so bent and frail. His large overcoat reached almost to the ground, and the fingers peeping through the sleeves were covered in gray woolen mittens. A hand clung to a little leather suitcase bearing the initials E.R.

One would have had to bend down or be very short to see the old man's face—a face that was dominated by a nose that would have flattered Cyrano de Bergerac's. He shuffled forward slowly until it was his turn to climb into a taxi. In guttural tones he told the driver he wanted to be taken to the bankers Daumier et Cie.

When the old man arrived at his destination he took time

sorting out which coins to pay with, then pushed himself slowly onto the pavement and stood gazing at the marble building. Once inside, he shuffled over to the girl behind the reception desk and said in stilted German, "I have come to see Herr Daumier. My name is Emmanuel Rosenbaum."

"Herr Daumier is in conference at the moment," said the girl, "but I will find out if another partner is available to see you."

The old man sank into a chair. He was unable to hide his surprise at the age of the boy who eventually appeared. "I am Wilfried Praeger," he said.

"Sit down, sit down," said Mr. Rosenbaum. "I cannot stare up at you for so long." The young partner complied.

"My name is Emmanuel Rosenbaum. I left a package with you in 1938, and I have returned to collect it."

"Do you have any proof of your identity, or any documentation from the bank?"

"Oh, yes," came back the reply, and the old man handed over his passport and a receipt that had been folded and unfolded so many times it was now almost in pieces.

The young man studied both documents carefully. He recognized the Israeli passport immediately. Everything seemed to be in order. He led Mr. Rosenbaum to a large and comfortably furnished room, and within minutes returned with Herr Daumier. "I don't think we have ever met, Herr Rosenbaum," said the chairman courteously. "You must have dealt with my father."

"No, no," said Mr. Rosenbaum. "I dealt with your grandfather Helmut. I saw your father only on the one occasion and was sad to learn of his premature death."

A look of respect came into Herr Daumier's eyes. "I wonder if you have any proof of identity other than your passport?" he asked politely.

Emmanuel Rosenbaum raised his head and, giving Herr Daumier a tired look, turned his wrist so that it faced upward. The number 712910 was tattooed along the inside.

"I apologize," said Daumier, visibly embarrassed. "It will take me only a few minutes to bring your box up."

The two men left Rosenbaum alone. They returned a few minutes later with a flat box about two feet square and placed it on the table. Herr Daumier unlocked the top lock while the other partner acted as a witness. He then handed over a key to Rosenbaum, saying, "We will now leave you, sir. Just press the button underneath the table when you wish us to return."

"Thank you," said Rosenbaum, and waited for the door to close behind them. He turned the key in the lock and pushed up the lid. Inside was a package about eighteen by twelve inches, covered in muslin and tied securely. Rosenbaum put it carefully into his old suitcase. He pressed the button under the table, and within seconds Herr Daumier and the junior partner returned.

"I do hope everything was as you left it, Herr Rosenbaum," said the chairman. "It has been some considerable time."

"Yes, thank you." The old gentleman managed a nod.

"May I mention a matter of no great consequence?" asked Herr Daumier. "Do you intend to continue the use of the box? Because the funds you left to cover the cost have recently run out."

"No. I have no need for it any longer."

"It's just that there was a small charge outstanding. But in the circumstances, Herr Rosenbaum, we are happy to waive it."

"You are most kind."

Herr Daumier bowed, and the junior partner accompanied their client to the front door, helped him into a taxi, and instructed the driver to take Mr. Rosenbaum to Zurich Airport.

At the airport, the old man was pleased to find that the passenger lounge was almost empty. He shuffled over toward the corner and collapsed onto a comfortable sofa. He checked to be sure he was out of sight of the other passengers in the lounge.

He opened the old suitcase and pulled out the parcel. His fingers wrestled with the knots for some time before they became loose. He then removed the muslin to check his prize. Mr. Rosenbaum stared down at the masterpiece *Man Gathering in Corn* by van Gogh—which he had no way of knowing had been missing from a Vienna museum since 1938.

Emmanuel Rosenbaum swore, which was out of character. He packed the picture safely up and returned it to his case. He then shuffled over to the girl at the Swissair sales desk and asked her to book him on the first available flight to Geneva. With luck, he could still reach Roget et Cie before they closed.

The BEA Viscount landed at the Geneva airport at eleven twenty-five, local time. A light drizzle was falling. Adam unbuttoned his raincoat and attempted to shelter Heidi beneath it as they ran across the tarmac to the immigration hall.

"Good thing I remembered this," he said to her. "It's my old army trench coat. It can hold maps, compasses, even an overnight kit."

Heidi laughed. "We're just going to a bank in Geneva, not out on military maneuvers."

The airport bus took only twenty minutes to reach the center of Geneva and the magnificent lake nestled in the mountains. The bus came to a halt opposite the massive single-spouting fountain that shot over four hundred feet into the air.

They stepped out of the bus, pleased to find the light rain had stopped. "First we must find our bank, so that we can have lunch nearby before going to pick up the booty," said Adam.

"How does a military man go about such a demanding exercise?" asked Heidi.

"Simple. We drop in at the first bank we see and ask them to direct us to Roget et Cie."

"Let's put your plan of campaign into action," Heidi said, pointing to the Banque Populaire on the far side of the avenue.

When they had crossed the road Heidi inquired of the doorman the way to Roget et Cie. They followed his directions, but the bank was not that easy to pinpoint. Finally Heidi spotted the discreet sign beside a high wrought-iron-and-plate-glass door.

"Looks impressive," said Adam. "Even when it's closed for lunch."

As the sun was trying to find gaps between the clouds they found a pavement café overlooking the lake. Both selected a cheese salad, and they shared a half bottle of white wine. Adam was enjoying Heidi's company so much that he began to tell her stories of his army days. She had to stop him and point out that it was nearly two. He reluctantly called for the bill.

When they had returned to the entrance of the bank Adam pushed open the heavy door and stared around the gloomy hall. "Over there," said Heidi, pointing to a woman who was seated behind a desk.

"Good afternoon. My name is Adam Scott. I have come to collect something that has been left to me in a will."

The woman smiled. "Have you made an appointment with anyone in particular?" she asked.

"No," said Adam. "I didn't realize that I had to."

The lady picked up a phone and held a short conversation in French. Then she asked them both to go to the fourth floor.

As they walked out of the elevator Adam was surprised to be met by someone his own age.

"Good afternoon. My name is Pierre Neffe, and I am a partner of the bank," said the young man in perfect English. He led them to an exquisitely furnished room. "Now, how can I help you?"

"My father," began Adam, "died last month and left me in his will a receipt for something I think you have had in your safe-keeping since 1938. It was a gift given to him by one of your customers." Adam hesitated. "A Mr. Emmanuel Rosenbaum."

"Do you have any documentation relating to this gift?" inquired Monsieur Neffe.

"Oh, yes," said Adam, digging into one of the deep pockets of his trench coat. He passed the Roget et Cie receipt to the young banker. Monsieur Neffe studied it and nodded. "May I be permitted to see your passport, Monsieur Scott?"

"Certainly," said Adam, delving back into his trench coat and passing it to Monsieur Neffe.

"If you will excuse me for one moment." Monsieur Neffe rose and left them on their own.

"What do you imagine they are up to now?" said Heidi.

"Checking if my receipt is authentic, I expect; 1938 was rather a long time ago."

As the minutes ticked by, Adam started to feel disappointed, then depressed, and finally began to believe it was all going to be a complete waste of time. Then Monsieur Neffe reappeared with another banker, whom he introduced as Monsieur Roget.

"Good afternoon," said Monsieur Roget, shaking hands with Adam and Heidi. "We have on file a letter from Monsieur Rosenbaum giving clear instructions that the box is not to be opened by any other than"—he looked at the piece of paper he had brought with him—"Colonel Gerald Scott, D.S.O., O.B.E., M.C."

"My father," said Adam. "But as I explained to Mr. Neffe, he died last month and left me the gift in his will."

"I would be happy to accept what you say," said Monsieur Roget, "if I might see the death certificate and the will itself."

Adam smiled at his own foresight and once more searched in his trench coat, before removing a large brown envelope. He took out copies of his father's death certificate, the will, and a letter marked "To Whom It May Concern," and passed them to Monsieur Roget, who read all three documents slowly. Monsieur Roget then spoke to Monsieur Neffe, who swiftly left the room, only to return a minute later and whisper in his chairman's ear.

Monsieur Roget said to Adam, "We have encountered one small problem, Monsieur Scott."

"And what is that?" asked Adam nervously.

"Monsieur Rosenbaum's account is one hundred and twenty francs in debit. That is the charge for housing the box over the past two years, since the deposit ran out. The bank's rule is that an overdraft must be cleared before any box can be opened."

Adam breathed a sigh of relief. He took out his wallet, signed a traveler's check, and handed it over.

"And finally," said Monsieur Roget, "we will need you to sign a form of indemnity for the bank."

Monsieur Roget passed over a long form containing clause after clause in tightly printed French, at which Adam only glanced before passing it over to Heidi. She studied each clause carefully and nodded her agreement.

Adam signed on the dotted line with a flourish.

"Excellent," said the banker. "All we have to do now is go and retrieve your box."

"I suppose it could be empty," said Adam once the two of them were left alone again.

"And it could be packed with gold doubloons," said Heidi.

When both men returned a few minutes later, Monsieur Neffe was carrying a flat metal box, about twelve by nine inches, and some three inches deep.

Adam was disappointed by its modest size but didn't show his feelings. Monsieur Roget proceeded to undo the top lock with the bank's key and then handed Adam a small, faded envelope with signatures scrawled across the waxed seal. "Whatever is in the box belongs to you, Monsieur Scott. When you have finished, perhaps you would be kind enough to let us know. Until then we shall remain outside in the corridor." Both men left the room.

"Come on," said Heidi. "I can't wait."

Adam opened the envelope, and a key fell out. He fumbled with the lock, which clicked, and then at last he pushed up the lid. Inside was a small, flat package, wrapped in muslin and tied with string. The knots took some untying, and then finally an impatient Adam tore off the string, before slowly removing the muslin. They both stared at the masterpiece in disbelief.

The beauty of the golds, reds, and blues left them speechless. Neither of them had expected the icon to be so breathtaking—Saint George towering over the dragon, a massive sword in hand, on the point of plunging it into the heart of the beast.

"It's magnificent," said Heidi, eventually finding her voice.

"I wish my father had seen it. Perhaps it would have changed his whole life."

"Don't forget he wanted it to change yours," said Heidi.

Adam finally turned the icon over, to find on the back a small silver crown inlaid in the wood. He stared at it, trying to recall what Mr. Sedgwick of Sotheby's had said that proved.

Heidi checked to see that there was nothing else inside the box. She then flicked down the lid, and Adam locked it with his key. He tucked the muslin around the masterpiece, tied it up firmly, and zipped the little painting into his trench-coat pocket.

Adam walked over to the door and opened it. The two bankers returned. "I hope you found what you had been promised," said Monsieur Roget.

"Yes, indeed," said Adam. "But I shall have no further need of the box," he added, returning the key.

"As you wish," said Monsieur Roget. "If you will excuse me, I will now take my leave of you. Monsieur Neffe will show you out." He shook hands with Adam and bowed slightly to Heidi.

"I hope that you will enjoy a pleasant stay in our city," said Monsieur Neffe as the elevator took its leisurely pace down.

"It will have to be very quick," said Adam. "We must be back at the airport in just over an hour."

The elevator stopped at the ground floor, and Monsieur Neffe accompanied Adam and Heidi to the entrance. The door was held open for them, but they both stood aside to allow an old man to shuffle past. Although most people would have stared at his nose, Adam was more struck by his penetrating eyes.

When the old man eventually reached the woman at the reception desk he announced, "I have come to see Monsieur Roget. Is he available?"

"What name shall I tell him, sir?"

"Emmanuel Rosenbaum."

The woman picked up the phone. When she had replaced it she asked, "Would you please go up to the fourth floor, Monsieur Rosenbaum?"

He took the elevator, and when he got out, another middle-aged woman accompanied him to the waiting room. He did not have to wait long before a smiling Monsieur Roget appeared, accompanied by Monsieur Neffe.

"How nice to make your acquaintance, Monsieur Rosenbaum, but I'm afraid you have just missed Monsieur Scott."

"Monsieur Scott?" the old man uttered in surprise.

"Yes. He left only a few minutes ago, but we carried out the instructions as per your letter."

"My letter?" said Monsieur Rosenbaum.

"Yes," said the banker, opening for the second time that morning a file that had remained untouched for almost twenty years.

He handed a letter to the old man.

Emmanuel Rosenbaum removed a pair of glasses from his inside pocket, unfolded them slowly, and proceeded to read.

September 12, 1946

Dear M. Roget,

I have left in your safekeeping a small icon of Saint George and the dragon. I am transferring the ownership of that painting to a British army officer, Colonel Gerald Scott, D.S.O., O.B.E., M.C. If Colonel Scott should come to claim the icon at any time, please ensure that he receives my key without delay.

My thanks to you for your help in this matter.

Yours sincerely,
Emmanuel Rosenbaum

"And you say that Colonel Scott came to collect the contents of the box earlier today?"

"No, no, Monsieur Rosenbaum. The colonel died quite recently and left the contents of the box to his son, Adam Scott. Monsieur Neffe and I checked all the documents, and we were left in no doubt that they were in order." The banker hesitated. "I do hope we did the right thing, Monsieur Rosenbaum?"

"You certainly did," said the old man. "I came only to check that my wishes had been carried out."

Monsieur Roget smiled in relief. "I feel I ought also to mention that your account had run into a small deficit. Monsieur Scott dealt with it."

"I am in debt to Monsieur Scott. Are you able to tell me the amount?"

"One hundred and twenty francs," said Monsieur Roget.

"Then I must repay the sum immediately," said the old man. "Do you have an address at which I can contact him?"

"No, I'm sorry," said Monsieur Roget. A hand touched Monsieur Roget's elbow, and Monsieur Neffe whispered in his ear.

"It appears," said Monsieur Roget, "that Monsieur Scott was planning to return to England shortly, because he had to check in at the Geneva airport by five."

The old man lifted himself up. "You have been most helpful, Monsieur Roget, and I will not take up any more of your time."

"It's Flight one seven one, and your seats are fourteen A and B," the man behind the check-in counter told them. "You will be boarding at gate nine in about twenty minutes. Have a good flight," he said, handing over their boarding passes.

Adam and Heidi started walking toward the escalator that would take them to the departure lounge.

"While we're here I must get my mother a box of decent liqueur chocolates," said Adam.

Heidi pointed to a counter that displayed row upon row of ornate boxes. Adam selected a large gold-wrapped box of Swiss chocolates, which the girl behind the counter gift wrapped and placed in a shopping bag. Then he checked his watch. "Not much else we can do except perhaps pick up some duty-free wine."

"I'd like to find a copy of *Der Spiegel.*"

"Fine," said Adam.

"Paging Mr. Adam Scott. Will Adam Scott please return to the BEA desk on the ground floor?" came booming out over the public-address system.

Adam and Heidi stared at each other. "Must have given us the wrong seat allocation, I suppose," said Adam, shrugging.

They returned downstairs and walked over to the man who had handed them their boarding passes. "I think you paged me," said Adam. "My name is Scott."

"Oh, yes. There's an urgent message for you," the man said, reading from a pad in front of him. "Please call Monsieur Roget at Roget et Cie on Geneva 271279." He ripped off the piece of paper and handed it over. "The phones are in the far corner."

"Thank you," said Adam, studying the message.

"I wonder what he can want," said Heidi. "It's a bit late to ask for the icon back."

"Well, I'm going to find out." Adam passed the bag to her. "Hang on to that, and I'll be back in a moment."

"I'll try and pick up my magazine at the same time, if I can find a newsstand on this floor," said Heidi as she gripped the brightly colored bag that contained the chocolates.

"Right. Meet you back here in a couple of minutes."

"Roget et Cie. Est-ce que je peux vous aider?"

"I am returning Monsieur Roget's call," said Adam, making no attempt to answer in French. "This is Adam Scott."

"I'll find out if he's available, sir."

Adam swung around to see if Heidi had returned, but as there was no sign of her, he assumed she must still be looking for a magazine. Then he noticed an old man shuffling across the hall. He could have sworn he had seen him somewhere before.

"Monsieur Scott?"

Hearing his name over the phone, Adam leaned back into the booth. "Yes, Monsieur Roget, I am returning your call."

"Returning my call?" said the banker, sounding puzzled. "I don't understand."

"There was a message left a few minutes ago at the BEA

counter, asking me to telephone you. They said it was urgent."

"There must be some mistake. I didn't leave any message. But now that you have rung, it might interest you to know that just as you were leaving, Monsieur Emmanuel Rosenbaum visited us."

"Emmanuel Rosenbaum?" said Adam. "I assumed he was . . ."

"COULD you assist me, please, young lady?"

Heidi looked up at the old man who had addressed her in English with a strong mid-European accent.

"I am trying to find a taxi and I am already late. I fear my eyesight is not what it used to be."

Heidi replaced the copy of *Der Spiegel* on the shelf. "They're through the double doors in the center. Let me show you."

"How kind," he said. "I hope it's not too much trouble."

"Not at all," said Heidi, taking the old man by the arm and guiding him toward the door marked *"Taxi et Autobus."*

"ARE you sure it was Rosenbaum?" said Adam anxiously.

"I'm certain," replied the banker.

"And he seemed happy about me keeping the icon?"

"Oh, yes. His only concern was to return your hundred and twenty francs. I think he may try and get in touch with you."

"BEA announce the departure of their Flight one seven one to London Heathrow from gate number nine."

"I must go," said Adam. "My plane takes off in a few minutes."

"Have a good flight," said the banker.

"Thank you, Monsieur Roget." Adam replaced the receiver. He turned toward the BEA counter and was surprised to find that Heidi had not yet returned. His eyes began to search the ground floor for a newsstand. Then he spotted her walking out the double doors, helping the old man he had noticed earlier.

Adam quickened his pace. Something didn't feel quite right. When he reached the automatic door he had to check his stride to allow it to slide back. He could now see Heidi standing on the pavement in front of him, opening a taxi door for the old man.

"Heidi," he shouted. The old man suddenly turned, and Adam found himself staring. He could have sworn it was the man he had seen at the bank. "Mr. Rosenbaum?" he questioned. Then, with a

TAXI

movement so fast and powerful it took Adam by surprise, the old man threw Heidi into the back of the taxi, jumped in beside her, and pulled the taxi door closed.

For a moment Adam was stunned, but then he dashed to the side of the taxi, only just managing to touch the handle as it accelerated away from the curb. The car's sudden momentum knocked Adam backward onto the pavement, but not before he saw the petrified look on Heidi's face. He stared at the license plate of the departing car; E-125 was all he could catch, but at least he recognized it was a blue Mercedes.

Desperately he was looking around for another taxi when a Volkswagen Beetle drew up on the far side of the concourse. A woman stepped out of the driver's seat, and a man joined her from the passenger's side. On the curb, the two of them embraced. As they did so, Adam sprinted across the road and, opening the door, leaped inside and slid into the driver's seat. He turned on the ignition, threw the car into reverse, and shot backward. The couple stared at him in bafflement. Adam jerked into first gear and set off at high speed, following signs to the center of Geneva.

He had to concentrate hard on remaining on the right-hand side of the road. He checked the license plate and the passengers of every blue taxi he passed, but there was no sign of Heidi.

Then he saw a Mercedes in the outside lane some considerable distance ahead of him. He pressed the accelerator harder and began to narrow the gap as he tried to fathom why the old man would want to kidnap Heidi in the first place. Could it be Rosenbaum? But he had wanted him to keep the icon, or so the banker had assured him. None of it made sense.

At the next traffic circle only three cars divided Adam from the taxi. "A red light, I need a red light," he shouted, but the first three lights on the approach road into the city remained stubbornly green. When one finally turned red Adam leaped out of the car and started running toward the taxi. But the light changed to green just before he could reach it, and the Mercedes sped away. Adam sprinted back to the Volkswagen. His decision to get out of the car had lost him several crucial seconds, and when he looked anxiously ahead he could only just spot the taxi in the distance.

When they reached the Avenue de France, running parallel

with the west side of the lake, both cars weaved in and out of the traffic until the Mercedes suddenly turned left and climbed up a slight hill. Adam threw his steering wheel over to follow it, and careened up the wrong side of the road, narrowly missing a mail truck meandering down toward him.

The taxi was only a couple of hundred yards ahead when suddenly it swerved into the curbside and screeched to a halt. Adam came to a stop directly behind it. He leaped out of the car and ran toward the parked vehicle. Without warning the old man jumped out of the taxi and sprinted off up a side street, carrying Heidi's airport shopping bag and a small suitcase.

Adam pulled the back door open and stared at Heidi. "Are you all right, are you all right?" he shouted. Heidi did not move. Adam put his arms around her and began to stroke her hair. Her head fell limply onto his shoulder like a rag doll's. Adam felt cold and sick and began to tremble uncontrollably. He looked up at the taxi driver. His body was slumped over the wheel.

Adam refused to accept that they were dead. He kept holding on to Heidi as he stared beyond her. The old man had reached the top of the road.

Why did he still think of him as an old man? He was obviously not old at all, but young and very fit. Suddenly Adam's fear turned to anger. He let go of Heidi and darted up the road after her killer. He moved as fast as he could, but the trench coat slowed him down, and by the time he too had reached the top, the killer was a clear hundred yards ahead of him, weaving his way through the traffic on the main thoroughfare. The man leaped onto a passing streetcar and stood on the steps staring back at Adam. He held up the shopping bag defiantly with one hand. The back was no longer hunched, the figure no longer frail. Adam stopped in the middle of the road, helplessly watching the streetcar as it disappeared from sight.

Behind him he could hear sirens. Ambulances trying to rush to the scene of the accident. Accident, thought Adam. They would soon discover it was murder. He tried to start sorting out in his mind the madness of the last half hour. None of it made sense. He touched the side of his coat pocket and felt the package that held the czar's icon. Why, why, *why* was the icon that important? What had the Sotheby's expert said? "A Russian gentleman had inquired after the piece." Adam's mind began to whirl. If it was Emmanuel Rosenbaum and that was what he had killed for, all he had ended up with was a large box of Swiss liqueur chocolates.

When Adam heard the whistle behind him, he felt relieved that help was at hand, but as he turned, he saw two officers with guns pointed toward him. He started to run, and turned into the first alley he came to. Once beyond it, he selected a one-way street. It was crammed with cars, and he was able swiftly and safely to move in and out of the slow-moving traffic.

In a matter of minutes he had lost the police, but he still ran on, continually switching direction until he felt he had covered at least two miles. He turned into a quiet street and halfway down saw a sign advertising the Hotel Monarche. It didn't look much more than a guesthouse. He stopped in the shadows and waited, taking in great gulps of air. After about three minutes his breathing was back to normal, and he marched into the hotel.

8

EMMANUEL Rosenbaum stood naked, staring at his image in the hotel-room mirror. He didn't like what he saw. First, he removed the teeth. He had been warned that his gums would ache for days. Then painstakingly he shed each layer of his bulbous nose, admiring the skill and artistry that had gone into creating such a monstrosity. It will be too conspicuous, he had told them. They will remember nothing else, had come back the experts' reply.

Next, he began on the lined forehead. As the lines disappeared, so the years receded. Next, the flaccid red cheeks, and finally the two chins. The Swiss bankers would have been amazed at how easily the sharp rubbing of a pumice stone removed the number on the inside of his wrist. Once more he studied himself in the mirror. The hair, short and graying, would take longer to restore.

Moments later he stood under a warm shower, his fingers massaging deep into the roots of his hair. Black treacly water ran down his face and body before finally disappearing down the drain. It took half a bottle of shampoo before his hair had returned to its normal color, if not its normal length.

In a corner of the room lay the long, baggy coat, the shiny, shapeless suit, the black tie, the off-white shirt, the woolen mittens, and the Israeli passport. Hours of preparation discarded in a matter of minutes. His back still ached from all the bending and crouching. He stood up, then touched his toes and threw his arms high above his head fifty times. He rested for one minute before completing fifty sit-ups. He returned to the bathroom and had a second shower—cold. He then changed into a freshly ironed cream silk shirt and a new double-breasted suit.

Before making one phone call to London and two more to Moscow, he ordered dinner sent up so that no one would see him. He had no desire to explain how the man who checked in was thirty years older than the man eating alone in his room. Like a hungry animal, he tore at the steak and gulped the wine.

He stared at the shopping bag but felt no desire to finish off the meal with one of Scott's liqueur chocolates. Once again he felt angry at the thought of the Englishman's getting the better of him.

His eyes then rested on the little leather suitcase that lay by the side of his bed. He opened it and took out the copy of the icon that Zaborski had suggested he should always have with him so that there could be no doubt when he came across the original.

A little after eleven he switched on the late night news. They had no photograph of the suspect, only one of that stupid taxi driver who had driven so slowly it had cost the fool his life, and then they showed the pretty German girl who had tried to fight back. The television announcer said the police were searching for an unnamed Englishman. Although the Swiss police had no photograph of Scott, Romanov didn't need one. It was a face he would never forget. In any case his contact in England, a man code-named Mentor, had already told him a lot more about Captain Scott in one phone call than the Swiss police could hope to discover for another couple of days.

LYING on his hotel bed, Adam tried to make sense of all that had happened. If Göring had left the icon to his father, and Göring's alias had been Emmanuel Rosenbaum, then a real-life Emmanuel Rosenbaum didn't exist. But he *did* exist; he had even killed twice in his attempt to get his hands on the czar's icon.

Adam switched on the bedside light, then pulled the small package out of his trench-coat pocket. He unwrapped it carefully. Saint George stared back at him—no longer looking magnificent, it seemed to Adam, but more accusing. He would have handed the icon over to Rosenbaum without a second thought to save Heidi.

By midnight Adam had decided what had to be done, but he didn't stir from his tiny room until a few minutes after three. Then he lifted himself off the bed, quietly opened the door, and crept noiselessly down the stairs. Outside, he checked up and down the street, then made his way to a phone booth at the corner. He pressed a coin into the box and waited for an operator.

"I want to make a reverse-charge call to London," Adam said.

"Yes," said the operator. "And what is your name?"

"George Cromer," replied Adam.

"And the number you're speaking from?"

"Geneva 271982." He transposed the last three digits. The police could well be listening in on all calls to England that night. He then told the girl the number in London he required.

He could hear the connection being put through. Please wake up, his lips mouthed. At last the ringing stopped, and Adam recognized the familiar voice that answered.

"Who is this?" Lawrence asked, sounding irritated but awake.

"Will you accept a reverse-charge call from a Mr. George Cromer in Geneva?"

"George Cromer? Lord Cromer, the governor of the Bank of Eng—? Yes, I will," he said.

"It's me, Lawrence," said Adam.

"Thank heaven! Where are you?"

"I'm in Geneva, but I'm not sure you're going to believe what I'm about to tell you. While we were waiting to board our plane home a man pulled Heidi into a taxi, and murdered her before I could catch up with them. She's dead, Lawrence. She's dead! And the Swiss police think I'm the killer!"

"Now just relax, Adam. I know that much. It's been on the evening news, and the police have already been around to interview me. It seems Heidi's brother identified you."

"What do you mean *identified* me? I didn't do it! You know I couldn't do it! It was a man called Rosenbaum, not me, Lawrence."

"Rosenbaum? Adam, who is Rosenbaum?"

Adam tried to sound calm. "Heidi and I came to Geneva this morning to pick up a gift from a Swiss bank that Pa had left me in his will. It turned out to be an icon. When we returned to the airport this Rosenbaum grabbed Heidi, thinking she had the icon, which doesn't make any sense, because the thing's only worth twenty thousand pounds."

"Icon?" said Lawrence.

"Yes, an icon of Saint George and the dragon," said Adam. "That's not important. What's important is that—"

"Now listen carefully," interrupted Lawrence, "because I'm not going to repeat myself. Keep out of sight until the morning, and then give yourself up at our consulate. Don't arrive until eleven. London is an hour behind Geneva, and I'll need every minute to see that the consul staff is properly organized."

"But—" began Adam.

"No explanations. Just be at the consulate at eleven."

"Right," said Adam. "And—" But the phone was only giving out a long burr. Thank heaven for Lawrence, he thought; the Lawrence of old. Strange that he didn't need to ask more questions though. It was as if he already knew the answers.

Adam checked the street again, quickly stole back to the hotel, and was in his bed by five minutes past four. He didn't sleep. Rosenbaum, Heidi, the taxi driver, the Russian gentleman who had visited Sotheby's. So many pieces of a jigsaw, none of them fitting into place. But the thing that worried him most was the conversation with Lawrence—the Lawrence of old?

THE two policemen arrived at the Hotel Monarche at twenty past seven that Thursday morning. They were tired, discontent, and hungry. Since midnight they had visited forty-three hotels, without success. They had checked over a thousand registration cards and waked seven innocent Englishmen, who had not come anywhere near fitting the description of Adam Scott. They still had three more hotels to check before they went off duty.

When the landlady saw them coming into the hall she waddled toward them. She loathed the police. Twice in the last year she had been fined and once even threatened with jail over her failure to register every guest. Her slow mind tried to recall who had booked in the previous evening. Eight people had registered, but only two had paid cash: the Englishman—Mr. Pemberton was the name he had filled in on the registration card—and Maurice, who always turned up with a different girl whenever he was in Geneva. She had destroyed both their cards and pocketed the money. Maurice and the girl had left by seven, but the Englishman was still asleep in his room.

"We need to check your registration cards, madame."

"Certainly, monsieur," she replied with a warm smile, and handed over the six remaining cards.

"Did an Englishman stay here last night?"

"No," said the landlady firmly.

"We will need to check your unoccupied rooms. I see from the certificate that there are twelve bedrooms in the hotel," the policeman continued. "So there must be six that are empty."

"There's no one in them," said the landlady.

"We still want to see for ourselves," the other officer insisted.

The landlady picked up her passkey and climbed the stairs, as if they were the final summit of Mount Everest. She opened bedrooms 5, 7, 9, 10, and 11. The old lady knew she would lose her license the moment they entered room 12. She turned the key in the lock. The two policemen walked in while she remained in the corridor, just in case there was trouble.

"Thank you, madame," said the first policeman as he stepped back into the corridor. "We are sorry to have troubled you," he added. He put a tick on his list next to the Hotel Monarche.

As the two policemen made their way downstairs the landlady walked into room number 12, mystified. The bed was undisturbed. "I wonder where he is," she muttered.

For the past hour Adam had been crouching behind a derelict coach in a railway yard less than half a mile from the hotel. He had watched the early morning commuters flooding in on every train. By twenty past eight Adam judged they were at their peak. He checked that the icon was in place and left his hideout to join the crowd as they headed to work. He stopped at a news kiosk to purchase a map of Switzerland with a detailed inset of Geneva.

There were still over two hours before he could present himself at the consulate. In the distance he could see the building he had picked as his next place of sanctuary. He steered a route toward it that allowed him to stay in contact with the largest number of people. His timing was perfect. He reached the front door as hundreds of worshippers were leaving the morning service.

Once inside St. Peter's Cathedral, he felt safe. He made his way down the side aisle toward the Lady chapel, dropped some coins into one of the collection boxes, and lit a candle. He then fell onto his knees, but his eyes never closed. Soon Adam realized there were only a handful of people left in the cathedral. Some old ladies in black filled a front pew, fingering their rosary beads. A few tourists were craning their necks to admire the roof.

Adam rose slowly, his eyes darting from side to side, and took a seat at the end of a pew. He lowered his head and whispered the Lord's Prayer as he opened the map to Geneva and began to study the road plan. He had located the British consulate, on the far side of a large garden square, by the time he reached *Deliver us from evil.* It was just over a mile away from the cathedral. Thirty minutes later Adam rose again and walked quickly down the side aisle behind a party of tourists. They shielded him out the door. He ducked under a shop awning at the side of the road, then crossed the road and headed up a one-way street. Two uniformed policemen came around the corner and walked straight toward him. He jumped into the first shop without looking and turned his back on the pavement.

"Bonjour," said a young lady to Adam. "May I help you?" Lissome dummies in panties and bras stood all around him.

"I'm looking for a present for my wife."

The girl smiled. "Perhaps a slip?" she suggested.

"Yes," said Adam. "A slip. Do you have one in burgundy?" he asked as he half turned to watch the policemen stroll past.

"I think so, but I'll have to check in the stockroom."

Adam had reached the next street corner long before she returned with "just the thing."

He managed the next three crossings without incident, but he could feel his heart thumping. Across the road was the garden square that had only been a tiny green blob on the map. On the far side of it he spotted a Union Jack hanging above a blue door.

He crossed the road and stood on the edge of the small park, fifty yards from safety. A policeman was patrolling the opposite pavement, but Adam suspected that was because there were several consulates standing adjacent to one another. He watched the officer. It took the man two minutes to reach the French consulate before he turned and continued his leisurely walk back. Adam ducked behind a tree in a corner of the park and selected another tree on the far side of the road, only yards from the consulate door, that would shield him from the oncoming policeman. He estimated that by walking at a speed that wouldn't attract attention he could cover the last thirty yards in under ten seconds. He waited for the policeman to reach the farthest point of his beat.

He checked the consulate door again, relieved to see there was no guard in sight. He looked up at the bay window on the first floor and saw two men staring out, as if waiting expectantly for someone to arrive. Lawrence had succeeded. In moments he would be home. Adam set off as the cathedral clock struck eleven. The policeman was now a few paces from the French consulate. Adam crossed the road at a measured stride. When he reached the streetcar tracks in the center he had to stop suddenly to let a car pass by. The policeman turned to start his journey back.

For several seconds Adam remained motionless between the streetcar tracks as he stared at the tree he had selected to hide behind. He took a confident pace toward the consulate. A tall man of athletic build, his head covered in a stubble of short fair hair, stepped out to greet him.

Adam would not have recognized him but for the eyes.

9

Number Ten Downing Street, London
June 16, 1966

WHEN Sir Morris Youngfield left the Prime Minister he still was unable to work out why the possession of any icon could be that important.

Leaving number Ten Downing Street behind him, Sir Morris marched quickly to the Foreign Office. When he walked in, Tessa, his secretary, was sorting out some papers for him.

"I want a D-four committee assembled immediately," he said to the woman who had served him so loyally for fourteen years. "And ask Commander Busch to join the team."

Tessa raised her eyebrows, but Sir Morris ignored her silent comment, as he knew he couldn't get to the bottom of this one without the Americans. Once more he considered the Prime Minister's instructions. Harold Wilson didn't get that many calls from Lyndon Johnson seeking his help. But why a Russian icon of an English saint?

As Romanov moved toward him Adam took a pace backward to allow the streetcar to pass between them. When the streetcar had passed, Adam was no longer to be seen. Romanov snarled at such an amateur trick, sprinted to catch up with the streetcar, and, to the astonishment of the passengers, leaped on. He began checking over the faces row by row.

Adam waited for the streetcar to travel another twenty yards before he emerged from behind a tree on the park side of the road. He swore under his breath. The policeman was now only a few paces from the British consulate. Adam looked back at the streetcar, which had just been passed by another that was heading toward him. To his dismay he saw his adversary leap from one platform to the other with the agility of a gymnast. With the policeman now right outside the consulate door Adam was left with no choice but to turn and sprint back in the direction he had come from. After fifty yards he glanced over his shoulder. Running toward him, the man he knew only as Rosenbaum couldn't have looked less like a helpless old man.

Adam jumped among the cars and buses and dodged pedestrians as he tried to lengthen the distance between them. At the first crossroad he saw a plump lady coming out of a phone booth. He changed direction quickly and leaped into the empty booth. Rosenbaum came hurtling around the corner and was twenty yards past the booth when Adam shot back out and down the road in the opposite direction. He figured he had at least five seconds before Rosenbaum realized what had happened. Adam ducked to the right, mounted three steps, and pushed through some swinging doors. He found himself in front of a small counter, behind which sat a young woman holding a small wad of tickets in her hand.

"Deux francs, monsieur," said the girl. Adam quickly took out two francs and made his way through another set of swinging doors. He stood at the back waiting for his eyes to become accustomed to the dark. It was the first performance of the day, and the cinema was nearly empty. Adam chose a seat on the end of a row that was an equal distance from two exits.

The film was *Exodus*. He was thankful it had just begun, because he needed some time to formulate a plan. Whenever the screen was bright enough he checked the map. He estimated that the nearest border crossing into France was only eight miles away, at Ferney-Voltaire. From there he could travel home via Dijon and Paris. Having decided on his route, the next problem was how to travel. He dismissed all forms of public transport and settled on renting a car. In between shows he remained in his seat to double-check the routes. Then he folded up the map and left the cinema by the exit least used in the past four hours.

WHEN Sir Morris entered the room he found the D4 committee already assembled. He glanced around the table at the handpicked men. On his left, the old war-horse Alec Snell, who had served at the Foreign Office longer than any of them, was touching his mustache nervously as he waited for Sir Morris to take his seat. Next to him sat Brian Matthews, a bright man with a chip on both shoulders. Opposite them was Commander Ralph Busch, the CIA representative co-opted onto the committee, who, after five years attached to the U.S. embassy in Grosvenor Square, considered himself more British than the British. At the far end of the table was Sir Morris' second-in-command. Some said he was a little too young, but then everyone except Tessa had forgotten that Sir Morris had held down his job at the same age.

Sir Morris settled in his seat at the head of the table.

"Gentlemen," he began, the only lady present being the long-suffering Tessa, whose existence was rarely acknowledged. "The Prime Minister has given this D-four his full blessing. And there is no time to waste. We have as part of our team a liaison officer from the CIA, Commander Busch. I am delighted that the American embassy has chosen him to represent them."

The man seated on Sir Morris' right bowed slightly. At five feet nine inches, with broad, muscular shoulders and a neat black beard, he looked every inch a sailor. Indeed he had been a PT boat commander during World War II.

"From the latest reports I have received," Sir Morris continued, opening the file in front of him, "it appears that Scott never reached the consulate this morning. We have learned," he added, consulting a note, "that the purpose of Scott's visit to the bank Roget et Cie was to pick up a bequest from a Mr. Emmanuel Rosenbaum. Further checking shows that a Mr. Rosenbaum arrived in Zurich yesterday morning and traveled on to Geneva in the afternoon. None of this would be of any great significance if Mr. Rosenbaum had not boarded the airplane to Zurich from"—Sir Morris couldn't resist a short dramatic pause—"Moscow. I think it is not unreasonable therefore to assume that Mr. Rosenbaum, whoever he is, works for the KGB. What still remains a mystery is why Mr. Rosenbaum should be willing to kill two innocent people for a relatively obscure icon. That brings my report up to date, but have you come up with anything in the last few hours?" he asked, turning to his number two.

Lawrence Pemberton looked up. "Since our meeting this morning, Sir Morris, I have spoken to Scott's sister, his mother, and the firm of solicitors who administered his father's will. It transpires that Scott was left with nothing of any real importance in the will, apart from an envelope that his mother says contained a letter from Reichsmarschall Hermann Göring." There was an immediate buzz around the table.

"Do we know the contents of Göring's letter?" asked Sir Morris.

"The whole letter, no, sir. But one of our examination entrants, a Mr. Nicholas Wainwright, was asked by Scott to translate what we now believe was a paragraph from the letter. It confirms a connection with Göring, although, so far, we don't know what it is. Scott told me last night that his reason for traveling to Geneva was to claim an icon left to him by his father. The icon was of Saint George and the dragon."

"Saint George and the dragon," said Matthews. "That's the icon that half of the KGB has been searching for during the past two weeks, and my team has been trying to find out why."

"And what have you come up with?" asked Sir Morris.

"Very little," admitted Matthews. "Only that the section leader in search of the icon is Alex Romanov."

There was a long silence before Sir Morris offered, "One thing is clear. We have to get to Scott first, and we must assume that it's Romanov who's after him."

"What do you imagine would be the outcome if Romanov managed to get to Scott before we do?" asked Matthews.

"A civilian up against one of the Russians' most ruthless agents? That's all we need," said Commander Busch.

Lawrence inclined his head toward the American. "I've known Adam for most of my life. If Romanov or this Rosenbaum come face to face with Scott, they'd better remember that he was awarded a Military Cross in Malaya."

"I wouldn't be confident of his chances," said Matthews.

"That's because you don't know him," retorted Lawrence.

Matthews lowered his eyes in order to avoid a clash with his boss. His boss! Lawrence was ten years his junior. A shortlist of two, and they had chosen the younger Oxford man to be under secretary. Matthews knew that as far as the Foreign Office was concerned, he had gone to the wrong school and the wrong university. He should have taken his father's advice and joined the police force. There were no class barriers there, and he would probably have been a chief superintendent by now.

"Are we allowed to know," interrupted Snell, looking straight at Busch, "why this icon is of such importance to both Russia and the United States?"

"We are as mystified as you," said the American. "All we can add to your current information is that two weeks ago the Russians deposited gold bullion in New York, to the value of over seven hundred million dollars, without any explanation."

"Let's get down to what we actually know," Sir Morris said, turning back to Lawrence. "What's the position now?"

Lawrence undid a folder with a red band around it and the words Immediate Action printed across the top. "We have seventeen agents in Geneva, and the Americans are flying in a further twelve today. With the Russians and the Swiss also roaming the city in search of Scott, I can only believe someone will come across him fairly soon. One of our biggest problems is the Swiss. As far as they are concerned, Scott is a common criminal on the run. We have started checking out all the obvious places: hotels, guesthouses, restaurants, airports, car-hire companies, and we are in constant touch with every one of our agents. So if Scott suddenly appears out of nowhere, we should be able to go to his aid at a moment's notice."

Lawrence looked up to observe one of the team carefully taking down all the details. "Added to that, the post office is intercepting every call made to Barclays Bank. If Scott does try to get in contact with me again at the bank or at my flat, it will be put through to this office automatically."

"Is he aware that you work for the service?" asked Snell.

"No. But it won't be long before he works out that the bank is only a front. After our conversation last night he is bound to become suspicious."

THE cinema door opened onto the busy pavement, and Adam slipped into the stream of commuters now returning home. Then he spotted a red Avis sign swinging in the afternoon breeze on the far side of the road. He safely reconnoitered the crowded crossing, but once his foot touched the far pavement, he froze on the spot. Just ahead of him in the crowd stood a man in a raincoat. He was continually looking around while speaking into an intercom. He must be an agent, but was he one of Rosenbaum's men, one of the Swiss police, or even British?

"Still no sign of our man, sir, and I haven't seen any of the KGB either," the man whispered into the intercom.

Adam, unable to hear the words, turned into a side road and almost knocked over a boy selling papers. *LE SOLDAT ANGLAIS TOUJOURS À GENÈVE*, the headline blared. Quickly he crossed another road, where he came to a stop behind a marble statue in the center of a small patch of grass. He stared at the building in front of him. It was a hotel, and he knew there would be no point in his trying to hide there.

He started to move away, but as he did so, a large empty touring coach drew up and parked outside. Smart blue lettering along its side proclaimed THE ROYAL PHILHARMONIC ORCHESTRA. Adam watched as some musicians walked out of the hotel and climbed onto the coach, carrying their instrument cases of assorted lengths and widths. When the next group of musicians came through the door Adam walked quickly forward and stepped past them into the hotel. The first thing he spotted in the crowded lobby was a double bass leaning against the wall. He glanced at the label around the neck of the unwieldy case. It read ROBIN BERESFORD.

Adam walked over to the counter and gestured to the clerk. "I need my room key quickly. I've left my bow upstairs, and now I'm holding everyone up."

"What name, sir?" asked the clerk.

"Beresford—Robin Beresford."

The clerk handed him key 612. "Thank you," said Adam. He walked over to the elevator and rode up to the sixth floor. When the doors slid open he was relieved to find there was no one in the corridor. He made his way quickly to room 612.

As he turned the key he said firmly in as good a French accent as he could manage, "Room service." When no one responded, he stepped in and locked the door behind him. An unopened suitcase had been left in one corner. Adam checked the label. Obviously Mr. Beresford hadn't had time to unpack. There was no other sign of the hotel guest, apart from a piece of paper on the side table. It was a typed itinerary.

> European Tour: Geneva, Frankfurt, Berlin, Amsterdam, London.
>
> Geneva: Bus 5:00 to concert hall; rehearsal 6:00; concert performance 7:30; encores 10:00.
>
> Programme: Mozart's Horn Concerto in D major; Brahms' Second Symphony; Schubert's Unfinished Symphony.

Adam looked at his watch. By the time Robin Beresford had completed the Unfinished Symphony, he would be over the border; but he felt safe to remain in room 612 until it was dark.

He picked up the phone by the bed and dialed room service. "Beresford, six twelve," he announced, and ordered himself some dinner before going into the bathroom. On the side of the basin was propped a little plastic bag with the words Compliments of the Management printed across it. Inside, Adam found a bar of soap, a tiny toothbrush, toothpaste, and a plastic razor.

He had just finished shaving when he heard a knock on the door and someone calling, "Room service." Adam quickly lathered his face again and put on a hotel dressing gown before he opened the door. The waiter set up a table without giving Adam a second look. "Will you sign the bill, please, sir?" he inquired.

He handed Adam a slip of paper. Adam signed it "Robin Beresford" and added a fifteen percent tip.

"Thank you," said the waiter, and left. As soon as the door closed, Adam's eyes settled on the feast of onion soup, steak with green beans and potatoes, and finally a raspberry sorbet. He suddenly didn't feel that hungry.

He still couldn't accept what he had gone through. If only he hadn't pressed Heidi into joining him. A week before, she hadn't even known him, and now he was responsible for her death. He would have to explain to her parents what had happened. But first he had to come up with some answers.

Adam forced himself to eat something. Then he lay down on the bed and began to consider the events of this nightmare journey.

"ANTARCTIC is in possession of an icon of Saint George and the dragon. But we know from our files of that period that that particular icon was destroyed when the Grand Duke of Hesse's plane crashed over Belgium in 1937."

"That may be what is written in your files in Washington," said Busch. "But what if your information is wrong and the icon was found by Göring but not returned to the grand duke? What if the Russians have now discovered the existence of the original icon?"

"Precisely. So you must be sure to get to Scott before the Russians do, or for that matter, the Foreign Office."

"But I'm part of the Foreign Office team."

"And that's precisely what we want the Foreign Office to go on believing."

" 'AND who's been sleeping in my bed?' said Mother Bear."

Adam awoke with a start. Looking down at him was a girl who was holding a double bass firmly by the neck with one hand. She was nearly six feet and weighed considerably more than Adam.

She had long, gleaming red hair that was in such contrast to the rest of her that it was as if her Maker had started at the top and then quickly lost interest. She wore a white blouse and a flowing black skirt that stopped an inch above the ground.

"Who are you?" asked Adam, startled.

"I'm not Goldilocks, that's for sure," parried the girl. "More to the point, who are you?"

Adam hesitated. "If I told you, you wouldn't believe me."

"Try me," she said.

"I'm Adam Scott."

"Am I meant to swoon, or scream and run away?" she inquired.

Adam realized that the girl couldn't have watched television or read a paper for at least two days. He switched tactics. "I thought my friend Robin Beresford was meant to be booked into this room," he said confidently.

"And so did I, until I saw you on my bed."

"You're Robin Beresford?"

"You're quite sharp for someone who has just woken up," she said. "But you haven't explained what you're doing here. Don't try any stories. I can see through a liar like a pane of glass."

"I should have a seat if I were you," said Adam. "It may take a while. What would you like first, the good news or the bad news?"

"Try me on the bad news," said Robin.

"The Swiss police want to arrest me and—"

"What for?" interrupted Robin.

"Murder," said Scott.

"What's the good news?" she asked.

"I'm innocent."

ROMANOV stood in the Russian ambassador's office in Geneva studying the group of men who had been flown in at short notice. They all had long records of service to the state, but only one of them, Valchek, was known to Romanov, and he worked too closely with Zaborski to be trusted.

"Comrades," Romanov began the moment they had all settled. "There is no need to remind you that we have been entrusted with a vital assignment. We must maintain a tight surveillance over Geneva in case Scott is still holed up somewhere in the city. My own guess is that, like any amateur, he will wait until it's dark, perhaps even first light, before he makes a run for it. The French border will be his most obvious choice. It offers him the opportunity to cross only one frontier before reaching the coast. If he tries to leave by plane, he will find we have the airport covered; if by train, we have the stations manned. But my guess is still that he will try to escape by motor vehicle. Just don't expect him to be roaming around looking like a tourist. Study your picture carefully and be prepared for him to try a disguise."

Romanov paused for effect. "The man who brings me the czar's icon need have no fear for his future prosperity when we return home." Hopeful expressions appeared on their faces for the first time as Romanov pulled out the duplicate icon from his coat pocket and held it high above his head for all to see.

"When you find the original of this, your task will be completed. And remember, comrades," Romanov added, "the only difference between this and Scott's icon is that his has a small silver crown embedded in the back of the frame. Once you see the crown, you will know that you have found the missing masterpiece."

Romanov looked at the silent men. "I underestimated the Englishman. He's good, and if any of you are hoping to kill him before I get to him, you'll have to be *very* good."

10

"NOT bad, Scott, not bad at all," said Robin when Adam had finished his story. "Either you're a superb liar, or I've lost my touch. Am I permitted to see this icon?"

Adam jumped off the bed and pulled out the package containing the czar's icon from the pocket of his trench coat. He handed the icon over to her. For some time she stared at the face of Saint George. "It's magnificent," she said at last, "and I can understand anyone wanting to possess it. But no painting could be worth the tragedy and trouble you've had to go through."

"I agree it's inexplicable," said Adam. "But Rosenbaum, or whatever his real name is, has been willing to kill twice to get his hands on it, and he's already convinced me that as long as I am in possession of the icon, I'll be the next in line."

Robin turned the painting over. "What does that mean?" she asked, pointing to the tiny silver crown embedded in the wood.

"That proves it was once owned by a czar, according to the man from Sotheby's. And it greatly enhances its value, he told me."

"Still, it couldn't be worth killing for," said Robin. She handed the icon back to Adam. "What other secret is Saint George keeping to himself?"

Adam shrugged and frowned, having asked himself the same question again and again since Heidi's death. He returned the silent saint to his trench coat.

"What was to have been your plan if I hadn't interrupted your sleep?" asked Robin. "Other than making the bed?"

Adam smiled. "I hoped to call my friend Lawrence. If he couldn't help me, I was going to hire a car and try to get across the Swiss border to France and then on to England. I felt sure that, between them, Rosenbaum and the Swiss police would have had all the airports and stations fully covered."

"No doubt Rosenbaum will have thought that much out as well," said Robin. "So we'd better try and get in touch with Lawrence and see if he's come up with any bright ideas." She stood and walked across to the phone. "Once I've got your friend on the line, I'll pass him over to you and then no one will realize who's phoning." Adam told her the number of the flat, and she asked the girl on the switchboard to connect her.

Adam checked his watch: eleven forty. Surely Lawrence would be home by now. The phone didn't complete its first two rings before Robin heard a man's voice on the line. She immediately handed the receiver over.

"Lawrence, it's me."

"Where are you?"

"I'm still in Geneva."

"We were waiting for you at eleven o'clock this morning."

"So was Rosenbaum."

"What does this Rosenbaum look like?"

"A six-foot, fair-haired, blue-eyed monster, who seems determined to kill me."

Lawrence did not speak for some time. "And are you still in possession of our patron saint?"

"Yes," said Adam. "But what can be so important about—?"

"Put the phone down and ring me back in three minutes."

The line went dead. Adam still couldn't fathom the sudden change in his old friend's manner. What had he missed during those months he had lodged with him?

"Is everything all right?" asked Robin.

"I think so," said Adam, a little mystified.

Three minutes later Robin picked up the receiver and repeated the number. After one ring Lawrence was back on the line.

"Only answer my questions," said Lawrence.

"No, I will not answer your questions," said Adam, becoming increasingly annoyed. "I want one or two of my own answered before you get anything more out of me. Do I make myself clear?"

"Yes," said a more gentle-sounding Lawrence.

"Who is Rosenbaum?"

Lawrence didn't immediately reply.

"You'll get nothing further from me until you start telling the truth," said Adam.

"From your description, I have every reason to believe Rosenbaum is a Russian agent whose real name is Romanov."

"A Russian agent? But why should a Russian agent want to get his hands on my icon?"

"I don't know," said Lawrence. "We were rather hoping you might be able to tell us."

"Who's we?"

Another long silence.

"Who's we?" repeated Adam. "You can't really expect me to go on believing you work for Barclays Bank."

"I work at the Foreign Office," said Lawrence. "I'm the number two in a small section that deals in . . ." He hesitated.

"Espionage I think is the jargon," said Adam. "Well, if you want my icon, you had better get me out of this mess alive."

"Where are you?"

"The Richemond Hotel."

"Registered in your name?"

"No. In the name of a friend."

"Right. Stay put until six a.m., then ring this number again. That will give me enough time to get everything in place."

"Is that the best you can do?" said Adam, but the phone had already gone dead. "It looks as if I'm stuck with you for the night," he told Robin as he replaced the receiver.

"On the contrary, it is I who am stuck with you," said Robin, and disappeared into the bathroom. Adam paced around the room several times before he tested the sofa. By the time Robin had come back out, clad in a pair of sky-blue pajamas, he had selected the floor as his resting place.

"Not very comfortable, is it?" said Robin. "But then British intelligence didn't warn me to book a double room." She climbed into the bed and turned out the light.

Adam slept intermittently, his mind switching between why the icon could be that important, how Lawrence knew so much about it, and, most crucial of all, how he was going to get out of the hotel alive.

ROMANOV waited patiently for the phone to be picked up.

"Yes," said a voice that he recognized immediately.

"Where is he?"

Four words were all Romanov received from Mentor in reply.

ADAM awoke just before he was due to phone Lawrence back. Suddenly he became aware of a strange sound coming from the corridor outside—two or three steps, a pause, then *whoosh.* A newspaper shot under the door, and the steps moved on. He didn't have to bend down to see that it was his photograph that dominated the front page of the *International Herald Tribune.*

Robin was still asleep. He silently picked up the phone and dragged it to the bathroom, closing the door behind him. He dialed the operator and repeated the number.

When the ringing stopped, he said, "Is that you, Lawrence?"

"Yes," came back the reply.

"Things have become much worse now. I'm still holed up in the hotel, but my picture is on the front page of every paper."

"I know," said Lawrence. "We tried to prevent it, but the Swiss wouldn't cooperate."

"Then I may as well give myself up to the Swiss," said Adam. "After all, I am innocent."

"I can understand how you feel, but your only chance now is to carry out my instructions to the letter and treat with suspicion every person with whom you come in contact."

"I'm listening," said Adam.

"Remember everything I say, because I am only going to tell you once. The Royal Philharmonic Orchestra is staying in the same hotel as you. They are going on to Frankfurt at ten o'clock this morning. Leave your room at five to ten, join the orchestra in the lobby, and then make your way to the front door, where you'll find their coach parked. We will have a car waiting for you on the far side of the road. The car is a black Mercedes, and you will see a man in gray chauffeur's uniform holding the door open for you. We have already arranged that no other car will be able to park on that side of the road between nine thirty and ten thirty, so you can't mistake it. Just get into the back. There will be another man in the car with you, and you will then be driven to the safety of our consulate. Do you need me to repeat any of that?"

"No," said Adam. "But—"

"Good luck," said Lawrence, and the phone went dead.

By seven Adam had showered and shaved, while Robin remained in a deep sleep. At ten to eight she finally awoke. She blinked at Adam, and a large grin appeared on her face.

"So you didn't murder me while I slept," she said. "Aren't you meant to have phoned London by now?"

"I already have."

"And what is the master plan to be?" she asked, rubbing her eyes on her way to the bathroom.

"I will be leaving with you," said Adam.

"Does that mean we're sharing a room in Frankfurt as well?" Robin asked a few minutes later when the bathroom door reopened, as if the conversation had never been interrupted.

"No. As soon as we're clear of the hotel I leave you at the coach and make my own way to a car on the far side of the road."

"At least we can have a farewell breakfast," she said, picking up the phone. "I'm nuts about kippers. How about you?"

Adam didn't answer. He had begun nervously looking at his

watch every few minutes. The waiter arrived with breakfast about fifteen minutes later, while Adam hid in the bathroom. When he reappeared, he showed no interest in the food, so Robin ate four kippers and most of the toast. Nine o'clock passed. A porter took away the breakfast trolley, and Robin began to pack.

When she had finished, Adam picked up her suitcase while Robin jerked the neck of the double bass onto her shoulder. She opened the door and checked the corridor. Two of her colleagues from the orchestra were waiting by the elevator. Robin and Adam joined them. They looked curiously at Adam, and Robin gave him a lewd wink. He sheltered behind the double bass as the elevator trundled down to the ground floor.

The doors sprang open, and Robin waited for her two colleagues to leave before she shielded Adam as best she could all the way across the foyer. His eyes were now fixed on the front door. He could see the bus, taking up most of the road, and several members of the orchestra already clambering on.

"Oh, I forgot," said Robin. "I'm meant to put this thing in the luggage compartment at the back of the bus."

"Do it later," said Adam sharply. "Just keep going until you reach the coach door." Then he saw the car on the far side of the road. He felt dizzy with relief. The car door was being held open for him. Another man was seated in the back, just as Lawrence had promised. Ten o'clock struck somewhere in the distance. The man dressed in a gray chauffeur's uniform, hat pulled down over his forehead, stood by the open door. Adam stared toward him as the man's eyes scanned the hotel entrance.

The uniform wasn't a good fit.

"Into the bus," hissed Adam.

"With this thing? They'll kill me," said Robin.

"If you don't, he'll kill me."

Robin obeyed, despite the adverse comments, as she lumbered down the aisle with her double bass screening Adam from the gaze of anyone on the far side of the road.

Adam slumped into a seat next to Robin, with the double bass between them. He wanted to be sick.

"Which one?" she whispered.

"In the chauffeur's uniform."

Robin glanced out the window. "He may be evil, but he's very good-looking," she said.

"Everybody's in," called a man from the front of the bus. "And I've double-checked, and we seem to have one extra."

Oh, no, thought Adam; he's going to throw me off the bus.

"My brother," shouted Robin from the back. "He's only traveling with us for part of the journey."

"Oh, that's okay then," said the manager. "Well, let's be on our way." He turned to the driver.

"He's started looking at the bus," said Robin. "But I don't think he can see you. No, you're all right. He's turned his gaze back to the hotel entrance."

"I didn't realize you had a brother," said the manager, who was suddenly standing beside them. The coach moved slowly out of the square.

"Neither did I, until this morning," mumbled Robin, still looking out the window. She turned and faced her boss. "Yes, I forgot to mention to you that he might be in Switzerland at the same time as the orchestra. I hope it's not a problem."

"Not at all," said the manager.

"Adam, this is Stephen Grieg, the orchestra's manager."

"Are you a musician as well?" asked Stephen as he shook Adam's hand.

"He's tone-deaf," said Robin, enjoying herself. "Takes after Father."

"What time are we expecting to reach Frankfurt, Stephen?" shouted a voice from the front.

"Must leave you now," said the manager.

"May I learn what's next on your agenda?" Robin asked Adam as soon as the manager was out of earshot.

Adam smiled. "I think Rosenbaum'll stay in Geneva for at least an hour, so with luck I'll get a fifty-mile start on him." He unfolded his map and ran his finger along the road the bus was traveling.

"That means you could make Zurich Airport before he has any chance to catch up with you," said Robin.

"Perhaps," said Adam. "But that would be too much of a risk. Whoever Rosenbaum is," he went on, cautiously not revealing the real name, "we now know for certain that he has a professional organization behind him, so I must expect the airports to be the first place he will have covered. And don't forget the Swiss police are still on the lookout for me as well."

"So why don't you come on to Frankfurt with us?" asked Robin.

"That's also too great a risk," said Adam. "When Rosenbaum has had time to think about it, the one thing he'll remember is this bus. Once he's found out where we're heading, he'll come after us."

Robin's eyes turned to the map. "So you'll need to decide where and when to get off."

"Exactly," whispered Adam. "I can risk sixty to seventy miles, but not a lot farther."

Robin's finger ran along the main road. "About here," she said, her finger stopping on a little town called Solothurn, near the French and German borders. "What will you do for transport?"

"I've little choice but to walk or thumb lifts," said Adam. "But I'll have to find a long stretch of road where I can see without being seen for about a hundred yards, and then thumb lifts only from cars with British plates."

"I assume the authorities are watching for you," said Robin. "How do you intend to cross the frontier with your passport?"

"That's one of the many problems I don't have a solution for."

Robin was silent a moment. "Will you contact Lawrence again?"

"Yes. I've got to let him know what happened this morning and warn him that someone must be passing information to Rosenbaum."

"Could it be Lawrence himself?"

"Never," said Adam.

"Your loyalty is touching," said Robin, "but what you actually mean is you don't want to believe it could be Lawrence. Just be wary of how much you let him know."

They sat in silence as Adam checked the map and went over all the possible routes he could take once he had left the bus.

"Got it," said Robin suddenly.

"Got what?" said Adam, looking up from the map.

"How we solve your passport problem," she murmured. "If you let me have your passport, I'll substitute it for the member of the orchestra who most resembles you. Whenever we cross a border, they only count the number of people on the bus and the number of passports, and as long as they tally, the customs officials don't check everyone individually. No one will notice a thing until we're back home in Britain on Sunday night."

"Not a bad idea, if there is anyone who resembles me."

"We'll have to see what we can do," said Robin, her eyes moving slowly from person to person. Gradually a small smile appeared on her face. "There are two of our lot who bear a passable resemblance to you. One is about five years older, and the other is four inches shorter. Let me have your passport," she said. Adam handed it over and then watched Robin walk up to the front and sit next to the manager, who was chatting to the driver.

"I need to check something in my passport," Robin broke in.

"You'll find them all under my seat in a plastic bag," the manager said, and continued his conversation with the driver.

Robin bent down and started to shuffle through the passports, as if searching for her own. She picked out the two possible substitutes and compared the photographs. The shorter man's photo looked nothing like Adam. The older man's could pass for Adam, as long as the officials didn't study the date of birth too carefully. She bundled up the passports, placing Adam's in the middle. She then put them back into the plastic bag under the manager's seat.

Robin returned to her seat. "Take a look at yourself," she said, slipping the passport over to Adam.

He studied the photo. "Not bad. But what will happen when you return to London and they find out my passport has been substituted?"

"You'll be back in England long before us," said Robin. "So send this one to the Royal Philharmonic Orchestra in Wigmore Street. I'll see that they return yours." Adam vowed that if he ever got back to London, he would become a life subscriber to the Friends of the Royal Philharmonic.

"I only wish I could take you with me," he said.

Robin smiled. "Frankfurt, Berlin, Amsterdam, just in case you get bored. I'll write down the hotels we'll be staying at. Can I have a last look at the icon?" she asked.

Adam slipped the painting out of his pocket, careful to shield it from anyone else's view. Robin stared into the eyes of Saint

George before she spoke again. "I lay awake last night trying to fathom what secret the icon held."

"Well," said Adam. "Did you come to any conclusions?"

"Yes," said Robin. "My first idea was that the crown on the back"—she turned the icon over and stared at the little piece of silver embedded in the wood—"indicates that this is the original by Rublev, and not a copy, as you have been led to believe."

"I've considered that," said Adam, "but it is still not enough to explain why Rosenbaum would kill indiscriminately for it."

"Perhaps it's not the icon he's after, but something else. Something hidden in or behind the painting."

"That was the first thing I checked," said Adam smugly. "And I'm convinced that it's a solid piece of wood."

"I don't agree with you," said Robin as she began tapping the wood all over, like a doctor examining someone's chest. "I've worked with instruments all my life, watched them being made, and this icon is not solid right through, though heaven knows how I can prove it. If something is hidden inside, it was never intended to be discovered by laymen like ourselves."

"Quite an imaginative little thing, aren't you?" said Adam.

"Comes naturally." She handed the icon back to Adam. "Do let me know if you ever discover what is inside."

Adam returned the icon to his trench-coat pocket.

"Two more kilometers to Solothurn," said Robin, pointing out the window at a signpost.

Adam rose from his seat. "I'll see you off," Robin said, and they both made their way up the aisle. When Adam reached the front of the coach he asked the driver if he could drop him off just before they reached the next village.

"Sure thing," said the driver, without looking back.

Adam turned and shook hands with the manager, saying, "Thanks for the lift." The driver pulled onto the shoulder and pressed a knob. The hydraulic doors swung back.

"Bye, Robin," said Adam, giving her a brotherly kiss.

"Good-bye, baby brother," said Robin. "Give my love to Mother." She smiled and waved at him as the door swung closed and the coach returned to the highway to continue its journey.

Adam was on his own again.

11

PROFESSOR Brunweld was summoned from his bed in the early hours of the morning on Friday and escorted to the Pentagon. They wanted his expert opinion, they had assured him.

Once they had handed him the document, they left him alone. He studied the clauses for over an hour, and then called them back. It was authentic, he told them, and if the Russians were still in possession of their copy, also signed in 1867, then his adopted country was in all kinds of trouble.

He began to realize how serious it was when they told him that he would not be allowed to leave the Pentagon until Monday. That didn't surprise him once he'd seen the date on the bottom of the treaty.

ROMANOV knew he couldn't risk standing by the side of the car for much longer. He was too conspicuously dressed not to be noticed by everyone who came out of the hotel. Three minutes later he threw his gray cap onto the back seat and instructed Valchek to get rid of the car and return to the consulate.

Valchek nodded. He had carried out Romanov's orders to kill the two British agents. Only one thing hadn't run according to plan. The dead chauffeur's uniform had been too tight for Valchek. Romanov thought he detected a smirk on Valchek's face when he realized who would be the chauffeur.

Romanov slipped into the shadows and waited for half an hour, by which time he was sure the plan must have been aborted from the London end. He hailed a taxi and asked the driver to take him to the Soviet consulate. Could he really have lost Scott twice? Once more, and Zaborski was going to require a very convincing explanation.

Something had happened outside the hotel that didn't quite fit. Romanov kept playing the last thirty minutes over in his mind, as if rewinding the reel of an old film, but some of the frames still remained blurred.

Once he was back in the consulate, Valchek followed him into his office.

"Tell me what you saw when we were at the hotel," ordered Romanov as he changed into his own clothes. "Do you remember anything unusual taking place while we were waiting?"

"Nothing in particular," said Valchek. "People entering and leaving the hotel—but I'm sure Scott wasn't among them."

"You are fortunate to be so certain. What happened next?"

"You told me to go back to the consulate and wait for you."

"What time was that?"

"It must have been about seven minutes past ten. I remember I checked my watch when that coach left."

"The coach?" said Romanov.

"Yes, the one that was being loaded up with musical instruments. It left about—"

"Instruments, that's it!" said Romanov. "Now I remember what was worrying me. Cellos, violins, and a double bass that didn't go with the luggage. Ring the hotel and find out who was on that bus and where they are heading." Valchek scurried away.

Romanov checked his watch: ten fifty-five. They were going to have to move quickly. He pressed the intercom by the side of the phone, saying, "I want a fast car and a superb driver."

As Romanov replaced the receiver Valchek returned. "The bus was hired by the Royal Philharmonic Orchestra, who are on a European tour—"

"Where are they heading next?" asked Romanov.

"Frankfurt."

ADAM strolled away from the village, having checked everything with a soldier's eye. The road was deserted but for a little boy who was relentlessly kicking a soccer ball. The boy turned when he saw Adam and kicked the ball toward him. Adam kicked it back, and the boy caught it in his arms.

Adam continued up the main road as it wound around a hill. There were only a few old houses. On one side was a dangerous ravine, with tree-covered hills rising in the distance, while on the other side stretched green fields in which cows with bells around their necks munched happily.

Adam went farther up the road until he came to a sharp bend. Standing on the corner, he could see down the hill for about half a mile without being seen. He soon became expert at picking out cars with British license plates as far as two or three hundred yards away. For twenty minutes he thumbed optimistically at seven English cars heading toward Zurich, but they ignored him.

By eleven twenty Adam decided he could no longer chance being seen on the road. There was no alternative left to him now but to try the ravine on foot. Cursing, he began to climb down one of the steep trails. If only he'd started earlier.

"FASTER!" said Romanov to the ambassador's driver. "We must beat them to the border." After they had covered one hundred kilometers, the three men began watching for the coach, but it was another thirty kilometers before Valchek was able to point and shout, "That must be them, about a kilometer up the hill."

"Force them off the road," said Romanov. The embassy driver swung out to overtake the coach and then cut across, forcing the coach driver to put on his brakes and swerve to the side.

Romanov jumped out of the car and ran toward the coach, his eyes already searching for anyone who might be attempting to leave. He banged on the door impatiently until the big doors swung open. Romanov leaped on. He took his passport from an inside pocket, flashed it in the frightened driver's face, and shouted, "Swiss police. Who's in charge here?"

Stephen Grieg stood up. "I am the manager, and—"

"When you left your hotel in Geneva this morning did you take on any extra passengers?" Romanov interrupted.

"No," said Grieg. "Except Robin Beresford's brother."

"Robin Beresford's brother?" inquired Romanov as he raised his eyebrows interrogatively.

"Yes," said the manager. "Adam Beresford. But he only traveled with us as far as Solothurn. Then he got off."

"Which one of you is Robin?" said Romanov, staring around a sea of male faces.

"I am," piped up a voice from the back. Romanov marched down the bus and saw the double-bass case, and then everything fitted into place. He stared down at the heavy-framed woman who now sat behind the monstrous instrument.

"Your brother is the one called Adam?"

"Yes," said Robin, trying not to sound nervous.

"Quite a coincidence," he replied. "The man I am looking for just happens to be called Adam as well."

"Common enough name," said Robin. "Perhaps you've never read the first chapter of the Bible."

"Six feet one inch, dark hair, dark eyes, slim and fit. Not a convincing brother for you," added Romanov, studying her.

Robin pushed back her red hair but didn't rise. Romanov could sense from the nervous expressions on the faces around him that it was Scott who had been on the bus.

"And where was your *brother*"—he emphasized the word—"intending to go once he had left the coach?" Romanov asked, tapping his passport against his other hand, like a baton.

"I have no idea," said Robin, still not changing her expression from one of disinterested politeness.

"I will give you one more chance to cooperate with me. Where was your brother heading?"

"And I'll tell you once more, I don't know."

"If you refuse to answer my questions," said Romanov, "I shall have to arrest you."

"On whose authority?" asked Robin calmly.

"On the authority of the Swiss police," he said confidently.

"No doubt you'll be happy to show me proof of your identity."

"Don't be insolent," Romanov said sharply.

"It is you who are insolent," said Robin, standing up. "You drive in front of our coach like a lunatic, burst in like a gangster, claiming to be one of the Swiss police. I have no idea who you are, but if you touch me, there are forty men on this coach who will beat you into pulp. And even if you manage to get off this bus alive, we are members of the Royal Philharmonic Orchestra of Great Britain, and as such are guests of the Swiss government. In a few moments, when we cross the border, we will become guests of the West German government, so you're about to get yourself onto every front page in the world. Single-handedly you will bring a totally new meaning to the words diplomatic incident." She leaned forward and pointed a finger at him. "So I'm telling you, whoever you are, in as ladylike fashion as I can, get lost."

Romanov stood staring at her for some moments and then

backed away as Robin's eyes remained glued on him. The coach driver closed the door the moment Romanov's foot touched the ground, and he quickly drove back onto the highway.

The entire orchestra turned around and gave Robin the kind of ovation normally reserved for the entrance of the conductor. It went unappreciated. Robin had collapsed back into her seat, shaking uncontrollably, only too aware that not one of the forty men on that coach would have lifted a finger against Rosenbaum.

Sir Morris Youngfield glanced around the table. Everyone was in place, despite the few minutes' notice he had given them.

"Let's hear the latest report," he said, looking at his number two, who was again seated at the far end of the table.

"Not good, sir, I'm afraid," began Lawrence. "Two of our most experienced agents were selected to pick up Scott at the Richemond Hotel and take him to the British consulate. No one at our Geneva office can be certain what happened, but our men never turned up at the hotel, and they haven't been seen since."

"And where do we imagine Scott is now?" asked Matthews.

"We've also drawn a blank on that," said Lawrence.

Matthews smiled at Lawrence's embarrassment. "We feel certain he must have boarded the coach with the girl," Lawrence added. "But he wasn't on it when we were waiting for them at the border. The orchestra is due in Frankfurt in about one hour, so we will be able to find out more then."

"Meanwhile, what else are we doing?" asked Sir Morris.

"Keeping a close eye on Romanov. One of our old hands recognized him, despite the fact that he's cut his hair very short."

"Do you think Scott will contact you again?" asked Snell.

Lawrence hesitated. "Almost certainly, if he's still alive," he said without expression.

Sir Morris stared at him but didn't comment.

"If Romanov is still in Geneva, Scott must still be alive," said Busch. "Because the moment he gets his hands on the icon, he will head for Moscow."

"Agreed," said Lawrence. "And we have men stationed at the airport checking every flight to the U.S.S.R. I suggest we assemble tomorrow at seven a.m. Scott may contact me before then."

Adam slipped and stumbled the last few yards down the ravine, before finally landing with a bump. His hands were cut and bleeding, his trousers torn. It had taken just under an hour. He sat trying to get his breath back and gazed across the valley ahead. He estimated the distance to the far ridge to be about two miles. At least the map had promised him there was a road, hidden from sight on the other side of the ridge. He reckoned he could cover the ground to the road in about twenty minutes. He checked that the icon was securely in place and then set off.

Romanov had hardly uttered a word since he had been unceremoniously forced to leave the coach. He knew the girl had called his bluff, but he couldn't afford a diplomatic incident, which would undoubtedly be reported back to Moscow.

Solothurn was about forty kilometers back in the direction they had come from. The driver could have completed the journey in about twenty minutes had Romanov not insisted on slowing down to check the occupants of each vehicle that traveled toward them, just in case Scott had managed to thumb a lift.

As soon as they reached Solothurn, Romanov instructed the driver to leave the car in the village while he and Valchek split up to see if they could discover any clues as to the route Scott might have taken. None of the locals whom they questioned had seen anyone resembling Scott that morning, and Romanov was beginning to wonder which border he should now head for when he turned around and saw the driver kicking a soccer ball to a little boy. Romanov ran down the hill and was about to remonstrate with him when the boy turned and kicked the ball hard at Romanov. As he picked it up, the boy gave a hopeful smile. Romanov held the ball high above his head.

"Have you seen any strangers this morning?" he asked in slow, deliberate French.

"Yes, yes," said the boy. "But he didn't score a goal."

"Where did he go?" asked Romanov.

"Up the hill," said the boy. To the child's dismay Romanov dropped the ball and began to run. Valchek and the driver followed after him.

"Non, non," cried the little boy, who followed after them.

Romanov looked back to see the boy pointing out over the ravine.

Romanov quickly turned to the driver. "Get the car. I need the glasses and the map." A few minutes later the Mercedes drew up by Romanov's side. The driver handed the glasses to Romanov, while Valchek spread a map out on the hood of the car.

Romanov focused the binoculars and began to sweep the hills in the distance. It was several minutes before his gaze settled upon a brown speck climbing the farthest hill.

"The rifle," were his only words.

Valchek ran to the trunk of the car and took out a sniper's rifle with a telescopic sight. He assembled the long, slim weapon and checked that it was loaded. He then raised it, and he too focused on Scott. As Romanov followed Adam's relentless stride with the binoculars, Valchek's arm moved with him.

"Kill him," said Romanov. Valchek was grateful for the clear, windless day as he kept the rifle sight in the middle of the Englishman's back, then slowly squeezed the trigger. Adam had almost reached the top of the ridge when the bullet tore through him. He fell to the ground with a thud. Romanov smiled and lowered the binoculars.

Adam knew exactly what had ripped through his shoulder and where the shot must have come from. He instinctively rolled over until he reached the nearest tree. And then the pain began. Although the bullet had lost a lot of its power at such a distance, it still stung like an adder's bite, and blood was already beginning to seep through his trench coat. He turned his head and gazed to where he knew Romanov must be waiting to take a second shot.

He looked back up toward the hill. Only thirty yards to the safety of the ridge, but he would have to run over the top, remaining exposed for several vital seconds. Even if he made it, Romanov would still be able to reach him by car within thirty minutes.

Nevertheless, that was his one chance. Slowly, very slowly, he crawled up the slope, thankful for the trees that he could still use as protection. Once he had covered ten yards, he knew he would be exposed. You can't hold a rifle up on your shoulder forever, Adam thought. He counted to two hundred slowly.

"He's going to make a run for it," Romanov told Valchek, "which will give you about three seconds. I'll shout the moment he moves." Romanov kept the glasses trained on the trees. Suddenly Adam jumped up and sprinted. Romanov shouted, "Now!" Valchek focused on the moving man and squeezed the trigger as Adam threw himself over the ridge. The second bullet whistled by the side of his head.

Romanov cursed, staring through the binoculars, knowing that Valchek had missed. He turned to the open map as the others joined him around the car. "He should reach that road in about ten minutes," he said, putting his finger in the middle of a small red line that ran between Neuchâtel and the French border. "Unless the first bullet hit him, in which case it could take him longer. So how long will it take you to get to that border?" Romanov asked the driver.

"About twenty-five, at most thirty minutes, Comrade Major."

Romanov looked back toward the hills. "Thirty minutes, Scott. That's how long you've got to live."

When the car sped away, the little boy ran home as fast as he could. He quickly told his mother everything he had seen. She smiled understandingly. Only children had such imaginations.

ADAM moved toward the road at a steady pace. He was anxious to stop and check the wound but waited till he reached the road. The bullet had torn through the outer flesh of his shoulder muscle. He was relieved to see that the blood had only made a small stain on his trench coat. He folded a handkerchief in four and placed it between his shirt and the wound. He knew he daren't risk a hospital. As long as he could get to a pharmacy by nightfall, he felt he could take care of the problem himself.

Adam checked the map. He was now only a few miles from the French border. Desperately he began to thumb at any car that passed. Unfortunately, there were few cars driving toward the border, and they all ignored his plea. Time was running out when a yellow Citroën drew up a few yards ahead of him.

The woman in the passenger seat wound down the window. The driver leaned across and said to Adam in a broad Yorkshire accent, "We're on our way to Dijon. Any use to you, lad?"

"Yes, please," said Adam.

"Then jump in the back with my daughter."

Adam obeyed. The Citroën moved off as Adam checked the back window; he was relieved to see an empty road behind him.

"Jim Hardcastle's the name," said the man, who had a large, warm smile perpetually imprinted on his chubby red face. His dark ginger hair was plastered down, and he wore a Harris Tweed jacket and an open-necked shirt. "This is the wife, Betty," he said. The woman in the front seat turned toward Adam, revealing the same ruddy cheeks and warm smile. "And sitting next to you is our Linda," Jim Hardcastle added. Adam stared at an attractive girl in her late teens whose first experiment with dark eye shadow and pink lipstick hadn't worked that well.

"And what's your name, lad?" said Jim.

"Dudley Hulme," said Adam, recalling the name on his new passport. "Are you on holiday?" he asked, trying to keep his mind off his throbbing shoulder.

"Mixing business with pleasure," said Jim. "But this part of the trip is rather special for us. I'm in mustard, you see, and we're on our way to the annual conference of the IMF. You may have heard of us." Adam nodded knowingly. "International Mustard Federation," Jim added.

Adam wanted to laugh, but because of the pain in his shoulder he managed to keep a straight face.

"This year they've elected me president, the high point of my career in mustard, you might say. Tonight I shall be making a speech of welcome to delegates from all over the world."

"How fascinating." Adam winced as the car hit a pothole.

"It certainly is. People have no idea how many makes of mustards there are." Jim paused for a second. "One hundred and forty-three. But British mustard is the best, I always say. Probably the same in your line of work. By the way, what is your line of work?"

"I'm in the army," said Adam.

"What's a soldier doing thumbing a lift in Switzerland?"

"Can I speak to you in confidence?" asked Adam.

"Mum's the word," said Jim.

"I'm a captain in the Royal Wessex, at present on a NATO exercise," began Adam. "I was dumped off the Italian coast with a false passport and ten English pounds. I have to be back in barracks at Aldershot by midnight Saturday." When he saw the look of approbation appear on Jim's face he felt Robin would have been proud of him.

"I was in the army in the last war myself," said Jim. "So where's the problem in getting you back to England?"

"The border officials have been briefed that eight British officers are attempting to get over into France. The Swiss love to be the ones to pull us in. Only two officers out of twelve made it back to barracks last year," said Adam, warming to his own theme.

"The Swiss won't pick you up, lad, believe me. I'll see to that," said Jim.

"If you can get me across the border, Mr. Hardcastle, I'm confident I will be able to make it all the way back to Aldershot."

"Consider it done, lad."

THE fuel indicator was flashing red. "How many more kilometers can we do when that happens?" demanded Romanov.

"About twenty, Comrade Major," said the driver.

"Then we should still make the French border. Go faster."

"Yes, Comrade Major," said the driver, who decided it was not the occasion to point out that they would run out of gas even more quickly if he was made to push the car to its limits.

The Mercedes touched a hundred and sixty kilometers per hour, and Romanov relaxed only when he saw a sign saying that the customs inspection stations were coming up in five kilometers. A few moments later the engine spluttered, and the car slowed to a stop.

Romanov did not even look at the driver as he jumped out and began running the last three kilometers toward the border.

"I'VE come up with an idea," said Jim as they passed a signpost warning drivers that the border was only two kilometers away.

"What's that, sir?" asked Adam, who could now feel his shoulder beating like a steady hammer.

"When it comes time to present our passports you put your arm round Linda and start cuddling her. Leave the rest to me."

Linda went scarlet. Adam looked across at the miniskirted, pink-lipped Linda and felt embarrassed by the predicament her father had placed her in. "Don't argue with me, Dudley," continued Jim confidently. "What I have in mind will work."

When they reached the Swiss border Adam could see that there were two checkpoints. Drivers were avoiding one line of traffic in which a row was going on between a customs official and an irate truck driver. Jim drove up straight behind the gesticulating Frenchman. "Give me your passport, Dudley," he said. Adam handed over the violinist's passport.

The argument continued in front of them. Adam remained alert, continually looking out the back window, waiting for the moment when Romanov would appear. When he turned back he was relieved to find that the truck in front of them was being told to pull over to the side and wait. Jim drove quickly up to the customs post. "Get necking, you two," he said.

Adam obeyed, took Linda in his arms, and kissed her perfunctorily, one eye still watching for Romanov.

"The wife, the daughter, and the future son-in-law," said Jim, handing over the passports. "What was the trouble about, Officer?"

"Nothing for you to worry about," said the policeman, leafing through the passports. "I hope it hasn't inconvenienced you."

"No, no," said Jim. "They didn't even notice." He pointed over his shoulder, laughing.

The policeman shrugged, and handing the passports back, he said, "*Allez,*" waving them on.

"Sharp-as-Mustard Jim, that's what they call me." He looked around toward Adam. "You can stop that now, Dudley, thank you." Adam felt Linda release him with some reluctance.

She glanced at him shyly, then turned toward her father. "But we still have to go over the French border, don't we?"

"WE HAVE already been alerted to look for him, and I can assure you he hasn't been through this post," said the senior customs officer. "If you want to double-check, be my guest."

Romanov went quickly from officer to officer, showing them the photograph of Adam, but none of them could recall anyone resembling him. Valchek joined him a few minutes later and confirmed that Scott was not in any of the waiting cars and that the Mercedes was being pushed into a garage.

"You seem to be right," Romanov told the senior official. "Could I have missed any of your staff?"

"Doubt it—unless there's a couple of them taking a break. If so, you'll find them in the bar near the French border point."

Four customs officers were in the bar. Two were playing pool, while the other two sat at a corner table drinking coffee. The Russians got some coffee and made their way over to the table where two of the border guards sat. Romanov pushed the photograph of Scott across the table.

"Have you seen this man today?"

Neither showed any sign of recognition, and the younger one continued with a story he was telling. Romanov sipped his coffee. Then he noticed how the young man's eyes kept returning to the photo. He asked once again if he had seen Scott.

"No, no," said the young officer a little too quickly. In Moscow, Romanov would have had a yes out of him within minutes, but he would have to follow a more gentle approach here.

"How long ago?" Romanov asked quietly.

The young officer hesitated. "Twenty minutes, maybe thirty."

"What make of vehicle?"

The officer hesitated again. "A Citroën. Yellow."

"Other passengers?"

"Three. Mother, father, daughter. He was in the back with the daughter. The father said they were engaged."

Romanov had no more questions.

"WHERE would you like to be dropped off?" asked Jim Hardcastle as he drove into the outskirts of Dijon.

"Anywhere near the center that's convenient for you," replied Adam. "How about the next corner?"

"Oh," said Jim, and he reluctantly drew the car up to the curb.

Adam kissed Linda on the cheek before getting out of the back. He then shook hands with Mr. and Mrs. Hardcastle.

"Nice to make your acquaintance," said Jim. "Good luck."

As the car moved off, Adam watched them disappear. He tried to wave, then walked quickly down a side street. Within moments he was in the center of Dijon, where he began to search for a pharmacy. Adam had to walk only fifty yards before he spotted one. He entered the shop tentatively and walked up to the counter.

"Do you speak English, by any chance?" he asked the druggist.

"Passable, I hope," came back the reply.

"I need some iodine, cotton wool, and a bandage. I fell and bruised my shoulder on a rock," Adam explained.

The druggist quickly put the order together, without showing much interest. "That will be twenty-three francs," he said.

"Will Swiss do?"

"Certainly."

"Is there a hotel anywhere nearby?" asked Adam.

"Around the next corner, on the other side of the square."

Adam thanked him, handed over the Swiss notes, and then left the pharmacy in search of the hotel. The Hotel Frantel was, as promised, only a short distance away. Adam flung his trench coat over his bloodstained shoulder and strode across the entrance hall as though he were a guest of several days' standing. He followed the sign to the lavatory.

Adam opened the door tentatively and found it empty. He locked himself in and let his trench coat fall to the floor. Slowly he stripped to the waist. He then ran a basinful of warm water.

Twenty minutes later the pain had subsided, and he even felt comfortable. He picked up his coat with his right hand and tried to throw it back over his shoulder. The movement caused the icon to fall out of the pocket and onto the tiled floor. As it hit the floor, the sound made Adam fear that it might have broken. He stared down anxiously and then fell to his knees.

The icon had split open like a book.

12

WHEN Adam returned to the Hotel Frantel an hour later, few guests would have recognized him as the man who had crept in earlier that afternoon. He wore a new shirt, trousers, tie, and a double-breasted blazer. The trench coat had been ditched, because the icon fitted snugly into the blazer pocket.

He booked himself into a single room in the name of Dudley Hulme and took the elevator to the third floor.

Lawrence picked the phone up even before Adam heard the second ring. "Where are you?" were his first words.

"I'll ask the questions," said Adam. "You must be aware by now that someone on your so-called team has a direct line to the Russians. It was Romanov and his friends who were waiting for me outside the hotel in Geneva, not your lot."

"We realize that now," said Lawrence.

"We?" said Adam. "Who are we? Because since I've been shot at, I'm finding it rather hard to know who's on my side."

"Shot at?" said Lawrence.

"Yes. Your friend Romanov took a shot at me today, hit me in the shoulder. Next time we meet, I intend it to be the other way around, and it won't be the shoulder."

"There won't be a next time," said Lawrence, "because we'll get you out safely if you'll only let me know where you are."

The memory of Robin's words—"Just be wary of how much you let him know"—stopped Adam from telling Lawrence his exact location. There was a long silence before he said, "I'm in Dijon."

"Give me your number, and I'll phone you back in an hour."

"No," said Adam. "I'll phone *you* back in one hour."

"Adam, you've got to show some trust in me."

"Not now that I know what it is you're all after. I can't afford to trust anybody."

Adam replaced the phone and stared down at the icon, which lay open on the bed. It wasn't the signatures of Aleksandr Gorchakov and William Seward on the document that worried him. It was the date—June 20, 1966—that read like a death warrant.

"Good night, sir," said the doorkeeper as the senior civil servant left the Foreign Office that evening. "Another late night for you," he added sympathetically. The man acknowledged the doorman by raising his rolled umbrella a few inches. It *had* been another late night, but at least they had caught up with Scott again. He was beginning to develop quite a respect for the man.

He set off at a brisk pace and hailed a passing taxi. "Dillon's bookshop, Malet Street," he told the driver before getting in.

He allowed himself a wry smile as he reviewed the plan. It had the double advantage of ensuring enough time for them to get their best men into position while keeping Scott well out of sight in a deserted hideaway. Pemberton had agreed to remain at his desk until all the loose ends were tied up, and he was sure that nothing could go wrong this time.

"Eight shillings, guv'nor," said the taxi driver as he drew up outside Dillon's. He handed over the money and added a tip. When the taxi had turned the corner he began walking away. In moments he turned into a side road and disappeared down some stone steps to a basement flat. He inserted a key in the lock, turned it quickly, stepped inside, and closed the door behind him. During the next twenty minutes he made two telephone calls, one international, one local, and then had a bath. He emerged from the flat less than an hour later, dressed in a casual brown suit and pink floral shirt. The part in his hair had changed sides. He returned to Dillon's on foot and hailed another taxi.

"Middlesex Hospital, please," he instructed the driver as he stepped into the back. He checked his watch: nearly ten past eight. Scott would be fully briefed by now, he thought. Poor chap. If he hadn't opened that envelope in the first place, the icon would have ended up with its rightful owner.

"Shall I drive up to the entrance?" asked the cabbie.

"Yes, please."

A moment later he strolled into the hospital, checked the board on the wall, as if he were looking for a certain ward, then walked back out onto the street. From the Middlesex Hospital it always took him about three minutes at a steady pace to reach Charlotte Street, where he stopped outside a house and pressed a buzzer attached to a little intercom.

"Are you a member?" inquired a voice suspiciously.

"Yes."

ON THE hour Adam phoned and listened carefully to all Lawrence had to say.

"I'll take one more risk," said Adam, "but if Romanov turns up this time, I'll hand over the icon to him personally—and with it a piece of property so valuable that no amount of money the Americans could offer would be sufficient to purchase it back."

When Adam put the phone down, Lawrence and Sir Morris played the conversation back over again and again.

"I think property's the key word," said Sir Morris.

"Agreed," said Lawrence. "But what piece of property could be that valuable to both the Russians and the Americans?"

Sir Morris began slowly revolving the globe that stood by the side of his desk.

"WHAT does that buzz mean?" asked Romanov. "We are not running out of gasoline again, are we?"

"No, sir," said the chauffeur. "It's the new calling device now fixed to all ambassadorial cars. It means that they expect you to check in."

"Turn around and go back to that gasoline station we passed a couple of kilometers back," Romanov said, tapping the dashboard impatiently. It would be dark within the hour. They had traveled about ninety kilometers and had seen no yellow Citroën going either way.

At the gasoline station Romanov ran to the phone booth. "I am answering your signal," he said when he was put through to the second secretary at the Russian embassy.

"We've had another call from Mentor," said the second secretary. "How far are you from Dijon?"

THE member stumbled about the dimly lit room until he came across an unoccupied table wedged up against a pillar in one corner. He sat down on a little stool and swiveled around nervously, waiting for someone to bring him his usual malt whiskey on the rocks. His eyes eventually became accustomed to the dim light thrown out by the long red fluorescent bulb above the bar. All he could make out were the same old faces staring at him hopefully. But he wanted something new.

The proprietor brought over the drink and sat down opposite him. The member never could get himself to look the man in the eyes.

"I've got someone who's very keen to meet you," whispered the proprietor. "He's leaning on the jukebox in the corner. The tall, slim one. And he's young." The member looked toward the blaring machine. A pleasing new face smiled at him. He smiled nervously back.

"Fine." He took a gulp of whiskey.

The proprietor walked over to the young man. The boy downed his drink, hesitated for a moment, then strolled across the crowded floor to take the empty stool.

"My name is Piers," the young man said. "Would you like to dance?"

"IT'S an emergency," the caller said. "Antarctic is in Dijon, and he's found out what's in the icon. He told Pemberton he was in possession of a piece of property so valuable that no amount of money we could offer would be sufficient to purchase it back."

"So where does that leave us?" asked Commander Busch.

"On our way to Dijon so that we can be sure to lay our hands on that icon before the British or the Russians."

"What about Antarctic, if we get our hands on the icon?"

"It's only the icon we're after. Once that's in our possession—Antarctic is expendable."

"I don't understand."

"We now know his father was the traitor who helped Göring to an early death. If the father would side with the Germans, why wouldn't the son side with the Russians?"

"Like father, like son."

"Precisely."

A FEW minutes after seven Adam knew it was time for him to leave. He had decided not to carry out Lawrence's instructions to the letter; he intended to be waiting for *them*, and not as Lawrence had planned. He locked the hotel room door and returned to reception, where he paid for the room and the telephone calls he had made.

Then he hitched a ride to the rendezvous site six miles out of town, off the Auxerre road.

He glanced at his watch. There was an hour and a half still to go before they were due, and by then it would be pitch-dark. He jogged over to the airfield and studied the burned-out buildings that ran alongside the road. It was like a ghost town, exactly as

Lawrence had described during their last telephone converation.

Looking across the two runways, he spotted the ideal place to hide, and he settled down to wait.

FLIGHT Lieutenant Alan Banks of the British Royal Air Force was thankful that the moon shone so brightly that night. He circled the little RAF Twin Otter aircraft around the perimeter of the airfield once more and studied the two runways carefully. The airport had been out of action for such a long time that none of the manuals included a ground plan of it.

"I can make a landing on the north-south runway more easily," Banks said, turning to the Special Air Service captain, who sat crouched in the back with his five men. "How near to that hangar do you want me to go?" he said, pointing out the window.

"Stay well clear, at least a couple of hundred yards," came back the reply. "We still don't know what to expect."

The six SAS men stared cautiously out the side windows. They had been briefed to pick up a lone Englishman called Scott, who would be waiting for them, and then get out fast. It sounded easy enough, but it couldn't be; otherwise they wouldn't have been called in.

The pilot swung the plane to the south and put the nose down. He smiled when he spotted the burned-out Spitfire that had been left derelict on the corner of the runway. It had obviously never made it home after the war. He descended confidently, and as the little plane touched down, it bounced along the pitted surface of the runway.

Flight Lieutenant Banks brought the plane to a halt about two hundred yards from the hangar, cut the propellers, and turned the lights out. The whirring slowed to an eerie whisper. They were early.

Adam watched the new arrivals suspiciously from the cockpit of the Spitfire, some four hundred yards away. His eyes never left the little unmarked plane as he waited for some clue as to who the occupants might be. A few minutes more passed before he saw six men drop out of the side of the aircraft and lie flat on their stomachs on the tarmac. They were dressed as Lawrence had said they would be, in SAS battle gear, but Adam remained unconvinced while he recalled the chauffeur's uniform Romanov had worn.

All six men on the ground hated the moon and the open space even more. The captain raised his hand, and they began to crawl toward the hangar, where Pemberton had said Scott would be waiting. With each movement they made, they became more and more confident that Pemberton's warning of an enemy waiting for them was unjustified.

A cloud briefly covered the moon, and a shadow was thrown across the airfield. The SAS captain checked his watch. Five minutes to go before the rendezvous. He was the first to reach the door of the hangar, and he pushed it open. The bullet hit him in the forehead before he had found time to raise his gun.

"Move, laddies," shouted the second-in-command, and the other four were up in a flash, firing in front of them and running for the protection of the building.

As soon as Adam heard the Scottish brogue he jumped out of the Spitfire and sprinted across the tarmac toward the little plane, whose propellers were already beginning to turn. He jumped on the wing and climbed in by the side of the surprised pilot. "I'm Adam Scott, the man you've come to pick up," he shouted.

"I'm Flight Lieutenant Alan Banks, old chap," said the pilot. "We ought to get going. My orders are to see you are brought back to England in one piece."

"But what about your men?"

"My instructions are to get you out. Their orders are to take care of themselves."

Suddenly the firing stopped. Years of night marches made it possible for Adam to see the dark figure running toward them. "Get going," Adam said.

The pilot moved the joystick forward, and the plane started moving slowly down the crumbling runway. He looked back to see a tall man whose fair hair shone in the moonlight.

"Faster, man, faster," said Adam.

"The throttle's full out," said the pilot as Romanov's bullets began ripping into the fuselage.

A third burst of gunfire came, but by then the plane had left the ground. Adam stared out his tiny window as the plane climbed steadily. Below, Romanov had turned to fire at someone who was not wearing an SAS uniform. "Where to now?" Adam asked, relief flooding through his body.

"I had hoped England, but I'm afraid the answer is as far as I can manage. Look at the fuel gauge," said Alan Banks, putting his forefinger on a little white indicator that was almost on empty. "Those bullets tore into my fuel tank."

Within moments the propellers on the left side of the aircraft spun to a halt.

"I am going to have to put her down in a field nearby. Just be thankful it's a clear, moonlit night."

Without warning, the plane began to descend sharply. "I shall try for that field over there," Banks said, pointing to a large expanse of land. "Hold on tight." Adam found himself gripping the side of his seat as the plane spiraled down.

As they touched the ground the pilot cursed. The wheels lost their grip in the soft brown earth, and the plane nose-dived. A few seconds passed before Adam realized he was still alive, but hanging upside down by his seat belt. He righted himself, pleased to find nothing broken, undid the belt, and clambered out of the plane. He searched around for a considerable time before he discovered Alan Banks some thirty yards in front of the aircraft, motionless on his back.

"Are you all right?" Adam asked.

"I'm okay. I must have been thrown clear of the plane. Sorry about the landing, old chap. Have to admit it wasn't up to scratch. We must try it again sometime."

Adam burst out laughing. "Can you walk?"

"Yes, I think so," said Banks, gingerly lifting himself up. "Damn," he said. "It's only my ankle, but it's going to slow me down. You'd better get going without me. That bunch back there with the arsenal can only be about thirty minutes behind us. Which lot are chasing us this time, by the way?"

"The Russians," said Adam, who was beginning to wonder if perhaps there was a second enemy. He touched the icon instinctively and was relieved to find it was still in place. The pilot's words had only made him more determined to get back to England.

"Which way?" he asked.

The pilot looked up at the stars. "I'll head east, seems appropriate, so you'd better go west, old fellow. Nice to have made your acquaintance." And with that, he limped off.

"I'M NOT sure how much longer I can last, Comrade Major."

"You must try to hold on, Valchek," said Romanov. "I know that plane isn't far. I saw it falling out of the sky."

"But at least, comrade, let me die a peaceful death on the side of the road rather than endure the agony of this car."

Romanov glanced across at his colleague, who had been repeatedly shot in the abdomen. Valchek's hands were covered with blood, and he held on to his stomach like a child about to be sick. The driver had been killed while attempting to run away, but Valchek was a different matter. No one could have questioned his courage. He had first taken on the British, and then the Americans, who had charged in like the 7th Cavalry. Now Romanov heard his comrade groan.

"Hold on," repeated Romanov. "Scott can't be far away."

Romanov noticed a gap in the trees ahead of him. He swung off the road onto a dirt track and drove as far as he could, until the thicket became too dense. He switched off the headlights and ran around the car to open the door.

Valchek could only manage two or three steps before he slumped to the ground. Romanov bent down and helped him to ease himself up against the trunk of a large tree.

"Do not waste any more of your time on me, Comrade Major. You should go while you still have Scott in your sights."

"But if the Americans find you, they might force you to talk."

"You know better than that, comrade."

Romanov rose. The bullet from his gun went straight through the back of Valchek's head. Romanov stood over him until he was certain he was dead. Valchek would probably not have talked, but this was not a time for taking unnecessary risks.

WHEN he awoke, he felt the familiar guilt. Once again he swore it would be the last time. It was never as good as he had anticipated, and the regret always lingered on for hours.

The expense of keeping up an extra flat, the taxi fares, and the club bills nearly made it prohibitive. But he always returned, like a salmon to its breeding ground. Once he had picked up a young man there, whom he had thought was safe. It was now so many years ago that he couldn't even remember his name.

But Mentor had never been allowed to forget the name of the young, aristocratic KGB officer he had found sitting on the end of their bed the next morning, or the look of disgust the officer had shown for both of them.

ADAM lay flat on his stomach in the bottom of the barge as it progressed at a stately pace down the canal.

The boatman stood behind the wheel counting the money for a second time. It was more than he could normally hope to earn in a month.

Adam listened anxiously for any unnatural noises, but all he could hear was the gentle splash of the water against the hull as the barge plowed its course slowly through the night. He knew they were not moving very fast, but he was grateful to be resting. He touched the icon, something he did frequently since he had discovered its secret.

The boatman's oil-covered face was not much cleaner than the old dungarees he wore. He smiled, took both hands off the wheel, and placed them by the side of his head to indicate that Adam should sleep.

Adam shook his head. Midnight had passed, and he wanted to be off the barge and away long before first light. But finally, curling up against the side of the boat, he rested his head on some old rope and allowed his eyes to close.

"THE Russians were able to get to Scott," said Sir Morris, "even though we didn't call a meeting of the D4. That icon must hold a secret that we haven't begun to appreciate."

"And if Scott is still alive," said Lawrence, "nothing is going to convince him now that we're not to blame."

"And if we're not, who is?" asked Sir Morris. "Because someone was so desperate to discover our next move that they must have taken an incredible risk during the last twenty-four hours. Unless, of course, it was you," said Sir Morris.

"Even if it was me," said Lawrence, "it doesn't explain how the Americans got there as well. Did you tell Busch?"

"No," said Sir Morris. "I told the Prime Minister, and to be fair, I knew the Prime Minister would tell the President. What I hadn't anticipated was how far the Americans would go without keeping us informed. More important: Do you think Scott can still be alive?"

"Yes, I do," said Lawrence. "I have every reason to believe that the man who ran across the tarmac to our waiting plane was Scott. The French police have informed us that our plane crashed in a field twelve miles north of Dijon, but neither Scott nor the pilot were to be found at the scene of the crash."

"And if the reports of what took place at the airport are accurate," said Sir Morris, "Romanov escaped, and they must have had a couple of hours' start on us."

"Possibly," said Lawrence.

"And do you think it equally possible," asked Sir Morris, "that they have caught up with Scott and now possess the icon?"

"Yes, sir, I fear that is quite possible," Lawrence said. "The BBC monitoring service at Caversham picked up extra-signals traffic to all Soviet embassies during the night."

"That could mean anything," said Sir Morris.

"Agreed, sir. But most revealing is that the Active Measures section of the KGB has booked pages of advertising space in newspapers right across Europe and America."

"Next you'll be telling me they hired an advertising agency to write the copy," growled Sir Morris.

"They won't need to," said Lawrence. "I suspect it's a story that will make every front page."

If it hadn't been for the ceaseless throbbing in his shoulder, Adam might not have awaked so quickly. The barge had suddenly swung at ninety degrees and started heading east. Adam looked at the boatman and indicated that the river was far wider now and could he ease them nearer to the bank so he could jump off. The old man shrugged, pretending not to understand, as the barge drifted aimlessly on.

Despite the dim light Adam could see the bed of the river quite clearly. He looked up helplessly at the boatman, who continued to stare over his head into the distance.

"Damn," said Adam, and taking the icon out of his blazer pocket, he held it high above his head. He stood on the edge of the barge and leaped into the water. His feet hit the canal bed with a thud and knocked the breath out of his body. The water came up to his waist.

He waded to the nearest bank, the icon still held high above his head, and clambered up onto the towpath. After an hour of soggy jogging he made out a light in the distance that he estimated to be under a mile away. As he got nearer he could see the outline of a large cottage. A little cobbled path led up to a half-open wooden door. Adam tapped gently with the knocker and stood directly below the light above the doorway so that whoever answered would see him immediately.

The door was pulled back by a woman of perhaps thirty, with rosy cheeks and an ample waist. She wore a plain black dress and a white apron. When she saw Adam standing under the light she couldn't mask her surprise.

Adam smiled. "*Anglais,*" he told her. "I fell in the canal."

The lady burst out laughing and beckoned him into her kitchen. He walked in, to find a man, evidently dressed for milking, sitting at a sparse wooden table. At the sight of Adam the farmer joined in the laughter.

When the woman noticed that Adam was dripping all over her spotless floor she quickly pulled down a towel from the rack above the fire and said, "*Enlevez-moi ça.*" She pointed to Adam's trousers and handed him the towel.

Adam removed his trousers, shoes, and socks, but the farmer's wife didn't budge until he had finally removed his underclothes and wrapped the towel around his waist. She picked up everything except his blazer and took them over to the sink while he stood by the fire and dried himself.

The farmer beckoned Adam to join him at the table, and Adam sat down, hanging his blazer over the back of the chair. A delicious aroma arose from the pan, where the farmer's wife was frying a thick slice of bacon cut from a joint hanging in the smoky recess of the chimney.

In moments she placed in front of him a large plate sizzling with eggs and bacon. "*Mangez*," she said.

"*Merci, merci*," Adam replied as she cut him a thick oval slice from the huge loaf of bread on the table. He began to devour the freshly cooked food, which was the first meal he'd eaten since the dinner he'd ordered at Robin's expense.

Without warning, the farmer suddenly rose from his place and thrust out his hand. Adam also got up and shook it gratefully. He remained standing as his host headed for the door, but the farmer waved him down with a further "*Mangez*."

As Adam finished the last scrap of food he tapped the jacket pocket almost automatically to make sure the icon was still safely in place. Then he pulled it out and studied Saint George and the dragon. He turned it over, hesitated, and then pressed the silver crown hard. The icon split in half, revealing two tiny hinges on the inside.

He glanced up at the farmer's wife, who was setting up an ironing board by the side of the stove and showing no interest in Adam's discovery.

Once again he stared down at the inside of the icon, which now lay open in front of him. The complete surface of the inside was covered by parchment, which was glued to the wood. The scrawled signatures in black ink and the seals gave it the look of a legal document. Adam had been surprised originally to discover that it was written in French, until he came to the date on the bottom—June 20, 1867—and remembered that long after Napoleonic times most international agreements were still conducted in French. Adam began to read the script again slowly.

His French was not good enough to enable him to translate more than a few words. Under *États-Unis*, William Seward's bold hand was scrawled across a crest of a two-headed eagle. Next to it was the signature of Aleksandr Gorchakov below a crown that mirrored the silver ornament embedded in the back of the icon. It had to be some form of agreement executed between the Russians and the Americans in 1867.

He then searched for other words that would help to explain the significance of the document. On one line he identified the words "*sept million deux cent mille dollars en or (7.2 million)*" and on another "*sept cent douze million huit cent mille dollars en or (712.8 million) le 20 juin 1966.*"

His eyes rested on a calendar hanging on the wall. It was Saturday, June 18, 1966. In only three more days the document would no longer have any legal validity. No wonder the two most powerful nations on earth seemed desperate to get their hands on it, thought Adam.

Adam wondered how the icon had come into the possession of Göring in the first place. Göring must have bequeathed it to his father unknowingly—for had he realized the true importance of what was hidden inside the icon, he would surely have been able to bargain for his own freedom with either side.

"*Voilà, voilà,*" said the farmer's wife, placing warm socks, pants, and trousers in front of Adam.

He snapped the icon closed and got dressed. He could think of no adequate way of thanking her for her hospitality, or her lack of suspicion, so he took her gently by the shoulders and kissed her on the cheek. She blushed and handed him a small plastic bag containing three apples, some bread, and a large piece of cheese. Then Adam walked outside into his other world.

13

The White House
June 18, 1966

"WHERE's our copy at this moment?" asked the President.

"Deep in the vaults of the Pentagon," said the Secretary of State. "Since the Yalta Conference our copy of the treaty has never seen the light of day. For fifty years we've believed the Russians' copy was destroyed at the time of the Revolution. Brezhnev must have come across something within the last month that convinced him their copy had only been mislaid."

"I don't want to be the first President in the history of the United States to hand back an American state rather than found one. Where do we stand on this legally?"

"Abraham Brunweld, the leading authority on documents of this period, has confirmed that the terms of the ninety-nine-year lease are binding on both sides. The lease was signed on behalf of the Russians by their Foreign Minister, Aleksandr Gorchakov, and for the Americans by the then Secretary of State, William Seward."

"Can such an agreement still be valid today?" asked the President, turning to his chief legal officer.

"It certainly can, sir," said the Attorney General. "But only if they can produce their original. Both the U.N. and the International Court at The Hague would be left with no choice but to support the Russian claim."

"There is a precedent for this," chipped in the Secretary of State. "The British will be facing a similar problem in 1997, when ownership of the New Territories of Hong Kong returns to the Chinese. They have already accepted the reality of the situation and have made it clear to the Chinese government that they are willing to come to an agreement.

"Also, in 1898," he continued, "the Russians obtained a lease on Port Arthur in northern China. The port was vital to them because, unlike Vladivostok, it is ice free all year."

"I had no idea the Russians had a port in China."

"They don't any longer, Mr. President. They returned it to Mao in 1955, as an act of goodwill between fellow Communists."

"You can be sure the Russians won't want to give this piece of land to us as an act of goodwill between fellow capitalists," said the President. "Am I left with any alternative?"

"Short of military action to prevent the Soviets' claiming what they see as rightfully theirs, no, sir," replied the Secretary of State.

"So one President Johnson buys the land from the Russians in 1867 and another has to sell it back in 1966. Why did the U.S. ever agree to such a cockamamy idea in the first place?"

"At the time," said the Attorney General, "the purchase price of the land in question was seven point two million dollars, and the price to purchase it back was set at ninety-nine times its original value, or in real terms, seven hundred and twelve point eight million dollars in gold bullion. At the time Seward had every reason to believe such a high premium would be impossible for the Russians to repay. In reality, years of inflation have made the asking price very cheap. And the Russians have already lodged the full amount in a New York bank to prove it."

"Now the land is worth that in annual oil revenue alone," said the President, looking out the Oval Office window. "Not to mention the chaos it's going to create in this country if the Russians get their hands on the original copy of the treaty. So what are the British doing about all this?"

"Playing it close to the chest, as usual, Mr. President. It's an English national who is thought to be in possession of the treaty at the moment, and they still seem quietly confident that they will get their hands on him and the icon before the Russians do."

"Meanwhile, we just sit and wait for the Soviets to move seven hundred and twelve million dollars in gold from their New York bank to the U.S. Treasury before midnight on Monday?"

"They must also deliver their original copy of the agreement to me at the same time," said the Secretary of State. "And they have only sixty hours left to do that."

AFTER leaving the cottage, Adam had walked to the nearest small town, but as soon as the early morning workers began to appear on the streets he opted for somewhere to hide while he considered his next move. He came to a halt outside a multistory parking garage and decided he was unlikely to find a better place.

He ran down the steps to the lowest level, tentatively pulled back the door to the basement, and found it almost empty. Two cars were parked in the far corner, and a thick layer of dust suggested that they had been there for some time. He checked the doors of the two cars, but they were securely locked. He crouched down behind one of them and began to plan how he could reach the coast by nightfall.

He was deep in thought when he heard a scraping noise that made him jump. He peered around the gloomy basement, and out of the darkness a man appeared, pulling behind him a plastic trash can full of rubbish. As the man came nearer, Adam could see that he was stooped and old and wearing a dirty, long brown coat. The cleaner stopped in front of him, spotted a cigarette pack, picked it up, and dropped it into the trash can. Satisfied that his task was completed, he dragged the trash can across the floor and pushed it outside. After about two minutes he returned, walked over to a wall, and pulled open a door that Adam hadn't previously noticed. He took off his coat and replaced it with a gray one. He then disappeared through the exit. Moments later Adam heard a door close with a bang.

He waited for some time before he stood up and crept around the edge of the wall to the little door. He pulled it open quietly, removed the long brown coat, tried it on, then headed back to his place in the corner. He ducked down as the first of the morning cars arrived. For the next hour he watched the cars as they continued to enter at irregular intervals. Tiresomely, all the owners carefully locked their doors and checked them before disappearing with their keys.

When he heard ten o'clock strike in the distance Adam decided that there was nothing to be gained by staying any longer. He had begun to make his way toward the exit when a Rover swung around the corner and nearly ran him down. He jumped to one side to let the car pass, but it screeched to a halt beside him, and the driver wound down his window.

"All—right—park—here?" the driver asked, emphasizing each word in an English accent.

"Oui, monsieur," said Adam.

"Other—floors—marked—*privé*," the man continued, as if addressing a complete moron. "Anywhere?"

"Oui," repeated Adam. "Bert ay merst paak you," he added, fearing he sounded too much like Peter Sellers playing Inspector Clouseau.

"Fine," said the man. He got out of the car and handed Adam his keys and a ten-franc note.

"Merci," said Adam, pocketing the note and touching his forehead with his hand. *"Quelle—heure—vous—retournez?"* he asked, playing the man at his own game.

"One hour at most," said the man as he reached the exit. Adam waited by the car for a few minutes, but the man did not come back. He opened the door and climbed into the driver's seat, then switched on the ignition and checked the fuel gauge: a little over half full. He revved the engine and drove the car up the ramp and out onto the road. It was only minutes before he was clear of the town and traveling up the N6 to Paris.

As the kilometers sped by, Adam began to wonder if it might be wiser to try a quieter road but decided, on balance, to risk pushing on to Paris as quickly as possible. When he finally reached the outskirts he proceeded on, planning to abandon the vehicle in a large public parking lot in the city. With any luck it could be days before anyone came across it.

He drove down the Rue de Rivoli and found a parking lot on a side street. He could hardly have picked a better place, as he felt sure it would be packed with foreign cars.

Adam backed the Rover into the farthest corner of the lot. He then wolfed down the cheese the farmer's wife had given him, got out, and locked the car. He had started walking toward the exit when he realized that passersby were amused by his ill-fitting brown coat. He decided to turn back and throw it into the trunk.

He was only a few yards away from the car when he saw a policeman checking the license plate and repeating letters and numbers into an intercom. Adam inched slowly back. He only needed to manage another six or seven paces before he would be lost in the crowd.

"*Alors!*" hollered the lady on whose foot Adam had stepped.

"I'm so sorry," said Adam, instinctively in English. The policeman immediately looked up and stared at Adam, then shouted something into the intercom and began running toward him.

Adam dropped the brown coat and swung around quickly, nearly knocking over the lady before sprinting off toward the exit. The lot was full of tourists who had come to enjoy the pleasures of the Louvre, and Adam found it hard to pick up any real speed through the dense crowd. By the time he reached the exit he could hear the policeman's whistle a few paces behind him. He ran across the Rue de Rivoli, through an archway, and into the Tuileries gardens.

By then another policeman was coming from his right, leaving him with no choice but to run up the steps in front of him into the Louvre museum. When he reached the top he threw himself through the door, ran past a group of Japanese tourists and a startled ticket collector, and charged on up the long marble staircase.

At the top of the staircase he turned right and ran into a special exhibition: through the moderns into the Impressionist room—Monet, Manet, Courbet—desperately looking for any way out. On into eighteenth century, but still no sign of an exit. Through the great arch into seventeenth century—as people stopped looking at the pictures and turned their attention to what was causing such a commotion. Adam ran on into the sixteenth century—suddenly aware that there were only two centuries of paintings to go.

Right or left? He chose right and entered a huge square room. There were three exits. He slowed momentarily to decide which would be his best bet when he became aware that the room was full of Russian icons. He came to a halt at an empty display case. A sign read WE REGRET THAT THIS PAINTING IS UNDERGOING RESTORATION.

The first policeman had already entered the large room. There were now only two exits from which to choose. He swung right,

only to see another policeman bearing straight down on him. Left: two more.

Adam came to a halt in the middle of the icon room at the Louvre, his hands raised above his head. He was surrounded by policemen, their guns drawn.

Sir Morris picked up the phone on his desk.

"An urgent call from Paris, sir," said his secretary.

"Thank you, Tessa." He took the call and listened carefully.

"*Merci, merci,*" Sir Morris finally said to his opposite number at the French Foreign Ministry. "We will be back in touch with you as soon as we have made all the necessary arrangements to collect him. But for now, please don't let him out of your sight. And if he has any possessions on him, please keep them guarded under lock and key. Thank you once again." His secretary took down every word of the conversation in shorthand, as she had done for the past fourteen years.

ADAM WAS MARCHED OFF TO A waiting car and yanked into the back by the policeman to whom he was handcuffed. There was a police car in front of him and yet another behind. Two motorcycle outriders led the little motorcade away. Adam felt more like visiting royalty than a criminal. Was it possible at last that someone had worked out he was innocent?

When Adam arrived at police headquarters he was immediately ordered to empty all his pockets. One wristwatch, one apple, some traveler's checks and some Swiss currency, and one British passport in the name of Dudley Hulme. The inspector asked him politely to strip to his underclothes. Once Adam had done so, the inspector carefully checked every pocket of the blazer, even the lining.

"Do you have anything else in your possession?" the officer asked in slow, precise English.

"No," was all Adam replied.

The inspector checked the blazer once again but came across nothing new. "You must get dressed," he said abruptly.

Adam put back on his shirt, blazer, and trousers, but the inspector kept his tie and shoelaces.

"All your things will be returned to you when you leave," the inspector explained. Adam nodded as he slipped on his shoes, which flapped uncomfortably when he walked. He was then accompanied to a small cell on the same floor and locked in. He looked around. A wooden table with two wooden chairs, a single bed with an ancient mattress on it, one small window. He took off his blazer, hung it over the chair, and lay down on the bed.

As the minutes ticked by, he made one decision. That he would demand a lawyer. An officer appeared half an hour later, carrying a tray laden with hot soup, a roll, a steak with all the trimmings, and a plastic cup filled to the brim with red wine. Adam wondered if they had got the wrong man or if this was his last meal before the guillotine. He followed the officer to the door.

"I demand to speak to a lawyer," he said emphatically, but the policeman only shrugged and slammed the door behind him.

Adam settled down to eat the meal that had been set before him, thankful that the French assumed good food should be served whatever the circumstances.

SIR MORRIS TOLD THEM HIS NEWS and then studied each of them carefully. He would never have called the D4 if he hadn't felt sure that Adam was at last in safe hands. Matthews continued to show no emotion. Busch was unusually silent, while Snell looked almost relaxed for a change. Lawrence was the only one who seemed genuinely pleased.

"Scott is being held by the police in Paris," announced Sir Morris. "I have contacted our military attaché at the embassy."

"Colonel Pollard," interrupted Lawrence.

"Colonel Pollard, indeed," said Sir Morris. "Who has been sent over in the ambassador's car and will bring Scott back to be debriefed at our embassy." Sir Morris turned toward his number two. "You will fly over to Paris tonight and conduct the debriefing yourself."

"Yes, sir," said Lawrence, looking up at his boss with a smile.

Sir Morris nodded. A cool lot, he considered as he stared around that table, wondering which of them served two masters.

Mentor smiled as Sir Morris left the room. His task had already been completed. So simple when you can read shorthand upside down.

A BLACK Jaguar bearing diplomatic plates had arrived at police headquarters a few minutes earlier than expected. The inspector, who was standing on the steps as Pollard jumped out of the car, looked at the flapping Union Jack on the hood and decided the whole exercise was becoming rather melodramatic.

Pollard was a short, thickset man dressed in a tweed suit and a regimental tie and carrying a rolled umbrella. The inspector took him directly to the room where Adam had been incarcerated.

"Pollard's the name, Colonel Pollard. British military attaché here in Paris. Sorry you've been put through this, old fellow, but a lot of paperwork had to be completed. Bloody red tape."

"I understand," said Adam, jumping off the bed and shaking the colonel's hand.

"Still, the problem's been sorted out now," continued the colonel. "The French police have been most cooperative and have agreed to let you accompany me to our embassy."

The inspector led them both back out into the hall, where

Adam had to identify and sign for his personal belongings. He wasn't surprised they didn't return Dudley Hulme's passport.

"Don't let's hang around too long, old fellow," said the colonel, beginning to sound a little anxious.

"I won't be a moment," said Adam. "I'm just as keen to get out of this place as you are." He inserted and tied his shoelaces before following Colonel Pollard and the inspector out to the waiting Jaguar. He noticed for the first time that the colonel had a slight limp. A chauffeur held the door open; Adam laughed.

"Something funny, old fellow?" asked the colonel.

"No. It's just that the last chauffeur who offered to do that for me didn't look quite as friendly."

Adam climbed into the back of the Jaguar, and the colonel slipped in beside him.

"Back to the embassy," said Pollard, and the car moved off.

Adam stared in horror at the flapping Union Jack.

14

WHEN Adam awoke, he was naked, and his arms and legs were bound by a nylon cord to a chair placed in the middle of a bare room. Pollard was standing over him. The moment the colonel was satisfied that Adam had regained consciousness, he left the room.

Adam turned his head to see all his clothes laid out neatly on a bed at the far side of the cell. He tried to loosen the cords around his wrists, rubbing them up and down against the wood of the slats, but his arms were bound so tightly that he could only manage the slightest friction.

The door swung open. Adam looked up as Romanov strode through, followed by another man whom Adam didn't recognize. The second man was clutching what looked like a cigar box as he took his place somewhere behind Adam. Pollard followed him.

Romanov looked at Adam and smiled, enjoying his humiliation. He came to a halt directly in front of the chair.

"My name is Aleksandr Petrovich Romanov," he announced.

"Or Emmanuel Rosenbaum," said Adam, staring at his adversary closely.

Romanov began circling the chair. "First I should like to congratulate you on having eluded me for so long, but as you will now realize, my source in London can work every bit as quickly as your friend Lawrence Pemberton."

"Your source?" said Adam.

"Don't be naïve. You're in no position to be asking questions."

Adam fixed his gaze on a brick in the wall in front of him, making no attempt to follow Romanov's circumnavigations.

"I think you have already met our Colonel Pollard," Romanov continued. "That's not his real name, of course, and indeed he's not a real colonel either, but that's what he always wanted to be in life, so when the opportunity arose, we happily obliged. He did serve in the British army, but only as a private soldier, I fear."

Adam's eyes remained fixed on the wall. "I confess, our mistake over the Union Jack was lax, but you must admit it is all too easy to fly your flag upside down. We must be thankful that you did not spot it until the car doors were safely locked."

Romanov stopped his endless circling. "Now I think the time has come for you to be introduced to our Dr. Stravinsky, who has so been looking forward to meeting you."

Stravinsky took his place immediately in front of Adam, the cigar box still tucked under his arm. Adam stared at the diminutive figure who seemed to be sizing him up. Stravinsky wore a badly creased gray suit, and a one-day bristle covered his face. His thin lips suddenly parted in a grin.

"It is a pleasure to make your acquaintance, Captain Scott," he began. "You could, of course, make our association very short by simply letting me have one piece of information." He let out a small sigh. "The whereabouts of the czar's icon."

Adam didn't reply.

"So it seems I must follow the normal procedure in such circumstances. You may have wondered," added Stravinsky, as if it were an afterthought, "why I am carrying a cigar box."

Stravinsky waited for Adam's reply, but none was forthcoming.

"Ah, no attempt at conversation. I see you have been through such an experience before. Well, then I must continue talking to myself for the moment. When I was a student at the University of Moscow my subject was chemistry. I specialized in one particular aspect of the science—scientific interrogation."

Adam feigned indifference as he tried not to recall his worst days in the hands of the Chinese.

"Torture, of course, is an old and honorable profession," Stravinsky went on. "The Chinese have been at it for nearly three thousand years, and even you British have come a long way since the rack. But that particular instrument has proved to be rather cumbersome for carrying around in a modern world. With this in mind, Moscow has developed something small and simple. So I will ask you once and once only before I open the box. Where is the czar's icon?"

Adam still made no comment.

Stravinsky put the box on the floor and opened it slowly. "First, I offer you," he said like a conjurer in front of a child, "a six-volt nickel-cadmium battery. Second," he continued, "a small pulse generator." He placed the rectangular metal box next to the battery. "Third, two lengths of wire, with electrodes attached. Fourth, a tube of collodion glue. And finally, two syringes and a vial, if it becomes necessary for us to progress to stage two in our little experiment, or even stage three."

Stravinsky placed everything in a straight line on the floor. "Now a few details about the nervous system. By sending a small electrical impulse to the end of a synapse, it is possible to pass a large electric message to thousands of other nerves within a fraction of a second. This causes a nasty sensation commonly referred to as an electric shock. This is known as stage one, and there is no necessity for you to experience it if you are now willing to tell me where I can find the czar's icon."

Adam remained impassive.

"I see you have not paid attention during my little lecture, so I fear we will have to move from the theoretical to the practical."

Adam began reciting to himself the titles of Shakespeare's thirty-eight plays. How pleased his old English master would have been to learn that after all those years Adam could still recall them. *Henry the Sixth, Part One*; *Henry the Sixth, Part Two*; *Henry the Sixth, Part Three*; *Richard the Second . . .*

Stravinsky picked up the tube of collodion glue, removed the cap, and smeared two lumps of it on Adam's chest. Then the Russian attached the two electrodes to the glue, taking the wires back and screwing them to the six-volt battery, which in turn was connected to the tiny pulse generator.

Two Gentlemen of Verona, Love's Labour's Lost, Romeo and Juliet . . .

Without warning, Stravinsky pressed down the handle of the generator for two seconds, during which time Adam received a two-hundred-volt shock to every part of his body. He gripped the seat of the chair and mumbled to himself, *Richard the Third, A Midsummer Night's Dream, King John . . .*

Stravinsky pressed the plunger down for another two seconds. Adam felt the pain instantly. The moment it was over, he felt violently nauseated, but he managed to remain conscious.

"Impressive," said Stravinsky. "You have definitely qualified to enter stage two, from which you can be spared immediately by answering one simple question: Where is the czar's icon?"

Adam's mouth had become so dry that he couldn't speak.

Stravinsky turned. "Fetch the captain some water, Colonel."

A moment later a bottle was thrust into Adam's mouth. He gulped half the contents down and spat what was left of the water toward his adversary. Stravinsky leaped forward and slapped Adam hard across the face with the back of his hand. Adam's head slumped.

"You give me no choice but to advance to stage two," said Stravinsky. "I only need inject an ingenious solution known as M and multiply the shock by a few milliamps to create a far more interesting effect." He took a syringe from the floor, jabbed the long, thin needle into the vial, and stood behind Adam.

Adam didn't move a muscle as he felt the syringe go into his back. Now he began to recite aloud. "*Troilus and Cressida, All's Well That Ends Well . . .*"

"You are a brave man, Scott," said Romanov, "but this is madness. Just tell me where the icon is, and I will send Stravinsky away and order the colonel to leave you at the British embassy."

"*Macbeth, Antony and Cleopatra . . .*"

Romanov let out a sigh and nodded. Stravinsky pushed the plunger down once again. Even the colonel turned white as he watched Adam's reaction. The pitch of the scream rose as Adam felt the volts reach the millions of little nerve ends in his body.

Stravinsky stared down at him. "Most impressive, Captain Scott. You have qualified for stage three."

Adam passed out.

WHEN Lawrence arrived at Orly Airport that evening he was looking forward to a quiet dinner with Adam at the ambassador's residence. He was met by the real Colonel Pollard.

"How is he?" were Lawrence's first words.

"I hoped you were going to tell us," said Pollard.

Lawrence stopped in his tracks and stared at the tall, thin soldier. "What do you mean?" he said.

"Simply that I followed your instructions to the letter and went to pick up Scott, but when I arrived at police headquarters I was informed that he had been taken away twenty minutes earlier by someone else using my name. We contacted your office immediately, but as you were already en route, the ambassador ordered me straight to the airport while he phoned Sir Morris."

Lawrence staggered and nearly fell. The colonel came quickly to his side. He didn't understand what Lawrence meant when he said, "He's bound to believe it's me."

WHEN Adam regained consciousness Romanov stood alone in front of him.

"Sometimes," said the Russian, "a man is too proud to show lack of resolution in front of the torturer, or indeed one of his own countrymen, especially a traitor. That is why I have removed Stravinsky and the colonel from our presence. But I can only stop Stravinsky from continuing to stage three if you tell me where you have put the icon."

"Why should I?" said Adam belligerently. "It's legally mine."

"Not so, Captain Scott. What you picked up from the bank in Geneva is the priceless original, painted by Rublev, which belongs to the Union of Soviet Socialist Republics. For fifty years the Soviet Union has only had a copy."

Adam looked in disbelief as Romanov removed from the inside pocket of his overcoat an icon of Saint George and the dragon. Romanov turned it over and smiled as Adam's eyes registered the significance of the missing crown.

"Like you," continued Romanov, "I only have this one on loan—but if you tell me where the original is, I will release you and exchange the copy for the original. No one will be any the wiser. After all, you cannot sell what belongs to us. This way, you'd make a worthwhile profit."

Adam didn't even bother to shake his head.

"Then the time has obviously come to give you some information you will be more interested in," Romanov said, extracting a sheet of paper from his inside pocket. He opened it slowly.

"This single sheet of paper reveals a sentence carried out in Moscow in 1946. The death sentence," continued Romanov, "pronounced on a certain Major Vladimir Kosky, the Russian guard in charge of the Soviet watch at Nuremberg the night Reichsmarschall Hermann Göring died. Major Kosky was found guilty of smuggling cyanide into the Reichsmarschall's cell on the night he died." Adam's eyes widened. "Ah, I see I have dealt the ace," said Romanov. "Now I think you will finally tell me where the icon actually is. It's a fair exchange. Your icon for my icon, plus the legal judgment that will finally vindicate your father's honor."

Adam closed his eyes.

Romanov was unable to hide his anger. He walked to the door and flung it open. "He's yours," he said.

Dr. Stravinsky reentered the room smiling and continued as if nothing had interrupted him. "I was never really satisfied with stage two," he said, "because the recovery time could sometimes take hours, even days. But then a solution was found—a rapid analgesic." Stravinsky removed another vial from the cigar box.

"This," Stravinsky said, holding up the little vial in triumph, "when injected into your bloodstream, will aid recovery so quickly that you may even wonder if you ever went through any pain in the first place. Then I can repeat the process every thirty minutes for the next week, if that is your desire."

Stravinsky stood in front of Adam and half filled the second syringe. Moments later Adam felt the needle, and the fluid entered his bloodstream.

In minutes he no longer felt sick or disoriented. The sensation in his arms and legs returned to normal, while the wish never to experience stage two again became acute.

"Coriolanus, Timon of Athens, Pericles." Stravinsky thrust down the handle of the generator, and Adam found a new level to scream at, as his body shook.

"Now, where is the icon?" Stravinsky shouted.

In the Louvre, Adam wanted to holler, but his words barely came out as a whisper. Stravinsky filled the syringe again and injected Adam with the fluid. Once again it was only moments before the agony began to subside.

Romanov stepped forward and, looking straight at Adam, said, "I feel Dr. Stravinsky and I have earned a little supper. When we return, he will repeat the entire exercise again and again, until you let me know where you have hidden the icon."

As they left, Colonel Pollard entered the room. He came over to Adam and offered him some water. Adam gulped it down and was genuinely surprised at how quickly he was recovering. But he doubted he could survive one more time.

"I'm going to throw up," he said suddenly. Pollard quickly undid the knots and Adam slumped to his knees. He threw up some spit and rested before the colonel helped him back up. As Adam sat down, he gripped both sides of the chair firmly; then, with all the strength he could muster, he jackknifed forward, swung the chair over his head, and brought it crashing down on top of the unsuspecting colonel. Pollard collapsed in a heap, unconscious, and never heard Adam utter the words *"Henry the Eighth* and *The Two Noble Kinsmen*—I'll bet that's one you don't know, Colonel. Mind you, not everyone thinks Shakespeare wrote it."

Adam waited for a few more seconds as he tried to measure what was left of his strength. He picked up the water bottle and drained it of its last drops. He then crawled across to the bed and pulled on his clothes. He was about to put on the blazer but changed his mind and stumbled like an old man toward the colonel, removed his Harris Tweed jacket, and slipped it on.

He made his way to the door, opened it an inch, and stared through the crack. All he could see was a dark corridor. There was a light shining through a pebbled pane in a door at the far end. He crept toward it and turned the knob slowly. Then he was outside and trying to get his bearings. In the moonlight he could just make out a high wall about twenty yards ahead of him. Summoning up every ounce of energy, he ran to the wall and clung to it, remaining motionless in its shadow. Slowly and silently he moved around the wall, yard by yard, until he reached the front of what he now felt sure was the Russian embassy. The great gates at the front entrance were open, and every few seconds limousines swept past him. At the top of the embassy steps he saw a massive man in formal dress shaking hands with each of his departing guests. Adam assumed he was the ambassador.

There were two armed gendarmes at the gate, who stood rigidly to attention and saluted as each car went by. Adam waited until a BMW, the West German flag fluttering on its hood, slowed as it passed through the gates. Following closely behind, he walked straight between the guards toward the road.

"*Bonsoir,*" he said lightly to the guards as the car moved forward. Walk, he told himself; don't run. They saluted deferentially. Don't look back. He kept his eyes firmly to the front.

Adam had ended up in a badly lit one-way street. "Do you search for a girl?" a voice said from the shadows of a recessed doorway. The voice had an unmistakable French accent.

"You speak English?" asked Adam, unable to see clearly.

"You have to know a lot of languages in my profession, *chéri.*"

Adam tried to think coherently. Although he had no money, the girl might lead him to safety. "Two hundred francs?" he asked.

"*D'accord,*" said the girl, stepping out of the shadows. "Take my arm, and if you pass a gendarme, say only, '*Ma femme.*' "

Adam stumbled forward.

"My apartment is just around the corner," she assured him. Adam was not confident he could get that far, and he took a deep breath when they arrived at a block of flats. He just managed to reach the front door.

"I live on the top of the house, *chéri*. Very nice view."

Adam said nothing, but leaned against the outside wall, breathing deeply. By the time they had reached the second floor, she almost had to drag him up the last few steps.

She strode into the flat, turning on lights as she went.

Adam staggered toward the only chair in sight and collapsed

into it. As she stood in the light of the doorway Adam was able to see her properly for the first time. Her blond hair was short and curly, and she wore a red blouse, a knee-length, skintight black skirt, and black mesh stockings.

She walked over to Adam with a slight swing of the hips and knelt down in front of him. "Would you please give me the two hundred now?" she asked without harshness.

"I don't have any money," said Adam quite simply.

"What?" she said, sounding angry for the first time. Placing her hand in his inside pocket, she removed a wallet. "Then what's this?" she said, handing the thick billfold over to Adam. He opened the flap to find it was jammed full of French francs and a few English pounds. Colonel Pollard was obviously paid in cash for his services.

Adam extracted two hundred-franc notes and handed them over. "That's better," she said, disappearing into the other room.

Adam checked through the wallet to discover a driver's license and a couple of credit cards in the colonel's real name of Albert Tomkins. He quickly looked around. A double bed took up most of the floor space. To his left was a small fireplace, with logs stacked neatly in one corner. With what strength was left in his body Adam pushed himself up, wobbled over to the fireplace, and hid the wallet among the logs. He lurched back toward the chair and fell into it as the door reopened.

Again the girl stood in the light of the doorway, but this time she wore only a pink negligee. She walked slowly across the room and once more knelt down beside him.

"I only want to rest a few minutes," Adam told her.

"*Les Anglais*," she said skeptically, and helped Adam toward the bed. Before she could cover him with a blanket, he was asleep.

When Adam awoke, the sun was shining into the room. He blinked as he took in his surroundings and tried to recall what had happened the night before. Suddenly it all came back to him. He looked around the room, but the girl was nowhere to be seen or heard. Then he remembered the wallet.

He sat upright, gathering himself for a few moments before standing up and trying to walk. Although he was still unsteady, it was better than he had expected. When he reached the fireplace he searched among the logs, but the colonel's wallet was no longer there. He went to the tweed jacket hanging over the back of the chair. He checked the inside pocket: a passport and some papers, but no wallet. He searched the outside pockets: a bunch of keys, a penknife, a few assorted coins. With a string of oaths he sat down and didn't move, until he heard a key in the lock.

The front door of the flat swung open, and the girl sauntered in, carrying a shopping basket. She was now dressed in a pretty floral skirt and white blouse. The basket was crammed with food.

"Where's my wallet?" asked Adam coldly.

"On the table," said the girl, pointing.

Adam glanced across the room to see that she had left the wallet in the most obvious place.

"It not necessary of you to 'ide it," she reprimanded him. "I'm not a thief." With this, she strode off into the kitchen.

Adam suddenly felt very small. "I'm sorry. I was stupid," he said to her, walking to the kitchen door.

"Not to think about it," she said. "*Ça n'est rien.*"

"I still don't know your name," said Adam.

"My working name is Brigitte, but as you 'ave not use my services, you can call me by my real name—Jeanne."

"Can I have a bath, Jeanne?"

"The door in the corner, but don't take too long, unless you like croissants cold." Adam made his way to the bathroom and found Jeanne had provided everything a man might need: a razor, shaving cream, soap, washcloth, clean towels.

After a warm bath and a shave Adam felt almost normal, if still somewhat fragile. He joined Jeanne in the kitchen. The table was already laid, and she was removing croissants from the oven. Adam spread one liberally with jam and devoured every crumb.

"Tell me, Jeanne," he said finally. "Are you still available for work? I would be willing to pay you another two hundred francs."

"Is it legal?"

"Absolutely."

"*Alors*, that makes a change. What am I expected to do?"

"For one hour I want every man in Paris to fancy you. Only this time you won't be available—at any price."

"SCOTT CONTACTED ME ONLY A few minutes ago," said Lawrence to the assembled D4.

"What did he have to say?" asked an anxious Sir Morris.

"Only that he was turning back the clock."

"What do you think he meant by that?" asked Snell, nervously touching his mustache.

"Geneva would be my guess," said Lawrence.

"Why Geneva?" said Matthews.

"I'm not certain," said Lawrence, "but he said it had something to do with the German girl, or the bank, I can't be sure which."

"Did you trace the call?" asked Busch.

"Only the area," said Lawrence. "Neuchâtel on the French-Swiss border."

"Good. We're in business again," said Sir Morris. "Have you informed Interpol?"

"Yes, sir, and I've personally briefed the German, French, and Swiss police," added Lawrence, which were the only true words he had spoken since the meeting had begun.

JEANNE took forty minutes to get herself ready, and when Adam saw the result he let out a long whistle.

"No one is going to give me a second look walking behind you," he told her.

"That is the idea, *n'est-ce pas?*" Jeanne said, grinning.

"Now, are you sure you know exactly what you have to do?"

Jeanne checked herself once more in the long hall mirror. "We 'ave rehearse like military exercise, four times already."

"Good," said Adam. "You sound as if you're ready to face the enemy. So let's begin."

Jeanne took out a plastic bag from a drawer in the kitchen. She handed it over to Adam, and he stuffed it into his jacket pocket. Then they walked down the stairs and out onto the street. Adam hailed a taxi, and Jeanne told the driver, "Tuileries gardens."

Once they had arrived, Adam paid the fare and joined Jeanne on the pavement. "*Bonne chance,*" said Adam. Then Jeanne set off to walk twenty yards ahead of him. Although he still felt unsteady, he was able to keep up her pace as she strode among the ornate flower beds. Her pink leather skirt and tight white sweater made almost every man she passed turn and take a second look.

Adam was still behind her when she reached the entrance to the Louvre. By the time she had reached the swinging doors, Adam was approaching the bottom step. She continued on up the marble staircase, with Adam still following discreetly.

Jeanne proceeded through the large, crowded rooms until she arrived in the gallery Adam had described to her so vividly. She strode purposefully into the center and paused for a few seconds. Some of the men began to lose interest in the paintings. Satisfied by the impact she was making, she flounced over to the guard, who straightened up his jacket and smiled at her.

"Where can I find the sixteenth-century paintings?" Jeanne asked innocently. The guard turned to point in the direction of the relevant room. The moment he turned back, Jeanne slapped him hard across the face and shouted at him at the top of her voice, "How dare you! What do you take me for!"

Only one person in the icon room didn't stop to stare at the spectacle. "I'm going to speak to the director!" she screamed, and flounced off toward the main exit. The entire charade was over in less than thirty seconds. The guard stared after his assailant in bewilderment.

Moments later Jeanne joined Adam at the top of the marble staircase leading down to the front entrance. As they walked back down the steps together Adam handed her the plastic bag. Then two attendants waiting on the bottom step stopped them.

"Madame, excuse me, but may I examine your bag?" the senior attendant asked suspiciously.

"Certainly, you can search her bag," said Adam. "You'll find an icon, quite a good one, I think. I purchased it in a shop near the Champs-Élysées only this morning."

He removed the czar's icon from the bag and handed it over to the attendant, who seemed surprised by the way things were turning out. He asked in broken English if Adam would mind if one of the gallery's experts were to look at the painting.

"Only too delighted," said Adam. "It would be fascinating to have a second opinion."

The senior attendant was beginning to be unsure of himself. He ushered them quickly into a little room and put the czar's icon in the middle of a table. Adam sat down, and Jeanne, bemused, took the seat beside him.

"I'll only be a moment, sir." The senior attendant almost ran out, while the other attendant remained stationed near the door. When the door eventually opened, an elderly man with a scholarly face preceded the senior attendant.

"*Bonjour, monsieur,*" the man began. He gave the icon no more than a glance. "Most interesting," he said. "But you do realize it's an inferior copy? The original czar's icon hangs in the Winter Palace in Leningrad. I've seen it, you know," he added, sounding rather pleased with himself.

You certainly have, said Adam under his breath as he placed the icon back in its plastic bag.

The old man bowed low to Jeanne and said as he shuffled away, "Funnily enough, someone else was making inquiries about the czar's icon only a few weeks ago."

The attendant accompanied the two of them to the exit, and they walked down the steps and into the Paris sun.

"Well, can I now know what that's all about?" asked Jeanne.

"You were *magnifique*," said Adam, not attempting to explain.

"I know, I know," said Jeanne. "But why you need Oscar-winning show by me when the picture was always yours?"

"I had left it in their safekeeping overnight. And without your bravura performance it might have taken considerably longer to convince the authorities that it belonged to me in the first place."

"You know, that was my first time in the Louvre," she said, linking her arm through Adam's.

"You're priceless," said Adam, laughing.

"That I'm not," she said, turning to face him. "Two hundred francs was our bargain."

"Correct," said Adam, taking out the colonel's wallet and extracting two hundred francs, to which he added another hundred. "A well-earned bonus," said Adam.

She pocketed the money gratefully. "I think I'll take an evening off," she said.

Adam held her in his arms and kissed her on both cheeks. She smiled. "When you next in Paris, *chéri*, look me up. I owe you one—on the house."

"I WOULD LIKE TO RENT A CAR, which I will be dropping off at the coast. I haven't decided which port yet," Adam told the girl behind the car-rental counter.

"Would you be kind enough to fill in the form, monsieur," said the girl. "And we will also need your driver's license." Adam passed over the colonel's license. He filled in the forms slowly, copying the signature off the back of one of the colonel's credit cards. He handed over the full amount required in cash.

The girl counted the notes carefully before checking the signature on the form against the back of the license. Adam was relieved that she hadn't spotted the disparity between his age and the date of birth. He replaced Albert Tomkins' documents and wallet in his inside jacket pocket as the girl handed him an ignition key.

"It's a red Citroën, parked on the first floor," she told him. "The registration number is stamped on the key ring."

Adam thanked her and walked quickly up to the first floor, where he handed the key over to an attendant, who drove the car out of its parking space for him.

The attendant returned the key, and Adam handed him a ten-franc note. Exactly the same sum as another man had given the attendant only hours before. That man had wanted to be informed if an Englishman who fitted Adam's description tried to hire a car. What had he promised? Another hundred francs if the attendant phoned within five minutes of seeing him.

15

The Kremlin, Moscow.
June 19, 1966

LEONID Ilyich Brezhnev entered the room, hardly allowing the other four men enough time to stand. Their faces were grim, resolute.

The General Secretary took his place at the head of the table and nodded to his colleagues to sit. On his right sat Marshal Malinovsky, minister of defense; on his left Andrei Gromyko, the Foreign Minister. Beside Gromyko sat the chief of the general staff, Marshal Zakharov, and on his left, Yuri Zaborski. Even the seating plan confirmed Brezhnev's obvious displeasure with the chairman of the KGB.

His eyes rested on Zaborski. "Your report, comrade."

Zaborski fingered a file in front of him, although he knew the contents almost by heart. "The Englishman Adam Scott was caught and later . . . questioned by Comrade Dr. Stravinsky in the privacy of our embassy in Paris, but he would give no clue as to where we would find the icon. After three hours, interrogation was momentarily suspended. It was during this period that the prisoner managed to escape."

"Managed," interjected Brezhnev. "Don't you realize that we had within our grasp the opportunity to turn the very land the Americans use for their early-warning system into a base for our short-range missiles? If we retrieve our icon, it will be possible to site those missiles less than eighteen hundred kilometers from Seattle, twenty-eight hundred kilometers from San Francisco, a mere four thousand kilometers from Chicago. If we fail to locate the czar's icon in the next thirty-six hours, we will never be given such a chance again. We will have lost our one opportunity to remove a star from the American flag."

Foreign Minister Gromyko waited until he was certain Brezhnev had completed his statement before he inquired of Zaborski, "If I may ask, Comrade Chairman, why was Major Romanov allowed to remain involved in such a sensitive operation after it was suspected he had killed researcher Petrova?"

"Because," replied Zaborski, at last looking up, "in my judgment there was no one who could have taken over Romanov's place at such short notice."

There was a timid knock on the door. All the faces around the table showed surprise. "Come in," shouted Brezhnev.

The great door inched open, and a secretary walked nervously toward them, deposited a Telex on the table, and almost ran out.

Brezhnev slowly unfolded his glasses before picking up the missive. Once he had read through the cable, he looked up at the expectant faces in front of him. "It seems an Englishman left an icon in the Louvre and picked it up this morning."

The blood drained from Zaborski's face.

The four men all began talking together, until Brezhnev raised his vast hand. There was immediate silence. "I intend to continue my plans on the assumption that we will still get to the Englishman first." Brezhnev turned toward his Foreign Minister. "Instruct Anatoly Dobrynin in Washington to demand an official meeting with the U.S. Secretary of State for late Monday."

Gromyko nodded as Brezhnev turned to the chief of the general staff. "See that our strategic forces in all zones are in a state of readiness, to coincide with the announcement of our diplomatic initiative." Zakharov smiled. The General Secretary finally turned to the chairman of the KGB. "Do we still have advertising space booked in every major newspaper in the West?"

"Yes, Comrade General Secretary," replied Zaborski. "But if we don't find the icon—"

"Then your last duty as chairman of the KGB will be to find a way to withdraw all the advertisements," said Brezhnev.

ADAM wound down the car window and immediately the warm summer air flooded in. He had decided to avoid the main road to Calais in favor of the road to Boulogne. He was confident that once he had cleared the outskirts of the French capital, he could average seventy kilometers an hour the rest of the way. But what he hadn't anticipated was running into a hundred or more cyclists, garbed in their various stripes of red, green, blue, black, and gold, bobbing along ahead of him. He honked his horn loudly as he passed a group of four men quite near the front, with the British team van driving just ahead of them.

"IT WAS foolish of you to contact me, Romanov. You're not exactly a hero of the Soviet Union at the present time."

"Listen, Comrade Poskonov, I don't have to be a hero any longer, because I may never come back to the Soviet Union."

"Be warned: Mother Russia has extremely long fingernails."

"And because of my grandfather's foresight I can afford to cut them off." Romanov leaned back at a desk in the Paris embassy and touched the gold medallion beneath his shirt. "I just need to be sure you don't let them know where I keep the scissors."

"Why should I remain silent?" asked the old banker.

"Because if I haven't got my hands on Saint George within the next twenty-four hours, I'll phone again with the details of how you can hope to collect a larger golden handshake than you'll get from your present employers."

The banker offered no comment.

The ambassador's secretary rushed into the room without knocking. "I told you, no interruptions," shouted Romanov.

"But we've located Scott."

Romanov slammed the phone down.

In Moscow, the old Russian banker wound the tape back. Poskonov smiled and listened to Romanov's words a second time, and came to the conclusion that Romanov had left him with only one choice. He booked a flight to Zurich.

"ROBIN?"

"Adam! Where have you got to?"

"I'm just outside Paris on my way back home," Adam said. "Are you sticking to the schedule you outlined on the bus?"

"Sure am. The orchestra is taking the ferry from Dunkerque at six thirty tonight. Can you join us?"

"No. I have to return by another route. But Robin, when I reach London can you put me up for the night?"

"Sounds like an offer I can't refuse," she said, and gave him her address. "When shall I expect you?"

"Around midnight tonight."

"Do you always give a girl so much notice?"

The young KGB officer assigned to tail Robin in Amsterdam was standing in the adjoining booth. He had caught most of the conversation, and he smiled when he recalled Major Romanov's words: "The man who brings me the czar's icon need have no fear for his future prosperity."

ADAM jumped back into the car and drove on until he reached the outskirts of Beauvais, where he decided to stop for a quick lunch. The ferry he wanted to catch was due to leave Boulogne at three o'clock, so he felt confident he would still make it with about an hour to spare.

He sat hidden in an alcove by the window, enjoying his lunch, and watched as the first of the cyclists pedaled through Beauvais.

The sight of the athletes reminded Adam that he was expected at his medical examination for the Foreign Office the following afternoon.

ROMANOV read the decoded message a second time. "Scott returning Geneva. Check German girl and bank." He looked up at the senior KGB officer who had handed him the missive.

"Does Mentor think I'm that naïve?" said Romanov to his colleague. "We already know from our agent in Amsterdam that Scott's on his way toward the French coast."

"Why should Mentor send you in the opposite direction?"

"Perhaps he's switched sides," Romanov said coldly.

He turned to the officer. "We know it won't be Dunkerque, so how many other possibilities are we left with?"

"Cherbourg, Le Havre, Dieppe, Boulogne, or Calais," replied the officer, looking at a map. "My bet would be Calais."

"Unfortunately," said Romanov, "Captain Scott is not quite *that* simple. As the motorway takes you direct to Calais, Scott will expect us to have that part of his route well covered. I think our friend will try Boulogne or Dieppe first."

He checked the timetable. "The first boat he could hope to catch leaves Boulogne for Dover at three, and then there's one from Dieppe to Newhaven at five. Assuming we can beat him to the coast, I think Captain Scott is once again within our grasp."

ONCE Adam had left the restaurant, it was only minutes before he began to catch up with the straggling cyclists as they pedaled on toward Boulogne. He remained in the center of the road to avoid the bicycles, but he had to slam his brakes on suddenly when an Italian and a British rider collided in front of him and the two men were thrown unceremoniously to the ground.

Adam spotted the British team van ahead and speeded up until he was alongside. He waved at the driver to pull over. The man looked surprised but stopped and wound down the window.

"One of your chaps has had an accident about a mile back," shouted Adam, pointing toward Paris.

"Thanks, mate," said the driver, who turned around and sped quickly down the road.

Adam drove on until he had passed all the leaders. Then a signpost informed him that it was now only thirty-two kilometers to Boulogne; he would still make the three-o'clock sailing comfortably. He began to imagine what life might be like if he could survive beyond tomorrow. Jogs in the park, Foreign Office interviews, even acknowledgment of the part he had played in delivering the icon into safe hands. The problem was that he hadn't yet decided who had safe hands.

A helicopter looking like a squat green bullfrog swept over him, and he watched as it turned and swung back. A few moments later it flew across his path at a considerably lower level. Adam gripped the wheel of the car as an impossible thought crossed his mind. As he did so, the helicopter swung back again and this time flew straight toward him.

Leaning over the top of the steering wheel, Adam stared into the sky. He could see three figures sitting in the helicopter cockpit. He banged his fist on the steering wheel in anger. He could sense Romanov's smile of triumph as the chopper hovered over him.

Adam swung off the main road toward a village called Fleureville. He pushed the speedometer well over ninety, causing the little car to skid along the country lanes. The helicopter likewise swung to the right and, doglike, followed his path.

Adam took the next right and headed back toward the Boulogne road, desperately trying to think what he could do next. Every time he looked up, the helicopter was there above him.

A road sign depicting a low tunnel flashed past, and as Adam entered it, for a brief moment he actually felt safe. He slammed on the Citroën's brakes and skidded to a halt about thirty yards from the end of the tunnel. He switched on his lights, and they shone brightly in the darkness. For several seconds he watched as cars slowed down before safely overtaking him.

He jumped out of the car and ran to the end of the tunnel, where he pinned himself against the wall. The helicopter was already turning back and heading straight toward the tunnel. Adam watched it fly over his head and moments later heard it turn again. As he waited, two hitchhikers passed by on the other side of the tunnel, chatting away to each other.

Adam looked across desperately at the two young men and shouted, "Were you hoping to thumb a lift?"

"Yes," they called. Adam staggered across the road.

"Are you all right?" one of them asked.

"No, I'm not," Adam explained simply. "I drank too much at lunch, and because of a cycle race the road is crawling with police. I'm sure to be picked up if I go on. Can either of you drive?"

"I only have my Canadian license," said the taller of the two youths. "And in any case we are heading for Paris, and your car is facing the opposite direction."

"It's a Hertz Rent A Car," Adam explained. "I picked it up in Paris this morning, and I have to return it by seven tonight. I don't think I can make it in my present state."

The two young men looked at him apprehensively. He added, "I will give you both one hundred francs if you will return it safely for me." Neither of them spoke. "My papers are all in order, I can assure you." Adam handed them over to the taller man, who crossed the road and used the car lights to study them before carrying on a conversation with his friend.

Adam could hear the helicopter whirring above the tunnel entrance. "We don't need the hundred francs," the taller one said eventually. "Do you want to come back to Paris with us?"

Adam hesitated. "No. I have to get to Boulogne."

"We could drive you to Boulogne and still have enough time to take the car to Paris."

"No, no. I can take care of myself, as long as I feel confident that the car will be delivered back as soon as possible."

The taller one shrugged, while his companion opened a rear door and threw their rucksacks onto the back seat. Adam remained in the tunnel while they started up the engine. He could hear the purr of the helicopter blades change cadence; it had to be descending to land in a nearby field.

Go, go, for God's sake go, he wanted to shout as the car shot forward and made a turn. They tooted as they passed him in the dark, disappearing in the direction of Paris. Adam was about to start walking toward Boulogne when he saw two figures silhouetted at the far entrance of the tunnel against the clear blue sky. Adam didn't move a muscle, praying they hadn't spotted him.

And then suddenly one of them, the tall, thin one, started walking toward him. The other remained motionless. Adam knew he could not hope to escape again. He cursed his own stupidity.

"Don't let's waste any more time, Marvin. We already know the traitor's heading back to Paris."

"I just thought perhaps . . ." began the one called Marvin, in a southern drawl.

"Leave the thinking to me. Now let's get back to the chopper before we lose him."

When Marvin was only twenty yards away from Adam he stopped, turned around, and began running back.

Adam remained rooted to the spot for several minutes. A cold, clammy sweat had enveloped his body the moment he realized his latest pursuer was not Romanov. If one of the men hadn't referred to him as traitor, Adam would have happily given himself up. Suddenly he became painfully aware that he had been left with no friends.

He did not move again until he heard the helicopter rise above him. Peering out, he could see the Americans heading in the direction of Paris. He staggered outside. What next? He had less than an hour to catch the boat.

Cyclists began to pass him again as he jogged slowly toward Boulogne. He even found enough strength to cheer the British competitors as they pedaled by. The British team van followed close behind, and Adam gave it the thumbs-up sign. To his surprise the van came to a halt in front of him.

The driver wound down the window. "Weren't you the fellow who stopped me back there?"

"That's right," said Adam. "Has your man recovered?"

"He's in the back—pulled ligament. Where's your car?"

"Broke down about a mile back," said Adam, shrugging.

"Bad luck. Can I give you a lift?" the man asked. "We're only going as far as Boulogne on this stage, but jump in, if it will help."

"Thank you," said Adam with relief.

The driver leaned across and pushed open the door for him. "My name's Bob," he said. "I'm the British team manager."

"Mine's Adam."

"Where are you heading?"

"Boulogne." said Adam. "And with luck I could still make my crossing by three."

"We should be there soon," said Bob. "The afternoon stage starts at three."

"Will your man be able to ride?" asked Adam.

"He won't be competing in this race again," said the team manager. "I shall have to leave him in Boulogne and complete the last leg myself."

Adam looked over his shoulder through the back window. He was thankful to see that there was still no sign of the helicopter as they drove into the outskirts of Boulogne. Bob took him all the way up to the dockside. "Thanks again," said Adam, jumping out of the van. "Good luck with the next stage."

Adam checked his watch: twenty minutes before the boat was due to sail. He walked over to the ticket office and bought a passenger ticket. He had just started toward the ship when a speck appeared in the sky.

Adam looked up at the gangway, now only yards away from him, then back to the speck as it grew larger in the sky. He checked his watch. The ship would leave in twelve minutes—time enough for his pursuers to land the helicopter and get on board. If he climbed on and the Americans followed, they were bound to discover him. But if they got on and he stayed off, that would give him time to reach Dieppe before the next sailing.

Adam jogged quickly back toward the large crowd that was waiting for the start of the next stage of the road race. As he did so, the helicopter started hovering, like a kestrel looking for a mouse.

"I thought you said you were desperate to be on that ship."

Adam swung around, his fist clenched, only to face the British team manager, now dressed in riding gear.

"Changed my mind," said Adam.

"Care to drive the van for us on the next stage?" asked Bob.

"Where does the next stage go?" Adam asked.

"Dunkerque," said the team manager.

Adam tried to remember what time Robin had said her boat left from Dunkerque.

"*Six minutes*," a voice said over the loudspeaker.

"Okay," said Adam.

"Good," said the team manager. "Then follow me."

They headed toward the van.

"*Quatre minutes,*" Adam heard clearly as Bob unlocked the van and handed him the keys. He stared at the two Americans, who were emerging from the ticket office.

"*Deux minutes.*"

Adam jumped up into the driver's seat and looked over toward the boat as Marvin and his colleague strode up the gangplank.

"*Une minute.*"

"Just get the van to Dunkerque and leave the keys at the British checkpoint," said Bob, and ran to the starting line to join his teammates, who were anxiously holding his bike.

"*Trente secondes.*"

Adam watched the gangplank being hoisted up as the starter raised his gun. "On your marks. Get set . . ."

The ship's foghorn belched out a droning note, and the two Americans started their journey to Dover. A second later the gun went off as Adam put the van in gear and headed for Dunkerque.

16

THE Royal Philharmonic coach trundled in with only ten minutes to spare, and Adam threw his arms around Robin as she stepped off. "It's good to see you," he said.

"Just couldn't keep away from me, could you?" she replied. "I thought you were going back by some mysterious route."

"I'll explain everything once we're on board," said Adam.

"By the way," said Robin, "a senior official of the Foreign Office returned Dudley Hulme's passport to him in Amsterdam. Which reminds me to give you yours back." She rummaged in her bag before taking out a dark blue passport and handing it to him.

Neither of them noticed the young KGB agent who had been trailing Robin. He stood in a phone booth on the dockside and dialed an overseas number.

ROMANOV and Tomkins waited expectantly. Romanov stationed himself so that he could look through the customs-hall window and watch the ferry as it sailed into Dover harbor. He had found the perfect spot behind a coffee-vending machine, from which he could observe everyone who entered or left the customs hall.

"Just in case he should act out of character for a change," said Romanov, "and fails to go in a straight line, you will cover the car exit. Report back to me if you notice anything unusual."

The colonel left Romanov and selected a place for himself on the dockside. Both men waited.

THE captain switched on his ship-to-shore radio and spoke clearly into the small microphone. "This is the M.V. *Chantilly* calling the Dover harbormaster. We have an emergency. A male passenger has fallen out of a lifeboat onto the deck and suffered multiple injuries to his arms and legs." Adam groaned as the captain continued. "I need an ambulance at the dock. Over."

"Everything will be all right, my dear," said Robin in a gentle voice that Adam had not heard before. "As soon as we arrive, they are going to take you straight to a hospital."

"I must get back to the bridge," said the captain gruffly. "I shall tell two stewards to bring a stretcher for your brother."

"Thank you," said Robin. "You have been most helpful."

"It's quite all right, miss. You might advise your brother in future to drink less before he comes on board."

"I've tried," said Robin, sighing. "You couldn't believe how I've tried." Adam held on to his leg and groaned again.

"Um," said the captain, looking down at the gash across Adam's shoulder. "Good luck."

"Thank you again, Captain," said Robin as she watched the cabin door close behind him. "So far, so good," she added. "By the way, your breath smells foul."

"What do you expect after making me swirl whiskey around in my mouth and then spit it out all over my clothes?"

ADAM was lifted carefully onto the stretcher, then carried out onto the deck by two stewards. They placed him gently at the head of the gangplank while a customs officer and an immigration officer ran up to join them. Robin handed over his passport.

"Does he have anything to declare?" asked the customs official. Adam couldn't stop himself from touching the icon.

"No. I wouldn't let him buy any more booze on this trip. I'll check his belongings through with mine when I leave the ship."

"Thank you, miss. Better see he gets off to the hospital, then."

The two stewards carried Adam down the gangplank. He waved gamely at Robin as they placed him in the ambulance. It shot out through the customs gates with its lights full on and bells ringing. En route to the Royal Victoria Hospital the attendant watched his patient's remarkable recovery with disbelief.

ROMANOV stood by the gate and smiled as the coach carrying the musicians emerged from the deep black hole of the ship. "Now I know exactly how Captain Scott hopes to get ashore, and we will be waiting for him when he least expects it. Go and hire a car to take us to London," he barked at the colonel.

As Romanov's eyes ranged up and down the coach he quickly picked out Robin Beresford. Just as he had anticipated, the double bass was propped up by her side, making it impossible to see who was seated next to her.

A few minutes later the colonel reappeared, red in the face.

"Where's the car?" the Russian demanded, his eye on the coach.

"I've booked one provisionally," said the colonel, "but they'll need your international license. I forgot Scott has got mine, along with all my other papers."

"You stay put," said Romanov, "and make sure Scott doesn't try to get off that coach." Romanov ran to the car-rental desk at the same time that Adam was being wheeled into a little cubicle to be examined by the duty registrar at the hospital.

"Nasty laceration," the young doctor said finally, cleaning Adam's shoulder wound. "Can you circle your arm?" Adam turned the arm in a full circle and straightened it out again. "Good. No break, at least." The doctor placed a large bandage over Adam's shoulder. "You can go now, but please report to your GP the moment you get back home."

ROMANOV followed the coach out of the main gate and onto the highway in the direction of London.

"Are we going to intercept them on the way?" asked Tomkins.

"Not this time," said Romanov without explanation.

ADAM WALKED OUT OF THE HOSPITAL, took a taxi to Dover Priory Station, and purchased a single ticket to London.

"When's the next train?" he asked.

"Should be in any moment," said the ticket seller. Adam walked onto the platform, keeping a wary eye out for anyone acting suspiciously. He didn't notice the dark-haired man in a blue duffle coat leaning against the newspaper stall.

The London train drew in, and Adam moved out of the shadows and jumped on, selecting a compartment full of young hoods who were apparently returning from a day at the seaside. He thought it would be unlikely anyone else would wish to join them. He took a seat in the far corner and sat silently looking out the window.

By the time the train had pulled in to Canterbury, no one had entered the compartment other than the ticket collector. Adam felt strangely safe in the corner, even when he noticed a dark-haired man in a blue duffle coat pass by the compartment door and look carefully in.

Adam was jolted out of his thoughts by a noisy claim made by one of the gang, who during the journey had given every appearance of being its leader. "There's a foul smell in this compartment," he declared, sniffing loudly.

"I agree, Terry," said his mate, who was sitting next to Adam and also began imitating the sniff. "And I think it's quite close to me." Adam glanced toward the young man, whose black leather jacket was covered in small, shiny studs. He pulled open the window. "Perhaps some fresh air will help," he said as he sat back down. In moments all four of them were sniffing. "I think the smell's getting worse," their leader concluded.

"It must be me," said Adam.

The youths stared toward the corner in disbelief—momentarily silenced by Adam's offensive.

"I didn't have time to take a shower after my judo lesson," Adam added.

A look of apprehension came over the four faces.

"I was thinkin' about taking up judo myself," said the leader. "How long does it take to get any good at it?"

"I've been working at it three hours a day for twelve years," replied Adam as he watched the man in the duffle coat pass by the compartment again. This time he stared directly at Adam before quickly moving on.

"Of course," continued Adam, "the only quality you really need is nerve, and no one can teach you that. You've either got it or you haven't."

"I've got nerve," said Terry belligerently. "I'm not frightened of nothin'. Or nobody," he added.

"Good," said Adam. "Because you may be given the chance to prove your claim before this journey is over."

"You trying to pick a fight or somethin'?"

"No," said Adam calmly. "It's just that at this moment I'm being followed by a private detective who is hoping to catch me spending the night with his client's wife."

The four of them stared at Adam with something approaching respect. "Then just point out this detective, and we'll sew him up for the night," said the leader, pulling up his fist with gusto.

"That might turn out to be unnecessary," said Adam. "But if you could delay him for a little when I get off at Waterloo East, that should at least give me enough time to warn the lady."

"Say no more, squire," said the leader.

"That's him," whispered Adam as the duffle-coated man passed by a third time. They all looked out into the corridor.

A few minutes later Adam slipped out of the compartment, leaving the door wide open. He started to walk in the direction opposite to that in which the man in the blue duffle coat had last been seen going. When Adam reached the end of the carriage he turned to find the man was now following behind. As the man passed the open compartment, two leather-clad arms shot out and he disappeared inside with a muffled cry. The door was slammed and the blinds pulled quickly down. The train drew slowly into Waterloo East Station.

ROBIN remained tense as the bus drew into Wigmore Street and stopped outside the Royal Philharmonic headquarters. A dark green Ford had been following them for at least thirty miles.

As she dragged her double bass off the bus she looked back to see that the Ford had stopped about fifty yards down the road. Romanov was standing on the pavement, looking like a caged animal that wanted to spring. Another man, whom Robin did not recognize, remained seated behind the wheel. She walked straight into the orchestra headquarters without stopping.

When the last musician had left the bus Romanov and the colonel searched the inside of the vehicle and the luggage compartment, despite noisy protests from the driver. Robin eyed them nervously from an upstairs window as the two jumped back into the green Ford and drove off.

THE colonel swung the car to a halt a few blocks away. Romanov jumped out, walked into a telephone booth, and started thumbing through the phone directory. Only one Robin Beresford was listed, and the address was the one that the young officer had read to him. He dialed the number and after ten unanswered rings smiled at the realization that she lived alone.

"What now?" asked the colonel, once Romanov was back in the car.

"Rather than waiting for Miss Beresford to come out, we will be waiting for her to come in," said Romanov.

ROBIN slipped out the rear of the orchestra headquarters about thirty minutes later and walked quickly to the corner. She kept telling herself that Romanov was not coming back, but she found it impossible to stop herself from shaking, all the same. She hailed a taxi and was relieved to see one draw up almost immediately. She checked the driver and the back seat, as Adam had advised her, then climbed in.

ROMANOV arrived at Robin's front door a few moments after she had hailed the taxi. The nameplates on the side wall indicated that Miss Beresford resided on the fourth floor.

The main door itself would have proved no problem to any self-respecting petty thief in Moscow, and Romanov secured entry within moments. The colonel followed him up the dark staircase.

Romanov slipped the Yale lock faster than Robin could have opened it with her key. Once inside, he said to Tomkins, "Settle down, Colonel. I don't expect the lady will keep us waiting too long."

THE TAXI DREW UP OUTSIDE the house that Robin pointed to. She jumped out and tipped the cabbie extra because she at last felt safe. It seemed ages since she had been home. All she was looking forward to now were a hot bath and a good night's sleep.

ADAM stepped off the train at Waterloo East a little after midnight and was pleased to find the underground still running. There were several stations between Waterloo and his destination, and even at this time of night there seemed to be a prolonged stop at every one. He waited nervously at each station, aware now that he must have caught the last train. He only hoped Robin had carried out his instructions faithfully. The train eventually pulled into his station at twelve forty.

The ticket collector was able to give him the directions he needed. It was a relief to reach his destination so quickly. He moved slowly toward Number 23. There were no lights on in the house. He opened the swinging gate and walked up the path, removed the bunch of keys from his pocket, fitted the Chubb one into the lock, and pushed open the door quietly.

A LITTLE after twelve ten the last train from Dover pulled into Charing Cross Station. As Adam was nowhere to be seen, Lawrence instructed his driver to take him back to his flat. He couldn't understand why the agent, whom he had handpicked, hadn't reported in.

HE OPENED the swinging gate and made his way up the path. Once he reached the house, he searched for the third stone on the left. To his relief the spare key was still in place. Like a burglar he pushed it into the lock. He crept into the hall and up the stairs. At the landing he opened his bedroom door.

As the colonel stepped in, an arm circled his throat, and he was thrown to the floor with tremendous force. He lay there, a knee in his back and his arm jerked up behind him, hardly able to move. The light flashed on.

"Don't kill me, Captain Scott, sir. Don't kill me," he implored.

"I have no intention of doing so, Mr. Tomkins," said Adam calmly. "But first, where is your esteemed employer?"

Adam pressed the arm higher before the colonel bleated out, "He went back to the embassy once he realized the girl wasn't going to return to her flat."

"Just as I planned," said Adam, but he didn't lessen the pressure as he described in vivid detail everything that would now be expected of the colonel.

The man's face showed disbelief. "But that will be impossible," he said. "I mean, he's bound to noti—ahhh."

The colonel felt his arm forced higher up his back. "You could carry out the whole exercise in less than ten minutes, and he need never be any the wiser," said Adam. "If you follow my instructions, you will be given in exchange your papers and wallet and a guarantee of no prosecution for your past treachery. But if, on the other hand, you fail to turn up by nine thirty tomorrow morning with the object of my desire, all those documents will be placed thirty minutes later on the desk of a Mr. Lawrence Pemberton of the Foreign Office. Remember," continued Adam, not loosening his grip, "spies—even unimportant spies such as you—at the present time seem to be getting anything from eighteen to forty-two years, at Her Majesty's pleasure."

"I'll get it for you, Captain Scott. You can rely on me."

Adam lifted the colonel slowly off the floor and then shoved him toward the landing. He pushed the colonel on down the stairs until they reached the front door.

"The car keys," said Adam.

"But it's a hire car, sir," said the colonel.

"And I'm about to hire it," said Adam. "The keys," he repeated, jerking the colonel's arm to shoulder-blade level.

"In my left-hand pocket," replied the colonel.

Adam put his hand into the colonel's pocket and pulled out the car keys. He opened the front door, shoved the colonel onto the path, then escorted him to the pavement.

"Now," said Adam, releasing him, "just one more thing, Colonel. In case you think of double-crossing me, I have already instructed the Foreign Office to place Romanov under surveillance and put two extra lookouts near the Soviet embassy." Adam got into the rental car. "See you at nine thirty tomorrow morning, Colonel. Prompt," he added.

The colonel stood shivering on the pavement, nursing his shoulder as Adam drove to the end of the road.

For the first time since Heidi's death Adam felt it was Romanov who was on the run.

"WHAT a great honor for our little establishment," said Herr Bischoff, delighted to see the most important banker in Russia sitting in his boardroom sharing afternoon tea.

"Not at all, my dear Bischoff," said Poskonov. "After all these years the honor is entirely mine. But now to business. Did you manage to get Romanov to sign the release form?"

"Oh, yes," said Bischoff. "He didn't even read the standard clauses, let alone the extra three you asked us to put in."

"So his inheritance automatically returns to the Russian people?"

"That is so, Mr. Poskonov. But what happens when Herr Romanov returns to the bank and demands to know what has become of his inheritance?" asked Herr Bischoff anxiously.

"I don't think that problem will arise," the Russian banker promised. "Now I would like to see what is in those boxes."

"Yes, of course," said Herr Bischoff. "Please accompany me."

The two men took the private elevator to the basement, and Herr Bischoff led his guest to the underground vault.

"Do take as long as you like," said Herr Bischoff, "but at five o'clock the great door is automatically locked until nine o'clock tomorrow morning. At four forty-five an alarm goes off to warn you that you only have fifteen minutes left." Herr Bischoff handed Comrade Poskonov the envelope with Romanov's key in it.

As soon as the massive steel door had been swung closed behind him, the Russian checked the clock on the wall. They had left him with over two hours to sort out what could be transported to Brazil and what would have to be left behind.

Poskonov opened the first of the large boxes and stared down at the twelve little compartments. He removed the lid of the first one tentatively, and when he saw the array of gems and stones that shone in front of him, his legs felt weak. He put both hands into the box and let the gems slip through his fingers, like a child playing with pebbles on a beach.

He hadn't realized how long it had taken him to go through the remaining compartments, but when the alarm went off, he was lost in a daydream, already enjoying his newfound wealth. He glanced at the clock. Enough time to check the other large box.

He turned the key and licked his lips in anticipation as he pulled the box out. Just a quick look, he promised himself, lifting the lid. When he saw the decaying body he reeled backward and, falling to the floor, clutched his heart.

Both bodies were discovered at nine the next morning.

ADAM sat on his bed at the Royal Garden Hotel considering the implications of his plan for nearly an hour. Then he picked up the phone beside the bed and dialed the number Robin had given him. It was answered by an elderly voice saying, "Mrs. Beresford."

"Good morning, Mrs. Beresford. My name is Adam Scott, I'm a friend of Robin's. I was just phoning to check that she reached home safely last night."

"Oh, yes, thank you," said Robin's mother. "It was a pleasant surprise to see her. She usually spends the night in the flat when she gets back late. I'm afraid she's still asleep. Would you like me to wake her?"

"No, no. Don't disturb her," said Adam. "I only rang to fix up a lunch date. Can you tell her I'll call back later?"

"I certainly will, Mr. Scott," she replied.

Adam replaced the receiver and smiled. Each piece of the jigsaw was fitting neatly into place. He put Tomkins' passport and personal papers into a large envelope. Then he removed the icon from his jacket pocket, turned it over, and carefully examined the little silver crest of the czar. He flicked open the colonel's penknife and began the delicate task of removing the crown.

Thirty minutes later Adam was in the elevator on the way to the lobby. He took his time selecting a new jacket and some gray flannels at the men's shop in the arcade. At nine twenty-three he settled his bill and asked the doorman to bring the green Ford up from the parking lot. He waited by the hotel entrance.

As the minutes passed, he began to fear that the colonel wouldn't turn up. If he failed to, Adam knew that the next call would have to be to Lawrence and not Romanov.

His reverie was disturbed by a honk on a car horn. The Ford

was parked by the entrance, and the doorman returned the keys to Adam.

"Thank you," said Adam and handed over one of the colonel's pound notes. He transferred the remaining notes to his pocket. Then he dropped the wallet into the large envelope, which he sealed.

He stood waiting anxiously for another two minutes before he spotted the colonel puffing up the slope to the hotel entrance. He was clinging to a small shopping bag.

"I've done it, Captain Scott, sir. I've done it," he said as he reached Adam's side. "But I must return immediately, or he's bound to notice it's gone."

He passed the shopping bag quickly to Adam, who opened it and stared down at the object inside.

"You're a man of your word," said Adam, "and as promised you'll find everything you need in there." He passed over his own package, along with the car keys, without speaking. He pointed to the hire car.

The colonel ran to it, jumped in, and drove quickly away.

Adam hailed a taxi. The driver pulled the window down and gave Adam an inquiring look.

"The Wood Workshop, Kings Road."

Adam spent twenty minutes looking around the shop while the craftsman carried out his unusual request. Adam paid him and then walked back onto Kings Road to hail another taxi.

"Where to, guv'nor?"

"The Tower of London."

EVERYONE was in his place for the D4 meeting at nine thirty, and Busch was on the attack even before Lawrence sat down.

"How did you manage to lose him this time?"

"I must take the blame myself," said Lawrence. "We had every port from Newhaven to Harwich covered, but the moment my man saw Romanov leave the quayside at Dover and follow the coach, he assumed Romanov must have seen Scott."

"But we were given a second chance when Scott got on the train," persisted Busch.

"My man was on the train," said Lawrence emphatically, "but

had only one opportunity to make contact with Scott while he was on his own, and at just that moment he was grabbed and badly beaten up by a bunch of drunken louts."

"So as far as we can tell, Scott, the czar's icon, and Romanov are still holed up somewhere in London?" said Matthews.

"It looks that way," admitted Lawrence.

"Perhaps all is not lost, then," suggested Snell. "Scott may still try to get in touch with you again."

"I think not," said Lawrence quietly.

"How can you be so sure?" asked Busch.

"Because Scott knows that one of us in this room is a traitor, and he thinks it's me."

"GOOD morning. Soviet embassy."

"This is Adam Scott. I need to contact Major Romanov."

"We do not have a Major Romanov working at the embassy."

"I'm sure you don't. But I'll wait. Wouldn't surprise me if you find him very quickly once he knows who is calling."

There was a long silence at the other end. Then, at last, there was a click, and Adam heard a familiar voice ask, "Who is this?"

"You know very well who it is," said Adam curtly. "I want to make a deal. I'll swap my icon—which, as you so vividly pointed out, is worthless to me—for your copy, which is not. But I require the papers that prove my father's innocence."

"How do I know you're not setting me up?"

"You don't," said Adam. "But you have nothing to lose."

"Tell me your number," said Romanov.

Adam complied.

"I'll phone you back at eleven," said Romanov, and hung up.

"How quickly can we find out where this number is located?" Romanov asked the local KGB operative, who sat opposite him.

"About ten minutes," the aide replied. "But it could be a trap."

"True, but with nineteen hours to go before the icon has to be in America, I don't have a lot of choice."

ADAM could do nothing about the middle-aged lady who was occupying his phone booth at the Tower of London. He had walked out to check the bridge, and she had slipped in.

He checked his watch nervously: ten forty-five. The talkative woman was on the phone another twelve minutes before she put it down and stepped out of the booth.

Adam began to watch the Beefeaters as they patrolled under the Traitors' Gate. Traitors' Gate—how appropriate, he thought. He had chosen the spot because he could clearly see the path leading to the drawbridge and felt he could not be taken by surprise.

When the phone rang, it sounded like an alarm bell. Adam picked it up anxiously.

"Scott?"

"Yes."

"I can see you clearly. I will be standing at the end of the bridge in less than one minute. Be sure you're there with the icon. If you're not, I shall burn the papers that prove your father's innocence in front of you." The phone went dead.

Adam stepped out of the phone booth and checked up and down the road. A motorcycle swerved to a halt at the end of the bridge. A rider dressed in a leather jacket sat astride the bike, but it was the man seated behind him who stared directly at Adam.

Adam began to walk slowly toward the end of the bridge. He put a hand in his pocket to be sure the icon was still in its place.

He was about thirty yards from the end of the bridge when the second figure got off the bike and started walking toward him. When their eyes met, Romanov stopped in his tracks and held up the small square frame. Adam simply tapped the side of his pocket and continued walking. Both men advanced toward each other, like knights of old, until they were only a few paces apart.

"Let me see it," said Romanov.

Adam slowly removed the icon from his pocket and turned it over. The Russian could not hide his delight when he saw the little silver crown of the czar embedded in the back.

"Now you," said Adam. Romanov held his icon away from his body, as if brandishing a sword. The masterpiece shone in the summer sun. "And the documents."

The Russian pulled out a package from within his jacket and slowly unfolded them. Adam stared at the official court verdict for a second time.

"Go to the wall," said Adam, pointing to the side of the bridge, "and leave the icon and the documents on it."

Romanov obeyed as Adam proceeded to the wall on the other side of the bridge and placed his icon in the middle of it.

"Cross slowly," called Adam. The two men moved back across the bridge, passing a couple of yards from each other until each had come to a halt at the other's icon. The moment the painting was within his reach, Romanov grabbed it, ran, and jumped onto the motorcycle. Within seconds it had disappeared in traffic.

Adam did not move. Although it had only been out of his sight for just over an hour, he was relieved to have the original icon back. He checked the papers that would establish his father's innocence and placed them in his inside pocket. Ignoring the tourists, some of whom had stopped to stare, Adam began to relax when suddenly he felt a sharp prod in the middle of his back. He jumped around in fright.

A little girl was staring up at him.

"Will you and your friend be performing again this morning?"

WHEN the motorcycle drew up outside the Soviet embassy Romanov leaped off and ran up the stairs and straight into the ambassador's office without knocking. "It worked out just as I planned," he said as he handed the icon over to the ambassador.

The ambassador turned the painting over and was relieved to see the little silver crown of the czar. "I have orders to send the icon to Washington in the diplomatic pouch at once."

He pressed a button on the side of his desk. Two men appeared immediately. One held open the diplomatic pouch while the other stood motionless by his side. The ambassador handed over the icon and watched it being placed into the pouch.

"There is a plane standing by at Heathrow Airport to take you to Washington," he said to the couriers. "You should touch down at around five o'clock, Washington time, easily giving our comrades in America enough time to fulfill their part of the contract."

The two men nodded, sealed the diplomatic pouch in the ambassador's presence, and left. Romanov walked over to the window and watched the official car drive the two men away.

"Vodka, Comrade Major?" The ambassador went over to a side

cabinet and took out two glasses and a bottle. "It would not be exaggerating to say that you have helped establish the Soviet Union as the most powerful nation on earth," he said as he handed over a vodka. "Therefore I think the time has come to let you know the significance of your achievement." He told Romanov of the briefing he had received from Brezhnev that morning.

Romanov was thankful he had never known how much was at stake. "But what is happening in Washington at this moment?"

"Our ambassador has already requested a meeting with the American Secretary of State at eight this evening. He is also setting up a press conference to follow that meeting."

"And we achieved it with only hours to spare," said Romanov. He shuddered at the thought of how close it had been, and downed his vodka in one gulp.

"You must join me for lunch, comrade. Although your orders are to return to Moscow immediately, the plane does not depart until eight this evening. I envy you the reception you will receive when you arrive back in the Kremlin tomorrow."

COMMANDER Busch barged into Lawrence's office.

"Romanov's got the icon," he shouted.

Lawrence's jaw dropped. "How can you be so sure?"

"I've just had a message from Washington. The Russians have requested a meeting with the Secretary of State this evening."

The phone on the desk rang. Lawrence grabbed it, as if it were a lifeline. "A Dr. John Vance wants a word with you, sir," said his secretary. "He said you had asked him to call."

Vance? Vance? Lawrence recalled the name but couldn't quite place it. "Put him on," he said.

"Good morning, Mr. Pemberton," said a voice. "You asked me to call you after I had examined Adam Scott? You wanted him to complete a physical for your department."

Lawrence was speechless.

"I've given him a clean bill of health," continued the doctor. "A nasty shoulder wound, but nothing that won't heal in a few days. He's fit enough to start work whenever you want him."

"Mr. Scott isn't there with you at this moment, by any chance?"

"No," said Vance. "Left about ten minutes ago."

"He didn't happen to tell you where he was going?"

"No, he wasn't specific. Just said something about having to see a friend off at the airport."

Romanov checked his watch. He had enough time to keep the appointment and still catch the plane. He thanked the ambassador and climbed into the back of the anonymous black car.

It was a short journey, and when the driver drew into Charlotte Street, Romanov stepped out and walked quickly across the road. He pressed the bell.

"Are you a member?" said a voice through the intercom.

"Yes," said Romanov, who heard a metallic click as he pushed the door open and walked down the dark staircase. Once he had entered the club, it took a few seconds for his eyes to become accustomed to the light. But then he spotted Mentor seated on his own at a little table in the far corner of the room.

Romanov nodded, and the man, nervously touching his mustache, got up and walked across the dance floor, straight past him. Romanov followed as the member entered the lavatory. Once inside, Romanov checked whether they were alone. Satisfied, he led the man into a little cubicle and slipped the lock. Romanov handed over an envelope containing one thousand pounds. Mentor greedily ripped it open and began to count. He never even saw Romanov straighten his fingers, and when the hand came down with a crushing blow on the back of Mentor's neck he slumped forward and fell to the ground in a heap.

Romanov yanked him up onto the lavatory seat; it took several seconds to gather the ten-pound notes that had fallen to the floor. Romanov then slipped under the large gap at the bottom of the door, leaving the cubicle locked from the inside. Sixty seconds later he was back in the car, on his way to Heathrow.

Adam arrived at Heathrow two hours before the Aeroflot flight was due to depart. He stationed himself with a perfect view of the forty-yard stretch Romanov would have to walk to board the Russian aircraft.

"BEA announce the departure of their Flight one one seven to Moscow. Would all first-class passengers now board through gate number twenty-three." Romanov left the departure lounge and walked the long corridor to the plane. He couldn't resist taking the BEA flight rather than Aeroflot, even though he knew Zaborski would frown at such arrogance. On board, stepping over the feet of the passenger next to him, he was thankful that he had been given the window seat.

"Would you care for a drink before takeoff?" the stewardess asked.

"Just a black coffee for me," said his neighbor. Romanov nodded his agreement.

The stewardess arrived back a few moments later with the two coffees and helped the man next to Romanov pull out his table. Romanov flipped his over as the stewardess passed him his coffee.

He took a sip, but it was too hot, so he placed it on the table in front of him. He watched his neighbor take out a packet of saccharin from his pocket and flick two pellets into the coffee.

Why did he bother? thought Romanov. Life was too short.

Romanov stared out the window and smiled as the plane started to taxi away from the gate. He was leaving London with only one regret. He had failed to kill Scott. He tried his coffee a second time: it was just as he liked it. He took a long gulp and began to feel a little drowsy. He leaned back in his seat. He would now take every honor the state could offer him. With Valchek out of the way he could even position himself to take over from Zaborski. If that failed, his grandfather had left him another alternative. For the first time in a week he didn't have to stop himself from falling asleep. . . .

Ten minutes later the passenger seated beside Romanov picked up the Russian's coffee cup and put it next to his own. He then put Romanov's table back and placed a woolen blanket over his legs. He quickly slipped the BEA eyeshade over the Russian's open eyes. He looked up to find that the stewardess was standing by his side.

"Can I help?" she asked, smiling.

"No, thank you. All he said was that he did not want to be disturbed during the flight, as he has had a very hard week."

"Of course, sir," said the stewardess. "We'll be taking off in a few minutes," she added as she picked up the two coffee cups.

Romanov's neighbor tapped his fingers impatiently on the armrest. At last the chief steward appeared. "There's been a call from your office, sir. You're to return to Whitehall immediately."

"I had been half expecting it," he admitted.

ADAM stared up at the Russian plane as it climbed steeply and swung in a semicircle toward the east. He couldn't understand why Romanov hadn't boarded it. Surely he wouldn't have taken the BEA flight. Adam slipped back into the shadows the moment he saw him. He stared in disbelief. Lawrence was striding across the tarmac toward the terminal, a smile of satisfaction on his face.

Epilogue

Sotheby's, London
October 18, 1966

"WE NOW move on to lot number thirty-two," said the auctioneer from the raised platform at the front of the crowded room. "An icon of Saint George and the dragon," he declared as an attendant placed a little painting on the easel next to him. The auctioneer stared down at the faces of experts, amateurs, and curious onlookers.

"I haven't felt this nervous since I came face to face with Romanov," whispered Robin.

"Don't remind me," said Adam.

"It is, of course, not the original, which hangs in the Winter Palace," continued the auctioneer, "but it is nevertheless a fine copy, probably executed by a court painter circa 1915," he added, giving the little painting an approving smile. "Do I have an opening bid? Shall I say eight thousand pounds?"

The next seconds seemed interminable to Robin and Adam.

"Thank you, sir," said the auctioneer, looking toward an anonymous sign given somewhere at the front of the room.

"How much did the experts say it might go for?" Robin asked.

"Anywhere between ten and twenty thousand," Adam replied.

"Nine thousand," said the auctioneer, his eyes moving to a bid that appeared to come from the right-hand side of the room.

"I still think it's amazing," said Robin, "that we let the Russians have the original icon back."

"Why?" asked Adam. "After all, it belonged to them in the first place, and of course the treaty had been extracted." He paused. "I think the really amazing thing is that Lawrence persuaded the Russians to let us have the copy in return."

"Even more amazing that you ended up with it," added Robin.

"Yes. As an example of diplomatic ingenuity, it was Lawrence at his most brilliant," said Adam, smiling.

"Ten thousand from the front of the room. Thank you, sir," said the auctioneer.

"What are you going to do with all that money?"

"Buy you a new double bass, get a wedding present for my sister, and hand the rest over to my mother."

"Eleven thousand. A new bidder on the center aisle," said the auctioneer. "Thank you, madam."

"No amount of money can bring back Heidi," said Robin quietly. Adam nodded thoughtfully. "How did the meeting with Heidi's parents turn out?"

"The foreign secretary saw them last week. At least he was able to confirm that I had been telling them the truth."

"Twelve thousand." The auctioneer's eyes returned to the side of the room.

"Did you see the foreign secretary yourself?"

"Good heavens, no. I'm far too junior for that," said Adam. "I'm lucky if I get to see Lawrence, let alone the foreign secretary."

Robin laughed. "I consider you were *lucky* to have been offered a place at the Foreign Office at all."

"Agreed," said Adam, chuckling to himself. "But a vacancy arose unexpectedly."

"What do you mean, unexpectedly?" asked Robin, frustrated by how few of her questions had been answered directly.

"All I can tell you is that one of Lawrence's old team was retired early," said Adam.

"Was that true of Romanov also?" asked Robin. "He can't have survived for long, once they discovered you had done a switch that ended up with Romanov giving you the original on the bridge."

"He's never been heard of since," admitted Adam innocently.

"Fourteen thousand," said the auctioneer, his eye settling on the front once again.

"What happened when you produced those court papers proving that it was not your father who had smuggled the poison into Göring's cell?"

"Once that had been authenticated by the Russians," Adam said, "Lawrence paid an official visit to the colonel of the regiment and furnished him with the conclusive evidence."

"Any reaction?" probed Robin.

"They're going to hold a memorial service in Pa's memory, and they have commissioned some fellow to paint his portrait. Mother has been invited to unveil it in the presence of all those officers who served with my father."

"Fourteen thousand for the first time, then," said the auctioneer, raising the little gavel a few inches in the air.

"She must have been over the moon," said Robin.

"Burst into tears," said Adam. "All she could say was, 'I wish Pa could have lived to see it.' "

"Fourteen thousand for the second time," said the auctioneer, the gavel now hovering.

"I suppose I will have to go to my grave wondering what treaty was inside that icon," Robin said. "It seems destined to remain the Foreign Office's best-kept secret."

Adam looked at the girl who had saved his life. "Alas . . ." he began, but just at that moment the auctioneer's hammer came down with a thud. They both looked up.

"Sold to the gentleman in front for fourteen thousand pounds."

"Not a bad price," said Adam, smiling.

"A bargain, in my opinion," said Robin.

Adam turned back to her. "After all," he said in a whisper, "imagine what the forty-ninth state would have fetched if *it* had come up for auction."

ABOUT THE AUTHOR

Jeffrey Archer's life story reads like one of his own best sellers. Born in Somerset, England, in 1940, the son of an army officer, he was marked for success while still a student at Oxford University. He was president of the Oxford University Athletic Club, and ran for Great Britain on the national track team. He even found time to persuade the Beatles to perform at a special charity concert that raised one million pounds for famine relief.

Jeffrey Archer

After leaving Oxford, he turned to politics and in 1969 was elected to Parliament, becoming the youngest member at the time. A promising political career stretched ahead, but in 1974 the crash came. A company in which he had invested heavily failed, leaving Archer facing bankruptcy, nearly half a million pounds in debt.

So, at thirty-four, he resigned his cherished seat in the House of Commons and started again from scratch. He had never written before, but decided to capitalize on his painful experience by turning it into a novel called *Not a Penny More, Not a Penny Less*. It was an instant success. Since then he has written five more best-selling novels, including *Kane & Abel*, which was made into a popular television miniseries. Archer's fame and fortune were restored.

He even returned briefly to politics. In 1985 Archer was appointed deputy chairman of the Conservative Party by Prime Minister Margaret Thatcher. A year later he resigned amid controversy. Perhaps in the near future his readers will find this story, too, retold between the covers of a new Jeffrey Archer best seller. The author, his wife Mary, and their two sons divide their time between homes in London and Cambridge.

PHOTO BY RICHARD OPEN

The Golden Cup

Three generations, one family—and the extraordinary woman at its heart

A CONDENSATION OF THE NOVEL BY

Belva Plain

Illustrated by Ben Stahl

New York City, 1891. Their love begins in a moment of breath-taking heroism: handsome young Dan Roth races into a blazing tenement to rescue a stranger while, from the horrified crowd below, Hennie De Rivera watches, transfixed. . . .

Dan is a penniless schoolteacher; Hennie is the daughter of transplanted southern aristocrats. But though they come from different worlds, they share a passion—for each other and for the cause of peace and social justice. Over the years their special love will bring both joy and heartache to Hennie. But her severest test will come when the gathering clouds of the Great War throw a deep shadow over the entire De Rivera clan.

One of America's most beloved writers spins a rich tale of love, idealism, world war, and the turmoil that can strain—but never break—the eternal bonds of family.

PART ONE
Hennie and Dan
1

All her life she would remember the somber autumn sky, how vast and high and cold it had been while the great wind raced from the East River toward Broadway. When she was very old, she would still marvel, as do we all, over the randomness of things, for if she had not happened to turn just that corner, in just that hour, her whole life would have been different.

The child whose hand she held would vaguely remember cries and lurid color, a blur of savage yellow, confusion and a terror only half understood.

And another child, the one who came to be born because she had turned that corner, would hear a tale of heroism, as it grew to become a family legend, until he was sick of hearing it.

The tenement burned. Out of its ruined heart there rose a spiral of flame; strong and fierce, it soared into the wind, and a bitter smoke poured over the rooftops. Powerful arcs of water shot from the pumps to the blaze, but the fire had power of its own.

And the sweatered and shawled residents, packed tightly on the street among the engines and great stamping fire horses, hardly moved, waiting to be told where to go. Fires like this one were common in that part of the city, yet these people were stunned into disbelief. It was too soon for anyone to have counted the full extent of his loss, the bedding and the pillows, the kitchen table, the change of underwear and the winter coat. That would come later. It was enough now to have gotten out alive.

There was a terrible, anguished shriek. The girl turned back at the sound. She still had the little boy by the hand. They had been hurrying through the street because she had not wanted the child to see anything so frightful. But the cry pierced her and she stopped at the edge of the crowd.

"What is it? Is someone hurt?"

"There's someone left on the top floor, somebody's baby."

Now the smoke came whipping out of the fourth floor. Soon it would reach the fifth and then the top.

"Can't live long in there."

"My God, what a way to die!"

The girl was unable to pull herself away. She could hear her own heart beat.

"You're hurting my hand," the child cried.

"Oh, Paul, I'm sorry. I didn't mean to hold you so hard." And she bent to button up his little velvet collar against the wind. "We'll go, we'll go in a minute."

But she was fastened to the place where she stood. Her eyes were fastened to the windows behind which the most awful death was taking place, the death of a child. She felt the trembling warmth of the little boy's hand. What if it were he?

Now with furious clangor of bells came the hook and ladder. Four horses clattered and charged, so that the crowd spread frantically apart to let them through. The ladder was dragged to the building and propped up against the wall, but the top of the ladder was still a full story and a half from the top floor. Had no one known it could reach no higher? A knot of firemen gathered on the sidewalk among the onlookers.

An innocent question: "Can't they go up through the next house and reach in?"

A scornful reply: "Who's going to try that, do you think?"

"And how get across? You can see the air shaft's too wide to step over. You think anybody will try to jump across, six floors up, with nothing but a rotting cornice to hold you?"

"No. Whoever is in there is a goner."

But now someone was shoving a way through the crowd. The girl had a glimpse of the back of a head of black hair and a checked woolen shirt. Standing on tiptoe, she saw a young man running. He plunged up the steps of the next tenement.

"He's going to try to get in through the other building," a woman said.

"I don't believe it. It's impossible! He'd be crazy!"

"Look there! Up there!"

The young man was at the top-floor window next to the burning building. Astride the sill, he swung a leg out into the air. A foot searched for a place on the narrow cornice. A hand groped the flat fake-classic pillar and drew back.

There's no purchase there, nothing to grasp, the girl said to herself. Her breath held in her throat.

The man was now almost hidden by the swirling smoke. He changed to a sitting position on the sill. For a moment he sat quite still; his long legs hung down. He wore green corduroy trousers. Then he twisted off from the sill, with his back to the street, his toes on the cornice, his hands on the sill.

Oh, let it hold! Let it not break off and send him smashing to the street!

The girl's neck ached; tense with the strain of peering upward, she felt herself in that young man's place. He probed now with one foot. He would need to slide to the edge of the building and then jump.

Come back . . . don't try . . . come back.

In the burning house the windows had begun to melt; the shattered glass fell with a musical tinkle. Cinders and shreds of burned cloth rained gently to the street.

His hand must have seized some small projection. Inch by inch he slid along the stone face, past the window. Now he seemed to be steadying himself, assessing his balance.

He leaped. The extended arm and the leg shot across the air space. The hand grasped; one could imagine the straining arm muscles and the fingernails going white. One foot jammed onto the cornice of the burning building and clung until the rest of the body, curving outward into space, could follow and right itself and steady itself.

The girl closed her eyes. I will be sick if he falls.

When she opened her eyes, he was inching himself toward the open window of the burning building.

Don't look down. If you look, you will fall.

He swung himself inside. A babble of relief and amazement broke out.

"My heavens, how brave!"

"The smoke will kill him."

"There can't be anyone left alive in there."

"Make way! Get back, get out of the way!" A dozen men were bringing up a net. They opened it and waited.

And then he appeared at the window. He was holding someone with a flapping skirt. Not a baby; a grown child, then. He let go. The body hurtled through the air, screaming, bounced in the net, bounced once more, and was lifted out. A great cheer went up.

Then the young man, flinging out his arms, jumped too. Another great cheer of relief and release went up. The crowd, thrilled and curious, pushed forward toward the hero.

They had cornered him. Close to the smoking tenement, he stood panting and coughing.

The girl was enthralled. She saw the vivid eyes, high cheekbones, the lock of waving hair, thick as a mane, that he kept pushing back off his forehead. His shirt was torn, and his hands were bleeding. She could see that he wanted to be left alone. I would not bother you so, she thought. Go home and rest, my dear, I would say. You are the most wonderful . . . Go home and rest.

"Well, sonny, what did you think of that brave man?" an old fellow asked Paul as they walked away.

"I could do that," Paul said gravely.

"That's the way to talk! Yes, sir, you'll make your mother proud of you when you grow up. How old are you?"

"Almost five," Paul answered.

They crossed the street and Paul whispered, "He thought you were my mother, Aunt Hennie."

It was not unusual for people to think Paul was her child when they were out together. She wished he were.

Who is this girl going home through the gathering afternoon? Her eyes tell of her that she is solitary and that she dreams. They are the distinguishing feature in a round, pleasant, otherwise undistinguished face. Leaf-shaped, they are the color of brown autumn, and they match the curling hair that escapes under the brim of her hat. She is eighteen years old and seems older.

Her name is Henrietta De Rivera. She lives with her family in a decent apartment house east of Washington Square's fine private brownstones. Her address is near enough to these to be respectable but too far from them to be fashionable.

Three days a week she walks to work as a volunteer at a settlement house downtown. She teaches English to immigrants, tries also to teach them to bathe, and tries not to mind their clothes, which are sometimes very dirty, for she understands how hard it is for them to find the time or place for cleanliness. Hennie does not feel superior; she feels, rather, a deep kinship. Indeed, the closest friend she has—and she has never had many—is a pupil in one of her English classes, an immigrant sweatshop worker named Olga Zaretkin.

"You must be tired, Paul," she said now. "We've had a long walk, but there'll be time for cocoa at my house before your mama takes you home."

They were passing through Washington Square. A lady stepped out of her carriage, holding a little white dog, and smiled at Paul.

"It's pretty here," Paul said. He was thinking, although he did not have the words, that he liked being here with Aunt Hennie. He loved it whenever he was allowed to visit with her. She was so nice! She was different; he could think of the rest of his family as "they" apart from "her," and could love them all, for no one was ever unkind to him, yet she was different.

Aunt Hennie was much, much better than Fräulein, his nurse, and better than his mother too, although he suspected he wasn't supposed to think that. Mama didn't scold, but she wasn't any fun. You could hardly ever get on her lap because of wrinkles: "Be careful, darling, you'll wrinkle my skirt." Aunt Hennie never said, "Don't bother me now" or "Later, Paul, I'm busy."

"Did you like that man?" he asked her now.

For a moment she could not think whom he meant. "The man who climbed up on the roof, do you mean?"

"Yes. Did you like him? I did."

"Yes. He was wonderful. But let's hurry along. They must be wondering where we are."

The tea service was out; Hennie's mother and sister were in the parlor. Florence must have brought the roses, Hennie thought. She never brought too many, only enough to create a perfection of pink and cream in a small silver bowl.

"Paul must have his cocoa," said Angelique, the grandmother. "And then you may take him home, Florence."

"This is such a lovely room, Mama," Florence said, apropos of nothing. "All your beautiful things. . . ."

Angelique shook her head. Her patrician face was still handsome, although the cheeks had just begun to sag. "They belong in a proper setting. Not here."

It was true. These portraits, these lace curtains, these Dresden dukes and duchesses bowing to each other on the whatnot were too grand for such ordinary rooms. They recalled high ceilings, columns, and verandas. They were from another place and life, the life that had stopped at Appomattox, eight years before Hennie was born.

How, then, could she still hear its cries and clamor in her head? It was because Mama made them so vivid. Papa, who had gone through four years of war, almost never spoke of it. Nor did Great-uncle David, who had gone through even worse, though, as Mama always said, on the wrong side. But how she clung to that war! She wore sorrow and anger like an old coat and could not throw it away. Perhaps in some peculiar way it protected her.

"Yes, it was a sorry day when we came to New York," Angelique said now. She stood up and went to the window. "Oh, when I think of where I grew up! Our lovely garden in New Orleans, with the fountain trickling." Her voice lamented that lost, privileged charm. "Lawns all the way to the river at Beau Jardin before the war. Parties and servants . . ." Slaves, but she would never use the word. And her swift hand dismissed the little parlor that Florence had so charitably praised.

"It's dark in here," Hennie said, finding it all unbearable.

She lit the gas; the blue flame hissed and jetted. The marble clock, the face suspended between gilt Corinthian columns, chimed the hour.

Florence stood up. "Come, Paul. Time to go home."

"We had a good time, Paul and I," Hennie told her.

"We saw a fire," Paul cried. "And gulls. They dive for fish in the river."

"We always have a good time," Hennie said.

"I know." It was never clear whether Florence minded or not.

From the window Angelique watched her daughter and grandson ride away in their polished black carriage with the coachman in brass buttons and the fine pair of matching grays. She sighed. "Your father is coming down the street," she said to Hennie.

In a moment the front door opened. Angelique turned from the window. "You're home early, Henry."

"There wasn't much doing downtown."

Too often there was not. Papa had been waiting to prosper ever since he and Wendell Hughes had come north and opened their office in the cotton district near Hanover Square.

"Not enough capital," he would say. "Not enough to expand as we ought. Oh, we're managing, but it's not what I had in mind. I sometimes feel I am failing you, Angelique."

Papa was gray: gray suit, skin, and faded hair. The sight of him pained Hennie. She watched him all through dinner. He ate silently. She wondered whether he heard half of her mother's and her brother's animated talk. Twelve-year-old Alfie could always amuse his mother.

"So Mr. Hemmings turned to see where the spitball came from. It hit the back of his neck, a real wet, squooshy one—"

Mama wanted to seem shocked, but laughter prevented. "Alfie, you are the limit! Now tell me, have you done your homework?"

Of course he hadn't. He would need to be reminded and prodded. But he is his mother's last darling baby and will always be, although a light mustache has begun to smudge his upper lip, and his nose will be bulbous. The twinkle of his eyes overcomes all.

When they went to the parlor, Papa laid his head on the back of his chair. He did that when he was tired, Hennie knew. They were two together, she and her father. It had been intended that she would be Henry, but she had turned out to be Henrietta instead. Still, she was tall like him, and she had his strong, separated teeth. That was supposed to be good luck, people said. Papa laughed at that and said he was still waiting.

Angelique picked up her knitting and said, "Florence and

Walter will be moving into the house on Seventy-fourth Street soon. Such a beautiful house, and right near the park, which is perfect for little Paul."

"Wonderful," Papa said. "Wonderful to think that their good fortune has come to them from the Werners and not from me."

It was a shame for a man to feel such bitter humiliation. Hennie could not look at him.

"We didn't even have her wedding at our house," Papa continued. It was the hundredth time he had said it.

"You know very well, Henry, we couldn't have had all those people in this place," Mama answered. "I don't know why you keep harping on it."

"The South was ruined, yet I married you in your own home, Angelique."

On the wall behind Papa hung his portrait. Proud he stood, in Confederate gray, with epaulets and braid, a small sword in his hand, a jaunty tilt to his head. Whenever he spoke of the South or of ruin, his eyes would go to the portrait. To him it was precious, but to Hennie it was only a warning that what he had lived through would have to be lived through by others, maybe by herself. Over and over again, to the end of time.

"As to the Werners," Mama said now, "it's an even exchange, and never forget that, Henry! The Werners got rich out of the war that made us poor. They may be in banking now, but the grandfather stood behind a dry goods counter, like all the German Jews, not too long ago. Don't think they aren't very much impressed by the De Rivera name, my dear!"

She was more impressed by the name than Papa, who owned it. What she meant was that, although among Jews it was infinitely better to be German than one of those poor Poles or Russians downtown, it was better yet to be Portuguese or Spanish.

This makes me shrivel in my skin, thought Hennie. So mean. And stupid too, because her own mother's family was German, as Uncle David likes to remind her.

Now Hennie reminded her. "Your own mother and Uncle David were born in Germany."

"Uncle David! Why do you refer everything to Uncle David?"

"I don't always."

"Well, you are so much like him," Angelique said, more mildly.

The family thought it was ridiculous that Uncle David should practice medicine among the tenements of the Lower East Side, instead of uptown. To Angelique he was an embarrassment. She made a mystery of his past, but Uncle David had told Hennie about it himself. He had been an abolitionist in the South before the war, had accidentally killed a man, and had had to flee north for his life. He was old now, nearly seventy. Hennie visited him often.

She got up. "I think I shall go to bed. Papa, Mama, good night."

"So early?" Papa said. "Don't you feel well?"

"I feel well, only sleepy."

But mourning had lain thick in the parlor, like dust. The woman frowning and knitting, the man with the newspaper dropped by his chair—it was as if they were both waiting for something. More money, so that they might be what they had been. But what they had been was nothing Hennie wanted.

In her own room she could shut the sadness away. She lay down in the dark. It was growing cold, with chilly air seeping around the edges of the bed, but the quilt made a warm pocket in which she curled, loving her little room.

Hennie had always known that she was not her mother's favorite, for no gift or smile or kiss can hide a truth like that from a child. Oh, her mother could be so gay with Alfie! He had personality, or rather, many personalities to suit the moment. Mrs. Hughes, the wife of Papa's partner—a hearty fool, in Hennie's opinion—called Alfie a young gentleman. Well, Mrs. Hughes wouldn't think he was one if she could see him mock her with his sputtering laugh, tucking two pillows under his coat behind and before.

And her mother could be so confidential with Florence! But Florence had always known how to tie a blue sash on an old white summer dress and turn herself into a beauty. When *she* had been eighteen, like Hennie now, invitations had piled up on the table in the hall. Walter Werner proposed to her two months after they were introduced, and married her on her nineteenth birthday.

So Hennie was caught between her sister and her brother, but none of that was any fault of theirs. It was simply that they were determined people and she was not.

"You only think you are not," her friend Olga had corrected her one day. "You have never tried to find out."

Their friendship was unexpected—or perhaps not unexpected, for Hennie needed to be wanted and Olga was honored that her teacher sought her out. Olga had piqued Hennie's curiosity. Married to a sweatshop worker like herself, confined to a drab life, Olga had not lost her eager imagination. As fast as Hennie lent books to her, she came back for more.

From discussion of Tolstoy and Dickens they came to the personal. Olga told of the horror of the Russian pogroms, of the long, hard months of the escape and voyage, and of the struggle in New York. Hennie told something about her family, and Olga came to understand her position in that family.

She had never visited Hennie's home. Their friendship was better left on neutral ground, removed from the tenements, to whose resentful occupants Hennie would seem to be a mere sightseer, and removed as well from the scrutiny of Angelique.

Hennie was wide awake. These random thoughts about her friend led now, possibly through a natural association of Olga's mean street with the one on which that afternoon's miracle had taken place, back to her own emotion. As never before in her life, she had been dazzled. She wanted to feel like that again.

In the gray shadows of the room his image floated—vivid eyes, a careless dark wave of hair. Absurd fantasy! What had he to do with her life? She was a foolish romantic. And yet there was so much happening in the world. Meetings, partings, lovers, life. Why not to her?

THEN one day she saw him coming out of Uncle David's office. He was running down the steps, tossing off his forehead that long, loose wave of hair that would not stay in place. He wore the same green corduroy trousers. It seemed to her touching, very masculine, not to know better than to wear such an ugly color. She watched him stride away, then turned and went up the stairs.

Uncle David had just made a pot of tea. "Sit down, have a cup," he said with a smile. "And so how are you?"

"Fine, Uncle David, fine."

"Tell me about the family. How are they all?"

"The same. My parents still worry about Alfie. He's not doing well at school and says he won't go to college. He wants to make money instead."

"Leave him alone, then. He's a perfectly sound young man who knows what he wants. They'll never make a scholar out of him."

"And Florence is moving. I saw the new house. It's lovely, right off Central Park West."

"Ah, yes, the Jewish Fifth Avenue. Well, good. That's what she wanted. It's nice to see people get what they want. And you, Hennie, are you getting what you want? How's your social life?"

She flushed. "Social life! It's stupid, Uncle David! People trading invitations . . ." And she mocked, " 'Have you been asked to the so-and-so's? What! You haven't? You—' "

Uncle David interrupted. "I of all people understand what you mean. But don't sneer at it all. It's not healthy to set yourself so apart." He spoke gently. "Be honest, Hennie. You make no effort. Is it possible that you don't feel pretty? Is that it?"

"I don't know exactly," she murmured.

"You'll be a fine-looking woman, Hennie. It's too early yet to see it, but it's there. Some women mature late." Leaning forward, he said, "Do you know, you remind me of your grandmother Miriam. She had endurance. Strength. Bravery."

A rush of words, unplanned, came suddenly. "Speaking of bravery, Uncle David, I saw something stupendous recently. I saw a man rescue a child out of a fire. He climbed up on the cornice six floors above the street. It was horrible. And so wonderful! He was offering his whole life for a stranger."

"Oh, I know who it was. I know him."

"Do you really? I thought I recognized him as I came in."

"Yes. Daniel Roth. He was just here. I took care of his burns. He's a very unusual man."

She remembered something. "Daniel Roth. I saw that name on the bulletin board at the settlement house. A Daniel Roth is to play the piano at our children's Thanksgiving festival. Do you suppose that's the same one?"

"Oh, yes. He plays piano pretty well, and it's the kind of thing he would do. He's a teacher. Teaches high school science downtown here. Something of an inventor-scientist too, keeps a little lab, lives above it." He paused, reflecting for a minute, unaware of Hennie's rigid, impatient attention, with her hands clasped around her knees.

Uncle David continued. "Oh, Dan's something special, all right. He's a fighter, a scrapper. Right now he's gotten mixed up with tenement reform." Here the old man waved his hand toward the window. "You know, it's an outrage, Hennie, that they permit these dumbbell tenements, with no courtyard, no light or air. But worst of all are the fires, like that one the other day. The stairway is right in the center and draws the fire up like a rocket. It shoots through the building. People don't stand a chance."

He talked on for another quarter hour; then Hennie said goodbye and stood to go. The Thanksgiving festival. I shall be there, she thought as she went out.

THE settlement house lay in the center of an irregular quadrangle bounded by Houston Street, the Bowery, Monroe Street, and the East River. Five old houses, once the homes of affluent merchants, had been renovated and turned into classrooms and workshops, where cooking, dancing, sewing, debating, carpentry, civics, and the English language were taught.

On this evening all the lights were on and the building was crowded. The assembly hall had been decorated with Thanksgiving symbols, pumpkins and dried speckled corn being part of the process by which the children from the ghettos of Europe were to be turned into Americans. On the stage a ten-year-old Governor Bradford, in black breeches and high-crowned black cardboard hat, bowed to Indian chief Squanto, played by a red-haired twelve-year-old only a year out of Minsk.

The piano was on the far side of the stage from where Hennie sat with Olga. The gas lamps were turned down as Daniel Roth came in.

He made a slight bow and struck the keys. He played the simple music with pleasure, looking up now and then to nod encouragement to a faltering child; he was enjoying himself.

When the play ended, everyone applauded and walked into the adjoining hall for coffee and cake. Hennie and Olga went in together.

Daniel Roth was standing among a group of buxom "uptown" charity ladies, and he looked as if he wanted to get away, just as he had when the crowd besieged him after the fire.

Hennie found herself approaching him, talking to him. "I'm Henrietta De Rivera," she began. "You know my uncle, Dr. David Raphael."

"I certainly do. He's one of my favorite people."

"He admires you too."

She would have liked to say something gay about the evening but could think of nothing more, and was confused.

The uptown ladies moved away. Olga moved away. The evening was ending. Children were fastened into their coats, and people were going home. She was alone in the room with Daniel Roth, who was looking down at her.

He said, astounding her, "Come out and have coffee or tea with me, will you? It's early yet."

Such things do not happen. Extravagant fantasies do not come true. In a daze she took the arm that he offered, and they went out onto the street.

It was a mild fall night, with a milky sky over the rooftops. He led her toward East Broadway.

"Do you live near here?" he asked.

"No. Near Washington Square."

"What brought you down here tonight, then?"

"I work at the settlement."

"One of those generous uptown ladies?"

"Not especially generous. I haven't any money to give. I just teach English to greenhorns."

"That wasn't nice of me. My remark about uptown ladies was sarcastic. I'm sorry."

She was beginning to feel uncomfortable with her hand in his elbow and made as if to remove it, but he tightened her arm against his side, imprisoning her hand.

"Your parents won't worry about your being out?"

"No. A group of us usually walks home together, so it's safe."

"You'll be safe with me, Henrietta."

"I'm called Hennie."

"That does suit you better. And I'm called Dan."

The darkening streets were still astir. Children spilled raucously over the stoops, and sewing machines whined like tired voices from open ground-floor windows.

"Listen," Dan said. "They're still working. I don't know where the strength comes from. Heat, cold, asthma, work and work."

"That's what Uncle David says."

"Yes, he knows. And cares. That's why he stays down here. It would surely be easier to move uptown."

"Is that why you teach here too?"

"Yes," Dan answered shortly.

Streetlamps glowed across East Broadway. Dan led Hennie into a café. "I'll bet you've never been in a café before, have you?"

"No." Nor out with a man, especially one to whom her parents had not introduced her.

They sat down. A waiter brought two glasses of hot tea.

"It's the Russian style to offer tea in a glass," he explained.

Her hands felt cold. She curved her palms around the hot glass, aware that he was regarding her with a studied gaze. She looked down, then looked back up. Something loosened inside her. "I saw you when you rescued the child at the fire," she said in a rush. "I wanted to go up and tell you how wonderful it was."

"Why didn't you?"

"I suppose I'm timid. And I saw that you wanted to get away."

"You're right, I did. Tell me, how old are you, Hennie?"

"Eighteen." She did not know whether that would seem too young to be interesting or too old to be as inexperienced as she must seem.

"I'm twenty-four. You seem older than eighteen. You're very, very serious."

"I guess I am. It's one of my faults."

"There's nothing wrong with being serious. Living is a serious business, especially around here. Did you know they found out there were three babies left in that building? They discovered the bodies after the fire had burned itself out."

Hennie shuddered, and he went on, "I get in a rage when I think of people getting rich out of owning such ratholes! I want to tear them all down!" He broke off. "Excuse me. I want to change the world. I make myself ridiculous."

She said gently, "You're not ridiculous at all."

"Yes, I am. I'm listening to myself talking too much."

"I like to hear you talk. Tell me about yourself."

"There's nothing much to tell. I was born in New York. In Yorkville, a German-speaking neighborhood. My father was a tailor. My mother died. I don't remember her."

"Tell me more," she said. "Tell me what you wanted to be."

"Be! Well, for a while there I had some grandiose ideas about music. When I was a kid, my piano teacher used to praise me, so I began to have a silly vision of myself at a concert grand, you know, dressed in white tie and tails—me, in a tailcoat!" He frowned. "Anyway, I got over that. Well, I didn't want to be a lawyer, and unlike half the boys in the neighborhood, I didn't want to be a doctor either. But I did like science. So I went to City College and now I'm a science teacher." He made a small, embarrassed grimace. "I do little experiments on the side. I have a lab in back of a machine shop, and a room upstairs."

"What kind of experiments do you do?"

"Well, it's hard to explain. They're based on the power of electrical resonance. I've got notebooks filled with ideas, most of them not much use, probably. Though I did invent something pretty good once. . . . I'm boring you."

"Of course you're not! What was the invention?"

"It was an electric arc lamp that could burn longer than the old ones. It's being manufactured. I got five hundred dollars for it. A friend of mine has a cousin, a lawyer, and he sold it for me. The five hundred came in handy right then, helped make my father's dying a little more comfortable." Dan's jaw tightened. Then he smiled apologetically. "I still have dreams that I'll discover something marvelous, like sending messages around the world by air. Crazy, you know."

"It's not crazy. You're only twenty-four. You can't tell yet what you'll do."

"At least I can do some good by teaching, I hope. There's so much intelligence here on these streets, waiting to be unlocked and set free! But one could do so much more in the school if the life outside were better. That's where science comes in, science and socialism."

"You're not a Socialist?" Hennie had never met a Socialist.

"My sentiments are. Not officially. I'm not with any party. I just try to do things that need doing."

"You really do remind me of Uncle David."

"Oho, that's a real compliment! I can't begin to tell you what I think of him. Honest, simple, good. He is rare. Rare."

"I think so too. In the family, you know," Hennie said shyly, "they think he's odd, a wild-eyed radical. But I don't find him so."

"Then your family must find you odd too, and radical?"

"I think they do. They love me, but I think they do."

"Is it lonely for you in your house, then? I imagine it must be."

"Yes. A little."

They looked eye to eye at one another. And Hennie had an extraordinary sense of startling reality, sharp and clear, as if she had just now awaked to that reality, which made trivial and insignificant whatever she had known until then.

Dan pushed his chair back. "Come," he said. "It's late, and I don't want your parents to be furious that I kept you out."

The night had deepened. It was beautiful, with fantastic dark blue clouds in the pale sky, a night to walk and walk and not go home. They passed a meeting hall. On the top step an orator was exhorting a small crowd.

"Christian mission to the Jews," Dan remarked. "I never could understand all this passion about religion. A lot of foolishness, don't you think so?"

"No. There has to be something." She looked up. The clouds were dispersing, opening the wide sky to a million stars. "All of that, and we down here, can't be accidents."

They had reached Hennie's building. A wind rose, rustling the last leaves from the trees. Dan looked down at her now.

"I wonder," he said slowly, "how anyone can believe in Him. Such misery. And the worst of all are the wars."

"Those are not God's fault, but ours," she said.

"Being a believer suits you, Hennie." He turned her face up to the entrance light. "Such a kind face. And lovely eyes, grave eyes. I want to see you again. May I?"

There was such a catch in her throat that she could only nod.

"I shall call on your parents. They will expect that. Good night, then, Hennie."

She fled upstairs. Tears came to her eyes, the softest, most bewildering tears.

He is like nobody else in all the world.

THE winter blossomed. The ice-cold sky reflected its pure blue in the snow meadows of Central Park, and the tinkling bells of jolly sleighs sounded in the streets, while snow sprayed under the runners. At the St. Nicholas skating rink Hennie whirled with Dan: a couple together, striding and sliding in rhythm.

Oh, enchanted city! Every passerby smiled approval. At the settlement her most rowdy, unmanageable children were really only normal rascals after all. People were so friendly, so good. One could love everyone.

At night Hennie sat at her window and dreamed. She had such longing for him, for his thick hair, his sad mouth, his rounded eyelids, his beautiful hands. Such longing.

"IT's been quite a while since you were here," Uncle David said one day in early February. "What have you been doing?"

She wanted to seem casual. "I've been seeing your friend Daniel Roth."

The old man's untidy eyebrows rose. "He came to call on you? Met your parents? Whatever did they talk about?"

"Oh, things. Nothing much, just the usual polite things."

But there had been questions, leading questions, and it had all come out about the tailor father and teaching school.

"So? Where do you go together?"

"Walking. Skating. We went to the opera. Heard *Rigoletto*. It was marvelous. Florence and Walter went with us. Walter insisted on buying the tickets, and Dan didn't like that."

"I should imagine not. He's independent." Uncle David paused, looking thoughtful. "I suppose you find him handsome?"

Hennie laughed. "Oh, yes. Don't you think so too?"

"I do. And so does every woman who comes in sight of him."

"What can you mean?"

"What I say. All the women run after him. I've known him

awhile, you see, and he has too much charm for his own good. Some people are born like that—as if they had a magnet in them."

"I don't see what difference that makes," she said. "What if women look at him? He can't help that, can he?"

"You see how it is, Hennie. There are men who can't resist. They can't be faithful to one woman."

"And you think . . ." Her voice was queer, falsetto. "You think Dan is like that?"

"Yes, I do. Don't go falling in love with him, Hennie."

She was silent, stricken, disbelieving.

"He won't do for you. I must tell you. Listen to me, Hennie, my dear. He loves women too much. That's his failing."

"After all the fine things you said about him!"

"They are all true. But what I'm telling you now is also true."

"Now you tell me! Why just now?" Something hardened in her. Fear or anger, or both.

"I never thought before that it would be necessary."

"You have no—no right," she stammered. "You're spoiling . . ."

"I don't want you to be hurt, that's all," Uncle David said gently. "Believe me, Hennie, I know that an unfaithful husband would break your heart." The old man gave her a smile, which she did not return. "Let me not make too much of this, though. A man comes to call a few times . . . that doesn't mean you'll be married. I only wanted to warn you. No harm done, I hope."

She would not look at him. She despised him. How dare he? A man was falling in love with her, she was sure of it. She drew herself up, smoothing her skirt; the womanly gesture reassured her.

Old man, old man, what do you know?

Oh, the damp first air of spring! Dan and Hennie rode a tandem bicycle through Central Park. They walked across the Brooklyn Bridge and watched the sailing ships come up the river.

"Imagine! Around the Horn from China!" Hennie cried. "What does it make you think of? Tea? Silk? Red lacquer?"

He bent down to her. Tall as he was, he always had to lean down. "Of you. I can see myself in your eyes. Did you know they've got green in them?"

"Dan! They're brown."

"But there's green all the same," he insisted. "Not like any other eyes I've ever seen. You're not like any girl I've ever known either."

She countered cheerfully. "How many have you known?" Banter, light and happy, while the heart pounds.

"Oh, dozens. No, seriously, Hennie, you're different from all of them. I'm in love with you. You know that, don't you?"

She wanted to prolong the marvel of suspense. "You hardly know me!"

"Five months, almost. That's long enough. Anyway, I know my own mind. The question is, do you love me?"

The wind almost bore her faint voice away. "I love you."

"Darling Hennie." His lips moved on her cheek. "We'll have good years together, a good life. Darling Hennie."

How wrong you were, Uncle David.

SPRING passed into summer. "You are seeing so much of Daniel Roth," Angelique remarked one day.

"Not just of him. I told you, there are always seven or eight of us together when we go walking or cycling."

Her mother looked at her doubtfully. "Well, of course I know you wouldn't go about with any young man unchaperoned."

Dan was not used to chaperonage. Among Lower East Side intellectuals, teachers, and writers, that sort of thing was ridiculed. So it had become necessary for her to lie at home.

Oh, if they knew what was going on! She thought of the rent-strike meeting where Dan had spoken with such passionate conviction, a hero of the platform. She had, of course, known her people in the classroom, but had had to imagine where they lived. That night she saw.

In these months she came to know every miserable street. Her sharpened vision picked out details that once had been only a blur. Listening to Dan, she felt a new surge of painful indignation.

One evening they walked through Bottle Alley and Mulberry Street. Rags blew on the clotheslines overhead; a hawker offered a worn coat for fifty cents.

"Look," Dan said, "at that boy reading there on the stoop. There's no place inside for him to do his schoolwork."

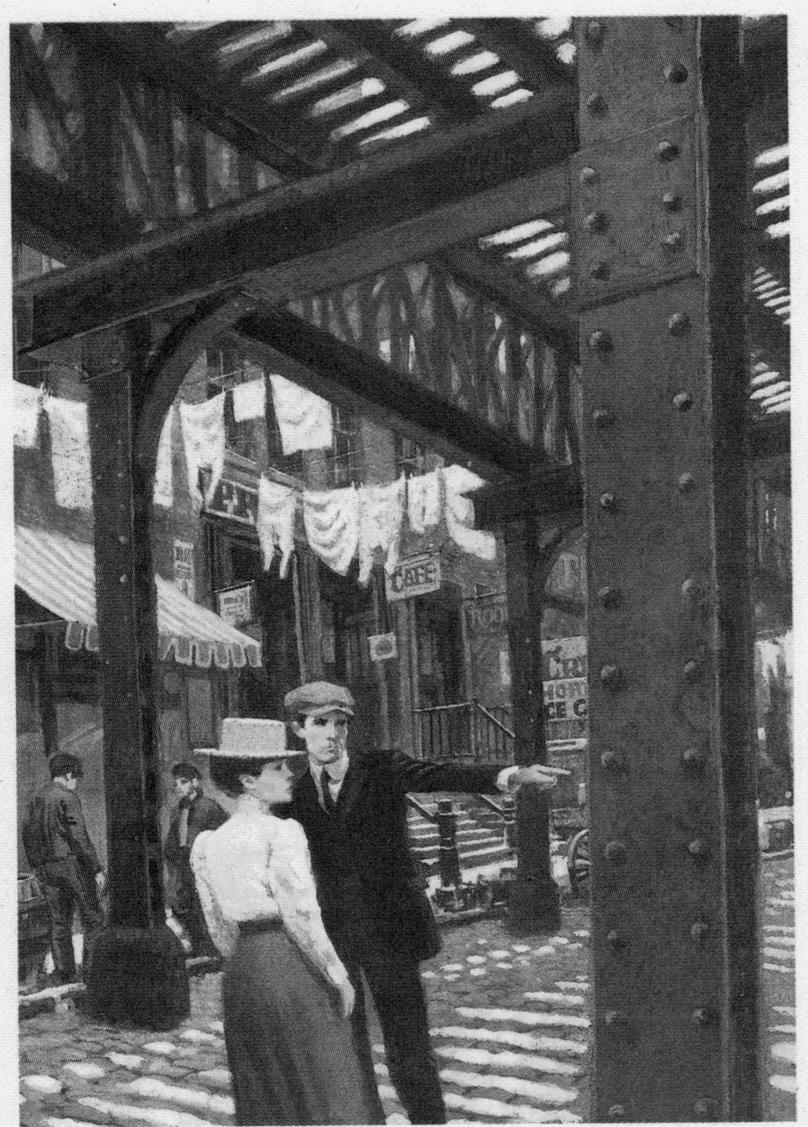
CAFE

Riding the Second Avenue elevated train, they could see into the second-floor rooms where the "sweaters" worked. "Like animals in stalls," Dan said.

Oh, it is wrong! Wrong! And Mama complains that it's not easy to be poor, as if she has any idea what being poor is.

"I wish we could go home together," he had said that night at her front door. "I'm so sick of always leaving you here. Kissing you quickly before anyone sees, walking home alone. It's such a waste. I wish we could be in a room together, with a closed door."

She had wanted to ask, Yes, when? But she kept still. Her eyes filled with quick tears.

"It's only money. I'm afraid of the future, of having nothing for you. Every damn thing is money." He had spoken bitterly. "Even love costs money in this world."

"We'll find a way," she had said. "I'm sure we will."

ALFIE came into her room. Thirteen now, he could say surprising things, showing a power of observation with which his parents did not credit him.

"I heard Mama and Pa talking about you last Sunday," he informed her.

Brushing her hair, she could see him in the mirror. "About what?" She turned quickly, knowing.

"You know what. About Dan. Pa said, 'Let the thing wear itself out,' or something like that. And Mama said, 'Yes, but it's been a year; he's wasting her time.' "

"Anything else?"

"Yes. Mama said that Florence could introduce you to lots of people, but you always say no. Do you?"

"I suppose I do."

"Are you going to marry him, Hennie?"

She had a need to talk about what had filled her all these months with such joy and such expectancy.

"Can I trust you, Alfie? I've not told anyone."

"I won't tell. Are you going to marry him, then?"

"Yes," she said softly.

"When?"

"I don't know. . . . Soon."

2

HENNIE put the book away. It was no use trying to concentrate. Her eyes, looking into the farthest distance, came to rest on the fringe of spring-green leafage that screened the stone gleam of the mansions on Fifth Avenue, across the park. The weather was fine and fresh; everything was new and beautiful. But she had a feeling of panic. She had known Dan for a year and a half now; days like this were slipping by and she was doing nothing with them.

On the opposite bench sat a young woman. It was plain, in spite of her concealing coat, that she was expecting a baby.

She's not much older than I am, Hennie thought. Yet someone wanted her enough to spend the rest of his life with her, and now there will be a child. . . .

A life made out of two. Dan and me. Hennie was shaken. Longing, and terror that it might never be—these shook her.

"I'm back, Aunt Hennie!" Paul sat on his little bicycle.

"Well, you had a long ride, didn't you? It's time to go home, you know. Time for your piano lesson."

Slowly they left the park. At the corner of Seventy-fourth Street they could see halfway down the block. Trunks were being carried out from the Werners' house and loaded onto a wagon.

"Look, Paul, there go your things on the way to the mountains! Aren't you excited?"

"Yes, and we're taking the canary this year. It will be riding all the way in the train, just the way we do."

Florence was at the front door as the wagon departed.

"What a mess it is going away." She sighed. "All the furniture to be covered and the windows boarded up for the summer. And only two more weeks to go. Well, come in, sit down. You must be exhausted."

"No, we had a nice time, Paul and I. It's a lovely day."

In the somber parlor the stained glass of an enormous chandelier spilled a wine-colored gloom over everything. In front of the sofa the tea wagon stood ready.

"I want cake," Paul said immediately.

"It's time for your piano lesson in fifteen minutes," Florence objected. "You may have cake after supper."

"I'm afraid I promised him cake now," Hennie said meekly.

"Oh, dear, you'll spoil the child. Well, all right, take a piece, then. But first go upstairs and ask Mary or Sheila to wash your hands. That's a good boy."

Florence looked at Hennie. "You should have a dozen children. You're the type."

Hennie gave the expected modest smile. A sudden physical weakness hit her, so that her hand, accepting the teacup, trembled. She felt like crying. It was fortunate the room was so dark.

"You really should come to the Adirondacks with us, dear."

Why is she so insistent? Why should it matter whether I go or not? But I do know why. And she knows I know.

"Walter's parents are so hospitable, they'll make you at home right away. They're really so good to us. I'm lucky to have in-laws like them. I pray you'll be as lucky, Hennie."

Yes, Hennie thought, I believe she does pray for me.

"Do come, Hennie!" Florence looked kindly at her sister.

Hennie collected herself. "I'm so busy at the settlement, you see. I've started a cooking class, and I hate to just abandon it."

Florence studied her teaspoon for a moment, then looked up frankly at her sister. "You won't go away because of Daniel."

"I guess so," Hennie said, beguiled into admission.

"What's happening, Hennie? I don't want to pry, honestly I don't. But I've had a hard time keeping Mama from exploding. She doesn't understand what's going on."

"Going on! Good heavens, I've known him a little more than a year—"

"Almost two, dear."

"Do they want marriage on sight?"

"Hennie, they don't want you to marry him at all. That's what they're worried about."

"You don't like him either. Don't deny it. It won't be any use, because I know you don't."

"I have been as nice to him as anyone could be, the few times I've been with him, and so has Walter. You can't say we haven't been."

"Yes, but he's not your style."

Florence did not reply at once. Then, laying her hand on her sister's arm, she spoke with a married woman's dignity and the authority of experience.

"Hennie, just remember, these are your best years. A girl hasn't got all the time in the world. Now, will you stay to dinner?"

Hennie stood up. "No, I can't." She had to go. Something was jumping alive in her chest. Something had to be done. She couldn't stay waiting this way any longer, waiting for something to happen. Why, why did he need to wait?

"Think about the mountains, anyway," Florence said at the door. "If you change your mind, let me know."

Hennie rode the omnibus all the way down Fifth Avenue. When the horses pulled to a stop at Washington Square, she stepped out into the fading afternoon. For a moment or two she stood beneath the green shimmer of the trees, holding an idea as if in the palms of her hands. She looked east toward home. She ought to go home. . . .

At last she made up her mind, and walked in the opposite direction with quick, decisive steps.

SHE has not meant it to happen this way. But then, neither has he. She has only meant to ask him what is to become of them and whether he really means to stay with her, because he has been so vague about it for so long and now this panic has taken hold of her. That's all she has meant.

But they come together. That which she has so long imagined and desired now happens.

He opens the door and is astonished to see her. Suddenly she is appalled at her own boldness, but it is too late to turn back.

"Will you come up?" he asks.

He opens the door at the top of the stairs and stands aside to let her go in. This is where he lives. His bed is the first thing she sees. She looks away, but the room is too small to avoid it. Between the bed and an ugly upright piano, there is just enough space to pass. There is a pile of clothing on a chair. He apologizes for the mess, and they both sit down on the edge of the bed. The sounds of the street drift through the open window.

He kisses her. The kiss is different from past kisses, softer, and also harder, because they are alone. She does not want it to end.

His hands quiver on the buttons that go all the way down her back. Piece by piece he takes off her clothes. She is warm, warm and weak, but she is strong too in the way she clings to him.

The last thing she hears is the sound of the organ-grinder, the opening bars of some banal, familiar tune that fades as quickly as it began, along with all the noises and voices in the world; everything fades, even the afternoon light; the circle draws in, shrinks to a single point where they lie.

Afterward she went behind the door to get dressed. Strange that the removal of her clothes had been so natural, while their replacement was embarrassing.

"Hennie, I want to tell you something," she heard him say.

He will tell me when we shall be married.

"I want to promise you that you needn't worry. I'm very careful. You won't become pregnant."

Why all at once this trembling shame? Because the consequences of all that sweetness could be so fearful. . . .

"Hennie, did you hear me? I said don't worry. Trust me."

"I will. I do."

AFTER that, it was arranged between Dan and Hennie that whenever she could find plausible time, she would come to him. The weeks flowed easily into one another. Hennie felt as good as married. Almost. And Dan was happy. He talked no more of longing to be in a room with her behind a locked door. Hesitating to mention marriage, since, after all, it was the man who ought to take the lead, or so the novels all said, she nevertheless brought up the subject on one of her visits.

"You see, I have to get some money ahead," Dan replied.

"I'm a simple person, Dan. You know that. I don't want a lot."

"Even so, we can't live here in this room, can we?"

Glancing at the narrow bed, the single chair, and the milk bottle on the windowsill, she had to concede that they couldn't.

"Darling, I wish it could be tomorrow. But I shall have to get a little ahead."

"How is that to be done?" she asked, keeping her tone steady.

"I don't know. True, I get a salary, but till I met you I saved very little. I always gave so much away, and now the need for giving is greater than it ever was."

"You're still giving?"

"Not much, though it's hard not to when I see my kids coming to school half asleep because they've been up late making artificial flowers. But I'm trying, I really am. Just be patient."

THE months revolved and fall came again.

When had she really felt the beginning of the drift? It was impossible to know precisely when. A drift is just that: gradual and vague, veering like a night breeze.

Women glanced invitingly and he responded. Nothing came of it really, except that whenever it happened, she felt left out and humiliated by her own jealousy. She knew one thing: never to let him know that she saw or cared, lest she become that ridiculous creature, a suspicious and possessive woman.

They had been at a beach picnic at the end of the summer; that had been one time. There had been a lively group of teachers with wives and children. It was a marvelous day, too cool for bathing but perfect for walking on the hard sand near the water's edge. . . .

We are in line, somehow arranged by twos, to the jetty and back.

I find myself with Mr. Marston, the Latin teacher. Dan is ahead of us with the daughter, Lucy. She is about my age and is as noisy as my brother, Alfie.

Mr. Marston keeps talking about his wife, recently dead. I am sorry for him, but my eyes are on Dan and the girl. The wind carries their voices away, all except her giggling treble, so I don't know what they are talking about, but I can see by Dan's enthusiastic gestures that he is happy. When she stumbles in the sand, he offers his arm, and they go on walking that way to the jetty and back.

It's time to eat. I sit on the rocks beside Dan. Lucy Marston wanders uncertainly, holding her plate, looking for a place to sit. Dan calls to her. He moves to make a place for her on his other side.

The girl has a lively energy that I don't have. She raises her arms above her head to stretch, and arches her back; her body is an invitation and a promise. If I see it, surely Dan does. I feel such a terrible, frenzied jealousy that I could smash my fist into her face. . . .

Was that day the beginning? Hennie dared not ask.

From time to time since then Dan had mentioned Lucy, but he mentioned other women too. So really it must be just a kind of game. A game of the eyes, of compliments and admiration. That was what Uncle David had seen and failed to understand.

Yes, Hennie assured herself. It is his way, harmless in spite of being painful to me. I will have to accept it. He must be loosely held, and then he will always come back.

And yet the second year was ending.

On the Sunday before Thanksgiving they went for an afternoon walk in Central Park. The day was hazy, the air warm and still, vaguely depressing in a season that ought to be brisk. People wandered slowly; children kicked at the piled leaves along the paths.

Suddenly Dan was staring at her. They had come to a stop in the middle of the path. "What is it, Hennie? You look miserable. What's bothering you?"

"A mood, I guess."

"Well, you're entitled to a mood. I'll forgive you."

Forgive me for what? she cried silently. Oh, Dan, won't you understand? I need to know where I'm going!

They went on again, speaking very little but breaking the silence now and then, when it became too heavy, with some desultory remarks about trivial things. They came out onto Fifth Avenue and caught the omnibus downtown.

"I forgot to tell you," Dan said. "There are some cousins of my mother's coming in from Chicago. Naturally, I'm obligated to take them around the city. So next week will be a busy one for me."

"Yes, of course," Hennie answered quickly.

When they got off at the last stop, she said, "You needn't walk home with me. No, really, I know you've got things to do."

"Actually, I can use the time. I've a pile of papers to go over."

He smiled. "Cheer up, Hennie. The world hasn't come to an end."

"I'm very cheerful, I'm quite fine. Don't worry about me," she said, walking away.

I will not look back to see whether he is looking after me. I will not. But I have lost him.

HENNIE was starved for food. Five times during one afternoon she went to the kitchen, raiding the icebox. She ate a chicken leg from the previous night's dinner, drank a glass of milk, and ate an apple. When her stomach was empty, she felt sick.

One morning she vomited. Oh, my God, it can't be! It's something else. Dan said it wouldn't be. So it isn't.

She had not heard from him for two weeks. She thought of walking downtown and playing a game, a dangerous game with herself: How far will I go toward his house before I turn back?

In the end she did go downtown, but to Uncle David's office. It was time to find out once and for all.

"FROM what you tell me," Uncle David said gently, "it's pretty clear what's the matter. But I shall need to look, all the same."

Burning shame. Where does one find the courage to do this?

"Just lie down and put the sheet over yourself. I shall step out. When you're ready, call me."

She lay quite still. The corset, the chemise, and the petticoats lay on a chair. She closed her eyes so as not to see them or the ceiling or anything. She called out.

When the sheet was lifted, cool air swept over her and she felt cold metal. Then the sheet was drawn up again.

"Get dressed," Uncle David said. "We'll talk afterward."

His voice was dry, without emotion, and she knew he was suppressing a terrible anger. So it was true. She forced herself to stand and put on her clothes. Tears poured; she wept without making a sound.

When Uncle David returned to the room, he said softly, "Don't cry." But the tears still slid down her cheeks. "Will you tell me about it, Hennie?"

She opened her mouth, but no sound came until, straining, she was able to whisper, "I can't."

"All right. I suppose there's nothing to tell. It happened, that's all. At least you love each other, and that's what matters."

Her tears stopped, but she still could not speak.

Uncle David's eyes rested on Hennie, touching her softly, softly. "You will have to be married," he said. "Right away. Does he know anything of this?"

Hennie shook her head.

"You must tell him today, Hennie. I'll say the baby came early. No one will question it. Now you're in this, you must brave it out."

"I don't know how I can do that, Uncle David."

"You will do it because you have to."

Opening the door, he reminded her, "Dear Hennie, the main thing is, at least you love each other. Just keep thinking of that."

SHE waited for Dan on the stairs outside his room. While he searched for the keyhole in the half darkness, she blurted what she had to tell.

"Dan, I'm having a baby."

The door slammed back against the wall. He threw his coat—she had mended a burn hole he had made in it at the lab—over the back of the chair. She followed him into the room.

"How do you know?" he asked.

"I went to Uncle David this morning."

He struck a match and held it to the gas bracket; a weak light seeped out into the dusky afternoon.

"What did he say? Was he in a rage?"

That we must be married right away. That the important thing is, we love each other.

"He didn't say very much."

"He must have said something." Dan looked down at the floor. "I should think he'd want to kill me."

"There wouldn't be much point in that, would there?"

He came to her. "Sit down here. Take off your coat. Maybe you should lie down. . . ."

She glanced at the bed and, moving past it, sat down in the chair at the window. She felt Dan's hand on her shoulder. "Don't be afraid, Hennie. We'll have to be married quickly, that's all."

His voice came to her as if it were an echo; she had a queer feeling of unreality. And as if another voice, not her own, were answering, she heard, "You don't want to."

"Hennie, I do! It's sooner than I— But we'll manage."

"All this time you said we couldn't afford it. And then you didn't talk about it at all anymore."

"I was afraid of the responsibility. The bills, the rent. I kept putting it off. Don't think I haven't felt guilty."

Hennie put her face in her hands.

"I'm not proud of myself. Hennie, don't cry. Please, I can't bear your tears."

"I'm not crying." She raised her head. Like death, he looked. This had brought him down. And she felt a vindictive triumph. "You'll get over my tears soon enough," she continued. "Miss Lucy Marston will help you do that."

"What in the name of creation are you saying? She has nothing to do with this! What can you be thinking? A pretty girl. There are dozens of them everywhere. Can't a man talk to a girl without somebody's thinking—" He faltered and stopped.

It would be good to believe him. Maybe it was the truth.

"We shall have to be married right away, Hennie," Dan urged, repeating himself.

"No. I don't want you to marry me because we 'have to.' " Something rose in her, something defiant and strong. "I'm worth more than that. I won't live with a man who will throw this up to me every time we have an argument."

"I would never throw it up to you. You have my word."

"Your word isn't good enough anymore."

He asked quietly, "Then what do you want? If you won't marry me, what will you do?"

She stood up and went to the window. "I don't know." She heard her own laugh, an ugly, broken sound. "Kill myself, I suppose."

"My God, Hennie!" He walked over to her, put his arms around her, and laid his cheek on her hair; his warm breath, his murmur, hovered over her head. "Don't talk about dying. Please. You terrify me."

Rigidly she stood, her body resisting his tight hold. Not a word had he said about the two weeks of silence, nor the indifference before that.

She became aware that he was controlling a sob.

He lifted her chin so that she was forced to see the tears in his eyes. "I never meant to hurt you. I blunder, I'm not as considerate as I should be. But I'll do better, believe me."

"I wish I could."

"You can! Trust me, will you? From now on?"

She was quite still, wanting, considering, hesitating.

Then his tears broke her. The great hard lump of grief in her chest broke open, shattered into little pieces. She wept. "I don't want to die! I didn't mean what I said!"

"Darling, of course you didn't. You're so lovely and brave."

He kissed her hair. Their tears ran together on her wet cheeks. His mouth came down on hers; they clung to each other. All the terror, the fear, the wrath and pride melted away into a merciful relief.

For long minutes they held each other. And at last Hennie smiled. Tenderly, with the familiar gesture, she pushed the stray wave from his forehead.

ANGELIQUE frowned. "I can't understand the sudden haste. Or why your father is going along with Daniel's insistence."

"Papa's happy for me."

"The whole thing's a puzzle. All of a sudden your father has such good things to say: he's so cultured; he's a scientist. Why?"

Hennie thought, It's because Papa knows how sad I've been. Or can it be possible that he suspects the truth?

Florence said, "If you'd wait until spring, we could have the winter to get properly ready."

"Florence, we don't want to wait."

"Well, then, we shall have to rush the invitations. You'll come down my stairs, Hennie—"

"I would rather have it very small, here at home. It would make Papa happy to have a wedding here."

"Perhaps you're right," Florence agreed reluctantly. "But at least let me help you with your clothes. Brocade would be best. We'll go on Monday. Begin on Broadway with Lord and Taylor.

Walter and I have decided to give you a check to start you off."

Hennie scarcely heard. All was being taken care of. She was being taken care of. She twisted the ring on her finger, the chip of a diamond that had belonged to Dan's mother. Incredible relief swept over her, like the gratitude of one who has been saved from drowning.

THE boy Frederick, named after Dan's father, was immediately called Freddy. He was unusually large and strong, Uncle David informed the family, for a seven-month baby.

They all came to the hospital—Hennie's parents, and Florence and Walter with little Paul.

"You won't take me to the park anymore," Paul told Hennie.

"Of course I will! Why shouldn't I?"

"Because you have him, and you won't love me anymore."

Everyone laughed except Hennie, who reached for Paul's hand. "I will love you both. You'll help me with Freddy, and he will love you. You will love each other all your lives."

"But you will love him more," Paul said seriously, "because he's yours."

How wise he is, thought Hennie, and did not answer, but held the child's hand until he left.

Then she was alone with Dan and the baby. Dan knelt to bring his face on a level with hers. He had brought roses and a little cloth cat.

"You and this boy." His voice wavered. "I don't deserve you."

She stroked his hair. "Don't say that. It's not true."

"Yes. These last months, being together, I've seen all the goodness in you. I'm ashamed of some of the things I've done."

Intensely moved, she said, "We're together, that's enough."

When Dan went home, she was left alone with the baby. A little mound under a white blanket, he slept on his stomach, revealing only half of a mottled face and some tan hairs on a naked skull. One hand lay above the blanket; the tiny fingers were trying to grasp the smooth sheet. For minutes, propped on her elbow, Hennie observed this marvel she had made.

He's here, she thought, and I'm here. We're a family with a future, and I know finally who I am.

3

It is the last night of the year, indeed the last of the century, and there is in the air the splendid tension that precedes a holiday, along with the regret that comes from leaving a familiar place.

Hennie looks around at the gathered family. We were together in the last hours of the nineteenth century, we will say, years from now; we will tell about it and there will be something elegiac in the telling.

All evening she has had a lovely sense of well-being. All is orderly in her home; there is enough of everything, but not too much. Only the elaborate silver tea service, one of several that Mama's mother had buried in the woods during the Civil War, looks out of place on the plain mission table.

"Mission furniture?" Florence had questioned when they bought it. "That square, homely stuff?"

"It's made for the people, solid and simple. That's why Dan likes it."

She has never wanted the things that Florence and Mama want. It is wrong to own so much that one doesn't need.

Dan has made their rooms cheerful. He has painted the walls and ceilings white, quite out of style. But fashionable dark colors close in on you, while white opens out to the world, to sun and air. The apartment is sunny. From the kitchen window Hennie can look down on the green yards around the homes on East Broadway, half a block distant. She has made curtains and Dan has built bookshelves. It gives her pleasure to watch the shelves fill up, for books are their one extravagance.

Her eyes move to the old upright on which Dan has begun to give piano lessons to Freddy. She wonders whether the boy is perhaps a musical genius. Dan says he has talent. Or is she merely the doting mother?

Fortunately, there is a large closet in the back hall where Dan, who can never part with anything, can toss his belongings; papers and pamphlets, along with every letter he ever received, spill out of shelves and boxes onto the floor. Hennie smiles to herself; the closet is a reflection of Dan—large, careless, free, and bold.

They have eaten well: turkey and turnips, potatoes, rolls and homemade jellies. Now, with dinner over, fruit and cake are to be served on the round table in the parlor.

"An excellent meal," says Angelique. "Too bad Florence and Walter couldn't be here, but they had a formal dinner to go to. There are some obligations one just can't refuse."

Alfie comes galloping down the hall with Freddy on his shoulders. Although Freddy is fair-haired, he is unmistakably Dan's son; the cleft chin, the rounded forehead, and the heavy-lidded eyes are Dan's. But he is small for five, and fearful.

"Did you know I saw elephants at the zoo?" Freddy cries. "They eat with their nose!"

"No," Paul corrects. "They only pick up the food with their long noses. The mouth is underneath, don't you remember?"

Freddy laughs. Paul is his favorite love. After him comes Uncle Alfie. He has no bond with any child of his own age; he is perfectly healthy, rarely sick, but he hangs back from play.

Alfie sets Freddy down. He is happy tonight, because he has brought with him the girl he wants to marry, the serene Emily, daughter of Henry De Rivera's business partner. The Hugheses' opposition to the marriage looms like a mountain. His own parents' opposition looms too, although it makes not quite as high a mountain.

Emily stands at the desk in the corner, where Uncle David is showing her a book of Mathew Brady's Civil War photographs. Her pale hair, caught high by a tortoiseshell comb, crowns her symmetrical Saxon face; she is placid and somehow ageless.

It is all too complicated, Hennie thinks, when it deserves to be so simple. Only wanting to be together! Yet some force in the world seems to want to keep people apart. In this case it is religion. But Alfie must not make Emily wait. It is the cruelest thing for a woman.

Hennie begins to cut the cake. "It's a Russian cream cake. My friend Olga gave me her recipe. I made an extra one to give to her. She has no place to bake, no place for anything really, since her husband died. Tuberculosis, as usual. She and her little girl, Leah, a darling child, have to board. I've never seen the place, but I can imagine it. Here, take this plate, Paul."

"I'll need a bigger piece than that," Paul complains.

"I don't know where you put it," Angelique remarks fondly. "It's a good thing you don't run to fat like your uncle Alfie."

Paul runs a finger inside his Buster Brown collar. His mother has made him wear his best clothes for this overnight visit to the Roths', complete with a Windsor scarf tied in a flopping bow, more suitable to his parents' parlor, certainly, than to this one.

Contained within the form of the twelve-year-old boy is the design of the man Paul will be. He has a thoughtful, formal expression, contradicted every now and then by his lively curiosity. People say that he looks aristocratic. How Dan despises the word! thinks Hennie. Nevertheless, it does describe Paul. One sees it in his posture and his steady gaze, so strikingly blue in the dark face.

Now Freddy challenges Paul: "I'll beat you at checkers."

They get out the board and lay it on the floor.

"Paul is so patient with Freddy," remarks Angelique. "But then, neither of them has a brother."

And why Paul hasn't got one, why Florence doesn't want more children, I'll never understand! Hennie's thoughts are bitter. In her place I would have five children. The time Dan said he would not let it happen, it did. Now we've been married for six years. We have been wanting another, and nothing happens.

Hennie becomes aware that Uncle David is looking at her.

"What are you looking at, Uncle?"

"At you. You've grown so pretty."

In truth, she has acquired a bloom, so that one is now more than ever aware of her rich hair and her leaf-shaped eyes.

"You do look well," Angelique agrees. "It's a wonder too, hard as you work here at home and at the settlement house too."

"I only do what I like," Hennie answers mildly.

The sound of Dan's laughter comes from the kitchen, where he is making lemonade and talking to Alfie and Emily. His laughter has a special note of gaiety that tells Hennie he is enjoying himself enormously.

He comes into the parlor carrying the pitcher and pours lemonade for Papa and Uncle David. He is good to them both, especially to Papa, who is growing old, going downhill faster than Uncle David, who is many years older still.

"That Alfie certainly knows how to pick a girl," Dan says. "She's a fine one, all right. Heads are going to turn when he walks in with her, wherever he goes."

Angelique reproves him. "Fine she may be, but hardly our first choice, as even you can understand."

"Oh, yes," Dan says. "And I'm sure you understand that your son isn't her parents' first choice either."

"Choice? They're in terror that something will come of it!"

Dan shrugs. "Perhaps nothing will. At his age a man can expect ten love affairs before he's through. If he ever is through," he adds mischievously.

Uncle David sets his glass down with a clink. "Any man worth his salt knows when it's time to be through." He snaps the words.

Dan makes no comment, but busies himself with the pitcher and the tray. Uncle David brings the glass to his lips. Over the rim his old eyes catch Hennie's briefly, then turn away.

What have they meant to say, those kind, clever eyes? Anything new that Hennie does not know? Or have they revealed only a flickering recall of words once spoken and never spoken since? Probably so. It is essential to her peace that any doubt be stifled.

The mantel clock strikes the half hour.

"Thirty minutes to go before the twentieth century begins," says Alfie.

"Oh, Freddy's falling asleep over the checkerboard," Hennie says. "Dan, he belongs in bed."

"Let him see this new year in. It's something he'll remember."

"Yes, you're right," Hennie agrees. "What a splendid century it will be!"

The clock lurches toward midnight. They open the windows and lean out into the freezing air. The city is almost as bright as day; every light must be ablaze. Down in the street a crowd is massed. Tin horns squawk and blare; whistles shrill and someone beats a drum.

Suddenly a tremendous shout goes up, as if every throat in the city has opened to hail the first of January.

"Twelve o'clock. Nineteen hundred," Dan says.

For a moment they are all stilled. Then there are kisses and toasts. Freddy is wakened and, held in his father's arms, is allowed a sip of wine. Coats are collected as the gathering breaks up. Alfie and Emily have embraced without embarrassment. Henry and Angelique have kissed each other decorously. Hennie and Dan, looking into each other's eyes, decide to wait until the house is quiet and they are alone.

THEIR bodies, joined and now released, have made a golden heat in the winter night. Dan laughs.

"How wonderful it is!" he says. "Do you ever think how really wonderful it is?"

"Yes, always," she whispers seriously.

She marvels that they have given one another so much joy, that she has given it to him, and can again, and will.

"Dear heart," he says. "You're so good for me. You make peace for me."

She *is* good for him. She knows it's true. And there is no doubt that she pleases him. A man can't pretend. If she were only sure that she is the only one. . . .

Stop it, Hennie. Stop it right now.

"I'm falling asleep," he says.

She closes her eyes. The warmth makes her drowsy at last. She seems to be seeing pink through her lids as sleep comes. Why, it's nine years since the fire that changed their lives! And still they love each other, and always will.

Of course they will. . . . Won't they?

4

BENEATH the pastel shimmer of the time that has come to be known as the Belle Époque, with its sensuous, curvaceous art and its exotic music, under all the lavish beauty, the bottom seethed, sullen and dark.

A long line of anarchists, beginning with the assassins of the Italian king, the Austrian empress, and the American President, brought terror to Europe and America. Socialists, suffragettes, and advocates of disarmament met and marched, petitioned and wrote. Crusading journalists and novelists exposed the corruption of the cities, the filth of the stockyards, the evils of child labor.

Rent strikes followed, and meat strikes. In New York City women shirtwaist workers struck for decent wages and conditions. Hennie knew some of the women from the settlement house.

"They're working seventy hours a week for less than five dollars," declared Hennie. "Do you know, Dan, they have to pay for the chairs they sit on. Pay for their needles and their lockers."

"They ought to unionize, of course," he said.

"Yes. But they all hope to get married and quit, so the union organizers haven't gotten very far with them. I ought to do something."

"You? What can you do?"

"I could picket, for one thing. I could at least do that."

IN THE second month of the strike the girls still marched outside the factory. Two by two they paced, carrying their placards; their defiant songs in Yiddish and Italian rang with vigor. Oh, it was cold! The January wind slashed around the street corner at which, after fifty paces, they turned and marched back.

Hennie came every day while eleven-year-old Freddy was at school. Whenever she could, she found her place beside Olga Zaretkin.

"You ought to take my coat," Hennie said one day. "It's a lot heavier than yours. You're shivering." The girl's thin coat was held up protectively around her throat, leaving her fragile wrists bare between sleeve and glove.

"Not at all! Why should you do that?" Olga was indignant. "I don't need—" The words were cut off by a spasm of coughing.

"Olga, your coat's like paper and you're sick."

There was no answer. They trudged, their feet squelching in the mucky brown snow. The wind fought with the placards borne high on flimsy sticks, trying to wrench them out of numb hands.

"Olga," Hennie persisted. "You shouldn't be here at all. You should be seeing a doctor."

"What good is a doctor if I can't make a decent living? Besides, I know what's the matter with me anyway."

Indeed, one did not need much knowledge of medicine to recognize tuberculosis. The pink-petal flush and the peculiar luminous beauty of the eyes were both as typical as the cough.

Olga is going to die as her husband did, thought Hennie. She

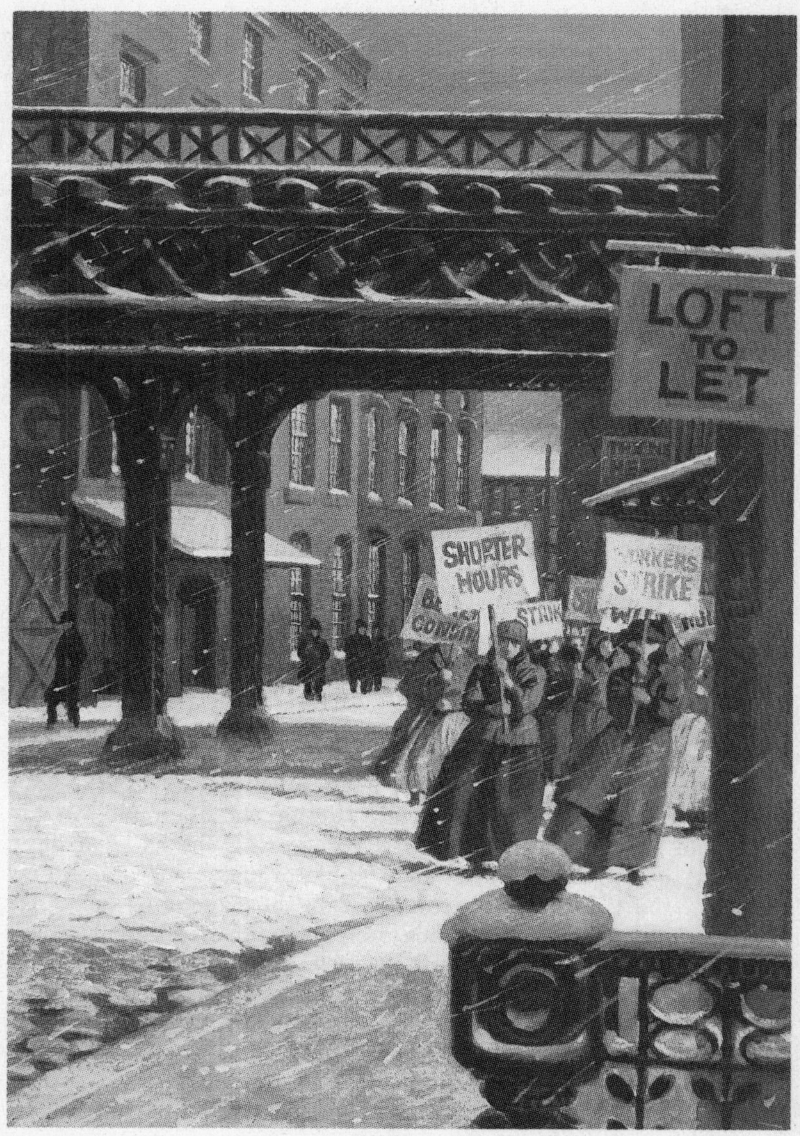
LOFT
TO
LET
SHORTER
HOURS

knows it quite well. In a few months she will be too weak to get out of bed. After that, the end will come slowly.

They walked the length of the block. One, two; one, two; turn at the corner and back. The second hour and the third.

"I worry so about Leah," said Olga. "She's only eight."

"No family here at all?" Hennie asked.

"Not here, not there. The ones over there are all dead."

She felt Olga's silence of recollection. It was necessary to speak, to make it bearable. "I haven't seen your Leah in so long."

"I wish we had a good place to live. It's not right for her this way, boarding with strangers. They're good people; they struggle, with five children. They sew pants—the whole family, even the children, work. Oh," Olga cried, "what will become of Leah?"

And now she looked Hennie full in the face, while her question hung in the cold air between them. Hennie had to look away from such terror, such anguish. "I don't know what to tell you, Olga," she said. "I wish I did. All I can say is, I'll try to keep an eye on her."

They turned again at the corner. The block seemed to be growing longer and longer. They moved mechanically, gasping with the cold. One by one the strikers had stopped singing and talking. Speech only used the energy they needed now to move their feet. The day wore on, the whole long, gray, unbroken day.

It shattered into a thousand pieces.

From around the corner, with savage, insane cries, came a dozen or more men. Company thugs they were, hired toughs. They fell upon the women, shoved them, beat them with clubs and bricks, with raw fists, swore at them, and scattered them.

In the confused, chaotic struggle Hennie was slammed against the factory wall, at the rear of the flailing mass. She had lost sight of Olga, but suddenly, through a tangle of knees and shoulders, she saw the familiar red woolen hat on the pavement and Olga sobbing on the ground. A man's knee pressed her down, grinding into her chest, while her frantic hands scratched at his face.

Hennie leaped. She tore at the man.

"You savage, you ape, you're not fit to live!"

She clawed him, kicked his ankles, and pulled at his shoulders to topple him, but he was too heavy and she couldn't move him. Then she felt a blow on the side of her head that knocked her to the ground. How long she lay there she did not know, but the brawl could not have lasted more than five minutes before the women were bested.

She awoke to find someone standing over her. A policeman. She stiffened. She knew that the police could be brutal.

But this one helped her, although not too gently, to her feet. "For shame," he said. "A lady. Or supposed to be."

Because of my good coat, Hennie thought, he takes me for what he calls a lady.

The toughs were gone, the battle over. Of course they always fled when the police came. Only a few of the women were left, the bravest; the rest had fled too. One couldn't blame them.

"I've got to arrest the lot of you," the officer said.

For some reason Hennie found herself the spokeswoman. "Why? What have we done?"

"Disturbed the peace. Brawling on the city streets, when you ought to be home tending to your families."

"It's not your business to tell us what we should be doing with our lives, as long as we're not breaking any laws. And we weren't," Hennie said hotly.

"Now listen here, lady," the officer mocked. "I'd advise you to step into that wagon, or you'll have another charge against you. Resisting arrest."

AT THE station house, the sergeant behind the high desk looked down at the bedraggled lot. One by one they were called before him. "I'll have to set bail. Two hundred dollars," he said.

From each woman in turn came a gasp.

"If you wish to use the telephone to contact your lawyer," he went on, "there's one at the desk, and Officer McGuire will assist you. Or you may use it to notify your families. There are bail bondsmen three doors down on this street."

"What family, what telephone?" Olga whispered to Hennie.

"We haven't got a telephone either," Hennie said, and addressing the sergeant, she asked, "If we have no telephone, is there any way we can get in touch with our families?"

"Give Officer McGuire the name and address. We will take care of it. Arraignment is before the magistrate at ten tomorrow morning." He turned to McGuire. "When they're finished with their contacts, take them right back."

"Back" was a cell at the end of a corridor. Hennie held Olga's sleeve to make sure they would not be separated. When one cell was filled with strikers, the remaining few went to the next one, which was already partly filled. The iron gate closed and the officer rattled the key, drawing it out with a final click. Final.

For a moment Hennie stood quite still, watching the dark blue uniform march away; then she looked around. She was in a gray cement room, fairly large, without a window. There were cots on one side, each with a filthy pillow and mattress. Around the other three sides ran a narrow bench.

She looked at the women on the benches: one prostitute, very young and pretty with a dirty lace-flounced dress, and two older women, typical of the homeless who sleep in doorways.

The prostitute stared at Hennie's swollen nose and cheek, which were turning black and blue. "Say, you got beat up! Who done it?"

"We were pickets at the shirtwaist factory."

"You'll be out of this dump in no time, then. A couple of hours."

"Why is that?"

"Because. The high-mucky-mucks'll get you out. They always get your kind out." And as Hennie looked perplexed, she explained, "You know, uptown mucky-mucks. Charity ladies. Ann Morgan. Mrs. Belmont. Don't you read the papers?"

"Yes. But it's late," Olga said. "If they come, it won't be before morning." She was coughing, holding a handkerchief to her mouth.

Looking at the cots, Hennie shuddered. "I asked the officer at the desk to tell Dan to get bail for you too, Olga."

Olga had sunk onto the bench, next to one of the older women. She leaned her head against the wall. Her closed eyes lay in dark blue hollows. Hennie sat down next to her.

The hours passed. Hennie's watch had been broken in the scuffle, and she could only guess the time. Where was Dan? Suppose they hadn't reached him? How hard would they try?

She waited. No matter what, even if she had to stay here all night, she mustn't panic. Mustn't. Wouldn't.

And then she heard his voice. From far down the corridor it rang, and at the sound of it her first tears came. Roughly she wiped them away, and was dry-eyed when he appeared. As the officer pulled open the cell door she raced out and flung her arms around Dan.

"I thought you would never come."

"Wait till we're outside and I'll explain. Paul's here, taking care of things at the desk for you and your friend."

"Olga," Hennie cried. "It's all right, you're free. Come along, we'll take you home." Together the three of them left the station.

"What have they done to you?" Dan was aghast, and Paul, who had been waiting at the street door, looked astonished.

"Do I look so awful?" Hennie said.

"Yes. I want to take you to a doctor right away."

"No, please, I want to go home. Nothing's broken. Paul, this is my friend Olga Zaretkin. My nephew, Paul Werner."

Paul bowed. Eighteen now, he was home from Yale, and in his velvet-collared overcoat, with his cheerful young face, he might have come from another continent to stand on this grimy street.

His sleek little auto was at the curb. He covered the women with a lap robe. "Where shall I take you?" he asked Olga.

She murmured, "You go down Grand Street, it's left around the corner, then you go— I'll show you."

These were the first words Olga had spoken in two hours, Hennie realized. How ill she is, she thought, and there is nothing to be done about it.

"When you didn't come home," Dan explained, "I went all over looking for you. I even went to your mother's. I took Freddy—"

"My mother knows?" Hennie cried.

"She does now. After I left her, she telephoned Paul, who'd just got home on his winter break. He picked her up and they both came to our house, just about the time a cop from the precinct arrived to tell me about you." Dan reached back from the front seat and grasped Hennie's hand. "Don't be afraid about tomorrow. The magistrate will give you a fine and you'll go home."

"This is the house," Olga said abruptly. They drew up in front of a tenement indistinguishable from the others on the street.

"No, wait here," Hennie instructed Paul and Dan, who were

both prepared to go inside. "I'll see Olga in and be right back."

The sewing machines whirred to a halt the instant they walked into the third-floor flat. Two men and two women in gray middle age and three pale boys stopped work. Seven pairs of eyes stared.

"So what happened to you? The strike again?"

"Let her sit down," Hennie said. "She's about to drop."

"You want some hot tea?" A woman, evidently the mother of the family, got up.

Olga began to struggle out of her coat. "Where's Leah?"

"I sent her for milk," the woman answered.

She brought tea. Olga warmed her hands around the glass and drank. There being no place to sit, Hennie stood. The light from the kerosene lamps was a sickly yellow. The air smelled of stale grease and unwashed bodies. I would lose my sanity if I had to live here, she thought.

Snow had begun to shower against the window, and Paul was waiting. She was about to leave when the hall door opened and a little girl came in, carrying a pail.

"Leah," said Olga, opening her arms.

The child, who had brought a fresh, pure cold into the fetid room, stood staring at her mother. "Mama! Are you sick again?"

Hennie said quickly, "Your mama's all right. She had to come home, but she's all right."

"Yes, I'm all right," Olga repeated, adding, "Don't worry, Leah," for the girl's large eyes had opened wide in alarm. "You remember my friend Hennie I always talk about?"

Leah looked closely at Hennie. "I remember you. You gave me lemonade once at the settlement house."

This was a child you would turn back to look at, Hennie thought. Something pulled you toward her, something immediately vibrant and warm. Reddish hair made a tiara of loose curls around her head; each silky cheek held a dimple.

The child was studying Hennie in return. "You came in the auto," she said.

"Yes. It's my nephew's," Hennie replied, and felt pain as always at the juxtaposition of wealth and poverty.

She put her hand on Olga's shoulder. "Try to take care of yourself." Foolish, futile counsel! "If there's anything I can do . . ."

Olga shook her head. "For me, nothing. Only for Leah." Her voice was filled with tears.

"I know. I promise."

Yes, there was something about Leah Zaretkin, eight years old. One of the golden ones, Hennie thought. You don't know how to describe what it is; it is just a sort of emanation, a bright glow.

And her heart went out to the child.

HENNIE dozed, and awoke with a painful throbbing in her nose and jaw, which had been pressed into the pillow.

In a chair next to the bed Dan sat and watched. He had called the doctor from the drugstore telephone, brought medicine, supper on a tray, ice bags, and warmed her with his enormous pride.

"I thought maybe you'd be angry," she said now.

"Angry? Yes, at the thugs and at the police. I'm only thankful you're not hurt worse." His eyes glowed with admiration. "You'll see, though, it will have been worth it. Oh, it won't be solved overnight! But eventually the law will regulate conditions. And it will be your courage that began it."

My courage, he says, Hennie thought. But I'm not brave. I was scared to death. Why do I do these things? Because I want to help and I know it's right. Yet there's something else. I want Dan to praise me. He loves me, but I want him to praise me too.

"I don't know why you don't fall asleep," Dan said. "The medicine's supposed to make you sleep."

"It's because I can't get that child out of my mind. If you could have seen her vivid little face, Dan, and that miserable room . . ."

"I know, I understand. But there's nothing you can do, so you really must try to stop thinking about her."

"You see, I sort of promised Olga that I would take care of Leah."

"How can you take care of her? You shouldn't have promised."

"Those people won't keep her when Olga dies. How can they?"

Dan's warm hand stroked her forehead. "We'll talk about it later. Close your eyes. Try. There, let yourself float away."

Hennie's eyes flew open. "We could adopt her. I don't mean legally or anything like that. I mean, just take her."

"Here? Into our family? Look, Hennie, your heart is wrung, I understand. But it's a big step. You'd better do a lot more thinking."

"I have thought."

"Well, think some more. It's been quite a day and I'm tired out. I'm going to go see how Paul and your mother are doing."

Dan opened the door. Quiet voices came from the parlor.

He hesitated. "I didn't mean to be short with you, Hennie. I only meant it's a staggering responsibility to take another child, a strange child. Frankly, I don't want to do it. But if you . . . well, you ought to be very sure you know what you're undertaking."

"Oh, I am, I am!"

And it seemed to Hennie, as she lay alone waiting for sleep, that the child's face was floating, beckoning so sweetly, so brightly there in the hazy darkness just beyond the window: I'm waiting for you, when it's time, I'm waiting.

PAUL was stretched in Dan's easy chair in the parlor. An amazing day! Wait till he told his friends! Bailing one's aunt out of jail. She'd been lucky today, though, and ought to be more careful; a picket had lost an eye a while ago in just such a labor brawl as this one. He'd read about it in the *Times*.

His grandmother and Freddy were sitting on the sofa talking, or rather, she was talking and Freddy was listening, fascinated.

"After the war," said Angelique, "came the yellow fever epidemic, when my mother died. After that, we came north."

"Tell me about it again," said Freddy.

A romantic. He feeds on these tales, Paul thought.

"We had a very old Negro butler named Sisyphus. He went outside when she died, and tacked the funeral notice, a card with a black border, on a tree in front of the house. It was raining. When he came inside, he told me, 'Going to storm bad. Always a storm after the death of an old woman.' Funny, my mother wasn't an old woman at all. The things you remember."

For a moment the grandmother and the boy were silent, each musing into some private distance. Then Freddy spoke abruptly. "I wish I'd lived then. It seems so brave and beautiful, like a story."

Paul felt a surge of anger toward his grandmother. "No, it wasn't, Freddy! It was a time of great wrong in a narrow-minded, backward place. You can be glad you weren't alive then."

"You weren't there, so you don't know," Angelique retorted. "It was a gracious culture."

Paul had no taste for futile argument. "Well, it's all theory anyway, since we can't turn time back. You know what the best time of anybody's life is, Freddy?"

"No. When?"

"I'll tell you: now. Yesterday's gone and tomorrow hasn't come, so now is the only time there is. Right?"

"I guess so."

Paul frowned. What was to become of Freddy, pulled as he was in two directions—whipped daily into a socialist fervor by his parents and at the same time enthralled by his grandmother's aristocratic, romantic pap?

He got up and walked to the window. Families! They bred you, fed you, and loved you, and baffled you so that you got to a point where you didn't know what to think.

"The snow's let up, Grandmother. I'll drive you home."

"Very well. Automobiles make me nervous, but I'd better get used to them. I'd better get used to a lot of things, the way it looks."

"I DREW a picture, Mama," Leah said. "Want to see?"

Out of her skirt pocket came a creased sheet of copybook paper. Carefully she unfolded it and presented it to her mother.

"It's a princess. Can you tell?"

"Certainly. You've made such a wonderful crown. Of course, she could even be a queen with that crown, couldn't she?"

"She's too young. She's a princess, waiting for the prince. And her dress is pink."

"It's lovely. You do make lovely pictures."

The mother sat with her chin in her hands, watching the child.

"I wish you would make me a pink dress," Leah said.

Olga trembled. Her child's simple wish, the slight petulance, the direct gaze, all turned a knife in her heart. With what was she to buy cloth?

"You're shivering, Mama! And it's hot here by the stove."

"I'm all right. It just takes me a while to get warm."

The child looked up sharply, as if to make sure that Olga was telling the truth. Then, seemingly satisfied, she said, "Will you make me the dress?"

Olga said gently, "I'll tell you, Leah darling. Pink is a summer color. It would look foolish now. But when summer comes, I'll see that you have a pink dress. I promise."

Dear God, somehow, I don't know how, she'll have it.

"I miss Papa," Leah said suddenly.

"I know. Oh, I know."

A silence came between the two of them. The face of the dead young man hovered before the widow's eyes, and perhaps it rose in the child's sight also, for now she wailed, "Oh, Mama, he'll never come back!"

"No."

"What if you die too? I'm scared. You could die too, couldn't you? You *are* very sick, Mama. I know you are!"

"Yes, I'm sick." Olga took resolve; one might as well face at eight what one would have to face at nine. "It's possible that I could die, Leah, my darling."

"I don't want you to! You can't! I'll have nobody then."

"Listen to me, listen carefully. You're a big girl, in third grade, and you can understand grown-up things. I'm going to write down the name and address of the nice lady who was here. Hennie Roth. And—if anything happens to me, somebody here will be kind enough to go to her for you."

"Why? Why?"

Olga steadied her wavering voice. "Because she promised me she would look after you. She'll take you to live with her, I'm sure. You'll have a good home there."

"But I don't want to live with her! I don't want to live with anybody but you!" The child put her face on the table and wept.

"Leah. You'll have dresses. Pink, and any other color you want. Toys too. Things I can't give you. Maybe even a dollhouse."

Out of the muffled, tear-filled mouth came an answer. "I don't want a dollhouse."

The little shoulders shook. Very, very gradually the sobs began to subside. Presently Leah looked up, wiping her cheeks with the back of her hand.

"Just remember you're a smart girl, Leah. You can make something of yourself. Fight for what you want, for what's right."

The child's dark, intelligent eyes seemed to comprehend something. Yet she muttered, "Still, I don't want to go there."

"Well, we needn't talk about it anymore just now. Take your dress off and I'll brush your hair."

Warm hair sprang and curled under the mother's fingers. And Olga, silently, rhythmically brushing that live hair, kept her anguish to herself.

DEATH came even sooner than might have been expected. It is merciful, thought Hennie. Her suffering is over.

They had come directly back from the funeral to collect Leah's possessions: a few clothes, a shabby doll, a drawing pad with crayons. Now, among the sewing machines that had been deserted so that their owners could go to the cemetery, they stood in the awkward attitude of people who are in a hurry to separate and are not sure how to do it without being abrupt.

Dan and Freddy stood apart in the doorway. Freddy was solemn. He had been scared—this was his first contact with death. Hennie hadn't wanted to bring him, but Dan had insisted that at eleven the boy was old enough to know realities.

Hennie opened her purse. "Who among you collected the money?" she inquired.

One of the men answered that he had, since they wouldn't have allowed the poor woman to go to potter's field.

"I have enough to cover the cost, with some left over for you people here." It was hard to keep her voice from breaking, and she finished quickly. "You were all so good to her."

The mother of the house grasped Hennie's free hand. "You're an angel," she said. "An angel."

"No, not I. It's my sister's money, hers and her husband's. When they heard about this, they wanted to do something."

"You hear, Leah?" The woman lifted Leah's chin, revealing the swollen, frightened eyes. "You're going with nice people."

Hennie took Leah's hand. It clutched hers tightly in return; the child knew enough to grasp a lifeline.

"Well, then," Hennie cried, feigning cheer, "off we go!"

They took the streetcar home. Leah's worldly goods were in a cardboard box on the floor between Hennie and Dan. Freddy and Leah sat across the aisle. Out of the corner of her eye Hennie watched the two. Look, now, she thought. Freddy is telling her something, making her smile a bit. She must be terrified. But Freddy feels for her already.

They walked home from their stop. The April day was lively; clouds and sunshine shifted in turns across the sky.

In Washington Square, pools of white and yellow jonquils rippled in a quick wind. "I never saw so many flowers before," Leah whispered, and stood still, gazing.

How eager she is! Hennie thought. And strong; she'll find her way in this new life before very long. And she urged gently, "Come. I'll show you the neighborhood tomorrow. Right now we need to get home so I can make dinner. Are you hungry?"

Leah nodded.

"Will you call me Aunt Hennie, dear, and tell me when you're hungry or whenever you want something?"

The child's eyes filled again. It is the kindness, Hennie knew at once; it always brings tears, especially on the sort of day this has been. So she said briskly, "Go on, you two. It's getting late."

Leah and Freddy went ahead. The boy chatted. "Once you learn checkers," they heard him say, "maybe I'll teach you how to play chess. I'm pretty good at it."

"I do believe he's happy to have her," Dan said.

"Then do you still think this is a mistake?" Hennie asked.

"Never mind what I think. I have to accept, it's done."

"Look how the sun glints on her hair! She's a charming little thing, you have to admit that."

"Oh, she's a charmer, all right. You're satisfied, and that's all I care about. I'll help you with her, do the best I can. Don't worry."

Hennie smiled. "I won't."

5

FREDDY is in his room after supper, supposedly doing his homework. Twelve math problems await him, but he can't think of numbers tonight. He can think only of what he has seen that winter afternoon. He lays his head on his arm and grieves.

It was such a good day in the beginning. Mr. Cox asking him to play the piano at Friday's assembly because the music teacher is sick. So Freddy rushes out after school; he has to tell Dad about the piano; he can't wait to see his pleased face. Dad wants him to be a real performer and keeps telling him he could be. He won't mind being interrupted at the lab with news like this.

He runs all the way, breathlessly arrives at the door of the lab, and rings the bell. Nobody answers. Dad must be there, though. He always is in the afternoons. Freddy rings again. Still no answer.

Maybe Dad's taking a nap upstairs? Then Freddy remembers that he has a key. Of course! It's in his schoolbag, along with the house key they gave him for emergencies.

He finds the key and unlocks the door. Dad's not in the lab. Ceiling lights blaze above the papers, the scattered plugs and fuses. So Dad's been here; he must be upstairs, then.

Freddy walks to the back of the building. He's about to mount the stairs when he hears voices . . . the sound of laughter, pealing soprano laughter. Whose? Not his mother's, he knows.

Then Dad's voice: "You're the funniest, most adorable girl. . . ."

Freddy is frozen at the foot of the stairs.

Dad's voice: "Oh, stay awhile. Come on, we've only begun. . . ."

Giggles. Silence. And sounds. Sounds. Freddy thinks he knows what they mean. He isn't sure, but he's been told things; the big boys talk in the bathrooms at school. Maybe he really does know, yet he doesn't want to; this is his father. His father!

He puts his hands over his ears and stares at the wall, shutting out the moment. Suddenly he picks up his schoolbag and walks, on tiptoe this time, to the front door, and lets himself out.

He drags himself home, feeling sick. He has to keep this to himself. He can't tell his father or ask him anything, ever. Ever! It would be awful. And maybe, after all, he was imagining things? No. No.

The woman, laughing. What right had she to be upstairs in that private room? He is furious at the unknown woman.

At supper his father is no different from the way he is every night, when he comes in and kisses Mama and talks about whatever is in *The New York Times* that day. But Freddy can hardly look at him. He lets Leah do the talking; he often does that anyway, because Leah is jolly and he likes to listen to her.

His mind touches Leah now. It's been almost a year since she came. She doesn't cry anymore. Maybe, though, death doesn't hurt as much as betrayal. Leah's lost her mother, but she has beautiful things to remember about her. Beautiful. Soothing. Not ugly, like today.

Freddy raises his head from the desk. I've lost something, he thinks. My father. Not altogether, of course not. But something I'll never get back, just the same. He'd better not ask me to play the piano for him tonight. He'd better not.

He sighs and opens the math book.

It was a raw night in darkest December, and the twenty-third wedding anniversary of Walter and Florence Werner. The entire family, even to the least important Werner cousin, was gathered, along with a few close friends. The house was warm and bright with celebration.

In the large, square dining room the company was enclosed as in a velvet box. The oak-paneled walls glowed in the light from half a dozen candelabra. Plum-colored draperies covered the windows; a plum-colored Oriental rug covered the floor. Under the ruby glitter of a Bohemian glass chandelier, the table, set for twenty-four, flashed with the white light of silver and diamonds.

At its head Walter Werner, in evening dress, began to carve an enormous roast. At the foot of the table sat Florence. In her sweeping ivory peau de soie and diamonds, Florence was stately; Walter, with receding hair and glasses, was not.

Hennie, to her own surprise, was enjoying herself. She ate and drank, observing her sister's triumph with pleasure. The old rivalry between them had long ago eased away; they were equals, two married women, two mothers.

It was heartening, also, to see what married life had done for Alfie and Emily. Never would Hennie forget that somber morning when she had gone with them to City Hall.

The Hugheses had chosen to be out of town. Henry and Angelique, to their credit, had consented to appear, although Angelique's expression as they stood before the marriage clerk had surely not been one to strike joy into the heart. All in all, it had been a sorry start.

Yet here they now sat, having survived marvelously. Living in an apartment on Central Park West, happy with each other and their little girl, Meg, whose arrival had produced between the hostile grandparents a kind of fragile peace.

Hennie's gaze slid from her brother and his wife down the table toward her own children.

Freddy seemed to be silent. He missed no nuance, however, and would make his private comments to her later.

Leah's robust laugh rang; her face was frank, gay, and bold. After nearly two years she was completely at home in the household and had become their own daughter—or Hennie's own, anyway.

Dan's reaction to Leah still troubled Hennie. "Don't you *like* the child, Dan?" she would ask.

"How can one dislike a child? But she isn't going to be a child forever," he would answer somewhat doubtfully.

Nevertheless, Leah had quickly put the slum experience behind her; she did her schoolwork well and filled the house with the schoolgirl chatter of her friends.

She's what I wanted to be and wasn't, Hennie thought.

Dan was absorbed with the partner on his left, one of the Werner cousins, a vivacious girl who was evidently having a wonderful time—as was Dan. His laugh had a distinctive timbre; it was the sensual laugh that Hennie recognized. He leaned to the girl, as if sharing some very private joke.

If only he wouldn't do that! Hennie thought. It meant nothing, but how were other people to know it? People glanced to see whether she was angry. She couldn't very well say to them, Mind your business, he really loves me and only me. She must pretend not to notice.

Dan hadn't wanted to come tonight. "At your sister's house," he had grumbled, "Paul's the only one who ever has anything worthwhile to say. He's the only man in the family I can really talk to now that Uncle David's in a nursing home."

Paul was talking quietly to his partner, young Marian—Mimi—Mayer. Freckled and fair and not quite sixteen, she was not destined to be a beauty, but she was already self-assured, with a definite elegance.

"The Mayers are like family," Florence always said with a prideful smile whenever they had to be introduced.

They have the simplicity of great wealth, Hennie reflected; or perhaps not so much great as accustomed and well worn. She was almost certain that the families had hopes that Paul and Marian would in time marry.

Paul's thoughts were random. Like Hennie and like Freddy, he was an observer. These dinners, these social games, he often found to be boring, and sometimes he even felt a sadness in what he saw. For instance, his two grandfathers . . .

His mother's father had little to say; he seldom did. His unfocused eyes, fixed on the opposite wall as he took the fork from his plate to his mouth and back again, were somber. He ate as though his mind were not there at all. The Werner grandpa, on the other hand, was the master wherever he went, even here in this house that belonged to his son. Paul wished that he liked the man more.

The meal continued for hours, but dessert was finally served and eaten. At last Florence stood up, and the party adjourned.

Between the double parlors the sliding doors had been moved back to make one room that extended the depth of the house. In the little bustle of finding seats Paul came up beside Freddy.

"Is it too awful for you?" he asked.

Freddy's eyes widened with surprise. "Awful? Why, it's so beautiful! You know I always love it here."

Paul's so lucky to live here, he thought. Everything in this house is perfect.

"How do you like the new portrait?" Grandma Angelique asked now.

Over the mantel sat Aunt Florence, looking as royal as the Princess of Wales. The ladies gasped.

Leah spoke up. "I saw a lady like you in a magazine."

"You did?" said Florence, turning kindly to the girl.

"Yes. She was wearing a tea gown, in France, I think."

The ladies smiled. Hennie's little protégée was learning fast, though how she knew about tea gowns was a mystery, since most certainly Hennie never wore one!

"We are having the entire house electrified," Florence announced as the women settled themselves around the fireplace.

"And you have a telephone too," remarked one of the cousins.

"A time of miracles," another lady said. "Goodness knows what will come next. They say that we shall all go up in flying machines before long."

"Impossible!" another cried scornfully.

The women's talk was dull, thought Freddy. But then the conversation turned to something interesting, as it always did when they lowered their voices to whisper. They were talking about Uncle Alfie and Aunt Emily.

"Alfie couldn't possibly have continued any longer in the business," Angelique said, "given the Hugheses' opposition to their marriage." Her tone brightened. "He has always been interested in real estate, you know, and now he has bought, with a couple of partners, a small building near Canal Street. Alfie says New York will be bigger than London, the capital of the world. He is putting everything into property."

"Your son never went to college, did he?" asked Mrs. Werner.

Freddy knew that old Mrs. Werner knew perfectly well that Alfie had not. She was a nasty old woman. Even Paul said so.

Angelique answered stiffly, her voice rising. "He was never interested in anything but business. He has a head for it."

"You can do a lot worse than have a head for business," pronounced Walter Werner, who had moved toward the women. "Work hard and do some good on earth, that's all that counts."

"Yes, work hard," repeated his father.

The men all brought up their chairs to form a semicircle.

"I myself went to the college of hard knocks," the old man went on. "My son went to Yale. How was he able to go to Yale? Because I first went to the college of hard knocks! My own father was a peddler, you know. I do not hide it; I am proud of it."

His wife, having heard too much about her husband's peddler father and preferring not to be reminded, interrupted him. "Play something for us, Paul."

Paul laughed. "I don't play! I stopped lessons years ago."

Florence intervened. "We should really hear Freddy play, Mother. He's the gifted one."

"Yes," Dan said, "he is gifted, more than he knows or will admit to. Why not play the new Mozart, Freddy?"

Freddy shrank. His horror of being conspicuous was visible in the eyes that he turned toward his mother.

Is it only the old, familiar shyness, or is there now, has there been lately, something new? Hennie wondered. Something sullen, even hostile, when he looks at Dan? Especially when Dan asks him to play? But why should that be? Sometime or other life ought to stop being so complicated!

"Do I have to?" Freddy whispered.

"I'll tell you what," Florence proposed. "While Freddy thinks about it, maybe Mimi will play something. Mimi?"

Mimi Mayer sat down cheerfully and played a simple piece poorly. The contrast to what Freddy could have done was absurd. Dan looked into space, avoiding his son.

"That was lovely," said Florence when Mimi had finished.

The girl shook her head. "Oh, I'm really stupid at the piano."

"Not as stupid as I am," Paul declared.

Mrs. Mayer shook her finger at Paul. "Now, now, we know all about you, Paul. You were one of the brightest scholars at your school. My nephew goes there now, and he told me you left quite a reputation behind you."

One of the cousins asked what school it was.

Walter Werner answered promptly, "Sachs Collegiate Institute. Very fine." He turned to Dan. "You should really consider sending Freddy."

"I wouldn't send him there if I could afford to, which I can't." Dan was in a mood. "I don't approve of private schools."

There was a moment's pause, until Florence said agreeably, "Oh, I think you must admit, Dan, even if you do teach in a public school—and I'm all in favor of public education—that there still are certain advantages. Smaller classes, more personal—"

"To say nothing of the fact," interrupted Grandmother Werner, "that the right young people meet each other there. They marry each other's sisters and they go through life together. It's a beautiful way to live. A community of friends."

The elder Werner nodded, smiling. "Yes, friends. Last winter when Randolph Guggenheimer gave his dinner at the Waldorf, I knew every man there. Unforgettable. The whole place made into a garden. What a display!"

"A display indeed," muttered Dan. "I find it disgusting." He came to stand beside Hennie. His eyes were dark and serious.

"Oh," Walter said, "most of those people, after all—"

But Dan interrupted. "They have earned it, I know. Just like Horatio Alger."

"Stupid books," said Paul. "Foisted on me almost as soon as I learned to read."

His father gave mild rebuke. "My son is too critical. There is a deal of truth in those simple stories, Paul. They wouldn't be printed or so popular otherwise."

"Oh, there are plenty of popular lies on the printed page," Dan cried out. "Look at the Hearst newspapers."

Hennie worried: He's had too much to drink. His face is bright pink. He can't drink; he hardly ever does, and now he's had wine at dinner, and brandy too on top of it.

She tried to meet his eyes but could not; avoiding her appeal, Dan stood tall above her. He wanted to arouse these men in what he called their penguin suits. He despised their suits and them.

"There are things in this city, I tell you, that would shock you if you heard they were happening in Calcutta or Borneo!"

Oh, why, thought Hennie, why must he do this?

"Last month, for instance," he continued. "It was not in the newspapers—too frightful, I suppose, or perhaps not something that the powers that be want the public to know."

He lowered his voice. "Last month a family froze to death. They had no money to buy coal or wood. The mother died of pneumonia, and lay dead for a week, decaying, while her children, too frightened to go for help, just waited. The baby died, and there was evidence"—Dan swallowed—"evidence of cannibalism."

Old Mr. Werner raised himself from his chair. "This is a disgrace," he cried. "In front of these ladies, these young people—your own son! It's disgusting, sir, unforgivable!"

"It is only reality," Dan replied evenly. "The world they live in. They might as well know what it is."

"Oh, please, Dan," Hennie said softly.

Florence fluttered. "Has anyone tried this marzipan?" She beamed a piteous smile to the room, the smile dying after a moment into a wordless plea: Can't someone stop this? And she began to cry.

Angelique put her arm around her daughter. "Don't, don't. It's not worth it. You!" she said. "You, Dan, you're not civilized."

Dan made a slight bow. "I'm sorry. It's hard to be civilized when you see the uncivilized things that I've seen. These wretched homes, the dispossessed— You can't imagine."

"Oh," Florence said, "we can imagine! Why do you suppose we give what we do to charity?"

To Florence, Dan spoke more gently. "Charity's not the answer, not the whole answer, anyway. What's needed are radical reforms. Tenement house reforms, from the bottom up. Reformers like Jacob Riis and Lawrence Veiller are still fighting, and so am I, in my small way."

"Still?" said Walter. "In spite of the tenement house act? I should think you'd all be satisfied now."

"Oh, it looked good enough on paper. But the old-law houses are still standing—you know that. Rotting away, and the tenants with them. Places like the Montgomery Flats, where I went the other day with Veiller."

Walter took off his glasses, wiped them, and replaced them. "What in particular took you there, may I ask?"

"Because the Montgomery is one of the worst tenements in the city. It should be torn down. You ought to go look at it, stumble up the dark, broken stairs and breathe in the smells! One dirty toilet, out of order, in a cold hall, for six families, when there's supposed to be one for each flat."

"I happen to know," Walter said deliberately, "the Montgomery was built according to regulations. It's a dumbbell flat, built to the letter of the law at that time and modified since according to the new law—"

Dan interrupted. "It's an evil place, Walter, no matter what you say. And worst of all, a firetrap, of which the owners must be perfectly aware."

"The owners are aware of nothing of the sort," said Walter.

The Werner cousins got up as a group, and the Mayers rose

with them. From the outer hall sounded the flurry of departure: "Delightful . . ." "Oh, my boots . . ." " Started to snow . . ." "Just a few flurries . . ." "Delightful . . ."

I want to go home, get out of here, Hennie thought. When will it end?

Walter and Dan still faced each other.

"Why, it's obvious to anyone who cares to think about it!" Dan said. "The owners don't give a damn!"

"You know a lot about the owners."

"Well, Veiller has looked it all up. They'll be surprised to see themselves spread over the newspapers when he has made his report to the legislature. We're not giving up. We want a new tenement act. And I'm invited to go along with him to Albany."

"So you are going to Albany to make an example of the Montgomery. Have you any idea who the owners are?"

"Oh, some sort of holding corporation. Veiller knows more about those things than I do."

"Oh, does he? Well, I'll tell you. The major stockholders happen to be my father and some of his friends. We took the property back on default of a mortgage." Walter patted his perspiring forehead with a handkerchief.

"I didn't know," Dan said.

Walter sighed. "I want to believe that. But it shows you what comes of meddling where you don't belong."

Dan shook his head. "I'm a citizen. I care very much what happens in my city, and I do belong."

"Be that as it may, you've got to get your people to stop whatever has been started."

"Walter, that's impossible. The report is already in the hands of the committee."

"It can be withdrawn."

"Veiller would never do that, and I could never ask him to. It would be dishonest, against the grain."

"Not against the grain to see the name of Werner smeared in some muckraker's journal? You would do that?"

Dan threw up his hands. "It would not be something I'd enjoy. You can't think it would."

"I think we have a question here of family, a family to which you happen to belong and to which you owe some loyalty. Are you telling me that you intend to go ahead with this disgrace and be damned to us?"

"I didn't say that! I said the report is in the hands of the committee in Albany and I can't call it back."

"Can't or won't?" Walter demanded furiously.

There was a long wait. Then Dan said very quietly, "Maybe some of both."

"You bastard," Walter replied, also very quietly.

No one moved. For a moment the silence was absolute, until Florence began to cry again.

"Stop it, Florence," commanded Angelique. "He isn't worth it and never was. I knew it the moment I laid eyes on him."

Hennie cried, "Mama! You've no right to say that! How can you?"

"Hennie, I'm sorry, I can't help it. My heart aches for you, and for Florence and Walter, to have this happen here in their home and on their anniversary, this happy night. What next?"

Henry De Rivera had been so silent in his corner that they had forgotten he was there. Now suddenly he shouted, "Stop it, will you? All of you! Damn fools! It's too much, I'm exhausted. No more, no more!" His face was dark gray.

"His heart! Look what you've done! Florence, get the brandy." Walter was distraught. "Lie back, Father. Mama is right, Dan, we've put up with you, your remarks— You think we don't know your opinion of us all these years? But now to upset this good old man who came here tonight, to my home for warmth and pleasure, and you— Oh, get out! Get out now. Now!"

"You don't mean that, Walter," Hennie cried. "You're not really telling us to leave your house!"

"Not you, Hennie, of course, not you."

Walter reached out to her, but Dan stepped between Hennie and the hand. "My wife goes with me, as any wife would, and when we go, we're not coming back. Leah, Freddy, get your coats."

Florence wrung her hands. "Is that true, Hennie? You will stay away from us all because of him?"

"Dan is my husband," Hennie whispered.

Dan placed Hennie's cape around her shoulders and, taking her elbow, urged her toward the door.

Walter followed. "If you'll turn from this course, it won't be too late. We can forget what's been said. I'm willing. Just turn—"

But Dan, without answering, had already opened the door and gone down the stoop to the street. In silence they hurried toward the avenue to catch the downtown trolley.

Hennie knew that this rift would never be made up, not with Florence, anyway. Parents were different; they would come around, but Florence owed allegiance to Walter, as Hennie did to Dan. When the news came out— Oh, she'd seen in the papers how reformers could blacken the names of the most respectable. How scandalizing for the Werners, for Florence! A wave of regret caught in her throat. Florence was good, she was a sister.

And Paul, she thought. I shall lose him too.

A light snow began to come down as they climbed into the trolley. They took their seats, and Hennie met Dan's troubled eyes.

"I'm sorry, Hennie. I had too much brandy."

"I thought so."

"I shan't use it as an excuse, though. I wasn't drunk. But those men! They were talking about the Boer War and all the money that was made investing in diamonds. I was thinking about what I've been seeing with Veiller. I was disgusted and angry."

He touched her cheek with his woolen glove. "Hennie?"

"Of course you're right. But tell me honestly, would you have tried to stop that report to Albany if you had known who owned the buildings?"

Dan hesitated. "Maybe I would have been tempted to for your family's sake. I don't know. But if you had seen that place . . . Such filth. And of course I always think of fire."

He stood in the poisonous smoke on the ledge under the roof while the crowd stared up and waited, hardly believing what they saw. No one else, Hennie thought, surely no one in that house tonight, has so much heart.

THE mills of the gods grind slowly, and seldom more slowly than in a democratic legislature. After long, tedious, and acrimonious hearings before investigating committees, nothing was produced in the way of new laws, only a reaffirmation of the need to enforce the existing one.

Owners were castigated for flouting the regulations; as always, outrage and shock were expressed at the wretchedness of the poor in the richest city of the world.

Flamboyant newspaper headlines brought misery into the homes of prominent and respectable people. RICH OWNERS RESPONSIBLE FOR CRUEL DEATHS BY FIRE . . . CRIMINAL NEGLIGENCE . . . EPIDEMICS . . . MILLIONS MADE OUT OF HUMAN SUFFERING ran the headings. The culprits were named: builders and mortgage houses such as Southerland, Van Waters, Werner.

In her white-and-yellow upstairs sitting room, Florence lay on the recamier sofa. The Sunday paper had brought on a sick headache, and the family had gathered to commiserate.

"I'm glad my parents are in Florida." Walter sighed.

Angelique's white hands trembled from her jet necklace to the black silk folds of her mourning skirt. "Yes, Florence, I'm thankful your father didn't live to see this. What he saw was enough! His two daughters estranged, and now this visited on poor Walter."

"What must people think?" Florence moaned.

"Pull yourself together, Florence," Walter rebuked. "The people we know will hardly believe a handful of sensational muckrakers. Criminal negligence!" he scoffed.

"I suppose," Florence remarked, "there's great rejoicing in my sister's house. They think they have defeated us, humiliated my husband and me."

No one answered. And Florence went on. "Oh, I don't want to make any more trouble than there is already. Mama, I know you have to see Hennie, she's your daughter. I will say one thing, though, to Paul. Neither your father nor I have made an issue of this, but how can you keep going to that house? We know you go there often. Don't think we don't."

"I haven't tried to hide it."

"But isn't it time to take a stand for who you are? You're a grown man!" Her tone was closer to a wail than to a scolding. "To go there and listen to them talk about your own parents . . ."

"They have never said one word about anyone in this house, Mother. They never talk about people anyway."

Walter was curious. "What do they talk about?"

Paul shrugged. "The Peace Society." It was their latest cause.

Hennie was even thinking of making speeches now, on its behalf.

Still, his answer was not quite true. Aunt Hennie always asked Paul what his mother was doing. Not, he knew, out of sly curiosity, but with regret. He recalled the two sisters at Grandpa De Rivera's funeral, sitting far apart in the temple, not speaking.

Paul wondered what it was that made people of the same flesh so different from each other. Freddy, for instance, now fifteen, was and would be different from either of his parents. So much was troubling that had not been before.

What most disturbed Paul was that—as his mother had just said, although with different meaning and intent—he was now of an age when he must know himself.

Finished at Yale, Paul would probably spend a year at the London School of Economics, get some international experience, and finally settle into the Werners' New York office. He wasn't sure how he felt about it all.

He knew he was orderly and responsible, essential traits for a banker. Certainly he liked everything to be planned; he would like to know right now what awaited him, whether good or bad.

He would like to know for others' sake too. Freddy's future was on his mind, for one thing. He had often discussed with Uncle Dan where Freddy would go to college. Uncle Dan insisted he would go to City College: "It costs nothing, and some of the best brains in the country have come from there."

Paul had conceded that this was so, but didn't Uncle Dan have to admit that a change of scene might be a fine thing too? Paul wanted to pay for Freddy to go to Yale. Paul had inherited money when he reached twenty-one. It was his, and he could spend it as he liked. But Uncle Dan still said no. What stubborn pride! Sometimes Paul wondered how Aunt Hennie put up with him. But she was crazy about Dan. She looked at him sometimes the way he'd never seen his mother and father look at each other. It was embarrassing. He supposed if there was such a thing as a perfect marriage, it was theirs.

In the very last row of the hall, Dan watched Hennie on the platform. He wore a look of total concentration. Concentration? He was enthralled.

"Once it was possible to have short wars, quick, gallant victories for individual heroes. A sort of contest of athletic skills, though bloodier! But now—now, because of all the marvelous new machinery we have invented, wars will be very long."

The voice dropped softly into a sigh, almost a whisper, distinct in the absolute stillness that, during the last half hour, no cough or shuffle or creak of chair had disturbed.

Dan felt a lump in his throat, watching her. He had actually sneaked into the meeting; this was her first big speech and she was nervous about it; she had made him promise not to come.

"I'll meet your eyes," she'd told him, "and forget what I was going to say for wondering how well I'm doing—or how badly. If I'm invited again, then you can come."

He hadn't been able to keep the promise and was glad that he hadn't.

"I recommend to you a book by a Polish businessman. Ivan Bloch is his name. It's a remarkable book."

She's read that? Dan marveled. She never told me! I haven't read it myself; I've been meaning to.

"It has a lot of technical detail about modern armaments, but he makes it understandable. Firepower is now so devastating that man will burrow into the very earth to escape it. There will be a long, long stalemate. And slaughter beyond imagining. Nations will lose their best young men by the millions. Not thousands anymore. Millions," Hennie repeated with awe. "It will be the suicide of nations."

The clasped hands rose; above them the face glowed, the beautiful eyes were enlarged and passionate.

If any single word could describe her, he thought, it might best be genuine. Never had there been anything calculated or spurious about Hennie. Women he had known, how different they were from her! Women one encountered here and there and everywhere, blended suddenly now, the faces all the same—lovely, dull, self-centered, ordinary. None like hers. Not one of them.

"It is always said that we need these enormous armaments for secure defense. The fact is that their existence only breeds more armaments on the other side. It is a dangerous game we're playing, with our preparations for wars that nobody can win. With all this in mind, men and women must speak out to their governments everywhere. It can be done. If we will it, we can."

A kind of music came from her voice. The greatest music is earnest, lofty, and hopeful, he thought, and his eyes filled. He was so proud. Recognizing the rise to a peroration, Dan got up swiftly before he could be observed, and left the hall.

6

HENNIE had an excellent memory for times and places, and so she was quite certain that it was at her brother Alfie's country house, on an unusually mild afternoon on a weekend in early spring, that Alfie first asked Dan about his vacuum tube. They were sitting on the terrace, from which height, above a bank of laurels not yet in bloom, they could just glimpse the four young people—Mimi Mayer and Paul, Leah and Freddy—playing tennis.

"A real family place," Alfie said, "that's what I wanted." A smile of genuine pleasure spread over his face, which was beginning to show chubby folds under the chin.

Once, they had gathered at the Werners', but now this would be the house at which the family would assemble. Brothers and sisters—except that when Hennie was there, Florence would not be—aunts and uncles, everyone to the farthest twigs on the family tree would come here to Laurel Hill.

Square and white, with green shutters and many chimneys, stood Alfie's house. An American flag flew from the pole on the side lawn. Ample fields ran to a background of sumac and wild-cherry thickets; behind these loomed the old woods, dark with maple, oak, and ash.

"This was all farms in the eighteenth century," Alfie told the family group. "It's said that Washington's army bivouacked down the road on the way to Trenton." He turned to Angelique and said mischievously, "I know you would have liked me to build something like Beau Jardin, Mama."

"Alfie! Don't you think I know you can't reproduce an antebellum plantation in New Jersey? Anyway, you've done wonders. For a man still in his thirties to have accomplished all this!" Angelique spread her arms. "I must say it was very, very smart of you to invest in Kodak. Everything you touch turns to gold."

Alfie was embarrassed. "You give me too much credit. The Kodak idea was Walter's." Then, turning to Dan, he said earnestly, "I know, we all know, how you feel about Walter, but—"

"And how he feels about me," Dan retorted.

"Yes, it's a pity." Alfie leaned forward. "But all I wanted to say is this. Walter knows some people—that is, there's a group that's bought a small company that makes electrical devices. I haven't the faintest understanding of such things, but these men are experts. They know what they're doing and I thought . . ." He fastened his gaze on Dan's eyes. "You've got all these inventions you're always working on. Paul mentioned a vacuum tube among other things. He said you felt you were on to something, that you were excited about it."

Dan shrugged. "Paul exaggerated. I don't know how it will turn out. The question is amplification, you see, and with a three-electrode vacuum tube—" He stopped short. "Wait a minute. You surely haven't got any foolish idea of connecting me with some project of Werner's, have you?"

"No *project* of Walter's. Only people I happened to hear about through him. This is a group with some money and a lot of vision. They want to get in touch with idea men like you, buy up patents and hold them, waiting for developments. That sort of thing."

Dan said quietly, "I'm a loner, Alfie. Not that I don't appreciate your good intentions, but I don't work well with other people."

"But you wouldn't have to work with anybody! Just patent your inventions, your tube, for instance, and turn it over to these people—with every legal safeguard, naturally. If they develop a use for anything of yours or they sell it, you'll get your share. And certainly I'd get you a goodwill payment at the start. Five or six thousand."

For a moment Dan made no reply. He examined the backs of his hands. Then he looked up. "Alfie, some things are hard to explain. What I believe is this. If anything good results from my fooling around in that lab of mine, if it's something that will make living easier or cleaner or safer, why, I'll give it away. I have enough. I have everything I need."

There was a silence. No one looked at anyone else. Then Alfie

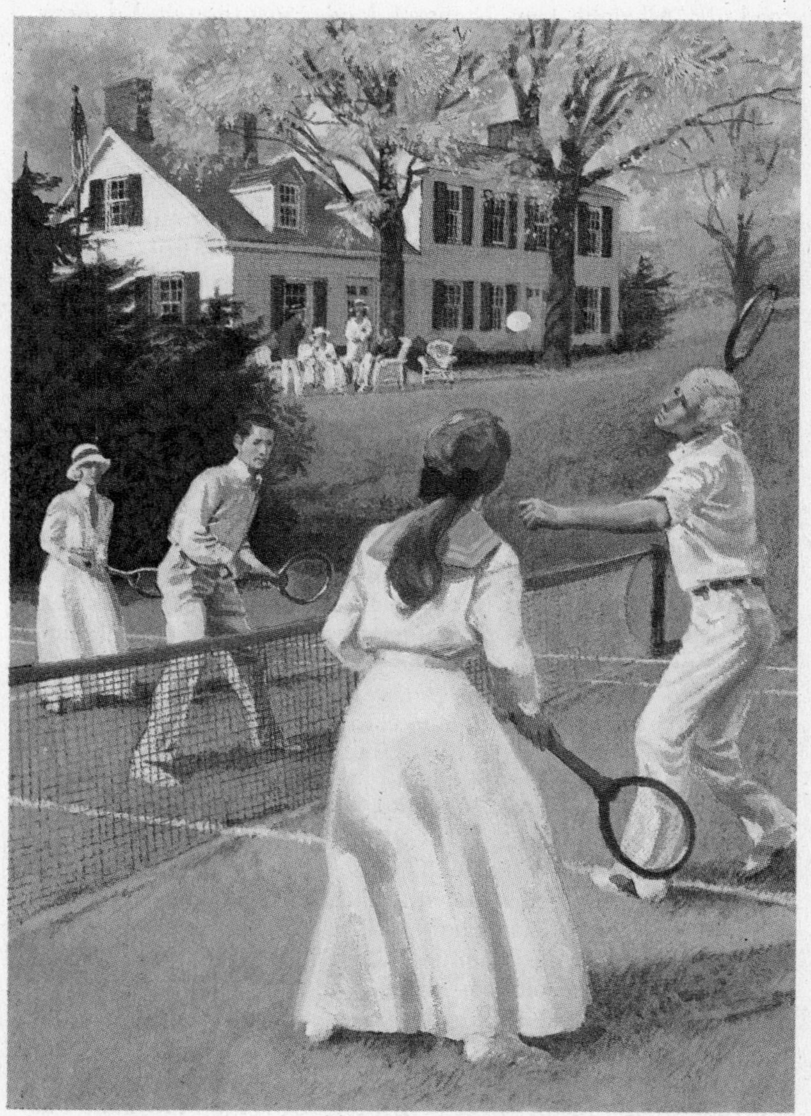

stood up. "All right, Dan. No harm done. I just thought I'd mention it. If you ever change your mind, let me know."

He doesn't understand; none of them do, Hennie thought. Dan might as well have been speaking in Turkish or Chinese.

HENNIE was enjoying the weekend. Reared in the city, she often felt drawn toward country things: the faint green light of reviving leafage and the barely audible buzz of a single bee, awakened by the unexpected warmth of this mid-April. She settled back to watch the tennis game. They played well. Freddy and Leah against Mimi and Paul. The girls ran gracefully, holding their skirts above their shoe tips with the left hand.

It was remarkable how quickly Leah had learned. She learned everything quickly. At fifteen she was as tall as Hennie. She was lively and, Hennie often told her, curious as a monkey. Her face with its round, busy eyes had a joyousness that made people look again and smile involuntarily.

"Good shot, Leah!" called Mimi.

A pleasant girl, Mimi, in a quiet way. Everything about her was of the best, from the crisp cut of her snow-white tennis dress to her manners. She was without hauteur, which was more than could be said of many young women brought up as she had been.

It was plain to see that Mimi and Paul would be married. It was a natural evolution; one had long seen it approaching. You saw a resemblance and a unity in them. Erect and purposeful, they seemed to know they would be winners, and not just in tennis. People like Leah and Freddy had to make an effort. Leah knew that already and did, but very likely Freddy wasn't even aware of it. Freddy, the innocent. . . .

"Hennie! You look half asleep!" Angelique's voice rang behind her. "I've been taking a walk with Emily and Meg. Such a darling child. You ought to have been with us, getting some exercise. Why else come to the country?" Angelique's tone managed to command and criticize at the same time.

"This is the way I like to feel the spring," Hennie replied patiently. "One gets so little of it in New York."

"If you lived near the park, you'd get all you want. I walk there every day." As a result of Alfie's generosity, Angelique since her widowhood had been occupying a small sunny apartment uptown near Central Park West.

She stood erect, shielding her eyes from the light, watching the game. Another cry came from the court, this time from Paul. "Beautiful shot, Leah!" He waved his racket in salute.

"You spoil that girl," Angelique said.

What if I do? I do for her what was not done for me. I want her to feel she is wonderful.

"As a matter of fact," Hennie said, "I don't spoil her. She's very grateful; she takes nothing for granted, believe me. She knows what she has and she loves us."

"She ought to, after what you've done for her."

"You really should approve of her, Mama. She fits your standards far better than I do. She has beautiful manners."

"I can see that she has raised herself out of the ghetto to learn proper ways," Angelique conceded. "And I must say her speech is excellent."

"Leah's bright. She loves life."

"Freddy is particularly nice to her, I notice."

"Why shouldn't he be, Mama? Anyway, it's been good for him, another young person in the house. And she admires him so."

"Let us hope it goes no further than admiration."

"Mama! Why do you talk like that?" Hennie got up, frowning.

"A terrible mistake is being made, Hennie, and that's why I must speak my mind. You know what I'm thinking—that you should let Paul pay for Yale and get Freddy out of the house."

"Why?"

"You know she has a crush on Freddy, don't you? And that she may turn his head?" Angelique's mouth tightened.

"The girl is fifteen years old."

"Fifteen. Quite so. I wasn't much more than that when I was married. And she's precocious. Watch how she looks at him."

"She admires him! It's childish hero worship."

Angelique sighed. "There are other reasons why Freddy should go to Yale. The education, the social experience he doesn't get at home. Yale, after all, compared to City College. How can you deny it to him?"

"It's against Dan's principles, and I happen to agree with him."

"Principles? Ah, yes, Dan's principles. We know all about those, don't we?"

For a moment Angelique stood regarding her daughter. A shadow of resignation, surprisingly tender and rather sad, passed unexpectedly across her face. "Well, I'll say no more. I think I'll go in for a little rest before I dress for dinner."

Hennie followed her mother's straight back across the lawn. The frustrations of family life! People thought they could say anything to you in the name of love. The righteous, well-meaning fist inside the velvet glove.

"THIS is a farm," Alfie liked to say. "We live simply here."

A cream-colored Oriental rug made a spacious island on the dining room's polished floor. Two lamps of Tiffany glass on the heavy sideboard contributed, with candles and the westering sun, to throwing a gilded light over the embroidered cloth and the Cornish hens on the flowered china plates.

"Paul, I hear you'll be going back to Europe soon," Emily said.

"Yes, I expect to have a busy summer." Paul hesitated and then, risking Dan's and Hennie's denial one more time, said to the table at large, "I've been hoping Freddy might come with me. It would be a great experience before he starts at City College."

Dan said, although Paul had not looked at him, "Hennie and I have already said no, Paul, although we certainly thank you."

"Going over on business?" asked Alfie.

"Yes. Father's given me quite a few commissions to carry out. He's growing tired of doing business abroad and he wants to break me in. I hope his confidence will be justified."

Alfie was interested. "Where will you be going this time?"

"London first, a short stay in Paris, and then Germany. I'm eager to go. I have such a dread feeling that everything's about to explode. This may be my last trip to Europe for years."

"What makes you say that?" asked Alfie.

"War," Paul said simply.

Dan's voice boomed. "Let them bleed themselves to death over there. We'll stay out of it."

"It won't work that way, Uncle Dan. The whole world will be in it if it comes."

"Nonsense! The laboring classes will refuse to fight. Why should a wage earner go to war to save his boss's investments?"

"It's not that simple," said Paul. "When the bands play, people don't think."

Alfie said, "If war does come, I agree with Paul that we'll be in it. Can you imagine what fortunes will be made?"

Dan shot him a look of outrage.

"I didn't mean," Alfie said, "that anyone would really want the money that comes from human blood. Who could?"

"Plenty of people," Dan answered. "Jingoes don't talk about that side of war, do they? Jingoes like Theodore Roosevelt. Only cowards hope to eliminate war, he says. Well, I'll stand up to any warrior type when it comes to cowardice!"

Freddy remarked softly, "What Roosevelt means is, one ought to be ready to die for principles. Some wars have to be fought."

"Rubbish," Dan answered succinctly. "I'll tell you one thing. If I were young, they wouldn't be able to make me bear arms. I would go to jail first. I would not fight."

"Well, I would," declared Freddy with equal emphasis. "I would be ready when called."

Leah, who sat across from Freddy, sparkled with admiration. Her round eyes widened and her lips parted.

Dan shook his head. "Freddy, you may be seventeen, but I tell you, sometimes you talk like a not too bright child."

"Let's hope these are all only words." Mimi's smile went around the table, making peace.

"Well," Alfie added heartily, "have a wonderful time, Paul, and think of us while you're drinking wine on the boulevards. We've never been to Europe, Emily and I. How about we set our sights on a trip, Emily? No use waiting. How about year after next? Meg will be eleven, old enough to enjoy it. Let's see, that will be the summer of 1914."

On that note they all pushed back their chairs and left the dining room.

NOT without some difficulty, Alfie had finally gotten a fire started in the parlor. Now he surveyed his relatives in the comfortable semicircle of sofas and chairs.

"Oh, I'm learning," he said, pleased with the crackling flame. "I'm learning country ways pretty well, don't you think, Emily?"

Emily smiled assent.

"I've studied a lot about cows, got three Jerseys to start with. I'll show you all tomorrow morning, if you don't sleep too late."

Two red setters lay down next to Alfie's chair. He stroked them, then lit a pipe.

The country gentleman, Paul thought kindly. If Alfie didn't have to make money, he would be content just living like this. He should have been born into the British squirearchy. He even looks the part, fresh-faced and ruddy. Some people really do miss being born where they belong: artists are born into commercial families and radicals are born to aristocrats. I? Where do I belong? I don't know, Paul thought critically.

Then something else occurred to him. "Have you made many friends in the neighborhood?"

Emily did not answer. She was doing needlepoint, while Meg, in smocked organdy, took instruction beside her.

Alfie said, "Well, it's only been a year. Far apart as we all are around here, I don't think most people know we've come yet."

They know you're here, all right, Paul thought. The only Jew for twenty miles around, I'll wager.

Meg spoke suddenly. "They know, and they don't like us."

"Why, Meg!" cried Emily, laying her work down. "That's not a nice thing to say. I'm surprised."

"You always tell me something's not nice to say. You said that when I didn't get into Miss Allerton's dancing class and I was upset."

"The class was overfilled." Alfie spoke in haste. "Your mother was right. You shouldn't go around spreading false tales."

"It wasn't false!" Meg was at the edge of tears. "The class wasn't full. Janice's mother told her they didn't take me because I'm—we're—Jewish."

Alfie made a deprecating gesture. "I don't for one moment believe it's true. The world's changing. All that nonsense is"—he sought a word—"medieval, that's what it is."

"Well, they don't like us here either," Meg mumbled.

"That's enough, Meg," commanded Emily.

And Meg, being well brought up, subsided, but not before Paul's sympathetic glance had met hers. The child's only nine years old, he thought, but she's more realistic than Alfie.

The clock ticked through desultory conversation; Emily put the needlepoint away; the evening ended. Alfie opened the door to let the dogs out, so that the scented air flowed in and lured them all outside.

High up, the swaying top of an ancient copper beech etched a pattern against a glitter of stars. Underneath, the earth, rank with leaf mold, lay in dark blue shade.

After a while Alfie called to the dogs, and everyone said good night. Only Leah resisted. "You can all go in, but I'm going down to the pond to see the starlight on the water. Who'll come with me? Freddy?"

For an instant Paul's eyes met Dan's frowning ones; then Dan's went blank and Paul looked away. They stood watching as Leah, with Freddy following, moved off down the slope and disappeared among the trees. Then they too went inside.

THAT night, upstairs in the black-walnut guest room, Hennie stood before the mirror regarding the brooch at the neck of her crackling taffeta dress. It had belonged to her grandmother Miriam and sparkled nicely.

From bed Dan studied her. "You're a good-looking woman, Hennie," he said.

"Am I?"

"I always tell you you are."

Yes, and I always feel and act surprised. I should take it for granted, the way Dan does his looks.

"What are you thinking?" she asked, for he was frowning.

"I was thinking that maybe Freddy should go to Europe with Paul. And maybe Yale would be good for him after all."

She had begun to brush her hair. Now she put the brush down and stared at Dan. "I can't believe what I'm hearing. You can't have changed your mind!"

"Maybe I have."

"I don't know what I think about his going to Europe, especially with Paul."

"Why especially with Paul? That surprises me."

"You know I adore Paul. But he's"—she hesitated—"a rich man's son all the same. I don't know that it would be good for Freddy, giving him expensive tastes."

"He has them already," Dan said darkly.

"And why on earth do you think Yale would be good for him?"

"Oh, a new environment," Dan said vaguely.

"My word, you sound like my mother!"

"Well, she could be right once in her life, couldn't she?"

"I feel as if you've struck me on the head!" Then she thought of something. "Where will you get the money? You surely won't accept Paul's?"

"No. I'll take Alfie up on that offer he made today. That's what I'll do. I'll take a five-thousand-dollar payment on my vacuum tube, assuming Alfie can do what he said."

"You've been doing a lot of thinking, keeping it from me."

"No, I decided everything right now, tonight. I think it would be good for Freddy, that's all," Dan repeated.

"Why? What's wrong with home all of a sudden? Have you been listening to my mother about Leah?"

"Can you imagine me going to Angelique for advice? No, I reached my own conclusions about Leah. I see things in her that you don't and probably can't see."

"What can't I see, in heaven's name?"

"That she's a rascal. Mark my words."

"I haven't the faintest idea what you're talking about. Leah's only a child! You make me furious. Sometimes you say the most unfounded, unreasonable things."

"Remember, it takes a rascal to recognize another one."

"That's disgusting, Dan. She's a good girl. I know."

"Oh, Hennie, you're an innocent, like Freddy. Don't you see how her eyes say, Come on?"

"I hadn't noticed," Hennie said coldly.

"I can tell. I know a thing or two about women."

Hennie stared at him.

"Don't look so wounded! You take everything I say so seriously." He caught her arm, pulled her down to him, and kissed her. "Don't be annoyed with me. Enough talking. Come to bed."

HENNIE IS ASLEEP, BUT DAN lies awake. Sleep, immediate and profound, usually follows after love, but tonight he is wide awake. The tall clock on the landing has struck the half hour, the hour, and another half hour, and only now has he heard the sound of footsteps on the stairs.

An hour and a half to watch the starlight on the pond? No doubt of it, Leah is the aggressor. This is by no means the first time he has seen it. A passionate young thing, she won't need to be courted or coaxed!

Yes, he has made the right decision. Best to send Freddy away to Yale, and let him go abroad with Paul this summer. Paul will do him good. Paul has his feet on the ground. . . .

At the far end of the hall the passionate young thing lies smiling up at the ceiling. The satin quilt is glassy smooth under her chin. Nice. Nice things in this house. Someday she will have a house like this, only better. Vividly she recalls the tenement and shudders. Never again. Never! Of that she is sure.

She dreams of a thin blond man caressing her. She likes thin blond men, romantic, elegant, and refined. Like Freddy. He is so terribly shy, though. Tonight at the pond she made him kiss her. It wasn't a very satisfying kiss, but he'll learn.

7

THE sinking sun hung like a gold balloon over the Hudson River and the Palisades. From the fourth-floor window Dan looked down onto Riverside Drive. He looked without seeing; his thoughts were elsewhere.

On the rumpled bed behind him the girl sat pulling on her stockings. She yawned, and complained in her whispery little voice, "Oh, I could fall back and not wake up till morning!"

"Why don't you? There's no reason why you shouldn't."

"Because I want to ride downtown on the bus with you. That's a whole extra hour to be together."

"You'll only have to ride back again alone," he objected, not feeling any need for an extra hour.

"Darling, I don't mind. I'm coming. Just let me fix my hair."

He glanced at the bedside clock. "Please hurry. I've got to go."

"Don't I know you're due home on the dot for dinner?"

The comb snapped through her blue-black hair. It was the hair against the whiteness of skin and the whiteness of the school nurse's uniform that had lured him in the first place.

Bernice was not beautiful, yet she had caught him and held him for a year now. Each time he'd been with her he'd been sorry afterward, counting the cost of the lies that were an unavoidable part of these Saturday afternoons and hating the guilt that fevered him when he walked back into his house. Each time he'd told himself that today had been the last. Each time by midweek he'd begun to think about Saturday.

She, for her part, wanted him permanently for her own, even though he had told her a hundred times that that was impossible.

"There!" she said now. "How do I look?" She had wound a flamboyant purple turban around her head.

"Pretty. That's a nice hat."

They went downstairs and crossed the drive to wait for the bus. When it came, it was almost empty, the flow of traffic being uptown this late in the day. They had the back seat to themselves.

Bernice raised his arm to settle around her shoulders, laid her head on his chest, and curved herself into him as if they were in bed. She had no self-consciousness at all, while he, on the other hand, was humiliated by public display. This time, though, there was no one behind them to see the display, so he relaxed.

The bus jolted and lurched across 110th Street and began its way downtown along Fifth Avenue. Bernice reached up and kissed his mouth. Her lips pulled softly, slowly.

The bus, nearing a corner, stopped to pick up a passenger. Alarmed, he tried to draw away. "Bernice! Not here!"

The passenger who had just climbed in, who was staring at them in total, absolute astonishment, was Leah.

A chill came over him. And with a queer, reflexive movement he jumped up. "Why—why, Leah!" he stammered. "Here, sit down, let me help—"

The girl was carrying two large dress boxes. She worked Saturdays in a dress shop and sometimes had to deliver last-minute alterations. "Thank you, I'll stay in front. I'm only riding six blocks."

She sat with her back to Dan. Her calm, straight back. While his heart pounded. Caught out. With a couple of million people running around in this enormous city. How was it possible?

"Who's that? You look just awful!" Bernice whispered.

He frowned furiously. "Not now."

At Eightieth Street Leah got out. He watched her cross the avenue, walking with head up, as if she meant business. A girl, hardly out of childhood. She had the power to destroy him.

"Who on earth was that?" Bernice pressed him.

"Leah. My adopted daughter."

"What rotten luck. You're afraid she's going to tell?"

"Of course I'm afraid! What do you think?"

He bit his lip and stared out the window. How to explain this away? The woman all over him, her mouth lingering. He was supposed to have been at an electronics exhibit this afternoon too. Leah would run to Hennie with the story the minute they were alone.

"I'm sorry, Danny. I really am."

No, you're not, he thought. You'd like nothing better than to have my marriage blow up. You think I'd marry you. I wouldn't. And you've no right to feel sorry about that either, because I told you from the start. I was honest with you.

"I wish I could help you, Danny."

"I don't want to talk. I have to think, Bernice," he said gently.

"All right. You know what? I'll get off at the next stop and take the bus home so you can think by yourself." She stood up. "Danny, I'm sure you'll work it out. Just let me know, will you?"

"Yes, yes, I will. Thanks."

He sat and pondered and shook internally all the way to his stop. Yet what was there to ponder? It all depended upon Leah.

AT THE supper table he pushed food around his plate. It gagged him. He had to be careful not to let his eyes meet Leah's. He felt like an interloper at his own table, an embezzler whose books were to be examined in the morning.

Hennie asked, "How was the exhibit, Dan?"

He couldn't look over at her. "It wasn't much."

"Really? That's too bad. I remember last time you said it was marvelous. So many new things."

"It wasn't much," he repeated.

When the dishes had been cleared away, Hennie said she had to take a box of old clothes over to the settlement house.

"I'll carry it for you. I have to go to the library before it closes," Freddy said.

So he would be here with Leah. Better so. Get it over with. Know where he stood. As if he didn't know already.

As soon as they had left, he knocked on Leah's door. "Leah, may I talk to you?"

"I'm doing my homework."

"It won't take long. Please open the door."

She opened it. Her slow gaze went from his face to his feet and back to his burning face. He felt stripped. Fifteen years old and she was commanding his future, enjoying her command.

"About today," he began. "Things aren't always what they seem, and this thing today was . . ."

The girl's eyes were fierce. "You're wasting your energy. You know that I know what this 'thing' was. Anybody would."

"Wait. Just let me explain—" What was there to explain? He said abruptly, desperately, "I love Hennie. Surely you've seen that? This had nothing to do with her. Nothing."

"I love her too," Leah said with scorn.

"I understand that your loyalty is to her, and that's only right."

"But you're afraid I'll tell her."

He didn't answer.

"If I didn't love her so much, I would. It's because I love her that I won't hurt her. Not now. Not ever. So you needn't worry."

"Can I depend on that, Leah?" he begged.

"If I say I won't tell, I won't. *I* don't lie."

He could have wept with gratitude. "You're a good person, Leah. I'll never forget. . . . It's only right for you to know that that woman today was . . . These things are sometimes a sort of accident, nothing that lasts. Not love."

"Then that makes it really disgusting."

Still they stood facing each other at the threshold of her room. The word disgusting had snapped through the air between them; now it lingered for a moment or two in his ears.

"It won't happen again, this sort of thing," he murmured.

"That's no business of mine. I have my homework now."

"Yes, go ahead. And thank you, Leah."

He went to the parlor, took a sheet of writing paper from the desk, and sat down. Not worth it, he thought. To risk my darling Hennie's trust and love! I always truly knew it wasn't worth it.

"Dear Bernice," he began. Clearly, kindly, and firmly he told her that they had come to the end. He sealed the envelope.

Done. Finished with her, the last and final. Finished with them all, so help me God.

8

June 17th, 1912

Dear Hennie and Dan,

Freddy and I have been here in the country for almost a week, staying with the Warrens, old friends, at Featherstone, which is what they call their place. We share a room, since the house is full. There's a fair assortment of guests, cousins, aunts, and uncles, and Mr. Warren's nephew Gerald, who, by good chance, is Freddy's age.

That will soothe my conscience when I return to finish up in London, leaving Freddy here. They've invited him, I suppose, because he'll be company for the nephew, and he wants to stay. He's enchanted by everything that's English. It has been a case of love at first sight. Last night he said to me, "You won't believe me, but I could stay here forever."

It's pouring this morning, that English rain you've read about, so that the countryside drips green. Everyone is either sleeping late or reading or writing letters. Freddy is writing in his diary while I write this.

I really think this trip is wonderful for him. One night after dinner he entertained—no, that's not the right word, I should rather say enthralled—everyone by his playing. He wasn't a bit shy, as he usually is. He played Chopin, perfect fare for a summer night in the country. I've never heard him play so well. I don't understand what holds him back at home. Everyone has taken to him, attracted by his modest ways and, of course, delighted by the way he expresses his feeling for England.

Next Monday I go back to London for more appointments, after which Freddy will join me there and we'll be off to Paris.

All my fondest wishes to you both,
Paul

June 22nd, 1912

The pages in my travel diary are filling up, which will please Grandmother Angelique. The book looks like her, impressive and expensive, with my name in gold: Frederick Roth.

Gerald has been taking me all over the countryside, on foot, on horseback, and on bicycle. He's the most wonderful companion. I've never known anyone like him. How can he know so much more and still be only my age? He's reading history at Cambridge; what they call reading is what we call one's major. He's got so many interests, knows flowers and animals, plays cricket and rides. What's so appealing is that he's so quiet and unassuming. That's probably the best definition of a true gentleman.

He has a girl. He showed me her picture. She's not as pretty as Leah. He talks about Daphne a lot. He says she's the real thing, not like other girls he's had, but spiritual, a real love.

June 26th, 1912

Last night they asked me to play again. I played "Eine kleine Nachtmusik." This is a group that would cherish Mozart rather than music with bravura flourishes. Mozart is music at its purest. Father once said it very well—that Mozart is simple as truth is simple. Very beautifully put.

I know my father is disappointed in me . . . in more ways than one, I'm afraid. That's why it has become so hard, almost impossible, for me to play in his presence. Also, I have some very uncomfortable thoughts, certain memories, when he's there.

July 4th, 1912

Tomorrow is the last day. Then I meet Paul in London and we leave for Paris. I want to go, yet I feel sadness at leaving here.

Yesterday we traveled to Glastonbury, Gerald and I, with two of his friends from Cambridge. We looked down on the Vale of Avalon, once a sea, they say, surrounding the Isle of Avalon, where King Arthur was taken by boat to die. It gives you chills, thinking of it. The great abbey is in ruins, with only the arch of a tower remaining, and grass growing on the base of what were once tall towers. It's said that Arthur and Guinevere are buried there. We stood listening to the silence. The only sound was the wind on the hill. It was awesome. I felt the ancient dignity and grace.

It's almost as if I had an English heritage, these old, old villages seem so familiar, with the peaceful fields around them. It's worth fighting a war, if need be, to keep it all like this.

Gerald and I had a long talk all afternoon. We talked about everything: Daphne, Yale, Cambridge, his home and my home. It was hard to describe mine. A good home, surely! But how to describe my parents? He wouldn't like them, because he'd sense they didn't approve of him, and I know they wouldn't. Especially my father. Oh, he'd resent everything here, the servants especially.

I asked Gerald whether he thought I should become a medievalist or a classicist. I'm sure I will specialize in history. Gerald says that I should give both a chance before I decide.

This visit has been a great influence on me. And I have found a lifelong friend, even though there'll be an ocean between us.

Paris, July 9th, 1912

Dearest Mimi,

The trip is almost at the halfway mark, and fine as it all has been, I miss you and am impatient to get home. I suppose that's really what loving is, if you want to put it at its simplest: just being at ease together, wanting to be together.

Someday, I hope, we'll see Paris together. Right now it will be fun to show it all to Freddy. He's so enthusiastic, such a nice kid. But I am glad to have gotten him out of England. He pines for it, or at least for that tiny part with which he seems to have fallen in love.

What rot they all talk there! I'm thinking of one night in particular, one wonderful summer night, and the picture those boys made in their white flannels, sprawled out in white wicker chairs, with the white lime blossoms overhead. And what do you think they were talking about, young Gerald and his Cambridge friends, while Freddy took it all in with his mouth hanging open? They were talking about how "the society has gone effete" from too much prosperity, and—believe it or not—too long a peace! It's time for sacrifice, they said; one needs to sacrifice for noble causes; we need new heroes like King Arthur's men. The crazy thing is, Freddy has been infected. He talks like an heir to British glory, poor boy. I see war looming in Europe and so do all these bright young men, but while I dread it, they actually welcome it! I'm frightened for them, fantasizing about a lost old world of honor and beauty that never existed except in their imaginations.

At this moment Freddy is writing in his diary. Strange, I've just figured out something about his aristocratic English sentiments. Far from being unlike his parents, Freddy is their mirror image! He romanticizes a past that never was, while they romanticize the future, a kind of socialist utopia, that will never be.

I don't know why I am rambling so tonight, except that I'm feeling lonesome and nostalgic. My mind goes back to those summers when you and I used to meet on the beach in front of my grandparents' house. Do you know, they used to make me be nice to you. When you were ten years old, you really were a nuisance! Then suddenly one day, when you were fifteen, I looked at you—and you were so lovely! All at once you grew up in my eyes. And in my ears.

Soft was her voice and low, an excellent thing in woman. Forgive the Shakespeare, please. I couldn't help it; it just fits.

Dearest Mimi, I'll write again very soon.

Paul

July 11th, 1912

What words are there for Paris? It seems to be all fountains, flowers, marble, and white stone avenues. Splendor.

Still, a part of me remains in England. Foolish, perhaps, after spending so few weeks in a place, to feel so attached to it, but I can't help it.

Last night we went to the ballet to see Nijinsky dance in *L'Après-midi d'un faune*. It was spectacular. I wished Leah could have seen it, she's so crazy about the dance. Little Leah! It's astonishing how much she's learned in just six years!

It's hard now to remember what it was like before Leah came. She has a way of making you love her, something like the way Paul does, when you think about it, though that seems ridiculous, Paul being so polished, while Leah—Leah bounces. That's the best way I can describe her. I guess what they have in common, what I feel, is their enthusiasm. And energy. And curiosity. They get something out of life every minute.

July 20th, 1912

The countryside around Paris is called the Île-de-France, and we picnicked there with a client of Paul's and his family. I must say the French know how to eat! We had chicken and salads and those long loaves of bread, still warm and crisp. Also the best peaches I've ever eaten, big as a baseball and sweet as sugar.

There were three daughters. They all talked in French. Paul did try to bring me into the conversation by speaking English to me and the one girl who knew it, but it still didn't work very well. What's wrong with me? The only girl I can really talk to is Leah, and that's because she loves me. I know she really does.

The best time I had was with their dachshund puppy. He was very affectionate and took my loneliness away. You wouldn't think a dog could do that. I don't know why we never had one. I told Paul I'd like to bring a dachshund home as a surprise for Leah. Paul says wait until we're in Germany and get one there.

I really want to do that. Leah will love it.

Munich, August 5th, 1912

Dear Parents,

Freddy and I are now settled in Munich for the next couple of days. We are not missing a thing here. Yesterday we went to Schwabing, the artists' section, where I bought two expressionist pictures that you will probably not like. They may appreciate in value, in which case I will have bought wisely; if not, I shan't mind, since they are to my taste.

Everyone has been most cordial, except for one rather nasty business this afternoon. At the conclusion of my meeting with

Herr von Mädler, the conversation, led by him, got around to the ugly subject of war.

"Surely we Germans don't want war," he told me. "But England is bent upon encircling us. They want to stifle us and keep us from our role as a great world power."

I didn't answer. I could feel only distaste for him, with his monocle and big belly.

"But if it comes to that," he went on, "we shall meet it. Our youth is strong, and war will ennoble it, make it stronger." Then he added, "You Americans will, of course, keep out."

I don't know what sort of answer he expected. I said only that one could hope it wouldn't come to that, that the peace movement was strong everywhere.

"Ach," he said, "the peace movement! Radicals, Jews—" I will give him credit. He blushed as he remembered. "Not your kind, of course, Herr Werner, you understand. Of course not. You know the type I mean. The lower classes, Russians, that sort."

There's a feeling of power in this country that's frightening. It's all mines and steel and energy. I saw the Krupp works when we were in Essen, acres and acres of black, threatening industry, storage tanks, railroads. At the Belgian frontier I saw new railroad tracks crossing and recrossing, coming from the heart of Germany. The Belgians want to be neutral, but it will not work. I don't think I am a pessimist, only skeptical and cautious.

Forgive me, I'm in a bleak mood. After a good dinner I shall be in a better one. People always are. So good-bye for the present.

Loving regards from Paul

August 8th, 1912

Dear Parents,

I've seen my last client, so I'm looking forward to some pure vacation before we start for home. It took a lot of research, but I have traced the whereabouts of Mother's cousins. I reached Joachim Nathansohn on the telephone last night. We had a long talk.

He sounds very nice. He's twenty-two, a graduate of Nuremberg, and a journalist. He lives in Stuttgart with his mother. His father died last year. I gather they are well off, since he has traveled all over Europe and speaks of wanting to see America.

How far we've traveled, he and I, from the peddler ancestor in that village that old Uncle David used to tell about!

Joachim suggested that we meet in Bayreuth for some opera and after that spend a couple of days in the Black Forest, at an inn where he always stays. It will be a strange meeting for us all.

Paul

Bayreuth, August 11th, 1912

Dear Parents,

What a day! Freddy and I met Joachim in the lobby of our hotel. He did surprise me. So German! Blond hair and bright blue eyes. He kissed us on both cheeks, shook hands, and actually had tears in his eyes. I had a few myself.

We sat across a table and stared at each other, and talked of the family. Joachim was saddened by what we had to tell of Uncle David, who had been the living link and kept up a loose correspondence with one generation after the other for so many years. Joachim knew only vaguely about the Civil War, and we told him about our people's part in it. He told about his grandfather who had been killed in the Franco-Prussian War.

Joachim is a religious Jew, not Orthodox but certainly not as free as our family either. He told me that he has little sympathy with the Zionist youth organizations that are springing up all over Germany. He sees no reason not to be thoroughly German while at the same time thoroughly Jewish in religious faith.

We talked almost all night and I'm almost asleep. I'll write probably once more before we leave.

Paul

August 17th, 1912

Dear Parents,

The Black Forest must be one of the most beautiful places on earth. It's like the pictures in my book of *Grimm's Fairy Tales* that Fräulein used to read to me when I was six years old.

Yesterday we went down to the village to buy Freddy the dachshund he is determined to bring home. He got the puppy and named it Strudel, so now three of us will be coming home.

I have to tell you that Joachim truly shocked me last night. We were at our inn, sitting on the balcony with a group of German men. It seems they all belong to the Pan-German League, whose slogan is, The world belongs to Germany. Every empire has its day; England is going downhill, as did Rome; and now Germany is rising. That's how they were talking. I didn't say a word until the other men had gone in, and then I remarked to Joachim that they were absurd, that the Kaiser was an idiot. He really stiffened, and almost rose on his heels to tell me that "we" don't talk like that about "our" Kaiser. I saw that he was really angry, so I apologized and said I understood how he felt (but I don't) and hadn't wanted to offend, et cetera. So we parted for the night with a friendly slap on the back.

Yes, it's a beautiful country, but I'll tell you, I don't like it. The German myth has corrupted Germans, even decent people like Joachim. All their endless philosophizing just covers up the truth, that they want England's colonies and control of the seas. And they will pull the whole world down, themselves included, unless something stops them.

So farewell to Germany and cousin Joachim. I'm glad we met and will keep contact, with no hard feelings, so that our family story may continue for more generations.

The train leaves early tomorrow, and on Friday we board ship for home. See you soon in New York.

Love,
Paul

PART TWO
Paul and Anna
1

IT WAS good to be back. There was something clean and wholesome in the American atmosphere, in contrast to scheming, cynical Europe. Paul was glad to be home, to be welcomed back by a dear American girl, with her straightforward ways, so different from the arch and subtle charm of European women.

Mr. Mayer was in his library reading the *Times* when Paul knocked on the door. "I wondered whether I could have a few minutes, sir? There's something I'd like to ask you."

He had rehearsed this scene, hoping it wouldn't be awkward.

Mr. Mayer laid the paper on his knees. "I believe I know what it is, Paul. I'll be very pleased if it's what I think it is."

Paul felt the smile spread over his face. "About Marian—Mimi—and myself. We've been . . ."

"In love," said Mr. Mayer. "And the answer is yes, of course, and God bless you both." The man's eyes were moist. "One thing, Paul. I'd like to wait till Marian's birthday in the spring to announce the engagement. We've a family tradition. We like our women to be twenty-one before we make things official. After that, you can get married as soon as you like. Does that suit you?"

"It will have to, sir," said Paul, who thought it an unreasonable tradition. "After all, it's only months away."

"Well, now, let's go find the ladies and open the champagne."

Mrs. Mayer kissed him and Mimi gave him the first public kiss, with her parents smiling their approval. He drew her closer, resting his cheek on her hair. Such a fine girl she was! A girl to be cherished.

They made him stay to dinner, during which Mr. Mayer discussed investments, sought Paul's opinion, and gave confidences exactly as if he were already a son of the family.

One Saturday Paul came home unexpectedly before noon. A dustcloth lay on his bed, the carpet sweeper was propped against the wall, and the new maid was reading. She had opened one of his art books on the desk and was engrossed in it, quite unaware that he had come in.

He had naturally noticed—as what man would not?—that the latest housemaid was remarkably attractive; her profusion of dark red hair would catch anyone's attention. He had also noted her musical foreign accent.

"She's Jewish, you know," his mother had said.

That was unusual. One was accustomed to Catholic peasants, whether Irish or Slavic, but not, for some reason that he had never bothered to examine, to either Jews or Italians. But he had thought no more of her. Maids came and went.

He stood for a minute now, watching her, until she felt

his presence and started. "Excuse me! I'm sorry, I—"

"That's all right, Anna. What are you looking at?"

"This—" She faltered.

"Oh, Monet."

A woman in a summer dress sat in a walled and fruited garden. The picture was green and gold; a breeze blew through the fragrant morning air; you felt how cool it was there.

"That's a lovely one. You enjoy paintings, Anna?"

"I have never seen any, except in these books."

"Well, this city is filled with museums and galleries. You ought to go. It doesn't cost anything."

"Well, then, I think I will."

There was an instant of silence, during which Paul felt clumsy. Then he asked, "So you like my books, Anna?"

"I look at them every day," she admitted. "I like to think there are places like that in the world."

The simple statement touched him. "I'll tell you what. Take any you want to your room. Take your time over them."

"You wouldn't mind? Oh, thank you."

Her hands were trembling, he saw, when she left with a book in one while the other pushed the carpet sweeper into the hall.

He mentioned the little encounter to his mother.

"A very nice person," she said complacently. "She's intelligent and learns fast. Goodness knows how long she'll last, though. She has a young man who comes for her on her days off."

Paul wondered what sort of man would appeal to her. He felt now that he knew something about her, and yet was conscious that this feeling was inappropriate; after all, he had had just five minutes' worth of conversation with the girl!

And then, coming home early on another Saturday and finding her dusting his room, he couldn't help asking, "How is your young man, Anna? My mother says a nice young man comes to see you."

"Oh," she said, "only a friend."

"Do you see him often?"

"Mostly on Sundays. He works Wednesdays, when I'm off."

"And what do you do on Wednesdays, then?"

"I've been going to the museums since you told me about them. Mostly the art museum on the other side of the park."

"You know, we never talked until last month. Isn't that strange?"

She had a little half-smile. "Not when you think about it."

He understood. "Because it's my family's house and you just work in it. That's what you mean, isn't it?"

She nodded.

"Well, that's wrong. People must judge others for themselves, not because of the work they do or—" He stopped.

"I know what you mean."

Her eyes were candid. Of course she knew. He felt the heat of embarrassment. "I'm hindering your work. Excuse me, Anna."

"No, I'm finished with this room. I have to go downstairs now."

He found, coming home now and then on an early half day, that he was anticipating her being still at work in his room. They began to have brief conversations, so he learned of her parents—dead in Poland—her brothers in Vienna, her first months in America.

Then it crossed his mind that he was waiting for these conversations, looking forward to them.

Good Lord, Paul, what can you be thinking of?

PAUL and Mimi liked to walk through the park on Sundays. On a certain Sunday in late winter, Mimi having gone with her family to visit a relative in the hospital, he took his walk alone.

He had almost reached Fifth Avenue when he saw a tall woman with red hair walking rapidly some yards ahead of him.

"Well, Anna! And where are you going?"

"To the museum."

"All by yourself on Sunday?"

"My friend couldn't come today."

"Do you mind if I walk a little way with you, then?"

"No. Please. I mean, yes, walk."

Where the next impulse came from, he never knew. "As long as we're walking, maybe you would like to go with me to the Armory Show this afternoon?" And he explained. "It's an exhibit of modern paintings, mostly from Europe. Everyone is talking about it, and since you like pictures, you should see it."

"Well, I—"

He interrupted. "It's worth seeing. At least, I thought so."

"You've seen it? Then you won't want to go again."

"On the contrary, that's just why I do want to go again. It's quite marvelous, exciting and new."

Still the girl hesitated. A blush flooded her pale skin.

He understood. "If we should meet anyone we know, I'll say we met by accident, which will be the truth. Come."

They turned toward Lexington Avenue. "It's on Twenty-fifth Street, a very long walk. We'll take the trolley."

"Can't we walk?" she asked. "I don't mind how far. I'm in the house so much. I like to be outside."

So they walked all the way to the armory, where she exclaimed at the vastness of the hall and the splendor of the fashionable people who were inspecting the sculptures and the paintings.

"Look here, Anna. This is a famous Cézanne."

"*The Poorhouse on the Hill,*" Anna read. "The beautiful earth! Round hills. It was flat where I came from in Poland. I should like to see hills someday."

Why did she make him feel so moved by her simple wish?

"Come over here, I'll show you something else. Marcel Duchamp, a Frenchman. It's called *Nude Descending a Staircase.*"

"It isn't beautiful, exactly," she said after a moment, "all those lines and squares, but it's—what do you say?—original. I mean, nobody has ever done anything like this before, I think."

"It's original, all right. And it's called cubism. What you called squares are cubes."

"Oh, yes, like little boxes. Over and over. But it moves, doesn't it? It's very strange. You look away and then you want to look again, to see her going down the stairs."

A few days ago he had stood in the same spot with Mimi. "That," she had declared, "is hardly what I call art. I don't even think it's quite—quite moral."

It's only fair to admit, Paul reflected now, that most American art critics share her opinion. And yet Anna, this uneducated girl, can accept the new.

She was still studying the picture. He stood behind her, looking not at the painting but at the thick hair coiled down her neck. How many shades of red there were in that glossy mass! There were tones of russet and copper, and where a few soft fibers lay free of the coiled mass, the red was touched with gold.

She turned to him. "It's getting late," she said. "Perhaps we ought to go."

"Yes."

Again Anna insisted on walking. How healthy she is, Paul thought, and strong! It grew cold as the afternoon darkened. Her coat was flimsy, a cheap gray wool, belted around her narrow waist with flair, but surely not warm enough. Paul's own coat was lined with fur.

"You know so much about art," Anna said. "Do you paint?"

"Goodness, no. But I try to learn what I can about it. Can't stick with banking all the time."

"Ah, yes, you work in a bank."

It seemed to him that she had frowned slightly, and he thought, I daresay she has the working-class concept of a banker as some sort of ogre who eats the poor. So his question came quickly. "You think bankers are bad people for lending money and making people pay for it?"

"Oh, no," Anna said. "How else would anything get done? I mean, towers like that," and she waved toward a tall construction rising across the park. "Nobody would have enough money to build one of those! He would have to borrow, wouldn't he?"

"Yes, of course, that's the answer," he said, clearly pleased. "You're a very interesting woman, Anna."

"You think that because you have never talked to anybody like me before." She spoke boldly, with a trace of humor. "An uneducated immigrant. I get so discouraged. Because although I've learned some things, I still think I don't know anything and never will. Or see anything. What I want is to see the whole world."

She made a pretty gesture, throwing her hands into the air.

"The whole world? That's a big order. But Anna, I have a feeling that you'll see the world. Wonderful places . . . Paris and London and Italy. The Alps, with snow on their peaks in the middle of the summer. You said you want to see hills."

They had come to the house. It had grown quite dark, and her bright hair gleamed under the streetlamp as, turning to him with one of the loveliest, curving smiles he had ever seen, she thanked him. "It was a beautiful time. I will think of it, and the Alps with snow, and all the pictures."

Then she went down the steps to the basement. He watched until she had unlocked the door, then tipped his hat and went up the steps to the front door.

THE next week a crazy thing happened to him. He was passing Wanamaker's when he heard two loud feminine voices behind him.

"Oh, look! Have you ever seen such a hat in all your life?"

"Gorgeous! It must cost a fortune, though."

He was drawn to look. In the window was a single hat, displayed like a jewel. On the silky straw brim lay a wreath of scarlet poppies and gold wheat. It was a hat to be worn at a garden party or to tea at the Plaza in the spring. Red hair gleaming under the wide pale brim. He shut his eyes for a moment and had a vision of the cheap coat so smartly wrapped, the curving smile.

He had hardly spoken to Anna since that day, staying out of his room when she was working in it. When she served him at table, he averted his eyes. She must think he was angry with her. . . .

He went inside and bought the hat.

All the way home, clanging uptown on the trolley, the big round box tied with a splendid ribbon lay on the seat beside him. Now that he had bought the thing, he was afraid of it. The motorman had to ask him twice for the fare, his thoughts were so terribly troubling. Good grief, what had he done? The girl would misunderstand. He was tempted to leave the hat on the seat.

Nevertheless, he carried it home. He waited for her in the hall outside his room, and intercepted her as she climbed the stairs.

"I thought you might like this," he said, extending a stiff arm with the box dangling by its ribbon. "Open it."

She didn't understand. "For me? Why?"

"Because I like to give presents to people I like." The words came more easily now that he had gotten started. "Here, let me," he said as her fingers fumbled. From its crush of tissue paper he lifted the marvelous hat. "Here! What do you think of it?"

"Oh! It's the most beautiful—" Her hands flew to her flushed cheeks. "Thank you, but really I can't."

"Why not?"

She raised her eyes. He hadn't noticed before that her golden lashes had dark tips.

"It wouldn't be right."

"Not right. But Anna, here I am, a man who can afford to buy a beautiful hat, and here you are, a beautiful girl who can't afford a hat. Oh, for heaven's sakes, give me the pleasure! Wear it next Sunday, with your young man."

"I shouldn't." The palm of her hand smoothed the delicate crown, around and around.

"Listen, you love it! He'll love it on you too. It's almost spring, Anna. Celebrate. We're only young once."

He spoke almost roughly. He didn't know how he felt.

"Well, good night," he said abruptly, and swung about and closed his door with a small hard thud.

A DULLNESS came over him. Spring had always been his time, but not this year. The days lengthened; there were ripe wet strawberries on the grocers' stands. Still the dullness lay upon him.

He had never known what obsession was, except for the dictionary definition, which could not begin to describe the horror of it. His inability to control his own thoughts was frightening. He hadn't known that it is possible to think of two things at the same time, to be alone with Mimi and at the same time to hear quite distinctly another voice, with a musical foreign accent.

This, then, was obsession. When would it end?

Early one Saturday morning he was coming up the stairs as she waited at the top to go down. It was impossible to avoid her.

"Well," he said, "your young man—did he like the hat?"

"I haven't worn it yet. It's too fine for any place we go."

"Well, make him take you out to tea and cake somewhere when you see him tomorrow."

"Maybe, but not tomorrow. He has to work this Sunday."

Her "young man." Paul had gotten a glimpse of him once as Anna and he were going in together at the basement door. A stocky fellow, with an ordinary face, nothing you would remember, except perhaps that he looked serious. What sort of man might he be? Did she allow him to kiss her or— And Paul had felt terribly angry.

The words came. He didn't will them; the words just came of themselves. "I'll take you to tea."

"Oh, no! Oh, no! It wouldn't be right."

She tried to go past him down the stairs, but he made no room. "What do you mean, not right? I'd like to sit down somewhere quietly and talk to you. There's nothing wrong with that. Nothing to be ashamed of."

"Well," she said. And there was that entrancing smile again.

"That settles it, then. Tomorrow."

He took her to the Plaza, where they sat in a corner behind a screen of palms. A waiter brought tea and wheeled a little cart from which they chose cakes.

"You look beautiful, Anna. Especially in that hat. You're the prettiest woman in this whole place, do you know that?"

"How can you say so? Look at that one in the yellow dress. . . ."

"She's just another pretty woman; the city is full of them. But you're different. You're alive. Most of these others are tired of everything, while you love life, you're not bored with it."

"Oh, bored, never!"

"And you've already done so much with your life."

"I? But I've done nothing. Nothing!"

"You've come across the ocean alone, and learned a new language. You're supporting yourself. I admire you, Anna."

They ate their little cakes. The violins began to play a waltz. "How I love the sound of violins!" Anna cried.

"Have you ever gone to a concert or the opera, Anna?"

Foolish question! How could she have done so? And when she shook her head, he thought of something. "I will get you an opera ticket. It will be a great thing for you, your first time."

There is a limit to the amount of tea one can drink. They came out to the sidewalk and stood for a minute watching the slow procession of Sunday walkers. It was still the middle of the afternoon, and the soft spring day had hours to go.

"We could ride uptown on the el," Paul proposed.

It was neither luxurious nor scenic, but it was an excuse to stay together a little longer. They walked westward toward Columbus Avenue, climbed the stairs under the black iron gloom, and came out onto the empty platform. Shortly a train came rumbling down the track.

"The express," Paul said. "We can ride as far as we want. If we like it, we'll just keep going."

She made no response, but sat where he indicated. On the narrow seat their shoulders touched; she could have moved away from the contact by leaning toward the window, but did not, and so they started off. When the train lurched around the corner, her whole body moved lightly toward his and back again.

He had never been so conscious of the nearness of another human body. He sat without moving, almost in a trance, mechanically reading the billboards that ran past. At the same time he was thinking, Everything that is solid and certain is speeding away, as if the train were careening toward a precipice and there were no way of stopping it.

Grime from the locomotive flew in at the windows and stung their eyes. Anna probed her eye with a handkerchief.

"This is no good," Paul said. "We'll have to go back."

Finally they came down onto the street. From there it was only a short walk home, where she would go back into the uniform of a maid and the distance would loom between them. He looked about desperately, and suddenly remembered.

"There's an ice-cream parlor up the avenue. We'll go there," he said; not, Would you like to go?

Still silent, although free of the elevated's roar, they walked together. Her heels clicked twice on the pavement to each step of his until, apologizing, he slackened his pace.

Still without speaking, they sat at the counter on the swiveling stools. Paul ordered two cherry phosphates.

"Well," he said. "Well. This is a far cry from the Plaza."

"Yes. But I've never been in such a fancy ice-cream parlor."

Paul became aware that he was staring into her face and she was looking back with widened eyes, as if they were astonished at each other or at themselves. They held the look.

Suddenly he was terrified. The sensation he had had in the el of rushing, rushing toward a precipice and being unable to stop caught at him again; his heart pounded, and he stood up.

"We'll go," he said, his voice sounding unnatural in his ears. "Now. It's really late. We'll go."

That night Paul lay awake, thinking. Mimi would be of age this week, and then the machinery that had been held back would be released: the birthday and simultaneous engagement, then the wedding.

Oh, Mimi, Mimi, how dear you are! But I don't want to marry you, not now, not yet.

Is it Anna you want to marry? Are you in love with her?

I don't know. I think so. I can't stop thinking about her.

You know you're in love with her. Why don't you admit it?

All right, all right, I'll admit it. And so, now what?

He needed so badly to talk to someone. But to whom? Any one of his friends would counsel him not to be a fool. Your family's maid. It doesn't mean anything; in no time you'll be over it.

A few days later Paul got Anna an opera ticket. The opera was *Tristan und Isolde*. Would Wagner be too heavy for a first experience? On the other hand, it was a love story of such poignance.

After the performance, late at night, he was waiting for her on the landing when she came upstairs. He had meant only to ask, Was the opera what you expected? But the words stopped in his mouth. In the dim light from the wall sconce she was radiant with happiness and awe. She glowed. She trembled and waited.

So there, in the quiet house, they came together. Quite simply, as if it were the most natural thing in the world. He kissed her hair, her eyes, and then her mouth. Her arms circled his neck. She was soft and firm, strong against him, and so tender.

How long they stood so, he could not have said.

"Oh, Anna. Sweet, beautiful Anna." And murmuring into her fragrant hair, he thought he heard himself say, "I love you."

For heaven's sake, pull away. Pull away before it's too late.

He released her. "Go to your room. Go. My darling."

And he went inside to his own room and lay face down on the bed. "It's no good, I'll have to talk to someone," he said aloud. He started up. Tomorrow was Mimi's birthday and the family dinner and— Oh, no, please, not the announcement!

I'll have to see someone. Hennie. I'll see Hennie.

PAUL sat on the sofa with his hands dangling between his knees and his head bent. He had been in Hennie's parlor for more than an hour.

"Are you horribly shocked?" he asked now.

"Surprised, not shocked," she said. "I have always thought it tragic when a person does something he desperately doesn't want to do, out of fear of hurting someone else. I don't mean ordinary things, but something to do with your whole life."

"Mimi's such a fine girl," he said into the vacant air at the dead center of the room.

"One can see that. But it's not fair either to Mimi or yourself to go ahead if you don't care about her."

"I do care about her."

"But not the way you do about Anna."

Paul looked down at his helpless hands. "Differently."

"Have you told Anna you love her and want to marry her?"

"I think I said I love her. But one doesn't have to *say*. One knows."

"Yes, yes." Hennie sighed. "I shall be sorry, whatever you do, since each of them loves you. It's terrible not to be wanted. It makes you feel worthless, not worth living."

He looked up, startled.

She was staring at the carpet. "I haven't helped you. I'm sorry."

"It helped to talk about it," he told her, although it hadn't. "I'd better go."

"I tell you what, Paul," she said rapidly. "I think you should speak to your parents today, before Mimi and her family come tonight. Tell them the truth, and then all of you can go on from there together."

"Tell them I'm in love with the maid?" he asked bitterly.

"The maid! Paul, that's not like you. I despise the concept."

"But it's a fact, Hennie. And you of all people should be able to imagine my parents' reaction."

"It would be very, very hard to tell them, I grant you."

"I feel as if I were on a bicycle. It has no reverse gear. You can't go backward."

"You can turn it around."

He looked down again. "I suppose I don't have your courage, Hennie. I never have."

"How do you know? You've never had to test it before now."

Upstairs in his room, he was dressed and ready. He stood before the mirror, talking to himself. Father, don't announce anything tonight. Give me time to explain. . . . I have to talk to Anna first. I don't know what I'm going to say. . . . She'll be at the table serving. . . . I've got to get downstairs and catch him, before he says anything. . . . Oh, Anna, help me. . . .

But the doorbell had rung. There were voices in the downstairs hall. He could hear happy-birthday greetings and Mimi's clear reply.

At the table he sat opposite her, with his father at the head, between them. She was dressed in summer blue; a wide collar made a lace frame around her slender face. She was an elegant young woman of refinement and means.

He wiped his forehead. Panic again. To escape someplace! Could he just push himself away from the table, pleading sudden illness?

A platter of vegetables appeared at his left and he looked down into a mound of beets cut like roses. The platter trembled. He looked up to Anna's eyes, looked not at them but into them; for an instant, a fraction of an instant, both pairs of eyes spoke.

"We German Jews have always been Republicans." It was his father speaking. "I know some turned to Wilson because he's an intellectual, but I'm not impressed by him."

Cordially Mr. Mayer brought Paul into the conversation. "And what do you think, Paul?"

"I voted for Wilson."

His father raised himself in his chair. "What? You never told me. What made you do that?"

"Because I think if there's any chance of keeping us out of the war that's brewing, Wilson is the man to do it."

"You keep saying there's a war brewing," his father objected. "I don't believe it."

The conversation continued in this vein throughout dinner. Finally the dessert was brought in and placed before his mother.

Paul's heart made a sickening lurch. The dessert. This will be the time for the announcement and the toast, if they're going to do it tonight. Don't, Father. Please, don't do it.

"Anna," his father said, "will you please call Mrs. Monaghan and Agnes? Ask them to come in and bring the champagne."

Here it came. Too late, too late to do anything.

Mrs. Monaghan brought the champagne bucket, and Agnes carried a tray of fluted glasses. Paul counted. There were glasses for everyone at the table and for the servants too. For her. Anna will raise her glass and drink a toast to Mimi and me.

His father stood up. "I don't need to tell you how happy we all are tonight," he began. "To begin with, it's Marian's birthday." He was almost chuckling with pleasure as he raised his goblet. "And we all wish her the happiest one, with many, many more. But also"—here his voice rose in emphasis—"the Mayers' announcement will appear tomorrow in the *Times*. Let's all now drink to Paul, our son, and to Marian, our Mimi, who will soon be our daughter!"

And he kissed Mimi in European fashion, one cheek and then the other. Mimi said something, Paul couldn't hear what; but there was a bubble of laughter, with everyone touching glasses so that they made crystal chimes.

His mother's voice sounded above the general murmur and buzz. "Now I can confess this is what we've all been hoping for since you two were babies."

And more laughter.

"I'll have a second piece of that cake," his father said, flushed with wine and excitement. "Where's Anna?"

His mother rang. She'll be coming in again, Paul thought, looking down at his plate.

It wasn't she, but Agnes, the kitchen helper who was clumsy and rarely served in the dining room. Something had gone wrong with Anna. He knew it and went cold, so that he shivered and tried to suppress it.

Somehow he got through the evening.

He awoke very early and left the house without breakfast.

In the office, on his desk, were stacks of papers he had neglected. Get to them, that's the thing, get to work, get the brain whirring. You have clients waiting. You are going to be married.

How was Anna today? Oh, Anna, I love you, believe me—

He got up. He had to get out of the office. He had to walk.

"What am I doing?" he said aloud when he reached the street. And all the time he knew perfectly well what he was going to do, what he had to do. He groaned and despised himself.

It began to rain. He descended into the subway and took the first train that roared in. For hours and hours he rode. He watched the white city faces as they passed in and out, and wondered what each might be hiding.

When at last he got out near home, the rain had turned to a downpour. He walked rapidly to get out of the wet, but when he reached the house he halted. What would he say to her? He wanted to turn around and walk away again, but instead he climbed the stoop with abrupt resolution and went in. His parents were already at dinner.

"So late, Paul! Good heavens, you're wet through! Why didn't you take a cab?" And without waiting for an answer, "What do you think, we've lost our maid!" his mother said. "Anna left today. Just like that. Imagine, without more than a minute's notice. Said she was sick, but I don't believe it."

"Too bad," said Walter. "She struck me as a fine young woman."

Anna gone. Where to? And in what condition?

He had a wild thought that he should go after her. And he had an absurd, humiliating vision of himself shoving his way through crowds, pushing down avenues and through mean alleys, searching for her. And after finding her, would he stand before her with nothing to say? Would she too stand there silently, despising him, pitying him, or pleading with him?

He was netted and trapped. He was a coward, a fool, a victim of rules and expectations and traditions.

Yes, blame everything but yourself, Paul! Will you ever like yourself again?

A WEDDING is an ancient mystery. The white bride comes slowly, pacing with the stately music, holding her father's arm. He raises the face veil for a kiss before he gives her to another man for protection and care. It is all so solemn, verging on tears.

Only the flower girl in crocus yellow, ten-year-old Meg, clutching her bouquet, grins up at Paul with frank enjoyment at being a part of the ritual. He gives her a slight smile in return and thinks of Freddy, who surely would revel in this pomp and circumstance, but who, understandably, has not come, because his parents were not invited.

The rabbi places Mimi's ice-cold hand in his. Words are being addressed to him and questions asked, to which the automatic answers "I will" or "I do" come to his lips. It must be almost over. Yes, it is.

The rabbi smiles and nods and the recessional starts up: Mendelssohn, with a note of triumph in it. They walk down the aisle. Women have wet eyes, looking at the bride. A photographer stands at the end of the aisle, waiting.

"Smile," he says.

Next is the reception line, then food and dancing; the orchestra lilts and crashes from waltzes to tangos and fox-trots. He dances with the bride, with his mother and her mother and all the bridesmaids one by one.

And it is over, the bouquet thrown, the blue garter revealed, and farewells said. Paul and Mimi are alone in the passenger compartment of the Mayers' Packard town car.

When Mimi reaches for his hand, he realizes that he has been too silent, even for a numb, bedazzled bridegroom.

"Well, it was a beautiful wedding," he says. "Your mother took care of everything."

The car drives them to the Plaza, where they will spend the night before the ship sails in the morning. In the suite there are flowers. And there is more champagne. He has had enough today, and Mimi agrees that she doesn't want any either.

Not knowing for the moment what to do, they both walk to the window to look out upon the park and the city lights. Then, smiling encouragement, he takes his suitcase into the other room to change.

When he returns, she is waiting for him, having gotten undressed for the night, although it almost seems as though she has gotten dressed instead, since the white negligee flows as voluminously concealing, as opulently lacy as the bridal gown.

She is so young, so frail, so scared. His impulse is to kiss her forehead, put her to bed as one puts a child to bed, and then go to sleep himself. Or go out for a walk in the mild, lovely evening. But now, wondering and expectant, she looks at him.

He moves to her and takes her loosely in his arms. Willingly she puts her arms around his neck. He lifts and carries her to the bed, as he is supposed to do, for this is their wedding night.

2

ON A fair summer afternoon, in a dull Bosnian town, the Austrian archduke and his archduchess, bowing with regal grace and serenely smiling to the populace from their open motorcar, were shot to death.

It was the work of an instant: the gun popped, bystanders screamed in horror, blood gushed on white silk, and all was over—except for the headlines that towered over the world, and the four years of war that came after.

For a month and more the diplomats rushed from one foreign office and chancellery to another, there to bluff and bargain, yet Austria mobilized and Russia mobilized. One by one the sovereign nations followed, until in the end almost the whole of Europe had been driven into the heart of the storm.

A terrible fear swept through America that she too would be engulfed by this madness. And millions of voices—especially women's voices—were raised now in a warning cry for peace.

Emotion was so profound that when the first peace marchers came down Fifth Avenue that August, there was not a sound from the crowd that watched. To the beat of muffled drums they came down the glittering avenue behind the peace flag with its insignia of the gentle dove; in rank after rank of quiet women they came, dressed in black like so many mourning widows.

Paul stood with his wife's arm linked in his.

"So awfully sad," Mimi murmured. "So helpless and sad."

He looked down. Under the fashionable brim of her hat Mimi's eyes were wet. She would want to wipe them, for public emotion embarrassed her, and he gave her his handkerchief. In a little more than a year of marriage they had evolved so many of these small, intimate signals without words.

He too was deeply moved by what they were seeing. This past month had been hard for any thinking person, but for one who knew and loved Europe as he did, it was appalling.

People were claiming it would all be over by Christmas. Nonsense, Paul thought, remembering the smokestacks and switching yards of Germany. And his cousin Joachim. No doubt he was already in uniform, to fight for his Kaiser. Well, God spare him. God spare us all.

"There's Hennie, there she is!" said Mimi.

"Where? Where?" Paul asked, startled.

"The third one in from this end, look where I'm pointing—"

And there she was, half a head taller than anyone around her, with chin up, stepping smartly.

Paul smiled. Good old Hennie! You couldn't keep her down.

"Well, now that we've seen her, let's go home," Mimi said. "If she and Dan are coming to dinner, I want to make sure that Effie does things right." The new Mrs. Werner was a meticulous housekeeper.

Their street was deserted. In this quiet area east of Fifth Avenue, there were few houses whose windows were not covered with gray boards; the owners were away for the summer. A fine dust lay over dry leaves on the trees that lined one side of the street, and a hot wind blew grit into their faces.

"Cross over to the shady side," Paul said. "You know, you should be on the beach keeping cool in the breeze, Mimi."

"As long as you're in the city working, I'll be here too. Weekends at the shore are good enough."

"You're very unselfish. Don't think I don't appreciate it."

"I'm happy being wherever you are, Paul. Don't you know that?" She squeezed his arm. Her eyes worshipped him.

"I know," he said, patting her hand, thinking, I don't deserve that you should say this to me.

HE WAS at the head of his own table. So the generations march on, he thought wryly, recalling first the Biedermeier table at his grandfather's house, and after that, the overstuffed plum-colored opulence of his parents' dining room.

This was a very different room. The brightly flowered linens gave cheer to the old English mahogany. On the sideboard there gleamed yet another silver tea service, the gift of Grandmother

Angelique. Between the windows hung Paul's prize, a small, radiant Cézanne, a landscape of billowing harvest fields cut into squares by rows of cypress trees.

Dan's forceful voice broke into his musings. "Incredible shock that the European masses flocked to the colors as they have. I never thought that the workers would forget their common brotherhood. It's been the most brutal disappointment of my life."

Paul felt like saying that he was tired to death of troubles, the world's and his own, that he just wanted to feel pure joy again. The inner conflict of this past year, the doubt and the guilt, had bled him enough.

Leah, who sat next to him, caught the troubled expression on his face. "This is a wonderful room," she said, changing the subject. "The amber tone—it's just right. Not too cool for a winter night, nor too hot, for instance, for today."

Paul smiled. "You have an artist's eye."

"Not really. Just a good eye for color. And fashion, of course. That's how I got my job."

She had begun to work in a fashionable salon a month or two before, after graduation from high school. Now Paul asked kindly, "Do you like your job?"

"Oh, yes! I'm at the bottom of the ladder, of course, but I'm learning. I'm allowed to baste, and I unpack the Paris samples that we copy. Wonderful clothes! They can transform a woman. Except that sometimes, when I peek into the salon at the customers and I see some of the old fat ones there, I think, Nothing will transform you, madame." And Leah wrinkled her nose in distaste.

Paul laughed. She was refreshing.

"America must stay out," Dan was saying. "No matter who wins, I tell you, it won't matter. The victor will lay down the terms of peace, and what will happen? The loser will harbor vengeance that will only bring about another war."

"Everyone doesn't think so," said Freddy, who was on summer vacation from Yale. "A lot of last year's seniors rushed to be commissioned in the British army."

"Besotted fools!" Dan cried angrily.

"No," Freddy argued. "German militarism must be crushed once and for all. I had a letter from Gerald this morning," he added, drawing it from his breast pocket. "It's an inspiration. 'I have the utmost faith that we are right. . . . It is an honor to serve, and we march away in glory.' " He swallowed. " 'I'm confident that I will come back. After all, if by some chance I don't, I can only say, *Dulce et decorum est pro patria mori.*' " Silently Freddy folded and replaced the letter.

"With all respect to your friend," Dan said, "that is the sheerest poppycock I've heard in a long time. Sweet to die for your country! When is it ever sweet to die for anything, pray tell me? Of course, if you say it in Latin, that makes it mean more, I suppose. A precious lot of idiocy you picked up in England, Freddy, not the least of which is this whole classics business."

Freddy flushed.

"I think," declared Leah, "it's absolutely wonderful that Freddy knows Latin and Greek."

"Devotion to a dead world, that's what it is."

"It's not a dead world," Freddy answered. His face was violently red. "When we talk of the classics—classical architecture, music, anything—we're talking of something that's pure and basic."

"It's escapism, that's the way I see it," said Dan.

"Freddy is an idealist. He's just like you, you know," Leah said. "His idealism is turned toward other ends, that's all."

Mimi, whose diplomacy could always be depended on, turned her soothing smile upon Dan. "Paul says you're working on something very interesting."

"Yes. Well, I've been working on some ideas about sound signals. Shortwave lengths reflect from solid objects. I've been thinking about how it could be applied to rescue fishing boats, for instance. Anyway, I threw that idea out to Alfie. Maybe those people he works with can use it. I don't want anything for it. I just want to know whether it's workable, and I'll be happy if it is."

"I don't know why you always say that," Leah challenged. "What's wrong with making some money out of it? Somebody else will, if you don't. I know I intend to make money. I'm going to open my own place one day when I've learned enough."

"You do as you think best with your life," Dan said shortly.

"Leah," Hennie intervened, "you've brought your notebook. Show everyone the fashion sketches you showed me."

Mimi stood up. "Yes, let's see. We'll have our coffee in the parlor and Leah will show us her sketches."

They were pencil sketches of graceful, attenuated ladies as portrayed in the more expensive, glossy fashion magazines.

"Very nice," Paul murmured, surprised by the deftness and style of the work. "These gowns are copies, I suppose?"

"Most of them, but I design my own too. This is mine." Taking one out of the folder, Leah passed it around. "It's a *robe de style.* I'd make it in blue moiré. I love the rippling pattern of moiré."

"It's lovely," Mimi cried.

Leah continued energetically. "And the ruffles would depend on who was to wear it. Now for some people I would have double ruffles, elaborate and flounced. For discreet types like Mimi, I'd have one around the back and another halfway down the waist."

"What would you do for Hennie?" Dan inquired. "What type is she?"

"No type. There's nobody else like her," Leah said very seriously. "She's beautiful even in that black outfit, as you can see."

It was so; the height that in her younger years had seemed unfortunate and awkward was now at forty a dignity. She had an unconscious presence, and even the lines in the forehead above the clear leaf-shaped eyes spoke of thoughtfulness and concern.

She said now, "The truth is, this black is beastly hot and what I'd love is to get home and take it off. I want to thank you all, though, for standing in the heat to support the parade."

When she got up, Dan put his arm around her, and she made a little gesture almost like a blessing.

"Family . . . you're all and everything."

Not all, though, Paul regretted, thinking of his mother, who should have been here among them.

When they were alone, Mimi and Paul settled down in the library, he at his desk, going over his papers, and she with a book.

Presently she put her book down and came to kneel on the floor beside him. "Paul, I can't concentrate. If we do get into the war, will you have to go?"

He didn't answer, only looked at her, and saw that her eyes were filmed with tears. She raised her arms to him and put her head on his shoulder; drawing her close, he stroked her back in a gesture meant to comfort. How she loved him!

"Don't worry," he said gently. "We won't be in it. Now, go on back to your book and enjoy it."

She stood up. "And you—you work too hard, Paul. You should relax in the evening. Shall I get your book from the night table?"

"No, no. I'll get it."

If only she wouldn't be so *good* to him!

He sat back down in the leather chair by the lamp, half turned away from her. His mind drifted.

Curious, whenever he saw Leah, how she could lead—in some oblique way—to Anna! One day when he'd gone into the kitchen of his parents' house, Agnes had told him that she'd heard from Anna, and that she was married to the man she'd been keeping company with. And he'd said, in his best dignified-employer manner, that he was happy to hear it and wished her the best luck.

The family had sent her a wedding gift from Tiffany's. Had he imagined that his mother had given him a queer look when she told him? They'd sent an expensive and handsome mantel clock for a place that probably had no mantel. A timepiece to tell the passing of drab hours. For what else could he provide other than drabness, that poor fellow he had seen that day with Anna? And she, with all the bright life in her, all the sweetness and heart and— It was wrong, all wrong!

Strange how his memory faded in and out. Sometimes it was so sharp and clear that he could see the gold wings of her eyebrows; then at other times it almost seemed as though he had imagined the tender, passionate, marvelous thing he thought he remembered.

Oh, but he knew what he remembered!

Dear God, let me be rid of the memory once and for all!

3

IN THE Roth household a truce had at last been called: there was no talk, except when Hennie and Dan were alone together, of the war. Decent living would have been impossible otherwise.

Freddy's face would blaze with aroused blood as he enumerated

German outrages. "Vicious and atrocious criminals! Savages, that's all they are!"

To which his father would retort, "They're no more savages than the others are! They're all the same. Can't you recognize propaganda when you read it?"

So a truce had had to be called.

Freddy came and went with the college vacations, carrying books, tennis racket, and sheet music, while all over Europe boys his age had discarded these for rifles and grenades.

When Freddy came home for the spring recess, a letter with a British postmark had just arrived and was waiting for him. He went into his room to read it. The supper was already on the table. From where she sat, Hennie could see down the hall to his room at the end. Something about the finality of his shut door disturbed her, and she got up to knock at it.

"Freddy, we're waiting. The dinner will get cold."

He didn't answer.

"Freddy! Don't you hear me?"

Then the door crashed open and he stood there with reddened eyes and choking voice. "They've killed him! The damned huns have killed him!" He waved the letter. "It's Gerald's mother. She says in his last letter he was in fine spirits. His commanding officer wrote that he died bravely. At Neuve-Chapelle, it was."

Freddy sat down on his bed with his head in his hands. After a moment or two he spoke again. "I'm sorry to make a fuss. But we were awfully good friends. And this is such a waste."

Leah and Dan had moved silently to Freddy's door. "Yes," Dan sighed. "All of it. A waste."

"Do you still deny that they're savages?" Freddy cried out.

"You've lost your friend . . . a terrible thing," Dan said quietly. "Come, drink a cup of tea, if nothing else. Talk to us."

They all went back to the kitchen table and Hennie served the meal. Freddy could not even swallow tea. "But he was ready for sacrifice. I have to remind myself of that," he said, his voice quivering.

Throwing up his hands, Dan cried, "Sacrifice for what? Of all the sentimental, revolting hogwash!"

"There's no talking to you," Freddy said, rising. "Maybe I'd better leave the table. Whatever I say offends you."

At once Dan's tone softened. "Sit down, Freddy. I have strong feelings and they're hard to control."

"Freddy has strong feelings too," Leah remarked. "Gerald was his friend."

"I understand that." Dan reached out to touch his son's arm. "I'm terribly sorry you've lost your friend. It's just that I view it as tragedy and can't see glory in it."

Hennie served the bread pudding and cleared the table. Her thoughts were confused and fearful. It was spring; by this time each year Freddy had already found a summer job, but so far now he had said nothing about work. She had not dared—why had she not dared? she asked herself—to question him.

When they were undressing for bed, she asked Dan, "Do you suppose he would enlist in the British army or do anything crazy like that?"

"He has another year of college. That's a comfort."

"And then graduate school. He's been saving money toward it, so he wouldn't, would he?"

Dan didn't answer.

HIS parents had gone to the theater. Leah was singing in her room, across the hall. Smiling, Freddy put down the Greek text to listen. It was an aria from *Aïda*. He thought of the festive day during Christmas vacation when he had taken her to hear it and of how entranced she had been. He had really wanted to take her someplace again during this vacation week, but exams were coming up and he needed every minute for study.

Closing his eyes, he lay back in the armchair. Concentration on Greek print strained them. Yet his skill with the wonderful ancient language thrilled him. He smiled, recalling all the discussions he'd had with Gerald about the classics. He missed Gerald with pain of loss and joy of remembrance. He wondered now what Gerald would think of Leah, who was so un-English in her blunt, lively ways.

She was bustling around in her room. Then suddenly there came a dreadful crash and an exclamation: "Damn!"

Freddy jumped up. Through the half-open door he saw her kneeling on the floor next to an overturned bureau drawer, the contents of which were strewn around her. She was laughing.

"What an idiot! It was stuck and I pulled it out too far!"

"Let me help you." He began to pick things up; then he looked at her. She had on a bathrobe, but it was unlike any he'd ever seen. It was blue, with feathery stuff at the collar and hem; when she leaned forward, getting up off her knees, it gaped open.

"What are you staring at, Freddy?"

"What you've got on. Those feathers," he said awkwardly.

"It's marabou. You like it?"

"It's beautiful."

He stood and watched her. She moved quickly, scooping the clothes back into the drawer. When she was finished, he picked up the drawer and replaced it in the chest.

"What are you going to do now?" she asked.

"Study some more, I guess."

"Haven't you studied enough? Take a few minutes off. I feel like having some tea and a piece of cake. I'm bored."

"You could have gone to the theater with the folks. They'd have gotten a ticket for you."

"But I would rather be here with you. I'll fix a tray and bring it to your room."

He waited for her, feeling a new kind of excitement. When had that begun?

A short time later she entered and plunked the tray on the desk. They ate without talking much, she because she was hungry and he because of the thoughts that were swirling in his head. He heard himself sigh.

"What's the matter, Freddy? Aren't you happy?"

"Sometimes yes and sometimes no."

"Well, that's only natural. One can't be happy all the time. Although *you* should be if anybody should. You've got everything."

"I've got everything?" he repeated in astonishment.

"Yes. To begin with, you're handsome. No, don't wave me away. You're smart and educated. You've got parents, a home that's really yours. Don't you know what that's worth?"

There was such confusion in him! The tension of being with

her in his own intimate room, his strange inner stirrings—all was confusion.

"I do know," he answered finally. "But things aren't usually what they seem."

A touch of irony twisted Leah's lips just long enough for him to recognize it.

"A trite remark," he apologized.

"That's not why I smiled. I was remembering when your father told me the same thing. For an instant you looked like him."

"You don't think I look like him, for pity's sake!"

"Not very much. But would it be so awful if you did?"

The conversation was leading toward something. It was as if each of them was hesitantly feeling a way toward some confession, some lifting of a mental burden.

"I've never understood how I really feel about my father. I've wanted to love him, but—there was a time I hated him."

"Why? What did he do to you?"

"Nothing directly to me. Something happened that a child shouldn't know. I was very young. I've never told anyone."

"You might feel better if you did," Leah said gently.

He bent his head. Things were swirling again. Then he felt her hand on his hair.

"I think I know what it was. You found him with a woman."

When, startled, he looked up, he saw comprehension.

"I've often wondered how much you knew about him," she said softly.

Her hand moved to his shoulder and lay there. He was sure he could feel the warmth of it through his sleeve; he was sure he could trust in anything she might tell him.

"I was riding on a bus a couple of years ago, and he was there with a woman. They were— Well, she was kissing him. He was scared to death that I'd tell your mother."

"And you never did."

"Can you think I would? She never knew. She never will. Anyway, I could swear he doesn't fool around anymore."

"How do you know?"

"We had a long talk afterward, he and I."

A composite picture took shape in Freddy's mind. His father is waving his arms on top of a burning house; he is kissing a woman, a cheap type with a painted face; he withers in guilt before Leah's tongue. . . .

"With me, it was what I heard," Freddy said finally. "It was in the room over the lab. I didn't see, I didn't have to see. I ran all the way home. For a long time I couldn't even look at him."

"Poor child!" Her breath was fragrant with lemon as she leaned to him. "You kept it inside of you all these years!"

"It would have seemed like shaming my mother to let anyone know."

"But you don't mind telling me now."

"No," he said, marveling. "You've taken the weight away."

"Freddy, don't you know that we're special people, you and I?"

They rose to stand only inches apart. Her arms drew him in. A crazy joy sprang up in him, while his heart drummed.

"I love you, Leah."

Her mouth drew him. It was sweet; he had never known such sweetness. He had no idea how long the kiss lasted. But when her lips released his, he had been gently propelled toward the bed.

In a dream and a dazzle he heard her whisper, "Now, Freddy, now."

The roundness, the whole secret softness—these were his to take. His nerves stretched, quivering. He wanted her.

"Not until we're married," he heard himself say.

"Freddy . . . I'm not afraid."

"Darling Leah, I can't do that to you. I should want you to remember all your life that you were a proper bride."

"I understand," she said. "You're very good to me, Freddy . . . and you really love me enough to marry me. You really do."

"Maybe I always have and wasn't old enough to know it."

He kissed her forehead. Her head came just to his shoulder. Just eighteen she was, and his own for life. He felt tender, responsible and older than his twenty years, as if youth and dependency had dropped away. How fast it had happened! An hour ago he'd been a schoolboy, and now he was a man, with a woman to care for.

He couldn't believe his luck.

CARRIE CHAPMAN CATT HAD founded the Women's Peace Party in Washington in January 1915; shortly afterward the New York branch was formed. Hennie had promptly joined, and had been elected an officer. She was full of proud enthusiasm.

"If women had the vote, you'd hear a different story," she liked to say. "We wouldn't vote money for guns, I guarantee. Women are not enthralled by power and force."

She went to all the meetings and spoke at many. She made posters and went about the city placing them in store windows. All this activity gave her a good feeling that in her own small way she was building peace.

Late one Saturday afternoon in May, she came home from a meeting to find Freddy in the kitchen with Dan, who, still in his topcoat, had apparently just come in. Freddy, kneeling, was filling Strudel's bowl.

"But how nice! We didn't expect you this weekend."

"I know. How are you, Mother?"

"Oh, fine! I'm late, and I suppose you're starved. But I only have to warm dinner. I made it all this morning."

"Don't make any for me or for Leah. She and I—"

"Leah!" Dan interrupted. "Have you come home to be with her or to give your parents a few hours?"

"To be with her," Freddy said quietly.

Hennie's heart sank. Don't let them quarrel again.

Freddy's hand had been caressing the dog, sliding over its long brown back while it ate. He looked up, then rose from his knees and said, "I love her. And she loves me."

There was a moment's silence. Dan sat down. "You don't know what you're talking about," he said roughly.

"I think I do. And I beg you, don't say anything that I won't want to remember."

Dan softened his voice, as if he had sensed something in Freddy that warned him to guard his anger. "I'm not going to say anything evil, Freddy. You ought to know me better than that. I'm only telling you that you're too inexperienced to be talking about love, that's all. Don't you see that you and Leah have almost nothing in common? You're at Yale, planning a doctorate. She works in a dress shop—"

"You astound me! You, the thoroughgoing democrat, to say anything as snobbish as that!"

"I don't mean it to be snobbish. I mean only to say that you're different, and will grow more so with time. Love between you makes no practical sense at all."

Freddy bent down and picked up the dog, set it on his lap, and held it close. "I'm sorry you think that way," he said slowly. "Because we were married just this noon."

The words seemed to come from far away. "You were married?" Hennie repeated.

"Yes. At City Hall." And Freddy swallowed hard. "Don't be angry . . . don't spoil things. Please. It's our wedding day."

Hennie's hand went to her mouth to stop her trembling lips. "Why didn't you tell us?"

"You would have tried to argue us out of it. So it was just easier this way."

Dan pounded his knees with his fists. "I call it a sneaky way of repaying your mother and me. I call it sneaky and foul."

"We didn't mean it to be. If you'll just let me explain—"

"Yes, do. I'd really like to know how you came to make what, I promise you, will be one of the worst mistakes you'll ever make."

"Keep it for some other time," Freddy pleaded. "Leave us a happy memory of a day we'll remember all our lives."

"Where, by the way, is the other half of this happy pair?"

"Leah ran out to get gloves. She lost hers in the cab. I hear her now."

Breathless and pink from running up the stairs, Leah appeared in the doorway. Seeing Dan and Hennie in a frozen tableau, she stopped short. "Well! I see you've heard our news."

Hennie's eyes swept over Leah: smart new lavender suit, lace jabot, knotted waist-length pearls, pert feather standing straight on the brim of the lavender hat. Leah smiled and waited.

"Aren't you going to wish us joy?" she appealed to Hennie.

A thought flashed through Hennie's mind. That fear, so many times examined and denied, that her son would find his way to the war, that fear was over now. Married, he was safe! She took Leah into her arms. "Of course we wish you joy! Yes, yes. I'm disappointed that you've done it this way, but I wish you joy!"

Leah said quickly, "We are planning to have a religious ceremony later. But right now there just isn't enough time. . . ."

Dan jumped on that. "What do you mean, not enough time?"

Leah turned to Freddy. "You haven't told them?"

"No, I was—"

Leah interrupted. "He dreads telling you. Freddy has enlisted in the British army. He only has a week. That's why we had to be married in a hurry."

Hennie's strength ebbed out and she sank down onto a kitchen chair. The room was dark as a cave, and it whirled. She put her head down on the table.

Her son's large warm hand cupped her head. It was the hand that had gripped hers on the first day of school, the hand that had charmed her as it rippled over the keyboard.

"Don't cry, Mother. I had to do it. It's sad that our principles aren't the same. All I ask is that you respect mine as I have always respected yours. I've done right, I know. This war is the last one. After this will come peace and freedom for all the world."

With this new outrage Dan jumped to his feet. "You've quit college! Thrown your education away! You couldn't have waited a year before going off to play the hero?"

"I'll make up the year when I come back."

Leah said softly, "You don't agree with Freddy's point of view, but I should think you might be proud of his courage."

Hennie looked at her son. He didn't age. She saw the child standing there, the slight, fair child with the lake-blue eyes. She began to cry.

Dan put his arms around her.

"Look what you've done to your mother," he shouted. "And you, Leah, what you've done to this woman who rescued you, gave you her heart and soul! You ought to be cringing in shame."

"If you don't want me here," Leah said, "I have some friends at work. I can live with them after Freddy goes."

Hennie got up and took Leah in her arms again. "This is your home if you want it. Surely you know that."

Suddenly Leah's voice filled with tears. "Whatever Freddy says. And if Dan wants me, I'll stay."

"I'd feel better if I knew she was here with you," Freddy said.

"You're my son's wife," Dan told Leah stiffly. "And as such, you're welcome here."

"We're going away for a few days," Freddy said. "Uncle Alfie's letting us stay at Laurel Hill. Paul's going to drive us there."

"You mean Alfie and Paul knew about this?" Dan demanded.

"Only this morning. I made them promise not to tell, and—and it wouldn't have mattered, because we'd have done it anyway, and they knew that."

A solemn silence fell over the little kitchen, and the four stood now in a circle, waiting for a way to break the circle, to say the final words and depart.

Leah spoke first. "It's half past four. We told Paul we'd be waiting downstairs."

Freddy picked up the bags. "We'll be back on Friday, so we'll say good-bye then. We won't say it now."

Dan opened the door. "No. Just—just be well," he said.

"IT WON'T last." Dan spoke bitterly into the dark. Numb and rigid, they had been awake, talking in bed, through most of the night. "Mark my words."

"They love each other, Dan, and must have for a long, long time. You were right when you said it could happen. I didn't see it."

"There are many things you don't see."

Hennie sighed. "Let us only hope they'll be as happy as we've been," she said, and moved closer to Dan.

AT LAUREL Hill, the peepers were loud in proclamation of spring. Wrapped in sweaters against the cool night, Paul, Freddy, and Leah sat on the terrace after a late supper.

"Listen to their music! What a wonderful night!" Leah exclaimed. "It's a pity Mimi won't come out."

"It's too chilly for her," Paul said. He stood up. "I'm going in too. We're driving back to the city in the morning."

"You needn't leave because of us," Freddy said.

"It's your honeymoon. You surely don't need our company."

"This house is enormous," Leah assured him. "We can rattle around in it without even seeing each other unless we want to."

She got up and walked to the edge of the terrace. "Look at the stars! The glitter's not cold at all. It seems to burn."

Stars, stars, lovers and stars! Paul thought. He turned away and went inside. Leah and Freddy did not even know that he had gone.

Poor Freddy, going off to war when he needn't go! What had possessed him? Was it because of Gerald, a compulsion to match his heroism? One thing was sure: Freddy was a romantic.

And Leah—what had possessed her? Drama perhaps? No, she wanted him, that was all. She loved him—or thought she did, which was the same thing—and had taken him while she could.

Paul went upstairs to the bedroom. Mimi was already asleep. Her needlepoint had fallen to the floor next to the bed, and he picked it up.

Vaguely restless, he walked to the window and looked out. A shaft of light from a lamp in the parlor below fell onto the lawn, where he could see two figures making a single shadow, so close was their embrace. In the depths of his body he felt a surge of longing, powerful and unfulfilled, as though their passion had been contagious.

He undressed and got into bed. His wife's face was calm in sleep. He made himself think about the client with whom he was to confer about a very important matter in the morning. His mind clicked carefully from point to point, clarifying his plan of procedure. After a while he was able to fall asleep.

PART THREE
Freddy and Leah

1

THERE is something about pregnancy, thought Hennie, that softens angers and resentments.

Angelique's first contempt for the marriage seemed to be forgotten at once as soon as Leah's condition could no longer be hidden from her. She became all sympathy; she bought sheets and embroidered gowns for the layette; she began to knit. Some basic instinct for survival of the race? Hennie wondered. Or was her mother simply mellowing with age?

As for Dan, once his first rage had come under control, he had reluctantly adjusted himself to Leah's new position in the household.

The winter was severe. By the fifth month Leah had stopped going to work. Now, in her seventh month, with her needlework on her lap and the little dog lying where the soft folds of her silver-gray skirt touched the floor, she was a Renaissance portrait.

"Read Freddy's last letter aloud again, do," Hennie said.

A sheaf of them lay on the table; Leah was in the habit of reading them aloud, skipping, naturally, intimacies. What was left were banalities, at least to Hennie's worried ears. Now that the letters came no longer from England but from France, all that mattered was that they should keep coming, to prove that he was alive.

"I'm in good spirits," he had written. "And very optimistic. It's a wonderful feeling to be part of this gallant army. The men are a staunch and plucky lot."

"He sounds so British," Dan had remarked wonderingly.

A quaver in Leah's voice as she read pulled Hennie's attention back to the moment. "He says, 'We underwent our first fire. It was pretty frightening, the noise alone could terrify you if you let it, but we got through all right and we're all safe. I'm glad I'm not a coward.' "

Hennie's mouth was dry with fear. The world was mad. She remembered a verse from Jeremiah: *Babylon hath been a golden cup in the Lord's hand, that made all the earth drunken; the nations have drunk of her wine, therefore the nations are mad.*

Here in this country Wilson talked peace and yet supported the buildup of a mighty navy. In Congress they said that only preparedness could preserve neutrality. To arm was the best way to keep out of war. Madness!

The War Department had organized a summer training camp for volunteers at Plattsburgh, in upstate New York.

"Paul's going," Angelique had informed her. "As an officer, of course." And when Hennie had expressed her shock, Angelique had explained, "He's not for war. It's that he wants for his own good to have some training if it should come. I suppose he hesitates to tell you because of the way you feel about it." And

then she'd said, "Florence has gotten active in the Special Relief Society. They're all for preparedness—a woman's counteraction to your group."

Hennie said aloud now, startling Leah, "They'll drag the whole world down, those preparedness people. They're growing louder and louder by the minute. Haven't you noticed how we pacifists are being attacked now in the papers?"

"Hennie, Freddy's over there," Leah said. "How can one be a pacifist? He may need our help before it's over."

Hennie had no answer.

LEAH's boy was born on a sunny morning during a late February thaw. Icicles dripped on the windowsill in the room where the baby lay in his bassinet, a magnificent affair draped in embroidered white organdy and blue satin bows. Mimi had brought it when the baby was two hours old.

"From Paul and me, with all our love," she had said with a wistful expression.

Leah, to Hennie's dismay, had gotten out of bed on the third day, and now, flat of stomach and nicely dressed in a flowered wrapper, sat in a chair by the bassinet.

"It's my peasant blood," she proclaimed. "I can't lie in bed when I feel this good. As soon as I can stop nursing, I'm going back to work, since you said you'll take care of him, Hennie."

Indeed she would take care of him! The boy was already the household king.

"Look at him, he's smiling," Dan said.

"Gas," Leah told him. "Only gas."

"He looks like you, Dan," said Alfie, who had come with Emily and Meg to see the new arrival.

Really he looked like no one, except that he did have Dan's black hair, and plenty of it. His eyes were large, he had a sharp little nose, and his chin was strong—a handsome baby.

"What are you going to name him?" Meg wanted to know.

"Henry, after his great-grandfather," Leah said. "We'll call him Hank. Would you like to hold him when he wakes up?"

"Oh, yes!"

Leah had a nice way with children, Hennie saw.

IN THE MIDDLE OF WINTER IN 1917 the German government warned of the start of unrestricted attack by submarines; not long afterward the threat was carried out. Unarmed American merchant vessels and their defenseless crews were torpedoed to the bottom of the sea, and even harmless fishing schooners went down.

Soon it seemed to Hennie that she and Dan stood almost alone against the onrush of war. One by one the old idols fell and went over to the other side. Samuel Gompers promised the support of the unions should the nation go to war, and Carrie Chapman Catt pledged the women of her peace party to help the war effort if need should come. Hennie mourned, and mourning, marveled that the world around her could be in such high spirits.

Getting and spending were everywhere: theaters were filled; on Fifth Avenue carriages were being outnumbered by Pierce-Arrows, chauffeur-driven; new shops were opening to meet the new need for glittering luxury, from platinum watches to silk shirts. Women bobbed their hair à la Irene Castle and did the tango wearing egrets on their little satin hats.

"They're making fortunes already," Dan said gloomily.

The Allies needed everything, as well as credit with which to buy: grain, tools, medicines, ammunition, cloth, steel, coal, iron, leather, powdered milk—they needed everything. The securities and commodities markets boomed; factory orders soared; warehouses were crammed. Everyone, from lawyers to shippers, felt the zest of expansion. A whole new crop of millionaires was born.

ONE evening Alfie rang the doorbell. Leah had just come in from work. In the kitchen Hennie was spooning cereal into the demanding mouth of young Hank, who, in shirt and diaper, was happily perched on his grandfather's lap.

"Have I surprised you? I couldn't wait till tomorrow."

Alfie looked around for a place to put his derby, but since every surface in the crowded kitchen was covered with something that belonged to Hank—bottles, bibs, stuffed animals—he held it in his hands.

"You remember, oh, I should guess it's three years ago, you gave me a plan for a radio direction finder for ships?"

Dan corrected him. "Not for the finder, just for part of it, a tube."

"Well, whatever it was"—Alfie smiled, relishing what he had come to say—"it's been sold! Finn and Weber Electroparts is putting it into production! It will make you rich, Dan, and it will make me richer. Look at this check."

Dan took the check over the baby's head.

"I don't understand this, Alfie. It says, 'Pay to the order of Daniel Roth twenty thousand dollars.' "

"What?" cried Hennie, dropping the spoon.

"Twenty thousand dollars!" Leah repeated.

Alfie relaxed, pleased and proprietary, as if he had given a beautiful, unexpected toy to a child.

"Well, Dan, it's just your share of the sale price, that's all. I took stock in your name as well as my own. Yours because the invention's yours, and mine for making the contact. There will be more to come. For tax reasons we'll take future payments mostly in the form of stock. . . ." Alfie paused. "You look perplexed."

"I am perplexed."

"Well, never mind. My lawyer will lay everything out for you, advise you on investing too, because"—and here Alfie chuckled—"you'll be getting a whole lot more of these nice checks and you'll want to handle them wisely, make them grow."

"All that money for this little tube! It doesn't make sense."

"Dan, it makes plenty of sense. That little gadget is worth a gold mine in the right hands, as you'll see."

"Whose hands? Who wants it?"

"The War Department, Dan, that's who wants it! You've got a government contract. And it'll go on all through the war that's coming, and after that too, because as Larry Finn explained it, radio direction finding is only in its infancy. Right now, though, they can already keep track of an enemy ship when they have two or more transmissions and—"

Dan raised his hand. "I don't sell my work to the War Department, Alfie."

Alfie stared. "Are you crazy? You don't sell—"

"No, I don't. If, as you say, this thing is to be used to find warships, that means sending human beings to their death at the bottom of the sea. And you think I want that kind of money?"

"Dan, war isn't a game. It's survival. People get killed. Good grief, your own son's over there fighting, and you—"

"Leave my son out of this discussion, please."

"What I'm trying to say is, a man's entitled to the fruits of his labors. Why shouldn't you be paid by the War Department or anybody else who can make use of your invention?"

"For the same reason that a man shouldn't get rich by owning firetrap tenements. Tenements, munitions, all those things are related. They're all exploitation, and I want no part of any of them. That's why I can't accept this."

The room was hot. Or maybe it was only Hennie's pounding blood. These two men, both decent but so different, and yet fond of one another, were now squared off like fighters in a ring. Her brother clutched his hat. Dan hugged the boy, who, sucking on a piece of zwieback, was half asleep.

"You've meant to do something wonderful for me," Dan said, "and I appreciate it. But you have to understand that I can't accept it." And he held the check out to Alfie.

"I'm not going to take it back," Alfie said, wiping the perspiration from his forehead. "Dan, the deal's made, the stock's issued in your name, everything's rolling. Why not take it for Hennie? Just sign it over to her."

Dan shook his head. "I don't mean to sound holy, Alfie, but Hennie's my wife. We're one." And he laid his hand on hers.

"I agree with Dan," she said proudly. "I don't want to make money out of war. We have to do what is right for us."

Alfie sighed. "You're a fool, Dan. A day may come when, God forbid, you get sick, and the day surely will come when you're too old to work. Then you'll regret this. Here's wealth being poured into your hands. Freedom from worry."

"We'll manage, Alfie. We always have. We don't need more. The answer is no and always will be."

The check lay on the table, yellow paper with neat black letters.

"Take the check back, Alfie?" Dan asked gently.

Alfie grabbed it. "Yes, I will. I certainly will!"

"Don't be angry, Alfie," Hennie said as he went to the door.

"Angry? No. Just flabbergasted and sorry for the lot of you." He took one last look around the room. "Okay, that's the way it is. Good night, Hennie." He kissed his sister and went out.

"I suppose you think I'm crazy too?" Dan asked Leah.

She answered frankly, "Yes, I do."

"I feel sad for Alfie," Hennie said. "He looked so crestfallen."

"I know. He's a good sort, Alfie. I can't help but like him." Dan got up. "Take Hank, somebody, he's asleep."

On April 6, 1917, America entered the war.

Paul came a few days later to say good-bye to Hennie. "I've enlisted, got my commission. Conscription's coming, so there's no use waiting." And he added thoughtfully, "Heaven knows, I'm not going with Freddy's spirit. What do you hear from him?"

"Not what we heard in the beginning, I can tell you. He's seen dead Germans, he says, and they look like us. I suppose it hit him hard. They weren't devils or subhuman after all. But his latest letters are just forms—postcards, actually, where they cross out what doesn't apply: I am sick in the hospital, I am wounded, I am well. So he's in the front lines, and that's all we know."

Paul was silent.

"To think the baby's walking and Freddy hasn't even seen him!" Hennie cried for perhaps the hundredth time.

"I wish I had one," Paul said. "I suppose going away like this makes you want one more than you ever thought you would."

They've been married four years, Hennie thought. Not since that day just before the wedding, when Paul had come to her in his despair and wild with pain—not since then had there been any mention between them of his marriage.

She ventured it now. "Paul, tell me, is everything all right between you and Mimi? Do you mind my asking?"

"It's all right. Mimi is a good girl."

Hardly a full answer! Clearly, Paul didn't want to talk about private things, yet he deserved the best. The beginning of his marriage had been so wrong. One could only hope that time had made a difference.

"That other— Anna. You've never heard anything of her?"

He looked up sharply at that. "No. Why should I?"

Flustered, Hennie made apology. "Of course you wouldn't have. Forgive me."

"That's all right."

For the first time that Hennie could recall, she felt clumsy in Paul's presence. At a loss for words, she said the first thing that came into her head. "I suppose Alfie's told you about Dan's turning down a fortune, a big War Department order?"

"Yes. He thinks Dan's very foolish. But you have to do what your conscience compels. Frankly, our firm has been financing Allied purchases on a large scale. Is that bad? War is bad, but we're in it, and they need supplies, so we make money." He brightened. "All I know is, my father's old relatives had better stop speaking German on the streets if they know what's good for them."

"It's not their fault. I'm sorry for them," Hennie said. "Sorry for everyone. For Mimi and for your mother, seeing you go off like this. I think of your mother so much, Paul."

He was still for a moment. Then he said, "None of it makes any sense, not quarrels or wars." Abruptly he stood up. "I must go."

"God bless you, Paul," Hennie said as he kissed her.

She stood at the top of the stairs, swallowing tears, and watched him run down.

2

As THE year passed, the country settled down for the long, long haul. Factories not essential to the war effort were ordered shut to save coal. Daylight saving, meatless Tuesdays, and days without gas all followed. Every blank wall was plastered with war-bond posters.

Hennie and Dan bought no bonds. They gave instead, more generously than they could afford to give, to the Red Cross.

"Contributing for bullets is one thing," Dan said grimly. "Helping the wounded in the hospitals is another."

This he dared say only to a few intimates who shared his beliefs. Otherwise, silence was the only prudent course. One didn't dare say that there might be such a creature as a good German. The German was the "barbarous hun," vilified in the movies and the newspapers. The local butcher, Schultz, who had provided meat to the neighborhood for the last thirty years, now called himself a Swede and changed his name to Svensen.

EVERYTHING FELL APART THE next spring. It would seem to Hennie later that it began with the death of poor Strudel.

Hank was in the stroller with a bag of groceries at his feet; the dog trotted on his short legs at Hennie's side as they finished their daily errands. On the way back, a few blocks from home, a cat sauntered out of an areaway to confront Strudel, who, furious at this temerity, barked and pulled at the leash to go after it.

"No, Strudel, no!" Hennie commanded.

Attention had been attracted. Four or five youths had been loitering at the curb. They now planted themselves in front of the stroller to block Hennie.

"Strudel!" one mocked. "What kind of a name is that?"

One of the louts grabbed the leash. "It's a German name, a kraut name. You ought to be ashamed of yourself, lady."

"Let go of that leash at once," Hennie said sharply. She looked around for help. The street was empty.

"An American shouldn't have a lousy kraut dog. What do you say, guys?"

"No. An American should have an American dog!"

He raised the leash so that Strudel dangled in midair.

Hennie screamed. "For God's sake, what are you doing? You'll kill him!"

"You think so, lady? Ain't that too bad."

Now from the rear of the group another youth came forward, holding a baseball bat. Strudel was wriggling, tortured and gasping for air. The fellow holding him smashed him to the pavement; the one with the bat raised it high and brought it down.

One cry sounded. Such agony Hennie had never heard in her life or could have imagined.

"There's your lousy kraut dog!"

She sank on her knees before the mess of bloody flesh. "Oh, oh, oh," she moaned. And heard feet go pounding away down the street as Hank began to wail.

A woman came running out of a house. "My God!" she said, and covered her eyes. A minute later a policeman appeared and put a hand on Hennie's shoulder.

"What can I do for him?" she wept. "He's in pain."

"Get up, missus," the policeman said kindly. "There's nothing you can do. The dog is dead." He knelt down. "I'll take care of everything. Go home now. Take the little boy home."

She bent to comfort Hank. How much had he understood? One could never know what memory might have been printed on his brain.

Dan was home early, and Hennie was thankful. When with a few choked words she told him what had happened, he made her lie down: he would give the news to Leah; she must just rest.

All that night she lay in his arms to be comforted.

"My darling, this is a disease, an epidemic. Thousands of men are dying as brutally as the poor little dog died."

"I know, but I haven't had to see them," she whispered.

Then, with visions of their son in both their minds, they said no more. And Dan made tender love to her, and she thought, You are everything; you make everything whole; without you it is all fragments and shards, all broken.

AFTER Hank's nap the next afternoon, Dan took him out. Hank was the only lure that could keep him away from his lab. He was a vigorous little boy. He loved to let Dan throw him up into the air and catch him; he loved Dan more than anyone. And Dan returned his love, with none of the hovering fretfulness he had shown to Freddy.

Hennie stood at the window, smiling, and watched them go down the street. For a long time she hadn't gone to the settlement house, now that she had Hank to care for, and she missed it. But there were new joys in her life that evened the scale.

Hank's toys were strewn on Dan's big chair. She put them back on the overcrowded toy shelf; then she thought of something she had long put off. Dan's hall closet, filled with the accumulation of years, was a space that could no doubt be better organized to make room for some of the toys.

She got a step stool and began with the top shelf, on which there were half a dozen cartons stacked with papers. Where to begin? Old miser, she thought. He never throws anything away! Receipted bills, check stubs twelve years old . . .

Her eyes caught something as she rummaged; a sheet of bright pink letter paper turned up among the nondescript rubbish.

"Darling Dan," she read.

Her heart skipped and staggered; she heard its frantic pulse in her ears. Her eyes flew down the page.

> Darling Dan, for in my heart, even though your letter broke it, you will always be my darling . . . you told me this year was the best year in your life, you told me a hundred times, and now you write that we can't go on together. . . . You told me you've never known a woman like me. . . . I know you've had *many* women, not being happy with your wife. . . . I'm broken up, I'm getting a job upstate. . . . I understand you can't get a divorce, I know you said you wished you could, but these women hang on so and make a scandal. . . . But why couldn't we have gone on as we were on our beautiful Saturdays . . . why?

Hennie went mad. The first thing at hand was the glass dome containing her wedding bouquet that Florence had had pressed for her. She smashed it against the wall.

Then she went numb. Cold seeped into the apartment. Outside, the day was bright and looked warm, yet the cold seemed to be coming from the poles to freeze her blood. She got a coat from the closet and, huddling in it, lay down on the sofa.

For a long time she lay with her head on her arms, listening as the silence thrummed. She needed to scream. But the neighbors would hear and call the police. If only she could go somewhere and scream! She could feel the screams tearing her throat until it hurt.

Oh, God, what have You done to me?

She thought of going to Uncle David in the nursing home. So you were right, Uncle David. You said there are men who can't be satisfied with one woman. Oh, I heard you, but I didn't want to hear you. . . .

Uncle David is senile. You can't go to him. You can't go to anyone.

She put her face in her hands and cried and cried.

The key turned in the front door.

"We had a fine walk," Dan said cheerfully. "This fellow attracts attention wherever he goes— Why, what's the matter?"

"I have something to talk to you about," she said coldly. "Take the child in for his nap."

In utmost alarm Dan obeyed. When he came out, she was standing in the center of the room with the pink letter in her hand.

"Take it. It's yours."

His face blanched; he sat down on the sofa.

"Oh, my God," he said.

"Yes. Oh, my God. I was cleaning the closet, not snooping. I never snoop. I had no reason to, or so I thought."

His color went faintly green.

"Do you want a divorce?" she asked in that same cold, thin voice, holding her head high.

"Are you crazy?" he implored.

"Well, you apparently told this—this *person* that you did."

He clasped his hands before him. "Oh, Hennie, Hennie, how can I ever explain this or make sense of it for you? Yes, I had an affair with her. I was stupid. . . . You must understand, a man lies to women like her. I never meant a word. Not one word."

"You tell me you lied to her but what you are telling me now is the truth. How can I know it wasn't the other way? Do you lie to all your women or only to me?"

Dan flung out his hands, palms up. "Believe me!"

"I always believed you, fool that I was."

"Believe me now. I never loved anyone but you. Yes, you. Why do you think I married you if I didn't love you?"

"Because in the circumstances you had to, that's why."

His voice was full of tears. "It was always sex, and nothing else. It never lasted. I never intended it to."

He was in pain, and she stood there tall above him, inflicting more. "You tricked them too, as well as me, then. You promise love and haven't any intention of keeping your promise."

"I'm ashamed, Hennie. I've done things I'm ashamed of. But I never tricked anyone. I told the truth, that I had a wife and would never leave her."

"Only that you were unhappy with her."

He groaned. "It was a way of talking, that's all."

"Oh, I see. What made you finally get rid of this one?"

Dan answered very low. "I realized I had to put a stop to that sort of thing, I had to grow up—too late I realized I might hurt you terribly, the last thing in the world I wanted to do."

"Tell me, how many have you had all these years? How many?"
"I never loved anyone but you, Hennie."
"Don't quibble. I asked how many times you've been unfaithful."
"Have I in any way failed you? In our daily life, in all the years, have I ever been anything but good to you?"
This evasion enraged her. "What an actor you are! To come home and make love to me, to keep telling me you loved me, when all the time you were saying the same things to heaven knows who else and how many—"
"It wasn't the same, ever!" Dan put a hand over his eyes.
"How you have shamed me! You and your women, lying in bed together, laughing at me and pitying me!"
"No, no! I never talked about you. I—"
The key turned in the lock. "They let me off early," Leah announced. And glancing from one to the other, she opened her mouth again as if beginning to ask, What's the matter?
"Don't worry, it's not Freddy," Hennie told her at once.
"Hank's still having a nap," Dan said.
"I'll cook dinner," Leah said quickly, rising to what she saw was a situation. "I never get a chance to."
Hennie responded, "Not for me. I don't feel well. I'm going to bed." And when Leah had gone into the kitchen, she said to Dan, "You can sleep on the sofa in here. It's comfortable enough."
Much later, when he came into the bedroom, she pretended to be asleep. When he whispered, she did not answer. Frozen, she lay and waited for him to tiptoe out. Then, alone in the silent room, she wept and shook, muffling her sobs in the blankets.

It seemed to Hennie now that a fog had wrapped around her, stifling, clinging, and damp. Her breath came hard; her legs and arms moved as if they were weighted.
Leah's presence was a fortunate barrier to another long confrontation with Dan. To Leah's credit, she kept up a pretense that nothing was wrong, going about her routine as always.
But on the first Sunday, after Leah had taken the boy and gone out, Dan came to where Hennie sat at the bedroom window. She had been looking out over the street.
"You sit there," Dan said, not unkindly, "as if you were waiting

to die. Your face is like stone." And he laid his hand on her head.

She jerked away, crying out, "Don't do that! Don't do that!"

He drew his hand back as though she had burned it. "I'm sorry." Even in pain his face was handsome. "Can't you forgive? If a person goes temporarily crazy, can't he be forgiven?" His voice was low and hoarse. "Will you? Can't you, Hennie?"

"I could forgive a love affair. It would be hard, but I could. What I can't forget is what you said about wanting to divorce me."

"But I've told you how it was. I don't know how else to explain it to you." He shook his head. "Give me a chance, Hennie, please?" With that, he went out and closed the door.

It did not get better in the weeks that followed. Instead something began to firm within her, something hard and sore. It was the knowledge that she could do without him.

He began to eat his meals out and come home late. In the evenings she would sometimes sit in the kitchen with Leah drinking coffee. Mercifully, throughout the first dreadful week or more, Leah asked no questions.

"Of course you see that something terrible has happened," Hennie finally told her in a voice filled with tears. "I owe it to you to say something about it, I know. But it's hard, very hard—"

Leah shook her head. "No, when it comes to owing, that's all on my side. You've given me everything." Her cool fingertips touched Hennie's hand. "I'd do anything in the world for you, anything."

The words and the tender gesture moved Hennie's heart. She nodded silently, then found her voice. "I'm sorry to be so mysterious."

"That's all right. But if you ever want to talk, I'll listen. I might understand more than you think."

Long after Leah had gone to her room, Hennie remained at the table, comforting her hands on the hot cup and staring into the gray air. What might Leah understand? I don't really care, Hennie thought. The question is, What's to be done about myself?

Then she heard Dan come in. He stood in the doorway behind her, waiting for acknowledgment. "What you expect of me is impossible, Dan," she said without looking up.

"I don't expect much, just that after all these years you might try to remember—"

"I remember all too well! Don't you see that's the trouble? Oh, it's so sad. I had so much love and tenderness to give you."

"You did, and you gave it." He sounded very tired. "Hennie, won't you try, really try, not to be angry at me?"

"It's not anger. It's far, far deeper." She threw up her hands. "I can't describe it. I want to go away."

"Go away? Where to?"

"Out of here. I can't live with you anymore."

Dan whispered, "If anyone's to leave, I will."

"All right, then. Let it be you."

"You don't mean it, Hennie. You can't mean it."

"I do. You and I can't stay here together."

"Hennie, you can't mean it?"

"Yes. Go away, Dan. Go away."

ANGELIQUE's shocked disbelief had turned, with the passage of days, to indignation. "Where on earth has the man gone?" she demanded.

"He's staying in his room over the lab," Leah answered. She glanced at Hennie. "He told me to tell you if you asked."

"I haven't asked," Hennie said.

So he had returned to the room where Freddy had been conceived. Suffer there! she thought. Mourn for your loss!

"The great benefactor of humanity walks out, abandons his wife after almost twenty-five years!" Angelique said contemptuously.

Hennie answered curtly. "He has not abandoned me. I sent him away."

"I don't understand. What is this all about? You won't talk. . . ."

Very quietly Leah said, "Sometimes there are things people can't talk about."

"Thank you, Leah," Hennie said.

"Well, since you won't talk, I don't see how I can help you." Angelique stood up. "It's getting late. I might as well go home."

"You won't stay for supper?" Leah asked.

"Not tonight. Maybe tomorrow. Let me know if you need me."

Angelique had been coming every day since Dan's departure.

She had not said, I told you so, which in the circumstances she could well have done. All of this Hennie appreciated.

Most afternoons Hennie took Hank to the park and sat there watching him play. Other women were there, watching other children, but she avoided them. And she felt that her loneliness must be visible to all, like those misty white halos around the heads of the figures in somber religious paintings.

She longed for a woman to talk to. Angelique was out of the question, and so was Leah. She had, these days, many memories of her sister. Through half-closed eyes, watching Freddy's child scrape with pail and shovel in the hard earth, she was at the same time seeing and hearing vivid moments out of an old life that now, oddly, seemed secure and good.

Florence comes into Hennie's room, swirling the ruffles of her first evening dress before the mirror. Florence wakes her at midnight to bring a napkin full of petits fours, filched from the party just for Hennie. Florence gives birth to Paul, and Hennie is the first to hold the baby when he has been swaddled.

What will she say to Paul when he comes back and finds what has happened in this, his second home, as he always called it? And what will she say to Freddy? He will be devastated.

Oh, it is better never to love anyone at all!

Summer came. The city smothered under a hot bronze dome. At night people slept on their fire escapes, burning citronella candles to keep the mosquitoes away.

One evening Alfie came to visit. "This heat," he said, fanning himself with his newspaper. "You look exhausted, Hennie."

"I'm all right." She had no wish for commiseration.

"Hennie, we're all so worried about you."

"Well, don't be. I'm all right, I tell you."

"Are you going to get a divorce?"

"There are no grounds for one. And anyway, I wouldn't want to make the effort."

Alfie clucked his tongue. "I'm sure I don't understand it all! I'd like to know what it's about."

"Why aren't you in the country?" Hennie asked, avoiding his gaze.

"We're going as soon as Meg's school is over. Meg takes all the honors in school, you know. She certainly doesn't get that from me."

Hennie had to smile. "No, she certainly doesn't. Give her my love. I haven't seen her in so long. Haven't seen anyone."

"That's just the point. That's why I've come. We'd like you to spend a week at our place. Cool off. Bring Leah and the baby, naturally. Do you all a world of good."

All that hearty jollity! She'd have to play croquet and sit through convivial dinners. Shaking her head, she demurred.

"I insist," said Alfie. "Make it the Fourth of July. You've never seen a bang-up country-town parade. We'll have just a small group. I'll ask Mama. Then there will be Emily's cousin, Thayer Hughes. He's an English professor, lost his wife a few years ago. A good sport. And Ben Marcus is coming; he's a young lawyer. I've been doing some real estate deals with him, and we've gotten friendly." Alfie was enthusiastic, trusting to his eagerness to keep Hennie from refusing again. "A very decent young fellow. He's got ulcers, or did have, so the army refused him. I think he feels humiliated because of it. So it's settled for the Fourth. I'll drive you out so you won't have to lug Hank's stuff on the train."

It was, as Alfie had promised, a real bang-up parade. The whole town and surrounding countryside had come to cheer. There were horse-drawn floats with Washington crossing the Delaware, Uncle Sam in white chin whiskers and stovepipe hat, Miss Liberty draped in red, white, and blue and carrying aloft an appeal for Liberty bonds. All was triumph and jubilation.

None of this, thought Hennie, has any connection with the trenches. And a trickle of cold dread seeped deep inside her, as if she had drunk ice water.

Beside her, little Hank rode high on the shoulders of Ben Marcus. The two had taken to each other. Well, of course! The child needed and missed a man. She wondered if it puzzled him that Dan wasn't in the house anymore to read a story at bedtime.

She liked Ben Marcus. He had a sharp, slender face; his hair was sandy red, with eyebrows and lashes to match. He had a keen look, not at all unpleasant; in his eyes there could be seen a readiness to laugh. Yes, she decided, she definitely liked him.

"You're thinking of your son." The gentle voice came from Thayer Hughes, who was standing on Hennie's other side.

"Well, yes, partly," she answered.

"You have just the one son?"

"One child. To my regret," she said.

"I have none and my wife is dead. I sometimes think loneliness is a sickness."

"That's as good a way as any of putting it."

"You and your husband are separated? Emily mentioned something."

"Yes," she said. "Separated."

She was not offended, as she might have been had some other person intruded on her privacy. For the man was mannerly, a true cousin to Emily. He looked like the popular image of a professor, thin and slightly stooped in his tweed jacket. His thick hair, just touched with silver, surrounded a face as serene as Emily's, with an added air of masculine authority.

"Would you care to walk back?" he asked her when the last of the parade had passed the firehouse and dispersed. "It's a good cool day for a walk."

"Why, yes, I would," she told him.

"It's going to pour before the day's out," Alfie warned. "Look at the thunderheads!"

"They're miles away," Thayer assured him. "We'll be home long before they get there."

So the two of them set out, while the rest of the party drove home.

They turned off the main road and down a lane. After a mile they took a shortcut through a hummocky field, and ended up at Alfie's gardens. To the left stood a grape arbor and to the right a row of raspberry canes.

Hennie paused; there was a sudden stillness in the air. "Feel how quiet it is," she murmured.

Thayer looked up at the sky. "I'm afraid it's the quiet before the storm. I miscalculated."

The sky had gone gray. Roiling clouds had come over from nowhere. Leaves flipped over onto their white undersides; a chill swept through the air, and branches, whipped by the wind, lashed dangerously about. The first rain spat. Thunder now split the sky; lightning sizzled and crackled.

"Here, this way," Thayer cried, pulling Hennie by the arm. "We can't make it to the house." A rickety structure stood hidden, squatting low in the shrubbery. "Here, into the gazebo. This'll be safe enough."

The octagonal gazebo had fretwork sides open to the weather, but by standing in the center, one could keep out of the rain, which was now coming down in torrents, flailing the earth.

Hennie smoothed her dampened hair, caught her breath, and, feeling a sudden awkwardness, found something to say.

"Alfie's been talking about fixing this up. It will make a nice quiet spot to read in. Don't you think so?"

"Yes, rather nice," he said. "Do you do much reading?"

"I don't know that you'd call it much, compared with what you must do. Right now I'm halfway through *Sister Carrie*."

Thayer's eyebrows went up. "Really? A banned book?"

"I know. It's supposed to be pornographic."

"Indeed. What's your opinion of it?"

"I feel sadness and pity. I think it shows that women's lives can be very, very hard. Unfair and cruel."

The man considered her a moment before he answered. "You looked very beautiful just now, saying that."

"Thank you." To her own ears she sounded shy and uncertain, like an awkward girl receiving a first compliment.

A terrible crack of thunder shook the little gazebo. Hennie drew her collar around her ears and closed her eyes.

Suddenly she felt Thayer's hands on her shoulders. She felt herself being turned around, and her eyes flew open. He was pulling her to him, so that the length of her body from shoulder to hip was held against his, a supple, hard, male body. There was a joining, a fitting, familiar and right; astonishing that it should instantly be so! She pressed closer. Warm, warm . . . His mouth held hers; she inhaled from his flesh a fine aroma of cologne and pipe tobacco. For a long, reeling minute they stood so.

Then something struck into the core of her brain and she fought loose. "No—not here!"

"Of course not here. But I can find a place tomorrow."

Something in her expanded, quivered. Wanting, knowing one ought not to want, being afraid of oneself. She found voice, murmuring, "Oh, no, I didn't mean that—what you're thinking. . . ."

The man's light, twinkling eyes were amused. "Hennie, save your energy. You know you liked it."

"But I'm not going to do it," she said.

"Why not?"

"I really don't know why," she answered wonderingly.

"I'll tell you. A thousand years of Jewish morality. Oh, don't be insulted, I'm not anti-Semitic! It is Jewish morality, though. It started with you people."

"I can't help that," she murmured.

"Or is it that you still feel you 'belong' to your husband?"

Now anger rose. "I don't want to talk about that. It's my business."

He bowed. "You're right. And I apologize." Flushing, he turned away to look out at the slackening rain, and she understood that he was feeling the humiliation of her refusal. She wondered what he was privately thinking: that she was a fool?

Thunder, moving away, made a distant rumble, and slow drops splashed from the eaves of the gazebo. Only a fine steady rain grayed the air; the storm was over.

Thayer said formally, "We can make a run for it if you're ready. I can give you my jacket to throw over your head."

"Oh, no, oh, thank you, I'm fine," she told him, and then, not speaking, they walked back through drenched grass to the house.

HENNIE took a long hot bath, then dressed for dinner. She stood before the tall glass and examined herself closely. Definitely she was looking better, far better, than she had for a long time. Maybe it was because of these few days of sunshine. Or could it be only because of what had happened this afternoon that her eyes were so clear?

It crossed her mind that it would be a fine thing if Dan could know about this afternoon. . . .

Your leaf-shaped eyes, he used to say. Like autumn leaves. The devil with Dan! But it was really irritating that he couldn't know she could do exactly what he could, if she wanted to.

Why hadn't she wanted to? A thousand years of morality, he'd said. She laughed. More like five thousand, Thayer. Was that the reason? Maybe. Part of it, anyway. And the other part? Oh, never mind about the other part. . . .

AFTERWARD she remembered the smallest detail of that evening. The mushroom soup had been too thick. The asparagus, of which Alfie was so proud, had been perfect, as were his further pride, his everbearing strawberries.

After dinner, as usual, the scatter rugs in the parlor were rolled away, for Alfie and Emily, who took lessons in ballroom dancing, liked to practice. Meg kept the Victrola wound.

In her awakened mood Hennie was almost exhilarated. She watched Alfie and Emily's complicated maxixe, then Ben's and Leah's jiggling turkey trot.

Thayer Hughes had sat down with Angelique on a small sofa at the farthest end of the room, making it clear that he intended now to keep away from Hennie. Angelique would be overwhelmed by this attention. She wouldn't discern the man's dry irony.

His sensual touch had been a delight: locked, warm, and curved—Hennie could feel it still. Strange, because she knew now she didn't like him. Yet she owed him something.

The music stopped, and Meg, serious about her job, went through the pile of records. "How about a tango this time?"

"Make it a fox-trot," Alfie told her. "I want to dance with Aunt Hennie, and unless I'm mistaken, she doesn't know how to tango."

"You're not mistaken," Hennie said.

"Well, are you having a good time?" he demanded as they began to dance. But before she could answer, he assured her that she must be, because she was looking more like herself.

"What do you think of that fellow Ben?" he asked next.

Hennie considered. "He's pleasant. Honest too, I would say."

"Turns out his younger brother was at Yale with Freddy. He remembers Freddy, met him a couple of times with his brother."

Strange that they had been talking about Freddy at the very instant the telephone rang. . . .

Alfie picked up the receiver. Looking surprised, he turned to the room to say, "It's Dan." Then for a few minutes he listened.

Meg shut off the Victrola and everyone waited. Hennie's mouth went dry, and her palms were wet. All the jollity seeped out of Alfie's face, like water disappearing down the drain.

"Legs?" they heard him say. "Yes. Well, I'll drive them back first thing in the morning."

When he hung up, he spoke softly, looking from Hennie to Leah. "Freddy's been hurt. His leg. Or legs, maybe."

Leah's hand flew to cover her mouth. And Hennie steadied her voice, but it came out like a croak. "How bad?"

"I don't know," Alfie replied.

He does know, Hennie thought, and can't bear to tell us.

3

THERE was nothing to say. On slat benches they made a semicircle around Freddy in the wheelchair: Dan, Leah, Angelique, and Hennie, with strained false cheer all vying to talk to him—or rather, at him—while trying not to see him.

Eyes wandered to the dazzling sky, the ivy on the walls, the hale young nurses pushing young men in wheelchairs—anywhere but to Freddy.

"Why didn't you bring Hank today?" he demanded.

Leah bit her lower lip; she had developed the habit just since Freddy had come back. "We thought perhaps he bothered you the last time. It's a long ride from New York, and he's so cranky when he misses his nap."

"How can you think he bothers me? Bring him!" Freddy said angrily.

Early fall winds were blowing from the north. In deference to the chill, a nurse had brought a blanket to cover what remained of Freddy's lower half, but the government-issue wool might as well have been transparent, so clearly could one imagine the stumps.

"Obscene!" Freddy cried abruptly, bewildering them all before they could comprehend. On the far side of the enormous hospital quadrangle, two teams in wheelchairs were playing some sort of ball game. "They keep trying to make me play, but I absolutely refuse. I was no athlete when I had my legs, so why should I be one now?"

There was no answer to that. And Freddy resumed, "Did you know I heard from Aunt Florence and Uncle Walter? They're coming to visit today. I guess it takes something like this to bring people together. It's rotten that people should behave like enemies over nothing. Nothing that matters a damn in the end."

Dan was staring straight ahead across the lawn. His lower lids were puffy, as though he hadn't slept. Well, of course he hasn't; who could? Hennie thought.

They hadn't spoken to each other during any of these visits. One might think that in the face of this new, far greater anguish, that other would be forgotten. On the contrary, it loomed larger. For what would it do to Freddy when he found out they had parted?

Hennie felt tears gathering again, and swallowing hard to stifle them, she said, "Uncle Alfie said to be sure and tell you they're expecting you in the country as soon as you—get better."

Freddy ignored that. "You haven't told me about Strudel. Does he get along with Hank?"

Leah and Hennie glanced at each other. Leah spoke first.

"I'm sorry. We hated to tell you. He caught pneumonia last spring and we lost him."

"Didn't you take him to a vet, for heaven's sake?"

"Oh, yes, but it wasn't any use. I'm sorry, Freddy."

"Well, I want another dog, then. A dachshund just like him."

Petulant, like a child, Hennie thought. Oh, my son, what's happened to you?

And Leah, what will happen to her? It's going to be very hard for her too.

Hennie wondered how it was that she was able to keep the tears from falling. Why, she had sobbed so that day when the dog was killed! It was strange too that when you were here with Freddy, you couldn't bear to get up and leave him, while at the same time you waited for the visiting period to be over.

THE hired car waited in the parking area. Leah took Hennie's arm without speaking. Angelique was crying into a handkerchief, and Dan was silent, walking with bowed head.

Somebody called Hennie's name. A woman was stepping out of a limousine and coming toward her. It was too much, all in one day! And something tore apart in Hennie's chest, so that at last she could sob, while Florence, sobbing too, opened her arms.

She heard Florence murmur, "Hennie, Hennie, I don't know what to say to you."

Don't say anything, only let me feel the comfort of your arms.

When minutes later they broke apart, they simply stood there looking at each other.

Walter grasped Dan's hand and cleared his throat. He had scarcely changed, nor had Florence, in her dark red suit, soft veiled hat, and pearl choker.

"Are you satisfied with the care?" Walter asked. "If there's anything I can do, let me know. I have a cousin who's quite a name in rehabilitation."

"I suppose they're doing here whatever can be done," Dan replied. His voice was thick. "But yes, when the time comes, I'll ask you. He'll need all the help he can get."

Walter cleared his throat again. "It's terrible . . . a wretched thing, unspeakable. Paul's still over there, you know."

"I know," said Hennie. "We—I think of him always."

"Oh," Florence cried, "this awful, awful war!" She caught Hennie's hand. "I wish—I wish we could turn time back and start all over. And do things differently. We want to help you, do whatever we can, only we don't know what. You'll come to us, will you? You and—"

But she did not say, Dan. So she knew. Of course. Mama would have told her in great detail.

"I will. Leah and I will come," Hennie replied.

"Do you want us to go in to Freddy now?"

"He expects you," Dan said.

Florence touched Hennie's cheek. "You'll manage, and God will help you."

"God," Hennie said. "What good has He been? Where is his great compassion and love that we are taught to trust in?"

Her voice rose, keening, as if, having forgotten for a few minutes what she was doing in this place, she had suddenly remembered. The earth reeled, and she heard Dan's voice.

"Hennie, don't lose your faith. Now is when you need it."

Counsel from one who had never been a believer! She looked

up, thinking for a moment that he might be ironic, but his eyes were filled with pity instead.

She looked away and, steadying herself, permitted Leah to help her into the car.

In a frenzy Dan had walked and walked, all the way downtown past factories and shops, coming at last into the district where money was made and lost, borrowed and lent—where money was king.

The rush hour had barely begun, but Alfie was an early riser; he would be in his office. Dan checked the scribbled address. Across the street it was, a tall building. Alfie was on the ninth floor.

The receptionist was arranging her pencils for the day. Dan pushed past her. In the wide front room Alfie sat talking to a thin young fellow. Who? Ben Marcus. Came to see Freddy at that place. Dan's memory clicked like a mechanical toy.

Alfie stood up. Immediate worry spread over his face. "Dan! Has something happened?"

"I want the money! I want every cent of it!"

"What are you talking about?" Alfie asked. "What money?"

"The money! All that stuff you—you sold. My stuff, those patents, stock—" Now Dan's mind stopped clicking; it was blinded in a surge of anguish. "It's not for me, I wouldn't touch the dirty stuff. It's for Freddy. For him, don't you understand?"

"Please," Alfie said, "calm yourself. I don't understand. I'm ready to listen."

"I want my son to get something out of the lousy war. They took his *legs*," Dan cried. "Something to compensate—" He put his head in his hands, then looked up bleakly at two pairs of pitying eyes. "Compensate. As if you could."

"No," Alfie said softly.

Suddenly Dan straightened, alert and alarmed. "You still have it? It's not all gone? Because I said I wouldn't take it?"

"It's in trust. You didn't think I could just throw a bundle of stock into the wastebasket, did you? Yes, it's there. And it's grown considerably since we last talked about it."

"Is it enough to keep him and his wife and child?"

Alfie smiled. "Enough to keep them pretty splendidly."

"How soon can I—he—have it? I want it all in his hands."

Alfie turned to Ben. "Tomorrow? Can you go over the figures that fast?"

Ben nodded. "Late this afternoon, as far as I'm concerned. The lawyers will probably need more time, for the trusts and—"

"We'll rush it. Ben's taken over as my accountant," Alfie explained, "and a good one too. His legal background's a real asset."

"It really will be all straightened out by tomorrow, Alfie?"

"Meet me at my lawyers'. Around four."

Some weeks later Alfie propped his elbows on Hennie's kitchen table. "Yes," he said, "you should see him. He's been like a madman ever since he came in demanding the money. Can you give me a sandwich or something? I'm starved. I haven't been home. He made me go look at the house he wants to buy."

Hennie cut bread and meat and spooned a helping of apple pudding while Alfie talked on in a disjointed rush.

"When your crazy husband refused to take his share, I took it in stock for him, and it's been piling up. It's worth over a hundred thousand dollars, and that's only so far. Freddy's a rich man, Hennie."

The words spun in the air and buzzed away with no real meaning. "Where is this apartment?" she asked.

"Not an apartment. A house. It's right off Fifth Avenue, uptown. I tell you, I'm staggered! It's fit for a king. He's going to put in an elevator," Alfie added triumphantly.

"How much does it cost?"

"The house? Hold on to your hat! Twenty-five thousand."

She was dazed. "So much."

It didn't make sense. His whole life Dan had worked in a classroom, six hours or more a day, besides the evenings at home marking papers. All of that had brought nothing compared with this tube he had played with; a gadget, a toy it had been, a game to satisfy his curiosity. Yet a shower of gold was the reward for it.

Alfie took a bite of the sandwich, then said, "Listen, the closing's early next month; then I can show you the house while Dan's at work. I'm to have a key. He's already been buying things right and left."

"What things?"

"Furnishings. Can you believe it of Dan?"

"He's furnishing a house for them and not asking Leah?"

Alfie shrugged. "He wants to do it his way. Says Leah can go to blazes if she doesn't like it."

HENNIE stood on the sidewalk between her mother and Alfie, staring up. The morning sun fell white upon the brick and limestone façade of an elegant Federal house. A pair of evergreens flanked the front door under a fanlight, and the brass knocker gleamed like a gold coin.

Alfie unlocked the door. It swung open onto a circular reception hall paneled in pale blond wood. The floor was marble; a dark red carpet covered the curving stairway.

Angelique took a quick breath, making quick appraisal. "That paneling! It's all hand carved."

"I tell you," declared Alfie, "the place is a gem. Come on up."

On the second floor, at the front of the house, three tall windows faced the street. It was beautifully furnished. A grand piano shone like jet in one corner, near a window.

"A Steinway. Nothing but the best," Alfie said. "He wants Freddy to play again."

The perfect instrument, thought Hennie, the one thing Dan had coveted and would have bought for himself if he had been able to afford one. The sight of it moved her to tears. If there was any possession that might bring joy to Freddy, this piano might. Here in this airy room he might make music again.

The doorbell rang. "Oh, that must be the girls," said Alfie. "I told them we'd be here." And he bustled away.

"Remember," said Angelique, "we have Alfie to thank for all this. Whatever else he may do"—like joining the Episcopal church, Hennie thought—"you have to admit he's the best-hearted man in the world. And as I always say, with the golden touch!"

There was no doubt about it, Freddy would need money. The government's pension would hardly support his family, even with Leah working. So it was understandable that Dan would take some of the tainted money he had refused before. But this grandeur?

Emily, Florence, and Mimi came babbling up the stairs. When they had made their greetings, Alfie took all but Hennie on a tour of the house. Left behind, she sat down on one of the new wing chairs. The sunlight played over the parquet floors, revealing an intricate golden grain. From the clock, there came a cheerful chime. Already the house was coming alive. Dan might have said that Leah could go to blazes if she didn't like it, but Hennie was sure that Leah would approve. Its costly simplicity was what she would recognize. Yes, it was beautiful.

The voices came back, still babbling their amazement.

"It's elegant, Hennie," Florence cried. "Really elegant."

Mimi inquired who was to take care of such a large house.

Alfie explained. "The couple who worked for the former owner will stay on. A Mr. and Mrs. Roedling. Swedish. The man will help Freddy, lifting and—" He stopped, glancing at Hennie.

"And Dan has bought a car. Mr. Roedling knows how to drive," Emily said. "There's to be a nurse for Hank too," she added in a disapproving tone, "since Leah will not give up her job."

"I've spoken to her about that," Alfie said, "but she likes her work. She says she doesn't want to be dependent on Dan's money."

Angelique made a correction. "But it's Freddy's money now."

A silence fell momentarily upon the little group, a silence that seemed to echo, making the empty house larger and emptier. Into it Mimi spoke again. "It seems as if Paul's been gone a hundred years."

"Surely the war will be over soon," Angelique said desperately.

"Oh, it surely will be. Any day now," Alfie assured them. "Well, shall we go?"

And they followed him, one by one, down the red carpet and out through the door of Freddy's sumptuous new house.

4

ON A cold day early in 1919, Paul and Mimi, having made their first visit at his parents' home, made their second one at Freddy's.

A fire snapped in the library, a snug enclosure of burnished ruddy wood, Oriental rugs, and lamplight. Freddie's man having brought a tray with tea things, Mimi poured and served.

The wheelchair had been drawn up near the fire. Its warmth had caused Freddy to throw off the plaid rug that had covered him from the waist down, so that now what had happened to him could be seen in its full horror beneath the pinned-up trousers. Stumps. He was half a human being. Paul couldn't bear to look and couldn't avoid looking. Mimi, more fortunately, was able to be busy with the tea things.

"You have Hank and Leah. They need you." Paul was ashamed of the cliché, yet what else was there to say?

"The thing is," Freddy said, "I'm of no use to the boy. He's a lively little kid, much more than I ever was."

I taught you to ice-skate, Paul thought, and said almost frantically, "But you are of use! There's more to life than sports. The real you is here, even though you've lost your legs."

"And Leah loves you," Mimi said.

"You've been wonderful," Freddy told her. "Your wife's come regularly, Paul, and brought me books." For a moment the old soft, dreamy look passed across his face. "And Meg comes after school. She's only fifteen, but we can talk. Your mother comes, and mine, whenever she's sure my father won't be here. Whatever all that's about! Do you know?" he demanded suddenly.

"I don't think anyone does," Mimi said.

"As if there isn't enough misery without making more. You knew that Uncle David died, I suppose."

"Yes. On Armistice Day," Paul answered.

"With all the crazy celebration in the streets and the whistles blowing. Do you remember New Year's Eve in 1899, Paul? Well, it was like that."

"Oh, I can remember," Paul said. "But can you, really?"

"Yes. I was lifted up to the window and my father said, 'He'll always remember this night.' "

Freddy's eyes were cast down toward the fire, which, flaring, made his pale lids almost transparent. What else was he seeing in the flames? No one spoke. The teacup clinked when Mimi put it down, jarring the stillness.

"The people who started this war ought to be shot! Wilson too, the whole lot of them," Freddy said suddenly.

Paul said nothing. The words that he could have spoken and

would not speak, because they would have been too cruel, came to mind: And what about you? With your great crusade and your scornful attacks on pacifists like your parents?

Now Freddy leaned forward and held Paul and Mimi with a blazing stare. "Do you know we fought three and a half months at Passchendaele? Fought in the mud, and lost a quarter of a million English boys. I learned to fight hand to hand. With grenades. They're more efficient than bayonets. I remember Gerald's letters, his mother's too. 'Gerald died a hero,' she wrote." Freddy laughed. "Oh, yes, a clean, neat, instantaneous death with a bullet through the heart!" He subsided.

Out of the corner of his eye Paul caught his wife's frail shoulders trembling. And he said very quietly, "Still, in spite of it all, you know, the world would be a very different place if the Kaiser's side had won."

"I can't say it would, Paul."

No, it probably wouldn't matter to him. Without legs, nothing would matter very much. Paul grasped futilely for something else to talk about.

He stood to go. "I'm afraid we've tired you."

"No. I'm just tired, that's all. You didn't do it."

Intensely shaken, Paul and Mimi went downstairs, out onto the street, where a cold wind was blowing.

"I keep remembering what he was like," Paul said. "All that poetry before he went away. What terrible innocence, I thought then. And now this bitter despair—it breaks my heart."

At the street corner they met Leah, hurrying home. Paul kissed her cheek, from which breathed a warm perfume.

"So you've seen him," she said. "Isn't it frightful? What's to happen?"

"Unanswerable questions, Leah."

"I know. He just sits there staring at nothing. Sometimes, oh, very rarely, he'll go to the piano and let his hands drift, not really playing anything. And here we are, only a few yards from the park, but he won't go there. He says people will see him and pity him." She sighed.

"We'll keep coming," Mimi assured her.

"I know. You've been so good, Mimi. I must say that people

really have been. Ben Marcus comes. He cheers Freddy a little, I think. And, of course, Dan comes. But that upsets Freddy some. He can't understand what's happened between Hennie and Dan."

"In spite of it all, you manage to look well," Paul told her. It was the only remark that came into his head.

"I have to. It's my job. That's the only thing that's going right. I've had a big raise and it feels good. Good not to be dependent on Dan. I have to live under the roof he paid for, I can't help that, but at least I can support myself."

The wind blew around the corner where they were standing.

"We're keeping you," Mimi said.

Leah held Mimi's arm. "No, it's all right. I desperately need to talk. I can't ever talk to anyone about this, you see. I can't be honest about my feelings, they're so ugly. I can't tell Hennie, can I, that the day I first saw Freddy in the hospital I had to run to the bathroom to be sick? I'm so ashamed of myself."

Mimi did not speak, and for the moment Paul could not.

"What's so awful is that sometimes I wish I could disappear," Leah continued. "Just vanish. When I think of all the thousands of days of my life that will be like this, I don't want to bear it, although I know I have to, and I will. And then I'm ashamed to be the least bit sorry for myself, when it's he who—" Leah's face collapsed for an instant into the ugly mask of grief. Then she straightened it. "I'd best go in. Thank you for listening."

She took a few steps and then turned back to face them. Her round, intelligent eyes appealed to Paul. "Are you shocked?" she asked.

Paul shook his head no. He supposed that the pity in him should all be kept for Freddy, and yet at this moment it overflowed for her.

FREDDY, having heard his father enter the house, swung away from the keyboard and propelled the wheelchair to the other side of the room.

"I heard you playing just now. Sounded like Debussy," Dan said.

"Only chords. Nothing much."

Dan sat down on the sofa, crossed his legs, and lit a pipe;

apparently he was settling in for a real visit. Well, why not? He owned the place.

"So. Enjoying the piano. That's great."

"It's a Steinway, isn't it? The best."

Dan didn't answer that. Instead he said, "Do you like this place, Freddy? The truth, please. I won't mind if you don't."

"Anyone would like it. Why shouldn't I? What makes you ask?"

"Then it must be my presence that you don't like. You hardly speak to me."

"I don't feel much like talking these days."

"Freddy, don't fence with me. You're too intelligent—we both are—not to know that something's been wrong, or not quite right, between you and me from far, far back."

"Why are you bringing it up now? Why today?"

"I don't know. It's not always easy to say why suddenly we feel compelled to say something that should have been said long ago."

"I've been upset about you and Mother." That was part of the truth, anyway.

"Naturally." Dan lowered his eyes. "It's a tragedy. If only I— Well, I can't. Can't do anything. Can't even tell you what it's about. She wouldn't want me to. Accept that, please."

He's weeping inside, Freddy thought.

Dan collected himself. "But there's more than that. You and me, I'm talking about. What is it, Freddy? I want to know."

He began. "It's never any one thing, is it? I always thought you thought I wasn't strong enough—"

"Go on."

"I'm not at all like you. Rescuing that woman in the fire, all that hero stuff."

"I never said . . ."

"I know you didn't. But it was there, all the same."

"Is that all? Anything else?"

The memory swelled in Freddy's throat, wanting to be spoken. His father was asking for it, asking. Give it, then!

"Well, there was a day, one day that mattered. I came to the lab after school to tell you something, and you weren't there. You were upstairs. There was someone with you. A woman. I stood and listened. Then I didn't want to hear any more. I ran home."

His father's face flushed. It looked scalded. He was staring at his fingers. "You never said anything."

"I couldn't."

Dan raised his head. His eyes were very bright, glistening. "Freddy, I'm not a bad man."

"I didn't think you were."

"But that day you hated me, didn't you."

"Maybe."

"You must have thought I didn't love your mother. I don't blame you. A child would think that. I loved your mother, Freddy. I still do. You can do things with your body that don't have anything to do with your heart. I don't say it's right. But can you understand what I'm saying?"

I'm expected to say I do. What he's asking for is forgiveness. Not mine to give.

"Mother never knew?" Freddy asked.

"About that day? No."

About that day, he answers. As to other days, he doesn't say, Freddy thought. That's what has gone wrong between them, then? So he's messed things up. Women go for him and he can't help himself. There were guys in the army like that.

"I think I understand," Freddy said. Comfort was in order now.

"Yes?" Dan spoke quickly. "I'm glad. And I want to say—that sort of thing hasn't been the pattern of my life. Just now and then my . . . weakness. But it was always—always Hennie."

"Doesn't she know that?"

"It doesn't seem so."

"It's all so sad. Everything is."

"At least you have Leah. That's something."

"Not that simple, Dad." He couldn't remember when he'd last called him that.

"I suppose it isn't, in the circumstances," Dan said.

"The truth is," Freddy said, "I've lost all my desire for Leah."

Neither spoke for a minute. Then Dan said, "If there's any way I can help by listening, talking . . ."

Freddy shook his head. "Please, not now."

"All right. But don't be too proud to ask advice." Dan stood up. He took Freddy's hand. "I'm sorry about that old business. Sorry about every unhappy minute I may ever have given you. I never meant to, Freddy. I hope you know that now."

"I do." Funny how the anger's vanished, Freddy thought. When he first came in, I was full of it. Now all I feel is the pulse in his hand, and I don't want to let go of it.

"Freddy . . . look, let's not pretend. You and I haven't always agreed, and I surely haven't been what you wanted or needed. But I always loved you, and I always will. And I'm glad we had this talk, and I want to have more talks from now on." Dan's lips grazed Freddy's forehead. "Hey, let me get out of here before I start crying like a woman. See you tomorrow?"

"Tomorrow. Come back."

The swift tread went down the stairs, two steps at a time by the sound of it. And Freddy felt the break of a small smile, the first he had felt in months and months. Rising from someplace close to the heart, it lumped in his throat, and warmed him and spread and filled him, softly, with its grace.

5

PAUL came out of Brooks Brothers and started on his way uptown. He had been feeling what he supposed was generally meant by the term well-being. He had bought new suits; the uniform, cleaned and camphored, had been put away.

There was an April feel in this last week of March—a soft, cool touch in the air, the sight of straw hats in store windows, the feel of walking again on streets that now, in the second month of his being home, were just beginning really to seem like home.

Having promised his father to pick up some papers at his parents' house for perusal while they were on a week's vacation, he swung west and north through Central Park. It felt so good to be back. He was still a trifle too thin, but Mimi was taking care of that, plying him with thick soups and home-baked rolls, mothering him as though he'd been starved, which was hardly the case.

The word mothering set his mind off in another direction. He could imagine Mimi worrying over a child as she now worried over him, fretting about wet feet and proper nourishment. She wanted a child so badly! And it was time, past time. Now that he was safely back, he hoped it would happen.

He came out onto Central Park West and entered the street of solid brownstones that, he supposed, would always be his symbol of home. There it stood, one out of an identical row. He fished in his pocket for the key and climbed the steps.

His mother had left a note on the silver tray in the hall.

> Paul, when you come for the papers, be sure to lock up carefully when you leave. The servants are away with us too.

He stood a moment in the dim hall holding the note. Then, mounting the stairs to the second floor, he went to his father's desk. As he picked up the folder he was to take, the doorbell rang. Now who on earth would be bothering on Saturday morning with the family away? He went downstairs. The curtain over the glass upper half of the door showed a vague shape, a woman undoubtedly, because of the wide hat.

Then he drew back. His heart lurched. He was seeing things! It couldn't be! He opened the door.

"Why, Anna," he said.

His heart pounded, pounded. He had a crazy thought: she had come to upbraid him, to call him the monster that he was. But after six years?

"I have an appointment with your mother," Anna said, looking past him down the hall.

"My mother?" he said. "My mother? She's not here."

"She told me to come this morning at eleven o'clock." Still the eyes looked beyond him.

"I don't understand. My parents are gone for the week."

"She told me to come at eleven o'clock."

Now he saw that her hands in their prim cotton gloves were twisting the strap of her pocketbook in distress, and grief pierced him as if someone had thrust a needle into him. "Come," he said. "She may have left a note. We'll go upstairs and look on her desk."

In the white-and-yellow sitting room he went to the neatly fitted little desk with its matching blotter, calendar, and appointment book. "Look, look here on the calendar! She's written it down. It's next Saturday. You're a week ahead of time."

There was absolute desperation in Anna's face. "I'm sure it was today," she said.

"Well, then, it's my mother's mistake. I'm really sorry." He spoke very gently. "May I ask you what this is about? Is there anything I can do?"

"I was going to ask whether she would lend us some money."

"Sit down, Anna. Tell me."

"But I'm keeping you. You have your coat on."

"Then I'll take it off. I'm in no hurry."

He noticed as she murmured that her accent was much less foreign than it had been. Well, six years had gone by, after all.

"My husband, Joseph, he's a painter, he works very hard. We have a little boy . . . he works hard for the boy's sake. He and an Irishman, a plumber, they work together on houses and they know a lot about building. They have a chance to buy a house."

The voice ran on, pausing for deep breaths like sighs, and he saw that the telling of her story was agony.

"If Joseph had two thousand dollars, he could buy the house, and they would fix it up and sell it. That's how you begin, he says. Oh," she cried suddenly, almost angrily, "I didn't want to come here and beg! Why should people lend two thousand dollars to a person they don't even know?"

"I suppose the only reason is that one wants to. And since I'm sure Mother would want to if she were here, I'll do it in her place."

Anna's eyes were astonished. She had almost surely expected to be turned down; certainly she could not have expected such quick acceptance. Oh, but he needed to do something for her! To give, to prove that he had heart and knew contrition.

"You have spirit and courage," he said. "That's why I want to."

His checkbook was in his pocket. He drew it out and took pen in hand. "What is your husband's name?"

"Joseph Friedman."

"Here you are. Two thousand dollars. When you get home, have him sign this. It's an IOU. You can mail it to me."

She stifled tears. "I don't know what to say."

"Don't say anything."

"My husband will be so grateful. He's really such a good man. The most honest, good man you could know."

Paul thought, What do I care about her husband? I've held her, told her I loved her, and now we're talking about her husband and two thousand dollars. I've carried her picture in my head the way one carries a snapshot in a wallet.

The room was too warm. She had unbuttoned the jacket of her suit. Two rows of spiral ruffles lay between her breasts.

"Tell me," he said, "tell me about your little boy."

"He's four years old."

"Does he look like you?"

"I don't know."

A smile curved her mouth. He had forgotten that her chin had a cleft, a shallow dimple.

"Red hair?"

"No, blond. But it will probably grow dark like his father's."

Something wrenched Paul's chest, almost taking his breath away: a sudden vision of Anna and that other man. He stared at her, at the tiny pearls in her ears and the silk strands of hair that swept past her cheeks, hair that that man could unwrap, loosen, and kiss whenever he pleased.

His heart began to pound again. And he heard himself say, "You're even more beautiful than you used to be. Do you know that, Anna?"

And he heard her answer, "Am I?"

Suddenly it seemed to him that as she sat there, on the feminine couch piled with pillows, she was waiting, entranced; that the same possibility which in this instant had shot through his mind had also shot through hers, a passing dart. . . .

He knelt by the couch and buried his face in her lap. Her hand smoothed his hair. And he raised his head, or was it she who, turning to him, raised his face? The kiss was the longest and the sweetest . . . His fingers found tiny buttons hidden under the spiral ruffles. In a minute all the encumbrances of her silks and his thick cloth were stripped away. He lifted her into the center of the couch and pulled up the quilt that lay folded there, to cover and enclose them. Her warm hair, released from pins and combs, fell over the pillows. Through half-open lids her eyes gleamed, and then closed, and his closed too as they soared together in that bliss which has no name.

When he awoke, they were still loosely entwined and she was still asleep. He slid away to see her better, to examine again the charming round of the shoulder where the quilt had been drawn away. He bent closer, as if to memorize the subtle structure of her face: the high bridge of the nose, the flat planes of the cheeks, the pure skin drawn over the bone, without flaw.

He got up, dressed, and folded her clothes, which lay in a heap on the floor. He went downstairs and stood for a long time looking out to the street. He felt drained.

Then he heard Anna flying down the stairs. Eagerly he went to meet her. But with a stricken expression she fled past him.

"Wait! Wait! Anna, you're not angry?"

"Oh," she said, "angry . . . ? No!"

"What is it, then?"

"What I've done! What I've done!" she cried out.

He wanted to understand, and thinking perhaps that he did understand, he said, "Anna dearest, you've done nothing wrong."

"Nothing wrong? I have a child. A husband."

He tried to take her hands, but she pulled them away. "You've done them no harm. My dear, my dear."

She fumbled with the latch. "I have to get out! Let me out!"

"Don't go like this. Please, sit down a minute, let's talk. Please."

But she was frantic. The latch gave, the door crashed open, and she flew past him down the steps. He started after her and then restrained himself. She was half hysterical and would resist him; there would be a scene and that would be worse for her.

Helplessly he watched her race away. Then he trudged back up the stairs. In his mother's sitting room he rearranged the quilt and pillows, and stood looking at the place where, only a few minutes before, Anna had lain, all fragrant, pink and white. In a storybook, he thought, one would read, It was like a dream. But this was no dream; it was real and true, the truest thing that had ever happened to him. He felt a lump, a sob, in his throat. And he thought, I will see her again. This isn't the end. It can't be.

He left the house and began to walk home through the park. He felt tense, stretched like a spring. He could not stop remembering how it had been.

Her face had been illuminated in that moment when she had

told him of her little boy. "Dark, like his father," she'd said, and once more that frenzy took hold, that unreasonable rage at the unknown man to whom she belonged.

But I am more fortunate than he, thought Paul. More powerful, since through sheer accident it happens that I do not have to ask anyone for money. I could do so much for her. . . . I can persuade her to leave him. I know I can. She can be persuaded.

He hastened his steps. His mind was sharply focused now.

There was so much grandeur and wonder in the world! And so little time. So long to be dead, and so many already dead in France, all young and able to love, who now never would.

Take it all while you can. Take life!

6

"Do come with us to the antique show," urged Leah. "Alfie and Emily go every year and it's fun."

Ben Marcus said, "I'll lift the wheelchair into the station wagon. No problem at all."

Freddy firmly refused. "I don't want to go, I said. But you all go. I don't mind."

Leah worried. "What will you do?"

"I'll read. I've three new books here on the seat."

"I'll take you for a walk to a different spot," offered Meg. "So you won't have the same view from this porch."

"Good idea, Meg," her father approved with cheer. "All right, then, you'll be company for Freddy. We won't be long anyway."

Down the gravel path they went, along the garden's edge and through the apple orchard. Strong young trees flanked the path in even rows, forming diagonal alleys as far as one could see.

Birdsong quivered in the trees, and the open air was laced by their swoops and darts. The dogs padded ahead, the tall setters prancing and the new dachshund puppy panting to keep up with them. For a moment, before his life surged back upon him, Freddy felt the marvelous wealth of spring turning into summer.

"Well, now, here we are," Meg said brightly. "This is a good shady spot where you can read. There's even a little breeze."

Meg placed the chair. Below, through a screen of moving leafage, the pond gleamed; flat as a silver plate it lay, decked with a ragged fringe of lilies. "There! Now you can enjoy your book."

"But you have nothing to read," said Freddy. "I don't think you'd like any of these books."

"That's all right. I'll just think."

She sat down and leaned her head against a pine trunk. Without seeming to watch Freddy, she could watch him. How unthinkable not to be able to run across a field, to have a whole life like this ahead, knowing that nothing would get any better! But at least he had Leah! And she was so lovingly careful of him, always fixing his pillows, fetching things for him.

Oh, how terrible it must be for her to have had the man she loves come home to her like this! It would never—how could it ever?—be romantic again.

The day drowsed. The dogs slept on their sides, twitching as they dreamed. There was hardly a sound, except for the flick of a turned page every minute or two.

Abruptly Freddy closed the book. "Come over here, Meg, and we can talk," he said. "You know, I remember when you were born. And the first day you got up and walked, it happened at my house. Your parents were visiting."

"I always loved going to your house. I love your mother."

"She loves you too. She thinks you're like her, inside."

Meg sighed. "And Leah. I wish I had a sister like her. She's so sweet and so pretty. Mr. Marcus . . . Uncle Ben—he told me to call him that—says she reminds him of Pola Negri. Once, when they were at the opera, he heard somebody whisper that's who she was."

"I didn't know they'd gone to the opera."

"Yes, before you came home. They saw *The Girl of the Golden West*, I remember, and Leah said it would have been better if it had been sung in English instead of Italian."

"That's probably so." Freddy's tone was oddly flat, and he looked very tired.

He was her responsibility. "Shall I take you back now?" she asked anxiously. "Would you like to rest?"

"No, let's stay. This place reminds me of a summer afternoon in

England. Oh, England was wonderful that summer! It was a paradise—a fool's paradise."

"Why was it a fool's—"

"Hush!" Freddy commanded sharply. Twisting his head to one side, he strained to see through the shrubbery.

Surprised, Meg followed his gaze. "Oh, that's Leah and Ben. They're back. . . ."

He turned on her. "Quiet, I said!"

Not understanding, she obeyed. The little breeze had subsided, and in the dead stillness voices carried distinctly across the pond.

"A magic spot, isn't it?" Leah said. "You would think you were miles away from another human being."

"I wish we were," Ben answered.

"I know, darling, but it can't be, so there's no use thinking about it."

Meg made a little sound in her throat. Freddy grasped her hand, hurting it. His expression was so—so awful! But rather than see what he was seeing, Meg stared at him.

When she did look back through the leaves, Leah and Ben were clasped together. Meg was frozen, horrified and fascinated. Their lips were fastened as if they did not want to come apart.

Now came Leah's voice again, high and clear. The two had separated. "Not here. Are you completely crazy?"

As the lovers walked out of the picture the voices blew away, but not before the man's voice was heard saying something about "New York" and "Tuesday."

Freddy let go of Meg's hand. Her fingers were numb, so that she had to rub them; a terrible fear washed over her. How could Leah? How could she? Then Meg remembered her responsibility.

"Shall we go back, Freddy?" she asked, not looking at him. And without waiting for his answer she turned the chair about and wheeled it up the path.

Suddenly Freddy flung out an arm. Meg stopped and came around to see what he wanted. Red blotches had come out on his forehead. He clenched his fist, and involuntarily she stepped out of his reach.

"Don't you ever, Meg, don't you ever say anything to anybody about this!"

"I won't tell, Freddy, I promise I won't."

"Well, see that you don't. Because if . . ." He did not finish. He let his arm drop to his lap and lowered his head. The books slid to the ground.

Meg picked them up and slowly, with great effort, pushed the wheelchair up the slope to the house.

From the porch, there sounded a pleasant babble and the clink of teacups. Leah's voice, cheerful and gay, rose over the rest.

"Goodness, where can Freddy be? Meg must have taken him on a sightseeing tour!"

HENNIE awoke from vague, oppressive dreams. A rooster crowed far away. It must, then, be almost dawn, she thought. A light rain began, then, turning heavier, struck at the windowpane. She lay still, listening, caught for a few moments in a trance of comfortable forgetfulness.

Reality swept back. In the room across the hall lay Freddy; Leah and Hank were in a room apart, for Freddy slept poorly and must not be disturbed. What was to become of him? The same constant, futile question. There was no answer to it. Or else there was an answer all too clear: fifty or sixty years more like this.

Sighing, Hennie fell back into half sleep.

When she awoke again, a swath of light lay across her face. The rain had stopped. There were voices below in the kitchen wing; the day had begun in Alfie's house.

The door to Freddy's room was being opened. Someone, either Ben or Alfie, was coming to lift him into the wheelchair and prepare him for the day. She thrust the blankets aside, got up, and began to dress. Freddy's door was opening again; they would be leaving to fetch his breakfast tray. She hurried, pulling her sweater on—

A terrible cry tore through the house like a gale wind and stopped Hennie's breath in her throat. Something went clattering, bumping . . . down the stairs? Thud and crash, smash as of ripping wood and screeching metal . . . And an animal howl.

She flung her door open; every door in the upstairs hall was open; people were screaming and scurrying. Hennie ran to the top of the stairs. Alfie and Emily were already halfway down.

And at the bottom, oh, almighty God! At the bottom, heaped and crumpled and broken, lay the wheelchair with its wheels still spinning, while Freddy . . . Freddy lay still. Sprawled, bloody and still, with his arms flung out.

Someone covered Hennie's eyes with a hand and forced her to turn away. Pinned to the wall, she fought to struggle free.

"What happened? How?"

"He was alone; he did it."

"Leah, don't look, get back!"

"Meg, go to Hank, close his door. Keep him away."

"Get the doctor! An ambulance!"

Alfie rushed back upstairs. "Somebody take care of Leah. No, Hennie, you can't go down, Ben and I will handle it. Hennie, no!"

"Help him," she heard herself whisper.

Alfie's voice was quiet and sad as he held her, still pressed against the wall.

"Hennie, he's dead."

MANY people came. From her bed she heard the house door opening and closing below; there was constant traffic on the stairs. People stood around her bed, and someone—it must have been a doctor—said, "Take this, it will make you sleep."

When she awoke, blinking, someone was sitting beside her.

"It's all right. I'm here," Emily whispered, taking her hand.

Hennie's speech was thick. "Where's Leah?"

"In bed too. The doctor gave her something."

"Poor Leah."

Hennie turned her face away into the pillow. A spasm shook her, but no tears. There was only a pressure inside, a terrible pressure that must be relieved if it was not to explode in her.

She jumped up, thrusting Emily away. "I have to go out!"

"You can't, it's raining again, you mustn't, Hennie—"

She was already in the hall, going down the stairs, past the spot where he had lain in his blood. But they had cleaned it; a silky golden Oriental rug lay on the floor at the foot of the stairs.

Emily beseeched her. "It's pouring, Hennie."

She ran out. The rain lashed her. She flung her arms around a tree, leaning her cheek on the bark, not caring that it scratched and hurt. Why, Freddy? We were caring for you as best we could. We would have cared for you always. Isn't life worth anything, even without legs?

Two hard hands took her by the shoulders. "You can't stay out here, Hennie," Ben Marcus said gently. "You're soaked through."

She allowed him to lead her back inside the house.

There was some sort of commotion in the living room; it stopped when Hennie and Ben came in. Dripping wet, she stood in the doorway. Then she saw that Alfie had a piece of paper in his hand and that Leah was crying.

"What is it? Give it to me," Hennie said, for Alfie had tried to hide it behind his back. "It's from Freddy, isn't it. Give it to me!"

There were only a few words, in Freddy's hand.

> I have lost everything. I hope you will be happy with Ben. He is more of a man than I am.

"What does this mean?" Hennie cried.

No one answered.

Meg shook, with tears running down into her mouth. "I didn't mean to tell! I didn't want to make trouble, but when they found the note, it just came out, what we saw yesterday at the pond—"

Leah spoke. "It's all right, Meg. You have every right to tell what you know."

Hennie looked wildly from Leah to Ben. "You—you two?"

Leah pleaded, "It's not what it may seem, awful as it is. The truth is that I would have stayed with Freddy for as long as either one of us lived. I would never have abandoned him."

A great hot hand clenched its fist in Hennie's chest. "Abandoned him?" she repeated. "You only killed him!"

"I would never have left him, I tell you!"

"You—do you think your lover would have waited forever? No, you would have left my son to wither! Have you forgotten? I took you into my family. You're a murderess!"

"You must believe Leah," Ben said. "Yes, I want to marry her more than I've wanted anything in my life. But we would never have hurt him, as much as we love each other."

Hennie ignored him. "Oh, Dan will want to kill you! He was right about you. He was right about you, Leah."

Her raging anguish mounted, and she moved toward Leah. Alfie caught her arms.

"Hennie, hysteria won't help. Come upstairs with me. Dan has been summoned. He's the father and must take charge."

"I don't want Dan," she sobbed as he led her stumbling up the stairs. "Not Dan. I want Paul. Get Paul for me."

"Yes, yes, we're trying to reach him. I've left a message."

"I'LL be out all day," Paul told his secretary at midmorning. "I've got about six stops to make."

His mind was prepared for the varied clients, bankers, lawyers, and brokers whose challenges he would meet. He was wound up, coiled tight. So he was glad of a day like the one ahead, in which he would keep moving.

He finished his last call at four o'clock. He knew he ought to go back to the office, where surely a desk piled with messages would be waiting, but the restlessness was upon him once more. He wanted the refreshment of open space and more motion.

At Fifty-ninth Street he entered the park. The sun had hidden behind a ceiling of cloud, and in the west the sky was livid. They must all be having a wet day at Alfie's place, he thought as he walked on through a soft gray mist.

Emotions that had been dammed up now came swirling back. The recurring images were dizzying and contradictory. Anna on the couch, eyes gleaming under lids like petals. Anna rushing down the stairs, wild-faced. So terrified.

But by now she must have calmed enough to think it over, to recollect and weigh. Surely in these weeks she must have been thinking and, just as he was, asking herself, What is to be done?

Everything, everyone, the whole world was conspiring to keep apart two people who only wanted to be together. From the beginning all had conspired!

To hurt anyone was the last thing he ever wanted to do, but there were some things one had to have, no matter what. And Anna was one of them.

For two months he had been puzzling, scheming, and discarding schemes. She had no telephone. A letter was obviously too risky. He'd even had a faint foolish hope, knowing better all the time, that Anna might make the first attempt. Oh, there must be a way; somehow it must be done. Carefully, oh, so carefully!

He left the park at Seventy-second Street and Fifth Avenue. When he opened his front door, Mimi was waiting in the hall. All the world's sorrow was in her face as she came to him.

"Darling, I don't know how to tell you. Freddy is dead."

7

PERIODICALLY during these last few months since Freddy's death, Paul had been going downtown to visit Hennie. The neighborhood was almost unrecognizable from the one he had known when he was a child. Gone downhill, it was poorer and dirtier. Anyone who could possibly do so ought to leave it. Certainly Hennie could, but she chose not to.

Paul and Hennie sat in the dim parlor. He had a feeling that the place hadn't been dusted. The shades were askew on the windows, and the potted ivy, once so exuberantly green, was dying.

"What are you thinking?" he asked gently, for Hennie, who had not spoken, was staring out the window.

"I was thinking of the funeral. The cemetery. Freddy. In the end it comes down to a simple grief. But I can only cry, Why? Was Leah worth it? Worth taking his life?"

Paul knew no comfort to give. Is life always worth living? How could he know otherwise when for him, in spite of everything that weighed so heavily now, the future loomed gloriously because he would make it be so? But it must remain a mystery for anyone who hadn't been where Freddy had been. Paul only knew that he was sitting here with a poor woman who wanted an explanation, and he had none to give.

"You're alone too much," he said abruptly. "Something has to be done about you."

"I long to see Hank," she said. "I haven't seen him since—since it happened. But I will not go to that house. I despise her, I can't look at her. That's one thing Dan and I have in common."

"You'll be surprised to learn there's been a great change. Dan visits there almost every day."

"I don't believe it! He's not forgiven her, has he?"

"I don't know anything about that. We haven't talked about it."

Forgiven her, he thought. So they had done, all of them in the family, if one could call a discreet silence on the subject of the "other man" forgiveness.

"Did you know Leah has given up all her widow's rights to the money?" he said now. "Everything has been put in Hank's name."

"I don't believe it," Hennie said again. "Leah loves money."

Once, Paul recalled, she had praised the girl for her ambition and industry. We see only what we want to see.

"Leah wants to move," Paul added. "But Dan won't allow it. He wants the house kept for the child."

"I should so like to see Hank," Hennie murmured as if she were speaking to herself. "He must have forgotten me."

"Do you know what I'll do?" Paul said. "I'll arrange a time when Leah won't be home and you can see Hank. And I'll meet you there."

HE HAD Dan's habit. Hennie watched the boy push back the glossy dark hair that fell like a bird's wing over his forehead.

Three-year-old Hank was on the floor with Paul, building a tower of blocks. Autumn sunshine fell over the corner in which they sprawled, warming the bright room, a child's world. Everything was proportioned to a child's dimensions, from the red chairs and table to the closet rods on which hung rows of little pants and jackets, and a velvet-collared overcoat.

"Let me show you how I can catch." Hank scrambled up and took a large ball from a shelf. He gave it to Paul. "You stand over there, Uncle Paul."

"Can you catch from this far away?"

"I can! You'll see I can!"

Paul tossed the ball and Hank caught it neatly. "I told you I could!" He shone with glee.

"Who taught you how?" Paul asked him.

"Uncle Ben. He takes me to the park and we play ball."

That stranger, Hennie thought. Taking his father's place. . . .

The clock struck. "It's time for my lunch," Hank announced. "When those two hands both stand straight up, that means twelve, and lunch. I'm hungry too."

"You're always hungry, you are, bless your soul." A neat woman of middle age, who wore a white uniform and moved briskly, had come in with a tray.

Paul made the introduction. "Mrs. Roth, Scotty. She's really Miss Duncan, but she likes to be called Scotty."

"Come, now," said Scotty, setting the tray on the table. "Here's your nice lamb chop, and Mrs. Roedling made ginger cookies. Now be a good boy and go wash your hands."

She had a nice face, this woman who had taken Hennie's place, who did for the boy what she had always done. Impulsively Hennie said, "I'm glad he has you, Scotty. Especially since he has a mother who spends no time with him."

"Oh, no," Scotty said, surprised. "His mother is wonderful. And when you consider that she goes to business— Why, I've been with families where the mothers don't do anything all day but go to luncheons and tea parties, and don't do half as much with their children as Mrs. Roth does."

Thus politely rebuked, Hennie flushed, and was about to sit down with Hank, disregarding the nurse, when voices came floating up the stairway. The voices belonged to Leah and Dan.

Hennie was furious. This was Paul's trick to get me here, she thought, following him as they skimmed down three flights of carpeted stairs. "How could you have done this to me?" she whispered angrily at his back.

"I swear I had no idea. There's been some misunderstanding over time. I swear it, Hennie."

Leah and Dan looked up from the foot of the stairs. Hennie had quick impressions: Leah, sober and delicate in slender dark gray, a kind of half mourning, and Dan, looming in an attitude of protection.

For a frozen moment no one spoke. Then Paul said, "We were just leaving."

Hennie moved toward the front door. She was shaking.

"You're not coming up to see Hank today?"

She heard Leah's question and Dan's reply.

"Tomorrow. I can't now. I only wanted to deliver these for you to sign. They're the final papers," he said. Then he called out, "Hennie," and almost automatically she turned around.

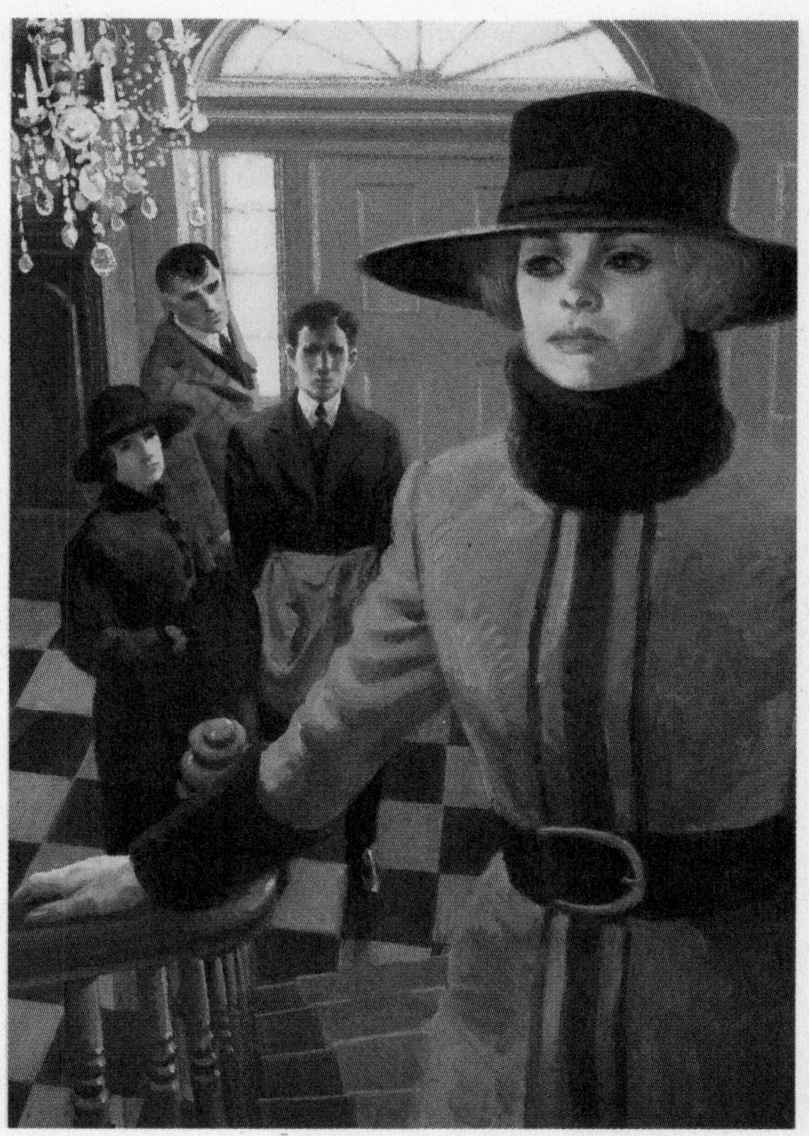

"Hennie, I think you ought to know that with these papers Leah is signing away her rights to everything, including this house. It's all to belong to Hank."

"Yes, admirable of her. Isn't that what I'm supposed to say?"

Leah said quietly, "I don't care anymore about your good opinion, Hennie. I know I've lost it. And life's too hard to struggle to be where you're no longer wanted." She gave a little shrug, a gesture of regret, wistful and rather charming; then she turned and went up the stairs.

Grand lady, Hennie thought.

The three walked eastward toward Madison Avenue; Paul went between Hennie and Dan.

"I'll never forgive you for this," Hennie muttered, knowing that Paul must have heard, although he went on talking to Dan.

It was Sunday. Women in furs and men in chesterfields and tall silk hats strolled and greeted and swung their malacca canes. And here was Dan in the same old winter jacket.

"Any place around here to eat lunch?" Dan inquired.

Paul said with some hesitation, "You can get a very nice lunch just a few blocks down. It's in a hotel, but . . ."

Dan grinned. "A bit fancy for me, you're saying, but we'll try it anyway."

"I'm not in the least hungry," Hennie said. Did he actually think she was going to sit at table with him?

"You need to eat, Hennie," Paul remonstrated. "And I'm hungry too. So come on."

He had a hand on her elbow, steering her down the street.

The hotel's lobby shimmered with flowers and smelled like spring, oblivious to the chill outside. Paul propelled her into the dining room and almost pushed her into a seat. Immediately a waiter came, hovering with pad and pencil. The two men ordered.

"I'm not hungry," Hennie said again.

Dan ignored her. "The lady will have a small steak, medium rare," he said. "A baked potato. And French dressing on the salad."

She was miserable and humiliated. Dan was trying to meet her eyes; she wouldn't allow him to. But he was not to be put off. "Well, Hennie, I hope you're surviving."

"I'm surviving."

"We're lucky to have Hank. He's all that's left."

The waiter brought rolls and butter. No one touched them.

"Well, isn't anyone going to say anything?" Dan asked.

Now she looked over at him. The vertical lines in his forehead were deep-cut grooves of anxiety. And she was moved to speak.

"Yes, I'll say something, Dan. I don't understand this business between Leah and you. After what she did to Freddy, how is it possible that you can forget? You, who never cared for her anyway? I can't begin to remember all the things you said—that she was all wrong for Freddy . . . And now it turns out that you were right. So I can't understand you at all."

"I wasn't right, and I wasn't all wrong either. I wonder whether you can understand that? Because with you things are either black or white, nothing in between. Would you, would any one of us, have expected Leah to turn down her inheritance?"

The waiter came back. In silence, impatiently, they watched him serve the food. When he had gone, Hennie said, "She took away my son's last reason to live, she broke his heart, and you make a saint of her because she doesn't want your money!"

"I make a saint of Leah?" Dan grimaced. "Hardly. But do you have to approve of a person one hundred percent to give him a chance? Fair is fair, that's all."

"So now it's you who've become a saint."

Leaning across the table toward Hennie, he spoke in a low, passionate voice. "Surely you know I'm not. Only try to remember what it is to be young, Hennie. This fellow Ben comes along. . . . Can't you feel for her? Flesh and blood, man and woman . . ."

"Don't make a spectacle of yourself," she warned.

"The flesh! You don't understand it! But I do!"

"Yes, well you do. Every woman you see . . . All the years, wherever we were, you thought I didn't notice. I've been so humiliated by your silly flirting—I hated the way you behaved."

"Why didn't you say so? Why didn't you kick me under the table or give me a dirty look?"

"I wouldn't lower myself."

"Ah, you see what I mean? You're not like other people. The average woman—Leah, for instance—would have spoken her piece, gotten mad, been honest about her feelings."

"Leah again. The woman who killed our son."

"Hennie, please," whispered Paul, who was miserable.

Tears came stinging. She pressed her lids shut. Damned tears again, here in this public place!

"That's not true," she heard Dan say. "He killed himself. Yes, she took a lover. But at bottom he killed himself because he despised living. He had no more desire for Leah, and I think he hated himself for it."

"And how do you know all this?" cried Hennie.

"I talked to him. And Leah told me. She had to let somebody in the family know how things were between her and Freddy, and I was the logical one, I guess."

"She lied! She lies to excuse herself! Do you believe this, Paul?"

"I don't think Leah lied, Hennie," he said very quietly.

"We've been too righteous, both of us," Dan said. "Even our own situation, Hennie. If I could have dared to tell you the truth in the beginning— I'm willing to wager you've never told anyone why—" And as Hennie, in spite of herself, gave him an intimate warning look, he added, "Paul can hear, as far as I'm concerned."

Dan looked steadily into her eyes. She looked back. Let him be the first to look away.

He turned to Paul. "I once did a terrible thing to Hennie. She can tell you if she wants to."

Flushing, Paul shifted uncomfortably in his chair.

"For a woman so practical in so many ways, my wife is a childish romantic. She thought I was a knight on a white horse, and I was only a fallible man."

"Please," Paul said. "I don't know what this is all about."

"You know something," Dan said. "Sometimes I think I don't know either. Anyway, I hope Leah marries Ben. Maybe they'll be luckier than we, and last their lives out together. He's a decent sort. He's lending her money to open a business of her own, and he loves the boy. He'll be good to them both."

"You hope she'll marry Ben!" Hennie cried. "And Freddy not five months in his grave. I don't care what you say, she left him when he needed her."

"You left me when I needed you, Hennie."

"I left you! This is outrageous!"

"Not here in this place," Paul remonstrated.

Dan touched Paul's arm. "You're right. It's not fair anyway, dragging you in."

"Paul, I must get out of here. I must," Hennie insisted.

Dan stood up. "Never mind. I'm leaving. Here's my share for the lunch." He drew some bills from his wallet, the same old wallet he'd always carried, Hennie saw. He looked down at her; she felt that every eye in the room must be on them.

"Wake up, Hennie." He spoke very quietly now. "Be human, learn to forgive. I don't care about myself anymore, but Leah—she's suffered, she's got courage, and she's the boy's mother."

Hennie watched him walk away.

SHE didn't stir from the apartment all that week. She slept, got up to eat some food, and slept again.

It had taken all that time for wrath to spend itself, and now there was only a tiredness so profound that she had no will. Occasionally she talked to herself, sometimes even actually speaking the words aloud; that's what happened to people who lived alone.

It has to be admitted that Dan has never been afraid of the truth. He used to say of Leah, quite frankly, that he didn't like her. Yet he was always fair to her. And now he defends her. He asks me to remember what it was like to be young. I'm not that old now, am I? Why should he think that I can't remember?

Leah said she would never have left Freddy. I didn't believe her. Still, maybe she wouldn't have. She was never a liar. So she would have stayed with my son and had her lover too. It's done all the time, isn't it?

What a terrible thing, to live without loving or being loved!

Why did you do that to me, Dan? I was so happy with you. Whatever else went on around us, still I was happy with you. That's where the center was. . . . You looked so lonesome walking away from Paul and me. I hated you, and still I could see how forlorn you were. Your eyes reproached me.

I have that look in my eyes too. I see what I am, and I'm afraid of what I see. I'm just forty-six, but I'm stern-faced and straight-lipped, a woman who knows no desire, only the memory of it.

And yet I have it in me still to desire. That day at Alfie's, that terrible day when we got the news about Freddy, there was that man Thayer, in the gazebo in the rain. I refused him. But with part of myself I didn't want to refuse. Because it was wonderful, yes it was, without even liking him. So it could have been that for Dan and that girl, couldn't it, just as he said it was? So long ago . . .

And if, like Leah and her young man, you do love, how much harder to deny, to refuse.

So Hennie spoke to herself as she paced the floor.

A ball rolled out when she chanced to bump into a chair. Hank's ball, left behind in the move. When she picked it up, she remembered how his hands looked, how the short fat fingers clutched.

She walked into the room that had once been Freddy's. Nothing had been changed in years. Dim in the lamplight, it looked like a tomb in which all the possessions of the dead had been stored to accompany him to the next world. She raised the shades to let in the daylight. It fell over the austere bed and over the table, where the last books he had been reading before he left still lay: a text in Greek and the poems of Emily Dickinson.

She stood there stiffly.

What am I doing?

Terror was at her back, lurking in the empty rooms. And she flung the window open as if to escape it. From the street below, life came sweeping up: a child crying, an ashcan clattering. And the peal of laughter. Even here, in this ugly place, the sound of laughter and life.

Oh, God, what have I done?

She went to the telephone. Her voice quavered and cracked so badly that the operator had to ask her to repeat the number. And when the connection was made, she could scarcely whisper.

"Dan. Please come back."

AFTERNOON sunlight, turning toward evening, lay over the bed where they lay. They had loved, they had slept, and now at last could let words flow as they wished, random and free.

"I'm so glad to be in this bed again, Hennie."

"Yes, yes, Dan."

"I'm thinking, Hennie, that maybe we should move away from here. We could find a small apartment uptown in Yorkville. We'd be only a few blocks away from the boy. What do you think?"

"I think I'd like it."

"I could give Hank piano lessons when he turns four. That's not too soon to start."

She got up on one elbow and looked at Dan. The grooves had been miraculously erased from his forehead; he looked boyish.

"Hello!" he said, laughing.

"You're home again! Aren't you hungry?"

"I haven't had anything since breakfast."

"Then I'll get up and make you something."

When they had eaten their supper in the kitchen, he in his old place and she in hers, he went to his usual chair and read the paper. She went to the desk and began to write.

After a while Dan put the paper aside and got up. "What are you writing?" he asked.

She covered the paper with her hand. "Nothing much. Clarifying my thoughts. I thought it would be good for me."

"Will you let me see it?"

She removed her hand, and over her shoulder he read:

> We own nothing and no one. Our children grow up and go away, and sometimes they die before we do. Yet we continue to live. For these few years are all we have. So let's take what there is, since we can't make more. I had a son. I had a lover too, a large man, brave and good, who has done good things in the world, and I have him still. I don't want to be without him ever again.

Dan pulled her from the chair and opened his arms. His eyes were wet. "Has it helped you to write it all out?"

"I think it has."

"Then tear it up and throw it away. Oh, Hennie, Hennie, it's a new start."

On the sidewalk outside the restaurant, Paul had parted from Hennie in deep distress. Such bite and bitterness in her! So unlike the Hennie he had known all his life.

And Dan so subdued . . . Paul had a quick flash at the front of his mind, an instant's recall of Dan standing high up someplace and people crying out, people clapping. Courage, Dan had.

Still, they were destroying each other. As if Freddy's death were not enough to bring them together. And yet how can I judge? Paul asked himself. Someone looking at me wouldn't guess the first thing about what's happening inside me.

A little boy, walking between his parents, went past with a sailboat in his arms; they were going to the park. *She* had a boy the same age. Her boy wouldn't be sailing a boat in Central Park, though. Paul didn't think there was anyplace to sail a boat in the part of the city where she lived. Then his mind recalled the address on Fort Washington Avenue from which the husband's IOU had come. He hadn't intended to memorize the address, but it had obviously stuck in his memory.

He walked on toward home. He looked at his watch; it told him that the afternoon still had a long way to go.

The garage in which he kept his car was just down the street from his house. He stood in front of it uncertainly. Suddenly the decision made itself, and he went in and asked for his car. He got behind the wheel, put on his driving gloves, and swung westward.

He went all the way up Broadway to where Fort Washington Avenue slanted up on his left. He was aware of his leaping heartbeat, but he kept going until he had parked the car on the opposite side of the street from Anna's house.

He glanced up at the house, wondering which of the windows were hers. Which was her kitchen? Did she sing while she worked? Which was her bedroom—their bedroom?

He felt like a thief, snooping and sneaking. He wanted to see her and was afraid that he might. It was foolish to sit there. And glancing through the rearview mirror, gauging the space to back away from the curb, he saw her.

She was walking up the little slope; her hand was lying in the crook of her husband's elbow; their little boy was pushing a tricycle. Paul ducked his head as they passed. He was shaking. They went ahead and crossed the street. The wind blew her hat loose and she took it off to refasten the pins; her red hair glistened before she covered it again. He saw her laugh, turning her mouth up to the man's answering laughter.

The three of them stood a moment with their faces turned to the sun. Then they climbed the steps of their house, the man, the woman, and the child.

Up there behind one of those windows Anna would be getting the supper ready. The husband would probably be playing with the boy. Paul wondered whether the real estate deal had gone through. The fellow was certainly ambitious; he was trying. He was thinking ahead for her and for their child.

How can you just walk in and blow the man and his hopes sky high? How can you do that? Take his home, take his child . . .

Paul forced himself to put the car in gear and move away. Oh, the turmoil! The turmoil! Hennie and Dan, Leah and Freddy, Anna and—

Anna wouldn't. She wouldn't do such a crazy thing, wouldn't make chaos out of order. No, Anna, sweet Anna, we don't belong in each other's lives.

He brought his car back to the garage and went home. Mimi had just come in.

"Well, how was your day?" she asked.

"Upsetting." And he told her about Hennie and Dan.

"I'm so sorry, darling. There's been too much trouble around you since you came home, with Freddy and all this business between Hennie and Dan. I know how much you love them. I'm sorry, darling. I hope they straighten themselves out."

Her eyes were wide with concern, and this concern gave her a look of extreme tenderness; he could imagine how she would look if he were ever to do anything to wound her.

"You'd think," she said now, shaking her head, "you'd think we might all have learned something at least from the war, if we didn't know it before."

"And what is that?"

"To be better to each other," she answered simply.

Something struck at his heart and he cried out, "Oh, Mimi, dear girl, I'll never hurt you!"

Her eyes were puzzled. "Hurt me? Of course you wouldn't."

He laid his cheek against her hair.

Choose life, that thy children may live. The ancient words from the prayer book shot through his head. Nourish and build, they meant. Heal, they meant. Inflict no pain. All that are born under the sun, let live to flourish under the sun, and disturb no peace.

8

THE birthday cake stood on the dining-room table between two crystal bowls filled with jonquils.

"Four candles," said Leah, "and one to grow on. There'll be a children's party tomorrow," she told Hennie, who stood next to her. "But today I wanted the whole family alone together."

She looked around the room with satisfaction. "And now Great-grandmother will cut the first piece," she said.

Angelique was pleased. She gave the first piece to Hank and beamed while everyone sang happy birthday.

"It's too bad," Dan remarked at Hennie's elbow, "that Uncle David couldn't have lived long enough to see this."

Hennie nodded. Uncle David would have been glad to know she and Dan were all right together. Yes, really all right this time.

"And special congratulations to you, Leah," Paul was saying now. "Would you ever have dreamed five years ago that you would be opening your own establishment on Madison Avenue?"

Leah answered promptly, "Yes," and everyone laughed.

"I'm to be known, in business, that is, as Léa. One has to be French to get anywhere in my business. But it's going to be really beautiful, thanks to Ben's generosity."

Ben grinned. "I'm not really all that generous. After all, it will be mine too, since we're being married next month."

"There's one clever girl," Alfie said to Hennie. "Never went to college either, any more than I did. It just goes to show you."

Meg had brought her plate of cake and ice cream and drawn up a chair next to Hennie. "I don't know what it goes to show," she complained when her father's attention had been directed elsewhere. "I've been accepted at Wellesley and I want to go, Aunt Hennie. Mother doesn't think that girls need college. She wants me to go to a finishing school in Switzerland. Worse than that, she'd like me to be a debutante. I'm not the type."

No, Hennie thought, regarding the girl's sweet, earnest face. You're not, any more than I was. And she said quietly, "I've always been sorry I didn't go to college. Maybe I can persuade your parents. Oh, they're opening presents, let's go see."

Ben was holding Hank aloft, carrying him to the library. The boy's arms were swimming in the air and he was crowing.

Leah's boy, Hennie thought with an instant's jealous dismay. Still, he had Freddy's luminous smile. She strove to bring back and never to let elude her even the most subtle detail of the living Freddy: the lake-blue eyes, the barely noticeable separation between the two front teeth. Remember those, not the bloodied body at the foot of the stairs.

Dan was on the floor opening toys. There were so many beautiful things! Trains and cowboys, wonderful books, and a huge stuffed kangaroo from Florence and Walter.

How strange it is, Hennie thought as always, to see Dan here in this rich room, with all the expensive presents. The money was coming in floods. Most of it was from Dan, but some would be coming now from Leah too, who would also, indirectly, be making money out of the war, out of a new class of rich women.

Money coming in floods. She hoped that it wouldn't affect the lovely child. Still, it hadn't changed Paul. And she glanced over at the sofa where he was sitting with his wife. The baby was due any day now. They looked very happy.

Paul caught Hennie's glance. He looked from her to Dan and back, and he was glad for them. Plainly their trouble was over. He watched them all; his parents were talking to Leah and Ben, and he smiled to himself, reflecting that his mother would be one of Leah's best customers.

Yes, this was a day to be glad of; the family was together and healed. And he thought of Freddy; he would be glad too, if he could know.

Hank was dancing, holding the kangaroo by the paws. And the thought of having a child of his own like him, very soon now, filled Paul with a gratitude that seemed too much to contain. He caught and held Mimi's hand.

Dan struggled up from his knees.

"A beautiful boy," Paul said.

"Yes, and he'll never suffer his father's fate." Dan sighed. "Thank God we've seen the last of the wars. Never again will young men go off as my son did, puffed up with false heroism." He sighed again. "We'll have the League of Nations this time. Did you know Hennie's been making speeches for it? I heard her the other night. She was marvelous."

"I had a letter the other day from my cousin Joachim," Paul said. "The first I've heard from him. He philosophizes. He had a stomach wound, got the Iron Cross too, but he feels fine again, and he's very optimistic. The country's a shambles, he says, but the German spirit will build it up like new."

The dachshund came in from the dining room with a stolen piece of cake and crawled under the piano, reminding Paul of the day they had bought that other dachshund. They'd carried it back to the inn in Freddy's pocket. A hundred years ago, that was.

"I'm optimistic too," Dan said. "Man is learning. Civilization is advancing." And he waved his arm around the room. "Yes, a better world."

Paul questioned himself: Why do I think he is naïve? Am I any wiser than he?

Mimi shifted on the sofa. Immediately Paul was concerned. "Are you feeling anything?"

"No, nothing yet." She smiled at him, and he thought he had never seen her look as beautiful as she was now.

It was growing dark. Someone turned up the lamps, and a tender pink light flowered. It circled the room to touch each member of the gathering, each so separate and distinct from every other, joined now in one of those rare, quick moments when amity and hope and love are fulfilled.

One's heart had to go out to them all.

ABOUT THE AUTHOR

"The relationship of people to their time and place is very important to me," says Belva Plain. As do her four previous best sellers, *The Golden Cup* paints a searing portrait of a family caught in a crucial moment in history. Not a surprising combination for a Barnard College history graduate who believes that "the family has been the most important thing in my life."

Belva Plain

Belva Plain began publishing short stories when she was twenty-five but waited until her three children were grown before she allowed herself the opportunity "to give a novel all the time and thought it needs and deserves." In 1978, at the age of fifty-nine, she wrote her first novel, *Evergreen*, which became an instant best seller. Though three other books come between, *The Golden Cup* returns to the world of *Evergreen:* this time she tells the romance of star-crossed lovers Paul and Anna from Paul's point of view, while *Evergreen* was all about Anna.

The author's own romance began when she fell in love with Dr. Irving Plain, an ophthalmologist, "because he looked so much like Charles Boyer, the actor." Their marriage lasted forty-two years, until her husband's death in 1982. But Mrs. Plain finds that "if you've had a good marriage, it gives you the strength to go on living and do creative work."

Her joy now comes not just from writing, but from being lucky enough to live "within walking distance of my two married daughters and six grandchildren," in suburban New Jersey. Methodical at her craft, she writes every day of the week but Sunday, and is now at work on a novel that will follow Paul, Leah, Meg and Hank through the Roaring Twenties and the Depression to the end of World War II. The world she describes so memorably in *The Golden Cup* is, happily for her many fans, not one she is ready to leave.

PHOTO BY JERRY BAUER

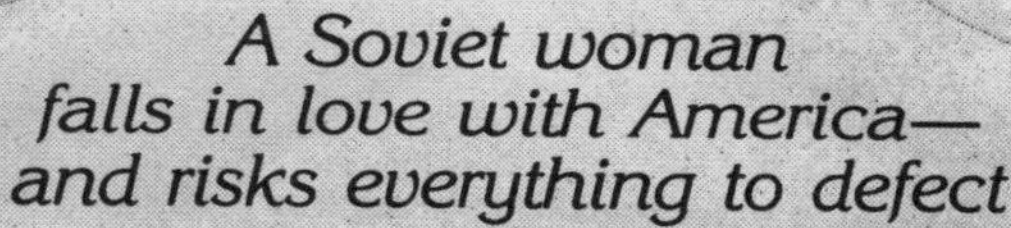

A Soviet woman falls in love with America— and risks everything to defect

Stepping Down from the Star

A CONDENSATION OF THE BOOK BY

Alexandra Costa

Illustration by Chet Jezierski

Her name was Yelena Mitrokhina, and she belonged to Moscow's privileged elite. She was the daughter of a Soviet air force officer, the wife of a well-placed Soviet official, and she taught at a prestigious Soviet institute. In short, she had the best that Russian life could offer. But then her husband was assigned to the Soviet embassy in Washington, D.C. And that's when Yelena discovered America—discovered opportunities she never knew existed, choices she never knew she had.

To be an American, to raise her children as Americans, became Yelena's dream. The question was, could she persuade her husband to defect with her? And could she act before the KGB put an end to her plans? Here, in her own words, is the remarkable true story of a courageous woman who risked everything for the chance to be free. . . .

Anastasia, tell me who you are,
Are you someone from another star?
—"Anastasia"

Chapter 1

ON THE morning of August 2, 1978, my husband, Lev Mitrokhin, left for work around nine, as usual. The Washington office of the Soviet copyright agency was on K Street, but first he planned to stop briefly at the embassy, one and a half blocks away. The weekly Aeroflot flight from Moscow had arrived the day before, and there would be mail for us there—both from our Moscow office and from our relatives. I asked him to call me as soon as he got to the office, to let me know if there'd been a letter from my mother.

My request was not unusual. Letters from home were treasured and eagerly awaited. Nor was it unusual for me to ask him to come home for lunch, as I had that day. I said I needed the car to run errands in the afternoon, and since we were the only people in our small office, nobody checked on his whereabouts or absences. Although we were formally attached to the embassy, where Lev held the diplomatic rank of first secretary, we ran the copyright agency more or less independently.

For me, however, that morning was anything but usual. The day had been planned weeks in advance, and it was crucial to my plan that I receive Lev's call—to make sure that he was in the office, a twenty-minute drive away, and that he would indeed return home for lunch. Today was the day that would change my entire life forever—even my name would change. I was defecting from my country and asking for asylum in the United States. The operation had been in preparation for months, and now I had less than three hours to change my mind if I wanted to.

Most of my belongings were already packed. We were scheduled to return to Moscow in September, and I'd been gradually sorting things out and putting them in boxes in preparation for our departure. Actually, I had been doing this not for me but for Lev. Whether he decided to defect with me or not, he would not have much time to pack. If he stayed, we would have to act fast; if he did not, he would be sent home on the first available plane. For myself I had only a couple of suitcases with clothing for me and the children, a box with a few of my favorite records and tapes, and some memorabilia from home.

The final packing did not take long, and I settled down to wait for Lev's call. Time moved so slowly. I picked up the newspaper, then put it down. I could hardly comprehend what I was reading. The children played quietly. They were mere toddlers—Kitty was three and a half and Konstantin one and a half—and I wished I had more adult company to help me pass the time.

There was a knock on the door. My heart leaped. Who could it be? The FBI had been renting an apartment upstairs for several months, and I was supposed to go there after I got the call; but no one was supposed to risk coming to my apartment. What if it was the KGB? What if they had found out after all, despite all the secrecy, despite all the planning?

Trembling, I opened the door—and saw Jim's smiling face.*

"Moving company, ma'am," he said. "Ready?"

"Yes," I said, sighing with relief. "Please come in."

"Lev is parking his car at the office," he said casually. "Won't be long now. Thought you'd like some company."

His cheerful mood made me feel better. Of course the FBI would leave nothing to chance. All Lev's comings and goings would be carefully monitored. These people knew their job.

We spent another half an hour drinking coffee and smoking. Despite Jim's cheerfulness, I felt that he was nervous, which was unusual. Jim always appeared to be easygoing; with his medium

---

*The events in this story are true. However, the names of a number of people, including FBI and CIA personnel, have been changed.—The Editors

height, sort of homely looks, soft brown eyes, and slightly receding hairline, he was the kind of guy you see on the street every day. He was rather tense now, though. After all, nobody had ever defected from the Soviet embassy in Washington before. It was a major operation for the FBI.

Finally the phone rang. It was Lev.

"No letters," he said. "Not much from the office either."

"Okay. I'll be leaving now," I answered, trying to sound as casual as possible. I'd told him the night before that I'd been invited to have tea with our neighbor, an elderly lady with whom I'd become friendly. "And try not to be late for lunch," I added.

"One o'clock," he said. "See you later."

I took a last glance around. Everything was in place. On the dining table two white envelopes leaned against a flower vase, positioned to catch Lev's eye as he came through the door. One was a letter to the embassy, with the formal announcement of my intention to stay in the United States; the other was for Lev, explaining my motives and asking him to stay with me.

My heart was pounding and I began to feel slightly faint. "Let's go," I told Jim. I picked up my son and took my daughter's hand; Jim picked up a basket containing the children's toys, baby food, and diapers. We took the staircase up to the second floor. Jim would get the rest of the things later.

The door to the apartment opened the moment Jim knocked. We'd obviously been expected. Several men were there. I knew one of them, John, my very first contact. It was comforting to see a friendly face. In the beginning I'd been a little scared of him. He was over six feet tall, and his round face with dark, penetrating eyes, closely cropped dark hair, and normally stern expression gave him a rather hawkish look. In time, however, I'd learned that those dark eyes could also be filled with warmth and laughter. I'd come to trust him completely.

The two men sitting at the dining-room table I had not met before. They were introduced as Larry and Craig. Larry was concentrating on something that looked like a portable radio and barely gave me a glance. He was very tall, with reddish blond hair and pale blue eyes. He fitted the image of FBI agents exactly—unsmiling, deadly efficient, and dangerous.

I sat at the table, and John brought me a cup of coffee. He knew I needed it, as well as a cigarette. "You look pale," he said.

"I don't feel well," I said. "I've got this terrible heartbeat, and I don't know what to do about it. I hope I won't faint."

"That's all we need," Larry said. "Why not take a sedative?"

Jim was going downstairs to pick up the rest of my things, and I told him where to find some. He was back in a few minutes, and I took the pills. Gradually the heartbeat subsided. By then Larry had finished his radio conversations. He smiled, and suddenly there was nothing menacing about him.

"Feel better?" he said. "Now, for the last time— Are you sure?"

"Yes."

Was I sure? At that moment I felt that I was.

The reasons for my defection were so many, so complex, that it was difficult to sort them out or to decide which was the most important. My marriage had been steadily deteriorating, my concern for my children's future back in the Soviet Union had been steadily growing—yes, those had both been important factors. But the primary factor was that after almost three years of living and working in the United States I'd begun to appreciate the opportunities that people had here for taking control of their own lives. I was thirty-four, well educated, and had had a good job back in the Soviet Union, but for several years before coming to the United States I had experienced a feeling that my life was following a predetermined pattern that was being laid out by somebody else. It was not until I came to the United States and started dealing with American businesses that the perception finally took shape. What was missing in my life was the ability to make my own decisions. It was simply not possible in the highly regulated, bureaucratic Soviet society. I wanted to become a part of the business world here—to try things on my own and maybe make mistakes but at least achieve something on my own merit.

My thoughts were interrupted by Larry's voice. "I'm still not sure about the letters," he said to Jim. "It would be better if she just left a note asking him to meet her outside, and then gave him the letter to the embassy. What if he calls the embassy first?"

"I know my husband better than you do," I said. "He is not going to call anywhere until he talks to me."

"While we're on the subject," Larry said, "are there any weapons in the house?"

"Only kitchen knives. Besides, if you think he will try to kill me, that's ridiculous."

"You never know," he said. "We'll have to trust your judgment, but we're not going to take any chances. Now, let's go. We don't have much time."

We went downstairs with the children to the main entrance. Out front was a taxicab. To my surprise we went straight to it.

"It's less conspicuous this way," John said, catching my puzzled look as we got into the cab. The car windows were open, but the hot August air inside was suffocating.

"Where are we going?" I asked Jim. It was eleven o'clock. I knew we would be back by one to meet with Lev, but that's where my knowledge of the plan ended.

"It's not far," he said. "We'll just take the children to a safe place and then we'll bring you back."

The drive was indeed short. Several miles west on Route 50 we pulled over to a motel. In the motel room were three people—two men and a blond girl in a nurse's uniform. She was introduced as Linda, a baby-sitter. One man was an agent; the other was from the Immigration and Naturalization Service. He had the papers that I had filled out a couple of months before: a request for asylum for myself and my children, and an application for citizenship. The man asked me to raise my hand and take an oath, and then to confirm that I was acting of my own free will. It was not until the man shook my hand solemnly and said, "Congratulations, you are now a permanent resident of the United States," that it finally dawned on me that this was the moment I had been waiting for during all those months of nerve-racking danger.

The INS man left. I gave instructions to the baby-sitter about feeding the children, and we left them with the agent who'd been in the room when we arrived. Larry, John, Jim, and I got into a car parked outside and drove back to the apartment building.

There was another car waiting for us in the parking lot at the rear of the building. Larry parked ours so it could not be seen from my apartment. It was only a few minutes after noon. We walked over to the patio. Through the door I could see my letters on the table. I could go back in, throw them away, and pretend that nothing had happened. Nobody in the world except me and the FBI knew how I had spent that morning. I could ask them to bring the children back and call the whole thing off.

As if he had read my thoughts, John took my hand. "Everything will be fine," he said. "Don't worry, we are with you." He paused, and then said, "What do you think he will do?"

"I just don't know," I said. This was not the first time we had tried to figure out what Lev would do when I told him of my decision. Although John assured me that my safety was their only concern, I knew that it would be a major political coup for the FBI if he defected. I did not have the answer. I had been married to Lev for seven years. He was a complex man, brilliant and unpredictable. There was a chance he would stay with me, but I also knew that his soul was deeply rooted in Russia. Other circumstances also would influence his decision; although I was taking our children, his beloved daughter from his first marriage was in Moscow.

Did I want him to stay? I did not have an answer for that either. Our marriage was faltering, but not dead yet. Whatever happened, it would be his decision.

One of the agents in the other car motioned to us to come back. He had received a message that Lev had left the office and was on his way home. I began to feel my heart flutter again. The other car was apparently equipped as a communications center. Messages began coming rapidly: crossed the bridge . . . five blocks away . . . two blocks away . . . pulling into the parking lot . . . went into apartment . . . found the letters . . . reading . . . coming out!

I gripped John's hand and went to face my husband.

Chapter 2

OUR assignment to the United States had been through an unusual route—Lev was not a professional diplomat. The opportunity had presented itself when, in 1973, after many years of pirating foreign books and films, the Soviet Union had finally signed the Universal Copyright Convention. The convention, which had existed for many years by then, provided protection of copyright and compensation for authors in all countries that signed it, and most countries had. But not the Soviet Union. There, books of foreign authors were translated, and printed in hundreds of thousands of copies, and the authors never got a penny for it—until the government finally decided it was politically expedient to go along with the convention.

Basically the decision was a by-product of détente, a gesture to show the Western world that the Soviet Union was a civilized country that complied with international standards. Shortly thereafter a new governmental entity was formed—the All-Union Copyright Agency, known by its Russian abbreviation, VAAP. The agency was granted the power to open foreign offices to handle all exchange of copyrighted material, to promote Soviet publications abroad, and to make recommendations on the choice of foreign works to be published in the Soviet Union.

The chairman of VAAP was Boris Pankin, a former secretary of the Central Committee of Komsomol—the Soviet Young Communist League. He had his own vision about who would represent his agency in key foreign countries. He did not want any bureaucrats. He wanted to have people who were thoroughly familiar with the culture of each country. He approached my husband, Lev, who had been his classmate at the university and later his deputy secretary of propaganda in the Komsomol Central Committee, to be the VAAP representative in the United States.

Lev had impressive credentials. After graduate study in philosophy, he had chosen a party career and had quickly risen through the ranks to a high position in the Central Committee of Komsomol. At that time he changed direction. He was contemplating a divorce from his first wife, which would immediately become an impediment to his career in the party, so he decided to go back to the academic world, which was more permissive in terms of people's personal lives. Two years later, by age thirty-six, he had a doctorate in the social sciences and was on the fast track again. For the next ten years he specialized in modern American philosophy and the history of political movements, published several books, visited the United States and England many times as part of academic exchanges, and became fairly well known in his field among the American academic community.

Lev was pleased with Pankin's offer but declined at first. At the time, he was a deputy director of the Institute of Philosophy of the Soviet Academy of Sciences, the most prestigious body for social research in the Soviet Union, and just then the social-research community was embroiled in a bitter factional fight between the old generation of dogmatic Marxists and the younger, more liberal social scientists. Lev felt that leaving Moscow then would give the old guard an opportunity to place their man in his critical position in the institute. He also had a personal reason for declining the offer—Xenia, his eleven-year-old daughter from his first marriage.

My own view was exactly the opposite. It was 1974. We'd been married for three years, and I knew the situation in his institute very well. I felt that the tide of euphoria over liberalization of the social sciences was ebbing. There was a confrontation brewing. It was safer, I argued, to sit it out in the cozy comfort of a foreign assignment until the dust settled.

On the personal front I had my own reasons for wanting to leave Moscow. Sonya, Lev's ex-wife, was making continual demands for more money. The Soviet law regarding child support is very clear: twenty-five percent of the ex-husband's salary to support one child, thirty-three percent for two, fifty percent for three or more. A quarter of Lev's gross income, coupled with Sonya's own salary, came close to what my father, an air force colonel, was making. It wasn't enough for her, though. Sometimes she used Xenia as a weapon. Lev would pay his weekend visit and have to run out to the grocery store because he found an empty refrigerator and Xenia told him that she was hungry.

Those Sunday visits took a heavy emotional toll on Lev. He would get moody and irritable and start drinking on Saturday in anticipation of the scenes he would have to endure the next day. Sunday night he would come back depressed and drink heavily. Monday was recovery day. We were expecting our first child, and I resented the fact that I had a normal family life only from Tuesday to Friday. Most important, I felt that the situation with his former family aggravated his drinking problem, and I hoped that removing him from that environment would help him.

In addition, I was worried about the future of my own job. Until then my life had been progressing smoothly. I'd grown up in a comfortably well-to-do family in Leningrad. Although my father was in the air force, he was never a field officer. From the beginning he was attached to the air force academy, based in Leningrad, and we lived on the same street the whole time I was growing up. After graduating with honors from high school in 1960, I was accepted by the University of Leningrad, where I majored in Scandinavian languages. For a year after graduation I worked as a translator at the patent bureau—a tedious but non-taxing job. Then I went to work at the Leningrad branch of the Institute of Philosophy, whose director was a prominent researcher in family sociology. He hired me as a research assistant, with the promise that I would have enough free time to pursue my graduate degree. Within a year I took my qualifying exams and started to work on my dissertation, comparing the effects of women's professional work on their family life, in the United States, Sweden, and the U.S.S.R. In 1970 I transferred my graduate study to the Moscow Institute of Sociology because I wanted to be closer to Lev, and there completed my degree.

For the past two years I had been teaching Marxism in a special institute for foreign students, where all subjects were taught in native languages. My degrees in Scandinavian languages and sociology, considerably reinforced by Lev's connections, had gotten me the job in this very privileged institution, which had its own foreign-goods store and commissary—perks that even my husband did not have. Another benefit of my work was the unusual degree of freedom permitted the instructors in teaching even such dogmatic subjects as Marxism.

Marxism is a mandatory subject in every college in the Soviet Union. The teaching is extremely rigid and consists mainly of standard interpretations of works by Marx, Engels, and Lenin. The students essentially memorize proper answers and a few quotations, and that is enough to get them through the exam.

That kind of teaching was not possible in our institute. Our students mostly came from Western countries and were very well informed on world events—and not necessarily from the Soviet perspective. They were all members of foreign Communist parties, but that did not preclude critical thinking on their part. In

Mother and me at age two months, 1944.

order to be believable, the instructors had to do some thinking as well. Although we could not deviate from the party line, we tried to avoid the most obnoxious dogmas and were expected to be able to defend our statements with logical reasoning in open classroom discussions.

We were encouraged to socialize with our students and spend some of our free time with them in the school cafeteria or during informal gatherings at their dormitories. And that eventually became my undoing. I became very friendly with a group of Brazilian students and began spending a lot of time with them, although I was not their instructor. One day my friend Marina, who had worked at the institute longer than I had, took me aside.

"Your Danes are complaining that you are neglecting them by spending too much time with the Brazilians. They'll get you in trouble, you know."

"My Danes are nothing but a bunch of snooty kids," I said. "Besides, we are told to be friendly with students."

"There are some rumors," Marina said, "that your relationship with one of the Brazilians is more than friendly."

I was stunned. Nothing could have been further from the truth. I was solidly and happily married. "That's ridiculous," I said. "Who is going to believe it?"

"The KGB."

I disregarded the conversation, but Marina was right. The Danes did complain at the end of the year. The head of my department, one of Lev's closest friends, warned me that the clouds were gathering over my head and recommended an extended leave after the baby was born. I thought a foreign assignment was an even better solution.

On top of all those reasons, I knew that since we were not professional diplomats, this might be our once-in-a-lifetime chance to spend several years in the United States—a country in which I had considerable interest. And to pass up the opportunity would be plain stupidity.

Finally, with help and cajoling from both families and friends, we reached a compromise—Lev would accept the post, and we would take Xenia with us to the States. We started preparations for our trip.

The first thing to do was to get as many tips as possible about life in the United States from our friends. We needed to know a

My father in 1952.

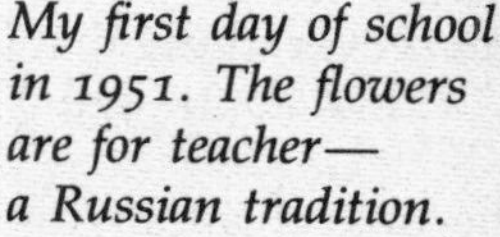

My first day of school in 1951. The flowers are for teacher—a Russian tradition.

myriad of practical, everyday things—what to take with us, how to behave in a strange country, what to watch out for.

Our friend Gennady had been assigned to Washington a few months before, and we knew we could count on his help there, but he was not planning to visit Moscow before our departure. Therefore we turned for advice to our neighbors, Eugene and Lilian, who had spent six years with the Soviet mission in New York. Although they had returned to Moscow in 1968, things could not have changed that much in a few years.

Lilian undertook the task of coaching me in practical household matters. "Do not take too many clothes," she said. "Take only enough to last for a few months, because you will have to buy a whole new wardrobe there."

I was surprised. I had always been well dressed by Moscow standards, and the store in our school had a good selection of foreign-made clothing.

"Don't misunderstand me, I am not saying that you look shabby." Lilian laughed. "It's just that you look . . . maybe too European. Americans dress . . . Well, you'll see it when you get there. Besides, clothes are cheap there, and if you sell most of what you have here for even half of what you paid for it, you will net a tidy amount of cash. Also sell your stereo system. You can't take it, because the United States is on different voltage."

At least I did not have to worry about furniture. We did not have any. Lev had left his apartment, with everything in it, to his former wife, and we were renting a furnished apartment from diplomats who were abroad. In theory, you cannot rent apartments temporarily in Moscow. Either you get an apartment from the state or you don't. There is, however, a booming business in private sublets, mostly apartments of people who are away from the city for a couple of years. We were paying about twenty-five times more than a state apartment would have cost us.

"Take all the dishes, pots and pans, and everything that is non-electric that you need for the kitchen," Lilian continued. "Those things are relatively expensive there."

As we talked, the basic philosophy became clear: anything that was inexpensive in the States but had high market value in Moscow had to be disposed of; things that were relatively expensive in the States had to be brought from home to conserve valuable foreign currency. After our three-year tour in the States we should have saved at least enough for a car.

Lilian went through the list of favorite shopping places where the prices were best. Orchard Street in New York City was the best source for buying gifts for relatives and goods for resale at home, but things there were too cheap and outdated to wear at the embassy. For better things, go to Hecht's. Always keep an eye on sales in good stores. Sometimes you can get real bargains. We spent days going through minute details until, armed with the long list, I set about rearranging my personal possessions and packing.

Eugene gave us a different kind of briefing.

"First of all, try not to follow any patterns," he said. "Your apartment and your car will be bugged—there is nothing you can do about it. If the bugs are removed, the CIA will get suspicious and you will only get more surveillance. Do not do anything to irritate them. They are just doing their jobs.

"Obviously you know better than to discuss any embassy business in the apartment," he continued. "But what some people don't realize is that the Americans can use your personal relationships and whatever family disagreements you may have either to blackmail you or to try to recruit you. So if you want to quarrel, go for a walk."

I was beginning to feel nauseated. "But how can you live in an apartment where you know that everything you do, everything you say, is heard by somebody else?"

"You get used to it," he said. "Besides, there are even some advantages." He recounted an anecdote, popular in the diplomatic community, about a wife who was constantly nagging her husband to buy her a fur coat. One day he came home and found a thousand dollars on his desk, with the note "For Pete's sake, buy her that coat!" We laughed, but an uneasy feeling persisted. Was it really such a great idea to live in the States?

"What about provocations?" I asked. "I've heard about people being lured into compromising situations and then photographed."

"Not too much of that anymore," he said, "although they won't miss an opportunity if you get yourself in a mess."

He told us several stories of diplomats who had been photographed drunk in public, or even in bed with prostitutes. "In most cases, however," he said, "those people got themselves in such situations by their own stupidity, and then later tried to blame it on CIA setups. But sometimes they still want to create an incident. So if you have a habit of stopping in a bar for a beer after work, change bars all the time. If you go to the same place, they may recruit the bartender to slip something into your drink and then create a public disturbance."

The more I listened, the more depressed I got. What kind of a place were we going to?

WE ARRIVED at Washington's Dulles Airport on August 24, 1975. Our friend Gennady met us at the airport. My very first impression of America was a feeling that I had stepped into a sauna. I was unaccustomed to the heat and humidity that are typical of Washington's summers. Although temperatures in Moscow occasionally reach ninety to ninety-five degrees, the climate is much drier and the heat more tolerable. It was a relief to get into an air-conditioned car—another alien thing, since Soviet-made cars do not have air-conditioning. The size of the car was impressive, and I thought that it must require quite an effort to handle it. Watching Gennady turn the steering wheel with what appeared to be just one finger, I could not help but ask him how he did it.

"It's not me." He laughed. "On cars of this size the steering and brakes are power enhanced."

The car slid smoothly out of the airport and onto the Capital Beltway. Things got more and more confusing. I expected to see an "industrially developed" country as traditionally described in the Soviet press: buildings crowding one another, heavy smog. Instead, I saw mostly open space, clusters of trees, occasional high-rise buildings and small houses, and very blue sky. I asked Gennady how far away from the city we were.

"We are *in* the city," he replied. He caught my puzzled look and added, "It'll take some getting used to, but we'll guide you through the first days. It happens to everybody who comes here for the first time. We all help newcomers to adjust."

The embassy had arranged for us to stay temporarily in the apartment of an embassy family that was on vacation in Moscow.

It was located in Riverdale, a Washington suburb. There were other Soviet families in the apartment complex, and everything was ready for our arrival. Gennady and his wife had even done some grocery shopping for us, and we found that the basic necessities were already in the refrigerator. On a coffee table was a box of disposable diapers—another new thing—for our baby daughter. Gennady only waved aside our offer to pay for the shopping. "Forget it," he said. "What are friends for?"

Within minutes, the apartment was filled with people from the embassy, each bringing something for the table, and we had a welcoming party. We were prepared, too. Before we'd left Moscow, we'd been told that certain simple things from home, such as black bread, salted herring, and smoked salami, were always in demand in the Soviet colony abroad, and we'd brought a generous supply with us. We put it all on the table, and I saw the nods of approval from the people around us. The party lasted several hours, with people coming and going. Although we were completely exhausted from the long flight, our friends explained that they were keeping us up intentionally in order to break the jet lag. Otherwise the eight-hour time difference would be felt for days. The trick worked—we slept soundly and got up at the normal Washington morning hour.

Gennady arrived soon after breakfast to take Lev to the embassy for introductions. Before they left, he said, "First thing you have to do is buy a car. Without it you are helpless here. I will make arrangements with our senior mechanic to take you to the dealership."

The men left. I cleaned up the apartment and tried to get familiar with the things in it. I figured out fairly quickly what a few containers on the kitchen counter were for. Most appliances were familiar. The stove did not look all that different from the one we had had in Moscow, although I would have to get used to the fact that I did not need matches to light it. Soviet stoves do not have pilot lights. The toaster was similar to the one I had used in Moscow. Earlier, Gennady had shown me how to use the coffee maker.

As I started to do the dishes I realized that nothing on the counter seemed to be dishwashing liquid. I took the soap from the bathroom and used that. It also seemed strange that there was no rack or some other place to put clean dishes to dry. I started looking in the cabinets and discovered that one of them had several rows of drying racks. I put the dishes in and called my new acquaintance next door, a woman named Valentina, to tell her I was ready to go shopping. She came over, and we started making a shopping list. I mentioned dishwashing liquid. "But you have a whole box of dishwasher detergent," she said, and pointed to one of the boxes that I thought was a laundry detergent. Seeing incomprehension in my eyes, she laughed. "Of course, I forgot," she said. "You know, after you spend several years here, you begin to forget all the things that do not exist back home." She opened what I had thought was a cabinet with racks. "This is a dishwasher. Here you don't have to do dishes by hand." And she showed me how to use the machine.

My first reaction was embarrassment. I was a worldly woman by Moscow standards. Our apartment had been well equipped; we had had access to many things that were out of reach for most of my countrymen. I had traveled to several foreign countries as a tourist. And yet I could not figure out some of the obvious, everyday things in this rather modest apartment. What next?

"Next" turned out to be the supermarket. At least half of the items simply did not exist in the Soviet Union. The produce and household-goods aisles were most confusing. I did not even know that so many varieties of fruits and vegetables existed on earth. The household goods took at least half an hour to go through, while Valentina patiently explained the merits of such things as plastic wrap, "quickie" floor mops, and myriad other items. I had already been introduced to the wonder of disposable diapers the night before, but the selection of baby food and instant baby cereals stopped me dead. In Moscow, having a baby meant hours of labor every day: washing diapers, cooking cereals, grating and mashing fruits and vegetables by hand. All of a sudden it occurred to me that having a baby here did not mean being tied up in the kitchen for half of every day. What a wonderful surprise! I realized that in this country you could have more than one child and still have time and energy for other things in life.

Another incredible thing was that I could buy everything in

one place, have it packed in bags, loaded into the car, and be home in an hour! In Moscow I often had to go to several different stores to do my grocery shopping: the bakery, produce store, general grocery store, and on and on. Even in larger stores that had produce and bakery departments, each one had its own counter and, naturally, its own line. Someday I would calculate how many years of my life I had spent standing in lines and doing household chores, but I already knew that this country was giving me the greatest gift I could dream of—my time.

But the most amazing thing was the profusion of color. Color, color everywhere. Things *looked* pretty. Soviet life is essentially colorless. The consumer products are generic and look the same everywhere. A bar of low-grade household soap is invariably brown; a better hand soap is always pink. A typical grocery shelf in the Soviet Union resembles the generic-brand section in an American supermarket—plain paper with dark lettering on everything. There is no need to make things attractive. If you need something, you buy it no matter how it looks. Things such as butter and sausage are not prepackaged at all. If the item is solid, it is cut, weighed, and wrapped in plain paper at the counter. For things that cannot be wrapped—such as sour cream—it is necessary to bring a container from home. All this weighing and wrapping at the counter is time-consuming and creates those infamous lines so often described in the Western press.

The scarcity of man-made color does have at least one positive effect. Russians are very appreciative of the beauty nature provides, and they try to make it a part of their lives as much as possible. The first fragile flowers appear on the streets of Moscow early in the spring, sold on the street corners by private entrepreneurs from the southern republics. From then until the end of fall there are tiny flower markets everywhere. The flowers are not inexpensive, since most of them come from private sources, but people buy them anyway. In Moscow it's not the migrating birds that signal the spring; it's people carrying the first bunches of yellow mimosas.

This lack of color partially explains the fascination Russians have with foreign goods. Not only are the products better, they also look pretty and brighten up your apartment. It is not unusual to keep containers from foreign-made hair spray in the bathroom, or a dishwashing liquid in the kitchen, long after the contents are used up, just for decoration.

By the time we got home from the supermarket my head was spinning from all the new information I was trying to absorb. And as though conspiring to finish me off, Gennady had already made arrangements for us to buy a car the same afternoon.

Buying a car in the Soviet Union is an experience that could rival anything Kafka ever put on paper. You have to live through it to believe it. It has to be planned long in advance, much as young couples in the States plan for their dream house. My particular encounter started in 1967. The local newspapers announced that on January 20 the automotive store in Leningrad, where I lived with my parents, would be signing up people who wanted to purchase a Soviet version of the Fiat 124, called the Zhiguli.

There was only one automotive store in Leningrad, a city with a population of four million. There was no need for another—the cars were allocated by quota throughout the country. This store's annual quota was six hundred cars.

The line started to form on the eighteenth. The sign in the store window directed people to the back door, where there was a large empty lot capable of holding crowds.

By the time we arrived on the evening of the nineteenth, our number in line was somewhere over twenty-five hundred. Volunteers from the line were keeping track of arrivals and conducting roll calls every hour. Anybody who missed the roll call was struck from the list. It was about twenty below and almost impossible to stay in place. People were bundled in several layers of clothing and used their ingenuity to keep themselves warm—some with coffee mixed with brandy, some with vodka straight from the bottle. Most came in families, with members taking turns out in the cold while the others warmed up in heated staircases of nearby buildings. There were only two of us—my mother and I—but we struck a deal with a couple next to us to take turns on the roll call so we could spend less time exposed to the cold.

By seven in the morning the crowd had grown to more than four thousand people. The store opened at eight. Sign-up cards were distributed quickly. All we needed to do was to fill in our names and addresses, hand the card over, have a number assigned to it, and go home. Within three hours our turn came. Our number was now 1856—apparently some people had left the line during the night. I was jubilant; in three years I would be able to buy a car. It did not matter that I did not have nine thousand rubles—I doubted that many people in the line did.

Once a year during the next three years, I received a postcard from the store requiring me to appear in person to confirm my registration. Finally, in 1970, notification arrived that I could purchase my car. By then I was living in Moscow, but my permanent residence was in Leningrad, so I was still eligible.

I did not have nine thousand rubles, however. After lengthy negotiations, my father agreed to lend me half the sum. I was planning to marry Lev, and he had the means to repay the debt. Under the worst circumstances, I could always resell the car. It just did not make sense to have gone through the registration process and not take advantage of it now.

The Soviet Union has no financial system from which people can borrow money—banks, credit unions, or anything like that. The only source of financing is friends, and money is constantly borrowed and repaid. It is always a gentleman's agreement, and no interest is charged. Primarily the habit developed from the fact that most major purchases cannot be planned in a timely manner but depend on supply and luck. It was not uncommon to get a phone call from a friend who was strapped for money and found herself in a store at a time when an imported refrigerator or piece of furniture was announced to be available for sale. Since most of those commodities sold out in a matter of hours, the only way to cope was to get a cashier's reservation, usually good for an hour or so, and start calling friends to see who had money on hand. A couple of times I had to catch a cab and deliver money to someone at the other end of the town. My friends did the same for me more than once.

It did not take long to collect the necessary amount, and soon I was the owner of a shining new Zhiguli. For two weeks I happily drove it around Moscow. Then Lev and I broke up. Angry and frustrated, I contacted a friend of mine who was not an unfamiliar figure in the Moscow black market and asked him to help me sell the car, splitting the profit fifty-fifty with him for his services as a mediator. Selling a car in the Soviet Union is an easy way to make a profit, since there are always people who want to buy one but cannot do so legally, either because they live in remote places where the allocation of cars is next to nothing or because they have illegal income, which quite a few Soviet people do, from moonlighting or taking bribes.

It took my friend only two days to find a buyer who was willing to pay nineteen thousand rubles for my Zhiguli, and I paid off my debts. Soon Lev and I reconciled and decided to get married. I had my fiancé back, but the car was gone.

Obviously, I did not expect to find anything close to that car-buying nightmare here, but I did not expect what I saw either.

Oleg, the embassy senior mechanic, who was in charge of car purchases, took us to an Oldsmobile dealership where the embassy bought most of its official cars. At the time I could not tell the difference between one car and another. I had seen American cars parked in front of the American embassy in Moscow, and they all looked the same to me—long, sleek, and elegant.

The salesman, introduced as Derek, greeted Oleg as an old friend. We walked to the new-car lot, and there I got my second shock of the day. There they were—rows of long, sleek, shining cars. Just walk in and pick one!

"I want a silver one," I managed to say.

The salesman started to explain the standard features of a Delta 88, most of which did not make any sense to me. Finally he said, "What options do you want on your car?"

Options?

I was saved from total humiliation by Oleg, who said, "We'll take it out of stock, and there is only one silver car." He then launched into price negotiations, which made me even more confused. At last the salesman started to write a bill of purchase.

"You can pick up the car tomorrow," he said.

"We'll pick it up in three hours," Oleg replied, and without listening to Derek's protests, he shook hands with him, took me to his car, and drove away.

"Why do we need the car today?" I asked. "I don't have a driver's license yet."

"You'll have it by the end of the day," he said. "The traffic department will simply issue you a license on the basis of your Soviet one. Of course, I will drive your car to Riverdale, and you'll need to practice a little, but I want to pick it up today so they won't have too much time to tinker with it."

He explained then that since the embassy bought most of its cars in the same place, a routine assumption was that the FBI would be notified as soon as we left, and be given the opportunity to go over the car and to plant bugs. The less time they had to do it, the less likelihood that they would plant anything too sophisticated. So everything Eugene told me in Moscow had been right—we could expect surveillance and intrusion in our private lives.

Oleg was right about the license procedures. It took less than fifteen minutes. I was not even given a driver's test.

My real test came the next morning. I decided to drive to the supermarket by myself.

It took me about twenty minutes to maneuver the car out of the parking space. It was twice as long as any car I had ever driven, and the responsiveness of the power steering and brakes was scary. It must have been a hilarious sight—the car was swerving, moving in fits and starts, and every time I hit the brakes it came to an abrupt stop. It took another twenty minutes to cross the street to the shopping mall. By the time I found a spot in the mall that had at least three unoccupied parking spaces on either side, I was drenched in perspiration and my hands were shaking.

Amazingly, I was not as scared on my way back. I even took a drive around the block and finally—the ultimate challenge—made a left turn at a traffic light. I arrived home proud and convinced that I was ready to face the American way of life.

My confidence was crushed the very next day. Kitty, my seven-month-old baby daughter, had developed a mild fever, probably from the change of food and water. I called the embassy and got the name of an embassy-approved pediatrician.

The doctor's office was on Connecticut Avenue, some ten miles from Riverdale. I looked at the map and decided to stick to major highways rather than try to find my way through the maze of streets. My plan was to take the beltway to Connecticut Avenue, and then drive a few easy blocks to the doctor's office. The route seemed to be easy and straightforward. How can you miss a major highway like the Capital Beltway?

Very easily, it turned out. I knew we were only a few blocks from the beltway and in which direction I should drive. As I approached what I thought was the beltway entrance, I saw a large green sign high above a major highway and happily set on my way.

I drove almost half an hour before an uneasiness began to creep in. In my estimate, I should have passed the Connecticut Avenue exit by then. The signs were now few and far between, and the highway seemed almost deserted. Kitty was whimpering; I had not anticipated a long trip and had not brought her bottle.

At last I saw a car on a road shoulder, pulled over, walked to the man checking under the hood, and asked him to show me where I was on the map. He looked at the map and said that it was the wrong one. I thought he did not understand what I wanted and tried again. Finally he looked at the license plate of my car, and between that and my broken English probably figured it out.

"Lady," he said slowly, "you are outside of this map. You are two miles away from Baltimore. If you need to go to Washington, you have to turn around and go about thirty miles back."

My initial reaction was panic. One of the first things we'd been told was to observe the twenty-five-mile limit on travel from the center of the city that was imposed on all Soviet diplomats. I'd heard a lot about American agents following our embassy people around. If they'd seen me, would I get in trouble, or would they believe that I'd simply gotten lost?

I thanked the man, made a U-turn, and began to drive back. Kitty was crying in full voice now and started trying to crawl out of the portable crib that was strapped to the front seat next to me. For a while I tried to keep her down with one hand while steering the car with the other. Finally desperation overcame me. I stopped the car and burst into tears. For a few minutes we cried together. Then by some miracle she quieted down. I put her back in the crib, started the car, and after ten more minutes saw the Riverdale exit. I decided not to tempt the hand of fate and to go home while I knew where I was. We never made it to the doctor's that day. And I realized that it would take many days and more mishaps to get used to the American way of life.

Chapter 3

WE STAYED in Riverdale for almost two weeks while waiting for the transfer of VAAP money from Moscow. I tried to learn as much as I could from my neighbor Valentina and to use my relatively free time getting used to my new family member, Lev's twelve-year-old daughter, Xenia. I had met her several times, years before, but since Lev's divorce, one of the conditions Sonya had set for his visits with Xenia was that he would never take her to our home or let her see me. So whatever I knew about Xenia I knew from Lev—that she was exceptionally bright, was attending a special workshop for talented children, was very good at clay modeling, and was trying her hand at writing short stories. I suspected that Sonya had not given me rave notices before Xenia's departure from Moscow, but I was hoping that the girl's natural intelligence would lead her to make her own judgments.

Things seemed to be going well. Xenia was polite, though sloppy, and I tried to excuse that by keeping in mind some of the details of her childhood. One of the reasons for Lev's divorce had been his resentment of Sonya's very active social life. From the age of three Xenia had been boarded out, coming home only on weekends. As a result she did not have much of a sense of family. I did not want to push her too hard, but I felt that, being a member of a family now, she should participate in the chores and other household activities. She seemed to be agreeable and intent on making the relationship work. Knowing how much Lev wanted her to be with him, I was happy that he no longer had to be torn between his past and present families.

My illusions were shattered very soon. It was exactly two weeks after our arrival. Aeroflot had one flight a week from Washington, and that morning I had given Lev letters to our relatives to drop into the embassy mailbox. I was surprised that Xenia did not have a letter ready for her mother, but that was up to her. After Lev left for the office, Valentina came to see me.

"Let's have coffee in my apartment," she said.

I took Kitty and went to Valentina's apartment. When we sat down at the kitchen table, I noticed that she had an unusually serious expression on her face.

"Xenia gave me a letter to send to Moscow in the embassy mail," she said. "The envelope was open, and a few words caught my attention. I think you should read this before it goes any further."

The letter was a complete shock. It was four pages long, and hatred poured from every word. She tried to find a bad side in everything I did. Her main complaint, however, and a revelation to me, was that her father was completely under my thumb, thus leaving her unprotected against a mean stepmother.

From what I read I deduced that Sonya had sent Xenia with clear instructions: ignore "that woman," listen only to your father, and anyway, it is all a temporary inconvenience. As soon as they buy you the things you need, I'll have you back—before the new year. That was another surprise. Lev had told me he'd reached a clear understanding with Sonya that Xenia would stay with us all three years in order to become fluent in English.

"What do I do?" I said.

"What you do," Valentina answered, "is show it to Lev. At the very least he'll need to explain to her that letters sent through the embassy mail are read by you-know-who and that she can cause trouble for him by writing such things. But if I were you, I'd send the girl home at the first opportunity."

"I can't do that," I said. "Lev is so happy to have her here." I briefly explained the problems we had had back home.

"It will be different here," Valentina said. "When the girl is three thousand miles away, he'll miss her; but he'll get over it. If she stays, she'll destroy your marriage."

What she said made sense except that, in practice, I did not have any choice. What bothered me most was the possibility that Lev had made a deal with Sonya behind my back about the line of authority in the family.

To my surprise he admitted doing precisely that.

"You mean," I said, "that if I want her to wash her hands, I have to tell you, and then you tell her to go and wash her hands?"

"Well, not exactly," he said. "But she does need to change a lot of her habits, and it would be better if it came through me. Meanwhile I'll find some pretext to talk to her about things that can be said or written, without letting her know that we kept this letter."

I did not like his attitude, but I decided to let it go for now. It was too early in the game; the girl was homesick and missed her mother. Maybe she'd come around in time.

THE Soviet embassy is very stratified according to rank. This stratification has little to do with snobbism but is mostly a result of differences in pay and allowances. The differences start with the ceiling on rent reimbursement, which determines who lives where. Most embassy officials with the rank of second or third secretary live in apartment buildings in Arlington, Alexandria, or Riverdale where rents are low. People are encouraged to find apartments in buildings where other Soviet families already live. For one thing, neighborly support and help are often important; another unspoken but clear reason is that living in clusters they can keep an eye on one another and, presumably, report any deviations from expected behavior to embassy security.

Senior officials live in a cluster of high rises in Chevy Chase, and that was where we were steered. We rented a three-bedroom apartment on the twentieth floor. Kitty was only seven months old and could share our bedroom, Xenia had her own room, and the third bedroom was to be used as an office. The size of the apartment was awesome by Moscow standards. In fact, we immediately got embroiled in a bitter bureaucratic argument with our Moscow office. The guidelines for living-space allocation that VAAP had issued for its foreign representatives had been fashioned according to Soviet housing standards, with no knowledge of or regard for the realities of living in a foreign country. Although our rent allowance was more than enough, the total area of our apartment was double the permitted maximum.

After an exasperating exchange of letters, with Moscow demanding that we move to a smaller apartment, Lev called on the embassy for help.

"Oh, no, not again," sighed Peter, a high-ranking embassy official who'd become a new friend of ours. "When will those idiots in Moscow get in touch with reality?"

Peter and his wife, Tamara, lived in a building across the street from us. We liked him very much and quickly became close. His advice was invaluable—he had been assigned to the embassy for more than ten years by then. "Don't worry," he said. "We've dealt with things like this before."

A few days later an official letter was sent from the embassy to the VAAP office in Moscow. In so many words the letter told VAAP to lay off and let the embassy decide what was appropriate for its members.

Gennady's wife, Alia, became my mentor in practical matters. Whether it was due to the fact that seven years had passed since our friends Eugene and Lilian had returned to Moscow or because of the differences between the Soviet communities in Washington and New York, a lot of their advice had turned out to be useless. Things were different from what they had told us. Within days I replaced the bulky four-wheel baby carriage I had brought from Moscow with a folding stroller, got a baby car seat, and became completely mobile—a luxury not attainable in Moscow when you have a young baby. I remembered how stranded I had been when Lev had taken a ten-day vacation with Xenia, leaving me alone with one-month-old Kitty. There was a grocery store within two blocks, but Soviet stores do not have shopping carts—you have to carry everything you buy. Nor could I take Kitty's carriage into the store; it was too large to pass through the checkout line. With a baby in my arms there was little I could put in a shopping bag, and within a few days I had been completely dependent on my neighbors to bring me groceries.

Other things had to go, too. The bed linens I had brought from Moscow were too small for our queen-size bed. Alia guided me through a big shopping trip to Hecht's, where we bought all the timesaving miracles of modern technology unknown in the Soviet Union—no-iron sheets, Teflon-coated pans, small kitchen appliances. "And now," said Alia, "we'll take care of your wardrobe."

Our start-up advance was rather limited, so there wasn't much we could do in that department. I had brought some of my better things with me. European look or not, they were well made and would suffice for a while. My immediate concern was Xenia. Her mother had sent her with one small suitcase and a simple instruction: "They'll buy you everything you need in the States, and don't hesitate to ask." The girl had nothing to wear but a pair of shorts and a change of shirts, and I knew it would take whatever was left of our first month's salary to get her even the basic necessities.

Despite initial difficulties, I was beginning to like life in Washington. Quite often, though, I had a feeling that I had been thrown into some kind of parallel universe where all meanings and values were reversed. The discrepancy in the cost of material items was just one small part of it. Even more bewildering was the difference in attitudes between people in the embassy and our friends in Moscow. We were used to long evenings with friends where conversations were often confined to gossip, rumors, and discussions of bickering in the institute. News of the world was incidental. In the embassy, nobody would start the day without reading the Washington *Post*, and Walter Cronkite's news program was sacred. Our embassy friends engaged in long discussions of upcoming presidential elections and how the outcome would affect Soviet-American relations.

One thing that puzzled me for a while was that all those lively political discussions and frank exchanges of opinions were taking place in our apartments. I remembered what Eugene had said in Moscow about bugging and finally decided to ask Peter about it.

"Oh, don't worry," he said. "They simply don't have the manpower to keep all of us under surveillance all the time. They do it on a rotating basis, and if something interesting comes up, they may put more resources into watching a particular individual. But"—he suddenly became serious—"there are people you should be careful with, and it's not the Americans. Be careful in the embassy, or you will have all the surveillance in the world, and it will be Soviet made."

I was also learning a lot. One immediate concern was the language. I was rather fluent in English, having taught philosophy in English back home, and I could read anything without a dictionary. However, understanding spoken American was another matter. I was amazed how many everyday words were different here from British English, which is taught in Soviet colleges. I had to get used to saying apartment instead of flat, call or phone instead of ring. My accent did not make things any easier. I decided that my best source was television.

I became an avid viewer, watching anything from *The Electric*

Company to *Kojak*. Besides being a feast for the eyes—color TV was a rarity in the Soviet Union—everything was so different: the programs, the totally new phenomenon of commercials, and especially the news. I was intrigued by the way the newscasters behaved. They actually talked to each other, made jokes. On Soviet TV the news is usually read by two somber-faced announcers, and there is much less visual material. Of all television programs, action shows became my favorites. There was nothing like that in the Soviet Union—pure entertainment, no propaganda. I did not even mind the commercials. I was still learning about a lot of things I saw in the stores, and commercials were helpful. It wasn't until much later that I learned that "new and improved" is a misleading phrase and that celebrities do not necessarily use the products they endorse.

Gradually, after the initial fascination wore off, I became more selective in what I watched. Some Hollywood clichés were irritating, such as the portrayal of Russians—always dumb and uneducated. The producers did not even trouble to make actors reproduce anything that sounded close to a Russian accent.

The only show that was markedly different at that time was *The Six Million Dollar Man*. I liked the spirit of the show, and several episodes where the main character dealt with his Russian counterparts were a pleasant surprise—for the first time I saw Russians portrayed as intelligent human beings, with human emotions, able to overcome their distrust of Americans and join forces at a critical time to save humanity. Maybe it was the still lingering spirit of détente, but it was pleasant to see Russians being treated as equals for a change. We tried not to miss any episodes.

I also started catching up on the movies that I'd never had a chance to see. I had been a movie buff all my life, but my knowledge of them reflected the strange system by which movies are chosen for showing in the Soviet Union. There are two criteria: cost and ideological suitability. The cost factor means that movies are purchased when they are already old and the licensing rights can be obtained for next to nothing. A five- to ten-year lag between the first release of the movie in the West and its showing in the Soviet Union is not unusual. The ideological factor dictates that the "socially significant" movies—those that show the deterioration of Western society—receive priority.

The combination of those factors gives the Soviet moviegoer a strange impression of the international movie scene. Among the names unknown in the Soviet Union: Clark Gable, Cary Grant, Charlton Heston, Rock Hudson, Clint Eastwood. The only movie I'd seen with Elizabeth Taylor was a totally forgettable one called *Rhapsody*. Jane Fonda is well known, but the only movie shown with Henry Fonda was *War and Peace*.

I would not have known about the great movie stars of the past myself if it hadn't been for a small movie theater in Leningrad that showed undubbed and very old foreign movies for educational purposes. Tickets were distributed at the University of Leningrad, where I studied. That was where I saw Cary Grant for the first time, in *Arsenic and Old Lace*, and Clark Gable in *It Happened One Night*. I still did not know who Rock Hudson was until I saw *McMillan and Wife* on American TV.

Watching movies or television was fun and a necessary language exercise. The other part of my discovery of everyday life in the United States consisted of getting to know things that simply do not exist in the Soviet Union: bank accounts, credit cards, car insurance.

We had to open a bank account for our VAAP operations. The account was opened in Lev's name, but since I would be doing bookkeeping and buying supplies for the office, I could also sign checks. Of course, this did not solve the problem of my personal shopping. The embassy does not permit its members to have their own bank accounts or credit cards. The ostensible reason is that all embassy members live in a precarious situation where they can be expelled on a moment's notice, thus possibly leaving the embassy with unpaid bills. A more practical reason, I suspected, was the fear that people would run up bills they could not pay.

Money brings out the best and the worst in people. Back home, Russians are normally very generous and hospitable people, ready to share the last they have with friends and often with strangers. That ingrained generosity is aided by the fact that Soviet money is looked upon as almost worthless. What's the use of saving money if there is nothing to buy anyway? Going abroad, Russians with a limited supply of money are suddenly confronted with the phenomenon of tremendous buying power, and their mentality often changes to reflect this new reality. Everything is instantly translated into the equivalent of Soviet black-market selling prices. While Americans think of a bottle of Coke as something that costs fifty cents, in the Russian mind the same bottle is one tenth of the cost of a sweater, and in those terms a bottle of Coke becomes very expensive indeed.

Black-market considerations aside, the incentives to save money are powerful. The Soviet government wants its citizens to bring home the money they earn abroad. Once people return home, they are not permitted to keep foreign currency, but they can exchange it for certificates that have the equivalent buying power in special diplomatic stores. Through such stores, Soviet diplomats can not only buy Western goods but also make a payment on a Soviet-made car, with immediate delivery instead of a long wait, and at a price of about one fifth of what a car costs in rubles. The same applies to cooperative apartments.

Stories about extremes in saving money abound in the Soviet missions. A most startling phenomenon is shoplifting. Although it is not widespread, there are a few incidents every year in which Soviet women are caught in the act. They usually blame foreign intelligence services for putting things in their shopping bags or purses in order to embarrass them. Most of the time the embassy takes the side of its employee or his or her family, but in some outrageous cases the culprits are sent home. One such incident involved the wife of a military attaché, who was stopped in the supermarket with a couple of pounds of meat stashed inside her dress. Nobody, including the embassy, would buy the story that it had been put there by somebody else without her noticing it!

Despite all the restrictions on credit cards and checking accounts, however, we were all warned not to carry too much cash either, because of the possibility of being mugged, especially in some areas of Washington, D.C. At the same time, we were advised to carry at least some cash because muggers might get angry if they found nothing. We were also told to surrender money without argument if stopped on the street, in order to avoid getting seriously hurt. Several Soviet diplomats were robbed in New York City but got off with the loss of a few dollars and some valuables.

The fear of being robbed partially explains why Soviet diplomats' wives go shopping in groups. I was just as scared of being mugged as everybody else, but group excursions did not fit my schedule. Lev left all the driving to me. Although he often bragged of how he had driven his father's car at sixteen, he refused to get a driver's license. I could not figure out why. Gradually, however, I started to suspect that my husband was far less comfortable with our life in the States than I was. My suspicions were confirmed when I received a canceled check from the bank for Lev's recent trip to New York. The check had Lev's signature on it but had been completely filled out by the hotel clerk.

I got permission from the embassy for Lev to have a credit card. But his card still did not solve my own shopping problem, and the rule about cash-and-carry continued to irk me. I had never liked rules that did not make sense. For many Russians, getting around the law is a national pastime. The Soviet bureaucracy is so vast that often the only way to get anything done is to find a way around it. Abroad, however, the risk of being discovered carried a potential penalty of being sent home if the offense was serious enough. We were watched much more closely here than at home. Still, I decided to take a chance. Soon I was in possession of a separate checking account and a bank credit card.

By the end of the first month, we had our apartment furnished, had bought a typewriter, had our stationery and business cards printed, and had gotten down to business. We sent an announcement to all the major publishers about opening our office, invited them to refer all copyright matters to us, and started regular mailings of VAAP catalogues and informational materials. Lev made several get-acquainted visits to New York, where he met major publishers, and we established a good working contact in Washington with the Copyright Office of the Library of Congress and with the Association of American Publishers.

I was enjoying my new job. It was essentially an executive secretary's job, but most of our contacts knew that I was Lev's wife and did not hesitate to discuss business with me if he was not around. I always liked doing things of an organizational nature. Having an office at home also helped—I worked part time and could easily manage both business and household duties.

My tenure, however, was short. Rumors started to circulate that we weren't doing much work. Soon we received a notice from Moscow that it was against the rules for a husband and wife to work together if one was subordinate to the other, which clearly was the situation in our case.

"What in the world . . . ?" Lev said when we got the notice. "We've been assigned to work together from the very beginning. There's got to be something else to it."

There was. Unknowingly we had broken an unwritten rule of embassy life by which a certain seniority is observed for embassy wives' employment. There are a limited number of jobs to go around, plus a lot of highly educated professional women who loathe sitting at home. Most of those jobs were with the Novosti Press Agency—doing the mailings, clippings, mild editorial stuff—but even that was a welcome relief from boredom. Because of the scarcity of positions, there was a waiting list of applicants. My coming with a ready job in my pocket had apparently caused complaints. Lev had no choice but to dismiss me and hire the wife of our trade attaché and neighbor, a woman named Natalie.

Chapter 4

In a way, I did not mind a break from work. The first thing I did was to take Kitty and fly to Moscow for three weeks in January. A co-op apartment that we had paid for before leaving Moscow was nominally finished. Lev's sister had the power of attorney, but she was working full time and could not deal with all the problems. The apartment needed to be fixed up, minimally furnished, and rented out. All of that required my presence. Besides, I was only too happy to leave Lev to deal with Xenia.

Since that fateful letter, we had kept an eye on her mail. She'd toned down her complaints after Lev had talked to her about possible repercussions, but she still asked her mother regularly to keep her promise and bring her back to Moscow by the new year. We'd bought her most of the things on Sonya's list, and she felt that she had kept her part of the bargain by tolerating me long enough to fulfill her mother's wishes. In a way, I sympathized with her—I would not have wanted to be in her situation.

Most of what Lev had dreamed about for Xenia did not materialize. His idea was that she would learn to speak English fluently. In Moscow she had attended a special school with early language education, and the language had been French. At first Xenia had refused to study English at all, claiming it would spoil her French accent. She had little choice, however, when school started. She did well, but still hated English and spent time at home going through her French textbooks. I suspected that the issue had a symbolic meaning for her—Sonya was fluent in French, while English represented me and our life in the States.

Lev did not seem to notice the tension. He did not spend much time with her—I drove her to school and took her shopping; he was content merely to have her around. Finally, at the end of November, I had brought up the subject with him.

"I think we should send her home during the winter school break," I said. "The idea of learning English is not working. She is miserable, she hates me, and it is beginning to get to me, too."

"Okay," he finally said. "I'll talk to her."

December came and went. I reminded Lev of his promise, but he kept stalling, saying he could not find the right moment. When school started again in January, I realized that he would never have that conversation. It was Lev's way of making a decision—by doing nothing and letting things take care of themselves.

Not that the pattern was unfamiliar. I still wondered sometimes how he ever managed to make the decision to marry me.

We'd met in 1969 at a conference in Leningrad. I was working at the Leningrad branch of the Institute of Philosophy then. The institute itself was located in Moscow, and Lev was the head of a department there and was attending the conference as chairman of one of the committees.

I was then twenty-five years old and already had one disastrous marriage behind me. When I was nineteen, I'd married a boy my own age whom I had met through my university friends. Leonid was bright, imaginative, and a little wild. Within six months we were wed, despite strong opposition from my family. My father was particularly unhappy with my choice.

I had never listened to my father, and I was not going to start then. Our relationship had always been quite distant. He was an older-generation dogmatic Communist whose philosophy was the front page of *Pravda*. We never had anything in common.

For once, though, my father was right. Leonid's wild imagination turned out to be an incurable form of schizophrenia, and nine months later I got a divorce on medical grounds. Devastated and disappointed, I started dating older men, with whom I felt more secure and comfortable.

Lev was the answer to my dreams. I was fascinated with his brilliance and erudition, his aura of power and secure knowledge that came from being in control of life. Our first meeting was unforgettable.

As the result of a snag, the papers submitted to the conference had been printed in quantities too small to provide copies for all the participants, and I had had to restrict the distribution to committee chairmen and authors. After the session started, I was sitting in a hallway with the few remaining copies, tired of explaining the shortage and certainly not looking my best.

I was ready to leave when a man came out of the conference room. I had never seen him before and was not prepared for what I was about to hear.

"What idiot invented this imbecile distribution list?" he said. "Anyway, I want my copy."

"I invented it," I said angrily. "Is your name on the list?"

He seemed taken aback that I did not know who he was. Finally I verified that he was entitled to a copy and gave it to him. He left without a word. I collected the remaining copies and hurried to the hairdresser's to prepare for the best part of the conference—the big banquet.

Later in the evening I caught a glimpse of him a couple of times, but I was constantly surrounded by people, talking and dancing. Close to the end, a friend from the Moscow delegation managed to get over to me.

"A friend of mine wants me to introduce him to you," he said. "Yelena, meet Lev Mitrokhin."

After a few months I transferred my graduate study to the Moscow Institute of Sociology and moved to Moscow. Lev was already separated and living with his mother and sister. We dated for almost a year. I was introduced to his mother, who had never liked Sonya and was hoping for a change in Lev's life, and to his younger sister, Tatiana, who was about my age. Tatiana and I became immediate friends; yet with all the support from his family, he still did not file for a divorce.

University days.

Exasperated, I started going out with other men, and after a while one of them, named Anatol, proposed to me. I called Tatiana for advice, and she came to see me in the apartment I was renting in the outer suburbs.

"What shall I do?" I asked. "You know I am in love with Lev, but it's been going on for almost two years, and there is no change."

"I know," she said. "My advice is to marry Anatol. You are not in love with him, but he is nice and dependable, and he is crazy about you. You'll be happy with him. I was hoping that a miracle would happen, but I don't think now that Lev would ever divorce Sonya."

"But why? He always says that he is not going back, and the only link between them is Xenia."

"That's true," Tatiana said. Suddenly she turned away to avoid looking into my eyes. "He will probably kill me for telling you, but the truth is that if he divorces Sonya, he will have to marry Irina, his mistress of ten years, and he does not want to do that either. I am sorry I did not tell you earlier, but he is my brother, after all, and I did hope that things would work out."

If a bomb had dropped from the ceiling and exploded in my apartment, I would have been less surprised. Slowly she told me the story. When she was four years old and Lev eighteen, their father, a general in the Soviet militia—the equivalent of a police commissioner—had been arrested on some cooked-up charges. It was 1948, and things like that were happening. Lev was a student at Moscow University. Although he was not expelled, his future was severely limited; with his father in the gulag and the stigma attached to the family, he could not continue his study of such a highly political discipline as modern Marxism and had had to change to the study of classical philosophy. Irina, his sweetheart, was seventeen and an obedient daughter. Her parents hurriedly married her off to the son of a politically reliable lawyer.

Lev's family fell on hard times; he continued his studies and moonlighted as a lecturer to support his mother and sister. His father died in the camp in 1952, several months before he was cleared of all charges. Lev's career went back on track; he completed his graduate study and went to work for the Central Committee of Komsomol. In 1960 he married Sonya, a provincial girl who was just finishing her studies at Moscow University. Soon afterward he met Irina again. She was not happy in her marriage. They started an affair, and Irina was ready to file for a divorce when Xenia was born and Lev decided to stay with Sonya because of the child. The affair with Irina continued, though, and when he separated from Sonya, Irina expected that she would file for divorce at the same time he did, and they would get married.

"The problem is," Tatiana said, "that it's sort of burned itself out, but he does not know how to get out of it. Neither Sonya nor Irina knows about you; both think it's between the two of them."

"Sure," I said bitterly, "like two dogs fighting over the same bone only to discover that a third has come along and stolen it from under their noses. Only I don't have the bone either."

We talked for another hour, when suddenly Lev showed up. He was high, as usual, but not quite drunk. My resolve to stay calm suddenly collapsed; I started crying violently. Tatiana called Anatol, who rushed over and took me away to his apartment.

I was determined not to talk to Lev again, but he managed to get Anatol's number and called me there. He was leaving for

Czechoslovakia the next day and asked me not to make any drastic decisions until he returned and we had a chance to talk.

A week later I went to the airport with Tatiana to meet him. He had called her from Prague and insisted that she bring me along. I could hardly recognize the man who got off the plane. He had lost almost ten pounds and looked sick. We drove to my apartment and he brought all his bags in from the taxicab.

"I brought a full set of glasses and dishes from Czechoslovakia. They are yours . . . ours, if you want. This will be the start of our household. But I want your decision now," he said.

I stayed with him. I loved him and he needed me. The next day he filed for a divorce from Sonya, and a year later we were married.

Now, packing for Moscow, I wondered whether he would ever have made any decision if I had not forced his hand by walking out with Anatol. I'd never regretted staying—Lev was a fascinating man to be with. After several years of marriage we still could talk late into the night; he always had interesting ideas and opinions about everything, and I had learned a lot from him. He also always seemed to be in charge of the situation back in Moscow, something that I had never challenged or questioned . . . until now. Whether his reliance on me in practical matters here had given me more confidence in myself or the strain of our family situation was showing, I don't know, but I was gradually losing my unquestioning admiration for him.

The first trip home is always a tremendous financial burden for any diplomat. Besides the natural desire to bring gifts for relatives, gifts are always brought when visiting friends in Russia—usually flowers or a bottle of wine—and someone coming from a foreign country is expected to bring something foreign.

I made a special trip to New York, where the Orchard Street district in lower Manhattan serves as a wholesale market for the Soviet community. Many stores there are run by Russian émigrés, who stock a variety of discontinued merchandise at very low prices. I went with a couple of embassy women who had been there before and steered me to the right places to do my shopping.

My final problem was to get enough supplies for Kitty to last her three weeks. She still needed diapers, and although she could eat a variety of regular foods, I was also bringing a full supply of fruit juices, vitamins, and enough baby food for the first few days in the Soviet Union to ease her gradually to Russian food. The rest of my suitcases were stuffed with gifts—fake-fur coats for Tatiana and my mother-in-law, which would cost a fortune in Moscow, fabrics for my mother, and household items for both families.

My feelings upon my arrival in Moscow were mixed. I was amazed how a few short months in Washington had changed my outlook. Familiar things looked different. Tatiana and her husband met me at the airport. After hugs and kisses we walked out to the parking lot. I looked at the line of cabs. I was used to all the taxicabs being Volgas—medium-sized sedans. All of a sudden all the taxis seemed to be compacts.

"When did they switch to the Moskvitch for taxis?" I asked Tatiana.

"They're Volgas." She laughed. "Don't you recognize them?"

"I guess I have lost my sense of proportion. Also, something is burning. Can't you smell it?"

Tatiana looked at me strangely. "You must be tired from the long flight. You are imagining things." And then, quietly, "Is it really that different?"

"Yes." I realized by then that what I thought was a burning smell was car exhaust. The pollution in Moscow is much greater than in Washington.

Finally we arrived at Tatiana's apartment. We quickly walked through the foyer to her rooms. Lev's family lived in an apartment they shared with two other families, with a common kitchen and facilities. They had two adjacent rooms: my mother-in-law occupied a walk-through—a small partition separated her sleeping quarters from the rest of the room, which served as a combination living-dining area—and Tatiana and her husband and their one-year-old daughter, Masha, occupied the other room. There were aahs and oohs as the gifts were unwrapped, but the thing that sent Tatiana flying to me with hugs was a supply of ready-mix baby cereals for Masha, and baby multivitamins. I had not forgotten how it was to have a baby in Moscow.

The next day I went out and faced Moscow reality—crowds everywhere, people elbowing one another to get through—in the subway, in the stores, on the streets. There was something strange and unfamiliar about the crowds, some persistent feeling that something was missing, until I finally realized nobody was smiling. I was so used to smiling people in Washington—on the streets, in the elevators, in the supermarket lines. It's not that Russians are unfriendly. They are the warmest and friendliest people in the world, but only inside their homes. Out on the street it's a fight for survival—you against the world.

And no color. Gray snow, smog, dirty buildings, drab clothes in subdued, practical dark colors.

I was home.

I TOOK Kitty to Leningrad, spent a couple of days with my parents, visited friends, left Kitty with adoring grandparents, and returned to Moscow to take care of the business at hand. Tatiana went with me to my new apartment.

It is very difficult for outsiders to understand the importance Russians attach to their housing. Living space is any Russian's most prized possession, and people go to extraordinary lengths to obtain it or to protect what they have. It has a lot to do with the fact that Russians cannot move freely from one city to another—they must have a residency permit to live in a particular city, which cannot be granted unless there is an available apartment and a ready job. The government thus controls population growth in the large cities, places very attractive to live because they have better supplies of consumer goods and a better choice of jobs. The population of Moscow, currently over eight million, would probably triple if people were permitted to move there freely, but the city's resources are limited.

The housing situation in the Soviet Union is a major source of jokes, but in reality it is more tragic than funny. Countless families have broken up because a young married couple has been forced to live for years with in-laws. Family members become bitter enemies who wage all-or-nothing campaigns against one another, trying to gain precious living space. Bribes, blackmail, and even anonymous letters to state authorities declaring the political unreliability of relatives are not unknown.

In our particular situation the only way Lev could have gotten a place to live from the state after leaving Sonya was to exchange their apartment for two one-room apartments. Such exchanges are permitted by law. That would have forced Sonya and Xenia to share one room, however, which Lev did not want to do. So he left her the apartment and we sublet from diplomats, until finally, using all his connections, he managed to get us the place in the co-op I was about to inspect. Unlike getting an apartment from the state, which is free except for a nominal monthly charge, co-ops have to be paid for, just like buying an apartment in the West; and they are expensive. A typical down payment is the equivalent of two and a half years of an average engineer's salary.

The visit was a shock. It was the first time I'd been in a brand-new apartment that came as is. Although it was an upgraded design and a hard-to-get-into co-op, the apartment was not ready to be lived in. It was the end of January, and the apartment was freezing cold. The heating system was obviously inadequate, and the window frames did not fit. Tatiana and I kept our coats on.

"You should have seen it in the beginning," she said. "Your mother was here when we received the key, and she stayed for several days. The heating did not work, the toilet was cracked, and there was almost an inch left between the front door and the floor. She found some men from the construction crew and had them fix some of it afterhours, for extra pay. But she could not stay long enough to take care of it all."

One thing was clear—the apartment would have to stay empty for a while. Nobody would rent it the way it was.

We went to visit my friend Alana, who lived in the same building. I was curious to see how she and her husband had managed, and wanted to ask her what could be done. When we walked into her apartment, we walked into another world.

Alana had had a crew of men working nonstop for two months. Everything had been replaced—sinks, tile, heaters, stove, floors. Alana was married to a talented psychiatrist, who worked in one of the most prestigious Moscow hospitals and had a flourishing consulting practice on the side. Money was no object for her.

"How much did it cost you to have it fixed?" I asked.

"Three thousand," she said. It was almost as much as our down payment.

If all the energy and ingenuity Russian people use for bettering their personal standard of living could be channeled into state enterprises, the Soviet Union would have as high a standard of living as any European country. The problem is that people have no incentive to work hard for the state, because their pay would not be any better if they did. Instead, they turn their considerable energy and mental resources to moonlighting. It provides a nice additional income—as can the illicit sale of scarce goods and materials. Store clerks, for instance, habitually hide better items and sell them to acquaintances for extra money. All this creates a "second economy," in which the state has no part.

Because of her husband's practice, Alana had enormous connections, and she offered to help me with my problems. I did not have enough money to do the wonders she had in her apartment, but she would find the workmen to take care of the most immediate problems—windows, heating, and plumbing—supervise their work, and then find a tenant. In return she made a list of things she needed from the States. It started with a supply of pipe tobacco for her husband and included quality cosmetics and baby toys. It was a fair trade.

I had to sell our collection of American jazz records, which I had left in Tatiana's care, and some of my own clothes to raise the money. I figured that both were replaceable back in Washington. Before I left Moscow, I gave Alana a thousand rubles, and was grateful that fate had placed her in the same building.

I returned to Leningrad to spend the remaining week with my parents, and gradually I noticed that I was counting the days left till my return to Washington. Suddenly I was thinking of Washington as home. I wanted to go back there, where people were happy and smiling, back to my action shows, my car, my morning newspaper that would tell me what had happened in the world, and my embassy friends who would talk about upcoming presidential elections instead of what was available in the neighborhood stores and the outrageous prices on the black market.

Why did it have to be that way? Russia is one of the richest countries in the world; its resources are almost unlimited, and certainly as great as those of the United States. The Russian people are hardworking—when they work for themselves. Yet everywhere I looked I saw a country that was at least twenty years behind the West in its development. True, it had been devastated by the war, but so had Germany. The problem was that the system actually discouraged the people from working.

Living in Washington, I had seen with my own eyes what people could do when they had an incentive to work. I felt sorry for my country, but I knew there was nothing that I or anybody else could do to change it. All I could do was to escape it for a while and live for whatever short time I had in a brighter world.

Chapter 5

WHEN I returned to Washington, I found Lev at his wits' end. Natalie, his new secretary, could not handle the job. She could not type, her English was on a grade school level, and after a couple of months in the office she still could not remember the names of our major publishing contacts. Letters had piled up, and I spent the first several evenings redoing most of them, simply because they could not be sent out the way they were.

The troubling pattern continued. Lev kept asking me to review Natalie's work, and I ended up redoing most of it every evening. Finally I said that I was unwilling to spend my evenings covering somebody else's mistakes. Lev wrote several letters to Moscow, spoke to senior embassy officials, and got me back as his assistant—on condition that we would open an office separate from the apartment and keep normal business hours.

We found an office on K Street, near the embassy. I had my own reasons for finding an office so close to the embassy. Lev still did not drive, and since I would be working only part time, he would have to depend on our neighbors for transportation. Besides, I was planning to take another leave at the end of the year. After careful consideration we'd decided to have another baby.

As I'd gotten acquainted with the people at the embassy, especially during outings to the embassy retreat on the Eastern Shore, I noticed quite a few babies. Once, I commented to Alia that it was strange that Moscow sent people with such young children on foreign assignment.

"Most of them did not come here with children," she said.

"They were born here. If a family wants to have a child, this is the time and the place to have it."

I talked to some of the young mothers. All said essentially the same thing—having children here was easy. The medical facilities were incredible, and good nutrition could build a foundation for years of future health.

Meanwhile, although I enjoyed being at work again, my frustration with it was growing. I often wondered why VAAP needed an office in Washington—the whole affair had been doomed from the beginning. Another agency existed to sell books printed in the Soviet Union directly to American booksellers. It was called International Book and had been in business for many years before VAAP, supplying Soviet art books, classics, and dictionaries.

Our task was much more difficult—we were supposed to sell manuscripts to be translated, published, and distributed through regular American channels, just as the work of any foreign author would be. Most technical translations were already handled by a small group of publishing houses that specialized in scientific works. That left us with Soviet fiction and books in nontechnical areas.

One of the problems was that VAAP sent tons of material to its foreign offices without making any distinction between different markets. The same books that were promoted in Bulgaria were sent to us. We once had a good laugh when we received a large shipment of books written by Soviet agricultural experts on modern methods of growing crops. Given the fact that only three years before, the Soviet Union had experienced severe grain shortages and since then had continually bought huge quantities of grain in the United States and Canada, I could only imagine how we would look if we offered those books to Americans!

In rare instances when we came across something really interesting, there were other obstacles. Most of the works of fiction that we considered good required a considerable knowledge of Soviet reality to be appreciated. They were clearly not suitable for the American mass market, and although some were eventually published for the sake of high art and good relations, most were money losers for their publishers.

We were not completely unsuccessful, though. Macmillan decided to publish a library of Soviet science fiction—over a dozen books in all. Soviet sci-fi is generally very good, one reason being that the authors can write unorthodox things under the guise of events occurring in some distant future and at some undisclosed place on earth. The best in the field were the Strugatsky brothers, Arkady and Boris, and two of their books were scheduled to be published first. The hitch was that Macmillan wanted the authors to come to the United States for a promotional tour. With the first book ready for release, VAAP stalled, clearly waiting for a decision in higher quarters, and finally the word came down—no tour. The science-fiction series was killed in its infancy.

One of the major frustrations of our work in the States was that Lev did not have real power to make any decisions on the spot. It was embarrassing to explain to our American contacts that everything we discussed with them had to be sent to Moscow for approval. A related problem was that we knew that some major decisions could not be made even by the VAAP chairman but, being ideological matters, had to go higher up to be decided by the Party Committee on Propaganda. There were other minor things, however, that were perfectly within VAAP's power to resolve, which still took us weeks just to get a reply on.

So there we were, dutifully shuffling papers, sending mailings, receiving polite refusals most of the time, and producing no tangible results. Although we established good relationships with many major publishing houses and were always received on the highest level whenever we traveled to New York to meet with publishers, all we could do was to recommend an occasional book that we deemed deserving of attention, maintain good public relations, and send everything to Moscow for a decison.

IT WAS the summer of 1976, and America was celebrating its bicentennial. I was glad we were here at that time. It was such a rare event to observe.

The way Americans celebrate national events is completely different from the way it is done in the Soviet Union. The most amazing thing was that so many people wanted to *participate*. There are two major holidays in the Soviet Union: May Day, which is the Day of Solidarity of All Workers of the World, and

Revolution Day, November 7. For each there's a demonstration during which the populace is supposed to show its support for the system and its leaders.

Watched on television, the demonstrations look impressive—huge crowds pass the main square of each city for hours, waving placards and flags and carrying portraits of Lenin and current Politburo members. Attendance at the highly regulated demonstrations is mandatory for anybody who cares about his or her career. A no-show can receive a reprimand, and it certainly goes on the record, indicating antisocial behavior.

In all probability some people would still go, even if attendance were not required. Loyalty to the state, especially among older generations, runs pretty high. Russians are no less patriotic than Americans. They love their country, and in a critical situation, such as war, they would rise to defend it without hesitation. But by making attendance a duty rather than an expression of human feelings, the system takes away whatever joy people have in feeling united with their country.

Therefore the bicentennial celebration was overwhelming to me because it was such a novelty. We watched the parade, with its colorful bands and floats, on television, but the uplifted mood in the city was hard to miss. People really *cared.* It was their country, and everybody was celebrating its birthday. Nobody sent people to the streets or to the Mall; they went because they felt they were a part of this country. It was their celebration.

I particularly remember the big gala televised that evening. When everybody in the audience rose to join the chorus singing "God Bless America," I felt tears in my eyes and, to my surprise, noticed that I was silently singing the words along with them.

XENIA had returned to Moscow permanently at the end of the school year. In the middle of August, Lev and I went on our first official vacation, to Moscow and then to the Black Sea. When we returned to Washington in the middle of September, Lev was in a depressed mood. The trip home had affected him more than I had anticipated. He had visited all his bright and talented friends, and he had discovered that there wasn't much they could talk about. Obviously the news of who was where, who was fired, who was promoted in the institute was interesting. And then—what? Suddenly he discovered that he had little to discuss with his friends of some twenty years.

Peter smiled understandingly when Lev mentioned his confused feelings at our welcome-home party in Washington.

"Welcome to the club," he said. "You have just joined an exclusive fraternity called Soviet Americans. We all went through that stage and by now are resigned to the fact that we will never be the same people we were before we came here."

"It's as if we were talking a different language," Lev said.

"Exactly," said Peter. "Your perspective has changed. By being a part of the embassy, you got used to thinking about things in more global terms. Your friends' concerns are confined to their own local world of internal politics. Unfortunately, I cannot offer you any consolation. You will feel like a foreigner in Moscow for many years to come."

I knew that what Peter was saying was true. I was also wondering how Lev would go back to doing what he had been doing for the past ten years—writing books about modern American philosophy. Even before our arrival here it hadn't been easy. A lot of material that he had originally included in his books he later took out, because he knew it would never pass the standards of ideological suitability. Now that he had actually lived here and seen the reality, how much censorship would he have to impose on himself, and how much inner conflict would it create in him?

My own professional future did not concern me very much at that time—our second child was on the way, and after that I had eighteen more months here. Why worry now?

By the beginning of December we had found a secretary to substitute for me in the office. Regina was competent and energetic, and I felt that Lev was in good hands. I took a maternity leave. After the sonogram my obstetrician insisted that the baby would be born before Christmas, but I disagreed.

"I do not expect a baby until the end of January, Doctor," I reassured him.

"That is impossible," he said. "Sonograms are very precise."

"Doctor," I said, "we do not have sonograms in Russia, but I

With my husband, Lev, at a Washington party.

can assure you that it is wrong. Maybe Russian babies are different from American ones."

The embassy has a full-time physician assigned from Moscow, but he is not affiliated with any hospital. Therefore obstetric care is referred to an American specialist. The doctor was nice and knowledgeable, and by then I had become used to his examinations. In the Soviet Union ninety percent of doctors are women, and I was uncomfortable at first because I wasn't used to a man examining me. But I adjusted to the idea. He finally became resigned to the fact that the sonogram was wrong but later insisted on checkups every two days, and at the end of January he decided to put me in the hospital.

The morning I was due to go to the hospital, I got up early and packed my suitcase. I would drive to the doctor's office, have my examination, and then go to the hospital, one block away.

As I was getting ready to leave I suddenly felt a familiar sensation. "I think my plans are changing slightly," I told Lev. "I am going to have the baby today. Maybe you'd better go with me."

"I can't," he said. "What am I going to do there? I'll be stranded with the car, and what will I do with Kitty?"

"You can call the embassy pool. They'll pick up the car. Then you take Kitty to a baby-sitter and go to work."

He was still hesitating. "You don't really know for sure. It could be just a cramp."

"I do know for sure." I was getting impatient. I was also scared and wanted to get to the doctor's office as quickly as possible. Kitty had been born in just one and a half hours, and it could happen again. "What if it starts for real while I am driving?"

"Nothing happens that quickly." He had made up his mind. "It's only a half-hour drive."

I gave up. I drove to the doctor's office by myself. An hour later I was in the hospital. A couple of hours after that I called Lev and told him that I would have the baby before the evening.

"Great," he said. "I'll stop by later in the afternoon."

"You know," I said, "you can come anytime. It's not like in Moscow. You can be with me here while I am waiting."

"What am I going to do there?"

"What other husbands do!" I shouted into the phone. "They stay with their wives to make them feel better. Only by now I am beginning to think I would really be better off without you!" And I slammed down the receiver. It was a useless outburst. If he had had to ask, he would never understand anyway.

I had plenty of time to kill. The room was comfortable. I was surrounded by monitoring equipment, but I recognized only one apparatus. I had seen it before in Moscow.

Like so many other things, the choice of the hospital in Moscow was a matter of connections. When I'd had Kitty, I hadn't wanted to take chances in the regular district hospital—Tatiana had told me some horror stories about unsanitary conditions there. My mother had substantial connections in the medical world, and so I was able to register in the maternity ward of the Institute of Gynecology of the Academy of Sciences in Moscow.

There, when things started to develop, I was strapped to some machine—I never learned its name—to measure the progress, I was told. The doctors were fascinated by the machine. From their conversations I gathered that it was brand-new, just arrived from Europe, and the hospital was one of the few in the entire Soviet Union to get it. That was the same machine that was a piece of standard equipment in every labor room in this rather average hospital in Washington!

I fully understood what other women in the embassy meant by saying, "It's easy here," when I was given an anesthetic. It's not that Soviet doctors are admirers of natural childbirth—I was given some kind of gas mask there that did not do much good—but they simply don't have such a modern marvel as epidural injection. My word, I thought, it's almost fun having a baby here!

Lev finally showed up shortly after five. Our friends Victor and Laura drove him to the hospital and waited in the car. My doctor came to my room to meet him.

"Well, you have about ten minutes together," he said. "We'll be taking her to the delivery room after that. I'll leave you alone now." He shook Lev's hand and left the room.

"In half an hour you'll know whether you have a son," I said. I knew that he wanted a boy. He often complained that he was constantly surrounded by women at home—his mother and sister and two daughters—and that he wanted a boy whom he could take fishing. His reply caught me by surprise.

"I can't stay," he said. "You know that Victor and Laura are going home next week. They planned to spend the whole evening shopping and asked for our car. They will bring me back after the stores close at nine."

I said nothing. It did not occur to him that he could stay and Victor could come back for him, and I was not going to suggest it.

Half an hour later, when the doctor took off his gloves and said, "Well, congratulations—you've got quite a guy here. I am going out to tell the happy father," I only said, "He is not there, Doctor."

He looked as if he were going to say something but changed his mind. Finally he said, "Well, I'll see you later, then."

Mercifully, I was left alone in the recovery room. Two other women were there, separated from me by partitions. I could hear their voices as they talked quietly to their husbands while I lay there crying. I was so happy to have a son. He was a big boy, over nine pounds, and if newborns have personalities, this one already showed determination. I wished I could share my joy with somebody. Eventually I was transferred to my room. Lev's arrival later went almost unnoticed. I said I was tired and needed rest.

The next three days in the hospital were the most restful I'd had in a long time. To me it felt as if I were on vacation in a luxury hotel. The TV, the phone next to my bed, visitors at any time, my baby whenever I wanted him, the nurse who answered the ring almost instantly, and, most important, privacy—all the things I had not had in Moscow.

The hospital in Moscow had twenty-four beds in each room. The hospital stay was seven days minimum, sometimes longer if complications developed, and no visitors were permitted. The only contact with the outside world was through the telephone—two pay phones for each floor. The first two days we were not even permitted to get up and therefore could not get to the phone, so the only means of communication was written notes. Notes and food packages were accepted for only two hours a day at the receptionist's window downstairs.

I am sure there were reasons for these regulations—the fear of infections, food allergies, and the desire to give us maximum rest during the time of recovery. The results were, of course, the opposite. We all suffered from anxiety and the lack of contact with our families, and none of us cared for the health foods that were permitted in the food packages brought by families. We all wanted to gorge on fancy foods to reward ourselves for the terrible experience we had just been through. Worst of all, we could see our babies only when they were brought in for nursing three times a day; the nursery in the ward was off limits to mothers.

Maternity wards in Soviet cities are instantly recognizable by the numerous men standing on the sidewalks and peering up at the windows, trying to catch a glimpse of their wives. The lucky ones who have wives in rooms below the third floor can even shout a few phrases to them. Most of the time, however, it's sign language. Each room had a long roll of string with a weight attached to it, more or less like a fishing line. When a husband on the sidewalk signaled that he had something to send, a lookout team would go to the door to watch for hospital personnel. Then the string was lowered out the window, the package tied to it, and it was pulled back into the room. Thank goodness my room was on the fourth floor, so it did not take long.

We all wanted to get out as quickly as possible, partly because of boredom but mostly out of concern for our babies. They were not well cared for. If the baby was fidgety during feeding time, it often went to the nursery still hungry and usually received no additional feeding. Diapers were not changed often enough. Practically all mothers told me that they brought their babies home with severe diaper rash or even sores.

Now all of that was just a fading memory. It was definitely easier to have babies in the United States.

Three days of relative solitude in a private room gave me time to think, and the thoughts were not always pleasant. I was deciding what to do with my marriage. My mother always told me that women should give more to a marriage than men because they have more at stake. I thought about where it had gotten her and where it had gotten me, and questioned the whole concept.

Both my mother and my father were students of architecture when the war started. My father was about to graduate, but Mother was only a second-year student. She never finished her education. The year I was born she contracted tuberculosis. The only cure was a change of climate and better nutrition. She spent the better part of the next several years in sanatoriums and she was not well enough after that to hold a regular job. Although my mother had a valid reason for not working, she felt guilty about not making a contribution to the family income. Out of that guilt, she threw her considerable talents and energy into her family and her husband's career.

And so I grew up in an atmosphere that placed the man of the family on a pedestal, with his slightest wish catered to immediately. He was *working*, I was told. But it was my mother who played the piano, sewed my dresses and knitted my sweaters, drove and fixed the car, and repaired things around the house. She also taught me all those skills and instilled the feeling that it was a woman's job to do everything and to leave her husband free for serious things such as work.

I do not know when her disenchantment started to settle in. Perhaps it happened when she found the receipts for expensive gifts to other women and then discovered a large sum of money hidden behind the books in the bookcase. She did not tell my father that she had found the money, and did not take any of it, but as soon as I finished high school she decided to get a job.

She became a secretary in a research institute. A year later she took a job as an editor at a youth magazine, and two years later she was writing her own stories and was accepted as a member in the Journalists' Guild. Finally she asked my father for a divorce. He would not give it to her. She did not want a messy scandal and stayed, living her own life, having her own friends—and her own money that she could spend on herself.

As I reviewed my own life and my own marriage I suddenly saw with alarm how perilously close I was coming to following that pattern. True, my situation was different. My mother had raised me to be self-sufficient. I worked from the moment I graduated from the university, obtained an advanced degree, and was fairly independent financially. Yet with all the differences between my mother's situation and my own, I was falling into the same trap. It was always my husband who came first—his moods, his wishes, his favorite things. I was doing everything possible to make his life carefree and happy, and what did I get for it? Driving myself to a hospital, already in labor, to have his baby.

As a sociologist I was aware that the reasons for this trend were deeply rooted in Soviet reality. Because of the housing shortage a young man often continues to live with his parents long after he is out of school, working, and financially independent, while his mother continues to provide all domestic services. When he marries, his wife takes over the housekeeping duties. Thus, many men go from childhood through advanced age without ever having to cook their own meals or do their own laundry.

All this made perfect sense in theory, but I found it difficult to accept. And the more I thought about it, the more I thought about Sonya. I had always believed without question what Lev and Tatiana had told me—that she was a gold digger, a poor provincial girl whom Lev had married out of pity and because, after he had lost Irina, he had not really cared about anything anymore.

Suppose she really loved him? That suggested a different scenario entirely, one that suddenly made a lot of sense. I knew that she was attractive, bright, and well respected professionally—many of our friends in Moscow had told me that. There were stories of her social life, but not until after Lev had started seeing Irina again. I imagined myself, with a newborn baby, finding out that my husband was seeing another woman. Wouldn't I run to somebody else for comfort?

There are lessons to be learned from ex-wives. I wished I had given them more thought earlier. Meanwhile, where was I going with my own marriage?

One thing was clear—I had to stay in it at least until our term in Washington expired. I owed it to my children to let them get as much as possible out of this wonderful country—good nutrition, medical care, colorful toys, a comfortable place to live. Therefore I had to continue living as if nothing had happened and to leave any scenes and explanations until our return to Moscow. I also needed to continue working on my English and my knowledge of this country. Both would be invaluable when we returned to Moscow, where I would have to start a life of my own.

But in my mind my marriage was over. From now on it was just a waiting game.

Chapter 6

THREE months had passed since my baby was born. I had returned to work in March. Regina had kept the work up to date during my absence from the office, and I was able to maintain it without extra exertion. In the morning I dropped Kitty and Konstantin off at the new embassy compound on Tunlaw Road, where the wife of a security guard took care of them, drove to the office, and then left after lunch. Lev stayed in the office for the rest of the day and caught a ride home with one of our neighbors.

One day I stayed at the embassy longer than usual. My business there had been finished for an hour, but I lingered in the dark, cool cafeteria, sipping my third cup of coffee. I was in no rush to get home. The apartment would be unbearably hot that afternoon—Washington was suffering from one of those heat waves that regularly strike it at the end of April, before the air-conditioning in apartment buildings is turned on.

It was past two o'clock in the afternoon, and most of the embassy staff were back at work in their offices. The only people left in the cafeteria were the embassy pool drivers who were waiting for assignments. The topic of conversation was a recent incident in which the trade attaché had been stopped on the New Jersey Turnpike, doing ninety miles an hour in his Soviet-made Lada. One driver said, "The guy should be given a medal for getting ninety out of that tin can. Still can't figure out how he did it."

The "tin can" was one of the five Soviet-made cars the embassy was permitted to have here, although they did not meet American emission standards. They were brought in for "promotional purposes" and assigned to embassy officials to drive. There were some nasty rumors that to avoid that "privilege," one of the high officials had procured a certificate from the embassy doctor stating that because of arthritis he had to have a car with power steering. With power steering, obviously, came air-conditioning and other amenities the Soviet-made cars did not have.

I thought lovingly about my own "ocean liner"—the Oldsmobile Delta 88, with all its comfort and gadgets. Only two years ago even its manual had been a puzzle full of unknowns. Speaking of comfort . . . "By the way, guys," I said, "my max switch on the air-conditioning is blown again. The service station near my apartment has tried to fix it three times already."

"Serves you right." Oleg, the senior mechanic, who was in his sixth year with the embassy, laughed. "Always take the car back where you bought it. We buy so many cars from them that we always get good service. Go to Derek. He'll take care of it."

I vaguely remembered Derek, who had sold me my car—a very tall and handsome man in his fifties. Probably even older. Unlike Russian men, Americans always look at least ten years younger than their age. "You mean every time I have a problem I will have to drive all the way to Arlington?" I complained.

"Well, you want to have that car fixed, don't you?" Oleg said.

"Okay." I sighed. "I'll go."

I left the embassy, silently cursed Washington weather as I went to my car, and gasped at the hot air that hit me from the air-conditioning vents. Then I drove to Arlington to fix my car . . . and to change my life forever.

It had not occurred to me to call Derek for an appointment, but fortunately he was in. I told him that Oleg had sent me, and explained my continuing problem with the car. He took the car to the service area and came back. "They'll check it right away," he said, and offered me a cup of coffee. In a few minutes the service department called and said they would need half an hour to fix it. I settled down to wait.

"Do you mind if I ask you a few questions?" Derek said. I did not mind, although I already anticipated the standard questions about life in the Soviet Union that Americans so often liked to ask. A conversation, even a dull one, was preferable to reading *Sports Illustrated*, the only publication in the waiting room.

"I was puzzled when you came in," Derek continued. "I've never seen a woman from the embassy bring a car in for service."

"My husband does not drive," I said curtly.

Derek shifted easily to questions about women in the Soviet Union. Do most of them work? Are they paid well? How do they combine the demands of job and the family? Standard fare. He was pleasant and listened attentively, and I found myself more involved in the conversation than I had expected.

When my car was ready, he brought it back to the entrance. "By the way," he said, "your car needs a tune-up, and the brakes feel sluggish. When was the last time they were inspected?"

I knew he was right. The car had had nothing but routine changes of oil and filters in two years, and it was probably time to do serious maintenance. "How long will it take to do it?" I asked.

"Oh, a few hours," he said. "I can drive you back to the embassy. Or"—he paused—"we could have lunch. I really enjoyed talking to you, and the Soviet Union is such a fascinating country."

I promised to bring the car for maintenance. Somehow the thought of getting away from home and having a long lunch was not all that unpleasant.

DURING the next few months I probably had the best-maintained car in the embassy. Everything that had not been fixed during the first two years suddenly required a special trip, and since the repairs were minor it was always, "We'll do it while you wait."

I scheduled my car maintenance to coincide with Derek's shifts. Whenever I came, he took time off and we went for a cup of coffee and my favorite cheesecake at a nearby Lum's restaurant, or we drove to a park on the Potomac for a walk along the river.

Our conversations had long since shifted from general interest in the Soviet Union to what seemed to be a genuine friendly concern about my problems. Since the incident with Lev at the hospital, I felt completely isolated; I could not mention my problems to anybody in the embassy for fear that the information would be passed along and we would be sent home as security risks. I could not discuss anything of that nature over the phone with my mother; besides, I did not want her to worry. It was no secret to anybody in or outside the embassy that Lev continued to drink. But our friends did not want to pry into my personal affairs.

Derek seemed to be an ideal person for a confidant. He was about thirty years older than I was, happily married, a good listener, and full of interesting and funny stories about his own life. In many ways he was what I had always wanted my father to be—a warm, understanding man who was genuinely concerned about my well-being. I felt completely safe in our friendship.

From what he told me, the early years of his life had been full of adventure. He'd worked as a stunt man doubling for Gregory Peck—the resemblance was indeed striking—and as a disc jockey, and had gambled quite a lot. One day he showed me his Paramount ID card, but it had a different first name printed on it.

"How do I know it's yours?" I said. "It has a different name."

I was just teasing, but he suddenly became defensive. "Everybody in the movies used assumed names in those days. But if you don't believe me, so be it."

"I do, I do"—I felt that maybe I'd gone too far—"although some of your tales seem pretty farfetched."

I was referring to his vague and somewhat hard-to-believe stories about his card-playing business. As he told it, he was an excellent poker player. He hinted that the stakes were very high and he regularly played with other people's money, for which he got a commission on his winnings. Those friends, as he called them, were rich and powerful. Because Derek was such a valuable investment, they maintained some sort of security around him and kept an eye on his comings and goings. That's why he always took me to the same restaurant, he said, so they would not get concerned about his whereabouts.

Most of the time I dismissed his ramblings about these friends as a ploy to impress me. But now I was concerned. If somebody was watching *him*, did that mean any danger to me?

One episode in particular got me worried. It was August, and by then I was worried that other people in the dealership were beginning to notice our frequent get-togethers. Therefore I changed tactics. I started calling Derek and meeting him at Lum's. After a while, however, I began to worry that the waitresses at Lum's had also seen us together too often, and one day I asked Derek to meet me at a little French restaurant across the street. As we were sitting there drinking espresso, a man suddenly stopped by our table. I almost jumped.

"Hi, Derek," he said. "Just wanted to remind you that we'll pick you up at eight." He glanced at me and walked out.

"I have a game tonight," Derek said. "He works for those people I told you about."

"But why did you tell them where you were coming for lunch?" I asked. All of a sudden I felt angry. "I am in a rather delicate position, meeting you like this. I do not want some shady characters to know about our friendship. If they are the kind of people you described, they can use it against me."

"I didn't tell them," he said. "They must have followed me here from the dealership."

For the first time, I did not believe him. In the back of my mind all the inconsistencies and evasions that had puzzled me in our conversations started to surface, and I knew that I had to make a choice. I could keep asking him questions until I was certain that he was lying, and by doing that destroy our friendship, or I could pretend that nothing had happened. I chose the second option. He'd become too much of a lifeline to me to give up. As long as the embassy did not suspect me of any wrongdoing, the situation was manageable.

THE summer of 1977 was coming to an end. Lev was in Moscow—he and Kitty had left in the middle of August. My parents had been begging for a chance to have their granddaughter for a while, and so he was going to leave her with them in Leningrad and take Xenia on a vacation trip to the Black Sea before the beginning of the school year. After that he had to spend two weeks in consultations with the VAAP staff. I stayed in Washington with Konstantin and in charge of the office.

Business was slow, as usual. VAAP had not changed its pace or procedures, and I wondered how long this could go on and whether the "consultations" for which Lev's presence had been requested had anything to do with our lack of progress. We had one more year to go on our three-year assignment, and the embassy had requested an extension of our stay—a fairly standard procedure for many people assigned to Washington. Peter kept reassuring us that our extension was inevitable.

When Lev came back from Moscow, there wasn't much to cheer about. His boss was under a lot of pressure to send a man with double duties—an intelligence operative. As business was slow, a KGB agent could easily handle our duties and something else, too. Still, an extension request from the embassy was not something to be taken lightly, and among high-level VAAP officials there were supporters for both sides.

"Meanwhile," Lev said, concluding his recital of events in Moscow, "we'd better be prepared to leave next September. It is time to start saving a little and making provisions for our future in Moscow." He was referring to the practice, prevalent among Soviet diplomats, of "taking a piece of America home."

We had already taken care of some important things, such as wall-to-wall shag carpets and major appliances adapted for European current. Small everyday household items had been shipped home in quantities sufficient to last for several years. But I had another dream. I wanted to keep my American car. Although it officially belonged to VAAP, the embassy practice was to replace cars after three years of service and sell them for the salvage value. Quite a few embassy drivers bought their cars. I brought up the question in my next meeting with Derek.

"I think it's crazy," he said. "You can't take all the parts with you, and too many things can go wrong."

"There must be a way," I insisted. "Other people do it."

" 'Other people' are professional drivers and mechanics. They can handle it. You will have nothing but a nightmare. Anyway, I have another solution for you."

"Which is?"

"Which is—why don't you leave the car here and stay to drive it?"

"You are out of your mind. I could never do anything like that."

"Why? You like living here, don't you? You said it yourself many times."

"Of course I do." I could not understand why he was pursuing such a dead-end subject. "As a diplomat, not a refugee. Besides, I have my children and their future to think about."

Kitty and Konstantin, 1977.

That was a mistake. The children gave him another opening.

"Precisely. You said yourself that this country is a much happier environment for the children."

"This conversation is not leading anywhere. What you are suggesting is utterly impossible, and I do not want to discuss it any further. Now, what can I do about my car?"

"Forget it," he said pointedly.

I was quite upset over the unexpected turn of the conversation. It was true that I had often said I enjoyed life in Washington. But to jump to the conclusion that I would leave my country was preposterous. I'd heard of people who had defected from the Soviet mission in New York. They'd usually been people with serious personal problems—or spies. I was neither. So what made Derek think that I would even discuss it?

An uneasy recollection of the incident in the restaurant stirred in my memory. Did this whole thing have something to do with his friends? Did they have photographs? Had they recorded our conversations? Our relationship was innocent enough, but even close friendship with Americans was taboo for us. Besides, I was often critical of the Soviet system in my conversations with him. Did they intend to blackmail me? But I had absolutely no access to sensitive information. So what would anybody gain by ruining me?

I went home and got on with my plans to build a nice nest in Moscow. The extension request had apparently been shelved in the Ministry of Foreign Affairs. We were going back next September.

LIFE went on without much happening until the end of October. Then I received a jolt. It was Tuesday night, and Lev came home about six in the evening, as usual. He had finally learned how to drive and turned out to be reasonably good at it.

"You are going to a special embassy women's meeting tonight," he said matter-of-factly. "Mandatory attendance. Better get ready. I'll feed the children."

"Do you know why they are calling a meeting on such short notice?" I asked, trying to sound casual.

"Have no idea," he replied. "Probably another campaign started in Moscow. Regular briefing."

At the embassy, I found with surprise that it was not a general meeting. Only about thirty women—wives of counselors and first secretaries—were present. Nobody had any idea what was going on. Even the wife of the embassy party boss was there. All of a sudden I felt cold.

The cold feeling grew into panic when I saw the embassy security officer, Vitaly Yurchenko, walk into the room. I knew that Vitaly's job was to prevent embassy personnel from becoming recruitment targets for American intelligence.

The room quieted, and Vitaly started to speak.

"Although it is easy to forget," he said, "we live here in a hostile environment. We are constantly watched by American intelligence services, who stand ready to seize the smallest human weakness and turn it to their advantage. We've been fortunate in that our embassy has been relatively immune from regrettable incidents that sometimes take place in other Soviet missions." This was a not-so-subtle reference to the Soviet mission at the United Nations, which had had several defections in the past few years.

"We are not completely immune, however," continued Vitaly. "Our enemies recently changed their tactics. It appears that they found a weak link in our defense—our women."

I froze. What was he talking about?

"We know that most of you make a tremendous sacrifice by being what you are. You are all well-educated professional women. When you come here, you abandon your careers in favor of your husbands', for the good of your country. We appreciate that this places a strain on you, and some of you apparently cannot handle this stress as well as the others. Our enemies play on your loneliness and isolation. Most of you are friends and keep each other company. But some are loners, who do not understand the importance of being on guard against enemies.

"The regrettable incident I am going to tell you about came to our attention only recently," he continued. "One of our women became very friendly with an American man who, for all we know, may be working for American intelligence."

He went on, describing how the woman had been seen taking walks with her American friend, engaged in long conversations. He still did not name the woman. He was talking, pacing in front of the first row, occasionally stopping and looking at one of us. Why did I have the feeling he was looking at me more than the others? Was he building up tension for a dramatic scene where he would finally say, "And this woman is one of you. Here she is!"? I wished there had been a mirror in the room so I could see my face. Was my horror plainly written on it?

I was so lost in my thoughts that I missed part of Vitaly's speech. I came back to reality when I heard a collective gasp.

"What did he say?" I asked a friend sitting next to me.

She repeated the name of the woman, who was already on a plane to Moscow. She was the wife of a second secretary.

Vitaly continued with the details. The woman had met the man in her apartment building. He spoke Russian reasonably well and was an avid reader of Russian literature. They'd struck up a friendship, which had grown into a full-blown love affair.

"What is amazing," Vitaly was saying, "is that apparently her Soviet neighbors did not think enough about it to report it, so we did not learn about it for a long time."

In the relief of hearing another name I almost forgot that mine might be next on the list. Gradually the horror of my own situation started to come back. It was only a matter of time till somebody found out about Derek and me. I was taking an incredible risk, and for what—just because I was lonely? I had to stop seeing Derek before it was too late—or was it already too late?

I KNEW I had to find a way to meet with Derek and tell him I could no longer see him. It wasn't anything I could do over the phone, but I didn't dare to go to the dealership openly anymore. I had to arrange a meeting in the evening, which presented another problem. What excuse would I give my husband?

It was almost two weeks before an opportunity presented itself. Gennady was coming back from a short business trip to Moscow. His family had already returned there permanently, as the older boy was starting high school. So I had promised to meet him at the airport. I knew it would be seven o'clock before we got to his apartment in Arlington, and it was its proximity to the dealership that gave me an idea. I called Derek from a pay phone and told him that I had to meet him after the dealership closed at nine. He promised to wait for me in the parking lot.

All embassy people returning from Moscow get a lot of visitors the night of their arrival. People come and go, making it an impromptu welcome party. Lev would be home with the children, and as one of Gennady's closest friends, I was expected to stay at the party several hours. In the middle of it I told Gennady that I had forgotten to pick up medication for Kitty and had to make a run to a drugstore in Rosslyn before it closed.

I drove to the store, picked up some cough syrup, and then drove to the dealership. Derek was in the parking lot at the rear. I quickly told him about the scare I had received at the meeting and said that I could not see him anymore, at least for a while.

I was ready to leave when he stopped me.

"I have to tell you something," he said. Suddenly his face had a serious, almost drawn look. "Leave your purse on the hood of your car and come over to my car."

His request was so strange that I laughed. "I won't leave my purse," I said. "Why? Do you think I have a tape recorder?"

I was joking, but he was serious. "Leave it," he repeated.

Reluctantly I obeyed. There was something urgent in his tone. I left my purse and walked over to his car.

"Don't panic," he said. "What I am going to tell you is unpleasant, but you have nothing to worry about."

I already knew. All my suspicions suddenly came together and made sense. "You are an intelligence officer," I said flatly. The shock left me drained of all emotion. My only thought was, There must be some way out. Nothing is final except death.

"No, I am not," he said. "But I was approached by intelligence agents after our second meeting. It appears they had some interest in you, and they asked me to encourage this relationship. I agreed. We were not friends yet, so it didn't matter."

"What difference does it make now?" I said bitterly. "I trusted you and you set me up. That's all there is to it."

"Not quite. In the beginning, yes, I did set you up. But as I got to know you I began to like you very much. I did not *pretend* to be your friend—I was and I *am* your friend. And I am not going to let anybody hurt you. You have to believe that."

"What can you do now? With your help they already have enough pictures and recorded conversations to bury me."

"Remember my friends—the ones I play cards for? They owe me some favors. And they have enough influence to end this."

"I won't trust your friends, or anybody for that matter, from now on. I'll figure some way to get out of it."

"Just remember," he said, "if you decide that you want me to do something, or if you need help of any kind, call me."

"Your best help would be staying away from me."

I walked over to my car and drove back to the party at Gennady's apartment. I stayed for another hour and then went home, replaying my conversation with Derek in my head, trying to find some ray of hope. All my life I had had incredible luck, which had pulled me through seemingly hopeless situations, but I knew that every lucky streak had an end. That night it ended for me.

Chapter 7

For the next two months I lived in a strange dual world. On the surface I was the same person to everybody around me, but the conversation with Derek remained constantly in my mind. I thought about it at home, in the office, at parties. A couple of times Lev remarked that my mind seemed to be wandering somewhere else when I talked to him. I blamed it on my tiredness. No matter how I tried, I could not stop thinking about my situation and its potential consequences.

Derek said that the intelligence agents had approached him because they were interested in me. That was the part I could not figure out. I had no affiliation with the KGB and neither did my husband. What could anybody possibly gain by blackmailing me? I remembered the time Derek had brought up the subject of defection. Was that the ultimate goal? What purpose would that serve? Besides, I was inclined to think that his remark had not been part of a preconceived plan. I had heard my other American friends say more than once that they were amazed how easily I fitted into the American life-style and that it was a shame that I had not been born here. I'd always regarded it as a compliment and had no reason to interpret it as an attempt to recruit me. Still, the possibility of defecting had occurred to me more than once.

I went through my conversations with Derek hundreds of times, trying to recall every word and every possible hidden meaning in everything he had said. Finally it became clear that this brooding was getting me nowhere. I simply did not have enough information to make a decision.

Then, in early January, 1978, I called him.

"Those friends of yours," I said. "I want to meet them."

"Why?"

"Because you said they could help me," I reminded him. "Somebody out there is sitting on a lot of compromising material about me, and I want to know what my options are."

"Okay. I'll arrange a meeting."

I did not hear from him for a week. Then he called and said that the meeting had been arranged. That very night, at nine, I was to come to the Holiday Inn in Rosslyn. It was already seven.

"I can't do that," I said. "Lev is in Chicago and there is nobody I can leave the children with."

"It's tonight or never. I'll wait in the parking lot until nine fifteen. If you don't come, I won't be able to do it again. My friends are very busy people. I can't ask them twice."

I thought feverishly of what to do. I almost never asked my

friends to baby-sit, and certainly never on a moment's notice. What kind of excuse could I offer?

I came up with an outrageous lie—a New York publisher had called who had been planning to be in Washington for a couple of days and to meet with Lev; but his plans had changed and now he had only a short stopover on his way to Europe. I had to meet him and pick up some important papers. With that I called Peter and Tamara, and they agreed to take the children for a couple of hours.

I barely made it to the Holiday Inn parking lot in time. Derek was waiting for me near the entrance.

"Park your car," he said. "We're going upstairs. My friend is waiting for you in a hotel room. I'll take you there."

A hotel room? In all the incidents with Soviet diplomats that I had heard of, hotel rooms figured prominently. God knows what they can do to you there when you are alone—drug you to unconsciousness, and then what?

"I am not going to any hotel room," I said. "A public place will do fine. Why can't he meet us in the restaurant?"

"Because he is a very important man and cannot be seen with you," Derek said. "And if I don't show up with you before ten o'clock, he will leave. So make up your mind."

I looked at my watch. It was quarter to ten. "All right," I said. "I don't know why I trust you, but I'll go."

I recognized his friend as the man who had stopped by our table at the French restaurant several months before. He was in his late thirties and introduced himself as John.

Derek launched into a long speech explaining my plight and how much I needed John's help. John then sent him downstairs to the bar, and I was left alone with him.

"So how can I be of help?" he asked.

I explained my predicament. I said that, granted, I had acted foolishly, but it was an innocent thing that could be blown out of proportion and ruin my life. What I wanted, I said, was to make sure that whatever American intelligence had on me would never see the light of day. Could it be done?

I was very nervous, and, strangely, he seemed to be nervous, too. I noticed that he broke several matches trying to give me a light for my cigarette.

"Yes, it can be done," he said. "I have certain connections. We can put some pressure on the people at the top to tell their underlings to forget it. The information would simply be archived, never to be used again."

"There is no guarantee of that. Somebody could dig up the archives a year from now, when we all think that the whole incident is over and forgotten."

"That's highly unlikely," he said dryly.

I was not convinced.

"By the way," he continued, "how come you attracted attention in the first place? Are you working for Soviet intelligence?"

"No." I laughed. "I honestly do not know why anybody would think that."

"I was told you move around quite freely," he said cautiously. "That would certainly suggest that you have some out-of-the-ordinary privileges or some other duties."

I explained that it had been because my husband was unwilling to drive. We talked for a few more minutes. Finally he called downstairs and asked the bartender to give Derek a message to come up.

"Don't worry," he said. "I will help you, just as Derek has promised. You are in no danger. Nobody is going to bother you."

We shook hands. Derek took me back to my car. As I drove out of the parking garage and made a U-turn I noticed another car making a U-turn behind me. I drove home, keeping an eye on my rearview mirror. The car followed the same route, sometimes falling behind and then reappearing. It passed me as I approached my building—a Volkswagen with diplomatic license plates.

I had been followed. The only question was, by whom?

I did not get much sleep that night. With Lev out of town I had all the time I needed to think. And the more I thought about the meeting that had taken place that night, the more it did not make sense. Something was very, very wrong. Mostly small details, but because of them the whole thing had a false ring to it.

First, there was something about John himself. He did not look or behave like the wealthy businessman Derek said he was. There was something military about him—maybe his haircut, maybe the way he was dressed. I could not put my finger on it, but I had met enough American businessmen by then to sense the difference.

And minutes after our meeting started John had received a telephone call from a "General Simpson's assistant." John had simply said to tell the general he would see him the next day. The brief conversation had appeared almost staged for my benefit—a reinforcement to make me believe in his status and influence?

The whole thing seemed to be so unprofessionally theatrical. Strangely, despite all the pretense, John seemed to be a nice person. He'd listened attentively, asked the right questions, and appeared to be understanding. There was something about his eyes. Honesty? Kindness? Concern? For some reason I wanted to trust him. He just did not seem to be the kind of man who would be associated with shady power brokers.

So who was he?

If my instinct was right, the only logical conclusion was that he was an intelligence agent. But if so, then why the meeting? Was it because they had finally discovered that I was of no interest to them after all, and now wanted to close the matter? Or was it a part of some plan to get me in deeper than before? I was back where I had started, with no idea what was going on.

My thoughts shifted to another part of the conversation. Just to cover all possible ground, I had asked John what would happen if I decided to stay in the States. His answer had surprised me.

"You should not consider it because you think you are trapped," he said, "because you are not. As I said, you have nothing to fear. However, I do think you should consider it for your own sake and for the sake of your children, simply because you would be happy here."

"I can't be happy in a strange country, away from home," I said. "Everything I know and love is in the Soviet Union."

"I don't agree with you. You love your children, and they are right here with you. You love your husband, and he could stay with you, too. But most important, you should do it for yourself. This country was built by people like you—people who were not afraid to take chances. They took risks and prospered. You would do well in America."

"Why are you saying I am not afraid to take chances? I am here with you precisely because I do *not* want to take any chances with my future."

"Maybe. But you have been taking quite a few by not following the embassy rules. You like to do things your own way, and if the rules do not make sense to you, you break them."

That was true. But to take a chance of such magnitude—that was something different. And yet the thought kept returning for days afterward. What would it be like, I wondered, to live in this country—as one of them? What would my life be like?

And always, another thought: What would my life be like if I went back?

NO MATTER which aspect of my life I considered, returning to the Soviet Union with divorce on my mind did not look very promising. First, the divorce itself. I knew I would face a long, protracted battle with Lev, who would not want to give me one. I doubted that I would ever be able to explain to him convincingly why I felt so put down by his attitude.

Assuming that I got him to agree to the divorce, it would mean my going back to a mundane and tedious job. Having an interesting career without Lev's support would be next to impossible. It is a common misconception that women are equal to men in that workers' paradise. It is not so. Maybe they have an equal opportunity to get heavy-duty construction jobs, but when it comes to professional life, very few women rise to a position of significance and power by merit alone.

And as for the children, I really did not want them to grow up in the Soviet Union. Of course, they were young and would adjust. Soviet children, growing up on a diet that is practically devoid of fresh fruits and vegetables, especially in winter, are not as healthy as American ones. Still, other children survive there, and so would mine. I could bring back a supply of vitamins, toys, and clothes to last them for several years, and then maintain it with things Lev got on his foreign trips, provided we stayed on friendly terms. He always brought things for Xenia, and I had no reason to believe he would not do the same for our children.

But there were other concerns. I would have to work. That meant the children would have to attend kindergarten and thus would be exposed to Soviet propaganda at a very early age. I remembered my friend Katrina flying into my apartment once in a smoldering rage.

"What's the matter?" I asked.

"It's Maria," she said. Maria was her four-year-old daughter, who'd just started kindergarten. "You won't believe what happened. She is making a present for her grandfather."

"So what?" I said. "She loves her grandparents. You know that, even though you don't like your in-laws."

"You miss the point," Katrina said. "The present is for Grandfather Lenin! She was told in kindergarten that she has two grandfathers, and Grandfather Lenin is the more important one."

If I went back, my children would be exposed to that sort of thing. They would have to be taught, gradually and carefully, that there were two truths—the official and the unofficial—to learn doublethink. And I would have to be the one to teach them to lead that life of lies if I wanted them to succeed in Soviet society.

As for myself, of course I would miss Washington. I would miss its carefree life, the Washington *Post, Time* magazine, television, movies, smiling and friendly people. But I would readjust to the Soviet system. Maybe I could even adjust to a life with Lev. After all, it would not be the first marriage to exist without love.

Question was, did I want that?

I had many thoughts at that time about how I would feel if I did defect. My family back home would probably not suffer any ill consequences, although they would have to sever ties with me. The Soviet Union has a long-standing policy that no relatives of defectors are ever allowed to emigrate.

The main problem was, how would I feel about myself if I defected? There was something distasteful about defection—even the word itself implies something wrong. I did not feel that I would be betraying my country—I did not have any big secrets to tell, and the system itself was certainly not something to feel loyal to. What was at stake was my loyalty to my friends. But that could be handled if I explained that my motives were purely personal, and if I kept things quiet, avoiding any public statements.

Yes, I could go back and adjust, but was it worth it? I had very little doubt that I would be happier staying here, that the opportunities this country presented were immense and that the things I could do here with my life and work were unlimited. I could finally *choose* what I wanted to be, what I wanted to do. I had little doubt that, even alone and with two children on my hands, I could manage to handle both my work and my family in a way that was impossible back home.

There was one unpredictable factor. What would Lev decide to do? He liked living in Washington, and there was no question that he could find a teaching job in a college engaged in Soviet research. On the other hand, he would have to sacrifice his established position and prestige in Soviet society and accept the fact that he would never see Xenia, his mother, or his sister again. I knew, of course, that taking the children with me would present him with a difficult choice. He was a good father to our children, but I knew that deep down inside, Xenia would always remain his favorite child. Everything being equal, he would choose her.

After two weeks of agonizing vacillation I called Derek and requested another meeting with John. It was quickly arranged. Derek did not even go with me to the hotel.

It was apparent that John expected some serious talking. After all, I had gotten assurances about my safety the time before. I noticed that he had ordered plenty of coffee to make me feel at ease. We chatted about this and that for a few minutes, while I gathered my courage to get to the point.

"I've been thinking about defection," I said finally. "But I have a few questions. First, what will I live on?"

"You'll be given a living allowance from the government," John said. "We will also help you find a job." He'd obviously expected my question and had a ready answer.

"I don't want just any job," I said. "I want to become a businesswoman. My degrees are useless here. I will need an American degree in business."

"I don't think that would be a problem," he said, smiling. "After all, it will be a bargain for the government. Once you get your education, you'll support yourself."

"And I would want no press coverage," I said. "It is a strictly personal decision. If I keep quiet, there is a better chance that the Soviet government will leave me alone."

"If your husband decides to stay with you, we won't be permitted not to capitalize on it. But if it's just you and the children, we can handle it."

"That brings up another interesting point. On my own I do not present as much interest to you as my husband would. So what's in it for you?" I wondered if they wanted me to spy for them while I was still with the embassy.

"It is our duty to help anybody who seeks freedom in our country," John said. "You don't have to do anything."

I decided to let it go at that.

"There is one more thing," I said. "I want to stay on at the embassy until our tour ends. And before that I need to make another trip to Moscow."

"That could be dangerous. The longer we keep it a secret, the greater the chance that something will go wrong. And the idea of a trip to Moscow is sheer lunacy. If somebody suspects you, you won't be able to return to Washington."

"I'll have to go. My parents want to see their grandson. I need to take care of some financial matters to provide for my parents, and for Lev's family in case he decides to stay here. And it will be my last chance to see my mother."

"Okay," he said finally. "If you insist. But I still think it's crazy. Call me when you get back."

Chapter 8

I FLEW to Moscow in early March, 1978, but first I made a couple of adjustments to our life in Washington. The first was to move from Chevy Chase. Our lease had expired, and the rent was going up in excess of our rental allowance. I jumped at the opportunity to move to another building, where no other Soviet families lived. John approved of the idea. Lev was surprised at my choice of residence but was finally sold on an enchanting backyard patio that came with a ground-floor apartment in a building in Arlington.

Another change I implemented was to put Kitty in an American day-care center. I checked with the embassy, and it was not unprecedented, although rarely done. My argument was that it would give Kitty an invaluable head start in English, which I could then easily maintain in Moscow. I did want her to have a head start in English, but for her new life in America.

My official excuse for a trip to Moscow was that, with our return scheduled for September, I needed time for a major remodeling of our apartment. I did, in fact, intend to do exactly that. There was a good chance Lev would indeed return, and it was the least I could do for him. Kitty stayed in Washington, but I took Konstantin with me to show him off. My father was tremendously proud that he finally had a male heir and took to his grandfatherly duties eagerly. I left Konstantin in Leningrad with his grandparents and returned to Moscow almost immediately, planning to hire workers for the apartment.

Alana had been as good as her word, and the most glaring problems with the apartment had been fixed. One room was filled with stuff I had shipped from Washington: a washer and dryer, carpeting, wallpaper, boxes with books and records. What I needed was a team of workers to repaint the walls, hang the wallpaper, and install the appliances. I immediately went to see my friend Andrei Mironov. I knew that he and his new wife had recently redone their entire apartment.

"It's impossible," he said after I explained my problem and he had made a few calls. "It's not a matter of money; it's the time it would take to get the team together and to do the job. These are the best moonlighters in Moscow and they are always busy."

"What about somebody else?" I asked. "Surely your man knows other people in the business."

"I already asked," Andrei said. "Nobody can do it faster. You should have called me from Washington in advance."

I knew he was right. I'd overestimated the flexibility of the Soviet second economy. Even though it was ten times more efficient than the official economy, the difficulty of getting supplies on the black market added to the time needed.

"Don't worry," said Andrei. "Let me know a couple of months in advance exactly when you are going to return, and we will have all the materials ready. Then the job can be done while you are living in the apartment, room by room. It will work out fine."

I thanked him for his help and promised to call him from Washington. If he only knew!

With the apartment problem beyond my control I set out to get together as much cash as possible and give it to my mother.

I did not want to dispose of any of the household items we had shipped from Washington; I still believed there was a greater chance that Lev would return rather than stay, and he was entitled to keep them if I defected. I did take one precaution: I moved everything that was easily movable to Tatiana's apartment and shipped some of the small items to Leningrad. I was afraid that if we both defected, our apartment would be sealed and possibly confiscated by the state, and all the contents would be lost. This way, at least some of it could be kept by our families.

The only things I could freely dispose of were books, records, my own clothes, and a few things I had brought home for resale. American paperbacks are accepted without limit by official Soviet secondhand bookstores at an equivalent of eight to twelve dollars each. Records are also very valuable and go for about fifty dollars for jazz to ninety dollars for pop and rock. Not many people can afford to buy many of them at once at such prices, and I did not want to dabble openly in the black market. I had a wholesale source for selling records, though—my old friend Anatol, whom I had almost married years before.

Anatol was running a booming private enterprise typical of the entrepreneurial Russians. Officially he worked as an electrical engineer. However, the bulk of his substantial income came from his private recording studio. He invested in Western records and in semiprofessional stereo equipment, and he made taped copies of his records for his clients. He was always on the lookout for new records, and he took all I had off my hands.

I brought the clothing I had to sell to an old acquaintance named Olga, who had a lot of friends interested in buying Western clothes. I named my price and left everything with her. Then I went to visit my friend Katrina. We spent several hours together catching up on her news. She said that after the dust had settled from her recent divorce, she had dated several eligible men. Her latest beau was a wealthy art collector. She insisted that we get together for a little party in the evening.

I was rather tired but promised to come. Later I called Katrina to cancel, but, almost in tears, she begged me to reconsider, saying that she would wait for me. She did, although I was more than an hour late. We drove to her friend's apartment, and it turned out to be a party for four—there was one other man besides Katrina's friend. The table was laid lavishly, and the host played records by Sinatra and Ella Fitzgerald. All of a sudden I started wondering why I was there and why Katrina had insisted on this party so much.

As the evening progressed, the men started to ask me questions about my life in the United States. There was nothing unusual about their interest, but the questions indicated that both of them were well informed about life abroad. I was usually sincere with my friends, but these two were strangers. Without any particular reason, I felt uneasy. Katrina's boyfriend talked with admiration about the Western way of life, occasionally asking my opinion as if he expected me to agree both with his adoration of the West and with his critique of the Soviet system. It could be that he felt that way; on the other hand, if they were KGB informers, it was a good way to ferret out my own opinions.

Much as I hated the thought that Katrina might have turned informer, I decided to play it safe with her friends and resorted to innocent double-talk: yes, that's true, but on the other hand, et cetera. At last I pleaded fatigue, and Katrina and her friend drove me home.

Within a couple of days I had completed all my wheeling and dealing and was ready to go back to Leningrad, except for the last and most difficult task. I had to get some papers out of the Soviet Union, but it is a criminal offense to take identification papers out of the country. My diploma and my birth certificate were no problem—they were in Leningrad. But the marriage certificate, which I knew I would need if I were to get a divorce in the United States, and Kitty's birth certificate were in my mother-in-law's safekeeping.

I kept delaying this mission, because I did not have any excuse at all to ask her for the papers. Finally, as the day of my departure for Leningrad approached, I came up with an idea. I told her that the management of our building had to update some records for our apartment, and I needed to make copies of both documents. Then I went to Leningrad, and when I returned to Moscow, ready to fly back to Washington, I told her that I had forgotten the papers in Leningrad. I hoped she would not check with my mother.

My stay in Leningrad was the most traumatic time of my visit. I hated to lie to my mother, but I had to do it for her own protection. I gave her all the money I had and told her that I was considering a divorce and wanted her to stash it for me for a rainy day. She was not particularly surprised; she knew I had been growing unhappy in my marriage. Nor was she shocked at my request. After she'd gone to work, she'd kept some money in her own account, building some reserves for the time when she could persuade my father to give her a divorce. We talked a lot, staying up late at night when my father was asleep, but even then I had to be careful not to alarm her unnecessarily.

Besides, she needed to talk to me even more than I needed to talk to her. My parents' marriage was deteriorating rapidly. She'd twice asked for a divorce, but my father had refused. She wanted my advice. I was glad she had so much to discuss, because it steered the conversation away from my own affairs. Or maybe she felt, with that sixth sense that only mothers possess, that it was better for both of us not to ask too many questions.

To this day I do not know whether she had figured my plans out, but all of a sudden she decided to go to Moscow with me to see me off to Washington. That was surprising. She usually did not feel well in the wintertime, and there was no need for the trip, since I was supposed to be coming back in a few months. She insisted, however, and I did not protest; I wanted to be with her as long as I could.

I'll remember the scene at the airport as long as I live. I lingered until the last moment, and when I got to the upper balcony reserved for international departures, I looked down at my mother. Standing there on the ground floor, she looked smaller than she was. I saw that her eyes were filled with tears, and I suddenly realized how much she had aged during the three years I had been in Washington and how much I would miss her. From now on I would see her only in photographs; our telephone conversations would have to be carefully controlled because somebody would always be listening. I knew it was the last time I would be seeing her. She would not be allowed out of the Soviet

Union, and I would never be able to go back and visit her. And I wondered again—had she guessed? Did she know it was the last time, too?

My return to Washington was almost routine. Everything was fine at home, and there was some good news: VAAP had decided to extend our stay for one more year after all.

I met with John, gave him my papers because I was afraid to keep them in our apartment, and told him I would be staying with the embassy longer than I had thought but my intention was unchanged. For a while nothing happened, until an event near the beginning of April changed the situation dramatically.

It was Friday, April 7, 1978. Lev was out of town, and I was home alone with the children when suddenly I heard a knock on the door. It was close to eight in the evening, and I did not expect any guests. As I opened the door I saw Vladimir, a young diplomat who was the ambassador's special aide. Vladimir was an ardent jazz fan, and he had a long-standing invitation to come and listen to some of our records.

"Just thought I'd take you up on your invitation," he said. I fixed him a drink and put a record on. He did not seem to listen, though. He looked very tired, and his face was almost ashen.

"Did you have a bad day?" I asked. "You look awfully tired."

He did not answer until he had fixed himself another Scotch. "Something terrible has happened," he said. "One of our highest-ranking diplomats in New York, Arkady Shevchenko, defected."

I was stunned. The name meant nothing to me, but the significance of his act could have serious repercussions in Washington.

"Did he know much?" I asked. "Know" was a commonly understood euphemism for "Is he going to blow a lot of covers?"

"Did he!" Vladimir said. "We spent the entire afternoon trying to figure out who is going to be expelled and how soon."

We talked a little more. Fearful of ever present bugging, he did not say much except the bare facts that would be in the newspapers later anyway. Vladimir soon left, and I stayed up late, trying to think about what this new development could mean for me. There would probably be increased security checks and increased surveillance from our own counterintelligence.

On Tuesday the story broke on the front pages of all the newspapers, but in the embassy there was little talk about the event. Most people behaved as if nothing had happened. Admittedly it was an unpleasant topic. The only person to whom I talked about it was Peter. He was bitter and angry.

"The s.o.b. would have been back in Moscow a long time ago if he weren't Gromyko's protégé," he said. "Everybody in New York knew he had family problems and was drinking heavily, and the security section requested three times that he be recalled, but every time Gromyko covered for him. At least those reports are on file, so nobody will lose a job because of this creep."

It was a disturbing preview of what my friends would say about me after I left. No matter how personal my motives were, I would be thought of as dirt for the rest of my life.

JOHN had a few more points to add to my worries. The most important one was that with increased security checks Lev might be identified as a security risk because of his drinking, and our stay in Washington could be shorter than I had thought.

"I want you to meet somebody to discuss your resettlement," he said. "It's time to begin detailed planning."

We were scheduled to meet the next Saturday in the apartment that he was now renting in the same building. I could not bring the children with me—Kitty was old enough to talk and later could have told Lev that we had visited another apartment. Lev was still out of town, so I took the children to the sitter, and half an hour later I was at John's apartment upstairs. He was not alone.

"Jim is a relocation expert," John said. "He will discuss with you the paperwork and the details of future arrangements."

A relocation expert? Who was he kidding? Even if John himself was who he said he was—a businessman—surely by now American intelligence was involved. Why was he still playing that game? Didn't they trust me?

"John," I said, "I've known you for some time. Why don't you level with me and tell me that Jim is from the CIA?"

"As a matter of fact, it's the FBI," Jim said.

I was quite surprised. Everybody in the embassy always referred to the CIA when mentioning surveillance. "I thought the

FBI was like the Soviet militia—to catch criminals," I said.

Jim explained to me that all counterintelligence inside the United States was FBI business. It turned out, however, that John was not with the FBI. Even now I do not know exactly who he was, but he was with me every step of the way.

The first thing Jim had me do was fill out some forms and write a formal request for asylum. He explained to me that the application for U.S. citizenship was a complicated and lengthy process, and that I would have to be sponsored by a Congressman to have it approved on an exceptional basis. They wanted to have the paperwork ready as soon as possible.

They were concerned about the Shevchenko affair and its possible repercussions in Washington. We agreed on a signal by which they would let me know when they needed me to contact John. I was always supposed to take the same exit from the parking lot. At the intersection there was a stop sign. The signal was a piece of metal tape wrapped around the stem of the sign.

"But I only drive by it in the morning," I said. "What if you need to contact me during the day?"

"If there is an emergency, we'll find you," Jim said. I understood; they would keep an eye on me around the clock.

A couple of hours later I had picked up the children and was on my way to the embassy's summer retreat on the Eastern Shore, knowing that I had made the first irrevocable step. Now it was not just conversation; I had signed the official papers requesting asylum. If the papers fell into the wrong hands and made their way to the embassy . . .

One good thing the Shevchenko affair did for me, however, was to provide me with an opportunity to open the subject with Lev and to test the waters as to what his decision would be. I brought up the subject carefully. His opinion of Shevchenko's actions was the same as the embassy's. I felt that it was dangerous to continue the conversation, and I quickly changed the subject. It was clear that Lev would have to be told only at the last moment.

THE events of the next two months proved that my worry was not unwarranted. First I got a telephone call from Katrina, in Moscow. That was not unusual; she was very impulsive and had called me a few times before when she felt low. This time, however, she sounded strained and her voice was artificial.

"Are you still having problems with Lev?" she asked, almost without a preamble.

For a moment I nearly lost my capacity to speak. "No, everything is fine," I managed to say. Katrina knew better than to talk about personal matters over international telephone lines, where every conversation was recorded. I remembered her friends in Moscow. So my instinct had been right—she had set me up for a KGB checkup, and now she'd been told to follow up. It also meant that the security check in the embassy was going on for real.

My suspicions were confirmed in a few days. Out of the blue we received a telegram from Moscow terminating our extension and ordering us to return to Moscow as originally planned, at the beginning of September.

"This does not make sense," Peter said when we told him about the telegram. "There is a VAAP delegation coming to the States on the ninth of September. It would be logical to use the opportunity to have Lev introduce his successor to his American counterparts. Yet they want you to return on the third."

It may not have made much sense to him, but it made perfect sense to me—we were being recalled to Moscow. Our original date of return was the earliest they could get us out inconspicuously.

Apparently the FBI was also concerned. One day in the middle of July I got a call from Derek while I was in the office.

"I have a buyer interested in your car," he said. "Why don't you give him a call? Here's the phone number."

There was no need to write down the number. What Derek was saying was that John wanted me to contact him—right away.

A few minutes later I ran downstairs to the pay phone. John answered immediately.

"Don't go to the airport today," he said.

Our friend Peter was flying to Moscow that afternoon and had asked me to accompany him to the airport and bring his car back.

"How do you know—" I began, then realized that they obviously knew all about it. "Why?" I asked instead.

"Just don't go. We have reason to believe that the KGB may want to put you on that plane to Moscow."

"I can't do that. Peter is our best friend. I have absolutely no reason to refuse."

John thought for a few moments. "You have a point," he said finally. "Well, all right, but under no circumstances go near the mobile lounge at the Aeroflot counter. Stay in the waiting area. If you see anything suspicious, take off your glasses and wipe them with a handkerchief."

I tried to joke. "I don't have a handkerchief."

"Use a Kleenex." He laughed. "Seriously," he added, "be careful. There will be people watching you, so don't take off your glasses just because your nose is itching, or you'll have a shoot-out on your hands."

As we entered the airport I kept looking around me, trying to see if I could spot the FBI. No such luck. Nobody was sitting on a bench, pretending to read a newspaper and darting his eyes furtively over the edge, as in the spy movies I had seen. If the FBI people were there, they had made themselves invisible.

I did follow John's advice to stay away from the lounge. We went to the airport bar, where Peter had a glass of beer and I ordered a cup of coffee. Then final hugs and kisses, and I left at the earliest opportunity.

I never learned what made the FBI think I was in danger on that particular day. Neither did I know until much later that the agents had an executive order signed by the President to hold the plane if I was put on it against my will. But although the airport scare turned out to be a false alarm, it did bring the realization that my double life could not continue much longer.

Two days later when I met with Jim and John, the decision was made. It was too risky to wait till the last moment. They were pulling me out on August 2.

Chapter 9

Now that the date was finally set, I could feel only one thing—relief.

As long as I could remember, I'd always hated uncertainty. Knowing that the plan had at last been set into action gave me a new burst of energy. I looked forward to that day, while simultaneously trying to use whatever time I had left to get my affairs in order. I made sure that all my own bills were paid and that the files and the bookkeeping in the office were completely up to date. That was particularly important, because any shortage in VAAP's money could exacerbate Lev's problems, of which he would have plenty if he decided not to join me. I did feel guilty about doing this to him, but I could only hope that the questioning would not take long and that he would soon be cleared.

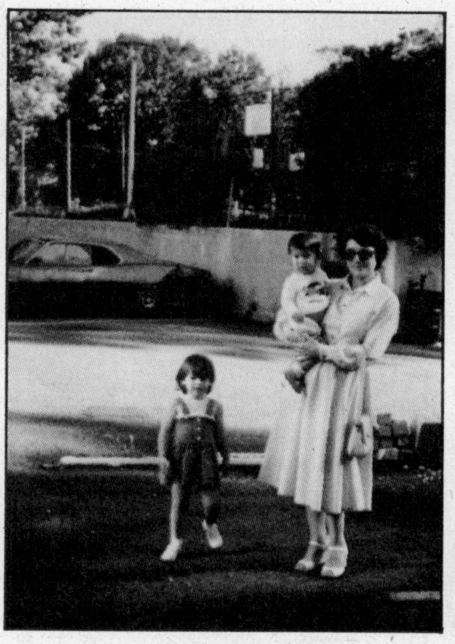

Lev took this picture of the children and me in the parking lot of our apartment building a few weeks before my defection.

I also tried to make the evening before the big day into something extra special, knowing that it could well be our last night together. I cooked his favorite dinner and set the table for two, with candles and music. He did not sense the mood, though. He ate his dinner quickly, had a few drinks, and went to bed early.

The next morning he went to work, and then all the hectic events of the next few hours followed: rushing between the apartment and the motel, taking the oath, leaving the children in the care of the FBI, waiting in the parking lot. Then they were all behind me. I was walking slowly toward the patio of my apartment, still holding John's hand. This was the final uncertainty that had to be resolved—was my marriage to continue or would I be a single woman?

Whether from the tension or from the heat of the August afternoon, I was beginning to feel light-headed. I kept holding John's hand as though afraid that if I let go, I would wake up and realize that it was not reality.

Then I came to my senses. Lev was standing on the patio, waiting for me to approach. He looked sad and angry.

"I want to talk to you alone. Let's go inside," he said simply. I looked at John. He shook his head. Once inside the apartment Lev could lock the door and refuse to open it, invoking his diplomatic immunity, until the embassy representative arrived.

"We can talk in Russian," I said. "Nobody will understand."

We stayed outside. What he said was predictable: I must have lost my mind, this was all a mistake, I should come back before the embassy found out—if *they* would let me. And why, why had I even thought of it in the first place? He was cool and controlled. Maybe the presence of other people restrained him from showing his emotions.

"You've read my letter," I said wearily. "I like this country. I want to stay here. I want the children to grow up here."

We went on for about half an hour, pacing the parking lot. Finally John said, "We have to go."

"What are you going to do?" I asked Lev. "I can't stay any longer. Are you coming with me?"

"I don't know," he said. "I need time to think. How can I get in touch with you?"

I looked at John. "I'll call you," I said.

John nodded. Then he asked Lev if he could speak with him for a moment. I went back to the car with Larry; John and Lev stayed behind. I could see Lev talking angrily. Finally John gave him a small piece of paper and returned to us.

"What was that?" I asked.

"Some phone numbers he can call if he wants to stay." I knew that the embassy had to be notified before the end of the day. That did not leave Lev with much time.

I looked back as we turned the corner. Lev was still standing on the patio, looking at me. He was a handsome man, I thought; his tan jacket and light blue shirt contrasted nicely with his tanned face and gray hair. Would I ever seen him again? And did I really want to see him again?

We went back to the motel to pick up the children. Linda, the baby-sitter, who turned out to be an FBI agent, was playing happily with them, and they obviously liked her. We took off again, heading west, and an hour later we were registered in a suite at a Sheraton hotel in Fredericksburg, Virginia, some fifty miles outside of the city and beyond the twenty-five-mile zone to which Soviet diplomats were restricted. Everybody seemed to be happily exhausted. We ordered some food and drink from room service and toasted our success. Then Larry went downstairs to make a call.

"Lev is still in the apartment," he said when he came back. "He has not made any calls. Just sits there."

"How much time does he have?" I asked.

"You'll call him at five. A few hours should be enough."

"You don't know my husband." I laughed. "Lev does not like to make quick decisions."

I was right. When I called from the pay booth downstairs at five o'clock, Lev complained that he needed more time to think. I had to promise to call later. Larry talked to somebody on the phone and finally said that they could keep it quiet till the morning.

I called again at ten p.m. To my surprise Lev was sober. He did not want to talk about himself; he wanted to talk about me. For twenty minutes he went through our marriage, reminding me of all the good things we had had together and how it could be great again if I returned. Eventually the pressure started to affect me and I began to cry. I told him I would call him early in the morning and hung up.

By six o'clock in the morning none of us had had any sleep except Linda, who had been sent to bed because she would have to get up early when the children woke. Larry got several calls from Washington—Lev was still in the apartment, no outside calls, the light had been on all night. Finally we went downstairs to the pay phone again.

The call did not bring any results. Lev told me that he had had a sleepless night, too, and although I managed to keep him from tearing me apart with reminiscences, he was still not ready for a decision. He needed another extension.

"I don't like it," Larry fumed when we returned to the suite.

"He's just stalling for time and putting pressure on Elena, that's all there is to it. We'll have to notify the embassy."

We talked about it some more, and I assured him that I could cope with the pressure. "He's always been that way," I said. "Give him more time."

The day went fast. John drove to Washington and returned in the evening. I caught a few hours of restless sleep. Late in the afternoon I called Lev again. He was hoping that I would come back and the whole thing would disappear like a bad dream.

"I am not coming back," I said. "I planned this for several months, and I am not going to change my mind now." I told him that we had gotten the final extension. At ten o'clock the next morning a formal letter would be delivered from the State Department to the embassy.

The second night was not as tense as the first. We'd already talked endlessly about what might have been going through Lev's mind and agreed that the odds were he would go back home. But there wasn't anything else any of us could do. Lev had been told that if he wanted to join me, he was to drive to the phone booth three blocks away from our home by ten the next morning and make a phone call. Somebody would pick him up.

Finally the morning came. We were up by seven. Larry had gotten several calls from Washington during the night. No change.

"You know," John said, "as a human being, I hope he will stay. It's terrible to lose a family like that. But as your friend, I hope he won't. You will be much better off without him."

All the months I had been seeing John I'd been awed by his seeming ability to read my thoughts. His way of saying exactly the thing I was thinking at the moment was uncanny.

Suddenly, a few minutes before ten, the phone rang. Larry answered, and a look of pleased surprise came over his face.

"Well, what do you know," he said. "We were all wrong. Lev loaded his things into the car and left the apartment. I guess you'll be seeing him soon."

I thought about something else, too. Just about then the embassy would be receiving the letter from the State Department. The finality of my action suddenly took shape and became real. I'd burned all the bridges; there was no return.

"Well," John said, "we might as well have a good breakfast. I'm sick of room service. Let's go have a decent meal."

We went downstairs in a cheerful mood. We'd gotten over the first hurdle. The children finished their breakfast quickly, and Linda took them upstairs. The four of us stayed, lingering over coffee. Now that the tension was over, we could relax.

"You know," said Larry, "I've learned more about you in these past two days than I have in all these months of watching you. But I still have one unresolved question in my mind."

"Ask it," I said. I was totally unprepared for what came next.

"Are you a KGB agent?" he said, deadpan.

"Of course," I replied, keeping an equally straight face. "And you are under arrest for kidnapping me and creating an international incident to embarrass the Soviet Union."

The roar that followed made people in the restaurant turn their heads in our direction. Still laughing, we went back to our room. Larry stopped by the phone to call Washington. When he came upstairs five minutes later, he was not smiling anymore.

"You won't believe it," he said. "He went back to the apartment."

In a few minutes we knew the story. Lev had left the apartment shortly before ten and driven to the phone booth. He walked up to the booth, stayed there for a couple of minutes as if lost in thought, then returned to the car and drove back to the apartment. What happened at that last moment I would never know for certain. I could only guess that some emotion had overcome his careful calculations and had driven him back—love for his family, fear, or just that mysterious Russian soul that keeps its people tied to their land.

Suddenly, for the first time, I clearly realized the dimensions of my own loss. Not only had I lost my husband and my own family, I had also lost something of myself, the identity that had been a part of me all my life. I would have to become a different person with a different name, a person without a country and without a past. Was what was left enough to get me through? Only time would tell. I started to cry.

Wisely, they let me go to my room and cry it out. When I came back, everybody was talking quietly. John handed me a drink.

"Don't think about the past," he said. "Think about the

future—yours and the children's. That's what you told me the first time we met—that you wanted a different future. Remember?"

I remembered. Gradually I relaxed. All the fears that had been on my mind during the past few months started to dissipate. I was safely away from the embassy; my children were with me. Lev was going home, and I had to start to plan for the future. The first thing I learned was that after all the formalities were completed, I would be turned over to the CIA, where a special relocation office would take care of my new identity, a place to live, and job training.

I was very surprised. It did not make sense to me that an agency whose primary purpose is foreign intelligence, rather than a domestic agency such as the FBI, would be undertaking a job search for me. But as I knew from my Soviet experience, governments often work in mysterious ways.

Meanwhile there was one more formality to take care of—an official meeting at the State Department with the Soviet representatives. Such meetings are almost routine, and their main purpose is to allow the other side to ascertain that its citizen is acting of his or her own free will. I was told that the embassy had requested the meeting, but that I did not have to go if I felt it would put too much strain on me. I wanted to go. The embassy had already filed a protest in which they had said that according to Lev I had been confused and appeared drugged during my meeting with him, and that he had almost talked me into coming back when the FBI agents had taken me away by force. Whether he'd actually said that or the protest had been concocted by the embassy was immaterial. I wanted to set the record straight and also, as much as possible, to leave my husband and my family out of it.

However, I did not particularly look forward to meeting my former compatriots. I knew that the embassy would try to put a lot of pressure on me. In such situations it was not uncommon to bring relatives in from the Soviet Union to make a personal appeal. Although I doubted very much that they would bring my mother, it was possible that Lev would be there. What I needed for the occasion was reinforcement, and as with many other women my reinforcement would be to dress to kill.

The problem was that most of my clothes were still back in the apartment upstairs that the FBI had been renting. All I had with me was the bare necessities. I told Larry about my dilemma.

"I need my white linen suit," I said. "I will feel much more comfortable and confident wearing it."

"Impossible," Larry said. "We can't go near the building. The KGB is all around it. Why can't we just buy you another suit?"

"I do not want another suit," I said. "I never feel comfortable in new clothes." I knew I was being unreasonable, but with all the familiar things around me crumbling by the minute, the suit was the last bastion of comfort I could cling to in a stressful situation. He understood, because the next day the suit was delivered to me.

The meeting was set for Tuesday, the eighth, and there was little we could do but wait. I could not make any phone calls nor visit any of my American friends. They were all known to Lev, and their houses could be watched. Everybody was certain that the embassy would be trying to find me and get me back.

Finally Tuesday came, and we went to the State Department. We came early so we would be in the conference room when the Soviet representatives arrived. I was beginning to feel panicky again. The FBI could not be present in the conference room—it was against the rules—but I knew I would feel much better if there was somebody I knew in there with me. A compromise was worked out. John was permitted to stay in the room as an observer.

The two representatives from the Soviet embassy were a man named Kavalerov, the head of the consular section, and a younger man I did not know. They did not bring Lev with them, and I wondered briefly if they were afraid he would ask for asylum right there at the meeting. Kavalerov was a portly, soft-spoken, middle-aged man who was well liked in the embassy. He sat across the table from the official interpreter, who sat by my side. The State Department official was at the head of the table; the younger man from the consulate was right across from me. I could not see John, who stayed in the chair near the wall behind me.

As soon as Kavalerov started to speak, I understood their game plan. He talked almost nonstop. In the most fatherly manner he told me that nobody held a grudge against me, that I had probably gotten upset over something, but that whatever it was it could be straightened out, and the embassy stood ready to help me. The translator was busy translating Kavalerov's speech for the record, and the State Department official, who did not speak Russian, listened to the translation. Meanwhile the younger man leaned over the table and with an impassioned face talked directly to me.

"Do you really think you can get away with it?" he said. "We'll find you anywhere. You think you can spit on us, you spiteful witch? You're pathetic. Cold-blooded, too. Don't you know what will happen to your parents? They are still there, and we can do whatever we want with them. Remember, we never forgive traitors. Sooner or later you will get what you deserve." He called me every dirty name in the Russian language. It was a typical good cop–bad cop routine, and with Kavalerov keeping the interpreter busy, nobody caught what the man was saying except me.

After about ten minutes Kavalerov finished his speech and asked me questions. I reaffirmed my decision to seek asylum. I also said that I had nothing against the embassy or the country itself; it was a personal decision, and I would not make any political statements to the press. When we rose to leave, Kavalerov said how much he regretted the mistake I was making.

"Your main mistake is that you think you know this country," he said. "But you don't. You've looked at it through rose-colored glasses from behind the embassy walls. Right now you feel like a hero because the people around you tell you so. But soon you will be useless to them, and they will throw you out like a used rag. You will never make it here on your own, and this country is not a heaven for people who have no means of supporting themselves. When you find that out, come back, and we will still take you, because Russia is where you belong."

I was disturbed by what he said more than I wanted to admit to myself. I had no idea what my future held; all my assumptions were based on John's promise that they would put me through school. What if they did not keep that promise?

We waited until the Soviet representatives left the building, and then went back to the car. As we drove out, Larry waved to some other FBI cars. They took off and followed us.

"Boy, you were real cool in there," Larry said. "John told me what was going on. And now—let's celebrate."

The "celebration" turned out to be lunch in a fast-food place in McLean. Other FBI people joined us; there were about twenty people there. Everybody was congratulating me, shaking my hands, hugging me. The mood was exuberant; it was *officially* over.

Except for one last thing I wanted to do. It was Tuesday, the day of the Aeroflot flight to Moscow, and I knew Lev would be on it. I wanted to say good-bye to him for the last time.

"Go ahead, call him," said Larry. "He's in the office. Just don't let him upset you."

A stranger's voice answered our office number. I was not surprised; I knew Lev would not be alone until he was on the plane to Moscow. I was surprised, though, when they called him to the phone. The conversation was short. Everything had already been said. I also knew he was restrained by the presence of the stranger, who was certainly listening on another extension.

"I just called to say good-bye," I said. He said nothing. "I just finished the meeting at the State Department," I said after a pause. "It's final now."

"Nothing is final." Suddenly he was speaking rapidly. "You could still come back. I was assured there would be no repercussions. We could forget this whole nightmare."

"No," I said. "I am not coming back."

"Have you thought about the children?" he asked. "Do you think it is fair for you to deprive them of their father, of their homeland, when they are too young to speak for themselves?"

"America is a free country. When they are old enough to make their own decisions, they may decide to return to the Soviet Union. But at least they will have a choice."

I hung up and went back to the table. I'd already separated myself mentally from him, and the conversation had not upset me. It had simply been a last gesture of goodwill. I felt that our seven years of marriage entitled him to it.

After the lunch most of the FBI people said good-bye to me, and I realized that for them it was the end of the assignment. The thought was slightly disconcerting. In the past few months I'd grown accustomed to the idea that they were always somewhere near, ready to protect me. Would the people about to take over be just as nice, as caring, and as protective as they had been? I thanked them all for everything they'd done for me, and drove back to Fredericksburg with "the bunch"—Jim, John, and Larry.

It was our last evening in Fredericksburg. We went out for dinner and spent most of the time reminiscing about funny episodes from the past few months, talking about my future, and having a good time. I knew I would miss them tremendously. They'd become almost a family to me, and at that moment there was nobody in this entire country closer to me than those people. I only hoped they would not fade out of my life as everything else had.

The next morning we packed and left the Sheraton to meet my new hosts—the CIA.

Chapter 10

THREE people were waiting for us in the car in the Marriott parking lot, two men and one woman. During brief introductions I learned that the men's names were Paul and George, and the woman's name was Barbara. Both men were in their late forties, medium height. Paul was rather distinguished-looking, with reddish hair and a small mustache, and smoked a pipe; George had dark hair and a slicked-back haircut. He was down-to-earth and friendly, while Paul had a more remote air that suggested authority. Barbara was a tall woman in her late twenties.

We returned to our car and followed the CIA car to a residential area in northern Virginia. I'd read enough about defectors to know that the first few months they usually lived in a safe house—a place that was secure and well protected.

My safe house turned out to be a town house, with three bedrooms upstairs and a comfortable living-dining room and a small kitchen downstairs. The woman who met us there had a simple lunch ready. She was Donna, the housekeeper, who would come daily to do the shopping and cook.

After lunch Paul outlined the plan for the next several months. As my case officer, Barbara would take care of all the paperwork, coordinate debriefing, schedule my time, and familiarize me with American life. I would also take professional aptitude tests and meet with a job counselor. George was Barbara's supervisor. Paul was the boss; he was not directly involved in day-to-day activities, but if I needed him, I could request a meeting.

The most pleasant surprise was that the bunch would stay with me for the next couple of weeks. They had to conduct the FBI debriefing anyway, and instead of coming and going every day, they'd volunteered to provide my protection as well. Linda would stay with me most of the time, with Jim and Larry taking turns in overnight stays. John would be there, too. How they'd managed it I don't know. But they'd figured out how lonely I would be without them and wanted to ease me into the new pattern gradually, for which I was eternally grateful.

The meeting went on for about three hours. Finally Paul rose. "I'll leave you with Barbara so you can get acquainted," he said. "Is there anything you want to ask before I leave?"

"Yes," I said. "My children are used to their own kind of food, and I'd like to take care of the cooking myself. It would also feel more like home to me."

"No problem," Paul said. "Donna will come twice a week to do your shopping. The rest is up to you."

"I'd like to do my own shopping as well," I persisted.

"That might be difficult," Paul said. "You will be busy during the day. Just give Donna a list of what you need."

The conversation was clearly over. Paul and George left. Barbara stayed to "get acquainted," but the conversation did not seem to hold together. She asked a few polite questions. Then she said she'd bring Social Security applications the next day and left.

"You didn't like her very much, did you?" John asked. As always, he was perceptive. "Your psychological profile said that you get along better with men than with women."

"That's not really true," I protested. "I get along with Linda wonderfully, and I have a lot of women friends."

"Let's agree that it's half true." John laughed. I knew he was right. Although I did have some women friends, they were generally older professional women who were secure enough to let other people be themselves. In my life in the States, however, I had discovered a certain category of women for whom I had little tolerance—those who were insecure in their newfound liberation and whose desire to assert themselves resulted in their bossing everybody around them. I did find it much easier to work with men, who were generally secure enough not to mind my independence.

Also, Barbara struck me as sort of cold. Of course, it was unfair to compare her with Linda. Linda was one of the bunch, a totally professional and well-trained FBI agent who simultaneously maintained the sincerity and the warmth of a country girl. She had more than once told me about her desire to get married and have children. I knew she would be a wonderful mother, but at the same time she firmly intended to stay with the bureau, the job she loved. No, I did not have any problems getting along with Linda, and maybe in time Barbara would turn out to be nice, too.

THE next two weeks were uneventful. Barbara showed up every morning with various forms and set up some appointments for me. Larry, John, and Jim came every day for a few hours of debriefing. There was little that we had not discussed during our stay in Fredericksburg, but they had to make some official records. The questions revolved mostly around embassy life and life in the Soviet Union. They usually brought sandwiches from a nearby deli for lunch, and in the early afternoon they left, leaving me with enough time to attend to practical details with Barbara.

My name was changed from Yelena Mitrokhina to Elena Alexandra Costa, and as resident aliens, my children and I were issued green cards with our new last name. I told the CIA that I did not want cosmetic surgery, but I did want to change my appearance. For occasional shopping trips I bought a blond wig, which changed my appearance dramatically. And I replaced my glasses with contact lenses; I'd always wanted them, but they hadn't been available in the Soviet Union. Barbara took me to her optometrist, and there I got a glimpse of how the agency operated. While we were waiting, the nurse came out and reminded Barbara about her appointment.

"Why did she call you Judy?" I asked Barbara. She seemed embarrassed. "She got me mixed up with my twin," she said.

I mentioned the episode to John, and he laughed. "I don't think she has a twin," he said. "The truth is, agency people never use their real names with defectors. Too many people go back, and some are simply sent to learn about our procedures and return."

"Why couldn't she just tell me that?" I asked. "Certainly I can understand precautions. But you always answered my questions. If you couldn't, you just said so, and I did not ask anymore."

"We work differently," he said. Thank goodness, I added silently.

All good things come to an end. In two weeks the FBI debriefing was completed and my friends had to leave. We had a final party, and they went on to other jobs. The agency took over.

I did not have much time to feel lonely. After a brief break the agency started sending their own people for debriefing. Two people came to go through my biography, two different people came to ask about Moscow life, and so on. Some of them spoke passable Russian, but I preferred to conduct the conversations in English—first because I needed the practice, and second because I felt it was less strain on me to speak English than for them to speak Russian, and that way we could accomplish things faster. I especially liked one woman, named Anna. Her Russian was fluent, and she was very knowledgeable about Soviet culture and literature. A couple of evenings she stayed on after debriefing and we had long talks. I became quite attached to her.

One of my minor problems was that although I was finally doing my own grocery shopping, I was still rather immobile. I did not have a car—or money, for that matter—because Barbara took me shopping and she paid at the checkout counter. This complete dependence on her began to get to me. Formally I was free; however, without money or a car I was homebound.

Just how precarious the arrangement was became clear during the Labor Day weekend. Everybody was off; there was no work scheduled. Barbara left late Friday afternoon to go out of town. I faced a long, long weekend.

Friday evening and Saturday went by without incident, but by Sunday afternoon I found myself running low on milk and diapers. I also began to feel lonely. It was the first time I'd been completely alone for more than a day since the defection. Everybody was having fun going to picnics and visiting friends. I missed my friends, both Russian and American. Was this the way I was going to spend the rest of my life—hiding? The future looked bleak and hopeless, and it felt as though the debriefing was never going to end. What was I doing here anyway?

Perhaps I would have come up with a surprising answer if I had spent another day alone. Fortunately, I did not get that chance. Linda called to say hello, and when I mentioned that I was alone and needed groceries, she came right over and managed to cheer me out of my silly thoughts. By the end of the day I was wondering why I had become depressed in the first place.

Anna was furious when I told her about my weekend. "That's how we lose people," she said. "Everybody gets depressed after a while, practically without exception. You should not have been left alone, and it's amazing you did not turn to the embassy in that state of mind. Quite a few people do, you know."

"The embassy is almost ten miles away, and I don't even have a stroller," I joked. The crisis was over. I had not really considered going back. I had no illusions about my future if I were to return home. Even if I did not end up in jail, I would be declared an unfit mother and my children would be taken from me. No, whatever I was facing here—the reality was not quite what I had expected—I would have to cope with it the best I could.

Anna was a senior officer, and she apparently voiced her disapproval. So did Larry. The next time I saw Barbara she was tight-lipped and colder than usual. I knew by then that this was her first assignment with the relocation office. Before that she had had mostly secretarial jobs in foreign missions. Now, apparently, she felt that I was blowing her chances for career advancement.

"I want to talk to you about a few things," she said. "I've been getting feedback about your complaints, and I want you to know my point of view. I am trying to prepare you to stand on your own two feet when you leave here. People can grow so dependent on us that they don't know how to handle their lives. What I am trying to do is really in your best interest."

"I'll be happy to stand on my own two feet as soon as you get me a car and some money," I countered. "I have lived in this country for three years, and although there are obviously some things I don't know, driving a car and grocery shopping do not fall into that category."

"We have our policies. You'll have a car when the time comes."

"I can understand that," I said. "But perhaps we'd better leave the building of my self-reliance until such a time comes."

Somebody else apparently disagreed with her as well, because a week later I had a car and a weekly allowance.

I went on with the debriefings. A couple of times a pleasant young man came to give me IQ and job-aptitude tests. A week later he came back with the results.

"Congratulations," he said. "You did extremely well. You have a very high aptitude for managerial jobs. You told me you were planning to go to business school. I think it's a very good idea."

Encouraged, I brought up the topic with Paul. "I have plenty of time in the evenings," I said, "and I would like to start getting ready for the exams. Barbara told me there is a Graduate Management Admission Test I need to take to apply to a graduate school, and if I get to it fast, I may be able to start in the winter semester."

"We'll get you together with a specialist who will suggest some suitable graduate schools," Paul said. "Meanwhile I'll arrange for GMAT materials to be brought to you."

"I know where I want to go," I said. "I want to go to the Wharton school of business." The Wharton School, at the University of Pennsylvania, had been mentioned to me as a good school, and it was within driving distance of Washington. I knew I would feel better if I could get to my friends there if I needed to.

"Well, that's just one possibility," he said. "I still think you should talk to our consultant. He may suggest some other schools you haven't thought about."

I had nothing against talking to a specialist. Meanwhile the materials arrived and I started studying. The debriefings were tedious but did not require a tremendous mental effort, and I was glad I had something interesting to do.

EVERYTHING went smoothly for a couple of weeks until an ugly incident blew my quiet life apart.

One day Barbara asked me if I would mind talking to a social scientist who was particularly interested in Soviet psychology. I agreed, and the next day she arrived with a man. Apparently they'd come in separate cars and just met outside, because they did not seem to know each other.

After a few minutes Barbara said, "Well, I'm going to leave you alone so you can chat." She left.

We sat down at the coffee table. The man started asking me questions and scribbling notes. As the interview progressed, I became more and more puzzled by his questions. They were all personal. Did I love my mother? Did I feel an urge to compete with her? Whom did I love more, my mother or my father? Finally I interrupted him.

"I don't understand what my feelings about my parents have to do with the state of Soviet psychology. Whose business is it whether I ever tried to compete with my mother, anyway?"

Now it was his turn to look puzzled. "It is my business," he said. "I am a psychiatrist."

"But," I said, "Barbara told me that you were a colleague interested in Soviet psychological research."

"I don't know what she told you. But a psychiatric evaluation of defectors is standard agency procedure, and that's what I was sent to do."

"Well, you are going to have a short working day today. The interview is over."

He left without saying good-bye, and I went straight to the phone and dialed Larry's number. "I am not going to take any more of this," I said flatly.

"Wait a minute. Cool down," he said. "What happened?"

Almost in tears, I explained what had happened. "Look, I've always cooperated with all requests. If there is such a procedure, then it has to be done. I just don't want to be treated like a child. Why can't she stop lying and level with me?"

He listened patiently to my outburst. "She is just inexperienced," he finally said. "I know you're upset, but things can be worked out. The agency is doing a good job, and you can't blame the mistakes of one person on the entire organization."

I knew he was right. The other people from the agency were mostly nice and helpful. It was just that Barbara was the one who held the most control over my day-to-day life.

I did not see Barbara for three weeks. George stopped by a couple of times to get my signature on some papers, and Anna continued her work with me. Then Barbara reappeared, but not alone. With her was a man who would almost single-handedly change the course of my life.

IAN WAS A godsend. He was an easygoing man, about my age, with a mop of curly hair and quicksilver dark eyes. He had been asked to give Barbara a hand, he explained, because she was swamped with paperwork and he had more time just now than she did. Within days he set things in motion. A promised consultation with an educational specialist materialized, a date for taking the GMAT was set, and he went through several dry runs of the test with me. He also got permission to invite me to his home to meet his family. At the end of October, I was invited to bring the children for trick-or-treating. I had no idea what Halloween was, but jumped at the opportunity to go out. It was the first time I had spent an evening outside of the safe house.

In Ian's yard at Halloween.

We had a wonderful time. Ian's son, Mark, was about Kitty's age and spoke a little Russian he had learned from his father. Mark and Kitty got along immediately. Konstantin was still too young to go out, and Ian, dressed as Dracula, took Mark and Kitty—for whom we improvised a costume on the spot—for a long walk, while I stayed in the house with Konstantin and Ian's wife, Charlotte. When Ian showed up with the children an hour later, Charlotte and I were still engrossed in conversation. I remember the feeling of warmth in their house and how welcome we were to participate in their family activities and family fun. I no longer felt isolated from the rest of the world.

It was years before I found out how Ian had gotten to work on my case and how much influence he had exerted over my future.

He'd happened to pass Barbara's desk and had seen the psychiatrist's evaluation of me, ready to be sent to other officials in the office. A few sentences caught his attention. He picked up the report and went to George. "Something's wrong here," he said. "Nobody's *that* bad." The report described me as a mentally disturbed, self-absorbed narcissist, almost a sociopath. George explained the tricky situation that had developed between Barbara and me, and Ian volunteered to take over the case. Even now, I tremble to think what would have happened if Ian had not stopped by that desk at that particular time.

In early November, Paul and George arrived to have a meeting with me. After general chitchat Paul got to the point. "Your debriefing is over," he said, "and it's time to move on to your own life. We have carefully considered your tests. They show a high degree of aptitude for executive positions. Therefore we've decided to send you to a good secretarial school. You can start in January, and in two years we'll find you a nice job as an executive secretary and you'll be on your own."

I was too stunned to speak. Finally, just to say something, I forced out, "Making what?"

"Oh, don't worry," Paul said. "We will supplement your income."

When they left, I sat at the table and started to cry so violently that Kitty ran over to me, scared. The darkest of thoughts went through my mind. All these months of danger, of walking away from my comfortable life with the silly notion that I could be something on my own, of leaving my mother without a chance to see her grandchildren ever again—and all for what? To learn typing and to stay on government welfare for the rest of my life?

Suddenly I wished I had never run away from the embassy. I wanted to be back in Moscow, with the people who loved me.

No, that was all wrong. I *had* friends here. They could not, would not, let me down. I picked up the phone and dialed Larry's number. He was still in the office. He listened silently to my recital and then said, "I'll call you tomorrow."

Somehow I got through the night. Before ten the next morning Larry called me. It was the shortest conversation of my life.

"Forget what happened yesterday," he said. "You are going to Wharton."

LARRY HAD SIMPLY TAKEN THE matter to his boss in the Washington field office.

"Our credibility is at stake," he'd said. "Business school is the only thing Elena asked for, and we promised her that. She is the first defector from the Soviet embassy here in forty years. If we go back on our word now, we won't see one for another forty years." His boss had agreed and had taken immediate action.

Apparently there had been dissent on the CIA committee that discussed my future, Ian being the most vocal opponent of the secretarial school. The basic argument of the proponents had been that with two toddlers on my hands I would never make it through the master's program.

"At least let her try," argued Ian. "That school is almost an obsession with her, and she is a very determined woman. If she fails, we can always send her to secretarial school, and by then she'll agree with us."

My supporters had been overruled, but by a small margin, and the pressure from the FBI had tilted the scale back in my favor.

Within a week my documents were prepared and sent to Philadelphia, and two weeks later I went there to see the school. I also visited Drexel University as a possible alternative. Though Drexel was impressive, it required that all undergraduate courses be taken before enrollment in the master's program. Only some of the courses I'd taken in Leningrad could be credited toward the program. Simple arithmetic showed that it would be two years before I could even start working on my master's degree.

I went to see the dean of admissions at Wharton with trepidation. If Drexel had presented such a problem, what would they tell me in one of the top business schools in the country? To my surprise the dean said that I could be accepted.

"We have a different approach here at Wharton," he said. "Our master's program is designed for people who don't have an undergraduate education in business. Two thirds of our students have liberal arts or technical backgrounds, and we are proud to be a truly international school. Your background will complement our student body."

I could start school the next September. Meanwhile he suggested

I take two mandatory courses, calculus and computer programming, during the winter semester, to ease the burden in the fall. He also suggested that a beginning accounting class in the undergraduate school would be helpful.

Walking on air, I returned to Washington after spending two more days in Philadelphia finding an apartment. There wasn't much to do now. The CIA had finished the debriefing and left me alone. Nobody came to my town house anymore except for an occasional visit from Anna, Ian, or the bunch.

The last two weeks in Washington were mostly spent going through the final formalities with the CIA. My legend—my new personal history—was worked out. To keep it simple, I was to tell everybody I was an émigré from the Soviet Union. The agency provided a previous address for reference and inquiries, and a business card with an address and telephone number in California to account for three years of previous job experience, should anybody want to check my background. I was told that my living allowance would be twelve thousand dollars a year. The agency would also pay for the school, day care for the children, and my medical insurance.

The amount was less than I had thought, but money was the last thing I wanted to argue about. I was too happy about going to school, and I had some small savings, which I could use in an emergency.

I spent my first American Christmas with Ian and his family. And I had a big farewell party the day before New Year's Eve. All of the bunch were there, as well as the CIA people.

Near the end of the party, Barbara told me she wanted to talk to me. We went to the bedroom, where we could be alone.

"I want to tell you that despite some misunderstandings, I do not have any hard feelings and I wish you all the best," she said. "Although you didn't like the way I did things, one day you will understand that I was right. People like you come here with exaggerated expectations, and it was my task to bring you closer to reality. You think you know enough about living in this country, but you don't. You still have a lot to learn."

"I appreciate your concern," I said. "It is true that there are many things that I still have to learn. But you don't teach adults by treating them like children. I hope you will keep that in mind. Meanwhile I wish you well, too."

I returned to the party, which continued well past midnight. Three days later Larry and Jim drove me to Philadelphia—a new person with a new name and a new life.

Chapter 11

BARBARA was right about at least one thing—I had a distorted view of American reality. My life at the embassy had been more sheltered than I had realized. I had not had to deal with such major issues as health care, insurance, and taxes. I also had not learned how to live on a shoestring.

The realization that I would not make it financially came with the first check. About twenty percent had been withheld for taxes. I sat there staring at the check. The amount was only thirty dollars more than Lev and I had been paid together, when our rent, the car, and medical expenses had been taken care of by the embassy. Now I had to pay for everything myself and still manage to feed and clothe myself and the children.

I'd rented an apartment in the suburbs, because accommodations on campus were expensive and because I was scared to live in the city. I had visions of street crime and filth, and I knew I would not dare let the children outside. The apartment complex had large lawn areas between the buildings, where the children could play. It did not take me long to discover that I had about three hundred dollars left in the budget after rent, utilities, and car expenses were paid. For the first time, I regretted that I had sold so many of my clothes trying to raise money in Moscow. It did not look as though I would have an opportunity to replenish my wardrobe for some time to come. I did not even have a winter coat.

There were still two weeks left before the start of classes. I found a day-care center that was on my way to the city. The center had an excellent reputation, and the children were well cared for.

I also got myself a life-insurance policy. Given my precarious past and uncertain future, it seemed a prudent thing to do. Getting the policy was the first in a series of incidents that showed me what a sloppy job the CIA had done with my paperwork.

Several days after I filled out the application, the insurance agent came to see me.

"I have a problem," he said. "I have to verify your income, but I can't find a trace of the company in California for which you worked. The income-verification form I sent to them was returned by the post office, and their phone doesn't answer. I wanted to talk to you before I turned your application down."

"I'll try to reach them myself," I said. "I'll call you later. Thank you for taking the trouble to come here and tell me about it."

I called Al, my CIA contact in Philadelphia, and told him about the incident. A week later he told me that everything was straightened out. I asked the agent to mail another form. This time it came back properly filled out and I got my insurance.

My next problem came when I went on my first date. The young man was delighted to hear that I was from Russia. He'd met some other people who had recently emigrated from the Soviet Union and found their tales fascinating.

"Which relocation center did you go through, Vienna or Rome?" he asked.

I did not know what to answer. Nobody in Washington had briefed me on normal emigration procedures. I had no idea even what a relocation center was. So much for my legend.

I pleaded a headache and went home. Was there anything the CIA had prepared for me that I could rely on? I decided to devise my own legend. I was going to tell people that I had married an American scholar in Moscow on a scientific exchange. I had had some friends in Moscow who'd married foreigners, and I knew that they did not have to go through normal emigration channels. Then we'd separated, the story would go, and he was now living in Europe. It was still shaky but would satisfy cursory curiosity.

The problem persisted, however. In some instances people who knew other Russians offered to introduce me to my former compatriots, assuming that I wanted to have the company of people who spoke my native tongue. I could not explain that a Russian émigré community, heavily infiltrated by the KGB, was the last place I wanted to be. Finally, exasperated, I decided my only way out was to hide the fact that I was a Russian altogether.

My accent was not typically Russian, perhaps because I had

studied Norwegian and had been fluent in it before studying English. In any case, for most people my accent was simply an accent. With my Spanish-sounding name and Mediterranean looks, which I had inherited from my Greek ancestors, I could easily pass for a Latin. I did not speak Spanish, which ruled out naming a Spanish-speaking country. Finally I decided I would pass myself off as Portuguese. Most people had no interest in Portugal, assuming they even knew where it was. The ploy worked. In all these years I have never met anybody who spoke Portuguese and could call my bluff, and the moment I said "Portugal" all further interest waned and there were no questions.

STUDYING in an American college was a fascinating experience, totally unlike anything I had been familiar with in Russia, where all courses are predetermined and mandatory. I was not enrolled in a regular program yet, just taking courses in accounting, calculus, and computer programming. But learning to deal with midterm exams, partial credits, and the grading curve was baffling enough. No relative grading is done in the Soviet Union. Either you know the material or you don't.

Accounting presented no problems. I had done the bookkeeping for our VAAP office and was familiar with the principle of double entry. It was the other two courses that seemed to present insurmountable obstacles.

I was good at math in high school; in fact, my math teacher was very disappointed that I chose to go into liberal arts, saying that it was a waste of my brain. However, calculus had not been a part of the curriculum.

With the help of several individual sessions with the instructor, I got on track in calculus. But computer programming left me completely baffled. No matter how hard I tried, the meaning of what I was doing seemed to evade me. The school had a DEC-20 mainframe computer, and the language we were required to learn was APL. I did not know until much later that APL is considered to be one of the most complex languages and is used only by professionals.

The course was driving me to distraction. I could not understand the concepts. I could not figure out why the programs I copied from the book worked, but every command I typed seemed to elicit only question marks from the computer or, worse, a message along the lines of "What do you think you are doing?" The whiz kids at the computer center had programmed it to recognize the most common mistakes and to respond with one-liners. After hours of futile attempts to get something out of that machine, my overwhelming desire was to kick the terminal, yell, "Why don't you shut up!" and walk out. It seemed I would never understand what was going on behind that screen.

That lasted almost eight weeks. And then something happened. I could not pinpoint an exact moment or an exact event, but all of a sudden everything became absolutely clear to me. I understood the logic of computer thinking and the most important law of dealing with one: You cannot make a computer think like a human being; you have to learn to think in its terms, which are nothing more or less than straightforward, ruthless logic. Like many people coming from a background in liberal arts, I had been trained in intuitive thinking, in dealing with concepts that could not always be defined. All of that had to go. Computers do not tolerate ambiguity. In a way they are like children: the fewer choices you give them, the better you can get them to obey you.

It was a personal triumph when I wrote a short program that ran from beginning to end and actually produced the same result that I had calculated by hand. It was also then that I found the love of my life—the computer. Although I did not have to use it often after I'd started the core master's program, my warm feeling for this beautiful machine stayed, and eventually I came back to it.

Other than the struggles and triumphs of classwork, my life was not much to cheer about. My children were still very young—two and four. Aside from day care, I could not afford a baby-sitter, which effectively cut off my social life. I dropped the children at their school in the morning and drove to my school. At five thirty I picked up the children, came home, and stayed there.

I had not made any friends in school yet. The students were basically divided into two groups: those who'd come right after college and those closer to my age. I simply did not fit with the first group; they were too young. Most of the members of the second group had families and went home after school, like myself. I also was constantly haunted by money problems. Even a small outing could make a large dent in my budget.

The most important factor in my reluctance to go out and make friends, however, was that I did not have much to talk about. Being a defector is even worse than suffering from amnesia. You know what your past is, but you cannot talk about it. Until then I had never realized how important the past is in our daily lives. When people meet, the way they build a conversation is to ask each other where they grew up, where they went to school, what their lives were like. Without that, what do you talk about? Ninety percent of all personal questions were ones I could not answer without sinking deeper into lies, and eventually I stopped trying.

I hated to ask the CIA for more money, but I swallowed my pride and presented Al with my budget, which, even cut to the bone, could not possibly be covered by my allowance. The first few months I supplemented it with my savings, but there wasn't anything left by now. Finally the agency agreed to increase my allowance by two hundred dollars a month, and it was enough.

At last spring came. I passed all my exams; nothing spectacular, but at least I did not fail. Now I had a whole summer . . . and not much to do. I decided to take a job and make some money to supplement my income and to take care of emergencies.

Mindful of the snafu I had had with the insurance company, I asked Al if he could help me. I needed a job with flexible hours, and it should be something I could continue to do on a part-time basis after school had started in the fall. I also wanted a job in which compensation was tied to results, rather than a straight hourly rate. I figured that with some extra effort I could make more money that way.

The obvious possibility was to find a sales job. The opportunity that presented itself exceeded all my expectations. Al's friend owned an Oldsmobile dealership about three blocks away from where I lived, and the sales manager there was looking for another person. He specifically wanted a woman, and I was hired.

I learned more about America that summer selling cars than in all the previous years I had lived here. This was real life, a make-or-break situation, and I could finally find out whether my dream of becoming part of American business had any grounds to it.

I was incredibly lucky. I had never sold anything before. I'd been told that I could be persuasive, but I knew that in order to succeed I had to believe in what I was saying. I doubt I could sell candy to a child if I did not think it was good. The Oldsmobile dealership was ideal for me. I was driving my third Olds by now, I loved the car, and I knew a lot about its features and how it compared with other makes.

It was a small but well-established dealership with an excellent service department and a good reputation. There were only three other salespeople, all of them older men who had worked there for years. As I'd found many times before, being a woman had its advantages. Men feel less threatened by a woman and they tone down the normally competitive behavior they display toward other men—that is, until a woman becomes competent enough to compete with them as an equal. I was no threat, as they knew I was there only temporarily. All of that added up to a willingness to help, to teach me the ropes.

I enjoyed the work itself immensely. I'd always liked working with people rather than with paper, and I liked the variety. Each sale was a different situation that required a different approach. There were some unpleasant surprises, of course. I take what people say to me at face value. In sales that does not always work. Jack, the sales manager, gave me a few invaluable lessons in that respect.

"You're too naïve," he often said. "You think that if people like you and they like the car, they'll buy it from you. That's a wrong assumption. You let people walk away, counting on the fact that they'll come back. That will get you nothing but lost sales. Always get a deposit."

"But it does not mean anything," I said. "If they change their minds, they can get the deposit back anyway."

"It does make a difference psychologically," he insisted. "It's the commitment in their minds that counts. Once they write a check, they feel that they have made their decision."

Most of the time he was right. I lost a couple of sales to people who spent hours with me and promised to come back. When I called them, they said they had bought a car someplace else.

I did sell five cars in the first month, though, and things looked

With the Olds outside our Philadelphia apartment.

bright. Then came the Arab oil embargo. By mid-July gasoline quotas were in effect, gas station lines stretched for blocks, and car sales slumped. The dealership could no longer afford to have four salespeople, and by the end of the month I was let go.

It was a strange and unfamiliar feeling—losing something through no fault of my own. Jack took pains to explain to me that it was nothing personal, just a business necessity, and as soon as sales improved, he would take me back part time, as promised. I understood that, but still the feeling of personal failure persisted. This was the other side of the free-market economy—if you are in the wrong place at the wrong time, there is nothing you can do about it. On balance, however, I came out of the experience clearly on the positive side. Besides making a couple of thousand dollars, I learned a lot of valuable lessons about business, selling, and people in general.

AT LEAST one other thing became easier that summer. I established a regular correspondence with my mother. I had talked to her on the day of defection and given her some instructions about the disposition of money and things I had left in her care. I'd also told her that she could not write me for a while, because I would not have an established address.

In the next several months I did manage to make a few more calls. For obvious reasons I could not say much, but the content was not important; all I needed was to let my mother know I was okay and to make sure that she was still there, at home, and that there had been no drastic changes in her life.

Finally we managed to establish a postal exchange through an intermediary, though typically it took a month between the date a letter was mailed and the date it was received.

At first my mother and I were very careful and simply exchanged short notes. We both assumed that the letters were opened and read on the Soviet side, and wrote nothing that could cause them to be censored or destroyed. Gradually my mother started to write more details, and the letters, with few exceptions, reached me. I was naturally curious about what had happened back home after Lev had returned. I knew that both families would experience a lot of discomfort and questioning, but did not know the extent until I got a letter from a Soviet émigré who'd recently gone to Israel. It had been mailed from there, and for the first time I learned the details of what my father had gone through.

Of all the people connected with me, he probably suffered the most. Not physically—he was not harmed or arrested—but he was my father, so it had been his responsibility to raise me as a good citizen. Even Lev could say that he had gotten me "as is" and had not been aware of what was deep in my mind. My father did not have that excuse.

He was already retired from the air force, but he lost his part-time coaching job with the marksmanship team at the air force academy. His retirement pension remained intact and he could still live comfortably, but his pride was hurt.

The worst blow he suffered was the loss of his membership in the Communist Party. For my father that meant the greatest dishonor a man could suffer. He had been a member of the party for forty years; it was part of his life, part of his identity. He appealed directly to the Central Committee in Moscow. In the process, of course, he had to denounce me as an enemy of the state—an understandable thing for which I never held a grudge against him. There was an investigation and endless questioning.

To the credit of the people who conducted the investigation, the truth prevailed. After about a year his party membership was restored and he was completely cleared. He also found another well-paid coaching job and was happy again.

Lev went through a similar process. He was in limbo for several months while he formally stayed on the VAAP payroll in Moscow. Finally he was cleared of any wrongdoing and resumed his job at the Institute of Philosophy. My mother, to avoid being accused of being unfair, had given him all the money I had left in her care. I had not been particularly worried about Lev. He was a survivor.

The person who felt the most personal loss was my mother. But as she wrote to me in September of 1979, she had a solution in mind:

> What a great joy—received two letters from you, full of photos. You look good, and the children are beautiful. Bless you for sending the pictures. They are my only real link with all of you.
>
> You write that Kitty is constantly asking to visit Grandma. Tell her something she can understand and accept, like that the planes from here can only take mail but not people. She must understand firmly the impossibility of my visit, at least for the next few years. I myself would give anything for the opportunity to see you, to touch you! I cannot stop thinking about the constant stress in your life; with two children you cannot relax even for a moment, and I wish I could be there to help you.
>
> I am going to get a divorce and apply for permission to join you. There isn't much hope, though. Rudolf Nureyev has been trying to get his mother out for eighteen years now. She is eighty years old, and many famous people petitioned on his behalf, but . . . no. So what can I hope for? And now, when you need me most, I am helpless to relieve your burden. I will keep trying, though.

Chapter 12

THE first year in school went fast. I made a few friends, most of them foreign students. I did not date, but I had company to go out with for a drink or to have at my place for a barbecue.

I also made friends with a few fellow immigrants who lived in my apartment complex—people who had been displaced from their normal surroundings, having either rejected their own society or been thrown out by it. We were all used to better and different lives and to an entirely different social milieu. Reza, a wealthy Iranian, could not get any of his money out of Iran and could not find a job here; Nellie used to live in a mansion and give parties to high society in Kabul, before the Communist regime took over Afghanistan. She was now supporting herself and her two teenage children on a small salary. My own life, of course, was vastly different from what I used to know. Yet we all had hope and were struggling to get back to our former level.

What I did not realize at the time was that my transition was permanent; even though I could improve my life somewhat, I would never rise to the status and social position I'd had in Moscow. I did not figure it out by myself, at least not then. I was still full of hope for a bright future and too naïve about the workings of this country. It was a Russian émigré I met in school who explained a few things about life here to me.

I met Aron by accident. It was the end of the second semester in school, and we were supposed to choose an area of specialization. I chose strategic planning. Some of its courses were taught at the Busch Center, a research facility that occupied an entire floor in one of the school buildings. Most of the students there were doing their Ph.D. studies, but some courses were offered for those working toward a master's in business administration.

I went to the center to talk to a prospective instructor about a course I was considering. The instructor was away, and I was steered to one of the Ph.D. students for information.

"You don't want to take courses here," he said. "Our philosophy is different from what they teach you in the M.B.A. program." He sounded snobbish and seemed to be trying to put me down.

"Your courses are listed in the M.B.A. catalog," I said.

"What we teach here is opposite to what they teach you there," he persisted. "In the M.B.A. program they teach you how to run corporations and to work for a capitalist society. Here we try to learn how to feed the hungry people of the world and to change the capitalist system that makes people suffer."

I could not believe what I was hearing. For a moment I felt as if I were back in the Soviet Union.

"I do not believe that your personal philosophy is shared by everybody in the center," I said. "I lived under socialism long enough to know that it does not work."

"Where are you from?" he asked.

"I emigrated from the Soviet Union," I said. "So don't tell me about the hungry people of the world. I've heard it all my life."

He suddenly smiled. "We have a Russian professor here," he said. "Come meet him. I am sure you will find a lot to talk about."

I did not want to meet another Russian, but I agreed. At least a professor would tell me about what was going on in this strange place.

The name on the door, Aron Kantsenelinboigen, seemed familiar. I was certain that I had heard it before. After we were introduced, I recited my conversation with his student.

"Well, Murjab does tend to take things to the extreme." He smiled. "What he meant is that our approach may be a little unorthodox. We do welcome M.B.A. students here, because we think that a different perspective will give the M.B.A.s a better understanding of how things fit together in society—from a global point of view, not just that of a single corporation. We hope to foster a sense of social responsibility, but we certainly do not advocate Communism. Being an émigré, like yourself, I took my stand when I left the Soviet Union."

Gradually we got involved in a long conversation. I remembered now where I had heard his name—he used to work for the Institute of Econometrics in Moscow. We both knew a lot of people in the social sciences back in Moscow, and for a while I felt as if I were back home, talking about the situation and personnel moves in social research in the Soviet Union.

I started to visit Aron frequently, dropping in whenever I had a couple of hours between classes. Conversations with him were refreshing and stimulating, bringing back memories of conversations with my embassy friends, though obviously he was far more critical of the Soviet system than they had been. Like many educated Russians, he could see both the good and the bad sides of the socialist regime, as well as the advantages and the shortcomings of the American system.

As time went by we became very good friends. Yet sometimes I intercepted a puzzled look on his face. I knew what was causing it. In our conversations I often mentioned people of his generation who held high positions in Moscow, usually referring to them by their first names. He was obviously trying to figure out how at my young age I had come to know all of them so intimately. In the end he probably decided that I was simply a name-dropper. I still did not dare to tell him about my past.

One day, however, he caught me off guard. I came to visit him and noticed that his office was filled with cardboard boxes.

"A friend of mine is emigrating, and he sent all his books in advance," Aron said. "His name is Vladimir Shlyapentoch. Did you know him?"

"Yes, of course," I said. "He was in the Institute of Sociology at the same time I was." Aron smiled, and I thought it was sort of an impish smile; he obviously figured he had called my bluff. Just then the door opened and a man came in. His jaw dropped in complete surprise, and I thought feverishly what to do next.

"Well, well, what do you know," Vladimir Shlyapentoch finally said to me. "Of all the people in the world, you are the last one I expected to see here. How is life on the CIA money? You must be doing quite well." His expression was hostile.

"You two know each other?" Aron said in utter astonishment.

"Certainly do," said Vladimir. "So, tell me—how much is the CIA paying you?"

Aron still could not comprehend what was going on.

"I have a class," I said to Vladimir. "May I speak to you on my way downstairs?"

I almost dragged him to the hallway. "What do you think you are doing?" I said angrily. "Aron has no idea who I am." I explained briefly the story of my defection.

"I am sorry," he said. "Everybody in Moscow said that the CIA offered you a lot of money and you sold out, and everybody is angry that you ran away like that and stole Lev's children."

"Someday I'll tell you more about my family situation at that time," I said. "Please do not believe everything you hear. And please try to smooth things out with Aron. He is a wonderful man and I'd hate to lose his friendship."

Vladimir promised to take care of that and not to tell Aron anything more about me. After some thought, however, I decided

I would have to tell Aron the truth. He'd heard enough to be very curious, and I also knew by now that I could trust him.

"I admit I had some misgivings," Aron said when I came to see him the next time and told him my story. "It just did not sound right—the things you were telling me and your age. Now, of course, I understand that all these people were Lev's friends and you knew them socially."

Actually I was relieved that the truth had come out. It had been difficult for me to watch what I was saying and to filter out references to my past. It had brought strain to our conversations; there'd always been a certain barrier that prevented us from being true friends. Now that barrier was removed and I felt free to talk about whatever I liked.

My friendship with Aron and occasional trips to Washington were the only bright spots in my life outside of school. Even the trips were not as much joy as before. Larry had been promoted and was involved in sensitive work; he'd been advised that his superiors would not be happy if he continued to see me. Nor could I see John. I did continue seeing Ian and Anna, who had apparently cleared it with the agency, and Jim and Linda, who were not as highly situated in the FBI as Larry.

I told Aron about my feelings of being misplaced and the lack of intellectual companionship. "Americans are not interested in anything outside of their homes and their careers," I said. "I do not meet anybody who is interested in the arts or in international politics—all the things that were so much a part of my world before defection. The students in school do not read anything except *The Wall Street Journal* and the business section of *The New York Times*."

His answer was profoundly true, and I wondered why I had not thought about it myself. "There are people in this country who are exactly the kind you are longing to be with," he said, "but we will never have the same position in this society as we had back home. When you finish school, it will be a little better. You will start work and start meeting people who will become your social circle. But in Moscow we were part of the elite, and your expectations reflect that. You'll have to scale down your expectations."

I knew he was right. My old life was over; it was only a matter of adjusting to the new one. Later I realized that part of my disenchantment was caused by another factor. Philadelphia is not Washington, and I lived on the Main Line, which is a very conservative and well-established suburban area with a rather closed local society. It was just the wrong place for a foreigner.

I hated Philadelphia and wanted to get back to Washington—its straight, planned streets, the open areas around the Mall, the river that reminded me so much of Leningrad, the scenic parkways that started my day with beautiful views. Therefore, I decided to forgo a summer job, much as I would have welcomed the additional income. I stayed for the summer semester so I could finish school half a year earlier.

I continued getting letters regularly from my mother. She went through a rather messy divorce with my father and was finally free to apply for emigration. She could not ask to join me. In order to send her a formal invitation that would serve as a legal basis for her application, I would have had to deal directly with the Soviet embassy in Washington, which was out of the question.

Meanwhile the emigration restrictions in the Soviet Union were tightening. In the late 1970s people emigrated in large numbers, since it was enough just to be Jewish and have a relative, any relative, abroad who had put in a legal request for unification of the family and sponsorship papers. A lot of such requests were issued for people who were barely related or not related at all, and the government finally caught up with the fact.

The grain embargo and the boycott of the Moscow Olympics brought disastrous results. Emigration was restricted to immediate relatives. Very few people had parents, children, or siblings in the West. By changing the eligibility rules, the government effectively brought emigration to a halt.

It was in this atmosphere that my mother, who is of Jewish descent, tried to get an exit visa. As I learned later from her letters, she found an ingenious way to deal with it. She said that her mother had revealed a family secret to her before she died—that she'd had an illegitimate child prior to marrying my grandfather, and that the child had been taken out of the country by his father shortly after the Revolution. The family had eventually moved to Israel. Mother said that she had kept this secret since 1966 because if she had told my father or me, it could have hurt our careers.

She further claimed that, by a miraculous stroke of luck, some friends had managed to locate my long-lost "uncle" in Israel, and she had gotten an official invitation to join him. I warned her not to raise her expectations too high. The story seemed farfetched to me. However, she did manage to get her application accepted.

It was my father who put an end to it. Since his reinstatement in the party, he had become particularly concerned about anything remotely illegal that could mar his newly reacquired reputation. He made a formal statement that in his opinion the request was fake and she did not have any brother abroad. The application was turned down. Mother appealed several times. Finally the emigration office in Leningrad refused even to talk to her.

From the beginning I had had no hope; the authorities certainly knew that I was the primary reason she wanted to emigrate. My father's statement only made it easier for them to refuse.

FALL semester started. For me it was the last one, and it was time to start thinking about graduation and a job. Interviewing season started in October. Even our small winter graduating class brought dozens of corporate recruiters to school. I had my résumé printed and sent out, and was invited to eight interviews—about average for any Wharton grad.

My immediate problem was that I had nothing suitable to wear for interviews. We had been given substantial coaching in how to "dress for success," and besides the fact that my clothes were old, nothing in my wardrobe even resembled a business suit. I could not afford to buy one, so the agency paid for it.

The interviews did not bring any results, though. Some companies sent rejection letters, but one recruiter was kind enough to call me and give me a hint of the problem.

"We cannot fit you anywhere," she said. "On the one hand, your degrees and age make you overqualified for entry-level positions. On the other hand, we cannot hire you into a middle-management position, because you have no work experience in this country."

I had a feeling it was the same problem with all the other corporations with which I interviewed. My grades were good—in my calculation I was somewhere in the upper third of the class—I just did not fit anywhere. I wondered quietly if being a single mother with two children, and a foreigner, had anything to do with it as well, but I just didn't know. The fact was that I was the only one of the entire class without a job.

Finally Paul, the boss of the Washington office, used a personal connection to get me a job with a management-consulting company in Washington. The arrangement he made did not add much to my self-esteem. Within the company, only Paul's friend knew my real story. The president was told that I had independent means, but that because of my late entry into the job market I desperately needed a job, any job, to gain experience; the pay was unimportant. He jumped at the opportunity. What other company could boast of having a Wharton graduate on the payroll for less than they paid a receptionist? The agency would continue my support.

I was grateful to Paul for finding the job for me; I knew I had no other options. Still, I was unhappy. From the beginning the idea had been that I would get my education and be self-sufficient. Now I was on agency welfare for an indefinite time.

"Don't worry," Paul said. "It's a fair arrangement now because you are a totally unknown quantity. After a while, when you prove what you can do, they will increase your salary. In a year you'll be completely on your own."

I agreed. I did like the people with whom I talked in Washington, and, of course, I wanted to return there. I was hired as an associate, but without clearly defined duties. Although I would be formally attached to the department headed by Paul's friend, I would be on loan to other departments to work on specific projects and that way would learn about different aspects of the company's multifaceted business: contracts with local governments for strategic planning and economic development, consultancies with associations, fund-raising for private schools. There was certainly a lot to learn, and I awaited the beginning of my real work eagerly.

I was expected to start in the middle of February. As it happened, I had a bad car accident at the end of January and was stranded in Philadelphia while the car was being fixed. Because of that I had to do my apartment shopping with the help of the Washington *Post* and the telephone. I finally found what sounded like a suitable apartment in northern Virginia. A friend in Washington went there to inspect the place and leave a deposit.

I was lucky. The apartment turned out to be nice. I made arrangements for Kitty's school—she was already in first grade—and day care for both children. On February 17, nervous and full of expectations, I started my first real job in this country.

Chapter 13

MY FIRST month on the job was confusing for me and, I think, for my employers. Nobody seemed to know what to do with me.

After shuffling and rearranging files related to school fund-raising, I was requested by the economic-development department to do some work on input-output analysis. The impressive name turned out to mean a simple recalculation of percentages on huge economic-data tables. A tenth-grade student could have done it easily. The work was tedious, and after a few days my wrist ached from the endless punching of buttons on a calculator. There had to be a better way of doing it.

Full of enthusiasm, I requested a meeting with the president of the company. The request was granted. It was a medium-sized company and everyone was on a first-name basis.

"How do you like your new job?" he asked.

"I do not know yet," I answered. "I haven't done anything that a high school kid couldn't have done."

"Well," he said, "there are always dull parts to a job. Somebody has to do it."

"Jerry, this is the kind of job people should not do at all. It is a job for a computer, and you do have one. Why isn't there a program that would do these recalculations?"

"Frankly, I don't know. All our programming is done by an outside firm. Why don't you get in touch with them and find out? If it can be done, I'll authorize your training. It might be a good idea to have this capability in-house."

Encouraged, I contacted the programmer. Yes, the computer

had the capability. Within two days the programmer came in, reserved a separate space on the disc for my work, brought three thick manuals, and set up a schedule for my training. An additional terminal was installed for me, and soon I was kept very busy indeed. The input-output analysis was followed by modifications to the accounting system, which was even more fun.

Gradually I started doing work for other departments. I was grateful to Jerry for going along with all this. I also realized that the arrangement Paul had made was working in my favor. There was no way Jerry could have afforded to let me spend so much time learning new things if my salary had cost the company more.

However, I knew I needed more money. In January 1982 I tried to bring up the question of a raise. I'd worked for the company for almost a year by then and felt the request was justified. It was turned down.

Unhappy, I gave my two weeks' notice and started to look for another job. One day, when I had just run through my bills trying to figure out which default would hurt me least, my phone rang. It was the manager of a Radio Shack computer center. "I have an opening," he said. "If you want the job, it's yours."

Doug was a maverick manager. His credo was that people could learn about computers and could be taught the basics of selling, provided they had the brains and enough education. As a result, the people who worked at the store were an interesting bunch. One had a Ph.D. in economics, another was a former professor of African studies, and a third had a master's degree in psychology. The base pay was low, but with good sales, people could make twenty-five thousand dollars or more a year.

Armed with a stack of manuals, I spent four days at a computer in the back room, working my way through the store's programs. They were not difficult to learn, and soon I was on the floor. I did need more help as I started getting into actual selling situations, but everybody was ready to give me a hand. By the end of the probationary three months my sales were well over the quota.

I liked my new job. The store was like family—there were only seven of us, including Doug and the customer-support representative. There was plenty of opportunity to learn as much about computers as I cared to. Soon I became proficient enough to be able to help my customers with the inevitable problems people encountered after buying their first computer.

An additional factor in my enjoyment was that I had gotten this job all by myself. I'd found an ad in the paper, gone to an interview, and been hired on my own merit. Whatever I was making was my own doing. I wanted to terminate my dependence on the agency as quickly as possible. Three months after I started working for Radio Shack, I called my Washington contact, Ken, and told him they could cut my allowance in half, hoping that within a year I would be able to terminate it entirely.

By November I was number three in sales in the Central Atlantic region. Then in January the store's sales slumped, and I decided to quit. I thought that I had learned enough about computers to find a more professional job, either with a company that sold more serious business systems or as a free-lance consultant. I knew from my customers that they often used consultants to help them set up programs and train personnel. I hoped that my former customers who had come to rely on me for help and support would hire me to do the same for them after I left Radio Shack. However, I grossly miscalculated. In the store my services were acceptable because they were free, but when people had to pay, they wanted a "professional" consultant. Nor could I find any decent job. Limited experience in retail sales did not count for much in companies that were selling equipment worth tens of thousands of dollars.

There was also another problem—many of these computer companies sold equipment to the government. I had read enough and talked to enough people to be afraid that, as a defector, I would not be trusted. If I took a job with a company that had dealings with the government and something happened that required an investigation, I would be an immediate suspect.

I still had enough money to live on, thanks to a free-lance data-processing project, but I was beginning to worry. The agency support had been cut in half at my own request; I was determined not to ask them to reinstate it unless I faced the real prospect of starvation. Fortunately, as had often happened in the past, an opportunity came along by accident.

I was in my old store buying additional equipment for my own computer. Doug saw me at the counter and came out of his office.

"Our customer-support rep is leaving," he said. "Want to come back as a CSR?"

I thought about it for a moment. It was not a bad idea. Being a CSR was a technical job that required constant learning and a very detailed knowledge of computers and programs. Building my expertise in technical support rather than sales could be very useful in the future if I decided to try consulting again.

Doug was happy to have me back. I made arrangements with the baby-sitter to pick up the children from school, in case I was delayed downtown in an emergency, and went back to work.

Returning to Radio Shack as a customer-support representative was probably the smartest move I'd made since I'd left school. My main duty was to help customers with whatever problems they had running their computers. Most of the problems were easy, but some required in-depth knowledge. It was a hectic job—the phone rang incessantly; people walked in with their questions. Not every Radio Shack center had a CSR, and I often took calls from other stores. My name was becoming well known among the customers. More important, I could take any time I needed to study the new programs, without worrying about my income.

All of that continued happily for about a year, and then I started feeling the familiar itch again. I was overworked; money was tight. It was time to move on.

This time I was more confident, not only because my knowledge of computers and my practical work experience were greater now. There was something else—I'd finally become convinced that "the land of opportunity" was not an empty phrase. This was the third time in four years that I was contemplating changing jobs, but I was not afraid to do it. Every time I'd done it in the past, things might have looked bleak for a while, but eventually something had come up. I simply could not believe that with all the possibilities open to me I would not get something better than what I was doing now. This country had so much to offer; it was up to me to find it.

I quickly landed several interviews. Most jobs were along the same line—technical support—but one offered a unique opportunity. It was with the House Information Services, a quasi-governmental organization that provided computer services to the House of Representatives. The position did not even require U.S. citizenship. The management was looking for a programmer to put together a data base that would keep track of the usage of their computer system. The task was extremely challenging; the person who would do it would have practically the sole responsibility for the project. The people who interviewed me were eager to go ahead; I was the only suitable candidate they had.

I was still concerned about my background. I'd run into a strange attitude toward Russians before—that it was safer not to have them around. I felt it was only fair to share my concerns with Rick, the project manager who was planning to hire me.

"Don't worry," he reassured me. "Although we have to submit it for approval to a House committee, we've never had our decision overruled yet. You are as good as hired."

Well, I wasn't. Rick called, angry and frustrated, to say that the application had been turned down in the House committee.

"I don't believe it," he said. "We tell them that we need you urgently, and what do we hear? That they can't hire a Russian in an election year—what if the press finds out? They told us to come back after the elections and there would be no problem."

I assured him that there were no hard feelings. It was just politics, I said. He was more upset about it than I was.

That my past was a handicap I had no doubts, and not just in the job market. It backfired seriously in personal situations as well.

I'd known Ron for a couple of years—we'd dated for a while; then we'd drifted apart. We remained friendly, though, and ran into each other occasionally, both being in the small community of computer professionals. Eventually we started dating again, and it was getting rather serious this time, until one night the dreaded question came up.

"You know," he said, "you never told me much about yourself. I only know that you went to school here and what you were doing thereafter. How did you come to be here in the first place?"

I told him. He listened with interest to my adventures and asked a lot of questions. One question bothered me, though.

"Is the CIA still keeping an eye on you?" he asked.

"You mean, like tapping my phone? No, I don't think so."

"You did have a problem with the House Information Services," he persisted. "Do you think the agency called there behind your back and told them not to hire you?"

"I have no reason to think so. Why are you so concerned? You don't work for the government."

"I'm undergoing a security clearance right now," he confessed. "I'm bidding on a large RCA contract, and they are heavily involved in defense research. In order to do my own work for them, I must have a need-to-know clearance."

We switched to another topic, but I had a feeling that the news disturbed him. Several days later he abruptly canceled a dinner we had planned. I never heard from him again.

The incident once more brought forth my years-long debate—was I right in hiding my past? I still tended not to tell people about my background right away. In my personal relationship with Ron it had obviously backfired. Yet I preferred to take that chance rather than be completely open with strangers.

Some of my friends knew about my past, of course. Just as with Aron, in Philadelphia, I found it very difficult to build a true friendship with somebody when I constantly had to watch what I said about my origins. My confession seldom brought any adverse reaction; on the contrary, my friends usually appreciated the difficulties I had gone through and admired my action. But they were few and trusted friends. I was not ready to make my background public knowledge. I still feared that the embassy might want to get back at me.

Technically my children and I could still be subject to Soviet law, in the eyes of which I was a criminal. My only hope was to get my American citizenship, but I had to wait five years for it from the moment my residence permit was granted. Citizenship would resolve the problem once and for all. Unlike some other countries, which permit dual citizenship, American law is unequivocal: an American citizen cannot be a citizen of another country. With citizenship I would be much better protected.

Now at last my citizenship was in the works. It was 1984, five years had passed, and the agency initiated the proceedings. I waited eagerly for the moment. It signified so much to me—

finally, the ultimate freedom; I would truly become a part of this country that I had come to love and admire so much.

I also hoped that with citizenship I would have more opportunity to try to help my mother. I still did not believe that she would be let out of the Soviet Union, but at least I could formally try. Mother has always been a sick woman, and now her health was deteriorating. I thought that if I were free to act, maybe I could get enough support from the U.S. government to get my mother's release.

The problem was that I could not go out and lobby for it. I did get in touch with Robert Kaiser at the Washington *Post*. I had read his book, *Russia: The People and the Power*, admired his knowledge of the Soviet Union, and decided he would be the right person to ask for advice. He was intrigued by my story and promised to keep our meeting off the record. He was not very optimistic about the chances of getting my mother out, however.

"We cannot lobby for you," he said. "We can run a front-page story and attract attention to your case, but then you would have to take over. Such an undertaking requires months, even years, of lobbying. If you are not ready to go public—which, by the way, is a mistake, because publicity could be your best protection—there is nothing anybody can do to help your mother." I knew he was right, and I was grateful for his advice, but until I got my citizenship the issue was moot.

By late fall my papers had moved through channels at the Immigration and Naturalization Service. The official date in court was set for December 20, just in time for Christmas.

The big event turned out to be almost an anticlimax. It was bureaucratic and dry. There were about a hundred other people in the courthouse receiving their citizenship the same day. We stood in line for almost an hour; then we were shepherded into the courtroom, where there was a roll call. The judge made a speech, followed by one from an elderly lady who represented the Daughters of the American Revolution. I had expected a more uplifting event.

"At least they could play the national anthem for us," whispered the man next to me. "They play it at every football game."

I agreed. For most people in the room this was a tremendously

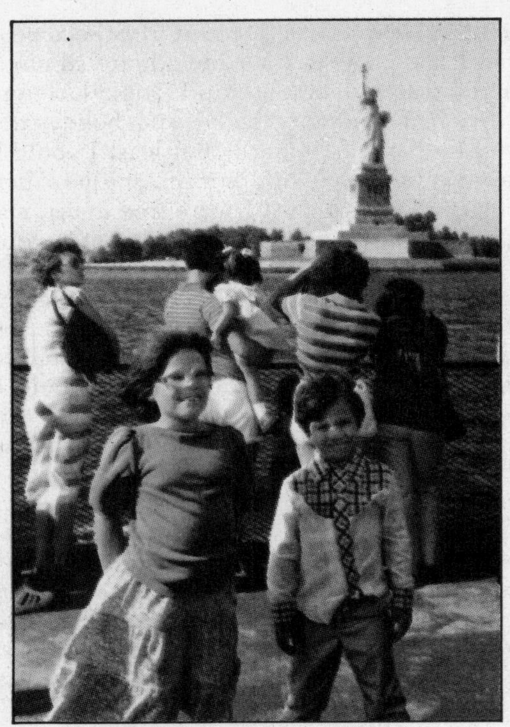

The children on a trip to New York City in 1985.

important turning point, an event that was very symbolic, the end of a struggle. Many had risked their lives coming to this country. Couldn't we be welcomed a little more warmly as its new citizens?

A YEAR and a half had passed since I'd left Radio Shack. My life seemed to have settled into a manageable pattern. The gamble had paid off. This time when I became a consultant, the customers followed me. Gradually I switched from technical support to systems development, specializing in accounting systems for small businesses, where my Wharton background and programming capabilities combined to my advantage. And I was finally running my own business. I learned what it means to be your own boss—if anything goes wrong, there is nobody else to blame. Weekends ceased to exist, for the most part, but I did not mind. This was what I had always wanted—to make my own decisions, to do my work the way I saw it. I'd paid dearly for this privilege, and I was not going to complain. This was what this country was about, and I loved it.

The children were doing equally well. At ten, Kitty was old enough to understand when I explained our family history to her. She and Konstantin became typical American kids—Barbie dolls, McDonald's, and pizza. Both did well in school, and it assuaged my guilt about not having given them enough of my time while chasing the American dream. They did not speak Russian at all, but developed some interest in Russia, which I encouraged. Too many people in America are completely ignorant about the Soviet Union.

I had changed, too. Success in business had brought me more security and more self-confidence. I even gave my good old dress-for-success outfits to Goodwill and stopped wearing conservatively tailored business suits. I felt that my reputation had become well enough established to allow a little more flair.

The past would not go away, though. It got back at me in ways that were unpredictable and could not be avoided. Once, I met a Russian émigré at a party at Anna's house. He was actually from Soviet Georgia, and his Russian was not very good, but it was still better than his English. We went out, and I quickly found myself forced to speak about Russia and life in Moscow. In addition, I switched to Russian to make it easier for him. It took me half an hour to get back my fluency. I had hardly spoken the language since I had left the embassy.

It was a mistake. Later that night I had a nightmare, the worst I could recall in many years. I dreamed that I was in Moscow, surrounded by Russians, speaking Russian. For some reason my mother was not there. I was searching for my children—the state had taken them away and given them to Lev, but he did not want them and had sent them to an orphanage. In my dream I was on my knees in a snow-covered street, begging my mother-in-law to tell me where my children had been sent.

I woke up in the middle of the night. The dream was still vivid, and I could not fall asleep again. I'd never analyzed why I avoided seeing Russians and speaking Russian. I had no problems speaking about Russia with my American friends, in English. It was as if English provided an impersonal touch to the conversation; I could talk about life there as if it were somebody else's life.

Now it seemed that the combination of speaking *about* Russia *in* Russian broke down the safeguards and brought the nightmare out of the deepest freeze of my memories. There must have been something still lurking there. Fear of reprisals? Guilt? What was there to hide after all this time? It was unlikely that the embassy would undertake anything against me now. I was formally divorced from Lev, and my children and I were U.S. citizens.

I remembered a book I had read recently, a memoir of another Soviet defector, Vladimir Sakharov, a former KGB officer who had defected to the United States long before. After years of hiding he'd come out into the open and was now giving lectures. He'd said he was sick of pretending to be somebody else, and even though he knew he was taking a risk by revealing his identity, it was the first time in many years that he felt free, just by being himself again.

Still, I continued to live my life in the shadows of my past until a sudden and unexpected event forced me to make a decision and helped me to take that final step.

Chapter 14

In early September, 1985, a small article in the newspaper caught my attention. It said that Vitaly Yurchenko, a high-level KGB official, had defected while on a trip to Italy and was now in the hands of American intelligence in Washington.

I read it twice. I could not believe my eyes. Vitaly Yurchenko was the embassy security officer who'd given us such a stern lecture about the dangers of American recruiting attempts, at that women's meeting at the embassy. What an interesting twist of fate! I'd never known Vitaly well, and after that memorable meeting I had avoided him like the plague. But he couldn't have been such a bad guy, after all, if he'd decided to take such a risk. He must have had a reason for it. I called Jim, the FBI agent who had set up my relocation.

"Do you think you could arrange for me to meet with Yurchenko?" I said. "Maybe I could give him a helping hand. I know there is life after debriefing, but he may not."

"Might not be a bad idea," Jim said. "Let me sound it out. You know he is out of our hands now."

The CIA would have him, and that was what worried me.

Jim called back a few days later. "The guys here think it's a good idea," he said cautiously. "We have to put it through channels, though. That will take a while."

I could only wait. The papers continued to publish reports on Yurchenko. He was apparently providing interesting information. The FBI made at least one arrest and was searching for another man whom Yurchenko had ostensibly pointed out. There was still no word from the FBI about my request.

I did not even know why I was so concerned. Perhaps it was that strange feeling of fraternity that people sometimes develop after they have gone through a disaster or a life-threatening situation together. It is the knowledge of something that other people who have not been through it cannot understand. Nobody could get through this experience without scars. If he had the same feelings at the safe house I did, he needed somebody like me—to listen and to understand. I could only hope that Jim would prevail and the permission would be granted.

It all came to a conclusion on November 5. I was driving home from downtown Washington. It was raining, and as usual traffic was crawling. I was listening to music on the radio. The six-o'clock news started. The first item was Yurchenko.

"Vitaly Yurchenko, the highest-ranking KGB official ever to defect to the United States, is back at the Soviet embassy," said the announcer. "We are awaiting more information from a news conference scheduled by the embassy for six o'clock tonight."

I immediately switched to an all-news station. Apparently, Yurchenko had been having dinner with one of the CIA people in a Georgetown restaurant, only a few blocks away from the new Soviet embassy compound, when he'd left on the pretext of going to the rest room and never returned.

What went wrong? I could only guess. Maybe he'd broken under debriefing. He was a KGB officer, after all, and his debriefing would have been much more intense than mine. It is only human to try to evade certain questions when personal friends are concerned. It is one thing to walk out on the system and another to point a finger at friends, knowing that it could endanger their lives.

Had he just become homesick? Possibly. Even after many years here I sometimes thought longingly about going to Leningrad, just for a few days, to see that majestic city, to touch the granite of its columns and embankments. And of course I missed my mother. It was November 5—two days before the biggest national holiday in the Soviet Union. Had that made his homesickness worse? I could guess forever and never know the truth. Whatever it was must have been serious, because going back was suicide. The KGB does not forgive its own. At best he would fade into the obscurity of an early retirement; at worst . . . I did not want to think about it.

It was six forty-five when I finally got home. I rushed to the TV set to catch the evening news. They televised part of the news conference. Vitaly looked somewhat drained but otherwise perfectly composed and even smiling. He read a prepared statement that said he had been kidnapped while in Italy, kept under drugs, and brought to the United States against his will, and that he had escaped at the first opportunity. I did not believe a word of it. I'd heard it too many times from every defector who returned.

The circumstances surrounding Vitaly's stay here would surface in the press later: stories about an involvement with a woman attached to the Soviet embassy in Canada, who refused to defect with him, after which he became difficult and uncooperative. All of that I did not know yet, however, and afterward I could only speculate, just like everybody else. And even if I had known, it probably would not have overshadowed what I felt—that the main problem had been his inability to adjust to being a defector. I remembered all too vividly my own loneliness, the despair, the guilt, and the second thoughts I had had. Vitaly's depression would have been a normal stage in the defection process, but somebody should have been with him, to tell him that he'd done the right thing and all these feelings would pass.

I went to the phone. There was no question in my mind where to call.

"What city, please?" said the operator's impersonal voice.

"Washington, D.C.," I said. "*ABC News Nightline.*"

At that moment I still did not think of myself as going out into the open. All I wanted was to share the frustration I felt that a man like Vitaly, a man of immense value to this country, had been lost, and the conviction that something should be done to prevent it from happening in the future. I needed somebody who would explain it to the world for me so that people would understand. *Nightline* was a logical choice. It covered its subjects in greater depth than the regular evening news; at the same time, it always got to major events quickly, and I was certain they would be doing a program on Yurchenko soon.

To the woman who answered the *Nightline* phone I probably sounded incoherent. I wasn't really sure what I wanted to say, and I was still afraid to say too much about myself. It was a miracle that she did not dismiss me as a crank; instead, she kept me talking until I was able to collect my thoughts and say that I had defected some years back, had gone through the same process as Yurchenko had, and that I felt that something might have gone wrong in his debriefing. They were planning to have a program on Yurchenko the very next day, and she would not let me go until I'd promised I would call back and talk to the producer.

In the morning I was more calm and rational. I called Bob Kaiser, who was now in charge of national news at the Washington *Post*. He had the same feeling that something must have gone wrong, and he asked if I would talk to one of his reporters.

I did not want to disclose my present identity—the fear was still there—so I told Bob to use my old name, Yelena Mitrokhina. It was also the name I gave to the *Nightline* associate producer, Tara Sonenshine, when I reached her at noon. Tara was elated that I called, and asked me to appear on the broadcast.

I agreed to go on the air. I still had my blond wig, and I knew that, coupled with dark glasses, it would make me practically unrecognizable. I did not have to disclose the name I was currently using. I felt that the issue of how a defector was handled was important enough to speak out about, but after one TV appearance and one newspaper interview I planned to go back to living my life quietly, as before.

I spent three hours with Patrick Tyler, the *Post* reporter, had my picture taken with the wig and sunglasses, went home, and returned downtown later for the broadcast. It was easier than I had thought. Ted Koppel was easy to talk to. His voice sounded so reassuring in my earphones that I almost forgot I was sitting in front of a camera that was sending my image to millions of homes. I talked about the stress and anxiety all defectors go through, and the critical need for support from people who are with the defector at that time, and how many things can go wrong if those people are not right for the job. After the broadcast I went home. It had been an interesting day. In the morning I would go back to my regular routine—being Alex Costa again. Meanwhile my frustration had subsided. I had done what I could to bring the problem to the public, and that was all I wanted to do.

Little did I know that fate had other plans for me. I'd started a chain of events that I could not control.

The next morning I was making breakfast for the children when my phone rang. It was my best friend, whom I had told the day before about the broadcast and the newspaper interview.

"Did you see the paper yet?" she asked.

"No," I said. I was hurrying to get the children off to school.

"Go and look. I'll talk to you later."

I went to the porch and picked up the paper. One glance told me what she meant.

My own picture looked at me from the front page. Everything was as I expected—the blond wig, the dark glasses—except for one little detail. The caption said that my name was Alexandra Costa, and the article emphasized that it was the name I had adopted after defection.

The next fifteen minutes were hazy. I gave the children breakfast and practically pushed them out the door. Then I ran to the phone and called Patrick Tyler at the *Post*.

"Have you seen the paper yet?" I almost yelled.

"No," came back a sleepy voice. "Hold on."

In a couple of minutes he returned. "What's wrong?" he said. "I don't see any problem."

"The name is wrong. I thought we had an agreement."

Gradually we both realized the misunderstanding. I had given Pat both names, one to use in publication and the other in case he needed to reach me to get more details. Because Bob Kaiser was aware of my intention to use the old name in print, I assumed he had told Pat, and I had not emphasized it clearly enough to him. Pat, in turn, had assumed that I did not want to jeopardize my family back in Russia and kept my old name out of print.

Pat was disconsolate, but I was not angry at him. His assumption had been logical, and if it was anybody's fault, it was my own. I should have made my wishes clear beyond any doubt.

I thought feverishly. Now the embassy had the name I was currently using, and it would only be a matter of time until they knew my address. My phone number was unlisted, but the phone company had the records—difficult to get, but not impossible. I called Ken at the CIA.

He sounded upset and genuinely concerned about possible repercussions. "We think it would be prudent to change your name again and move you to another city," he said. "We cannot guarantee your security if you stay here."

"I don't want to move," I said. "I don't think the embassy would really go after me after all these years. I am much better protected from a legal point of view now, and I don't see what they would gain except a lot of bad publicity. Besides, it took time to build my business. If I move, I would have to start from zero. The last thing I want to do is go back on agency welfare."

I did promise to keep my eyes open and let him know at the first sign of anything unusual. I also asked him what I should do with the media. By then Tara had called me with a list of people who had contacted *Nightline* and wanted to talk to me. I had taken down the numbers—*Time* magazine, Cable News Network, UPI—but had not returned any calls yet.

"Return the calls," Ken said. "Since you don't want to move, publicity is your best protection."

It was the same thing Bob Kaiser had told me. But what about my business? How would my clients react? Was the disaster with the House Information Services and my breakup with Ron indicative of what was to come? Right now the damage was limited to one broadcast and one newspaper article. Perhaps my clients were early risers who went to bed by ten; but there was less hope that they would overlook the front page of the *Post*.

The issue resolved itself quickly. I began receiving call after call. Some people had seen *Nightline*. Most had not recognized me in disguise—until I had started to talk. My voice was instantly recognizable by anybody who knew me well enough.

Nobody was apprehensive; nobody canceled appointments. Their sentiments could be summarized in a few words: "We are concerned about your safety. And we hope that being a celebrity won't prevent you from continuing to work for us. We need you."

The morning that had started with panic was becoming a celebration. It was as if the burden had suddenly been lifted from my shoulders. All the fears disappeared. For seven years I'd been living on my star, silent and lonely, afraid to set foot outside of my little private domain. I'd stepped down from it and found the world ready to greet me with open arms and a smile.

My throat was beginning to hurt from nonstop talking. I went to the kitchen and made myself a cup of an old Russian remedy—half tea, half milk, with a dash of baking soda. The day was not over. I had a long list of calls to return.

ABOUT THE AUTHOR

In the years since her defection, Alexandra Costa's fondest wish has come true. She and her children are living their lives as free Americans: free to make choices, to develop their talents, to follow their dreams. Alex's daughter, Kitty, is now twelve. She likes to cook and shows considerable talent as a cartoonist. Konstantin, ten, is an avid skateboarder and computer enthusiast. "He'll probably end up in some high-tech field, like me," his mother speculates. *Star Trek*, roller coasters, vacation trips to Disney World, and weekend-long games of Monopoly are all a part of their very American lives—and Alex Costa wouldn't have it any other way.

When asked if she has any regrets about her decision to leave the land of her birth, she shakes her head emphatically. "There are only two things that I miss. One is my beautiful city of Leningrad. The other is my mother." Although she and her mother frequently exchange letters, gifts, and photographs, both women are resigned to the fact that they will probably never see each other again.

But Alex Costa has neither the time nor the inclination for brooding. Most days she is too busy running her computer-consulting business, making sure that Kitty and Konstantin have enough clean socks, and decorating the new town house she recently bought in a Washington suburb. She is also hard at work planning her next book—an espionage thriller set in Russia. Asked whether she is dating, she smiles enigmatically, then confesses that she is. But more than that she will not say, except to add that her current gentleman friend knows about her past and is not troubled by it.

Does she still harbor fears that the KGB might try to kidnap her and put an end to her new life as an American? "Mostly not," she says. "I doubt they'd bother with me now." But just in case, she has drawn up a notarized document stating that if she ever appears at a news conference saying she has decided to go back to the Soviet Union, her American friends should assume that she has been coerced by the KGB. "I renew that statement every year," she says. "And I will renew it every year for as long as I live."

PHOTO BY SOREN NORING

A Deadly Presence
A CONDENSATION OF THE NOVEL BY
Hjalmar Thesen
Illustrated by John Thompson

Imagine a jet-black leopard
on the prowl.
He is sleek, powerful,
moving sinuously
through the deep shadows
of the jungle,
nearly invisible
but for a pair of brilliant
emerald-green eyes.
Then imagine
that the leopard is injured,
hobbled by a cruel trap gun.
His normal food supply—
the swift rhebok
and bushbuck—
easily elude him.
The leopard faces starvation.
But he discovers that
there is one prey animal
with no natural defenses.
It wanders alone in the jungle.
It is slow, awkward
and abundant.
It walks on two legs. . . .

1

THE eagles circled slowly, and from their great height they could see across the entire width of the coastal plateau with its blanket of forest and slashed river canyons. They could see the town and its lagoon, all grasped in the embrace of enveloping hills that ended in massive twin headlands between which the open sea poured and receded each day, like the breathing of a great sea creature. The pale green farmlands and red and white houses and red roads ended only at the blue barrier of the mountains, and if the eagles had cared to look into a small field at the mountain base, they might have seen two men standing over a bush from which something white protruded.

The sheep lay belly upward at the far end of the field, where the forest began to slide down into a steep mountain valley. Its hind legs stretched up stiffly from a tangle of dry bush that seemed to have reflowered with buds of wool and smears of blackened blood. Immediately behind where the men stood, the forest rose up in a wall and grew quickly darker among the stems of thorn and pioneer trees.

The two men didn't touch the carcass of the sheep at first. They walked into the forest and tramped about, seeming to measure and calculate. Eventually the bigger of the two men leaned his shotgun against a branch and, with a hand axe, cut the tops off two stout saplings. After this they tied the shotgun to the still living poles and then began to build a small enclosure of sticks and brushwood some thirty feet in front of the looming gun barrels. When this was done, they adjusted the gun's position carefully, one man aiming and the other, flat on his chest at the entrance to the little enclosure, looking up at the twin barrels through a chink he had made between the leaves.

He grunted. "Up, down, up a little more, too much; yes, that's it. Here, you come and see."

He crawled out, and they changed places. Satisfied at last, the two men returned to the sheep and towed it back between them into the forest and over to the enclosure. They pushed it into place through the narrow opening. While the big man wrestled the dead sheep into its final position, the other began to unroll a spool of nylon line. The big man took it from him and began to spin it in an intricate pattern from the triggers of the shotgun back to a small pulley wheel that he nailed to a tree trunk, forward to a second pulley and, finally, down to the enclosure and then across its entrance, eight inches from the ground. The men then made some adjustments to the tautness and angle of the nylon web.

When they were satisfied, the smaller man went to the entrance of the enclosure and crawled inside. He touched the taut line tentatively. "It should work with pressure both across and upward, I suppose."

His companion was squinting down the barrels. "If he comes, he will come in low on the ground, under that top branch, and when he braces to pull at the sheep, he will push against the line. Try with your hand. Push the line upward slowly."

There was a waiting tension of silence and then the sudden metallic click of a firing pin.

"Fine," said the larger man.

After the gun had been loaded and the safety catch slid forward, the men stood back to look, trying to imagine how it would be when darkness came, and at last they went away silently, as though a little ashamed of what they had done. A flock of sheep parted for the men as they walked back toward a small truck at the far end of the field. Behind them, the flock returned to their ceaseless nibbling of the trampled grass.

NOT FAR AWAY, AT THE BOTTOM of a gorge, a woman sat on a hot rock that shaped the course of the river. As she dried her hair, sunlight tingled on the bare skin of her arms. A breeze moved the treetops high up on either steep side of the valley, but no breath of it reached down to ruffle the glass-black surface of the pool around her. Below where she sat a thin fall of water dribbled, and apart from this, there was no sound other than the birdcalls that pierced all the gorge from near and far. Her feet just under the surface in the shallows gleamed a pale gold, like the pebbles and the sand.

She sat with her knees up and dried her hair in the sun's full warmth. With a blue towel she rubbed the long black tresses that cascaded over her shoulders. When she turned her head full into the sun, the comparative paleness of her skin under the dark canopy of hair made a startling contrast. At last she sat without moving, letting the sun do its work unaided.

From the beginning Jean Mannion had adapted well and quickly to farm life here at the southern end of the continent of Africa. Perhaps this was not so surprising in view of the fact that her widowed father had given her a privileged apprenticeship through the game farm he had owned up north, in the heart of the big game country. Her brother, John Avery, four years younger and away at school, had missed much of this, to his constant regret. Then, with their father's death, it had all ended. Jean had married a year later, and when she thought of Simon Mannion, as she did now, here by the pool they had enjoyed so much together, she could feel her heart squeeze until she heard herself make a small sob, tears flooding her eyes. She had loved him very much, and he was around her everywhere.

She wiped the tears away almost angrily, as she had done many times before. Simon was dead, killed in a car accident six months ago. She would never see him again; she had to keep reminding herself of this fact and accept it without pain if she could.

Simon had left Longlands to her. Soon after his death her brother had finished his army service and he had come to stay with her. Superimposed on his old boyishness, there was now a sometimes comic adulthood that had helped her over a bleak threshold and into a slow rekindling of interest in the farm.

Buying the sheep had been John's idea, and the disappearance of five of them had filled him with indignation; he thought that they might have been stolen. But then they found the partly eaten ewe, and John brought Japie Kampmuller over from the neighboring farm. It was he who had declared it to be a leopard kill. And it was he who had suggested the trap gun.

Japie Kampmuller, kind and avuncular, had been one of the pallbearers at Simon's funeral, at Jean's request, and as though mindful of the honor she had done him in recognizing him as a special friend, he had become her willing adviser and protector in his own bluff way. She had not known him well before this. He had been to her only another member of the local farming community, seldom seen in anything but khaki and sweat-stained hat; a large, dark-complexioned man, loud in laughter and speech. She guessed his age at about fifty.

Longlands was just under fifteen hundred acres and had had many owners. The poor soil made farming difficult, but the countryside was beautiful, and Jean could well afford to be merely a checkbook farmer.

The farm was one of many on the plateau running east and west between mountain range and sea. There was only one point on the farm from which it was possible to look out over the sea, but when the west wind blew, the roaring of breakers would thunder in a continuous roll, like heavy guns firing far away. The coast was a resort area, and the wilderness sometimes seemed like nothing more than a scenic backdrop.

At first, when monkeys invaded her orchard, Jean had been indignant and surprised, and when wild boars and porcupines dug up her bulbs, she found it difficult to imagine the creatures themselves snuffling in the moonlight outside her window. Anything as large and dangerous as leopards, she felt, belonged to the bushveld far to the north. In fact, she did not entirely believe that the five lost sheep had been killed by leopards and secretly wondered whether her dogs had been loose on those nights. She had seen to it since then that they were safely locked away in the kennel each evening.

She looked up suddenly. The depths of the ravine were about to lose the sun, and bird sounds changed in anticipation. Perhaps in her subconsciousness too there stirred an ancient remembering of the dangers of darkness soon to come, for now she stood up in a single graceful movement and turned to look behind her, then all around her. She began to dress. Across the pool, not a hundred feet from her, the leopard, which had stiffened at the first movement of the still figure on the rock, sank down again among the ferns and gazed unblinking, ears flat against her skull, tail moving gently from side to side.

The leopard had been puzzled by the figure on the rock, for it had made no sound. Years of experience had taught her to know the sounds that invariably accompanied fresh human scent. With the supersensitive hearing of her kind, she could pinpoint a single mumbled word or the scraping of a match, mark the place and direction, and slink away unseen. Another puzzling thing had been that the figure had remained almost motionless. But now the potential enemy had declared itself with movement. The leopard heard the soft hiss behind her, the excited intake of breath, and knew that her two-year-old cub was watching over her shoulder.

The girl finished dressing, oblivious of the watching animals. She flung the towel over her shoulder, shook back thick strands of wet black hair and started toward the path.

The leopard was just over seven years old, and apart from a scar that chipped her right ear and ended in a small gash over her right eye, she was immaculately glossy and well muscled. She was exceptionally large, and the dark black rosettes on her tawny back and legs contrasted strongly with the pure white fur of her belly. Now, as the last of the light dappled the forest floor with black shadow and white-gold sun dots, she was the embodiment of all camouflage.

Making no sound, the leopard and the fully grown cub rippled in single file up the slope of the darkening forest toward their temporary lair. Pausing at the base of the cliff, the female looked up for the first time, her eyes huge and intense; she gathered herself, steadied her tail and went up the broken rock face in a series of effortless bounds that carried her under a rocky overhang high above the trees. The cub joined her a few seconds later, and for some time they sat together gazing out over the ravine, listening to the night begin.

The female's association with the cub was one of habit more than of fond maternal unity. He had been born in this same lair as one of a litter of four, and for three months she had suckled them. After that she left them in the lair as she hunted in tireless efficiency up and down the valley. At that time there had been a plentiful supply of porcupines, whose own rich diet of tender roots and bulbs nourished her litter. The cubs grew rapidly, and finally, after a hundred hunting lessons on grasshoppers and frogs, on mice and on small antelope, the time had come when her long task was over. First one cub and then another had found itself looking around after the pursuit of a mouse only to discover that its mother had gone. At last a single cub remained, and he followed her with dogged determination. One cub was no problem to her, and soon she hunted with him on almost equal terms.

When the female was ready to mate again, her attitude toward the cub changed swiftly. She snarled at him and cuffed him viciously, but it was not until one afternoon, when a big male lay glaring at him across a glade in the forest, that the cub knew real fear. The male came straight toward him, past his mother, with an ominous rumbling growl, and the cub turned and fled. When the mating was over, he found her again in the rock shelter; she licked him in greeting and life for him returned to normal.

In his behavior the young leopard was no different from any other of his species, but there was one thing that set him apart and made him a strange and unusual animal: from head to tail he was almost jet black. Seemingly darkest of all was the mask of his face, but perhaps this was only because of his eyes, which burned so bright against their dead-charcoal background. In the light that filtered down through the leaves of the forest, they were pure emerald green, but when at night they reflected the naked flame of a fire, they burned red and disembodied against a doubling of black. He was a striking example of melanism.

The territory that the female and the young male occupied was not hers alone, but by an intricate and mutually effective system of timing, she and the others, including two fully grown males, seldom allowed themselves to clash. The scent of another leopard revealed the time of its passing and the direction it had taken, and in the overlapping territories the intricate pattern of scent and counterscent preserved the delicate balance, at least as long as food remained plentiful.

But already there were signs that the game in these forestlands were dispersing. The wild pigs had disappeared from the twin valleys; the bushbuck had grown wary. So had the monkeys and baboons. To survive, the predators had to roam farther, and the ripple of their wider-ranging population was beginning to lap over the disciplined perimeter of civilization. As had happened many times before in many places, civilization had begun cracking down, pushing the boundaries back even farther than before.

In all her wanderings the female had never before killed a sheep. Since the sheep grazed at the very edge of the forest and were without speed or horns or cunning to protect them, she could have taken one whenever she wished. But it was the young male that had taken the first of the five sheep, as a hunting exercise, and only after he had dragged the carcass down into the thorn thicket had the female joined him in eating. The meat was good, but the wool, which they first had licked away from the belly, was unpleasant.

Lying now with the male on the floor of their rocky overhang, she licked his mask and ears with thorough maternalism, and he submitted, eyes closed and head bent in cublike bliss. Destined soon to weigh nearly one hundred and fifty pounds and, together with his three-foot-long tail, to reach more than eight feet in length, the cub was already as heavy and as thickset as his mother.

In the soft light of the setting sun, the west-facing shelter glowed a rosy rock red. It was further lit by the sheer brilliance of the female; the width of her back, with the massed irregularly shaped black rosettes, each with a center of rich rufous yellow richer than the tan background, seemed to gather all the light to itself and then scatter it out to explode on the surrounding stone. On her outstretched legs the spots were solid black and round, and running downward to her paws they became first teardrop-shaped and then elongated dashes. She lay with one foreleg over the cub's shoulders, cradling his head with the other.

Across the valley they saw the lights of the farmhouse come on and heard the dogs barking—a familiar pattern by now. From very far off came the faint twanging of a guitar and the hum of a car, but these last were sounds of no consequence except that they may have belonged to the realm of the two-legged creatures.

The valley had long been a lake of darkness when they rose to their feet and went together up through the narrow chimneylike passage that formed a rear exit to their den. They were hungry now, and at the edge of the forest their next meal awaited them.

Following close behind one another, the two leopards picked their way unerringly through the black night until they came to the open land where the sheep grazed. Ignoring the scattering flock, they skirted the field close by the forest and entered the trees again below a small dam. Sheep on the wall of the dam sheered away in a dim white wave with no sound other than the scuffling of their hoofs.

The leopards moved swiftly now, closer to the ground. Their progress became almost completely silent: each padded paw touched the ground outer edge first, as lightly as a feather. The smallest breeze trembling the fine hairs in their ears told of every change in wind direction, so that prey animals alert for enemy scent could be approached unawares; mask whiskers, each a quivering nerve center of ever sensitive feelers, measured gaps and detected obstacles with unerring accuracy.

Stopping at the place where the dead sheep had been, the leopards cast about, sniffing and suspicious. But the scent of the carcass was positive and it led them directly to an enclosure nearby. Here the scent of man was strong, but this was no novelty. The female had visited many campsites in her lifetime, stepping over old fires and knowing the scents that were peculiar to such places: freshly cut wood, tobacco, coffee.

The young male circled the corral of brushwood, his belly close to the ground and his long tail lashing in anticipation, while the older animal settled down on her paws in the gloom and watched. The male, with infinite caution, was approaching the carcass uphill and sideways, for it was easier to pull down and there was a handy sapling close by to use as leverage. He was angled halfway in when the night exploded. To the unprotected eyes of the female, the brilliant flame that leaped from the darkness, lighting for a second every leaf and twig around her, was a blinding stab of pain in her head. In the brief instant before her reflexes sent her bounding away, she saw the male cartwheel over the bank to disappear in a tearing and snapping of branches. She floundered through the thorns, while the echoes of the blast still rolled down the valley. Half an hour later she was safely back under the shelter of the overhanging rock, concerned only with the fact that she was still hungry.

She settled down to wait for the cub. The pattering of a small stone in the darkness below brought her instantly to full consciousness, and then almost as quickly she relaxed, knowing that the cub was on his way up to the shelter; but there was something wrong—the sounds were clumsy and did not tally exactly with the pattern in her memory. Further, she could smell blood and fear.

The cub struggled over the lip of rock and settled down to lick himself while his mother watched from a corner of the rocky platform. When she finally came to help the cub lick the gaping wound that ran from his right shoulder blade, then along his back to the end of his rib cage, he submitted warily and lay with his head on his paws, blinking into the darkness, confused and weakened from loss of blood.

The cub had been lucky in his angled approach up the bank. From any other direction the cylinder of compressed shot that had flashed at him out of the darkness would have caught him between the shoulder blades. Still, the ragged wound was deep and it had bled strongly. Far more serious was the damage to his right hind paw. He had reached up with his hind leg to gain leverage when he gripped the carcass with his teeth, and the ribbon of pellets had sheared away three of his toes and more than half his paw.

When dawn came, the female grew restless. She paced the rock platform with quick, nervous movements and made a high, moaning sound that was strangely like the mewing of a domestic cat but far more resonant. Then, with a brief backward look at the shelter, she went up the stone chimney and set off toward the fading stars that crowded the tops of the distant mountains. She traveled swiftly, alone. In a short while she would give birth to a new litter of cubs, and instinct was driving her on to safety and survival. The memory of the trap gun with its terrible sound, the blood spoor that led to the shelter, and the wounding of the cub had all combined to trigger a circuit in her brain that now signaled danger; and nothing was more important than the safety of the new life she carried.

Once, when the black leopard paused in his licking to rest and listen, he heard his mother far away on the opposite slope; her deep coughing grunts seemed to command all the still forest to greater stillness, and the forest obeyed.

2

AWAKING from indolent outdoor sleep is one of the pleasures of life. To lie down on soft forest grass within the sound of the sea and under a canopy of leaves with the sun dappling through is to invite a glide just below the waking surface, like that of a fish in warm, shallow water, and one smiles when one awakes.

This is what Clifford Turner did; he smiled and stretched, his legs reaching out rigid and his arms brushing the dry leaves near his head. Then, throwing his arms and shoulders forward, he rose swiftly and began to scamper almost recklessly down the cliff path toward the beach. Along the way he stopped to gaze out over the great ocean that had no end but the ice packs of the Antarctic many thousands of sea miles away. Then, jumping down into the last patch of sunlight, he went quickly through the tunnel of green-and-black forest that led to the entrance of his camp.

The cave in which Turner now lived had been well chosen by its previous occupants. Set amid the same soaring red cliffs that ran the whole length of this rocky part of the southern coastline, the cave was not much more than one hundred feet above the beach and was accessible from higher up only by means of the old river cleft in which it was situated; however, without the logging road that hugged the coast a farther three hundred feet above, the beach and cave—separated from main highways by a strip of almost impenetrable coastal scrub forest—would have been inaccessible to all but the most enthusiastic forester.

The cave itself was not too deep and accordingly fairly well lit by the sun, even at this hour of the late afternoon. On one side there was a trickle of water that flowed down through moss and fern into a small stone basin, and in front was a screen of trees that made an efficient wind barrier. It excited Turner to hold in his hand a small bone implement from the cave floor and to know that long ago, perhaps a thousand years or more, another man had sat in that same place with the same sea sounds in his ears.

But now the cave was different. In a corner under a shelf of rock there was a camp bed, neatly made up with blankets and a white pillow. On the rock shelf above was an assortment of rucksacks, kerosene lanterns, boxes of provisions and pots and pans. On a flat surface nearer the mouth of the cave was a fireplace surrounded with stones, a folding table, three folding canvas chairs and a kerosene pressure stove. The dusty central area of the cave had been covered with pieces of driftwood from the beach.

On the table there was a neat pile of typed sheets held down by a stone, and beside the pile a booklet entitled *Notes on the Southern Cape Leopard* by Clifford Turner. Beneath the table was a portable typewriter, and beside it was a briefcase.

Turner put the teakettle on the stove, whistling as he did so. He was tall and angular, with broad shoulders, giving the overall impression of muscular leanness, which was accentuated by the clothes he was wearing—faded blue jeans, heavy boots and a khaki bush shirt with all its buttons undone. His brown hair was long, a thick mane down the back of his neck, and the three days' worth of stubble on his chin and the deep tan of his face made him look older than he was.

Cliff Turner had been in the district off and on for over a year. Although solitary by nature, he was by now known to a wide spectrum of the population, if only by reputation. A student of modern philosophical zoology, he was greatly absorbed with the question of the place and responsibility of mankind as an animal species in the limited habitat of the earth's surface. His research grant from the department of conservation had been a lavish one, and he had accumulated a remarkable weight of fact about the leopard in this southern Cape region. His work evoked a variety of responses locally, not all of them favorable. Among the farmers, his research was viewed with reactions ranging from positive encouragement to good-natured ridicule to outright hostility.

He went about his business with cheerful indifference on the surface, but he had a special regard for the great cats of the world and for leopards in particular. Increasingly he tended to believe that here in this coastal strip of mountain and forest, in spite of its trailer parks and hotels and apparent tameness, was a reservoir of leopards, a sanctuary where the animals could more than hold their own. However, an outdated zoological map showing the distribution of the leopard had quite specifically shown this region as having few if any leopards at all. So in a way he was like a miner or an explorer discovering new and unsuspected riches.

He preferred to work alone and out of the public eye. Few people, even among his academic colleagues, appreciated better than Turner the difficulties involved in studying this most skillful and secretive of all the nocturnal hunters. His two Colored assistants, products of indigenous Hottentot and white ancestry, occupied a cabin near the cave. With their help, Turner was slowly perfecting a system of photographic identification that was yielding a pattern of new information. Each of his five units consisted of twin flash cameras linked through an activator to two small electronic-beam packs having battery lives of close to a year. By means of these cameras, he was building up an extraordinary record of the nocturnal life of the leopard, together with an ever growing gallery of individual animals. Thus far he had clear color photographs of nineteen distinctly different animals, and so he had reason to be pleased with the progress of his study program.

His first task each morning was to check the camera stations and to move and reset those that were due, in accordance with a detailed and previously planned pattern. In the gorge country this was not always easy. There had been times when a whole day had been spent in positioning only one unit. Such a day could involve forging a pathway through the forest, carrying the delicate equipment, baiting with scent derivatives, adjusting the cameras and the beam trigger mechanisms, and then staggering back up to the Land-Rover. But the results were beyond Turner's most optimistic expectations. They showed that he was not only field testing an aspect of wildlife management but producing a visible census as well. Adding to his satisfaction was the knowledge that none of the creatures were being hurt.

When he had finished his tea, Turner made his way up to the

forest road directly above his cave, then walked to the nearby cabin, where he kept his Land-Rover, as well as petrol, tools and various pieces of equipment. A routine stop during most days was at the Rooikrantz forestry office six miles away, and this was where he was headed now.

By arrangement with the forester Machek Prewalski (known as Mike to his friends), the office acted as a receiving depot for Turner's mail as well as for telephoned leopard reports from the surrounding district. At first this telephone link had been regarded by the area's farmers as a sort of complaints center, with hoped-for swift action from the authorities. After a while, when it was discovered that Turner actually liked leopards, the reports had dwindled. But he had made good friends in many quarters. What was more, by gentle diplomacy in two languages—English and Afrikaans—he was teaching a lesson of basic ecology that was beginning to make sense to even the most backward farmer. But the leopard remained a stock killer, and even a potential hazard to human life—a problem animal in governmental wildlife circles. The only reports that Turner dreaded were those of a wounded beast, often the result of a trap gun, for such a leopard became one of the most dangerous animals in existence.

He turned the Land-Rover into the oak avenue that led to the forest station and pulled up in the courtyard outside the office.

Inside, he found Polly, Mike's wife, standing in front of a mirror, arranging her hair. As he came in she turned, startled, upsetting a pile of papers that slid from a table.

"You gave me a fright," she said accusingly. She was still an attractive woman, very dark with almost violet eyes, but her hair was showing streaks of gray.

"Sorry, Polly," he said, "I didn't mean to barge in like that." He picked up the papers in silence.

"John Avery phoned," the woman said. She crossed to a small table on which there was a gas hot plate with a blue coffee jug and cups. "He says he's wounded a leopard. He wants you to phone."

Turner jerked his head up to look at her to see if she was serious. "Damn!" he said in sudden vehemence. "That young man is an idiot. What the devil has he done now? Probably set up a trap gun."

"Take it easy, Cliff. Have some coffee."

Turner ground the handle of the telephone savagely and nodded his thanks to the woman as she handed him a cup. He gave a number to the operator, then hung up to wait while she put the call through. He sat on a corner of the table, sipping his coffee and frowning. "Pure mischief on John's part, this," he said. "I bet old Kampmuller was there too. A new game animal for him."

"But a thing like that *can* be dangerous, Cliff. What about all the people up there?"

"Now it will be dangerous all right." He paused. "It may be dead, of course."

She put down her cup. "Why are you so crazy about leopards in any case?" she asked. "What good do they do?"

He looked at her for a while. "I'm in favor of life, that's all." Then he grinned crookedly. "Perhaps you're right. Maybe I am going a little crazy. Could I have some more of that coffee?"

She refilled his cup. Out beyond the open door the courtyard had become a brilliant rectangle of sunlight. The room was silent.

"When is Mike due back?" Turner asked after a while.

"Do you want him, or are you just making polite conversation? He's a big fool, that's what Mike is. He's out for the day and that suits me fine."

Turner smiled. He had seen enough of their domestic battles and inevitable reconciliations to be able to be merely amused.

The telephone shrilled stridently, and he went across to it with relief. He said, "John? Yes. I'm here. In the office."

He listened, then said, "A trap gun, what sort? Rifle, shotgun?" He drummed his fingers impatiently on the table. "Twelve gauge. Okay, I'm coming." He told Avery to contact Paul Stander, the conservation officer. Then he put the receiver back in its cradle.

"You're going to have to go and look for the leopard now, aren't you?" Polly asked.

Turner sighed. "I suppose so."

He rose, managing a smile. "Thanks for the coffee," he said.

Then he drove away in the Land-Rover, his expression one of deep sadness. He looked at his watch, calculating the time he would need to collect his shotgun and set about a task that was the antithesis of all his work and inclination, and very dangerous.

Cliff Turner and John Avery entered the forest in single file and as silently as they could. On the outer fringe the trees were small and sparse and the soil was dry and dusty. But as they went farther in, the forest grew both darker and damper. It seemed quiet, with only isolated birdcalls from far and near, and Turner, walking behind, was glad that there was not a breeze to rustle the leaves overhead and drown the sigh or grunt of a leopard about to lunge forward.

By the time they reached the site of the trap gun, their eyes had grown accustomed to the gloom. Here the three mongrels that Avery had borrowed from his farm laborers began to show fear, and for the first time Turner began to believe that they were in fact dealing with a leopard. The hounds minced around the trap-gun site as though the ground were too hot for their paws. Their bony tails no longer wagged, and their necks and noses were stretched out toward the repellent and yet fascinating scent.

The twigs and leaves that formed the roof of the pen where the dead sheep lay had been cut in a jagged pattern by the pellets from the trap gun, and it was difficult to imagine how an animal the size of a leopard could have escaped a mortal wound. On the ground in front of the opening there was a scattering of short dark hair, small pieces of bloodstained skin and two almost complete claws. The two men crouched over these in silence, for there seemed little to add to what the sad scraps told them. John Avery was wearing a deerstalker cap and when he stood up, a thorn hooked into it and lifted it neatly off his head. Turner glanced up but did not smile as Avery retrieved this incongruous headgear. With infinite care Turner and Avery went down the bank, following a path of disturbed ferns. Among a bower of arum lilies they found a copious spoor of blood. The drops stood out clearly against the green. Very slowly the men began to follow the trail.

At the end of an hour Turner paused and relaxed his hold on his shotgun. His fingers were stiff and cramped with tension. Close behind him, John Avery breathed heavily. The dogs had disappeared; the blood trail was still there, but it was growing fainter. From the clues they had seen so far, Turner was beginning to believe they were seeking an animal that had been slightly wounded and was waiting for them. Smears of blood on branches and roots some distance above the ground seemed to indicate places where the great cat had purposefully rubbed shoulder or flank in an effort to relieve the pain of a deep surface wound. There was also the print of a paw clearly outlined in blood on a broad lily leaf. A grazing wound was the only possibility. Considering the angle of the entrance to the pen and the close range of the shot, anything but a graze would certainly have killed the animal. A whole paw blown off? No, there would have been far more blood. In his imagination Turner followed the wounded animal in its dumb, disbelieving flight from shock and pain, and he was filled with anger.

John Avery's face glistened with sweat; he looked about him continuously, his eyes swiveling from side to side, huge with excitement. For himself, Turner still hoped that the great cat would avoid them and recover. But he would have given much for a glimpse of the rare animal.

The spoor took the two men slowly down toward the river and then up again, steeply, onto rocky outcrops and moss-covered boulders. The spoor was fresher here but confusing. There were two sets of prints—one clotted and drying, the other still wet and not more than an hour old. The fresh trail led straight up toward the cliff that was becoming visible through the trees. The two men followed it. Emerging from the last of the trees, they stood looking up at the brilliant blue sky against which the gray cliff angled. John Avery expelled his breath in a sigh of relief. Turner felt it too. At least here in the open sunlight their odds were somewhat better and for a moment they could relax.

"I think that's where he's gone," Turner whispered. "Do you see that crack up there, above that little lip of rock?"

John Avery swallowed loudly. "Looks like it. What do we do?"

Turner did not answer immediately. "That fresh spoor changes things a bit. He's been up there all night, but he came down and went up again, and not long ago either. So he's probably not too badly hurt. If we go straight up, we're asking for trouble. I think we should detour around this cliff and have a look from the top."

The detour around the base of the cliff was long and uncomfortable. But at least, in spite of their struggles through the steep thorn jungle, they were relaxed, without the sense of danger.

Turner knew that without hounds and fresh spoor the chances of catching up with their quarry were rapidly fading to nil. In this forest, if the leopard was not badly wounded, he would simply slide away into the shadows, and they would never catch even a glimpse of him.

At last the two men reached the top. They approached the edge and looked cautiously into the valley, but the solid green slope of treetops beneath them made it difficult to know at what point in relation to the leopard's shelter they had emerged. They moved slowly along the rocky border. They had reached a comparatively open place when the black leopard came out to meet them.

Turner was alerted by the soft slither and tinkle of sand and gravel and swung around in time to see the black shape close beside him on the lip of the cliff. As he swung his shotgun the leopard was already moving. A guttural snarl of intense ferocity punctuated its spring, and then Avery moved into Turner's line of vision. Avery staggered back, and the leopard, shockingly dark against the white stony background, appearing hardly to touch the ground, swiveled its long body and flicked a paw at Avery, sending his shotgun clattering away. Then the leopard disappeared into the dense thickets behind. Cliff Turner hurried over to his companion. Avery was gritting his teeth and struggling to get up from a small gap between two boulders. He stretched up to take Turner's hand. "My God!, Cliff! What was that?"

"You all right, John? Did he get you at all? You okay?"

"No, the thing went straight over my head; but it's black."

"Yes, black," Turner was saying, and his voice held wonder and almost uncontainable excitement. "It's a black leopard, John, a great beautiful black leopard, can you believe it!"

3

A COMBINATION of market center and small coastal resort, the town of Knysna was once again playing host to hordes of tourists. As they did each year, the cars with loaded luggage racks, towing trailers or boats, came like migrating flocks and settled in a noisy, colorful throng as close as they could to the water's edge. From the parks and hotels, vacationers scattered in all directions, filling beaches and parking areas and turning the great lagoon estuary into a playground of fluttering, brightly colored sails, with water-skiers and anglers and speedboats drawing a maze of white wakes across the green water.

Jean Mannion parked the Range-Rover in the shade of a large oak tree and was soon walking quickly down the main street, amid Friday end-of-the-month shoppers and window-shopping tourists. In spite of being a comparatively recent local resident, she was stopped and greeted by a number of people. This was one of the pleasures of coming into town, and in addition to her errands—including buying toothpaste and shotgun shells for her brother—she managed to conduct a fair amount of extraneous business. She made an appointment with the veterinary surgeon to have her dogs inoculated; she arranged for a bulldozer to come and make a new dam; and she was invited to a Sunday lunch party.

By late afternoon, when she had finished making her rounds, a new flood of humanity was pouring into the town. Now the shops were filling with factory workers, men in jeans and overalls, women with small children, old-age pensioners and truckloads of forestry workers. They were predominantly light-skinned Colored people, with here and there the darker-faced Xhosa, and she watched them with some concern. A sudden shower of rain was coming down hard, and she wished it would stop for them, for an hour or two at least, to let them get home dry. As if in answer, the shower ceased as quickly as it had begun.

She had climbed into the Range-Rover and was about to start the engine when Cliff Turner loomed up through the rain-streaked windshield, and she gave an involuntary start. He came loping toward her and grinned as she opened the window. He was out of breath and his hair was wet.

"Hello, Jean. I saw you get into your car. Thought I was going to miss you, so I ran." He breathed deeply. "Good exercise. I was going to the yacht club for a drink. Do come with me."

She frowned very slightly. "I haven't been to the yacht club for a long time . . ."

The sentence was unfinished, but he knew that she meant since Simon's death; he added quickly, "Or coffee somewhere?"

She said firmly, "No, the yacht club is fine. Why not. We could sit outside, couldn't we? I've been wanting to ask you about that leopard you and John saw."

They sat on the small covered veranda of the yacht club, barely aware of the noisy throng inside. The water stretched away blue in front of them, with here and there the movement of boats and windsurfers, lonely as drifting feathers. She sipped her drink and listened to Cliff.

"Everyone seems to know about black panthers. I suppose they caught the public imagination a long time ago, in the days of the explorers, but it's a misnomer really. The melanism—the black coloring—is rare but can show up in both jaguars and leopards. A so-called black panther is simply a jaguar or a leopard with a predominant melanistic gene. It's generally recessive, so that a black leopard mating with a normal spotted one will usually produce spotted offspring. But black-to-black mating might give one black cub out of, say, a litter of three."

"So black is rare?"

"Very rare indeed, especially around here. The African black leopard is more a tropical, central-African phenomenon. This far south, well, it's almost unheard of—one of the first recordings, I should think, of an almost pure black, not even faint spots as far as I could see."

"That makes it even worse about John's trap gun," she said.

He was silent and drank from his glass. Then he said, "Don't worry, they're tough creatures, nine lives and all that. They have been known to recover from the most dreadful injuries. Their problem is to be able to keep eating—catching prey. But they can adapt. They'll even make do with beetles and frogs and lizards for a while, if they have to."

"And people?"

He laughed. "Almost never. I'm no expert on man-eaters, but it does require an unusual set of circumstances, of which possibly one could be a hunting disability. But there would also have to be a chance beginning, like, say, in India with a very dense population and a few unburied bodies around, to sort of get the taste. All I can tell you for certain is that there has never been a case here."

Jean was silent, looking out over the water as Turner filled her glass with white wine, her face in profile, the line of straight black hair sweeping in a soft curve down the side of her face and covering one shoulder like a shining shawl.

"It's peaceful here, don't you think?" Turner asked her.

She tucked the dark line of hair back behind her ear and turned to him. "Yes. But I must get back," she said.

"I wish you wouldn't go. We could have supper somewhere."

"I'd like that, Cliff. Really. Sometime, but not tonight."

He was searching for a way to keep her as she collected her bag and scarf, but he knew he was helpless. "I do wish you'd stay."

She smiled, looking at him appraisingly. "All right, a moment longer. I may as well finish the wine."

She had been aware of the sudden tension in his face, almost sadness. Now relieved and pleased, he poured from the small bottle too eagerly, spilling the wine on her arm and then standing, looming over her protectively, blotting with his handkerchief, holding her hand. A small party of visitors came filing through the door, exclaiming about the flamingo-pink glow around them as the sun went down over the hills.

For the second time in his life the black leopard had known fear, and when the two-legged creatures came so close, his anger had changed swiftly to an adrenaline-triggered survival instinct that obliterated even the pain of his wounded paw. In his plunge to safety he would certainly have mauled these creatures who stalked him, for they were large and he was wary of them. Now in the cool forest he moved slowly on three legs. From time to time he stopped to lick the bleeding stump of his injured back leg, and after each period of licking he sat still, listening for alien sounds.

The black leopard was hungry and thirsty, and weak from loss of blood. He was not conscious of any immediate danger beyond the pain and stiffness in his shoulder when he moved and the dull ache in his lower leg. Against the dark green of the forest undergrowth, his camouflage was perfect, but in the shaft of sunlight that flooded over him as he moved, lighting the jet-black hide to a gloss that was silver-tipped with shine, there was also a flash of red; the wound in his shoulder and back was still oozing blood.

Near a clump of bracken there was a patch of exposed earth

where a wild pig had shoveled experimentally with his nose, and upon this there was the clear outline of the forepaw of a full-grown leopard. With it was a scent that the cub knew from instinct offered his only chance of survival. Slowly he began to follow the route his mother had taken upward into the mountains.

By late afternoon he was on the plateau of dense, high forest, and here the going was comparatively easy after the steep-sided valley country he had crossed. But the cub could not hop on three legs for any distance before his lacerated back muscles ached intolerably from the unbalanced posture. He crossed a small stream, drank, and smelled the overhanging fronds of tree fern where his mother's scent hung damp and strong. From here he emerged into an old grass-covered logging road. It was open and more dangerous, but it was also easier to travel.

As he rounded a bend in the road he stopped in momentary shock. Ahead were three men—three foresters with two ridgeback dogs. The dogs were bounding playfully ahead, and they came upon the black leopard before they or he had had any choice between attack and flight. The bitch in the lead, after first bounding back with a yelp of terror, had collided with the dog behind her and snapped at him savagely. But now she was standing her ground, fangs bared, both throat-rumbling and whining, chest close to the ground. For the dogs there was no alternative; they knew only that here before them on equal ground was an ancient enemy and that to attack was close to death and to run was to trigger an attacking response.

The black leopard was afraid, but now in this instant of suspended animation, with the dogs in front of him and the tall creatures openmouthed and motionless beyond, his fear changed swiftly to an overwhelming panic. Because of his wounds, he knew that he could not outrun the dogs. A shout of fear came from one of the men, and in that moment the triggers in the leopard's dazed brain flashed the quick message to kill.

His ears flattened against his skull; his eyes became slits, the pupils dilated; his long tail lashed twice; and before the front man had turned to run, the leopard's hind paws, one a mere stump of bloodied skin, were gouging the earth as he reached full-clawed for the dogs. The bitch he killed with the muscled strike of his claws into her skull, and the other, as he gathered stride and skidded around, was disemboweled in midair, the tawny body flying upward toward the men. The men were running, and the leopard, half blind with the killing drug in his veins, bounded between them, striking as he passed, clearing a way.

When the road before him was empty of all but man sound, he swung off, crashing through the familiar underbrush, slowing only when he collided with a sapling and was forced to lie panting on his side. Even now he listened, ears swiveling to the sounds behind him. But the man sounds faded, and there was no baying of dogs, and when the night came he rested where he was, on the soft dry leaves.

Long before the dawn of the forest he was awake and licking the dirt patiently from his wounded paw. For many minutes there was no sound but that of the rasping of his tongue as he cleaned the upper fur of dried blood; then a lourie began to croak. Soon all the birds of the forest were awake; they were lacing the valleys with sound, and the leopard moved on.

Those hours of deep, exhausted sleep had served the leopard well and enabled him to get himself out of the last steep spur of mountain forest, through the macchia jungle and up into the wet, glittering rock faces on the southern side of the range. On the old wagon road, the scent he followed was still detectable in the damp sand, but once over the crest, where the sun blazed down, it evaporated in the smell of aromatic scrub bush. He faced a vast, empty valley—a bowl of sunlight on rock and green veld and silver-ribboned mountain streams. Going slowly downward toward a rocky scree, he found shelter from the sun under a ledge of rock, with a stunted tree in front and some dry grass beneath. There he lay, panting, drained of all strength or will to go farther.

When darkness came at last, he was sufficiently revived to begin to take an interest in his immediate surroundings and the possibility of food. This quite natural reaction to a new area was quickly confused by a sudden pain as he stood on a sharp stone, and then, for the first time since his wounding, he gave voice to his misery; it was a low, moaning cry that changed eerily to a deep coughing and ended as a sad meowing. It was the sound of approaching death, and it filled all the valley with a kind of sorrow that only the wild places could know and feel for the passing of something of great beauty and great strength.

All through the early night the cub called at intervals. Far away, near the bottom of the valley, where frogs fell silent at her passing tread and water tinkled softly, the female heard the sound and stopped to listen. This was no mating call. Following the sound, she moved uphill, and many minutes later when she was close, she began to call in answer. She approached the cub's shelter cautiously, her mouth half open as she smelled the air. The two animals touched noses very slowly and grunted a kind of contented greeting; then, as he laid his head on his paws, the female began to clean the wound on the cub's back.

Early in the morning the female led the way down to the river gorge, and before the sun was up, the two leopards were in her rock shelter overlooking a black pool that was thickly surrounded by jungle growth and protected on its far side by a steep cliff. The cub lay exhausted. As the light grew in intensity there was nothing to be seen in the shadowy shelter but the stark white point of a fang and a patch of silver sheen where some reflection of the sun's coming touched wet black fur; and then the spots on the female blurred for an instant as she moved and slipped downward into a rocky bush tangle and vanished.

She returned at dusk fully gorged and round of belly, to regurgitate a steaming mound of rhebok meat onto the shelter floor. Half crawling, the cub crossed to the meat and began to feed.

For a week the female hunted on the mountain slopes until the leading ram of the herd of rhebok took the last of his does up over the ridge to comparative safety. By then the cub was recovering rapidly. Even the stub of his hind paw, licked and bitten clean of ragged flesh, was hardening, and the wound on his back was shrinking into a long red-gray scar. On the tenth day in this place the female moved to a nest she had made down the ravine and gave birth to a litter of two cubs, both spotted. Eventually she brought them back to the original shelter and when, blind and hungry, they suckled from her, the black cub joined them without complaint from his mother.

They made a strange group: the spotted female lying contentedly on her side; the black cub, as big as she, crouched suckling at right angles to her; the two spotted cubs tucked in beside him. But he was drinking more than his share and the female grew restless. Four days after the cubs were born she took the black leopard hunting with her for the first time. As he followed her up into the full glare of the sunlit slope he limped still, but a gloss was coming back to his hide, and his head, alert and quick, moved at every small sound the mountain made.

4

CLIFF Turner was enjoying the drive as a passenger in the back seat of Jean Mannion's car. He looked at the forest walls streaming by on either side of the road and smoked his cheroot in a state of blissful well-being. His lonely cave seemed a long way off; and then as suddenly as he had become conscious of his contentment, he was aware of a twist of longing or loneliness, he was not sure which, and for a moment he contemplated leaving his primitive headquarters. In any event, he would have a party, he thought; yes, that was it. Leaning forward, he said, "How does the idea of a beach party appeal to you two? Down at the cave. Would you come?"

Jean, who was driving, turned her head. "Thanks. We'll come. What a splendid idea, Cliff."

"You'll arrange a moon, of course," said John Avery, who was sitting beside his sister in the front seat.

"Of course," said Turner.

They drove in silence for a while.

"This thing we're going to tonight," Avery said, "is it a forestry affair or nature conservation or what?"

"Both, I think." Turner sat forward again. "After the symposium we had on Wednesday, everyone thought it might be a good idea. You know, nature conservation and government forestland; get together socially; cooperation and all that."

"And the meeting on Wednesday," Jean said, "it wasn't about leopards in particular? I mean, you weren't in the hot seat?"

"No, I had to read a paper, that's all." Then he added, "Actually, it was a bit hotter than I would have liked, with those two foresters getting mauled."

"How are they?" the girl asked.

"Barnard's still in the hospital. The claw wounds were deep, right across his back. But Dick Barker was only caught on the arm. He was lucky. They both were, for that matter."

"Do they know about the trap gun?" Jean asked. "I mean about its being John's?"

"They know it was a trap-gun wound," Turner said. "And they know where it happened, but it won't go any further than that. Actually, the law is a bit confused when it comes to protecting stock or possibly even human life against dangerous animals. But as of now, a trap gun will be very suspect, and from now on, too, leopards will be protected animals, in this region anyway."

"Well, I'm sure you're pleased about that," Jean said. "I am."

"Yes, I'm glad. And I'm glad you are. But it's going to mean headaches for the conservation officers. I'll have problems too."

"And we farmers and stockmen are going to have problems," John Avery said petulantly. "Us, Kampmuller and all the others."

Cliff Turner sighed in the darkness. It was going to be a long evening. He let sufficient time pass to defuse any potential acrimony. Then he said gently, "Your sheep probably won't have much more trouble, John; the place isn't completely overrun with leopards, you know." He was about to remark that in his opinion leopards would kill sheep only if nothing else was available, but thought better of it.

He wished that the black leopard had remained hidden in the mountains and valleys of this wild, sparsely populated country, as it could easily have done. Leopards suddenly had become a local political issue. Japie Kampmuller, who was something of a force in church and politics, was leading a faction against leopard conservation. The black leopard had polarized opinion to a degree that seemed quite out of proportion to the actual danger.

They parked the car behind a string of others and walked down a muddy road toward the forestry lodge, which sat on a grassy promontory overlooking a long sweep of forested valley. Jean held her brother's arm as she stepped over the puddles, lifting her calf-length, russet-colored skirt with one hand. She wore a belted jacket of dark evergreen, and a green silk scarf over her long black hair.

Outside the lodge nearly a hundred people were gathered.

Jean Mannion normally drew attention wherever she went, and in this group she represented a kind of sophistication that seemed to please everyone.

Turner stood at the edge of the crowd and watched her over his glass of wine. When she smiled, her eyes seemed to glow with an intense darkness, and to him she was beautiful. He turned away with an effort and began to arrange other faces and names in his mind. A wooden dais had been set up on the grass, directly overlooking the forest, and here a small official group chatted together, most apparently enjoying their proximity to the cabinet minister. Four of them Turner knew as representatives of conservation and forestry and one or two others he knew only by sight.

As darkness fell and the lights came on, accentuating the complete isolation of this hillside lodge in the midst of the wilderness, the crowd drew together, the wooden benches filled up, and an expectant hush fell.

The regional head of forestry began to speak, first in Afrikaans and then in English. The minister followed in Afrikaans for a good quarter of an hour. Turner observed thankfully that the minister did not mention leopards at all. He turned his head and noticed Dick Barker standing at the back under an awning, with his injured arm heavily bandaged and in a sling. There were three other speakers, but their speeches were mercifully short, and soon people were released to fill their glasses and join the line for the buffet supper.

Turner made his way across to Barker, who was talking with Japie Kampmuller; he wanted more information from Barker about the leopard's attack, and he also wanted to confirm Kampmuller's predictable reaction. In spite of the fact that they represented diametrically opposed points of view in most things, Turner liked Japie Kampmuller and found his jibes amusing.

"Hello, Cliffie," Kampmuller shouted, draping a massive arm over Turner's shoulder. "You see what your cat's done now, hey," he said, inclining his head toward Barker.

"Messy job," Turner said, grinning at Barker. "I'll have to start the creature's training again; he missed the jugular completely."

Kampmuller began to wheeze, and then laughed so heartily that he doubled up with a coughing fit. Turner gave Dick Barker a lopsided apologetic grin and was relieved to see that the slightly shocked expression had gone from the man's face.

Kampmuller recovered from his coughing fit and wiped his eyes with a handkerchief. "Dick says that black animal charged them. Someone could get killed like that."

"The leopard was badly wounded," Turner said. "And you know how dangerous a wounded leopard can be. Dick here and the others were just unlucky to have been in his path. Normally he would have heard them and given way."

"But when *you* saw it," Kampmuller persisted, "didn't it nearly get hold of John Avery?"

"We were following a blood spoor. That's looking for trouble."

Kampmuller said, "How do you know the thing wasn't waiting for you?"

Turner laughed. "Waiting for what? To eat us, I suppose?"

"Could be," Kampmuller said quite seriously. "It could be a man-eater."

"A man-eater!" Turner echoed incredulously, for in all truth he had not seriously considered the possibility.

"You know, I worked in Zambia once," Kampmuller was saying, "and a leopard killed fourteen people in one year, before it was shot."

Turner said, "Look, I'm not disputing the fact that man-eating leopards have been known to exist, but why here all of a sudden? I mean, there's no reason for it."

"People have disappeared in the forest, haven't they?" Kampmuller said, raising his eyebrows. "And this black thing, he's acting funny. And you said yourself he's big."

"He's a huge thing," Barker said with surprising vehemence. "And I'm telling you, when he came for us he was out to kill. You could see it in his eyes."

Kampmuller laid a large hand on Turner's shoulder. "Protected or not, Cliff," he said, shaking his head slowly, "if that thing comes to my farm and I can get a shot at him . . ."

He left the sentence unfinished as a tall, thin man approached and greeted Turner. He wore steel-rimmed glasses on a bony nose, and his slightly graying hair seemed to grow at varying unruly angles around his head. Turner introduced him as Dr.

Williams, from Cape Town. Williams shook hands with Kampmuller, then smiled at Turner.

"Your black leopard has achieved rather spectacular notoriety," Williams said, speaking slowly and enunciating each word with pedantic clarity. "An unusually well-substantiated sighting, I should say." He looked at Barker. "Your arm," he said. "You were one of the party that was attacked. You saw the animal quite clearly?"

Barker was silent for so long that Turner felt forced to give him a lead. "Dr. Williams is a zoologist, Dick, and black leopards aren't common in this part of the world." He knew that Williams wanted eyewitness corroboration, a scientific double check.

Barker grinned shyly. "I saw him clearly all right, Doctor. He was nearly on top of me."

"Must have been quite frightening," the tall man said solicitously. "What particularly struck you about the animal?"

"Well, sir, it was his eyes, you know, and his teeth. Because his mouth was open," he added lamely.

Turner suppressed a tremor of mirth. The forester had been so shocked at the sight of the leopard that the specific color of the animal had been relatively unimportant.

"And the tail," Barker said.

"The tail?" Williams cocked his head slightly.

"Yes, sir, the tail. It was long, you know, and it hit me on the cheek as the animal jumped past. That was the worst, because I didn't feel the claws on my arm. There was this thing like a snake hitting me hard on my cheek. Just like a big black snake."

"The tail was black, you say?"

"The whole animal was as black as charcoal, only shiny."

Williams rubbed his chin. "Very unusual so far south." He looked out into the dark valley below. "Wish I could have seen him; he must be beautiful. You'll try and get a picture, Cliff?"

Turner nodded. "I've moved the equipment, but it's a long shot."

"I know," Williams said. "Now I'd like to go and find another glass of this excellent wine."

Cliff Turner drifted from one group to another, finding nothing to hold him. When he saw Jean again, he gazed at her for a moment in surprise, as though he had never met her. The lamplight was soft on her face, casting high shadows around her cheekbones. His hand trembled as he lit a cigarette. While the match still flamed, she looked up and then directly at him. She waved, and he saluted her with a slow, open hand before turning away.

5

THE black leopard left his mother and her litter only when she made it clear to him that he was eating more than his hunting presence was worth and that he was no longer welcome. Since then, it had rained for three days—a steady, hissing downpour—and he had eaten little besides dung beetles and lizards. To kill rhebok or baboons on these open, stony slopes, he needed that final surge of speed at the end of a stalk, and his wounded paw had let him down three times in succession. Now the stump had started to bleed again. A trail of droplets followed him down the old, rutted wagon road; drop by drop it stalked him still, like the shadow of death close behind him, but not yet close enough to dull the star-green gems of his eyes.

He passed the creature smells of the Kampmuller farm when night was darkest, with all his senses beamed toward the dogs that barked and rattled their chains in the little village of improvised houses, where the Colored laborers lived. The dogs were telling him that they were frightened individuals and no hunting pack, and he circled slowly in toward them until the outlines of roofs and chimneys became clearly visible in the starlight. He slipped soundlessly over the bare, trampled earth in front of the first house, and the dog tethered to its porch by a length of chain barked in a high, yelping frenzy.

He killed the dog in one swift movement, as easily as a domestic cat would catch a cornered mouse. Then, bending, he took the animal quite gently in his jaws and turned away toward the shadows. As his speed increased, the dog's chain rattled behind and then jerked to a sudden stop. Thrown momentarily off balance as the dog was torn from his jaws, the leopard turned to retrieve his kill. A new sound was coming now from the house, and with it light, yellow and bright, and the scent of the tall, two-legged creatures whose mark was on all dangerous things. A moment later he was engulfed in a scent streaming from the open door of the house. His lips drew back in a mask of fear and tension as a figure loomed toward him. Acting from instinct alone, the black leopard rose from his pool of deep shadow, and with a hissing intake of breath he sprang upward at the creature's head.

Two sets of claws fastened upon the man's shoulders, the great inner talons driven to the hilt under the enormous power of the forelegs, and almost simultaneously the gaping jaws closed on the man's throat. His neck snapped. Around them, dogs still barked. Slowly the leopard disengaged his jaws from the warm, hairless neck, for he sensed that his prey was dead. Then, grasping the shoulder with his teeth, he began to drag his burden away toward the forested valley below.

As the deeper darkness of the scrub forest closed about him, the leopard heard sounds far behind but rising in intensity, and he went on. In spite of his hunger he stopped only when the first glimmer of dawn hazed the patches of open sky between the treetops. With claws and teeth he stripped the clothing from the body. Then he ate. In the middle of the day he rested on a shaded ledge some distance away, and when night fell once more, he returned to his feast. By the following morning, when the louries began to croak to each other again, he was sated at last. He went down to the river to drink, then up into a rocky cliff on the opposite side of the valley. Here, in the midday haze of baking rock and small, white jasmine-scented flowers, he went to sleep.

He was awakened in the late afternoon by the clinking sound of metal on rock, and almost at the same time his slitted pupils detected movement on the opposite cliff a quarter of a mile away.

CLIFF Turner knew that the so-called hunting party had no hope at all of even a glimpse of the leopard, but it was the sort of gesture that had to be made immediately. Leopard it certainly was, and the drag marks and drops of blood had been easy to follow all the way down to where the mutilated corpse lay.

The whole affair had come as a shock and an unwelcome challenge to the ordered life of the district. Of the party of seven who now stood on the rocky ridge where Turner and Avery had first encountered the black leopard, the only one patently aglow with excitement was the reporter from the local newspaper. The two policemen, creaking with leather and perspiring in the heat, carried their holstered service revolvers. Of the other weapons in the party, Turner would have pinned most faith on Sergeant Botha's 9-mm Walther pistol in the unlikely event of trouble.

Martin Botha was a craggy-faced man of massive strength whom Turner knew well and liked. His hair was gray-flecked, but black, bushy eyebrows seemed to underline the unfailing vitality that had long been the scourge of the district's petty thieves, drug peddlers and wife beaters, all of whom both respected and feared him. In off-duty hours Botha was a sad, gentle man and a grower of orchids; he was also a deadly shot with his pistol.

Kampmuller carried a .375 rifle and wore a bush hat with a leopard-skin band. The hat annoyed Turner; he thought it arrogant and aggressive. Kampmuller had got over his initial obvious satisfaction at having had his morbid suspicions justified. Mostly he was upset about the death of the man Charles Witbooi, who had been an employee of long standing and a good tractor driver.

John Avery wore his deerstalker cap and carried Simon Mannion's expensive English shotgun; red-faced in the heat, he was clearly acting the part of the nonchalant old-hand leopard tracker. Last was Hendrik Witbooi, brother of the dead man. Ten minutes after the leopard had vanished into the night with its prize, Hendrik had been on the scene, comforting his hysterical sister-in-law, who, seeking her husband, had found only the dead dog and the smear of blood on the ground. Hendrik Witbooi had run along the dark path to the farmhouse and alerted Kampmuller, who had come in his truck. Only then, in the scalding whiteness of the headlights, had they found the leopard's spoor.

Now it was Sunday. Turner had seen the spoor and the toeless print among the normal ones, and so he knew that the black leopard had in fact lost almost an entire paw to the trap gun.

After establishing that the leopard was nowhere nearby, the party spent the remainder of the afternoon finishing the unpleasant business of retrieving the corpse and handing it over to the man's anguished relatives and friends in the little village. Then the body was taken away in an ambulance.

When the party returned to the spot where the corpse had been found, Turner looked up at the trees and said to Botha, "There's only one way of working this, you know. Wait for the leopard tonight, up in one of the trees. I'll bring that dog he killed. If he comes back, the dog will keep him occupied for a while."

Botha scratched his head and puffed his pipe. "Man, Cliff," he said, "that would be a devil of a job. I'm not sure about that."

What he was not sure about was sitting all night in a tree with a man-eating leopard in the neighborhood.

"Don't worry, Martin," Turner said. "I'll ask Paul Stander to sit with me for company. It's really his department, I suppose."

Jean Mannion, charged with tracking down Paul Stander, the conservation officer, had succeeded, after a great deal of effort, in finding him at a friend's house, where he had been spending his day off. To Turner it was a moment of great relief when Jean drove up with the uniformed officer. Sergeant Botha's relief matched Cliff Turner's, if for different reasons. Botha was a good policeman and a good friend, so that although stalking a man-eating leopard was hardly his business, he would not easily have left Turner to tackle the job alone. Now that Stander had turned up, the situation was under control.

John Avery and Japie Kampmuller both volunteered to join Turner and Stander in their all-night vigil up a tree, but Turner had been adamant; from the point of view of noise alone, four men would be a ridiculous number. However, Avery and Kampmuller worked hard helping Turner and Stander erect a rough platform, and Jean drove back to the farm to collect such things as flashlights, white tape and new batteries, as well as a thermos of coffee, some sandwiches and a hip flask of brandy.

"Be careful, Cliff," she said. "Come for breakfast in the morning."

Then at last Turner and Stander were alone. As arranged, they worked in the silence of sign language. Turner fastened a strip of white tape to the barrel of his shotgun and attached a small cylindrical flashlight underneath. Stander tied another flashlight to an overhead branch. After painstaking readjustment, they seemed satisfied that the beam would center roughly over the area where the dead dog lay.

Soon there was nothing left to do except shift occasionally on the hastily nailed boards and hope that there would be at least one position that might prove bearable through the night. The evening shadows closed around them, and there was not air movement enough to stir even a single leaf. Stander's .308 rifle was already cocked and so was Cliff Turner's shotgun, for even the faint metal click of a safety catch might be too loud. Turner began to breathe with his mouth open, as this tended to silence his steadily thumping heart.

The explosive bark of a bushbuck left ten seconds of almost complete sound vacuum in the surrounding area, and then one by one the little noises came back to remind them how much soft slither and crackle and tiny sound there had been. The breathing of the two men quickened, Stander's only just audible. Turner felt his trigger finger fluttering against the guard as the minutes slowly ticked away across the luminous dial of his watch. The tension of such unbearable excitement could not be sustained beyond the full quarter of an hour that they sat like statues in the tree, and excitement it was. For both of them this was a new experience, and it was still difficult for them to believe that they were dealing with anything more than a marauding animal that would die in a blast of light and sound as it touched the bait.

As his taut nerves relaxed, Turner sorted out the facts and probabilities in his mind once again. The leopard had probably killed the man as a result of an accidental fear reflex. There was every likelihood that this would prove to be an isolated instance of man killing. On the other hand, the chance remained that the leopard, having found a new prey that was easy to overpower, would strike again if the opportunity occurred.

Turner looked up. In the darkness Paul Stander's face was only just visible. From below there came no sound. Turner felt a chill of fear, a kind of superstitious dread, as he thought of the sinuous black creature, ears flattened, snake-headed, stalking silently through the night, pupils dilated to unearthly size, great paws hiding their sheathed claws. As a scientist, he knew that the black leopard was identical in all respects to its spotted fellows. Yet the thought of a true man-eater caused the hairs on the backs of his hands to prickle against his skin—a predator hunting men and women in preference to all other prey, becoming wise to the ways of man, wise to his defenselessness, wise to his methods of retaliation. Was it the man-eater of Panar, in northern India, that had killed four hundred people? And closer to home in the north of Africa, the Chambeshi leopard that had killed thirty-seven in one year?

The smallest of rustling sounds came from below and to the left. The two men silently turned to each other as though for confirmation. The source could be any of a host of smaller animals, and besides, the night had hardly begun. Turner was thinking about this when Stander gave a wild, strangled cry and seemed to fling himself backward, grabbing a branch as he went, so that the whole tree and platform shook violently. His rifle muzzle flashed in a deafening blast a second later, and by then Turner was already half swiveled in his perch and gazing into the face of the black leopard. Turner saw only luminous green eyes and white fangs, but he smelled the taint of the leopard's breath, and he was climbing, one paw fastened into Stander's back and the other already reaching up. Turner struck downward with the butt of the shotgun, feeling the impact and then the give as the butt slid over the animal's head; there was a tearing sound as Stander lurched forward and a soft thud as the leopard dropped away into the darkness, then silence again.

Stander shouted, "Good Lord!" and both men scrambled up from the platform to stand erect, clinging to the central branch.

Turner's flashlight and gun barrels scanned the forest floor, reaching into tunnels of green. The leopard was gone. Turner turned toward Stander. "Paul, are you all right?"

"My God, Cliff, it was coming after us. The thing's mad."

"Turn round, Paul, let me see."

Stander felt his back with his left hand and turned slowly. The thick jersey he had tied around his waist by its sleeves was ripped to shreds and so was the back of his shirt; his leather belt was neatly snapped in two and hanging, but otherwise there was not a mark on him.

"No marks, Paul. Nothing. He got you by your belt. But watch it, man, he could come back," and Turner flashed his lighted barrels down again on the open space below. He said, "I can't believe it. He's taken it, he's taken the dog."

They gazed at the place in silence. There was nothing they could do but wait for morning. There was no question of climbing down and going back to the settlement. They drank the brandy over the next three hours and smoked and talked and hoped the two flashlights would see them through the night. They were no longer hunters, but the hunted. Dawn was a long time coming.

They shifted their positions on the platform and after that were silent. In a short, vivid period, when he slept briefly and awoke with a start, Turner dreamed that Jean Mannion ran before him, beckoning him on. But she was a dark spirit, all that was lovely and unattainable, and she was wearing only the skin of the black leopard. She smiled at him mockingly, it seemed, and ran effortlessly with long strides, her black hair streaming behind her.

6

IT TOOK three weeks for the newspapers to abandon the subject of the leopard attack and black leopards in general, and they did so reluctantly. They had been able to resurrect old stories of people in the area who had vanished without trace. There was also one hysterical report of a strange spoor, which Turner investigated with the local correspondent—only to find that the tracks were those of a Great Dane belonging to the correspondent's next-door neighbor. Turner moved a camera unit to the valley that bordered Jean's farm and Kampmuller's, and results during the period were two genets, a lynx and a badger. Jean was delighted with this minor wildlife census, and leopards were forgotten by all but Turner and Paul Stander.

On the night of the next full moon Turner gave his cave party. He and his two assistants spent an afternoon carrying down glasses, boxes of meat and drink, extra lamps, and firewood. They tidied the cave as best they could, and Turner set up the battery-operated record player he had borrowed. The brilliant afternoon sky confirmed that it was going to be one of those warm, still nights that had often made him sad in a nostalgic way, because he had no one with whom to share such beauty: the gleaming breakers, the gleaming beach, the silver shawls of retreating water washing the smooth shoreline.

When the thirty guests had all arrived, there was still plenty of room in the cave. Light from carefully hidden candles and oil lamps shed a soft radiance over the rock walls and the high-domed roof, giving the illusion of a great medieval hall warmed by fire glow. Glasses of wine twinkled like ruby-flashing fireflies. Most of the guests were dressed for the beach.

Down by the sea there was an additional lighting effect, for with each wave a rippling fire of phosphorescence glowed a magical green, waxing and waning in explosions of light.

After a while the entire party moved to the beach. The water was creamy and warm. It seemed to Turner that the only guests not swimming now were Kampmuller and the forester Mike Prewalski, two silhouettes by the bonfire on the beach. Paul Stander and John Avery, leaping high with each wave, were competing for a bottle of wine, and near them somewhere he could hear a girl's laughter. Turner himself was content to walk in the shallows and think of Jean, who was somewhere nearby. He moved slowly away down the beach, wading in the swirl of sound and foam, seeking her as he had been doing unconsciously for so long.

By the dark mussel-studded rocks of a small cove he saw her, her water-streaked hair black as a seal's skin. When he called to her, she turned and then stood slowly, seeming to rise up out of the foam in a gesture of both fear and welcome. Suddenly he could see, in a small explosion of green fire, the whole symmetry of her body. Green rings of fire formed around him as he moved toward her. She stood trustingly before him. He was filled with a sense of glorious elation that echoed the radiant night in a crescendo of sea sound. They stood almost touching, accepting. Her face was turned up toward his, and he brushed her mouth with his lips, tasting salt and strawberries and the sweetness of her breath, and his hands lifted, meeting hers halfway and then moving on as hers did, to touch warm shoulders and hold and caress.

She drew away but very slowly, making it easier for him.

He said, "One day. Please promise me, if you can."

"One day, perhaps," she whispered. "I'm going back now. Let me go first." She untwined his arms and sank down into the water and the darkness, and foam swallowed her.

Turner plunged forward, scattering the water into a white fan with his knees, and flung himself into a cauldron of foam, so that his joyous shout was drowned in bubbles.

When the leopard went back to the remains of his two-legged prey animal, he was alerted to suspicion by the changes that had taken place. His meal appeared somehow to have been transferred upward into the branches of a tree and to have had its place on the ground taken by the dog. In the tree, without the anchoring claws of his wounded hind paw, he lost his balance when a second two-legged creature struck him on the head. The deafeningly loud blast and the light shafts swinging through the leaf canopies above him fitted in with the voice noises he was coming to associate with the appearance of the two-legged animals. On his way back across the clearing he picked up the dog; he ate it not a hundred yards from the creatures in the tree. In his subconscious mind he now gave them pride of place in his meal preference, supplanting monkeys, but at the same time he would instinctively never again tangle with more than one at a time.

He moved eastward through the remainder of the dark hours and spent the following day dozing under an overhanging rock, high up on the lip of a river gorge. When another two days and nights had passed, the leopard grew restless with hunger. He came down into the gorge, then began to move toward the flat farmland and plantations above, seeking the paths that his prey used.

In time, with summer nearing an end and all the beaches and the roads filled with activity, the black leopard made two more human kills. One occurred in an isolated area and went undetected. The next was an old shepherd who lived alone and who was not seriously sought for ten days after he had been dragged away into the night. The owner of the farm missed the old man on Friday, when he had not come to the little shop to collect his pay and buy his groceries. The following Monday afternoon the farmer climbed into his truck and inquired among his other laborers, but no one knew where the old man was. The farmer was fond of the old shepherd, and believing that he might have died somewhere up in the foothills of the mountains or that he lay injured in some rocky place, he searched the area with five men and found him at last. Shocked and saddened by the tattered remains, he telephoned the police.

THE leopard followed the little group of Colored children for over a quarter of a mile, sometimes stopping to sniff at the footprints left by their bare feet and once sitting down to watch as they threw stones at a signpost. He was more curious than hungry as this little herd of smaller-than-usual prey creatures dawdled and sang. He followed the children out into a dusty open place, and turned back only when a window flashed the afternoon sun into his eyes and a dog began to bark. He stayed close by the houses that night, and early in the morning went back to the path and lay, chin on paws, under a wild olive tree. The children were the first to use the path that morning, as usual, for school began early.

The children were quieter this time, not yet fully awake, and the last of them, a boy, came on more slowly, dragging his bare feet in the sand. The leopard heard the boys and girls coming long before they were near him, and when the first five passed in a tight group, he was crouched flat on gathered muscles, tail straight out on the ground behind and eyes hugely green with anticipation. The boy neither heard the splayed paws striking the sand behind him nor felt the single blow that killed him, but the knot of children turned when a girl screamed, and saw the great black beast standing there in the path—the boy beneath him. The girl had paused to scold her brother, telling him to hurry. She had seen the shape, a blurred black shadow, bound and strike with a flashing white-tipped paw, and then stand stock-still and lift its head to gaze at her with green eyes.

THE children ran into the schoolyard, crying and shouting about *'n Swart ding* (a black thing). The teacher rose angrily at the noise, and called them and the rest of the class into the school.

"*Stilte,*" the teacher shouted in Afrikaans. "Be still. What's the matter with you?" But a moment later he realized that something serious was amiss and began to question the hysterical children.

The group of five led the teacher back down the path but would not go near the spot where the boy had been attacked. As the teacher came near to the place, the children shouted and pointed. There was no sign of the boy, but then the teacher saw the pool of blood, the spoor, the drag mark that a dangling foot would make. A sick knot began to form in his stomach.

"A black thing?" he asked the children. "A baboon, a dog?"

"Like a big black cat," came the reply.

SINCE the night the black leopard had killed the man on Kampmuller's farm, Turner's study program had come to a halt. He knew it was time for him to get the strange creature out of his mind and move his cameras away from the valley below Jean's house, but it was difficult; he saw Jean often, and although he was seldom able to speak to her alone, without her brother, John, her very proximity, the perfume she wore, the sound of her voice were becoming Turner's only store of value and need. She was not the sort of woman who would allow herself to fall into a casual affair. Turner knew this; he knew how deeply in love she had been with Simon. Things were suddenly muddled and meaningless in his life, and even the task of writing his monthly progress report became a chore.

It was a Thursday afternoon when he heard the news about the leopard's latest attacks. He had driven to the Rooikrantz forest station to collect his mail, and when he arrived, both Mike and Polly Prewalski came out of the office to meet him.

"That leopard has killed a little Colored boy," Polly said. "And an old man too, they say."

"No!" Turner said, climbing out of his truck. "When did you hear this?"

"The police station phoned, and Paul Stander. The boy was walking to the Bosnek school when the thing pounced on him."

"The old man was a shepherd over at Engelsmansplaas," Mike said. "They missed him for more than a week; there was very little left of him, they say."

"What about the boy? Did they find anything?"

"They haven't looked yet. It only happened this morning."

Turner rubbed his chin in the sudden silence while husband

and wife looked at him, and he wondered whether the icy trickle of fear he felt was visible in his eyes.

"You must phone Sergeant Botha," Polly said. "And Paul Stander too; he left a message and a number."

Mike ushered Turner into his office with a little bow. A small, thin man with an old, sad, rather wise-looking face, Mike Prewalski was a Pole, who often gave way to periods of quaint formality. He referred to Turner as Doctor, and it seemed that he had once known nobler, grander days. He gave the impression that he was only waiting for a call to new emergencies that could suitably extend his resourcefulness.

With a flourish, he offered Turner his own office chair and nodded toward the telephone. Turner phoned Martin Botha, but the sergeant was not available. He next phoned the forest station at Bosnek. Paul Stander was out, but had left a message that Turner would find him at the Bosnek Colored Primary School.

Turner put the phone down. "Thanks, Mike. By the way, that leopard has a distinctive spoor—the right hind foot is badly damaged, may be gone completely. Anyway, there are toes missing. On muddy ground it should show up quite clearly."

"You may rely upon me. I have a shotgun and I shall set a trap." He made it sound as if the whole business was as good as over.

Polly suddenly said, "Hey, that thing mustn't come here. There are a lot of people here, you know."

Turner smiled. Her belligerent tone indicated that in her eyes the leopard was a part of his wildlife nonsense that had gone awry and that was now likely to inconvenience her personally. Then the smile vanished as he thought suddenly of Jean and the forest pool where she liked to swim. He could not remember whether he had warned her not to go there again. In his restlessness he stood up quickly and left.

When Turner arrived at the Bosnek school, Paul Stander, Sergeant Botha and a Colored policeman were leaning over the hood of Stander's truck. The police van was parked near the school building, surrounded by adults and children of varying ages, and a man was standing beside a large thornbush branch in the path farther down. Turner greeted the men and lit a cigarette.

"We thought we'd wait for you, Cliff," Paul Stander said. "Mr.

Abrahams over there, the teacher, is keeping the spoor as fresh as possible, but it was already trodden on when I got here."

Turner propped himself up against the door of the truck. "So what's the story, Martin? What's next?"

Consciously or not, Turner was casting himself in the role of unofficial assistant, and Botha was not altogether prepared for this. He scratched the back of his head and frowned.

"It seems certain it was the leopard. The children saw it."

"It's him, all right, Cliff," Stander said. "The spoor is clearly visible. Shall we go and have a look?"

They stood around the brown bloodstain and looked down over the valley in silence. From this high point, the valley was a river of scrub trees that flowed down into the vast forest beyond. In the farthest distance, they could see the hard line of the ocean.

"I've been thinking of getting the department's hound pack up here," Paul Stander said musingly. "This spoor will be cold by the time they get here, but it's better than nothing. In the circumstances, I think I might be able to keep them for a few weeks."

"Ready for the next killing, you mean?" Turner said.

"Something like that."

DURING the week that followed, Cliff Turner moved his headquarters to the Bosnek forest station. He had an office with a telephone, and a forestry-service hut that contained three bunks as well as a fireplace, a small kitchen and even gas-heated hot water. After the cave, this was luxury indeed.

The move had been prompted by his superiors in Cape Town, who felt that the cave existence was not good for the image of the department; the cave scene had featured prominently in one of the city newspapers. The visiting reporter had been good at his job, and his article had resulted in a wave of public interest in the man-eater itself and leopards in general. The black leopard had focused attention on the future of its species in a hostile world. Kampmuller too had been interviewed, and the whole tenor of his statement was one of righteous indignation that there were men actually spending public money to protect such dangerous creatures. Unfortunately for him, he had also implied that the black leopard was dangerous simply because it was black.

Turner's balanced scientific viewpoint on the same page, accompanied by photographs of the cave, was by contrast a masterpiece of diplomatic objectivity. Turner had made certain that the reporter understood all aspects of the problem, and he had fed him a steady, easily digestible stream of information, always slanted toward ecology and the ecosystem.

The first caller on Turner's telephone was Kampmuller himself, delighted with his new status and congratulating Turner as a fellow celebrity. His second caller was Paul Stander, telling him that the dogs had arrived—a pack of six crossed beagle-foxhounds that had hunted jackal and caracal lynx in open country with great success. Turner said he wondered how they would get on in the forest, and Stander said he didn't know. There was a third call that day, from the forestry-service director himself, announcing his intention to pay a visit soon. "Damn that leopard," Turner muttered to himself as he hung up.

He sat at the desk and idly drew pictures on the notepad. He circled a telephone number with a leafy rope and turned the two zeros into the barrels of a shotgun. He drew a sunflower emerging from one barrel and from the other a jagged flash of lightning. He squared off this picture and then drew an almost perfect leopard head, which he colored black with his ballpoint pen. Under this head he wrote, "Jean Jean Jean Jean Jean."

7

Mike Prewalski had been a zealous but largely unfulfilled hunter in various parts of the world for most of his nearly sixty years, and now, as an official in a forest reserve, he sublimated this instinct by an awareness of the spoor and the sometimes-visible wildlife around the forest station. It had rained steadily for most of Friday night, but the rain had stopped shortly after breakfast on Saturday morning as he and Polly set off in their Volkswagen. Polly's parents had settled at Mossel Bay, a town sixty miles away along the coast, and this was where he had left her. He had stayed for lunch, then had driven home alone through a brightly washed afternoon.

Now, back at the almost deserted forest station, he drove up through the oak avenue, parked his car in the lean-to garage and set off across the mule paddock toward a row of beehives near the green-black forest wall. As he crossed the patch of bare black earth where the mules rolled, he noticed the fresh bushbuck spoor. He marked the animal down in his mind as the big ram he had seen earlier that week, and he was about to move on when more spoor, like that of a very large dog, leaped into focus. The prints, and there were only four of them, were almost perfect: two forepaws intact and two hind paws—one with its four toes intact, the other with only one toe visible and the remainder a blurred depression. The tracks were easily the size of the palm of his hand, and Mike sank down on his haunches to examine them more closely. The three complete impressions were rounded, cat round, and they were little more than six hours old.

Mike crouched over the last print. As he stared at it a small muscle in the corner of his mouth began to twitch. He smiled and looked up and around him slowly. His very blue eyes seemed to dilate, making his face suddenly more boyish, eager. The tracks were almost certainly those of the black man-eater, and he saw his visitor as a prize of a sort—something to his credit whichever way he looked at it. Either he phoned Turner and became the bearer of important information, or he remained silent and acted on his own.

He rose slowly and chewed a cracked nail. The old, experimental walk-in cage trap was still in his storeroom, where it had been left after a research project. Dismantled as it was, its five sections could easily be transported and joined together with light chains. His mind raced ahead. With the help of two laborers, he could set up the trap before nightfall. He thought of the Land-Rover for transport; his shotgun and a few cartridges; a flask of strong coffee; sandwiches; his good flashlight, with extra batteries; and a hip flask of brandy. All of the important ingredients were available. If he failed, he would report the spoor early on Sunday morning and no harm would have been done. He turned and walked rapidly toward the cluster of laborers' cottages.

What he proposed to do was to use himself as bait, live bait, secure inside the cage but ready with his flashlight and shotgun for the time when the leopard came.

He and his two Colored helpers drove to the place he had selected: an open glade beside a disused road. The site was more or less in line with the direction of the spoor and little over half a mile from the forest station. Here they erected the cage, sides and top chained together and strengthened in places with baling wire. It was only when Mike carried his gear into the trap that the two laborers showed hesitation. Tom Windwaai, the tractor driver, was genuinely concerned. He told Mike that the leopard might catch him. Peering out through the mesh, Mike laughed and waved his battered silver flask and said that if he drank enough brandy, he might even catch two leopards. The men fell back, laughing nervously. They were awed by his bravery.

After they had driven off, Mike knew that he should have asked them to come for him in the morning. But no matter, morning would bring light again and the road would be safe; he would leave his departure until well after the sun was up.

When the last of the evening bird chorus died away, Mike unfolded a canvas camping stool, put on a thick army greatcoat and poured the first generous tot of brandy into a plastic mug. From this moment on, the flask kept him both optimistic and excited. A wood owl stationed above him up in the total blackness woke him from a doze with its mournful "Whoo, you," and he once heard the startled bark of a bushbuck and the crackle and leaf-swish of its sudden flight. Nerves tingling, he swept the flashlight beam all around him as soft sounds came and went.

At four o'clock in the morning he drank the last of his coffee and ate the remainder of his sandwiches. After this he dozed at intervals and then awoke with a start to the blast of a dog baboon barking a warning. With his pulse drumming and his mouth dry he listened to the panicking baboons crashing away, a mad medley of barking and frightened yells fading into the distance.

Mike strained his eyes, peering into the slowly lightening gloom of the forest, and breathed deeply to still the trembling that shook him from head to toe. He knew that there was a leopard close by, and the hair of his head prickled and a shiver rippled down the length of his back. For a full half hour he was almost motionless, cradling the cocked shotgun in arms that began to ache on the insides of each elbow. Then the sun came through the trees at last and with it calls of the birds. Mike put the shotgun down and stretched himself out beside it, yawning and smiling with the relief of lying flat for the first time. As far as he was concerned, the vigil was over; it had been a good try. Now he would sleep for a while, and then he would walk back to the station in full daylight and phone Turner.

THE black leopard was not actually awakened by the man's snoring, but he opened his eyes wide. He circled the cage for the fourth time since he had come upon it and then went back to his dry-leaf bed. When the two-legged creature moved at last, the leopard's whole body stiffened. His eyes became hooded slits of intense concentration, recording each motion with tiny pupils. It was only when the two-legged creature began to stride away from the trap that the leopard rose from the ground in one swift movement and followed. Crouching—head and body in line close to the ground, ears flat back, mouth slightly agape—he flowed like a long black shadow through the undergrowth. Even as his speed increased, his passage was almost soundless.

TOM Windwaai rose from the bed he shared with his wife and stepped outside his wood-and-iron shack. He noted with satisfaction that the weather was going to be good; there was no sign of wind in the pale dawn sky and no cloud in the west. He stretched and yawned, then washed his face and the back of his head under the tap of a rainwater tank, and rinsed his mouth. He thought of Prewalski in the cage, and for a moment he paused, debating whether he should walk over to the station, get out the Land-Rover and pick him up. But this would take time, and the low tide would not wait. The boss would only have to walk half a mile, after all, and fetching the cage could be done later.

The black iron wood stove in the kitchen was only just warm, and there was a pot of coffee standing on it. Tom Windwaai lit the Primus stove, and while he waited for the coffee to heat, he put on his trousers and took his fishing-tackle bag from a wall peg.

When the coffee was ready, he poured out a mugful. The liquid was black and strong and sweet, and he dipped a doughnut into it and chewed slowly. There was a faint snoring coming from the room where his wife still slept. He was contented and at peace with himself.

He got up, pulled aside the tattered curtain that served as a door to the main bedroom and took his hat from one of the knobs of the old iron bedstead. Then, with rod and reel in hand, he stepped out into the weak sunlight and set off toward the path that led through the forest and down the cliffs to the sea.

The low tide yielded enough red bait for his needs, as well as a few mussel worms and three red crabs. Having chosen his spot, Tom settled in, as rock anglers tend to do, surrounding himself with discarded clothing, overflowing tackle bag, floats and knives, assorted hooks, a long gaff, a lunch box and a bait basket. He tied his crab carefully to an outsize musselcracker hook, then heaved a long cast toward a patch of light green water, which indicated a sandy bottom beneath. A long wait for a musselcracker but a gamble that Windwaai could never resist.

It was four o'clock in the afternoon, and Tom was down to his last crab, when the long-awaited moment came. There was a tremor along the nerve ending of nylon, like a current of energy flowing from one life force to another. Then there was a decisive knock, enough to twitch the tip of the rod sharply, and in the next instant the whole rod bent and the reel began running taut and hissing against its brake. Tom gave a great bellow of triumph, and for the next quarter of an hour stood firmly in that rare mixture of suspense and excitement that only the angler knows. Deep below him, the fish sought the dark rocky places while the nylon hummed in its teeth, following it inexorably over reefs and ridges and holding it at last.

Tom began to reel the musselcracker in. Soon the first living blue and silver of the fish flashed up through a lens of green water. Then the musselcracker came up slithering and bumping against black mussel-covered rocks, and the fight was over.

High up out of reach of the water, Tom sat listening while the thirty-pound fish banged out a last rhythmic tattoo with its tail on the sun-hot rock surface beside him. Then, unmistakably loud and clear, there came another sound—pealing yells of hounds giving chase—and in another moment six dogs came loping out into the sun, droop-eared with fatigue, their pink tongues showing, their bodies black and tan and white against the pebble background of the beach. Then they disappeared one by one into the fringe of trees under the cliff.

Now Tom remembered Prewalski's night in the walk-in trap. While he thought of the leopard he watched the fringe of trees above the driftwood line, but no hunter appeared. He collected his gear and his catch and left.

When Tom reached the forest station, the collection of vehicles told him that something was wrong. Eight or nine assorted cars and trucks here in the gravel courtyard on a Sunday afternoon would have been strange enough, but the presence of the stark white ambulance filled Tom Windwaai with dread.

He wanted to inquire about the trouble, but law forbade his mingling with the whites here, so he withdrew to the group of laborers under the oaks.

They confirmed his worst fear. "It's old Prewalski," he was told. "That black leopard got him. He's dead."

THE leopard heard the truck doors clicking shut and he heard the voice sounds and the metal rattle of chains, but it was not until he caught the faint yelp of a dog that he began to move away. His instinct was to go north, toward the high forest, but that way led past the danger sounds that were mounting all the while in his brain.

He was still moving slowly down an open path when the now ominous silence behind him exploded into a blast of baying hounds, and with one long bound he plunged off into the undergrowth. For a hundred yards or more he traveled at a fast trot, his shoulder blades sliding like pistons under the black hide, ears flattened and head close to the ground, with eyes adjusting to the gloom, so that the smallest black hole through leaf and thorn thicket became a tunnel into which first head and then body flowed.

In one open patch he broke into a sinuous canter, and to any watching eye he would now have been only a black speeding blur. Then abruptly the forest ended. The leopard moved more slowly here, and as the hounds bayed again closer, the leopard was suddenly afraid. Seeking the lifesaving trunk of a large tree and finding none, he plunged downward over rock faces baked hot in the sun, hardly aware of the sea below. Grunting at the muscle-tearing impact of each downward bound, and with the hounds sounding directly above him, he leaped onto a sandy beach in a dangerous panic. Swerving sharply to the right, his paws throwing up a fan of sandy grit, he began to mount upward again into the twisted gorse and broken rock until, with a final running bound, he cleared a sheer ten-foot face and lay, dizzy and tongue lolling, on a narrow ledge high above the white-foamed rocks and the sea.

With every breath he took, his head sank lower until there came a blessed moment when his chin rested on one muscle-padded forearm and his eyes slowly closed to slits. The sun still beat hot on this narrow west-facing ledge. His erect ears were the only indication that he was not asleep.

He listened intently now for the hounds. Finally he heard them—the scrabbling of claws on stone, the rustle and slap of bony tails on brush, the rattle of pebbles. He lifted his head and opened his eyes wide, for the sun was setting and his ledge was now in the shade. From directly beneath came a chorus of baying. The leopard drew back his lips in an involuntary snarl, but the sounds came no closer.

After many minutes had passed, there was a new sound—a snuffling and whining, first to one side and then the other as the pack leader sought a way up. After that came a rain of gravel and small stones from above, with an almost continuous chatter of excited two-legged creature sounds now close by. The leopard's eyes were adjusting with each gradation of fading light, so that the mosaic of gray and black around him—slope, hollow, outcrop—remained as clear as it had been in the bright sun. With the strength of his muscles restored, he reached up with both fore-paws into the single cleft at the far corner of the ledge, and satisfied, he sank back, stood free on his two hind legs for a moment and vaulted upward in a series of rippling, clinging leaps.

The group of two-legged creatures had no time for anything other than shouts of alarm before he was on hard ground and past them, heading this time into scent that was familiar and heavy with distant running water.

From halfway down the steep, forested sides of the gorge he could still hear the occasional clamor of a hound. But the sound was static; there was no pursuit. He began to move more slowly, following the contour of the river, always upward toward the mountains. But long before midnight the terror of the hounds had faded from his memory and he began to drift westward, through the dim starlit corridors of high forest, toward the twin ravines that marked the western limit of his territory.

INSIDE the forest station, Cliff Turner offered his condolences to Polly Prewalski, who sat weeping in one corner, with her parents looming protectively over her. Moving away, he thought of Mike, trying to imagine how the man's long night must have passed. In his own mind Turner was certain that Mike had found fresh evidence of the leopard's presence. The laborer Tom Windwaai was quite sure that Mike had said nothing about fresh spoor or an actual sighting, and yet Turner could not believe that Mike would have gone to such lengths without some evidence that the leopard was in the vicinity.

There had hardly yet been time for the reality of the man's death to affect Turner personally, as a friend, but it was beginning to now. He thought of the flattened grass inside the cage and the scattered litter of possessions only thirty yards away, where the beast had struck: the khaki greatcoat, the canvas knapsack and, significantly, the still loaded shotgun, unfired and uncocked. It was not difficult to deduce that the leopard had waited for Mike to emerge and then had taken him unawares from behind. The body had been feasted upon.

Turner shuddered, knowing too well those hollow, dead hours of predawn, the terrible suppressed hysteria, the panic that could dispel rational thought. But Turner did not believe that Mike had fled from the security of the trap in panic. He would remember him as a brave man, though perhaps foolhardy. Mike had underestimated his quarry, but at least he had proved that they were dealing with a situation that was quite beyond anyone's control. Man-eater was a word so removed from normal reality as to be difficult to grasp in an age of supertechnology. Yet the fact remained that no life in the enormous area of plantation and forest was now safe, and there was nothing anyone could do to prevent the creature from striking wherever and whenever it chose.

8

TURNER's alarm clock woke him at five o'clock in the morning to a thunder of rain on the corrugated-iron roof of the forestry hut. After cutting off the strident ringing with a slap of his hand, he sat up and groaned. The rain was coming from windless skies in a steady, drenching sheet that would obliterate whatever faint traces of scent might have remained for the hounds to follow.

He switched on the electric kettle and sat on the edge of his bed and rubbed his forehead. He wished he had more faith in the hounds. In any event, they could not stay on in the district indefinitely, waiting for that single chance they needed.

Martin Botha had told him that there had been a flood of people from outlying families who were in a panic and reporting missing relatives and friends. How many were dead and how many just missing was impossible to guess, but Turner had no doubt now that the leopard was a deadly presence, far more dangerous than he had at first believed. Analyzing his emotions about the black leopard was difficult. To save his own life or anyone else's, he would obviously shoot to kill if he could, without a second of hesitation. Well, perhaps he would be tempted to take just a second longer—to see the animal, to observe him. The forest without the excitement of this rarity somehow would be a poorer place. Did he actually feel sympathy for the animal? Yes, unequivocally. It was not the leopard's conscious evil nature that caused him to kill; it was civilization that had impinged; it was the human urge to protect wealth that had crippled him.

He prepared a cup of steaming coffee, then sat on the edge of his bed again and sipped it, allowing the full horror of Mike Prewalski's death to flood over him. It was no bad dream after all and must be faced sooner or later. It seemed the least he could do to mourn the man for a moment and remember all his willing enthusiasm from the earliest days of the cave camp. Turner's thoughts drifted down from the cave to the beach below and to that night in the phosphorescent surf, with Jean warm against him. But this memory brought only a sense of frustration. That night had been so full of promise, and the promise had come to nothing but a firm, if gentle, rejection.

With no further desire to go back to sleep, Turner dressed, and as his head cleared, his thoughts began to center around the large walk-in trap that Mike Prewalski had used. It had been a good idea marred only by Mike's fatal error, and the error need not be repeated. Moreover, with a scheme that he was turning over in his mind, it might just be possible to catch the leopard alive.

He made breakfast and phoned Paul Stander. Outside, the rain slackened, then stopped altogether, leaving trails of drifting mist.

With the help of a team of laborers from the forest station, Paul Stander had the walk-in trap dismantled and delivered to an engineering workshop in Knysna before midday, and by late afternoon the modifications were complete. The trap was now longer by the addition of a new wire-mesh cell that was only just big enough for a man to sit up in. Turner and Stander had discussed having a sliding trapdoor inside the cage that would open into the cell and that could be tripped at the same time as the door of the main cage. That way the human bait would be irresistible. But for that one critical moment nothing would separate the human prey from the leopard as it entered. They had abandoned this approach to avoid the risk of mechanical malfunction.

"And what if you fall asleep?" Paul Stander had asked.

"I'm not going to fall asleep."

"You could faint, you know, or be paralyzed with shock."

"Fear, you mean," Turner had said, grinning. "Okay, we'll cover the whole thing. But the trigger must be manually operated. We can't risk losing him to anything that he can touch or feel."

"It's going to be difficult to know when to pull the lever," Stander had mused. "If the door came down on him halfway in or even on his hindquarters, he'd be out again in a flash."

WHEN the rain in the forest ceased its roaring avalanche and the trees had lost their last curtain of heavy dripping to a sudden shiver of wind, the leopard came out of his warm leaf bed and stretched himself. He ambled along an old grass-grown logging road through a waking forest, the sun slanting in, gold and mellow. At one spur of a gorge, directly below a rocky outcrop, the main river of the twin valleys showed itself in glimpses as a narrow black band that twisted away to become only a series of black or amber pools at its upper reaches. Farther on, the forested slopes on either side hid the river completely and curved out of sight. From these hot upper regions of the plateau, with the sun mounting higher, he made his way slowly downward. As the river drew nearer, the trees began, and then there were tree ferns and a smell of dampness and at last the river itself.

He drank among the dappled shadows of an overhanging branch, then set off upstream at a loping walk and did not pause until he reached Jean Mannion's long-neglected forest pool, almost five miles away from his point of descent. The familiar rock overhang where he had sheltered with his mother was only a few hundred yards away in the cliff above, and the Mannion house was little more than that distance over the curve of the hill.

The leopard lapped from the black water three or four times, but languidly, as though tasting it only, and his head moved in a series of small jerks as he sniffed the green peppermint-scented undergrowth around him. He began to move slowly upward into the forest, tasting as he went.

There was only intermittent bird sound in the forest now, with the sun directly overhead, and the leopard moved uphill without another pause. He crossed a rockslide under the cliff, and looked up only when he was directly below the jagged cleft that led upward through stunted trees to the old shelter high above. He gathered himself, tail raised, then propelled himself onto the ledge. He inspected the area until he was satisfied that there was no danger—no gusty hiss of puff adder, no arched scorpion's tail—then threw himself on his side with a grunt of satisfaction.

He rested and slept at intervals throughout the afternoon. Then, by the faint blue light of a moon in its last quarter, the leopard went up the rock chimney behind the shelter and, skirting the grazing lands, made his way toward the houses occupied by Kampmuller's farmworkers. He ignored the barking of the dogs and kept well hidden in shadow, inspecting each dog and each cottage in turn with huge eyes. Light shone from the windows of one of these houses, and he was drawn to it partly because he associated the two-legged creatures with light and partly because of the volume of sound that came pouring from it. The sound was that of his prey together with a discord of guitars, mouth organs and small drums. He circled the cottage with every sense alert, crouched low on the hard, bare earth, and sniffed at each door in turn. He did this three times, and finally in frustration reached up to scratch and pluck at a chink of light that flowed from a shuttered window. There was no change in the volume of sound, and after a final prowl, which encompassed a henhouse and a small outbuilding, the leopard turned away.

The molded curve of the open hillside with its covering of tough grass was tinged with yellow light and smelled of sheep. He went under a fence, hardly touching the bottom strand of wire, and was immediately aware of dog scent heavy on the wet air, intermingled with the aromatic essences of an orchard. Here the earth was soft, soundless. Directly ahead, the Mannion house loomed on the hilltop like a rock outcrop, stark and silent against the skyline. He crossed a patch of lawn—familiar, remembered—then smelled the musty drifting air of a swimming pool and lapped the water experimentally. He spent a far longer time smelling a towel that was draped over the back of a chair, and a pair of sandals on the grass nearby, and then walked slowly around the house, glancing up at windows and doors as he went.

9

JEAN Mannion stood on the upper balcony of the airport building in the town of George, about forty miles from Knysna. She stayed just long enough to watch the jet scream its course down the runway, then take its graceful leap into the sky. It was taking her brother, John, to Cape Town. He would be away for four days, the last two at Stellenbosch, on their cousin's farm. She would now have four days alone, and the thought was enough to set her pulse tapping a little faster.

During the last two weeks she had not seen much of Cliff Turner, though he had phoned at least four times—twice he had spoken to John and twice to her when John had been out, but she knew quite clearly that it was she he hoped to hear. In this knowledge and in their long, rambling conversations, carefully guarded because of the party line, she knew that their relationship was a strong bud waiting to flower and under her control alone. And yet she experienced a twinge of guilt. For now, as she drove home from the airport on the coastal road, she thought about Simon and found that for the first time she could remember him without pain. She did not believe that he would have wanted her to remain single in honor of his memory, and she knew that she had no real reason for guilt. Nevertheless it was there.

She drove slowly, trying to see the coast through the eyes of a stranger and finding that its beauty required no exaggeration. It was honeymoon, vacation country. The first long beach, butterfly yellow, burst into view around rock walls as the road descended to sea level. It wound past summer houses, which were emptying now as the season raced to its end. Over dunes and past lakes with still, masted yachts; past yellowbill ducks and the pink flush of migrating flamingos. She passed a dark river flowing down from the forest and mountains, and then she saw the great open estuary of Knysna itself; she would be home in twenty minutes.

On her way in through the farm gates she spoke to Henry, the foreman, and assured herself that all was well. She drove slowly along the red-graveled road that wound through the pasturelands toward the house, then stopped the car where a bunch of Aberdeen Angus steers stood in a field of ryegrass beside the road. She got out and, resting her hands on the top strand of the fence, studied the cattle.

They seemed fat and glossy enough, and she was satisfied that she had kept strictly to Simon's dipping schedule. But she was afraid of the future and her own ability to be the kind of farmer she would like to be. She knew that the tough, sour veld, which now lay beaten momentarily beneath the green, exotic cover, would work tirelessly and timelessly to reassert itself and that worms and ticks would continue to wage their relentless war on the cattle. John, with his two years in the army now behind him, must go to university soon. For her father's sake she could and would see to this. But she could not guarantee to live alone on

Longlands forever and farm it as Simon would have done. Just as there was nothing static about the land, there was no stopping point in life.

Against the flushed sky there was a line of birds, colorless, slow wings beating in the dying light, soundless. The geese stood out clearly along the wall of the dam, white dots catching the last of the light, and she knew as she stood there that she was saying good-bye to Simon.

Outside the house it was dark and quiet, and she stood listening to the chorus of frogs and crickets beginning again. Now suddenly she was lonely. She went in and switched off the outside lights and locked the door. She paused by her telephone for a moment, then turned purposefully away toward the kitchen, where she made herself an omelet and poured a glass of wine.

Cradling her Siamese tomcat in her arms, she watched a single program on television. Then, after a long, hot shower, she went to bed. She left a half-finished thriller on the table beside her, wanting to go on but just a little afraid; the suspenseful story was too close to home, if for no other reason than that she now had on her bedside table Simon's Colt .38 automatic. The pistol was old, but it worked and she could use it.

It was well after eleven o'clock when she turned out the light. She lay in the dark for a while; then she forced herself to turn on her bedside light again and get up to lock the bedroom door. She also closed and locked the double windows that overlooked the front lawn and the great abyss of the twin valleys, black and silent below. The single window near the bed she left slightly open. The night air streamed in, and there was no sound but the far-off floating, falling notes of crowned plovers, alarmed.

A FLOOD of cool air was streaming slowly down the side of the hill and over sheep-nibbled grass, and it was heavy with scent. There was the mushroom odor of early autumn and the tang of ripening oranges and the dog smell that lingered near the house on the crest of the hill. But the scent that dominated all others was the warm, bloodlike smell of the two-legged creatures—the one scent that caused the leopard to open his mouth a fraction, to taste with his tongue and to blink his eyes in anticipation.

A deep black shadow in the predawn darkness, he flowed, changing shape as wire fence and furrow dictated, and crossed the short grass of the courtyard. Here, with the dog scent intensifying, he paused and changed direction, taking his own smell away with him around the house and out of reach of the silent kennel. He stopped at a window and stood with his forepaws on the sill, ears turning as he listened to the sounds of the house: the rhythmic ticking of metal that was a clock; the purring of a refrigerator; and gentle, much softer, as soft as living tissue, the breathing of his sleeping prey.

The kitchen door was ajar, a stream of warmth, and he went in, more cautiously now, whiskers bristling, shoulders hunched, testing each footfall with the unfamiliar feel of the cold tile floor. His pupils at full intensity, he followed his tasting tongue, recording the change of temperature from tiles to wooden floor, feeling the softness of carpets and at last becoming conscious, by some nameless sense, that his quarry lay less than his own length away from him, behind a closed door.

Normally a sound sleeper, Jean was mildly surprised to find herself wide awake, with the pale beginnings of dawn seeping into the bedroom. The luminous dial of her clock showed a few minutes after half past four, and her heartbeats seemed quicker than usual. She knew that something specific had waked her, and imagining a burglar, she lay still in the gray darkness, with her eyes wide open. The sound, when she heard it again, was more a sense of something moving than noise itself—a stealthy, sibilant rustle. Then came a distinct thump, which at first sounded like her Siamese tom as he strutted beneath a chair, striking his arched, quivering tail against mahogany legs. But the Siamese was fast asleep on the end of her bed. She tried to remember whether she had locked the kitchen door. The sound could possibly be that of a burglar in stocking feet. She was thinking very clearly now, and in the darkness she reached over to the bedside table, her fingers tickling her watch and the alarm clock, and finally closing on the butt of the pistol. She drew it toward her slowly and sat up against the headboard, with the gun across the tops of her knees.

A sudden low, growling howl close beside her made her twitch with shock, and the weapon in her hand trembled. The Siamese had left her bed and was now beneath it, making an eerie sound, a wild, keening note. She breathed deeply, and the pounding of her heart seemed to drive the exhaled breath from her lungs in a series of small, audible puffs. When the cat's wailing faded, she listened intently, the whole range of her hearing concentrated on the inside of the house, but she could hear nothing, and after a long while she began to breathe more normally.

The butt of the pistol was warm as she uncurled the fingers of her right hand and flexed them. She heard the far-off sound of plovers again and the ticking of the alarm clock, and then suddenly these comforting sounds were totally eclipsed once more by the menacing presence that seemed to whisper and breathe, sharing the darkness with her. It was as though some long dormant sense had awaked in her, opening a door in her brain to reveal the ghosts of terrors from a vanished time: the frozen winds of an ice age, the snuffling of a cave bear at the bouldered entrance, the very breath of some great feline hunter.

But the snuffling at the door was real, and the soft slither of a padded paw. The door creaked, and then for a long time in the timeless darkness that began to change to gray there was no sound. She was half relaxing when the door handle banged down with a force that seemed capable of wrenching the frame from its hinges. The door bulged and rattled, and the whole house echoed with the shock of fear. An empty gray sickness passed over her in the absolute silence that followed.

She remembered the pistol and drew back the hammer. The click was loud, and as though the sound had waked the dogs, they began to bark hysterically in their kennel thirty yards away. She could feel the trigger, cold and metal-hard against her finger, but she drew her left hand across the weapon to reassure herself that the hammer was cocked. Yet now the door on her left no longer radiated danger. It was as though the aura had gone from there and moved away, drawing her eyes and ears after it, through the kitchen door and then slowly around the house, to the narrowly opened window, a square of lighter gray in the gloom of the room. And even as she watched, the window rattled and the whole length of a thickly muscled foreleg reached through, hanging,

feeling the darkness with hooked, seeking claws that glinted white in the half-light. It hung there, disembodied. Then Jean saw the head—the domed black outline, flat ears breaking the curve with small points—and she pulled the trigger.

The pistol bucked in her hand. The explosion was deafening in the still room. Only half hearing her own whimpering sobs, she fired again, gripping the weapon tightly with both hands, aiming and firing until the window was empty of all but white sky. The dogs still barked furiously, but they were not howling now; and then sweetly, faithful to the dawn, a robin started his little piping song, and Jean began to cry with long, aching gasps.

The sunlight crept up until a yellow bar touched the corner of her wardrobe. Eventually she allowed her eyes to stray from the window long enough to see that it was after six o'clock. The telephone was in the living room, and she knew that it was important that she contact either Cliff Turner or Paul Stander quickly. She knew now that they had not been exaggerating the danger of the leopard, and she remembered how close she had been to ignoring Cliff's warning of the danger of the forest pool.

It occurred to her then that she might have hit the leopard with one of the shots. Perhaps it was lying dead outside her window, with a bullet through its head. Curious and even a little excited, she got out of bed and slowly approached the window, the cocked pistol held steady in a two-handed grip in front of her. But when she looked out through the glass, there was nothing there. She opened the window and, leaning out, searched the courtyard and the lawn beyond for any sign of movement or unnatural shadow. She knew that her next move should be to unlock the bedroom door and get to the telephone. But what if the leopard was lying in wait somewhere in the house?

She dressed quickly—slacks, a shirt and sandals—and then remembered the dogs, which were still restless and whining. She decided that they could help her. At least the bright open space outside held less terror than her own living room. With heart pounding and the pistol hampering her movements, she climbed out the window, dropped to the ground and ran to unlock the kennel. The dogs streaked out, a howling, galloping pack. They tore around the yard, then inside and all around the house. When they came out again, she let them run, ranging for a full minute, and then called them back and locked them in the kennel once more. She walked slowly into the kitchen, into the shadowy living room, laid the pistol down on the telephone table and called Cliff. She heard his voice with a feeling of overwhelming relief, knowing only when she replaced the receiver that he had said, "Stay where you are. Shut everything, lock yourself in. I'm coming."

10

TURNER and Paul Stander in their khaki and boots looked out of place in Jean's bedroom with its carpets and gilded furniture. They were examining a bullet hole drilled in the window glass.

Turner said, "You couldn't have missed by more than a hand's width." He pointed to a splintered hole in the wooden frame. "That one was close too." Next he looked up at the ceiling and smiled. "The less said about that one the better."

She pulled a mock cross face and punched him softly on the arm. Then she noticed the truck outside in the drive, with its assortment of metal-and-mesh panels and its three attendants. "Is that a trap of some sort?"

"Yes, a trap," Stander said. "We think it's going to work; we hope."

"This has been a stroke of luck," Turner said. He put his hand on Jean's shoulder. "Rough on you, I know. You've been very brave."

"Brave," she said laconically. "You should have seen me. I was nearly sick with fear."

Over coffee they told her how the trap was to be baited and sprung, making it seem a safe and simple matter.

She was aghast. "Cliff, you can't do that, you can't possibly."

"The leopard can't get in, there's no way. No heroics on my part, I can tell you. But keep it to yourself, Jean. Paul and I are acting rather on our own, and if this doesn't work, we may get it in the neck for not calling the hounds in straightaway. Anyway, the idea is that Paul will stay with you tonight. I'll be in the cage. We'll have a radio link between us, and maybe you might ask us to have breakfast with you in the morning."

They put the cage together on the flat land close to the place where John Avery and Kampmuller had set their trap gun. By early afternoon all was ready.

At half past five Cliff and Jean had half an hour together alone when Stander took the three laborers back to Knysna. They watched the truck until it was out of sight, then went into the house without speaking. In the cool intimacy of the living room, Jean crossed to the window and Cliff followed. He put an arm around her shoulders and said quite softly, "You've had a bad time. I'm sorry."

She turned toward him, and their mouths met tentatively at first, then more strongly, more urgently, until there was no reticence between them.

THE birds of the coastal forests have a pattern of calling that is like a clock measuring the waxing and waning of daylight. In the morning the louries are first awake, like raucous children rousing the woodland from sleep. After them the chorister robins chime in, and the Cape robins and the Cape thrushes, and then the cuckoos and shrikes and the paradise flycatchers, all awaiting their cues. Evening is a more solemn affair—unlike the excited, crowded greeting of the day—for there is always the lurking danger of the night ahead. The cuckoos are first, and then the shrikes, and then the sweetest of all, the chorister robins, their short repertoire ending in a silence for the owls to fill.

Turner, in his cramped cage, heard all these, and now he could also hear the owls hooting eerily. Again and again he thought of Mike Prewalski; each time he tried to twist his mind away. Simon Mannion's pistol lay fully loaded and cocked beside the white top of a thermos flask. In this confined space the pistol was a better weapon than a shotgun or rifle, but it was only a safety backup; its use would mean a dangerous disruption of the plan. The two-way radio link was Stander's idea, and it worked well. Turner did not think that the sound would be a deterrent; he even believed that it might be an additional lure.

"Are you still receiving loud and clear?" he asked Stander after a while.

"Clear as a little bell, Cliff. Over."

Turner said, "Sounds orchestral. About a million frogs have just awaked again. You can probably hear them. Confirm again that you can hear when I talk at this level. Over."

"We can hear you fine. We hear the frogs too. Here's Jean."

Jean leaned over the instrument. She said, "Hello, we're missing you. Paul is looking after me very well. All the doors and windows are shut; I hope you've remembered to shut yours. Over."

"That was nice," Turner said. There was a pause; then he said, "There is something moving around out here. Some porcupines have just made off in a hurry."

Jean and Paul looked at each other expectantly. A long silence followed; then Turner's voice came again. "I can sort of sense something else here. I don't want to use the flashlight. I'll check with you again every half hour unless something happens. Over."

Paul sighed and looked at his watch. "It could be a long night," he said to Jean. "You can get some sleep if you like. I'll wake you."

Jean stretched. She went to the window and stood staring into the darkness. There were no lights visible in the whole expanse of the valley. She imagined herself in the cage, with the black leopard outside, and shuddered, so that her shoulders shook.

"I'll stay here with you, Paul. I'd rather, but I may curl up with a book on this settee."

At half past four in the morning Turner's voice sounded tired. "I'm a bit worried about the flash, Paul. If it goes off at the moment I happen to be blinking my eyes, I may not see it." They had rigged an electronic-beam unit in the cage, about three quarters of the way along the side from the door, using one of Turner's cameras. If the leopard set off the camera, he'd be well inside, and that would be Turner's signal to release the cage door.

"I was a fool not to bring a rifle," Turner went on. "He may be lying just off to one side here, waiting for me to come out. But don't come for me until I give you the all clear, and then don't get out of the truck. And bring your .375, not a shotgun; the range may be too far. How is Jean? Over."

"She's fine. She's asleep. Snoring, actually, but very delicately. You shouldn't worry about not seeing the flash; you'll detect it right through your eyelids."

Turner's voice changed now to a scarcely audible hissing whisper. "He's here. I'm sure it's him. He's cruising around. I'll leave this thing on."

"Jean," Paul whispered urgently. She sat up, quickly alert, and was at his side in an instant. "He's left the channel open on his side. He says the leopard is close by. I'm not sure how he knows; could be imagination, but I thought I'd better wake you."

Suddenly the receiver erupted with a deafening crash and then Turner's voice, an incomprehensible bellow, and, above all, the terrible roar of a big animal, blending peal upon peal with a pounding, metallic rattle.

"We've got him, we've got him." Turner's voice was choked and breaking. "My word, what an animal. What a wonderful, beautiful thing."

His voice was drowned by a snarl that seemed to rattle the receiver and another loud crash of metal.

"It's all right, it's holding," Turner shouted. "You can come now. But keep clear; put the headlights on him."

Paul and Jean stood staring at each other, eyes wide with excitement.

There was a softer but intense snarl. Then Turner again, "Poor old beast." They distinctly heard his voice break as the receiver clicked off.

They hugged each other, and Jean was wiping tears from her eyes as they ran together out toward the truck. They drove in silence, tense with expectancy. The headlights of the truck probed and waved over the dipping, twisting track, and then they were through the open gate and out into grazing land. In the faint dawn light, the cage stood out clearly at the end of the field, and long before they had expected, they saw the brilliant green points of eyes winking open and shut as the animal moved.

After Stander switched off the engine, they sat quite still.

The leopard was silent too, pacing up and down, its head low, ears flat back and great muscled limbs rippling behind the bars and mesh.

"He's right," Stander said softly. "That's the most beautiful animal I've ever seen."

He climbed slowly out of the truck and circled around behind it toward where Cliff Turner was now emerging on hands and knees from the back end of the cage. The leopard whirled with a snarl and crashed against the mesh, and then lay flat, his breath rasping in and out.

The two men came and stood at the window of the truck, where Jean sat. There was nothing to say. She looked at Cliff Turner's face, bony and haggard in the dim light, and he seemed remote, a stranger, almost beautiful—long jawline and straight nose prominent.

"And now, Paul," he said at last, "what do we do with him? What happens to him?"

Stander rubbed his chin. He said slowly and gently, as though forced to break bad news, "Well, we can't let him go again, can we." Then he added, "They'll want him dead, I suppose."

After a while Turner said, "There must be another way. I can't think now." He paused again. "You can't see in this light, but he's lost almost the whole of one paw."

"You don't have to make excuses to me, Cliff, and that won't affect the issue in any case. No one could risk transferring him to a game reserve. It'd be far too dangerous."

"What about a zoo?" Jean said.

Stander said, "Maybe. Nothing wrong with that."

They looked at Turner. Stander said, "Come on, man, cheer up. We should be celebrating; it's been a fantastic success. Look, pull some strings; who was that old zoology professor, that Williams fellow? Surely he'll want to look at him. That would be a delay at least."

Turner said suddenly, "You're right. We can try. But we'll have to keep an eye on this old boy. Half the district will be here soon, and I can just see old Japie practically howling for a lynching party."

Turner telephoned the forestry-service director at home in Cape Town at seven o'clock and was mildly surprised at the relief and pleasure his news evoked. He passed the phone to Stander, who came in for his share of praise as well. Then Turner spoke to Dr. Williams and was relieved when the suggestion about a zoo was accepted and understood. Both the director and Williams promised that the necessary contacts would be made. Finally,

Turner passed on the news of the capture to the local head of forestry and the police.

The first cars began to arrive soon afterward, and others kept streaming in all morning: forestry officials, the police, the mayor of Knysna, Kampmuller and other local farmers, two reporters and a large contingent of local Colored families.

It was important that the offending animal should be seen, but Turner and Stander were relieved when three uniformed parks-board men arrived in a large specially equipped truck. De Villiers, the leader of the parks-board group, was visibly awed by the great black cat. He crouched over his medicine chest, and when he was ready, he walked straight up to the side of the cage, knelt quickly and squirted the contents of a syringe directly into the leopard's wide-open snarling jaws. The physical impact of the leopard's weight against the mesh rocked the cage, and De Villiers flinched, but the dose had found its mark. Everyone settled down to wait.

For a while the drug had no noticeable effect on the leopard's alert movements. Then slowly he began to sway drunkenly and to stagger, his head moving in jerks, eyes staring, searching. When the cat at last slid down near the side of the cage, the men were ready: the tip of the drooping tail protruded for a moment through the mesh, and the men seized it, dragging the feebly pawing animal toward them. They held the black tail long enough for De Villiers to slide his needle under the skin and depress the plunger, administering a stronger dose, which would keep the big cat manageable for hours.

The men then raised the door of the cage, and there was a loud, wailing cry of alarm from the onlookers, who fell back, pushing and tumbling. When the men staggered out with their burden, the cat's forepaws were still paddling the air in a slow, swimming motion. They lowered the animal onto a plastic sheet and covered his wide-open unblinking eyes against damage from the sun. Now they measured and probed and examined, and soon it was all over. They placed him carefully in the truck and drove away in a cloud of dust, leaving the last of the crowd to disperse and Cliff Turner and Jean Mannion to be driven thankfully back to the farmhouse by Paul Stander.

CLIFF, FULLY CLOTHED BUT without his boots, lay asleep on Jean's bed and awoke startled and disoriented to the ringing of an alarm clock. He turned it off, noticing as he did so the cup of tea and the note in Jean's handwriting propped against it. The note said, "Have gone to the forest pool. Join me if you like," and at the bottom of the blue notepaper there was a single small *x*.

He drank the lukewarm tea, then put on his boots and started down the hill. It was hot and humid outside, with the hint of a thunderstorm in the black clouds gathering over the mountains. But Cliff walked briskly, feeling refreshed after his first untroubled sleep in weeks. With each step he was intensely aware of waking to full consciousness, as though he had shed a great physical and mental load.

Jean was lying in the sun on a lichen-covered rock in the middle of the pool, an island of white light against the background of dark water. Cliff stripped to his shorts, waded into the water and swam silently toward her. For a moment she lay with her chin resting on top of her hands, watching, smiling at him. Then she climbed down, long-legged and graceful, and slipped into the water to join him.

To the pair of black eagles circling an air current high overhead, the pool was only a small window of intense darkness in the green forest, but the tiny movements of the swimmers alerted them, and they tilted their great paddle-shaped wings to sweep in a wide, descending arc, so that the lofty silence around them was filled for a moment with a sibilant hissing of wind through quivering feathers. To their eyes the converging heads below came quickly into sharp focus, and the eagles turned away, their flying shadows flashing unseen across all the unchanging secrets of the wilderness beneath.

ABOUT THE AUTHOR

Creating a memorable animal character—in this case a black leopard endowed with beauty, cunning, strength, and speed—is challenge enough. But evoking a reader's understanding and sympathy for a leopard that *attacks and eats humans*—well, that takes a very special kind of art. As a writer, Hjalmar Thesen honed his skills by producing a newspaper column and three previous novels. His affinity for nature and wildlife goes back further still.

Hjalmar Thesen

"Nature has been a lifelong hobby and study of mine," he said recently, speaking on the phone from his hilltop home in Knysna, South Africa. "Since childhood I have lived fairly close to the wild parts of this country, and one automatically becomes very involved with all the creatures that inhabit these areas."

His family operated a forestry and sawmill company in South Africa for a hundred years, and Thesen was one of its directors until a recent merger. Since then he has been absorbed in establishing a game farm. The preserve covers five hundred acres and is surrounded by an eight-foot-high fence. He has just completed stocking the land with zebras, ostriches, and several varieties of antelope, including a very rare one, the bontebok.

So far no leopards have threatened the game preserve, but caracals, a type of lynx, occasionally prey on the young antelope. Rather than shoot these invaders, Thesen traps them in a walk-in cage, much like the one used in the book, drives them away from the farm, then lets them go. "I only hope they don't come back," he adds.

Hjalmar Thesen describes his game-farm work as "more creative than writing a book." Fortunately, though, he hasn't given up writing. A novel with a conservation theme is in the works.

ACKNOWLEDGMENTS

Page 2: from the collection of Jodie Richardson.

Page 371: "Anastasia" by Alfred Newman and Paul Francis Webster, © 1956, renewed 1984, Twentieth Century Music Corporation. Rights assigned to CBS Catalogue Partnership. All rights controlled and administered by CBS Feist Catalog Inc. All rights reserved. International copyright secured. Used by permission.

Pages 380, 381, 405, 417, 429, 451, 467, 477, 494: courtesy of Alexandra Costa.